A Life Entwined

A Life Singular
Book 3

Lorraine Pestell

First published in Australia in 2014
Second edition published worldwide in 2016

© Lorraine Pestell 2016
http://lorrainepestell.com

The moral right of this author has been asserted.

All characters, places and events in this publication, other than those clearly in the public domain, are fictitious and any resemblance to real persons, living or dead, is purely coincidental.

Paperback ISBN: 978-1-925151-12-1
E-book ISBN: 978-1-9251510-4-6
Amazon ASIN: B00LLB9LIO

Other books in the "A Life Singular" series:
Book 1 – A Life Singular
Book 2 – A Life Found
Book 4 – A Life Lived
Book 5 – A Life Tested
Book 6 – A Life Loved
Book 7 – A Life After

For Mike,
who always helps me see things more clearly

The author supports two not-for-profit organisations which provide invaluable assistance to Australian children in need:

EdConnect Australia (formerly the School Volunteer Program)
(http://EdConnetAustralia.org.au) "We're harnessing the wisdom and skills of older generations to enrich the learning experience of young people who are at risk of falling by the wayside in an often over-burdened school system."

The Smith Family *(www.thesmithfamily.com.au). "The Smith Family is a children's charity helping disadvantaged Australian children to get the most out of their education, so they can create better futures for themselves."*

Prologue

At her uncle's house, looking forward to Christmas with her younger brother and the rest of their family, Freya was thrilled to find a book that she had been desperate to read for a number of years. The romantic story of Lynn Dyson Diamond and her handsome husband had fascinated the little girl for as long as she could remember, rendered ever more alluring after her mother insisted she was too young for the rather adult themes explored by the bestselling autobiography. Several of the youngster's friends had read it, mostly in secret too, and the pre-teens had spent hours at school and during sleepovers reliving its expedition through the spectacular life of Australia's most famous heroes.

Delighted to have been left with the house to herself while her mum treated all the boy cousins to an afternoon at the beach, and after checking that her aunt was absorbed in her gardening, the eleven-year-old's temptation had been far too great to resist. The book had fairly leaped off the shelf into her hands, and by the time Christmas Eve two-thousand-and-eight finally arrived, the avid reader had successfully snatched enough time here and there to immerse herself in the novel's hidden treasure trove and make it to the end of Act One.

Freya found her mind constantly returning to the love affair between her favourite superstars, who had both passed away before she was born, and she could hardly wait to find out how they had weathered their separation. It was as if Christmas had arrived early when, most unexpectedly, another fortuitous opportunity had opened up while her mother was frantically wrapping last minute presents to go under the tree. She smuggled herself into her uncle's study, closed the door and curled up in his comfortable, leather executive chair.

The studious and creative child had been through a great deal in her eleven tender years. She had inherited her father's intelligence, but luckily not his fierce temper and tendency for aggression. Her mother had avidly consumed Jeff Diamond's powerful autobiography when her marriage had ended, recognising in it many of the traits her former husband shared with the author and which had eventually led to their divorce. It was mostly for this reason that she had forbidden her daughter to read it, and although the young girl had been spared the specific details leading to this conclusion, somehow the telepathic signals had been nagging in the back of her mind.

And so it was that every night over the balmy Queensland holiday season, Freya planned to retrieve "A Life Singular" from under her mattress, and every morning she would make her bed exceedingly tidily, so that her mother wouldn't feel the need to touch it. The magic of this heavy book surpassed her every expectation, and the curious child devoured page after page as the tragic love story unfolded. There were some sections she didn't yet fully comprehend, and a great many more with which such a girl couldn't help but identify.

A new act, Freya's eyes recalled excitedly from that morning, parting the pages at her bookmark. Exactly how did the extraordinary boy from the south-west of Sydney turn himself into one of the biggest stars the world had ever known? And how did his broken heart manage to survive the nightmares alone? Her heartbeat quickened. She needed to know so badly...

Overture, Act Two

Having dabbled in a wide variety of art forms during his long and illustrious career, Jeff Diamond had spent many nocturnal hours arriving at the most compelling way to structure his autobiography so as to do justice to their extraordinary story. He wanted people not only to read it, but to understand it and to learn from it. To be energised by it, and even to love it. Above all however, he hoped his crowning glory might mobilise a whole new generation of inspired world-changers to embark on lives yet more singular than his own.

Furthermore, remembering how adamant Lynn had remained throughout their time together about constantly widening their reach, the author was determined to make the finished book appeal as much to their detractors as to their fans, and even more so to those who remained disinterested in bringing about a better world. What would he need to do to attract people who rarely visited a bookshop or library, and then to draw their gaze to this book among all the others? And which first impressions ought it to register in order to engage the public enough to lift the memoirs of this particular pair of national treasures down from a crowded shelf and take them home?

The eye-catching cover, with its composite of colourful photographs artistically arranged, was sure to beguile their fans; particularly females of all ages, who had always clamoured for glossy magazines and picture books featuring the couple and their family. Indeed, their feeding frenzies in recent years had occasionally crashed Stonebridge Music's computers after certain announcements, when they surged to download pictures by the tens of thousands from the celebrities' website! For the cover galley and a collection of special photographs inset chronologically into four separate sections, Jeff had worked with the publisher's graphic artists to create a visual design that would convey an irresistible yet accessible image of supreme happiness and triumph over adversity. Given his own lowly beginnings, he most certainly didn't want the life he and Lynn had enjoyed to seem beyond the reach of ordinary folk.

Part star-studded musical marathon, part feat of endurance; part comedy, part tragedy; their life singular had twisted and turned so many times and at breakneck pace around a succession of achievements and setbacks. To say that things had gone according to plan was both a truism and a falsehood, Jeff realised, as he sat staring at the list of chapters inside the front cover. Yes, he and Lynn had found each other and hung on to their rollercoaster of a partnership through thick and thin, which had always been the master plan. But on the other hand, one could hardly say the unfolding melodrama hadn't thrown up its fair share of unforeseen challenges along the way.

'Dramatic structure,' the billionaire author explained to his faithful personal assistant and publicity guru. 'Plain, old-fashioned dramatic structure's what it's ended up as.'

Cathy Lane laughed and shook her head. 'I know I should remember that from my school days, 'cause I loved English, but I can't. Another coffee?'

'Yeah. Great, thanks,' Jeff nodded, tossing her an arrogant smirk. 'Would I care to enlighten you?'

The longstanding employee and her husband had invited the widower to dinner, knowing his daughter was out of town. They were endeavouring to continue Kierney's good work by monitoring his eating and drinking, maximising the former while reining in the latter to a level tolerable by all parties. Having known the great man since the early nineteen-seventies, the woman with the sunny disposition and natural flair for marketing whom Gerry Blake had recruited to handle the superstar's explosive showbusiness career had learned very early on that excess was a vital part of Jeff Diamond's character. She remembered sharing a joke in the office, shortly after meeting Lynn Dyson for the first time. Never had she seen more love shine from a person's eyes than when the beautiful star had said of her leading man, "To deprive him of his vices is akin to stealing his soul."

'I'm sure you would,' Malcolm sniggered, refilling their wine glasses and unknowingly ruining the romance for his wife.

Peeling the cellophane from two slim-line cigars, the intellectual smiled and handed one to his host. The December evening was warm in Camberwell, and dinner had been eaten outside on the deck of the couple's expansive period home, purchased of course with the spoils of their long association with one of the world's richest celebrities and quite the most generous of men.

Leaning forward to accept a light from his friend, Jeff led the couple once more along the path of enlightenment. 'One story, many subplots, woven into three acts and with five stages in all.'

'Oh, how boring and mathematical,' Cathy whined. 'Not at all arty-farty. So Act One is your first period together, when Lynn was still at school. Act Two is your time apart, and Act Three is the rest?'

The writer blew a long plume of smoke into the darkness overhead. 'No. Well, Act One, yes. Dramatic structure's how you build the story so that you don't leave the audience behind. Explaining what's going on without giving too much away too soon and spoiling the ending.'

The faithful employee frowned when she saw her boss catch his breath, knowing full well how the ending had already been spoiled for him. As usual, Jeff had read her mind and gave her a grateful wink. His reaction was not one of regret though, on this occasion, since his present discomfort came as the result of a sharp twinge in his left pectoral muscle; the one adorned with the bigger of the eternal couple's twin tattoos, through which he regularly received assurance that their happy ending was still to come.

'Exposition, followed by rising action, leading to the climax,' the handsome man continued, eyebrows raising suggestively, 'then falling action and finally the *dénouement*. The unknotting. Untangling, I guess, which I always thought was a weird word. It suggests that endings have to be tidy, or somehow that the plot can only end when everything's clear, straight and ordered. To me, that'd leave nothing left to be decided. Such a concept leads me to picture everything disconnected, and that's not an ending I'd ever look forward to.'

'So why not five acts?' Malcolm interjected, cutting himself a large chunk of melting brie and attempting to scrape it onto a cracker. 'You guys certainly had enough rising and falling action to flesh out all five stages. Look at this cheese, hon'. Bloody warm summer evenings! Sounds like you need more than three.'

'Yes, mate,' Jeff replied. 'I laboured over that for a while too. But in the end, I went back to basics, mainly because I want people to recognise where they are at any point in the book. I think, even if you're not into plays or symphonies, most storytelling art forms use standard dramatic structure, more or less. People are familiar with it innately, so artists should only deviate from it if they want to confuse. Stir things up a bit...'

His audience nodded obediently.

'If people watch TV or listen to pop songs, it's still a three-act gig. Everything works towards the climax, doesn't it? Then it's downhill from there, and the credits roll or the DJ moves on to the next track.'

All three friends laughed out loud, the consummate performer once more in his element. The Diamonds' life had been chock full of climaxes, enjoyed both in private and in public, and it was nigh on impossible for the Lanes to discern where falling action might have given way to a new patch of rising action. For Jeff however, the climax had always been as clear as day. And judging by the sweet stinging in his chest, so had it to Lynn.

'Our high point was always going to be our twenty-fifth wedding anniversary,' he croaked, sniffing back tears and attempting to stem their flow by dragging hard on his cigar, 'if she was still here... But now, I don't know. I still haven't decided. Maiastra in 'ninety-three or Live On Earth at the beginning of 'ninety-five?'

'But why your silver wedding?' Cathy blurted out, herself overcome with emotion by a memory of the intimate and very splendid occasion she had attended at the turn of nineteen-seventy-six.

The widower smiled and rubbed his chest again. 'Because I finished my groom's speech with an invitation for everyone to get together again in the ballroom at Admin, to mark twenty-five years from that amazing day.'

'Oh, yes. I remember that. Only I always thought of it as just a party invitation. And a bit of a dig at the Dysons for doubting your commitment to their daughter! But after all the accolades you achieved on the public stage, why would you choose that to be the climax of your autobiography?'

'Ah, y'know... It was all of those things too, Cath. Symbolic, in a typically pretentious kind of way. You know me. Always want to have the last word. Make a statement, as per the phrase coined by my fallen angel. The date's creepy though, don't you think? First of the first, two thousand and one? The very start of a millennium.'

Malcolm frowned. 'Never thought about that before. Who picked your wedding date?'

A shiver ran down the great man's spine. 'Lynn did. Jesus! And she said it too... A new beginning. New Year's Day's always been significant for her. The Dysons have their big, annual pow-wow on that day, and she originally chose it because her family were guaranteed to already be around. Well, I always thought that was why she chose it anyway... The whole damned command performance was arranged in less than three months. She was in one hell of a hurry!'

'She wanted to make sure you didn't change your mind!' Cathy laughed.

'No chance,' the handsome man shook his head. 'Not in a million years.'

The hairs on the back of Jeff's neck stood on end as the gradual realisation hit him, and he exhaled as tears flowed from his eyes without warning. It appeared that he was undergoing an enlightenment of his own... Had Lynn known all along? Maybe she had. His tattoo was lending no clues at this present moment, but perhaps now wasn't the time or place. He couldn't bear the thought of having to endure this living purgatory for another four years. Surely it wasn't his destiny to stick around until the turn of the century? Feeling his heart rate accelerate, the man who had been left behind was imbued with a renewed sense of purpose for the next sections of his book, suddenly anxious to obtain a better explanation for this latest kink in their ethereal plotline.

'We only realised the significance of the date our silver wedding would fall on several years later,' he continued, 'and it freaked us out. Oh one, oh one, oh one. Like time was starting again.'

'Who for though?' asked Cathy, sneaking a dubious look at her husband.

Their dinner guest shrugged. 'Never got that far. And now we'll never know. We'd planned to go to extremes, like give it all away and kick off something completely new. But we hadn't put much thought into it by the time Lynn left for greener pastures. Therefore by its nature, the book has to be somewhat anti-climactic too. The loss of great things to come.'

'Premature ejaculation,' Malcolm chuckled under his breath.

'Mal, please,' his wife moaned. 'That's in awful taste. For God's sake! I'm sorry, Jeff. My husband can be so uncouth.'

The widower pushed his chair back and stood up. He saw the funny side of the vulgar comment, but it had cut to the quick nonetheless. Excusing himself for a visit to the bathroom, he squeezed Cathy's shoulder to let her know he was not too offended, having played his part in encouraging the corny, schoolboy humour with his own *double entendres*. He walked back into the house, listening to raised voices and the agitated clattering of plates and cutlery.

'Hey, angel,' he checked if Lynn was following him. 'I'm still causing trouble. Some things never change, huh? Did you know about oh one, oh one, oh one? What does it mean? Anything? We would've talked about it. You didn't know, did you?'

Again no sensation was forthcoming, and Jeff smiled. 'I take that as a no. Thanks, angel. Shall we go home soon?'

By the time the billionnaire returned to the table, a fresh cup of coffee had been placed next to a large measure of whisky in a heavy tumbler. He grinned and toasted his hosts, before scooping two blocks of ice into the glass and swirling them around. The clear peal of high quality crystal was unmistakeable, expressly meant to reinforce an appreciation for the couple's strained hospitality.

'To climaxes, in whatever form we can get 'em!'

The Lanes simpered in gratitude and raised their glasses to the magnanimous superstar, who proceeded to lift a flame to his extinguished cigar and reinstall himself on the other side of the table. His rugged good looks and haunted expression sent Cathy's pulse racing. How she had loved this man for so long and from such close quarters, watching his wildly successful career take him from bad-boy rock star to a revered leader of worldwide stature. He seemed a little less lonely these days, she thought. More resigned to his new solitary life.

'D'you remember when I made that series of philosophy programmes?' Jeff coaxed his chief publicist from her trance.

'Oh, yes. The year before last?'

The celebrity nodded, flicking ash into the ashtray, dragging hard and letting out another long, provocative waft of smoke. 'Nietzsche and I don't agree on everything, but his idea of the best view being from the top of the mountain is what I'll aim for with the book, I think. The idea of a high point being high not least owing to the effort and hardship we endure to reach it. Does that make sense?'

The others nodded, although the billionnaire suspected that he had lost them to the lateness of the hour and to liquid spirits proofed at a high percentage. Cathy succumbed, as she inevitably did, to the super-octane sex appeal oozing from the man across the table, acknowledging with some solace that he was at last growing back into the classy yet unpretentious bespoke tailoring which had been his trademark for two decades.

'I don't agree with his view on alcohol though!' he added.

Hearing the ice crunch between her guest's teeth, she laughed. 'No, obviously!'

'A sober philosopher's got to be treated with suspicion, don't you think?'

'I suppose so,' Malcolm grinned. 'Was Nietzsche teetotal? I didn't know that.'

Jeff smiled. 'So they say. Because he was so sickly, apparently. He went up into the Swiss mountains and wrote about the evils of alcohol, but I'm not sure if he never touched it. The passage of time makes room for some hypocrisy. For fuck's sake, I'm banking on it! The thing that annoys me so much about him though was that he always complained that no-one took him seriously, but he didn't change the way he looked or behaved to improve his chances.'

'How do you know?' his loyal employee squealed like a girl. 'You say the strangest things sometimes.'

'Cheers! Kind of you to say so,' the forty-four-year-old cocked his head. 'It's well documented. It's also reported that women were repulsed by his monster moustache. So if you need to get laid, why not shave it off, Herr Nietzsche? He was surprisingly obtuse for an intelligent man. Whatever... Enough of this shit! You're tired, and I should let you get your own rocks off. What's on next week, boss?'

Sighs that could have been born out of relief or embarrassment blended with the smoke hanging in the air, causing the celebrity to smile again. A desk diary had appeared at the table on the verandah at the same time as their recent round of drinks, and Jeff recognised it as his assistant's method of keeping track of the Diamonds' movements. Despite having supervised the conversion of Stonebridge Music's office to electronic recordkeeping, Cathy still insisted on maintaining a paper version of their busy schedule. The star's private diagnosis for this uncharacteristic duplication of effort was that the physical article was kept as much as a souvenir as for any practical function.

'Yes. Sorry. Do you mind?'

The widower took the large black book out of the woman's outstretched hand and leafed through the pages until he reached the current date. A folded newspaper cutting fell out and drifted across the table on the breeze, coming to rest next to the ashtray. Jeff retrieved it and flattened the page to reveal a photograph of himself as a much younger man, alongside two columns of copy. The headline read "Free Radical", and the browned paper and old-fashioned typeface led him to date it from the early nineteen-seventies.

'Why's this in here?' he asked.

Cathy was caught unawares, feeling her face redden, and she hurriedly held her hand out for the flimsy piece of paper. 'I found it while I was sorting through some old files. Magazine articles we hung on to, you know. I like the photo'. Do you remember that being written? Just after you'd launched Childlight, I think.'

'Mate! Look how young you look!' her husband exclaimed, looking over his wife's shoulder.

'Yes, and how happy. Do you want it, Jeff?'

The billionnaire shook his head, feeling another deep tingling in his chest. 'No, thanks. You keep it. I *was* young and happy then. That was when we'd first got back together after Lynn had been in the US. Literally days after, I reckon, judging by the cocky expression on my face. That was the onset of my absolute invincibility period.'

'And you were so different from the Jeff Diamond we'd known up 'til that point,' the middle-aged office manager gave her boss an impish smile. 'The girls here in the office were quite disappointed. You went from one hundred percent sinner to almost saintly in the matter of a few weeks.'

'Sorry about that. I sure did,' the superstar chuckled. 'You're not wrong there.'

'I know I'm not!' Cathy affirmed. 'Do you remember the time Gerry let on that you had five dancers in your hotel room? The girls were shocked but they wouldn't stop talking about it either. I had to send a couple of them home because of their hysterical chatter.'

'Oh, yes? Wish I'd been there then!' Malcolm perked up. 'I've never heard that story. Tell me more.'

Seeing Jeff smirk, clearly about to indulge her lecherous husband, the publicist cut him off. 'I said you had to be careful, I seem to remember. It was right at the start of that huge tour, wasn't it? In 'seventy-three. You'd just come back from the US leg and were going straight off to Japan. Gosh, you were such a big, big star, Jeff. I just couldn't believe I was working for you and how lucky I was to be hearing all these real, live rock'n'roll stories straight from the horse's mouth.'

'Yeah,' the widower sighed, knowing he ought to play along with his host's reminiscences, even though he had no desire whatsoever to recall those awful months of desolate debauchery. 'I said Gerry should learn not to tell tales, and I told you I was tired. I remember that really clearly, for some reason.'

Cathy nodded. 'And you also said, "It's not in my nature to be careful."'

The exhausted man shook his mane of greying hair, which was cut quite a lot shorter than in those days. 'Most probably! Sounds like the sort of dumb-fuck thing I would've said back then.'

The kindly woman carried on, memories coming thick and fast. She was keen to lift Jeff's mood before he went home, with Kierney away overseas and the grieving husband returning to an empty house. With any luck, a light-hearted conversation about the good, old days would give him sufficient motivation to keep writing until the alcohol wore off or he managed to fall into some much-needed peaceful slumber.

'I said something about calling your mother too,' she continued, angling the corners of her mouth downwards, 'not knowing she was no longer alive. You really were the proverbial wild child. Oh, and I remember wondering out loud about who was going to tame you, to which you said you weren't going to be tamed by anyone. But you knew you were lying then, didn't you?'

Her employer nodded with a wry half-smile. 'Yes, I did. I was hanging out to be tamed, but I was hardly going to tell you that, was I? You were like a bloody schoolteacher sometimes. Gerry and I used to call you "Matron" behind your back!'

A hearty guffaw burst from Cathy's husband's chest. 'Good on ya, Jeff! That's priceless! I'm going to use that one.'

'On your own head be it, darling,' the stern woman couldn't help but laugh at the unbecoming term of endearment from her good-looking charge. 'You were always such a nice guy, JMD, even when you were off your face with drugs and booze. Like when I suggested you get a driver, because then you wouldn't have to worry about getting caught or having a crash...'

Malcolm left the table, taking a few empty glasses with him and still sniggering about the nickname with which this colossus of a superstar had labelled his wife. He would never understand what made Jeff Diamond so great and he certainly didn't envy his current situation, yet there remained a residual jealousy between them for the close relationship the star shared with his long-serving assistant. He could hear the two of them continuing the conversation while he trudged through to the kitchen.

'Yep, and I remember telling you, "I'm not worried. *You* are!" I have to get going soon. Thanks for dinner. It's been great catching up. And before you say it, I won't get caught tonight, just like I never got caught then, Matron.'

'OK. Yes,' she capitulated, with a brief glance over her shoulder to make sure they were alone. 'The smile on your face made me swoon then, exactly like it still does now. I loved you, Jeff. Really loved you. But we all kept our distance because you said you weren't interested in being loved.'

'Yeah. I lied about that too.'

'Oh, God,' Cathy sighed. 'You always came across as so bulletproof. No-one knew you were caving in inside. None of us did. We just thought you were making the most of your rock star privileges, and none of us wanted you to break our heart.'

The tall celebrity leaned towards his assistant's tear-streaked, smiling face and kissed her cheek. 'That's right. Also exactly like now. G'night, Cath. Thanks again, and see you on Monday.'

***

Act Two's overture was to be dark and brooding. The long exposition of Act One had been mostly joyous writing, save for the last few chapters and with the promise of significant rising action to come. Act Two would see writer and reader revelling in unbridled good cheer for the majority of its scenes, but for now Jeff was obliged to languish in those long, Lynnless days of drink, drugs, decadence and despair. With both children out of the country, the large house they were renting in the riverside suburb of Burnley South echoed with the same emptiness that resided in his heart.

Part of him wanted to omit the interminable stretch of time he had endured while counting down the months and waiting for his dream girl to return to Australia from the Californian college sentence handed down by her parents. After seven months of sublime happiness, Bart and Marianna Dyson had concocted a new plan for their elder daughter, in order to turn her attention away from the revolutionary ideas espoused by her first love, the dissident boyfriend who they were convinced was going to lead her in the opposite direction from the path they envisioned for her.

The author sighed, rolling his chair in towards the desk and waiting for the computer to boot up. It would be wholly inappropriate to skip over these lonely episodes in their life singular though, wouldn't it? After all, these represented the inaugural, auspicious steps on his own all-important path to "someoneness". Act One had concluded with his first album about to be released, with twenty songs telling the story of his journey thus far and offering scant glimpses into the bleak past of a damaged teenager who had fought for everything he had ever possessed. Act Two would see the fight transfer to saving the love of his life from a forced extinction.

The autobiography's prospective readers must not be cheated of any secrets from this formative period. Many of the instant superstar's fans had been following him from the very beginning, as the battered box of lever arch files which Cathy had recently delivered by car served to prove, stuffed full of letters, photographs and the odd piece of lacy *lingerie*. Pledges of undying love from hysterical females, numbering in their hundreds, were interspersed with a much smaller smattering of genuine admiration for electrifying stage performances and powerful music which had moved men to join his fan club too.

Now with a teenaged daughter of his own, Jeff had grudgingly come to appreciate the stance taken by Lynn's parents a little better, especially faced with the type of antics and resulting hearsay that his early years of fame had borne witness. He trusted Kierney's choice of partner implicitly these days, as he watched her heading towards legal majority and becoming more focussed on a promising career as a human rights lawyer. However, it hadn't always been so. He had spent many nights fretting over her whereabouts and wondering who had their hands on her beautiful and blossoming body;

understanding all too well how hard it must have been for his parents-in-law to see their naïve, blonde Melbourne Academy student misappropriated by a loudmouthed and arrogant non-entity from Sydney's west.

Yet even in the doting dad's most apprehensive moments, while waiting for their gorgeous gipsy girl to return home from a night out in the city or having agreed to camping weekends in Ocean Grove, his patient wife had continually reminded him that he was only being protective, and not controlling, as her own father had been during that time.

It was actually fortunate that Kierney was away when the author pieced together this part in her parents' history. The seventeen-year-old was hungry for information about the years before she and her brother had come into existence, and had asked reams of questions while reviewing the chapters that constituted the opening act. What was it like to meet a soul-mate? How did he feel when he found out he was the first man to touch Lynn Dyson? Why had he agreed not to contact her after she left for America? Had he believed they would get back together eventually?

'No, angel,' Jeff pointed out to Lynn now, just as he had to his persistent daughter. 'I didn't really believe we would. I wanted to. More than anything. But I didn't expect I'd ever see you again. In those first few months, flying around the world, shooting up on a regular basis and swallowing all manner of grog like it was going out of fashion… There was a time when I convinced myself you'd never want to talk to me ever again.'

Jesus! It certainly was going to be painful to resurrect those memories and admit to recognising the deeply flawed personality he would assume in the process of becoming rich and famous. Nevertheless, the diligent scribe couldn't shy away from providing an honest and complete account of how stardom had befallen him and how he had somehow managed to escape alive and more-or-less intact to arrive on the other side. He groaned aloud. Was there no end to the parallels to be drawn with his present circumstance?

Enough feeling sorry for himself… There was work to be done. Jeff lit another cigarette and twisted the stopper out of a half-empty bottle of *Rioja* that had been left sitting on the desk before he went out to dinner. Where to start? How about the panic attack during his first trip on the New York subway, watching people hanging from the handrails, swinging from side to side like carcasses in a butcher's cold store? That had been a wake-up call, no doubt about it! The momentary shock to the system had made him realise in no uncertain terms what a difficult transition this new era was destined to be: the way the past would interfere with the present wherever he went, his overactive and tormented mind poisoned still further by illicit substances and a dearth of sleep.

Even now, in nineteen-ninety-seven and as a stable, middle-aged man, the storyteller's blood pressure immediately dished out a dizzy spell as he remembered the flashbacks he had suffered in the packed train carriage; those of his mother hooking her toddler son onto the straps which hung from the ceilings of Sydney trains and leaving him to dangle his three-year-old feet a metre off the ground.

The twenty-year-old, novice rock star had clearly visualised, much like his older self could now, this cruel, spaced-out woman who had given him life but not much more cackling as he shouted to be let down. After several minutes of having his cries for help ignored, surrounded by gaping passengers, the boy had ended up letting go and crashing to the floor. He also remembered a kindly, old man beckoning to give him a cuddle, from which he could have benefitted equally at forty-four and at twenty as well. He still heard his mother's screeching voice calling the compassionate gentleman every name under the sun, and could feel his skin repelling her frenzied fingernails when she had snatched her confused son against her legs.

'That old bloke probably wanted to take me home,' the lost boy whispered to Lynn's ghost. 'I know I was willing him to. He knew he couldn't, I guess, and I only cottoned on to that much later. I hated him for years for not taking me with him. I often used to look back and wish I'd pulled him up out of his bloody seat and off the train at the next stop. He would've been arrested for kidnapping. Shit! What you don't know as a little kid, huh?'

In the quiet luxury of his current environment, Jeff put his head in his hands, desperately trying to rid his mind of the hallucinations. One of Lynn's most famous anthems had already begun to play in his ears, helping him on his way. Somehow she always knew when he needed a kick along, and this time was no exception. He was becoming stronger, no doubt.

'OK. You're right,' he shook his head in dismay, rifling through a pile of papers until he found what he was looking for. 'Leave it behind, I know. I found that quote, angel. The one I was going to start with...'

The ancient soul had long been an authority on French literature, once leading his wife to wonder whether her mystery man had spent time in Paris during the eighteenth or nineteenth century. Such was his affinity with the characters and events from that time that he found himself able to spout forth quotations galore without effort. However, before he could commit any excerpts to the pages of their autobiography, he insisted on verifying their accuracy with the original texts.

'*Alors... Ecoute-moi,* angel,' he coughed, his heart steadied by Lynn's smiling, ever-attentive face staring back at him from the photograph on the desk. '"What is reported of men, whether it be true or false, may play as large a part in their lives, and above all in their destiny, as the things they do." That was the one. I think I pretty much had it right, but that's it, *mot à mot*. Pretty apt, as it turned out.'

As he typed the sentence into the computer, Jeff couldn't help but laugh. Quite apart from the misinterpreted notoriety which triggered the *omega* of the Diamonds' long run in paradise, on countless occasions throughout his long career in the public spotlight he had been forced to restate his case, saying he was as often misquoted as quoted. And therefore misunderstood. Interviewers and news hacks hadn't quite known what to make of him when he first burst onto the rock music scene in October of nineteen-seventy-two. A musician who had plenty to say about the world, as many others before him and after him, yet far more eloquently than most.

'I found another one too, baby,' he continued, feeling his tattoo itch again. 'Another Victor Hugo. "*Monsieur*, you are looking at a plain man, and I am looking at a great man. Each of us may benefit." I wish I'd had that in my arsenal when talking to your dad. You're probably glad I didn't though, I s'pose.'

Lynn and her charismatic first love had been given no alternative but to break up by her parents, who had forged a road to greatness for her on the tennis court and in Hollywood. They enrolled her into a sports program at a prestigious Los Angeles university, and the couple had been issued a total embargo on contact during this period. Hence, after a tortuous goodbye which had lasted for several weeks, Jeff had been left to his own devices in Melbourne while his beautiful best friend was off making movies and winning Olympic medals. And to his own vices, as it turned out.

It had taken every last ounce of strength for the scarred twenty-year-old to pick up the pieces and turn himself towards his own rock music goals, having grown dependent on everything that his relationship with Australia's favourite schoolgirl had given him. With the help of a youthful but no less esteemed Gerry Blake, who had reluctantly agreed to be his manager, the smouldering, dark-haired singer-songwriter had rocketed to stardom within a matter of months, and along with this newfound fame came a plethora of adult adventures and an outrageous lifestyle which allowed him to seek refuge in the dark underworld of drugs, alcohol and orgies.

But how had Lynn fared during this two-year separation? Their combined life story needed to be balanced not only to include his own hard luck tales. While documenting Act One of their autobiography, Jeff had delved deep into his wife's diaries and unearthed the young woman's most intimate thoughts and souvenirs of her foray into their all-consuming affair, discovering a number of untold secrets. Following the same course for Act Two would necessarily contain many more harrowing revelations for the forty-four-year-old widower, since he feared she may have adjusted far better to their fate than he had.

And at least from an outside viewpoint, Lynn Dyson had taken America by storm. Appearing on television almost weekly, recording hit after hit and starring in blockbuster movies soon became her new kind of normal. That much her husband had found out over the years, being treated to insights long overdue once they had reunited and snubbed their noses at stuffy Australian society. Jeff Diamond had become a respected powerhouse of national pride during those same months, being credited with status and public adoration only rivalled by the fondness the country had always held for its returning handmaiden.

Against all precedents, the hottest celebrity property to have emerged from the southern hemisphere in the early nineteen-seventies had not been a sun-kissed, blond stereotype, as personified by the Dyson family. A boy of recent immigrant stock from Sydney's run-down western suburbs had climbed to the top of the pedestal and had taken up residence in the nation's psyche, by dint of a slew of well-chosen words on subjects dear to the average person's heart. He had gladly assumed the mantel of cult hero in a country which heretofore had hardly been an incubator for dissidents and rebels worthy of export onto the world stage. Like Clive James, Robert Hughes and Germaine Greer a decade earlier, Jeff Diamond was doing his bit to put the huge continent with the tiny, predominately white population on the map of cultural coolness and awaken its social conscience.

Yet as much as the surviving writer of an autobiography destined to be snapped up by millions around the world ought to speak of the successes which the couple's fans yearned to revisit, "A Life Singular" must also set out the many personal challenges endured by its subjects for all to see; for no other purpose than to serve as counterpoint for the acclaim and affluence best remembered by followers and sceptics alike.

'Two sides to every story,' Jeff murmured. 'At least. D'you remember when you asked me why I didn't publish "The Runner" under a different name, angel? To separate it from the music?'

There was no reply. The bereft husband lit another cigarette and walked over to the window, looking out over the lawn. 'It wasn't separate from the music. I told you that everything came from the same source, and you answered with something incredibly profound. Remember that, baby?'

The image of Lynn's radiant face filled his mind again, bringing a smile to his lips and tears to his eyes. 'Thank you. You said, "You're so fiercely honest." "Not honestly fierce?" I joked back, and you shot me a scolding look, like I'd insulted your intelligence. Then you said, "No. I mean fierce, as in proud. You know... *Fier*."'

The great man leaned both hands against the glass and bowed his head until the heat in his forehead met the chill of the windowpane. The benevolent lion to which his wife had once likened him in a letter from the dead was tonight unable to summon his patented noble roar. Lynn had understood the strain of a virtuous pride born from humility, and they had both pursued its quest over their entire, momentous journey. The inked muscle on his chest gave another short twinge, causing him to gasp at its strange, optimistic pain. The other half of their famed pantomime lion was telling him to get moving. Time was closing in, and she was as impatient as he was to chronicle their phenomenal alliance.

'I liked that idea then and I still like it now. It's what Act Two's theme is, I reckon. Fierce honesty, and bugger the consequences. By the time we got to the end of Act Two, I'd gone from the plain man to the great man, and I only have you to thank for that. *Celui-là, tout le monde le saura, Lynn.* It will be reported.'

***

At six o'clock in the morning on the fourth of November nineteen-seventy-two, Jeff Diamond embarked upon his first overseas promotional tour. A car was booked to pick him up at eight and take him to Tullamarine Airport, and his passport was ready for its first real workout. He felt particularly worse for wear, like a real rock star in fact, but for very non-rock-starrish reasons. The previous night had seen him finish the rest of the year's university assignments which would fall due while he was away. He had tried to steal some sleep early, before midnight, but had awoken violently less than an hour later. Dragging himself round the streets for his last run on Australian soil for a few weeks, his brain finally kicked into some positive momentum.

It was now nearly two months since Lynn Dyson had left for California. The first four weeks or so had settled into a bearable sort of half-life. Memories of their tearful farewell remained fresh and raw in his mind, and the student was determined to do as much as he could to push the next two years past quickly. However, as the long nights stretched into the second month, he found himself descending into the same dark places he had visited in his mid-teens.

The old adage was definitely true: the higher you climb, the harder you fall. Jeff's lifestyle regressed to the same state of depravity that he had known from before he moved to Melbourne, although suddenly on a much bigger and more destructive scale. Back then, he used to crave any vice he could lay his hands on, relying on friends or using the little money he could spare from part-time jobs and running errands for local businessmen and minor neighbourhood villains. These days however, since he had slammed his tired body into the big-time, and with the success of his first few records, people already lined his path with temptations of every description, and he willingly succumbed to them all with a familiar, jaded desperation.

Sobering up under a cold shower and squeezing the very last drops from a shampoo bottle, the twenty-year-old cursed his ludicrous situation. He had kept himself together fairly successfully during the months he and Lynn had passed off their relationship as something close to normal, but as soon as their irregular dates and secret *rendezvous* had dwindled out of his calendar, so had the accompanying range of wholesome activities which sustained life, such as shopping, eating and laundry. All vestiges of organisation now seemed pointless, and fortunately for the new star in the making, apparently they no longer mattered.

Fear of losing control gripped him without warning, and Jeff lost his balance and fell against the tiled bathroom wall. What was he doing? Was he ready to start jetting all over the globe? He whose sole adventure up to this point had been a weekend in New Zealand? For as long as he remembered, he had yearned to travel the world and see for himself all the wondrous sights about which he had only read or heard second-hand after friends' holidays. He and Gerry had recently been briefed by record company officials as to the requisite security measures and round-the-clock schedules while on tour, drilling into the young man that this was his career to win or lose.

These perfectly reasonable words of caution were received with authentic civility at the time. Later however, the two friends had shared a laugh at the forthright tone of their messengers and pondered how often the well-meaning lecture must fall on deaf ears, judging by the reputations of established stars of the Swinging 'Sixties. It was intriguing to imagine The Rolling Stones and The Who sitting through similar sermons! Perhaps publicity companies had learned a few costly lessons in dealing with these pioneer rock'n'roll bands, the pair concluded. A far cry from MAC's innocent touring stories which Lynn had shared with her former boyfriend, as high school students chaperoned wherever they went and surrounded by clean-living role models.

Would these very sensible pieces of advice still hold as much weight once the manic traveller was out of the country, no longer sober and seeking comfort in the company of nameless females? Or when he was caught prostrate and pouring with sweat in the middle of the night, haunted by nightmares and desperate for distractions? The new star pictured himself being rushed from place to place, weary and hyped-up; a truly lethal combination. Fraying at the edges, as his dream girl had once alleged.

Christ Almighty! Lynn had understood him so amazingly well. He would never know how or why, Jeff guessed, but was thankful for the brief flash of love they had shared. In his more lucid moments, he managed to let go of the obsession with maintaining some sort of telepathic connection across the miles. She was not his saviour, his lighthouse or his angel. She was a talented teenager destined for great things who had been tempted by his charms temporarily. If her parents hadn't seen fit to split them up, it may not have been long before she had lost interest in his attention and idealism and grown tired of the incessant mood swings, addictions and disturbing patterns of behaviour. She was his dream girl again, pure and simple. That would have to be enough to see him through.

The spring morning air was cool as it slithered in through the draughty Richmond bathroom window. Jeff had showered the night's dark clouds from his head as best he could. His daylight self was genuinely looking forward to the next episode of his early career, intent on putting Lynn to the back of his mind and enjoying all the amazing opportunities that this wondrous, new life was throwing at him.

Since his first single had been released in September, the newcomer's rise to stardom had been nothing short of meteoric. Despite all the times he had heard artists decry the term "overnight success", having spent years plying their trade in local pubs and clubs before being scouted by a roving agent, his first album had four singles lined up, two of which went to Number One in many countries almost as soon as they were allocated air time. What was more, on top of popular adulation, critical acclaim abounded.

The new sensation's record company immediately put him on the road in Australia, delighted that their good-looking discovery could talk as well as sing. First up, he had played three sold-out nights at the Festival Hall in West Melbourne, with a band quickly assembled from session musicians and friends of friends. These were followed by similar excitement in Adelaide, and then the other east coast centres of Sydney and Brisbane. Fans flew in from Australia's more remote state and territory towns and also from New Zealand, such was the star's instant appeal, prompting the executives to squeeze in a few nights in Auckland and Wellington too.

By mid-November, the second album would already be pressed and scheduled to hit the shops for the Christmas rush. Jeff Diamond became the proverbial "talk of the town" before he had really had time to think about it, and he chastised himself mercilessly for feeling so low, knowing how lucky he was. Whether by chance or not, he had risen far above Sydney's poorer suburbs and the poverty-stricken, crime-ridden community in the midst of which he had brought himself up. He now had a regular stream of money flowing in from royalties and television appearance fees, not to mention offers to act in films or collaborate with other well-known songwriters.

His old friend did a sterling job of handling the sudden star's growing financial stockpiles, and the twenty-year-old was already in a position to buy a city apartment outright. They had also set up a company called Paragon Holdings, aimed at providing seed capital for any new business ventures that happened to take their fancy. This was one of the most satisfying aspects of Jeff's newfound investor status, since he loved sharing ideas with innovative people who, like himself, had a vision for a better future.

The two ambitious mates had opted for this deliberately arrogant and tongue-in-cheek name after rather too many whiskies and with more than a passing gibe at his former girlfriend's father. "Paragon: an outstanding example," the Macquarie Dictionary revealed, after they had spent a few hours playing with various nouns of power and substance. The Dysons would soon see exactly what sort of a man Jeff Diamond was, with a social justice shopping list commensurate with the level of income he was generating of late.

Another few months and the Aston Martin would also be within reach, and Jeff had begun closely monitoring the design plans of the British car company. The nineteen-seventy-three model of the V8 was planned as "Series 3", a twin carburettor machine. His advisers had steered him away from an impulsive "Series 2" purchase because the factory had capped production at less than three hundred cars, thereby signalling it to be a comparative disaster. The musician was convinced to wait with negligible impact, given the modest amount of time he would be in Melbourne to drive it over the next year or so.

Accountant and client sat for hours over cash-flow projections and investment strategies, the numbers composed of so many digits that the younger man frequently lost sight of the fact that the money actually belonged to him. He had laid down strict ground rules for his new manager very early; one: fifty percent of all earnings after tax and expenses were to go to a variety of not-for-profit organisations; two: each year Gerry was to calculate a suitable pension amount in case the new chart-topper's popularity dried up the following year; and three: none of the many new family members and long-lost friends whom he had suddenly gained was to receive anything, save in exceptional circumstances. Those circumstances were to be decided by Gerry in an objective and independent capacity, chiefly because Jeff didn't trust his guilty conscience not to give in.

Between Blake & Partners, his record company and the music publishers, a whole army of people were now at the photogenic celebrity's beck and call: a clothes stylist, hairdresser, personal shoppers, footwear consultants, image makers, a producer-arranger, musical instrument maintenance people, fan mail readers and answerers, someone whose sole purpose was to RSVP to party invitations... The list was endless, and he eagerly lapped up any new tips and tricks that came his way. Jeff Diamond, the stray Catholic Argentinean Polish Jew, had turned into a marketer's dream, and the offices were soon besieged by salespeople left, right and centre, all trying to sell him the biggest and brightest of everything.

The university student's first purchases in this deluge of wealth consisted of a washing machine and two televisions. His infrequent trips to the local launderette after appearing on prime-time had become fraught with danger, regularly accosted by curious patrons perving on his clothes. It was a peculiar invasion of privacy that went far beyond the day-to-day whispers, nods and shouts from passers-by to which he had grown accustomed upon meeting Lynn. The televisions were for the sleepless nights in his flat; one for the lounge room, to fill the space that had been vacant since he moved in, and the second for the bedroom, to hypnotise his mind into relaxing sufficiently after each nightmare to return to sleep until the next one.

Performing on stage and in television studios hadn't fazed Jeff at all. In fact, it came as a surprise to everyone, including the man himself, how naturally the cap fit. But it shouldn't have been a surprise. He had performed in front of Lynn, and nothing could ever make him more nervous than that first evening in the ballroom in the Dyson Administration building. As it soon became apparent, the newcomer's stage presence was electrifying. Men and women alike clamoured for concert tickets, and some of Australia's most reputable musicians had competed to audition for his first international tour.

And the girls... There were so many girls! Women of all ages, in fact. As if the handsome man's "sexual mercenary" moniker had ever been justly deserved, roles were certainly now reversed. His services off-stage were every bit as popular as his crowded dance-card of public engagements. Wherever Jeff went, they screamed and mobbed him for autographs or simply to touch him, and as soon as this new kid on the block was spotted with a woman at a nightclub or restaurant, the following day's newspapers would be splattered with all sorts of make-believe nonsense which he and Gerry found highly amusing. These flamboyant antics often led him into considerable hot water though, and his bemused business manager began to set aside a serious provision for legal fees.

So why, with everything going so well for him and no end in sight, did Jeff still feel so wretched? It was perilous for him to slow the pace, because immediately he took his foot off the gas, his mind would plunge into the depths of despair. He kept on running away from himself as fast as possible, knowing full well that at some point he would need to rest. There was no way to keep up such a frenetic pace indefinitely or he would burn out, so the tortured soul forced himself to suffer the consequences of a night every so often when he fought with and very nearly gave in to his suicidal tendencies.

The songwriter's intensely personal lyrics and evocative melodies spoke to his fans of anguish and loneliness, yet somehow the songs took on a surreal distance during concerts. He often found himself on the verge of breaking down on stage, only managing to save the situation with humour or by looking into the crowd and finding an attractive female face on which to focus. As the musician's confidence grew in his ability to perform songs inspired by Lynn, he agreed to include material that until then only they, or indeed only he, had heard.

Not long before this decision, "Donna Jade" had been released. Jeff hadn't wanted to launch this track as a single, but his record company was convinced that it had an enormous hit on its hands. The musician had warned his team of the likely consequences, and sure enough, within a few days of the song's radio *début*, the face of his ex-girlfriend, Donna Watts, was plastered all over the media. Always one to steal any available limelight, the minor celebrity television reporter went public with their brief relationship from when the newsworthy singer-songwriter had just turned sixteen. The woman after whom the track was named had been nearly thirty years old at the time, and the public latched onto the story with keen interest. What made it worse for Jeff was that he had initially dismissed the name of the song as merely a good cadence.

This had been the first time the magnetic star's fans had turned cool, prompted by the stories Donna spread about his unfaithfulness and lack of respect for her feelings. He knew there was no point in trying to defend his teenaged self, because on the face of it, most of her complaints were absolutely true. Luckily however, both the press and his fans possessed short memories for bad news about their idol, and the damning indictments on Jeff's character soon faded. The spurned woman ended up dropping her case in exchange for a percentage of the song's proceeds, and her former lover secured a gagging order through the courts, thanks to Gerry's gun lawyer.

So today, on this warm November morning and with the limousine driver waiting down in the street, Jeff steeled himself for yet another first day of the rest of his tumultuous life. By the time the airport terminal buildings came into view, a mindless conversation with the driver had turned the morning's depression into a dull overlay on top of a positive and excited outlook. He barely remembered how he had felt that morning, once the aeroplane took off for New York and the breakfast beers began to slip down nicely. The restored, re-energised and re-anaesthetised Mister Life-and-Soul was back.

Glamorous flight attendants jostled each other to secure gossip about the musician's tour plans and other snippets of personal information. Where was he going? Who would he be seeing? And when might he be flying with the airline again? The red-blooded artist lapped up their friendliness eagerly, feeding his fantasies with visions of how far they might be persuaded to go for their apparently delectable new customer.

The twittering young ladies also wanted to know why the star was flying in the rear section of the aeroplane instead of in First Class, which was another ground rule he had been at pains to hammer home to his travel agent.

'I'm a cheapskate,' he admitted. 'It's a waste of money, and the beer tastes the same from any seat.'

Transiting through Los Angeles on his way across the huge North American continent, Jeff allowed his fantasies to wander to the well-known Australian beauty currently in residence. The pair was physically closer than they had been for two months; so close that he could almost feel her presence in the cold anonymity of the airport. He felt foolish scanning every single face in the halls and corridors, just in case she also happened to be flying somewhere on this very day, but he couldn't help himself. No gratuitous allocation of painted smiles or straining uniforms would ever compensate for the ache inside.

What if the traveller were to break his promise, defy the Dyson family and go in search of his dream girl? She wouldn't be too hard to find, once he had managed to sweet-talk the office staff at UCLA. Would Lynn be pleased to see him or angry that he had contacted her? Both, the decent man imagined, so he changed his mind. He was a man of his word. But for Christ's sake, it was so painful to consider the missed opportunity.

By the time Lynn Dyson's first lover climbed the steps up onto his connecting flight to New York, the sun was already setting over the west coast city, and with it the beam of his metaphorical lighthouse swept away from the heartbroken man. He sat down heavily in his seat with his waiting complimentary glass of champagne and forced himself to concentrate on the many happy conversations he and the blonde songstress had shared, when she would answer his never-ending questions about this trendy entertainment industry hub to the best of her sixteen-year-old ability. She had always assured him that he would know for himself before too long. She had been right, and yet setting foot in America without her had predictably failed to live up to the great expectations of those precious and fervent discussions.

How the tired man longed for those slow, sensuous, breath-filled kisses he had perfected with his beautiful best friend, which had spoken of love over lust and with a taste of passion beyond the sexual. A shudder ran through his body at the memory of Lynn's angelic blue eyes harbouring so many sinful pleasures. He pictured them opening on the verge of orgasm, only to close again once the sensation overtook her. How many more bleeding hearts would she leave behind before he saw her again? Or might he soon read in the newspapers that she had found a connection even more arresting with someone else?

The prospect of spending his entire US tour in such a state of desolation was neither appealing nor constructive. This was far too special an experience to squander. He was hot property these days; the man of the moment. Wasn't it every man's dream to have an endless flow of nubile companions hanging on his every word? He needed to snap out of morose melancholy and be grateful for this enviable position for which most men would give their eye teeth.

There had to be a way of kicking the Lynn Dyson habit, or at least dulling it to a point where the feel of her soft, warm skin ceased to linger on his lips day in and day out. Something to replace the hankering for her tight grip around his biceps, her desperate words of encouragement no longer hauling him out of a nightmare. These memories had to go too. Neat Scotch whisky warmed the inebriated poet's lungs and filled them with an amber light; a beacon calling love back. It didn't come. He hadn't expected it to. Only hoped.

Jeff hypnotised himself by staring endlessly at clouds being swallowed by the jet engines and cursed the depth of his feelings. Why couldn't he take a leaf out of Gerry's book, never becoming attached to anyone? The fun-loving Irishman only took two things seriously: work and sport. Indeed, the younger man had been much the same until Lynn had come into his life; seldom thinking twice about a woman once their hard-core encounter came to an end. These days however, for the duration of each inconsequential affair, memories of sweet and sensuous lovemaking would run rampant in the cultured Australian Romeo's head, riding on a stranger's touch and listening to someone else's rapture, before releasing the sluice gates of emotion as soon as he retreated to the solitude of his hotel room.

The upside to this inner turmoil, of course, was that new songs coalesced through him faster than ever, and the performer's stage shows became raunchier and less inhibited as he perfected his beguiling art form. The Jeff Diamond brand became synonymous with superb showmanship. His concerts were more than a dynamic set of hits played loud to crazed audiences. Whether rocking with a guitar slung across his body or screaming into a microphone, the Pied Piper had them laughing, crying, gasping and swooning on command, and *impresarios* from Tinseltown to The Big Apple stormed the office of Stonebridge Music's US representatives to book his time. He played by their rules, did as he was told and set about studying his new industry meticulously. He was keen to develop the skills and contacts that would enable him to strike for showbusiness self-determination, having learned the ropes from the best.

The price tag on the new star's time was increasing exponentially too. His face was in demand on camera and in magazines, and fans of all types and ages gorged themselves on his music. To think he had feared being overambitious by ordering a pressing of fifty thousand units for his first single! This quantity regularly sold in a twenty-four-hour period in the USA during October. What would Marianna Dyson think of him now?

Wallowing must be kept to a minimum from now on, the philosophical student decided. Once he landed in New York, his feet would barely touch the ground for a month. There would be little time to think about feeling lonely and wronged. Nothing vital had been taken from him, had it? He was neither the first nor the last person to suffer a broken heart, and he was physically fit and sufficiently in control of his faculties. Just a quick tune of the heart strings, and he would be fine.

The sight of Manhattan Island from the dusky sky was absolutely incredible. Jeff took a moment to reflect on the possibility of a different genetic manifestation of himself being born in this city, had his grandparents and father not left their first port of refuge after World War II for Australia. The well-read student was familiar with the striking skyline from pictures at which he had marvelled as a child. He fancied New York to become a second home, if this fantastic, new career of his continued to soar, looking forward to finally being able to visit such iconic sites as Washington Square and the State Library, and soaking up the essence of knowledge and innovative spirits which must surely hang in the air around Cornell and NYU.

The rapacious musician could hardly wait to be granted a batch of free hours to wander the famous streets and breathe the same air that filled the lungs of so many personages of influence and notoriety. He arrived for an appointment with his US publisher in the Brill Building and spent a good hour scanning the walls of gold discs, photographs and memorabilia in the corridors and offices.

Poking his head into an empty writer's room, the boy from Canley Vale sat at the piano for a few moments and stared out of the window while his fingers toyed with a brand new melody which had obviously been anticipating his arrival. Yet another in a long list of childhood dreams to come true.

As a supplement to these experiences, the modest twenty-year-old struggled to come to terms with the level of interest everyone was taking in his growing popularity. He found it disconcerting at first and would often steer the conversation away from himself. However, this aspect of his naïvety soon left him too. This was *his* promotional tour after all, and therefore it was better than good that people in this important city were engaged. He was here to sell Jeff Diamond, so he did what Jeff Diamond did best: charmed the pants off every last one of them. The many years spent analysing people's responses to his actions had turned the young man into a fine spin doctor, and the wordsmith soon had the Americans eating out of his hand.

Every journalist tried to seek out the story behind the songs, caught up in the expressive lyrics which unlocked the imagination of even the hardest heart. They would ask the typical questions about personalised content, and Jeff would describe his material as mostly "scenariographical". No-one had a clue what he meant by this, but his replies to each sycophantic interviewer were accepted without further interrogation as long words spoken by a charismatic foreigner with a strange accent, in which case they had to be right! Their blank looks and overt fawning left the clever songwriter smiling on the other side of his face.

Walking past a newsstand on his third night in The Big Apple, the Sydneysider flashed a double-take while glancing at the magazine rack. There was his headshot on the cover of this month's edition of "Rolling Stone". *Howzat!* He remembered the issue was imminent, but it was nonetheless a big deal to actually see copies for sale. His initial impulse was to buy twenty to send to everyone at home down-under, but such a childish act would have been decidedly uncool. Cringing at his own duplicity, he resolved to ask his publicist to complete this task for him the following day...

One kiosk attendant recognised the good-looking star as he walked by, hollering after him in true New York fashion. Flattered by the man's exuberance, Jeff posed for a photograph with the magazine and its seller, and provided him with an autograph to boot. The lessons he had learned while observing his beautiful best friend's generosity towards her fans now stood him in excellent stead while interacting with his own.

That night, the "flavor of the month" performed live on the Johnny Carson Show, overtired from jet-lag and loaded up on caffeine and a few other residual substances. The seasoned *compère* made reference to the fact that another Antipodean native by the name of Lynn Dyson had appeared on his show just a few weeks prior to promote her forthcoming movie. Giving nothing away, the newcomer's only reaction was to say that everyone loved Lynn in Australia, which of course was perfectly true. He then went on to perform a string of his recent hits to the noisy studio audience, who went wild with applause and chanted his name until the closing credits rolled.

Jeff requested that the limousine driver allow him to walk the last few blocks back to his hotel after the late-night show. He had no intention of going to bed in the city that never slept. Wasn't he the man who never slept? Feeling completely at ease on the streets, he must have taken every turn at least once in SoHo and Greenwich Village, attempting to list all the songs to have been written behind each door and at the top of each staircase over the last fifty years. Downtown Manhattan was an inspiring place, full of every kind of person, vehicle, noise and smell he could imagine.

Feeling tired and sentimental at the end of a very long day, the famous loner allowed himself to wonder whether his dream girl might also have set eyes on this month's copy of "Rolling Stone". What would she make of his success? If he were permitted, he would certainly give her much of the credit, since it had been she and her friends who had taught him about recording, and he had honed his performing talent from watching their televised concerts. Yet he was also content that his success had not come off the back of Lynn's fame, safe in the knowledge that she would never wish to take anything away from her former boyfriend's achievements.

The following morning's reviews raved about the latest raw yet sophisticated talent to win admiration from the American public. "The Australian Elvis", Jeff had read reluctantly. No, he resolved. He would refute this epithet publicly. He was too much of a Presley fan to accept such an accolade at this early stage, he announced to the waiting press, stopping short of adding "if ever..." Quietly, he thought back to his casual dismissal of Lynn's idea that he might send his compositions to the man himself. Funny how much more likely a scenario this had become, less than a year after the wild idea had been floated.

Was he already so different from the computer science student who had chased Lynn Dyson down the corridor to ask her out? Or, cast into the limelight at the piano in the grand ballroom which already seemed far less enormous and almost provincial, had the nervous songwriter simply been unusually self-effacing on that wonderful evening?

***

With applause still ringing in his ears, security men dressed from head to toe in black hustled Jeff Diamond and his four band members down the steps at the side of the stage, along a corridor lit with bright fluorescent tubes and finally into a series of dressing rooms. They had flown to San Francisco, after another brief stopover in Los Angeles, to perform his final sell-out concert on American soil.

Ripping off his sweat-drenched shirt and slumping down onto a chair, the exhausted but elated superstar stared at his own face in the mirror and marvelled at how his life had changed in the space of a few, very rapid-fire weeks. He slid his hand into his toiletry bag, freeing the lid on the compartment at the bottom, and pulled out a small bag of pre-mixed tobacco and cannabis. Echoing through the bowels of the stark concert hall were the bizarre, ear-splitting sounds of women screaming and men's raised voices, the latter presumably trying to keep order in the ranks of the former. The similarity of these noises with those of his nocturnal torturers would wreak havoc with his nerves after every gig. He spread a generous amount of leaves onto some papers, rolled them up and lit one, and within a minute or so, having stashed away the remaining joints, he drifted into a pleasant distraction as the drug hit his brain.

Australia's newest export, who was still breathing hard after well over two hours of exertion, cracked the top off yet another bottle of beer just as the door opened behind him. Stealthily, he secreted the joint on the edge of the Formica table top, hidden among items of clothing. A burly guard hurried to admit the star's manager along with his two flabbergasted sisters, who had been overjoyed to receive an invitation for a quick trip to the West Coast to see their old friend in action.

'Is it OK if I let Jack and Tammy in?' Gerry asked, gazing at the ripped carton in a crate of watery ice, wherein only five bottles remained. 'Have you drunk all those already? You should take it easy, mate.'

'Yeah, I know. Thanks. Sure, come on in. Fucking crazy, isn't it? Grab a beer, sit down and watch me strip, ladies.'

The visitors' brother let out a caustic laugh, helping himself to three bottles and passing two of them across to the awestruck women. His sisters would not be offended at the arrogant remark. They had known Jeff Diamond far too long for this to be an issue. He pointed at the door, referring to the hubbub still rumbling and fizzing on the other side.

'All that's for you, mate. It's totally manic out there. You've got to front up to the press in a minute. Are you ready, or do you want us to get out for a while?'

'My God, Jeff! All those women out there!' Jacinta interjected in a frenzied screech, fanning herself with her programme. 'You were absolutely amazing, by the way. I can't believe it was you up there. Our Jeff. Wow! How does it feel?'

The performer nodded and slugged back some more beer, suddenly remembering the half-smoked spliff which was probably burning the table by now. 'Great! Cheers, guys. Tonight was a good one. Did you enjoy it? Chuck me that black shirt, Tam, please?'

Gerry's younger sister reached behind her to lift a folded shirt from a suitcase and pass it to the half-naked man in their midst. Her eyes were ready to pop out of their sockets, scanning from his lithe, hairy torso to the day's dark stubble on his chin, and finally to the long waves of black hair which fell in unruly, damp curls beyond his shoulders. Jeff offered the joint around, winking his thanks, and the bottle almost slipped out of her hand as she gladly accepted.

'Shit!' Tamilla cursed. 'Jeez, Jeff, you were amazing. Thanks for making Gerry your agent. We had the best seats. They're crazy, your fans! Completely mental. And almost breaking down the door when we got here. How the hell are you going to get out?'

Jeff leaned forward in his chair, first to Jacinta and then to her younger sibling, giving them both kisses. Both women swooned, making no effort to hide their attraction to the dark, smouldering musician who had turned them on from afar with the beat of his rhythm guitar, his deep voice and the gyrations which perambulated him nimbly from one side of the stage to the other.

Gerry looked on, as if a penny had just dropped. 'You've slept with both my sisters, haven't you, you scumbag?'

His friend cocked his head. 'How long have you known?'

The accountant scowled, unable to maintain a straight face, while the women looked from each other to the men in a moment of tipsy awkwardness. It had taken quite an effort to hide their irregular trysts with their brother's handsome best friend, and Jeff had been sworn to secrecy that neither Gerry nor their parents should ever find out. As far as they knew, the older generation remained none the wiser, and that was for the best for all concerned!

'Forever, mate. You're such an animal. I'd be an idiot not to get that you couldn't spend a whole night at our house without taking advantage of the local merchandise. Just tried to put it out of my head, I guess. Are you ready for the journoes?'

Shirt buttoned to halfway, hair somewhat tamed by a quick comb, and yet another stubby emptied in less than five seconds, Jeff Diamond was about as presentable as he was going to get. Jacinta saw him pop a tiny white pill into his mouth, along with four paracetamol tablets, all washed down with another large glug of beer. Giving him a scolding look, the woman received a sly wink but no further explanation. Their sinful *compadre* was saved by a knock at the door, accompanied by a shrill cry shouting a five-minute warning for the press briefing.

'Jesus! "Merchandise" is a tad degrading, mate. These are your sisters, remember? Jack and Tammy are here to protect me from them out there,' the lothario instantly redeemed himself, raising his arm chivalrously to allow the excessively preened and primped young ladies to exit ahead of him. 'Let's get this over with.'

His manager encouraged everyone out of the room after another loud rap on the door, herding his errant flock. They made their way down the narrow passageway until they reached the source of the commotion. The songwriter shouted to his drummer, Martyn Bailey, who was a few paces behind them, then hung back until they could all walk into the hungry pack of wolves together.

The media conference was a long, drawn out affair. The new celebrity was becoming accustomed to the types of questions he was likely to face, which were duly drilled at him and Gerry like a barrage of machine gun fire. Only ten-word answers were required, and this suited him perfectly. Elaborating on his private life seemed both unnecessary and distasteful, beyond the platitudes which sold newspapers and magazines.

Midway through the quick-fire question and answer session, having watched their sexy intellectual run rings around television reporters and newspaper journalists alike, Gerry ushered his siblings out to a waiting Towncar. The women were wild with excitement, again unable to quite believe that the skinny boy their brother had befriended at a school sports camp had suddenly turned into a superstar. Clearly revitalised by the cocktail of stimulants he had ingested since coming off stage, the Blake sisters exchanged exasperated glances at the change which had come over the young heartthrob who used to play the piano for them as teenagers.

A large crowd of concert-goers were still hanging around outside the venue, determined to catch their idol's attention when they attempted their getaway. As soon as Jeff and the band appeared, surrounded by their entourage of roadies and friends, the fans surged forwards en masse. Remembering the grace and generosity Lynn had always shown to her adoring public, the chart-topping rocker steeled himself for signing autographs on all manner of body parts and letting them take photographs of each other draped all over him.

He shrugged at the sisters' incredulous expressions. Of course it boosted his ego... Too right, he enjoyed it... This was exactly what he had signed up for, wasn't it?

Later on, relaxing back in a sumptuous leather armchair and talking to Jacinta and Tamilla while his manager disappeared to settle the bill for dinner, Jeff came clean about the extent of the favours his lustful fans had been known to do for him. As he recounted some of the nights he had spent in New York and Florida, once more the women's faces were conflicted, multi-coloured canvases of curiosity, jealousy and horror.

'They're bloody desperate to please me. It's weird. Intent on putting on a show for me,' he condoned the groupies' behaviour. 'I'd be happy just to rip their clothes off and get stuck into it, but they come in in twos and threes, premeditated and pre-medicated. At first I used to object, albeit pretty half-heartedly, but now I'm getting used to not denying them their wish to entertain me. I guess I've entertained them for the last couple of hours, so now it's their turn. And then we get stuck into it.'

These titillating stories had Gerry excited at what lay in store. His friend had promised him some groupie action this evening too, once the ladies had retired to bed. Apparently, the few minutes the superstar had spent indulging his fans after the show were also long enough for him to have made correspondingly indulgent arrangements for the fortunate few to meet him at his hotel. With any luck, a gaggle of giggling and teetering hotties would be waiting for them in the bar, having already loosened up with a few expensed bottles of champagne.

'Do they strip?' Tamilla asked, with more than a little contempt in her tone. 'Right in front of each other?'

Jeff scoffed. 'Yeah, and the rest. You've got to start hanging around, mate. I'm prepared to share the booty. Plenty to go around. I could call up some agencies to get you girls hooked up too, if you want? Ever been in on a full-on orgy?'

The North Sydney private school girls were by no means virtuous Catholic *immaculati*, yet the fearsome idea of a rock musician's alcohol-fuelled love-in was a little too daring even for them. While they were clearly inquisitive, neither sister particularly wished to witness her brother or her erstwhile shared lover engaged in torrid, soporific fornication with numerous other women, deciding to tend to their jet-lag in their room with their own ice bucket of champagne instead.

'Good decision,' their famous friend's voice was laced with sarcasm. 'You might like it too much.'

The party was in full swing inside the luxurious suite that had been reserved for the celebrity's party, and from behind the door, the Melbourne accountant could hear his mate yelling. He pushed his way past several heaps of writhing limbs which loosely resembled copulating couples until he found several band members surrounded by empty bottles and further evidence of narcotics freely available. Never had he imagined an accountancy degree and an unlikely friendship with a boy born west of the Harbour Bridge would deliver him into such a dangerous type of heaven.

'Gez!' Jeff held out his own half-empty beer bottle. 'Get down here! Brandi's been beside herself, waiting for you to get back. Haven't you, baby?'

A voluptuous brunette immediately made an attempt to scramble to her feet, falling back onto the sofa and squealing in apparent amusement. She was clearly relieved to discover Jeff Diamond's manager was not a portly, fifty-something bore, instantly attracted to the virile Irishman. In contrast, Jeff's own female blanket, still relatively lucid, lunged to assist Brandi back to an upright position, having been requested to greet the illustrious Mister Blake in a more appropriate fashion.

Gerry helped himself to a generous whisky and soda and rolled himself a joint, settling down to catch up with his spaced-out client and their new collection of amorous best buddies, who would of course be interchanged as soon as the Diamond tour party rolled into the next town. He too was full of wonder at his situation, but such reservations were summarily dismissed since he had no wish to remain the last man standing now that his responsibilities were fully discharged.

'Jesus! It's too hot in here, man,' the singer roused everyone out of their comfortable muddle. 'Let's get the air-conditioning blasting. Where's the weed? Marty, over here, mate.'

Reaching For The Stars

The inaugural promotional tour next took Jeff Diamond to northern Europe, starting in rainy London. Again stealing time to himself late at night, he ended up hopelessly lost almost every time he left the hotel. After the sensible grid pattern of Manhattan, the twisting labyrinth of streets around the West End and down towards the River Thames was much more of a challenge to the tourist. Despite this time-consuming hurdle however, he found London oozing a sophistication to match New York, or perhaps even to surpass it. He was introduced to some very interesting Bohemians in the eclectic shops and art galleries of Carnaby Street, and was again excited to be soaking up the sensual vibes of this cultural hot-spot.

Dream after dream came true on the wide-eyed man's travels, passing through Amsterdam and visiting the famous bars, coffee shops and nightclubs about which he had read a thousand times. Plenty of glass doors in this city, the dreamer was glad to see! And then on to Paris and Madrid, where he wooed his audiences still further by having no trouble conversing with them in their own languages. He had instinctively developed a Midas touch with the crowds, which was both a blessing and a curse.

Jeff had expected to feel more at home in Madrid, due to his fluency in Spanish, but it was the French capital city which had been the surprise package. Meandering around the streets near the intersection of *les Boulevards Saint Michel* and *Saint Germain*, he stumbled across an eclectic cluster of bookshops and cafés surrounding *La Sorbonne*. Students and professors of all ages and grades of eccentricity sat in the open air, wrapped up in jackets, gloves and colourful scarves, with their cigarettes, *cafés simples* and *cognacs*, discussing philosophy and women. Strangely, he had never felt so much at home. This was his sort of place, and the closet intellectual vowed to return as soon as an opportunity presented.

After Madrid came Rome, Frankfurt and Berlin. The diligent linguist's Italian sounded too much like his mother tongue to appeal to the locals' sensibilities, and his German was by no means proficient enough to prevent the proud natives from answering him in English. This led the Australian to stick to his second language in these countries, not wishing to risk the embarrassment of inadvertently saying something he shouldn't. No matter though... He was an instant success wherever he went, with his swarthy

Mediterranean looks, dynamic stage presence and passionate music. He also found the Italian girls especially amorous and was reluctant to leave Rome so quickly.

As the months clicked by, the tormented soul recognised that he was better off on the road. In fact, as if back in his teens, he spent as much time away from home as possible. That way, when he finally touched back down in Melbourne, the long absences made sure he was beginning to crave familiarity. He liked having dinner with Suzanne for old times' sake, and catching up with his university friends for a game of basketball or a few drinks at one of the many live music pubs in Fitzroy or Carlton. By this time, the bad boy simply wished to act like a normal person again for a while and to leave his excessive consumption patterns behind. After six weeks overseas, the irrepressible performer's body was exhausted with endless travel and constant substance abuse, yet his mind was replete with a multiplicity of cerebral fodder which he set about processing slowly and methodically in order to appreciate the magnitude of his new experiences.

Returning home again in mid-December nineteen-seventy-two, the rock star found a cryptic message left by Gerry on the answering machine in his dark and lonely Richmond flat.

'Mate! GB here,' it went. 'Come into the office when you're back on deck. Something big to show you.'

Something big? Jeff was intrigued. When he reached the prestigious Collins Street address late the following afternoon, jet-lagged and listless, the indomitable business manager met him in the newly renovated reception area, positively brimming with excitement.

'What's got into you?' his friend asked, feeling doubly tired at the level of energy being expended around him.

'We're going for a bottle of wine,' Gerry told his client with an air of mystery and grabbed him by the arm.

Down in Rosati's, the money-spinning regular asked for the wine list and stood at the bar, contemplating its many pages for several minutes, while his famous buddy fended off some eager female fans. The accountant laughed, initially jealous, before sarcastically agreeing with the *sommelier* that such a level of attention could easily become quite suffocating. Jeff rolled his eyes in frustration, grateful for his mate's refreshing but predictable humour. After an amusing exchange at the celebrity's expense with the bartender, whom he knew from Blake & Partners' Friday evening drinking sessions, his manager placed an order.

'Elvis here's buying me one of your finest bottles of Grange Hermitage. 'Sixty-four or -five, if you have it, please, Vito.'

'Am I?' Jeff asked, giving his friend an irritated glare. 'Since when?'

The accountant put his arm around the songwriter's shoulder and led him to a nearby table, where they sat down opposite each other. Jeff crossed his legs and lit cigarettes for himself and his cheerful drinking partner, waiting to hear his excuses.

'Since about two weeks ago,' his manager informed him, slipping a few folded pieces of paper from the inside pocket of his suit jacket and flattening them out on the table in front of his client.

'What's that?' Jeff enquired, glancing down.

Before the older man had a chance to respond, the restaurant manager brought out a dusty bottle of the oldest Grange vintage he had been able to find in their cellar, a "'Sixty-two", and presented it to the dark-haired star for examination.

'Looks expensive,' the half-hearted celebrity joked.

Gerry huffed his objections in his own inimitable fashion. 'He can afford it. I cook his books.'

'Go on then...' his friend smiled at the shocked expression on the haughty man's face. 'Open it up and let him try it. Thanks.'

'This,' the businessman continued, expansively waving his right hand over the top page like a magic wand, 'is official confirmation that you, my good man... my best mate... are now a millionnaire.'

After a short pause, Jeff exhaled sharply. He picked up the papers and stared at the figures in each column, taking a few moments to work out what they represented. His manager couldn't wait for him to examine the balance sheet in detail, eager to propose a toast.

'To Jeff Diamond, rich bastard!' he announced with aplomb, lifting both their glasses into the air, clinking them together and offering one to his friend.

The songwriter took the long-stemmed goblet and spun the rich, red liquid round a few times, sniffing its bouquet like a professional and admiring the way the fine legs of syrupy liquid clung to the sides of the glass. This information was worth celebrating, he had to admit.

He toasted his manager in return. 'Cheers, mate. Sorry to be a bit slow to catch on. This is good.'

'This is good?' the incredulous man echoed. 'It's more than fucking good.'

Jeff laughed. 'Yes, OK. It's very fucking good. Thanks, Gez.'

As accountants went, the one across the table was about as excited as they could get. He reached forward and shook his old buddy heartily by the hand, almost sending the precious bottle flying. Both men lurched to save it, which Gerry did by a whisker.

'Jesus! That was close to a disaster. You're welcome, mate, but it's your money. Look at this...'

Gerry took back the papers momentarily and leafed through them until he found the transaction he was looking for. 'November the twenty-ninth,' he explained. 'Your balance had been tipping over the million-three mark consistently for a fortnight or so, and here... See?'

Following his friend's finger to the entry on his statement for that date, Jeff exhaled and rubbed his hand across his forehead in disbelief. The entry for this particular day read one million, five hundred and ten thousand dollars, give or take a few cents here and there. The rock star nodded but said nothing. In truth, he didn't fully understand his own indifference either.

The businessman continued regardless. 'So I got the girls to do a bit of digging around for outstanding expenses and did a proper cash projection, took a tax position as at the end of November and... Hey presto! Millionnaire!'

The younger man sat back and savoured the dark claret. It was absolutely delicious, and was becoming all the more delicious as the afternoon's news sunk in. His first rational thought was to imagine the looks on Alan and Ruth's faces when their irregular client could present them with a cheque large enough to fund The Fellowship's entire happiness chart research program, not to mention the rich assortment of new musical instruments he could purchase on behalf of the combined Fairfield High Schools' orchestra. And he mustn't forget Alberto's boxing club... The list of good causes was endless, but finally possible to address.

'How does it feel?' Gerry asked, seeing the cogs turning in his friend's tired mind.

Jeff shook his head. 'I don't know, mate. Great, I guess. Weird. Does it include your fee?'

Scoffing, his manager was undaunted by the brooding singer's lack of enthusiasm. 'This is not going to go away, you know,' he insisted, stubbing out his cigarette and refilling their glasses. 'This is only the beginning. I've got contracts on my desk from all and sundry, waiting to be booked in and signed. You are a *bona fide* star, mate. You are a serious money-making machine.'

A serious money-making machine? Yes, that was about right. The expression summed up how he was feeling quite well. Entirely unwittingly, his closest friend had hit the nail on the head. He was going through the motions, putting very little of his heart and soul into anything other than the few hours he spent on stage, where he could immerse himself in the power of the music and pretend to feel the semblance of goodness preserved within his lyrics.

The singer realised with a *frisson* of disappointment that his thoughts hadn't immediately turned to how Lynn might react to her former lover reaching this exalted milestone. So why was that? Simple, the philosopher rued. She would be pleased for him, no doubt. She would know how helpful this money could be for setting his many plans in motion, but she had never been the one to seek material benefit from their relationship. His elevation to rich rock star status was unlikely to impress her one *iota*, beyond the implicit recognition for the talent she had believed in so wholeheartedly.

'Thanks,' Jeff shrugged. 'I'm fried. Give me twenty-four hours, and we'll hit the town properly. I'm really grateful for all your hard work and looking after all this for me. It's just not that important, I suppose. Not the numbers. It's more what I can do with it that'll get me going. Sorry, mate.'

***

As Jeff rounded the corner from the kitchen, he could hear his children laughing. It was a welcome sound, since the house had been deathly quiet while they had been away. However, the frivolity was suspended as soon as they became aware of his arrival. Two synchronised heads turned to see him walk across the floorboards, revealing two angelic faces which then swung back and burst into more fits of laughter.

'Look at this, *Papá!*' Kierney cried out. 'It's so funny!'

The father crouched down and carefully edged three mugs of coffee onto the table, taking care not to spill any on the video cassettes and empty cases that were strewn everywhere. The kids were doing well. Sharing progress of their parents' autobiography as it took shape had been one of his most ingenious preventative treatments, sure to stave off any long-term psychological damage from what they were soon to go through.

Looking over his daughter's shoulder, he could just about make out the grainy footage of one of his early concerts playing on fast forward and with the sound muted.

'What are you up to, guys? You look guilty.'

Still chuckling, Ryan set the tape in motion, this time reversing at speed. 'This is hilarious, Dad! I wish we could get the sound backwards too.'

The three remaining Diamonds stood between the coffee table and the couch, while the long-haired band played with earnest looks on their faces, launching jerky, *staccato* attacks, almost as if the instruments were in control of the players. They each tried to guess which silent song they were watching, and it wasn't until the camera panned round to reveal a set of bongos that the superstar put the pieces together.

'This is "Leeway Sunset",' he announced. 'One of the bongo drums broke that night, if it's the gig I think it is. Rome? What does the case say?'

Kierney lifted the empty video sleeve and read the handwritten label on the back. 'It doesn't. Just "Nineteen-seventy-two, Europe", and then the band's names. Do you want to see yourself on fast forward? That's what we were laughing at when you came in. You look like you're on speed.'

'I was,' her father retorted with a shameful shrug. 'Well, the old-fashioned version, at least. Is this going to be the order of events for the rest of the night? If it is, I'm going to do some more writing, because I'm not much into analysing my own performance at this point in my career, if you know what I mean.'

His dark-haired daughter sat down next to her father and cradled her coffee mug in both hands. Her brother disregarded the question, insisting on rewinding further and then stopping for more track quizzes, backing his tall frame up a few paces and perching on the arm of the chair. The vision was amusing, Jeff had to admit, and he slapped the sportsman's back with a friendly force.

'You're easily pleased, aren't you?'

'Haven't you ever done this, old man?' his son taunted. 'What did you spend your student years doing? You missed out. Look at all the good, clean fun you could've had...'

Their dad shook his head. 'Contradiction in terms, mate. No such thing as good, clean fun.'

'You had big hair before the 'eighties,' Ryan continued, pausing the tape at a frame where the rocker was front and centre, looking raw and unkempt in a dark, satin shirt and tight, black pants. 'Look at you!'

'Big everything. Goes without saying, of course, boy.'

'You wish.'

'Whatever. Move it on.'

The seventeen-year-old grumbled. 'Shut up, guys. You had bigger hair than *Mamá* back then, and bigger sales.'

'Shush, *pequeñita*,' the widower urged. 'Yeah, probably. Let's not go there. Although I'd be lying if I said it wasn't a competition between us in those big-charting years. We were very competitive with each other for some peculiar reason, where neither of us was the slightest bit bothered by anyone else's chart positions. We never understood that about ourselves.'

'With the exception of body parts, I'm guessing,' Ryan gave a suggestive snigger.

Jeff raised his eyebrows as if to say his son's comment was accurate enough but that it would be advisable to refrain from any further commentary along these lines. The younger man laughed, throwing the empty cassette cover down onto the coffee table. As his sister took a seat on the floor in front of the others, the tape rolled on to show a scene from outside the concert hall, where fans were lining up to gain backstage access.

'Oh, my God! Look at those girls!' Kierney brought the men's attention back to the television, pointing at a sea of black and white faces belonging to females who were screaming at the top of their lungs, clutching T-shirts and programmes from their night out and with tears streaming down their faces. 'They're literally hysterical.'

'It was madness,' Jeff agreed. 'A noise like nothing I'd ever heard before. The venue was so old that my dressing room reminded me of a spray-painted dungeon, below ground and with only a long, narrow window at the top. There was even a security grille over it, I think. It was like being in a jail cell with a pack of dingoes waiting to mob me the moment I stepped outside. From that far away from the crowd, it honestly sounded like some sort of primal howling and screeching.'

Lighting a cigarette, the father tossed the packet into his daughter's lap to see if she also wanted one. Kierney flipped the lid, peered in at the white sticks for a few seconds, before deciding against it and throwing the packet over to her brother. He also passed up the offer, agreeing that it was too close to bedtime. During this familiar ritual, the footage had changed from the manic scenes outside to a press room inside, where a small group of fans had been invited to meet their new idol.

Jeff leaned forwards, wondering if he would recognise any of these original devotees. A mixture of young men and women, he watched his twenty-year-old self sign autographs and pose for photographs with this lucky few, who had presumably won their privileged audience with the headline act in a competition. He heard Kierney sniff in mild disgust when the arrogant, young Diamond looped his arm around the best looking woman and offered her a beer. Of course, the star-struck fan was mesmerised in the moment, accepting the drink eagerly and fawning all over the handsome star. Several of the others appeared downcast and thwarted that they were not receiving such undivided attention.

'So how did you choose?' Ryan enquired, also keen on checking out these excited females, even though they would now be old enough to be his aunties. 'First come, first served?'

'Ry!' his sister exclaimed. 'Gross-out or what?'

Smirking, Jeff put a steadying hand on the young woman's shoulder. 'Other way round, mate, don't you think?'

'*Papá!*'

'C'mon, Kizzy. Lighten up. It's late, and we're just mucking around. It was the era of free love. Easy pickings for me. It wasn't pretty, but it didn't need to be. There were no expectations. They wanted a piece of me as a souvenir, and I got me a piece of ass for the night. That's all it was. OK? I was the master of cheap and nasty back then.'

The willowy teenager shuffled backwards and levered herself up onto the couch beside her father. Resting her head on his arm, she tucked her legs up underneath her and snuggled into his warm body. Jeff curled a long arm around her and kissed the top of her head. His kids had watched recordings of both his and Lynn's concerts many times over the years and had heard various backstories, the versions becoming more honest and less sanitised as their youth gradually evaporated.

'I shared the spoils with the band. And Gerry, when he stuck around. We'd do our thing, then I'd leave 'em asleep in the hotel room and go back to mine.'

Ryan stood up, stretching and yawning. 'Doesn't sound at all bad to me,' he grinned. '"The Roughs" need to step up band practice when I get back to uni'. I want me pieces of ass after every gig too. Can't believe you're actually using that phrase with us, after all the lectures about respecting women! Close your ears, sis.'

'So cold,' the rock star's drowsy daughter moaned. 'I guess girl bands do the same thing. Just there weren't many girl bands in those days, Papá, were there?'

'No. That's true,' Jeff continued, satisfied that his life had turned out so differently in the end. 'And yes, it was very cold. Simple and meaningless. We all enjoyed ourselves for a short time. They got to brag about sleeping with the singer in the band, while I moved on to the next town and next batch of girls. Sorry, guys, but that's just how it was.'

The proud father gathered up the empty coffee mugs and the ashtray. In a few days' time, the trio would be driving out to Lynn's parents' enormous farm at Benloch for the first Christmas without their mother. None was particularly looking forward to masquerading in a party mood with their grandparents and extended family, yet each knew they had a part to play in ensuring everyone managed to enjoy the festive season.

'One more example of the relentless passage of time,' the grieving husband thought aloud, wondering if his children might be mulling over the same notion. 'Sometimes it sweeps you up in its wake. Other times it leaves you behind, and you have to scramble to catch up. But none of us can ignore it. I'm going to the study for a while. This little retrospective interlude is the perfect segue into the chapter I'm currently working on. You guys alright?'

'Dad?'

Jeff wheeled around at the sudden serious tone in his son's voice. 'Yeah?'

'So while you were getting it on with all those women and living the rock star life,' the nineteen-year-old began, 'did you talk to anyone about the shit you had going on inside? You know, the depression and suicidal thoughts?'

'Jesus, mate. Where's this come from? *Sientete.*'

The young man shook his head. 'No. It's all good. I just wanted to know how you managed to live two lives in parallel. I asked Mum once how she dealt with being apart, but she wouldn't tell me. S'pose she thought I was too young. It was a few years ago.'

'She dealt with it a whole lot better than I did,' Jeff nodded. 'She had the ability to rationalise things, whereas I was just a mess. Resilience, I guess. Like you two.'

'It comes from being loved when you're a kid,' Kierney offered. 'Helps you to know you won't always feel this bad. That's what you missed out on. *Mamá* told me that.'

Tears immediately formed behind the father's eyes, and he sniffed them back. 'Yep. I think you're right, *pequeñita.* 'I didn't want to talk about it to anyone, mate. It was easier to force a smile and behave like an idiot, because that's what was expected of me. On the few occasions when I opened up a bit to Celia, she'd always say, "But you shouldn't feel that way."'

Both children laughed at the showman's impression of Gerry's prim and proper mother, who had taken it upon herself to become the young man's surrogate parent. Jeff shrugged as if to accentuate how straightforward she thought his problem was to fix.

'"Oh, OK. Thanks, Celia. I won't then,"' he continued the story. 'Your mamá was the first person who didn't say that to me. Instead, she said, "How awful that you feel that way." She wanted me to feel better just as much as Celia did. She just knew it wasn't something I did on purpose; that I could turn on and off at will.'

All three Diamonds stared at each other while the missing fourth family member sent a private message to her wistful husband, causing him to scratch the skin over his heart. 'That's the big difference when you need support. I remember the look of complete sorrow on her face. All you have to do is acknowledge its validity. You'd don't have to fix anything, because most of the time, you can't. *Buenas noches a los dos.*'

Kierney wrapped her arms around her father's waist and leaned her head into his chest. Wiping the tears from his eyes, he hugged her back. Slender fingers moved his hand off his shirt and stroked the fabric covering the "JL" tattoo.

'That's so beautiful, *Papá.* And *Mamá. Buena escritura.*'

***

The movie which Lynn Dyson had been filming for the last few months was set for release at Christmas. "Reaching For The Stars" was a typical schmaltzy Hollywood musical; an idyllic story of growing up in America in the nineteen-forties, full of post-war positivity and a dream-like innocence. The part of Barbara had been written especially for her, and the precocious starlet had fallen back into acting easily, despite privately admitting that she had well and truly outgrown the childish, chintzy plot. Her co-stars, also big names in their own rights, were seasoned professionals and took the stunning, blonde seventeen-year-old under their wing in the studio and during the rare outdoor scenes. Lynn had been a keen student, respectful of the director's wishes and very popular with everyone on set.

Her character's "romantic interest", Dominic, was played by another former child-star making his debut in an adult role. Carson Wright fell instantly head over heels in love with the well-known Australian singer and sportswoman, his obligatory Hollywood ego unable to understand why she was not interested in him. He feverishly wined her, dined her and showered her with gifts until Lynn finally had to confront him and put a stop to his attempts at winning her affections. The producer had even pulled the leading lady to one side to air his concern that the on-screen relationship might suffer as a result of the youngsters' lack of involvement off-screen.

This unexpected allegation served as an interesting lesson for the young Australian beauty. No wonder so many actors had such short-term relationships, she realised. Thrown into a situation where they were required to be on heat while playing their roles, it was sometimes hard to distinguish fact from fiction when she and Carson were spending such long and irregular hours in each others' company, full of pretence and in so many compromising positions. Moreover, the rest of the cast and crew, and soon the ever-attentive press as well, took it for granted that the good-looking pair would become the next showbiz scoop.

It was with a mixture of amusement, frustration and sadness that Lynn imagined her former lover's outspoken opinion on this issue. Jeff would unquestionably hook up with his co-star without a moment's hesitation, easily able to consider the relationship as inconsequential outside the context of the movie. Such an arrangement appeared to suit everyone in the here and now, so why the hell not? His deep, expressive voice spilled into her ears from her forlorn heart, as she imagined the man who dominated her vivid dreams night after night gently goading her into enjoying the fun for what it was. It would also help pass the time, she imagined him telling her, echoing her own words back. Should she relent and keep the peace, for the sake of box office triumph? Everyone would be satisfied with her life's new veneer, as her worldly lover had so aptly put it.

Back in Melbourne, Jeff rolled his eyes in disgust when he read the synopsis of Lynn's new film in the entertainment section of The Age. Evidently, her overprotective minders were determined not to honour her advancing adulthood, despite the polite protestations she would doubtless be insinuating. The sundered lovers had spoken many times about the various directions in which she wanted her career to head, and this certainly wasn't one of them. He hoped she was suitably scornful of her casting, but couldn't be sure now that he no longer lent a supportive ear, acting as the disreputable influence her parents had sought to purge from her life.

Nevertheless, the humble student who up until recently had shared the sexy, new film star's most intimate aspirations would love to have secreted himself into a cinema under the cover of darkness and feasted his eyes on his dream girl once more. He might have been prepared to swallow his pride under the circumstances, yet without his certain someone to protect him from the movie monsters, Jeff couldn't bring himself to step inside a theatre.

46

At least the twenty-year-old had the perfect excuse for why he hadn't seen the blockbuster hit when Gerry and his sisters pressed him. The stern critic simply told them it was a ridiculously frivolous plot and he was disappointed that Lynn had been enlisted. Jacinta and Tamilla had rushed to see it anyway, since romantic musicals had always been "just their thing", and once again the ruthless duo set about teasing their brother's longtime friend by describing Lynn Dyson's on-screen kisses and bodily entanglements in infuriating detail, knowing full well how jealous it would make the hot-blooded male.

Christmas nineteen-seventy-two came and went in a muddy fog. Jeff had been invited to the Blakes' family home in the North Shore suburb of Mosman, like he had every season in recent times. This year though, the affluent family's wayward extra son had turned down their invitation, using his travel schedule as an excuse. Truth be told, he knew he would be lousy company, and didn't care either to dampen the happy family's spirits or to suffer the endless taunts of the catty siblings. He had also heard that the entire Dyson family was flying across to spend the holidays in Los Angeles with Lynn, and this news hit the heartbroken young man particularly hard when picturing their happy festive reunion.

The now famous musician was undecided about the whole Christmas concept. Without any firm religious beliefs to fall back on, two days of gluttonous eating, drinking and merriment were crass and wasteful on the one hand, seeming to have developed in recent years into a competition to see who could spend the most on gifts. However on the other hand, there remained a magic the loner envied when families came together to celebrate. He preferred the idea of the American Thanksgiving holiday, which had fewer religious overtones while still acknowledging the importance of surrounding oneself with loved ones.

The other, more private reason why Jeff was not looking forward to the holidays was the fact that Lynn's Christmas Special was being regularly advertised on television, and it was clear from the publicity that she was living life to the full over in California. Over the last few weeks, she had been pictured dating a prominent star of the screen and had given interviews which revealed to the jaundiced sceptic that she was changing a lot during this sabbatical from Melbourne. He hoped her conspicuous affairs were as superficial as his were, but he had his doubts. He knew women too well to believe his own spin.

For all the newspaper columns and magazine articles describing The Australian Elvis' many steamy assignations, he hadn't found a single one in the least bit fulfilling. Had he used up his one respecting sexual relationship and was therefore now being punished for wanting more? He sorely missed the intimacy he had shared with Lynn and the natural touch they had perfected, knowing exactly how to entice, enflame and then pacify each other at every moment. He also craved the exchange of witty banter, the endless words of love and the small tokens of affection that had made life so special, none of which he had the slightest desire to repeat with anyone else.

Night after night, the southern hemisphere's most eligible bachelor found himself in someone else's bed, too often anticipating a strong hand to reach round the back of his head as he came inside the latest beautiful stranger. He longed for the feeling of Lynn running her strong, piano-player's fingertips down his spine, forcing him to struggle to maintain control until he had satisfied her. What he would do for a massage of his tired shoulders from his beautiful best friend, and to feel the slow, kneading strokes travel along his neck to the most susceptible sinews just below the hairline. Yet the magic sensation never arrived, and neither did he want it to arrive as soon as he focussed his eyes back on whomever he was with.

Other frequent memories of their supremely choreographed, bare-skinned confluences were those enjoyed after a night out with the most beautiful woman in the world, painted nails running the length of his engorged penis as she shifted similarly painted lips back and forth, her tongue hidden from nothing but his eyes. These images were easy enough to reproduce, and indeed Jeff's frazzled body begged his mind to reproduce them on an alarmingly regular basis, such was his rampant dependence. However, the truth was unavoidable. Applied to Lynn Dyson, these colourful adornments were merely symbols representing something much, much deeper; something unique and powerful that neither she nor he had fully understood, and which were now lost to them both.

And to cap it all, if a nameless woman happened to trigger a sensuous suggestion of those heady times, the seasoned addict was scarcely able to prevent himself from recoiling. He was unable to stomach his soul being invaded, despite his insatiable physical needs, as if someone were venturing into his dream girl's exclusive domain. Only when he was blind drunk, high on amphetamines or mellowed by cannabis... or all of the above... did this missing element not matter quite so much. The loss seemed insurmountable in the rare sober moments, invariably pushing him to seek another high.

The lonely superstar arrived back in Melbourne a few days before the city shut down for the holidays, sitting alone in his dark Richmond flat and wondering what sort of sexual relationships his gorgeous ex-girlfriend was enjoying these days. Did she look back on their special moments together as lost forever, or were their recall as pervasive to her as they were to him? Did she also expect to be touched the way he had touched her? Was she getting what she needed? Perhaps she had found something even better. Jeff Diamond had given Lynn Dyson a thorough education, including how to ask for exactly what she wanted. Much to his *chagrin*, Miss Irony rarely missed an opportunity to admonish him. His gorgeous schoolgirl songstress would be a superb partner now.

Craving company of any kind in the lead-up to Christmas, Jeff had gone straight from a one-day international against Pakistan in Gerry's corporate entertainment box at the Melbourne Cricket Ground to a gala event at the National Gallery of Victoria, celebrating a tour by the Paris Opera Ballet. The tearaway rocker had no real idea how he had ended up on the guest list for such a glittering *soirée*, especially since the Australian ballet's patron was none other than Marianna Dyson.

The Victorian Premier and his wife, who confessed that their daughters were his biggest fans, had made an unexpected beeline for the swarthy singer, and they were soon sipping cocktails in front of a painting by Sidney Nolan, discovering a common appreciation for Wassily Kandinsky's work. The elderly couple's task for the evening was to chaperone the principal dancer from the grand, old French company, and they had been begged to introduce her to the famous rock star.

'From the ridiculous to the sublime,' he told them, after describing his day first in English and then again in French for the benefit of the diminutive and delicately sculpted visitor.

He had said the very same thing to Lynn a few months ago while standing in the very same spot. The irresistible opportunity to revisit this memory and test their invisible elastic connection was aided by another tiny, white pill slipped down in the taxi between the two venues, later serving its purpose when it dulled the disappointment he felt on receiving not one hint of a response.

'What's the difference between an art critic and an art *connoisseur*?' the handsome charmer posed to the dignified party at his side, who all shrugged politely.

The rueful philosopher sighed and forced a smile. 'Both know what they're looking at, but only one understands why.'

This was how he had answered his sixteen-year-old muse. Back then, his thoughtful reply had triggered an in-depth exchange about the underlying sensuousness of art appreciation, laden with bubbling chemistry that set both lovers' passions alight in the very public arena. He was not surprised when only blank stares and a few more placatory grins came his way this time. Jeff could see Lynn's parents out of the corner of his eye. Paranoia suggested they were scrutinising him closely, but he was wise enough to realise this was most probably due to the effects of the drug on top of an afternoon of drinking. Who cared? He was no longer beholden to them in any way.

Don't drink too much, the twenty-year-old imagined escaping from the elegant woman's mouth. He raised his glass to the all-Australian couple on the other side of the hall and gave Lynn's mother one of his highest-octane smiles. The gracious lady flinched slightly, clutching her own champagne flute, before turning to Bart and suggesting they walk off in the opposite direction.

After a few paces however, Jeff noticed Marianna turn briefly. Had she only just noticed to whom he was speaking, or about what? Or even that he was speaking French? Perhaps she had secretly been impressed. Perhaps not. He watched her re-join her husband, who was sensibly keeping his distance. Feeling hot under the collar all of a sudden, the young man sensed the room closing in on him as panic invaded his senses. There was no invisible elastic connection after all. Who was he kidding?

The rock star spent that night in a hotel room with the prima ballerina, where she danced for him and with him, nude but for his tie knotted around her waist. He surrendered willingly to her lithe, supple frame and star-struck advances, finding the asinine discourse strangely comforting. There were worse ways to kill time, and for once he could proffer his own, genuine observations about Paris.

In the end, Jeff rode out Christmas Day and Boxing Day in a drunken and drug-induced stupor with a bunch of international students from RMIT and Melbourne University who couldn't afford to fly home for the festive season. They dubbed it their "Orphans' Christmas", and the displaced Sydneysider fitted right in. He paid for some typically classless entertainment recommended by one of the others, which he found as funny and titillating as he could through the hazy *mélange* of drugs. By the time he returned to his apartment, Melbourne's richest student was too far gone to care that he had broken all the promises he had made to himself after his mother died concerning substance use and abuse.

On Wednesday the twenty-seventh of December, with time having slowed to an absolute crawl, Jeff penned a song entitled "Broken" while straightening out after his Christmas bender. This was a cracker of a song, destined to make him a lot of money, yet he knew he would never be able to perform it live. It joined the swelling ranks of potential chart-toppers that weren't even candidates for singing in the shower without breaking down, but which would go on to be multi-platinum hits for other artists.

And thus on Thursday the twenty-eighth of December, the millionnaire hermit tuned in to Lynn's TV Special in the privacy of his rented flat. It was the torture he deserved after the debauchery of the last few days. With the lyrics of his plaintive ballad still lying on his coffee table, he did his best to match his spirits to those of the show's bubbly host by blocking out the taste of her kisses and the pain of their absence tearing him in two. Her soulful voice melted his tired heart, which skipped a beat each and every time her blue eyes looked directly into the camera.

Good sense kicked in halfway through the self-inflicted emotional agony, and Jeff started to wonder exactly why he was putting himself through this misery. Just forget her, he told himself. He was on one hell of a ride without her these days. He didn't need her any more. His body was telling him so, with not a shred of recognition rising from below the belt. For the first time since the blonde beauty's departure, he found himself wishing they had never met.

How did the saying go: better to have loved and lost than never to have loved at all?

Bullshit, he thought. Utter bullshit.

Gerry flew home from the Blake family Christmas in time for New Year's Eve, and things immediately took a turn for the better. Jeff had come through the lowest point of his life so far, and the concentrated accumulation of inorganic chemicals had eventually cleared out of his system. He made a promise to himself that he would take it easy over the next round of celebrations, secretly admitting it was a false hope. Gerry's younger sister had flown down from Sydney to spend New Year with her brother and their now super-famous childhood friend. She decided during this trip that they should all go skiing in the French Alps or Switzerland in February, and to her surprise, both men agreed.

Tammy had been shocked to see the dark and dashing sex symbol looking so unhealthy and had quizzed the star's manager as to why he had let his client get into this state. Her brother, as usual, had noticed nothing, both because his mate was a good actor and because Gerry only really cared about Gerry.

***

Jeff took heart from his stumbling, tenuous recovery during January. He had arranged to spend some time in Canada, as the guest of a fellow songwriter with whom he had swapped demo' tapes over recent months. They rented a log cabin in the hills way north of Toronto and wrote some high quality material which the Canadian folk singer would later release in a series of mainstream albums. Both men were nocturnal beings, drinking rye whiskey well into the night while turning their ideas into music. Douglas would then sleep all day, leaving the Australian free to conduct his business over the telephone during working hours or to run in the clear, clean mountain air in an effort to reclaim some much needed fitness in preparation for the rigours of his next tour.

Also while in the stunning, rugged landscapes of Alberta, the generous benefactor with an ulterior motive made contact with a leading psychiatrist whose work on addiction he had admired after reading articles in a medical journal found in a waiting room somewhere or other. Such was the life of the rock star of the moment, who could no longer easily go out on his own, thereby necessitating him to spend an inordinate amount of time waiting for other, lesser mortals to convey him from place to place.

Professor Sarah Friedman was fascinated by Jeff Diamond's story, or rather the pieces of his story he chose to impart, and they worked together and played together in the name of science. Their project was a shining example of a using relationship, which the only guitar-toting honorary doctor of Toronto University would often quote in years to come when speaking to audiences far and wide. The rank outsider needed a professional accreditation to give validity to his theories on psychological trauma and addiction and to attract supplementary funding for the treatments' clinical trials. The academic, on the other side of the transaction, was over the moon to secure a walking, talking case study with an absolute passion for making sense of himself.

Miss Irony came to call yet again during this fascinating interlude in the onslaught of fame and fortune. Being immersed in the research over a three-week sabbatical, Jeff felt the happiest he had been since Lynn's departure, both because and in spite of coming face-to-face with his own "below the line" issues. This fact didn't surprise him, since the intellectual stimulation he found with Sarah was as close as he had come for a long while to enjoying female company beyond sex. Nonetheless, he caught himself on more than one occasion expecting too much, crashing down in flames when he recognised that the scientist could never give him what he had enjoyed with Lynn.

Or was his mind merely insisting she couldn't? Try as he might, the frustrated lab rat was unable to entertain the prospect that he might be about to replace the girl of his dreams and settle for a worthy substitute because it took him partway back to the paradise he had glimpsed.

To her credit, Sarah took the time for her handsome and intelligent subject to cross these hurdles without pressing him for the reasons why. Their research didn't depend on knowing the details of each atrocity to be visited on patients, since the list of damaging events was very long and wide-ranging.

'That's good,' Jeff smirked, ''cause I wasn't going to spill my guts about that anyway. You're right. We don't need to know how, just what was the result and how do people work around it.'

The handsome celebrity slipped off the side of the bed and reached down for his clothes. Pulling on some shorts and slipping a T-shirt over his head, he turned to locate his cigarettes. He could feel Sarah's eyes following him all the while, and his head filled with melancholy and regret. It was a bad idea to get this close, even in the name of science, but she was an attractive woman, and they had spent the whole day together.

He walked over to draw the curtains on the distant, frozen landscape and dragged hard on his cigarette. 'You know, we should've done this in Queensland. Or even in LA. I'm not used to being so cold in January, spending so much time indoors.'

Turning away from the window, Jeff strode purposefully towards his suitcase and slipped his hand into a recessed pocket in its back wall. Sarah watched him carefully, wondering what he was looking for. It made her a little nervous when she thought back to his references to a violent adolescence. With great sleight of hand she saw him pop something into his mouth, before their eyes met and he continued to speak.

'It still blows my mind, you know, that less than six months ago my practical knowledge of the world was limited to its lower east side. Eastern Australia and South Island New Zealand, I mean. I never did get the whole "western society" nomenclature. Australia and New Zealand are about as far east as you can get, and we're still considered a western society. We're west of the US, I s'pose, if you don't factor in time. Go west and skip a day.'

Feeling the drug take hold of his senses, the tall man flopped down onto the end of the bed.

'You're ranting,' the professor issued an ingenuous critical observation. 'You're getting high, aren't you?'

'And only the capital cities, at that!' the superstar went on with a grin. 'Hope so.'

Sarah knew she should disapprove. 'What was that? What did you just take?'

Jeff shrugged. 'Nothing you need to be worried about.'

'We could take a walk,' the professor suggested, marvelling at another substantial mood swing taking place. 'What's wrong? This was your idea.'

Jeff sighed. 'Yeah, I know. Can't walk and work at the same time. Let's spend an hour or two here, and then we'll go grab a drink somewhere dark. I'd prefer to get all this junk out of my head before it turns into a song instead.'

The psychiatrist laughed out loud. What was the point of coming on all high and mighty with her superb lover? This conundrum of a man never ceased to amaze her with the constant dissonance between his words and actions. Jeff Diamond was a blatant hedonist who also wanted to change the world, all seemingly enacted by a perfect match of left and right brain function. Such an altruist, but also supremely self-absorbed; fun-loving one moment, spitting chips the next. Attentive and keen to please her in bed, yet he couldn't wait to put some distance between them immediately afterwards. And intelligent. So unbelievably intelligent.

'Sexy and smart: my favourite combination,' her self-assured bedfellow cocked his head, as if reading her mind. 'Say it, whatever it is, or leave it alone.'

'Shoot! Alright,' the sophisticated woman acquiesced, dressing quickly. 'I can see through you, you know. And I can mess with your head just as well, so leave it out, buddy. Let's keep the trauma causes as categories. We'd never manage to list them all anyway in the time we've got. It'll only trip us up later, when we're more under pressure. You said that the day before yesterday, and I thought you were nuts, smart-ass!'

'I am nuts,' her sarcastic chief lab' rat chuckled. 'Jeez, you're good, doc. Remind me to fuck you again tonight. So which categories do we have so far?'

The professor fastened a patent leather belt around her waist and rolled her eyes. 'I wish I could just say, "Go fuck yourself," but I won't. And you know it, don't you? You're a bastard, Jeff Diamond, but a fascinating bastard who also happens to be bankrolling my research, so I have to force myself to be nice to you.'

Picking up a sheet of paper from the circular, teak table, Jeff straddled the chair next to the tall brunette, leaned in and kissed her pouting lips. 'I'm sorry. I'm an asshole, as you Canadians say. Feel free to say whatever you want. I deserve it, and you're gorgeous. Now, categories... "Under six years of age, was I cherished by my parents and family just by virtue of my existence?" No. Can't say I was. I was the happy event that shouldn't have happened. My sister was too, but my parents were excited the first time. After a while, when my dad hardly ever came home anymore, for my mum I was just that kid who looked like a miniature version of her bloody husband. So strike, I guess. Next?'

Sarah wrote feverishly, only looking up when Jeff drew breath. 'Wow. That's a pretty horrible way to grow up. I'm really sorry to hear that.'

'Not your fault, I assume. It was a classic case of "more of the same",' the musician gave her a wry smile and a half-hearted impersonation of his mother's attitude. '"Ah, boy child..." *Yadda, yadda, yadda.* It just left me with an abject ambivalence towards my own flesh and blood. But you know, Sarah, I wasn't the only one. And as we've seen these last few days, there's people way worse affected than me.'

'This is interesting,' the professor raised her hand and looked into troubled eyes. 'Where's your grammar gone all of a sudden? Have you been listening to yourself over the last minute or so?'

'What? No, obviously not. Go on...'

'Jeff, it's like talking about this time in your life has caused you to regress to the speech patterns of someone much younger and unschooled. One moment you're saying "abject ambivalence towards my own flesh and blood", and then you can only find the most grunting of vocabulary. It's a fascinating response.'

'If you say so, doc,' the sexy superstar hid his distress with humour, his oft-used deflection technique. 'Mahatma Gandhi said something like "Happiness is when what you think, what you say, and what you do are in harmony." Did you know that? He was onto it too, babe. What's category number two?'

'Gandhi? Really?' his research bedfellow murmured with a modicum of impatience at the capricious attention span which the fast-acting drug brought to her serious data collection exercise, directing her eyes back to the notepad. '"Were you provided with adequate food, clothing, shelter and medical care?" That should be easy enough to answer.'

Jeff nodded. 'Yeah, to begin with. We had some sort of home nurse come after I was born, I think. So my grandmother told me a while back... I don't even know why we were talking about it. I was probably caught complaining about something, and she pulled me up on it.'

'Hold on for a sec'. You said, "to begin with",' the doctor jumped in when her rueful subject paused. 'Slow down a little. It wasn't always that way?'

The twenty-year-old shook his head. 'To tell you the truth, I don't really remember. I know we... my sister and I... used to take money from our mother's purse and buy groceries. Whatever we felt like. Nothing very nutritious! Smokes, if there was any change left over. And I know Lena used to steal clothes, but maybe not until she was older. Six and under we're talking about, aren't we?'

'Yes. What about your living arrangements?'

The superstar scoffed loudly, lighting yet another cigarette. 'My living arrangements? I don't remember any living arrangements. The opulent surrounds of our flat? The maid who came to clean up, and the cockroaches that loved to climb six flights of stairs? Get outta here! It's not like we had any sort of routine, I can tell you that much.'

'I mean your house, or wherever you lived,' the longsuffering woman teased. 'You know exactly what the classifications mean, so don't get all hard-done-by on me! Did you feel safe? Did the roof leak? Were you too cold, too warm? Did you have size-appropriate clothes?'

Jeff tipped the chair backwards and stood up. To the psychiatrist's astonishment, beads of sweat were visible on his forehead, and his breathing had become erratic. Could a panic attack really be induced simply by talking about this man's childhood home? Indeed, their discussion appeared to trigger all manner of negative reactions, the most unhelpful of which was anger.

'All of the above,' his tone was almost mocking. 'Absolutely nothing about my living arrangements was safe. I can assure you of that. Jesus! This never gets any easier. I'm sorry. Clothes though? I guess they were OK. I wouldn't have cared about that.'

Sarah felt great pity for the quivering mess which was now pacing round the table, as if he were endeavouring to pluck up the courage to sit back down again. 'Is the agitation due to what you just swallowed? Or solely from having to talk about this? OK, sorry. Don't answer that if you don't want to. How old were you at that time?'

'Don't know. Seven or eight? I was in worse shape talking to the last shrink, so the pill's probably helping. Hope so, otherwise you're in for a real treat, baby! I do remember having to spend a day indoors because all my clothes were in the wash at the same time. In fact, I think I took them to the local launderette and told the woman my mum'd be back with the money. Then I realised I didn't have anything else to wear. Can't even remember how we got it all back!'

The songwriter's eyes suddenly darted upwards, staring out of the window. It had hit home exactly how much easier it had been to talk to Lynn; that somehow she had made him feel less ashamed. He had all but forgotten those sunny afternoons spent sitting on the edge of the dam, pausing between bouts of love- or music-making to answer another of his dream girl's empathetic questions. Anxiety had always reared its head, but in her company, its effects seemed to diminish quickly after the first churn of his stomach.

Dismissing the happy memories, the human case study picked up their questionnaire again. 'Come on. What's left? "Were you given opportunities for education and developing talents?" Yes, but not at home. At school, when I went after them. I'm an anomaly on this front, Sarah. I always went looking for information, even before starting school, so I can't tick this box. But this last one's a big joke… "Were you given age-appropriate boundaries, enforced without demeaning your value?" Fucking hell! Yeah, "Fucking hell" is what you should write down against this one.'

The long index finger of Jeff's left hand reached over and stabbed at the end of the professor's notes, coming to a discouraged rest on the paper. Her hand closed over his and squeezed it down until its palm was flat on the notepad. It was best not to press further on this issue. Instead, she read out the more specific categories for the six to eighteen age group: children who were subjected to abuse of any kind, whether verbal, emotional, physical or, of course, sexual; and also whether the children witnessed the abuse of others.

'Yes, yes, yes, yes, yes,' Jeff murmured, his head in his hands. 'But I can't give you any details. You have to understand. I'm sorry. I'm not prepared to put this into words. But yes, all of this happened to my sister and me, and my mother. And even to my dad by people who came to despise him. It was one unholy mess, and that's no exaggeration. We saw things and were made to do things that kids just aren't supposed to be a part of. It wasn't healthy, physically or mentally.'

Sarah gripped his clammy hand in hers, moved to tears. 'Gosh, I'm so sorry, Jeff. I had no idea things were so bad. I thought maybe one or two episodes of violence, but never that you lived in that type of environment permanently. It's OK. I don't need you to tell me. I'll write it up later.'

'Cheers, gorgeous,' the rock star breathed deeply and freed his fingers from her grasp. 'The adult onset categories here don't really apply to me. Any that do only build on what went before, so I can't honestly say that any specific trauma arose after I was eighteen. I pretty much lived on my own from fourteen onwards, so managed to stay away from any further shit.'

He retrieved the questionnaire for a final scan down the list of typical events which caused long-term symptoms in adults: relationship break-up, business collapse, unexpected bereavement, domestic violence.

'They're much of the same core categories, but with a more adult slant,' the doctor smiled. 'Rape, physical trauma, war and catastrophic events.'

'It's only one category, if you think about it,' Jeff offered, lighting a cigarette and offering the packet to his companion.

'What's that?'

'Breach of trust in the world. It lets you down... You know, when it's not exactly how Louis Armstrong promised.'

Again, the handsome celebrity looked away, fighting back tears. He had lied about not incurring further damage as an adult, hadn't he? His mind pictured precisely where he was when Lynn had spoken this most *à propos* phrase, prising the guitar out of his hands and beginning to sing the song. It had indeed been a wonderful world for that brief period. His memory recalled the curvaceous instrument sitting across irresistible brown thighs, on a rug surrounded by eucalypts and willows by the dam at Coldwater Creek, and he steered his line of sight upwards, past her hidden breasts and those sportswoman's shoulders until they reached her smile, her blue eyes and long, golden hair blowing in the breeze.

On that particular afternoon, he recalled, the ambitious songwriter had just finished giving "Do As I Say" its *début* in front of his Number One Fan; a song which would go on to earn him a magnificent and perpetual income. Six months later, its framed double-platinum disc currently leaned up against the wall in his empty Richmond flat.

'Are you OK?'

Jeff jumped at the sound of Sarah's voice, half expecting to hear another's. 'Yep. I'm thinking of a very special time that's now gone, that's all. What's next?'

The telephone rang beside the bed. Both occupants went to answer it at the same time, but Jeff gently pressed down on his roommate's shoulder until she was seated again. It was Gerry calling from Melbourne, clearly excited about the news he needed to impart.

'Mate!' the celebrity shouted. 'What? Sure am. It's only cold if you go outside, you idiot.'

Sarah laughed loud enough for the indomitable accountant to pick up, and he was both surprised and apologetic that he had not expected his client to have company.

'Why not?' Jeff exclaimed. 'What time is it? That doesn't matter. Party time, mate!'

It transpired that Gerry was calling to make sure his friend was the first to know that Michael Parkinson, the British chat show host, had booked the musician for a whole hour-long episode. It was a big deal, his manager continued, since it would be only the second time an entire programme had been devoted to a single personality.

'I met him at the SCG,' the half-naked singer reminded his manager. 'We sat next to each other at the cricketers' breakfast. You should've been there too, remember? You had to cancel for some client thing.'

The academic looked on in surprise, listening to the subject of her very testing research behaving like a regular buffoon with his transpacific correspondent. The erstwhile sweat-drenched and angst-ridden patient had transformed again, full of the joys of spring. Once the call had been terminated, her curiosity got the better of her, and she asked him how he managed to switch *personæ* so seamlessly.

The young man chuckled, a little ashamed. 'Yeah, someone else used to wonder about that too.'

'The one you were thinking about earlier? A woman?'

The doctor was jealous, and Jeff smiled. 'The very same. My guardian angel.'

'What happened to her?'

By the impish expression on the rock star's face, Sarah was frustrated to be toyed with again, yet she was interested to find out more. This arrogant upstart had wormed his way into her affections with no difficulty, and it was unnerving to discover a hint of heartbreak in this man who had women lining up in their hundreds wherever he went. Calmly dressing in a fresh, crisp shirt and donning his leather jacket, he stood tall and faced his determined inquisitor.

'I let her go,' Jeff answered, his eyes briefly giving away the very smallest of hints. 'Let's go for a drink. We can do the rest there. Bring your notebook. You need a drink.'

'*I* need a drink?' the woman gasped. 'You're a priceless fuck, Jeff Diamond, and an extreme arsehole.'

The tired musician laughed at a poor rendition of the mildly obscene Australian label, holding the door open for her to exit ahead of him. Once they were out of the lift and walking through the hotel foyer, Sarah asked him to describe his state of mind while talking with Gerry over the telephone or while joking with her and the concièrge while he had made their dinner reservation.

'Don't give me any sympathy,' he admitted without pathos. 'It's all an act. The whole fucking thing, recently. I have no idea who I am, doc. Years of practice at making life up.'

After a pleasant evening dining on seafood and steak, washed down with two bottles of wine and a few cocktails, Jeff walked his attractive colleague back to the hotel. Surprising her yet again, he left her at the lift doors, confessing his intention to stay out for a few more drinks. Sarah unwillingly accepted this dubious excuse, realising she should not expect to retain the attention of such an imperious man for any length of time.

The celebrity returned to the freezing night air, armed with the addresses for several local nightspots supplied by the helpful staff. Within an hour, he had met up with a new playmate, bought her two quick drinks and slipped her one of the special mouthfuls which always assured pleasant entertainment. Forethought had already seen a second hotel room booked, and then a third for good measure.

Jeff respected the eminent and flirtatious professor too much to use her so artlessly in his drunken state, though nowhere near enough to spend the night with her. Or with anyone else, for that matter. He knew he would be quizzed by Gerry as to why he had expensed so many rooms, already imagining the ebullient Sydney accent bellowing in his ear: "You rented three rooms in the same hotel on the same night? What the fuck were you up to?" Grimacing as the lift doors closed on him and his latest guest, he stifled a chuckle. "What the hell was he doing? Hide and seek?" he could hear the executive laughing with his PA, as he was entitled to. Indeed, what was he doing?

The next morning, over a languid breakfast and nursing a hangover, the twenty-year-old faced the maternal scolding of his research fellow, whose ego had been dented by his rejection, apportioning little sympathy for the seediness of his morning after.

'What was the most important lesson you learned during your teens?' she asked, pen poised to take dictation.

Jeff smiled, feeling the bile rising both physically and metaphorically. 'To inhibit animal behaviour, particularly when off my face with drink.'

Sarah's eyes met his, and her intriguing bad-boy winked. He was forgiven. Women always forgave him. It was such a pity that it counted for so little, since he was unable to forgive himself. He poured another cup of coffee and dropped in six lumps of sugar. Stirring vigorously, taking his frustrations out on the tepid liquid, he provided the explanation that her gaze demanded.

'Twisted, malformed instincts still take me by surprise all the time, so I'm learning every day. My mouth's easier to control than my fists, which might surprise you! And it's dangerous. I had absolutely the wrong role model for violent behaviour in my dad.'

While they were talking, a member of the hotel's reception team approached their table, red-faced and flustered at having to interrupt a serious conversation involving her most favourite superstar. Jeff's breakfast companion excused herself to take a telephone call from the university, leaving him with his meal and his thoughts. What he had omitted to pass on to the researcher was that his sister had suffered a far worse fate than he had during those early years in Canley Vale. Three years older, Madalena Diamond had escaped the worst of their parents' physical abuse, since both families' cultures held females in subordination and therefore with fewer expectations. However, she had certainly suffered a great deal of sexual abuse, and at the hands of the worst of Sydney's underworld. Her brother's graphic depictions would doubtless have reduced the professor to tears at the thought of a young boy bearing witness to such demeaning acts, let alone hearing about the screams from behind the bedroom door and the guilt he still carried from not being able to do anything to help.

Furthermore, he refused to confide in Sarah that their father had actively discouraged his son from intervening, sometimes hitting him and other times booting him down several flights of concrete steps from their squalid, second-floor flat. These were atrocities he was likely to keep to himself for the rest of his life. Madalena would never hear these details, and certainly Gerry wouldn't either. The fewer people with access to this information the better, not least to minimise the chances of it slipping into the wrong hands. Such salacious gossip about Australia's hottest new star would no doubt spread like wildfire across a globe which was hungry for scandal.

For the remainder of this study, the team in Toronto was more interested in the way victims reacted to trauma and how they sought to compensate for their losses through addictive behaviour. Jeff and his fellow guinea pigs, who came from all walks of life, swapped experiences of rejection, shame and insecurity, finding they commonly addressed these by shrouding the traits they perceived as defective. All patients admitted to feelings of anger, resulting from resentment of a life which had dealt them such a raw deal. The danger of this implicit fury, kept firmly obscured by their masks, was that it tended to cause severe depression in virtually the whole sample, along with suicidal tendencies in many.

Of course, across the board, altering their state of mind with alcohol or other drugs became the easiest method of convincing others that there was nothing wrong with them. In addition, several reported a dependence on anything that could bring a sense of personal power, particularly sex. Listening to these stories of dominance and revenge were frightening, making it clear to Jeff and Sarah that reliable evidence existed to support the reasons why the abused often showed a propensity for becoming abusers themselves, and therewith an urgent imperative to find a way to rehabilitate them. Shivers ran down the young man's spine as he remembered the time he had been a hair's breadth away from raping Lynn Dyson, forevermore to be known as "the tennis skirt episode", and felt thankful that so far he had known when to stop. So far...

The longer the study continued, and the more data they collected, a second stark difference became apparent between the millionnaire who was funding the program and the other participants: an unfailing resolve to be the instigator of lasting change. This was the phenomenon which was explicable to the philosopher only by the deeply-held belief in reincarnating souls which he had only ever shared with one person. Why, otherwise, was he the only one among his cohort not to be beset by an inferiority complex? Quite the opposite, in fact.

Jeff had known for many years that he stood apart from the rest, constantly at pains to play this useful characteristic down. It had been evident right through school and again in the present day, as demonstrated by the velocity with which his career had taken off. Whatever drove him, whether from within or without, was a force greater than Jeff Diamond. This man was only the nineteen-fifty-two vintage of an old soul passing through, with the misfortune to be delivered into the world as the second child of Pavel Diament. The nobody from Canley Vale harboured a need inside far stronger than the mere desire to turn such misfortune into a monumental vat of good fortune. Perhaps the same need that had seen him seek out Lynn Dyson.

No wonder the rising star felt so compelled to deliver tangible results from this piece of research! He had long held the suspicion that he was born preordained with this outlandish responsibility, and thankfully he had now garnered both the financial and intellectual means to do something about it.

As he had suggested to Lynn all those months ago, Maslow's Hierarchy had served its expected purpose nicely, and the patience and perseverance of this peculiar partnership was soon rewarded, with Doctor Friedman totally unaware of her financier's private commitment. The result was a seminal work linking the triad of trauma, mental illness and addiction presented to the

Committee of Reactive Disorders, which would go on to achieve worldwide critical acclaim. Jeff remained relatively anonymous as its unqualified co-author, but nevertheless he was very proud of his contribution and anticipated it as a trigger for accelerating further research into new treatment patterns, including a better understanding of the requirement to supplement psychological therapies by fulfilling oft-neglected basic needs: sleep, exercise, relaxation and healthy nutrition.

It would prove difficult to pursue his own treatment plan once the rock star headed back out on the road with his bombastic, beer-swilling band. He was also eager to work on the more sophisticated layers of the hierarchy, such as learning to stay in a positive frame of mind and to do his best to control his environment, the groundwork for which had been laid during his time with a certain Australian tennis player. He smiled when he remembered the sixteen-year-old's amiable efforts to wean him off excess alcohol and her pointed criticism of the amount of time he spent in nightclubs and pubs instead of "recharging".

The stakeholder plan which his former girlfriend had encouraged him to maintain had certainly undergone a considerable workout in recent months. Some new names had been added, and others demoted. The same name remained steadfastly on the top row. No surprises there! Jeff wondered if his name might have cracked a mention on Lynn's plan now that her parents weren't able to oversee it quite so closely... Regardless, the ambitious celebrity was confident that he was putting his newfound fame and fortune to good use, which left him feeling a good deal happier than if he were simply amassing further fame and fortune and having it stagnate in some Swiss bank account.

On the night they put the final touches to their paper, the professor and the rock star shared a celebratory dinner at the Panorama restaurant in Toronto, overlooking spectacular city views. Sarah took the opportunity to proclaim her love for him and begged him to stay for longer, unaware of the unbroken bond which Jeff shared with an ex-girlfriend. The announcement did not come as a surprise to her dinner companion, who had watched many similarly-infatuated women dissolve into distraught tears. Even though her offer was rejected with great compassion, the shoe was firmly on the other foot, and blame was cast unfairly once again. Callous though it seemed, the lovelorn musician felt strong and satisfied with his ability to be honest and not simply cave in and prolong a relationship for the sake of not being alone.

The songwriter recalled the sorry situation into which he had tumbled several years earlier with Donna Watts, determined not to make the same mistake again. Theirs had been a hostage situation, in which neither party had been acting rationally. Similar to his mental state upon meeting Sarah, he had been in such a desperately low place that he sought refuge in the attractive television reporter; someone he could hang onto and let drag him up and out of the abyss. In those days, he had been too immature to stop himself latching on, and both suffered the consequences when they discovered that neither was the saviour they had expected.

Jeff understood what was happening this time, with another four years of self-awareness under his belt, and broke the dependency soon enough. However, his reliance on Lynn remained fully intact, confident that she was the key to helping him rise above the trauma and its exhausting after-effects. He had always known this, hadn't he? Therefore, departing for the Swiss Alps with Gerry and his kid sister, the rock star made the transition to Mister Life-and-Soul once more, ready to serve out the rest of the sentence Bart Dyson had imposed upon him.

Lynn would be proud of him. Hopefully.

Distribution Of Wealth

In Saint Moritz, surrounded by the affluent jet-set who insisted on the new celebrity's attention, assuming with a different kind of inbred superiority that theirs was the lifestyle he was after, Jeff Diamond committed to taking some time out. At first, it was just like old times, except for the pleasing fact that he was paying for the Blakes rather than the other way around. Tamilla had recently turned twenty-two years of age and was a breath of fresh air for her dark-haired travelling companion; fun in bed and sophisticatedly salacious in the bar. And she wouldn't be asking him for anything more, since she was as much of a hedonist as her brother.

Unfortunately however, the star's plan for meaningless romps with a fun-loving friend quickly turned sour. More than simply an aphrodisiac, the newfound notoriety which besieged the grown-up version of her brother's best friend acted as a powerful magnet for the spoiled Sydney socialite, who spent the entire trip stuck to his side and posing for the cameras. Why was it that all these erstwhile carefree women got away with being so possessive, and yet he had never been further removed from the one he really wanted?

Gerry took the adulation in his stride, amused by the lengths to which some people would go to be seen with his handsome client. All he saw was Jeff enjoying himself, fighting off overt advances and accepting drinks bought for him by total strangers. Concealed was the paradoxical loneliness which lurked just beneath the surface, as the star struggled to put on his happy face time and time again. They would host a party in their hotel suite every night, word spreading like wildfire through the well-connected skiing fraternity.

This time, Tamilla stayed for the orgies, protected from the worst scenes by her chivalrous hosts. She was introduced to threesomes, foursomes and moresomes, occasionally finding herself across the enormous bed from her own brother! Conversations each lunchtime, which substituted for breakfast due to the long, wakeful nights, would include extensive *post mortems* and agreements on the level of detail appropriate to be passed on to Jacinta, who was obviously missing out on all the fun.

The young woman repaid her gallant gentleman for his hospitality in her own special way, by teasing and torturing him incessantly that Australia's most eligible female export would never be coming back to him. She showed him articles that she had torn out from women's magazines and brought with her from Sydney, showing Lynn out partying with clean-cut Americans and looking unlikely to give the famed playboy another thought. The more Jeff assured his tormentor that her tactics weren't working, the more it encouraged the feisty minx to needle away. Frayed patience stretched to the limit, the tired man's resolve finally cracked, and he confessed to being inclined to agree, but that he owed it to himself to wait and see.

This was the first time that Tammy had seen her brother's handsome and gregarious buddy close to tears, and she realised she had pushed him too far. She apologised profusely, but it came too late to save the twenty-year-old's sanity from taking another nosedive. Using rehearsals for the new tour as his excuse, he bid farewell to the Blakes, flew home the following morning and shut himself inside his apartment for the three days remaining.

Absurd in its irony, his next stop was Los Angeles, home of the Lakers and Lynn, yet by now the coincidence held surprisingly little significance for the young man in need of re-energising again. He poured his heartbroken angst into writing and recording, producing mesmerising performances for another series of sell-out concerts and also becoming firm friends with the two front-men from the Vultures. Greg Marlow and Phil Steyn were both proud patriots, yet shared the Australian's critical perspective on their countries' insularity and narrow-mindedness, particularly when it came to the conflicts in the Far East. This was a dangerous view which Jeff had dared to voice at home too, and the musicians' combined powers of reasoning yielded a portfolio of potential hits laced with anarchic ideas and cultural commentary for both sets of performers to hold in store.

While in Los Angeles, the Sydneysider happened to be in town and playing the well-known Troubadour Club at the same time as another new sensation, a talented British singer-songwriter by the name of Tex Fletcher. Swapping rehearsal schedules, the unlikely pair struck up an instant friendship while their respective roadies bumped equipment and instruments in and out. Tex was primarily a composer, and hence became an outlet for the countless poems that had come to Jeff as lyrics with no melody. Another lucrative collaboration partnership was born, and with it yet another unrequited love. Tex, in his late twenties, had been experimenting with his sexuality and was upset to find that Jeff was definitely but most compassionately not gay.

Their professional relationship survived in spite of this rejection, largely because in opening up to the amateur counsellor, the older man had revealed a similar fragility carried from childhood paternal abandonment. This discussion provided the Australian with an ideal follow-up research project into the human condition. Why were so many artists, musicians and songwriters also troubled souls? Which came first, the psychological imbalance or the creativity?

He had found kindred spirits in several other writing partnerships too, and became driven to understand why certain musicians did not present as fellow sufferers, such as the members of The Rolling Stones. He was fascinated by the circle he now inhabited, which was as vice-ridden as the one he had grown up in and yet was endowed with all the trappings a man could ever desire. Week after week, he recognised new like-minds and vital songwriting collaborators who would feed each others' intellects long into the future, not to mention the common addiction to sex, drugs and rock'n'roll which had drawn them together in the first place.

Were some stars purely in it for the money or to churn out material for art's sake, or only for vain, narcissistic success? Indeed, as Jeff forced himself to admit, the lovely Lynn Dyson was among these types. Songs did not typically come to her as a result of deep thought or mental crisis. Hers were manufactured on demand; a skill honed in the music department at Melbourne Academy rather than while drinking and smoking in a darkened bedroom, drowning out screams from the other side of the wall or having been woken by the second brutal nightmare in as many hours.

Jeff Diamond was, once the glamour and adulation subsided, heading for an even more dangerous time. The bright onset of the northern hemisphere spring coincided with the anniversary of his meeting his dream girl, and the chasm widened still further between his vibrant stage persona, who strutted like a peacock and held his court spellbound at endless parties, and the disillusioned, sleep-deprived shell of a man who lay squinting in the sunlight that streamed through his hotel window each morning. He foresaw the impending disaster only too easily, though elected to deny the warning signs for many weeks.

No longer gratified by the usual suspects of alcohol, barbiturates and marijuana propelling him out of the doldrums, the impervious risk-taker allowed the Vultures' guitarist, Ray Smart, to introduce him to cocaine. Whoa! What a buzz this gave him! Instead of dulling his senses and reducing the heartache, it rendered him utterly oblivious to pain. Riding on its powerful high, the new rock star believed he was indestructible and even managed to convince himself that Lynn had never mattered. Jeff likened the freedom he hit upon when spiced with cocaine to the elation he had experienced when first confessing to his former lover about his damaged youth, and then magnified ten times. It was as if nothing could touch him. Everything was totally cool. Until he came down, that was...

So the rock star didn't come down. What was the point? The first half of nineteen-seventy-three was consciously lost to endless depravity and self-indulgence. It seemed that wherever he went in the world, the party people would sniff him out, quite literally... Jeff Diamond became known as a very popular drawcard for anyone who sought their fifteen minutes of fame, always willing to share the limelight and frequently making the headlines, either through his larger-than-life public appearances or the antics in which he luxuriated behind the scenes. Moreover, back in Australia, his friends remained blissfully unaware of his precarious lifestyle, only hearing reports of soaring success and watching the money pouring in.

In late May, having wrapped up a third album in New York and after a brief detour to Toronto to receive a horizontal update on Sarah Friedman's research paper, Jeff returned to Melbourne with a view to completing his bachelor's degree as quickly as he could. Autumn had taken the sting out of the midday sun, matching the superstar's demeanour, dog-tired and bored with the hype. In his personal mail, which had been set aside for him while he was away, he found an invitation to his own twenty-first birthday party. Shit! So caught up was he in this extreme, decadent way of life, that his actual life was passing him by. The invitation was from Celia Blake, who with her son's help had booked a function room at a swanky Melbourne hotel on her extra child's birthday, which conveniently fell on a Saturday this year.

Since putting his studies on hold, the millionaire undergraduate had travelled high on amphetamines to prevent the embarrassment of nightmares, played high on cocaine to counteract the exhaustion and taken refuge in prolonged bouts of tranquilising sex while mellowed out on marijuana. Regardless of the substance consumed, a side order of alcohol remained the perfect accompaniment, topped off by a cigarette or two. His life had become a pageant of parallel, concentric circles, navigating from gig to interview and from cocktail party to bare-skinned *bacchanalia*.

Twenty-one years old, the old soul mused, re-reading the embossed and silver-edged invitation. Only twenty-one? He felt at least double that, and then some.

Jesus, Jeff thought, *what a mess!* He had leaped headlong into the very hedonistic and self-serving types of recreation he had sworn his rich and famous alter-ego would never entertain. Who the hell did he think he was? At home, his true friends cared enough about him to organise a birthday celebration, and there he was pissing his days away with the type of friends that were swallowed, snorted, smoked or injected. These were good companions in the short term, but he was so much better than this. The hollow celebrity resolved to drag himself out of this quagmire of chemicals and regain some perspective.

It was a lesson Jeff appreciated he had learned just in time. As he came crashing down from months of delirium, his senses were regularly scuttled by horrific images of his mother's drug-ridden body, disgusted at his own behaviour. How could he have discounted these familiar perils so easily, and how could he show such little respect for her memory? Let alone for himself. Through cocaine he had managed to disassociate himself from his own nightmares and phobias in an effort to find a way out, but he knew this was only lifting him from the frying pan into the fire.

And all the money the new millionaire had wasted feeding his reckless habits... Silently, back in his Richmond hideaway, the young star ate some humble pie and calculated how much more he could be ploughing into worthy causes if he had stayed on the straight and narrow. It was a frighteningly large sum, and the final kick to spur him towards cleaning himself up.

Having made this overdue choice, the superstar songwriter found his journey back to healthy habits to be surprisingly easy. Once back in Melbourne and free of jet-lag, slipping back into his old environs again, RMIT's most famous student threw himself into physical exercise of any kind: running, tennis, swimming, basketball and soccer. His university mates welcomed him back with open arms, glad to have someone so interesting to hang out with and, more importantly, to attract the fairer sex.

Therefore, by once more applying the disciplines he had sorely neglected, Jeff Diamond managed to fix his daylight self pretty well. Mister Life-and-Soul gradually began to like the someone he had become, rationalising the happy memories of Lynn with the good fortune of his newfound importance. With no fewer interruptions to his sleeping hours however, he set about using the long nights to put the finishing touches to his first novel, in an effort to kick his various addictions. Entitled "The Runner", the story was set in Auschwitz in World War II and centred around a character loosely based on Joseph Mengele, with also a fair resemblance to Bart Dyson thrown in for good measure. A British publishing house picked up his proposal on first hearing, and negotiations followed soon afterwards with Paramount Pictures to create a screenplay to be scheduled for the following year.

With the exception of a full night's sleep, it seemed there was nothing the new sensation couldn't accomplish.

***

From her secret hideaway overlooking San Francisco Bay, Lynn Dyson followed the burgeoning career of her enigmatic ex-boyfriend as closely as she could get away with without arousing suspicion. Her fellow college students, mostly North Americans, automatically assumed Australia to be such a small place that everyone must know everyone. This afforded their very own superstar the convenience of answering truthfully but noncommittally when asked if she had met the talented and altogether delicious Jeff Diamond.

The sporting star loved to read reviews of his sell-out concert appearances, picturing the confident new artist walking out on stage, arms aloft, and looking out over a sea of faces. She could well imagine the new levels of pride and power he must now be enjoying and hoped he could derive some much needed inspiration from his adoring fans. How excited the persuasive, would-be activist must be to now have a voice and some financial resources with which to start the projects he had foreshadowed so passionately.

It hadn't taken the photogenic orator long to take the entertainment world by storm, wielding his superior intellect regularly in television interviews and magazine articles. Lynn was often moved to both laughter and tears when she read between the well-chosen lines he provided to innocent journalists who knew no better than to take the handsome pretender at face value. Not unlike her own uncertain response in those early days, she admitted.

Jeff Diamond was now a force to be reckoned with, which pleased the young woman a great deal. She missed him acutely, even though her new life was replete with new friends, and she frequently caught herself daydreaming whether his rapid rise to stardom had caused him to leave all thoughts of their mighty fine few months behind. He was constantly pictured with pretty women on his arm at nightclubs and industry events, creating mixed emotions in his former lover. Overall, Lynn was happy that her troubled black stallion seemed to be enjoying his fame and fortune, but she also wished she was free to share it at least in some capacity, so long as their relationship could have endured while their individual ambitions and very different paths diverged.

The most fulfilling part of the rock star's success was the ability to spread money around to wherever it was needed most. Gerry, through their new management company, had employed an expert not-for-profit tax accountant specifically to manage his friend's ever-growing charitable fund. This torrent of inward-flowing cash was fifty percent of a significant amount, even after less than half a year at the top of his game. Paragon Holdings was in the process of splitting into two organisations; one seeding new profit-making ventures; and the other opening up channels to those less fortunate. The Diamond Celebration Foundation was soon on the map and with the grandest master plan imaginable.

On a flight from New York to Paris in early February nineteen-seventy-three, Jeff had been seated next to a pair of dynamic and entrepreneurial humanitarians working in Nicaragua after a devastating earthquake. Recognising who he was, they seized the opportunity to explain their dream of setting up an organisation which could fly makeshift schools, complete with teachers, into remote places and help to save lives in disaster situations. Jeff was captivated by the innovative idea and, as impulsive as ever, he instantly committed a huge sum towards their cause.

'What the fuck have you done?' Gerry had jeered down the telephone. 'You haven't got that sort of money lying around in petty cash, you idiot.'

"No sweat, mate,' was the traveller's casual reply. 'This needs doing, and I can help make it happen. It's exactly why I'm doing this shit. I'll make it up to you. Couple of months, max'.'

Such was Jeff's confidence in his own performances and the endless stream of new material he was generating that he insisted the investment go ahead. Nominally apolitical in its manifesto, the outspoken and charismatic media star launched a therefore deliciously political mission in his favourite European capital within a few weeks of this original, mile-high conversation.

The celebrity's confidence in his manager, friend and trusted adviser was beyond impeachment too. With every new development in the celebrity's accelerating career, Gerry Blake rose to the challenge admirably, coming up with ever more creative options for dealing with the obscene dollar amounts which continued to funnel into Blake & Partners' offices in the form of large cheques and international money orders.

The expansion within the prime Collins Street real estate knew no bounds either. Stonebridge Music was already a substantial entity in its own right, requiring independent floor space and someone to preside over it. The able accountant suggested Jeff might like to find an experienced impresario and entertainment industry veteran to take care of his artistic interests now that he was part of the "major league". The loyal Sydneysider wouldn't hear a bar of that particular song however, determined that their business relationship would remain as strong as their friendship for as long as the fun-loving businessman wanted to be involved with his mate's crazy world.

Theirs was the ultimate professional match, each living and learning through each others' expertise, and the one never straying onto the other's territory. Gerald Blake Senior and other well-credentialed partners in the Sydney Head Office were occasionally called upon for advice, but largely the two *amigos* made their own way.

One of their better decisions was to recruit an energetic graduate of the Melbourne Business School to oversee Stonebridge Music. Primarily installed at first as an administrator, within a few months Cathy Patterson had proven her worth several times over in the specialist fields of marketing and event management, and quickly earned herself the third *amigo*'s stripes.

As their individual reputations grew, more and more Australian celebrities knocked on Stonebridge's door, seeking representation from the hot, new team in town. Collaboration personified, Jeff made sure he introduced Gerry as a matter of course to every possible connection for the other side of the office, the mainstream accountancy practice. Business was booming, whether at the Board table, in the cocktail lounge, on the terraces of the MCG or in the bedroom. Gerry and Cathy lapped up every new experience voraciously, and their top-notch signing was stoked to see his friends benefitting from the outrageous success he appeared to be able to garner with comparatively little effort.

Regularly at the end of the night, the two red-blooded males would part company in the hallway, heading to separate hotel rooms with their chosen playmates, having shared a warm handshake and a last drunken joke. Not once did the happy-go-lucky manager ask his client how he was travelling, for which the musician was grateful since it meant his sordid secrets stayed safe. The older man touched neither the hard drugs nor the money; only occasionally making reference to the dangers of the former and the delights of the latter, and the younger made sure his mate was amply rewarded for the mutual trust and confidentiality which underpinned their partnership.

More to the point, the accountant never dug deeper as to why his biggest client frequently expensed two hotel rooms per night when away from his home town. Fortuitous indeed, for he would never have understood the tortured soul's *modus operandi*. Of course, one room was for the girl or girls to sleep in after they had partaken in sufficient cavorting, while the other was where Jeff spent the remaining nocturnal hours entertaining the ghoulish characters inside his head. The private man would explain it as a desire to retreat for the solitude of his own company, to write songs or his screenplay, both reasons being incontrovertible substitutes for the truth.

The prosperous rock star, conversely, never quite understood the Scrooge-like pleasure Gerry had inherited from his father at seeing the numbers on each ledger growing larger and larger, and much less the almost frenzied compulsion to squirrel as much as possible away from the taxman's hungry clutches. Notwithstanding these differences of opinion, the twenty-year-old most definitely valued the opportunities provided by these sizeable balances to kick off project after project. Two boyhood friends from different sides of the railway tracks, who had long sparred over their opposing political views around taxation and social welfare, were these days no longer testing hypotheticals. Jeff insisted in no uncertain terms that he pay every cent of his share to the Australian Tax Office, and Gerry counter-asserted in his own indomitable fashion that his nemesis was a lunatic of both stark and raving proportions.

The complex human being slowly making his mark on the world was busy turning dreams into reality. He saw his role at The Fellowship morph iteratively from customer to counsellor to generous benefactor, depending on his state of mind on any given day. A grant from the Diamond Celebration Foundation funded a new centre, replacing the dilapidated community hall off Church Road with a purpose-built facility complete with creature comforts, as well as taking on additional paid support staff. The most pleasing aspect of all was to witness the rollout of the treatment plan trials he himself had played a significant part in defining, and then to watch them yield positive results right in front of his eyes.

It irked the young star somewhat that among his growing legion of fans, vehemently thirsty for any new musical material and as much salacious or romantic gossip they could lay their eyes and ears on, precious few were interested in looking beyond the music and the party antics which gave rise to his high profile public persona.

Those who knew how much effort he put into these more sober activities chose to admire him silently, and consequently it was extremely edifying to receive a letter of thanks or an encouraging telephone call once in a while. Whenever such correspondence arrived, it gave Cathy and the team in the office the rare excuse to treat their magnanimous and humble boss to a little flattery, and each one brought him renewed hope that he could survive yet another month to close in on Lynn's distant return date.

Night after night, fighting his obsessive death-wish, Jeff would plead with whomever might be listening to send his guardian angel back to help him. Neither fame nor fortune, nor even his growing compendium of accomplishments could help him endure the long, dark nights without descending into the deepest, darkest depression. Only his beautiful best friend had the power to calm his jangling nerves when the nightmares struck, and only her memory could give him the strength to carry on when morning reared its ugly head.

With each turn of this ridiculous but lucrative merry-go-round, the best mates' loyalty to one another never wavered. They lurched from business to pleasure, frequently mixing the two far too thoroughly, in every corner of the globe and totally in step with the master plan. Two closer friends there could not have been, even though neither took the time to stop and think about it. Money poured in hand-over-fist and was repurposed in myriad ways without delay. The Diamond machine careened along in perfect working order, and they were the envy of all their associates and rivals.

***

On a promotional tour of Europe for the latest blockbuster movie to come out of Hollywood, leading lady Lynn Dyson came across an article in The Economist magazine. She had picked it up quite by chance while waiting to be ferried between television stations, idling in a similar limbo scenario to that in which her ex-boyfriend had discovered Sarah Friedman. There was a picture of two French educators standing next to a tall, dark and devastatingly handsome man whose face she recognised only too well.

The report filled her with joy at the realisation that Jeff's dreams of changing the world were beginning to come true. Regularly through the media, Lynn learned of the many frivolous exploits fuelling her former lover's playboy reputation, so much so that she had begun to wonder whether he was now so caught up in the showbusiness scene that he had forgone all the altruistic ideals he had espoused during their time together. The optimist refused to believe her ambitious intellectual would sell his worthy goals short for the sake of rock'n'roll, but also had a fair idea of how much his warped mind would command indulgence.

The star's contribution to "Enseignants pour la Paix", translated to "Teachers for Peace", was suitably understated in the article, as only he would have had it, but nevertheless it had restored the intelligent young woman's faith in her errant black stallion, guessing that his commitment to this novel cause was significant. That night, in a luxury London hotel, she had cried herself to sleep for the first time in six months, steeped in a mixture of pride and regret.

How Lynn longed to pick up the telephone and congratulate her good friend personally. She would love to know if being involved with such a worthwhile project was giving him the satisfaction he had envisioned, and to learn how many more similar activities he had kicked off, about which she was as yet unaware. He probably didn't even have the same number these days, the teenager presumed, as tears sprang to her eyes once again. The four-pointed tour of the pokey Richmond flat never ceased to bring a smile to her face, and a shiver ran down her spine as memories flooded back of his strong hands steering her shoulders until she had come full circle.

The studious film star refused to believe that Jeff had forgotten her and all the happy times they had shared. Even though she had been dating casually whenever her schedule allowed, not a day went by when she didn't relive their steamy encounters or picture him staring at her lovingly from the couch while they constructed a new song. She had trusted his eloquence completely. Surely Mister Life-and-Soul's heart still harboured at least some of the emotions he had expressed so openly?

When the pair had first parted, the Olympic athlete had jumped every time the telephone rang, feeling hopeful that her passionate rebel had chosen to ignore her parents' ruling. It both surprised her and disappointed her that she hadn't heard from him, at times sure that her own integrity would not be as strong. As the months had gone by, she found a certain peace of mind in the fact that his touring and hectic recording commitments were helping him to push her to the back of his mind. She should do the same, but she had never expected it to be such a heart-wrenching challenge.

A week or so after the "Enseignants pour la Paix" launch had been announced, Gerry informed his biggest client that a quarter of a million US dollars had been donated to the charity anonymously. The money had been credited directly into the fund by an Australian bank, yet its source remained undisclosed.

'Two-fifty thou'? You're kidding?' Jeff had exclaimed in response. 'Who from?'

Gerry was about to tease his frequently wasted friend as to whether he still possessed the mental capacity to understand the meaning of the word "anonymously" when he twigged that Jeff was playing with him.

'Very funny, mate,' the accountant barked. 'John Paul Getty? Kerry Packer? Santa? How the hell should I know?'

Not prepared to suffer further derision from his business manager, Jeff decided against airing his sneaking suspicion as to who the mysterious contributor might be, fervently hoping he was right. Not many people gave donations of this magnitude without wanting to be identified at least to the recipient organisation. There would need to be a very good reason why someone would seek to slip under the radar in that way. He knew of someone with such a reason.

That night, in a similarly luxurious Sydney hotel room, the almost twenty-one-year-old lay on the bed, staring at the picture he carried in his wallet and willing it to speak to him. He thanked Lynn's image for her generosity and wished her well. She had reached out to him in an exquisitely noble and selfless way, and it had bolstered his strength no end. Instead of hitting the town after his television appearance, he had spent the late evening hours in wild fantasies of the beautiful and compassionate celebrity who continued to occupy his every lucid thought.

The elder Dyson daughter would turn eighteen in a mere three months' time, and Jeff wondered if this might trigger a change of heart from the States-side superstar. This was highly unlikely, since they had discussed the possibility at length before she departed, and he had been left in no doubt that she intended to weather the imposed expatriation without resistance.

Their invisible elastic connection was stretched to its absolute limit, so paper-thin that the lovesick songwriter could barely feel it, yet taut enough to set his teeth on edge with its resonance. At least he was now convinced that she still thought of him in a positive light, which was a most unexpected bonus at the halfway point. His faith had been restored, whether for real or in his imagination, in the most magical way.

Despite this rare cheerful mood however, in the early hours of the morning the tormented man kept his regular appointment with his demons, who once more warned him not to venture towards happiness. He oughtn't to get too optimistic, they had threatened. He didn't deserve it. He hadn't done enough yet...

Family members who were at most distant memories gradually came out of the woodwork as another by-product of Jeff Diamond's new status as a household name. His mother's siblings and their children, along with a number of other cousins far removed, began to appear out of nowhere on hearing their relative's name linked with vast sums of money and notorious celebrity. Keen to muscle in on a piece of the action, they contacted the superstar's record company one by one, eagerly proclaiming their connection.

On one particularly morning while her boss happened to be in town, an office clerk at Stonebridge Music opened a glossy envelope addressed to her favourite heartthrob. It was a wedding invitation from a bride by the name of Graciela Mercedes Moreno, and the dizzy secretary gossiped excitedly to her colleagues. Between them, the women came to the conclusion that it had been sent by one of the good-looking musician's many female conquests around the world, only silenced by Cathy's stern glare and a tacit request to stow the card back in its envelope and safely into the folder, along with the rest of his salaciously personal correspondence.

'Interesting...' Jeff mused aloud to his manager, as they sat in the Boardroom at Blake & Partners a few days later. 'My cousin wants me to go to her wedding.'

Gerry looked up from the endless pages of bank transactions which they had been reconciling. 'Cousin? Girl cousin? Is she hot?'

'Maybe,' his friend replied with a shrug. 'Haven't seen her since she was nine or thereabouts. Some guy obviously thinks so. Pregnant, I'd guess.'

The older man noticed a scowl on the celebrity's face. Despite having known him for almost a decade, the Irishman had gleaned almost nothing about his mate's immigrant family. He only knew there was a sister somewhere in Sydney's west, since teenaged boys were wont to check for the existence of any easily accessible females.

'I didn't even know you had any cousins.'

'Yeah. Quite a few,' Jeff confirmed. 'Catholic family. What do you expect? There are some I haven't even met. I'll be damned if I'm going to this just to serve as some hired exhibit.'

Tossing the wedding invitation across the table towards his manager, the disgruntled musician moved quickly on to the next item in the pile. Nonplussed by the venomous tone in the other man's voice, Gerry shook his head.

'Just tell Maria what you want to say in the response, and she'll decline it on your behalf,' he instructed, businesslike and only half concentrating. 'We'll send her a cheque for a million dollars. That's what she's really after.'

The millionnaire let loose a bitter, smoky chuckle. 'You're not wrong! Unbelievable, huh? They never lifted a finger to help my mum, that bunch of money-hungry, Argentinean *derrochadores*. They can all go to hell.'

The accountant nodded, scanning the wording in the invitation. 'Fair enough! Not too keen on them then?'

'Fuck, mate. Leave it,' his sarcastic friend scoffed. 'D'you wanna go instead? You're welcome. I doubt they'd notice you weren't me. You could have a lot of fun with it.'

Gerry scribbled a note to Maria requesting a polite decline and placed it with the invitation on another pile. It was only a bloody wedding invitation, he thought to himself. Sometimes Jeff's tendency to overdramatise annoyed him.

'No, thanks,' he replied. 'That's beyond my brief. Beer?'

As the days went by, with the late autumn weather turning colder and wetter in Melbourne, the lonely man suddenly realised the invisible elastic connection to Lynn had vanished again. Blaming himself, as he always did, the sickened obsessive became convinced that he had taken his eye off the ball, given all that was going on in his life. He had made the mistake of relaxing into the resurgent bond engendered by her donation, which in itself could not be substantiated and might just as well be a figment of his imagination, and carelessly he had let it slip away.

To add insult to injury, that same night he dreamed that he had attended his cousin Graciela's wedding after all, and with Lynn. It had been the most beautiful dream, during which they had danced the night away while his estranged family looked on in disbelief. His very own Bond girl looked hot, her eyes devoured him, and her hands were all over him, letting him know how much she had missed him time and time again. Their lost love reinstated itself steamily under the covers until this beacon of retribution ludicrously transformed into the usual nightmare, as any pleasant dream invariably did, leaving Jeff soon wide awake, cursing into his whisky and utterly dejected.

***

'Lynn, it's Dad,' Bart Dyson announced into the telephone from his study, at home in the sprawling Benloch mansion. 'How are you?'

'Hi, Dad. I'm fine. And you?' his daughter replied from her college room, looking out into a thick fog rising off the river.

The seventeen-year-old was immediately filled with a foreboding feeling, always suspicious when her father rang her directly. Social calls were normally initiated by her mother, who would wait until they were almost finished before then passing the receiver to her busy husband for any final words.

'I'm very well, thanks,' his booming voice answered. 'Do you have a few minutes for a chat?'

The young woman's heart sank. Her instincts were right. She had already guessed the reason for his call.

'Yes, Dad. What's up?'

Bart cleared his throat. 'Lynn, I've been informed that you requested a withdrawal from your term deposit account sometime last week for a charitable donation.'

'Yes, I did.'

'Access to that account is supposed to be for emergencies only.'

'I know, Dad,' his daughter answered with contrition, 'but I transferred the money back in the next day, from the trust.'

'It was a significant amount of money, my girl, wasn't it?' her father continued, sounding angry.

'Two hundred and fifty thousand,' Lynn agreed with gutsy pride, aware she was pushing her luck. 'Dad, what's the problem? It's my money.'

'Don't you think this is something you should have discussed with me or Mum first?'

'Probably, but I needed to do it quickly,' the teenager defended herself. 'I'm sorry. I should've told you.'

'No,' the Olympian snapped. 'You should have asked us. *Asked* us, Lynn. Do you understand the difference? You can't go throwing that sort of money around indiscriminately.'

The singer's hackles rose. 'I didn't throw it around indiscriminately,' she insisted. 'It was a donation to a worthy cause. Well, at least *I* think so.'

All the way from California, the teenager could sense her father bristling on the other end of the line. It was too much to hope that the powerful man, with his army of advisers, wouldn't be on top of the type of news covered by The Economist, and also hardly surprising that he would be able to deduce from her timing exactly where her withdrawal had been credited. She had already guessed what he was about to say next, and guilt flooded through her.

'A worthy cause it might well be, but here's how it is... Firstly, you're still under eighteen, and strictly speaking we are still responsible for you.'

That'd be right, Lynn thought. Like they were responsible for sending her to the other side of the world on her own...

The forthright sportsman continued. 'And secondly, I expect you to be honest with me about whether you know who's behind this particular worthy cause.'

'Yes and yes,' she replied without hesitation, bursting with an indignation now fuelled by surging emotions and evoked by the visualisation of her handsome orator at his most potent. 'Dad, I know I'm still a child in your eyes... and legally too... And I'm sorry I didn't discuss it with you first. I didn't, precisely because I knew you would ask me the second question.'

'As I thought,' Bart murmured under his breath. 'I'm very disappointed. I thought you were better than that, Lynn.'

The Australian beauty hated to think that she had let her parents down but was also angry at her never-ending inability to act for herself. She knew her father was right. It had been an impulsive act motivated more by bitter anguish and to make up for the sweet, sublime intimacy she missed, than by a desire to see temporary schools erected in war-torn places. Her father mustn't know this though.

'Dad, I'm sorry,' she said again. '"Teachers for Peace" is a fantastic idea. You have to agree, don't you? I can't kid you that I would've donated such a lot of money if I hadn't found out that Jeff was involved, but the money hasn't gone to him. I haven't contacted him, and the donation was given anonymously. It went through the bank and with no connection with California or anything.'

The well-respected statesman appreciated his daughter's candour but refused to understand her position. As far as he was concerned, it had shown immaturity and a careless disregard for her family and for their resources. He and Marianna had not raised their children to be cavalier with money, regardless of how worthy the cause.

'Jeff Diamond's long since forgotten about you, my girl,' he responded in a slightly more compassionate tone. 'Look at his appalling behaviour. Never out of the papers. Does he look like a man who's pining for you? You're not that naïve. Surely all the publicity hasn't escaped your notice?'

'No,' Lynn gulped.

She could hardly deny this. Jeff's affairs were front page news, his image regularly gracing the gossip columns with his arm around one red-hot woman after another. She resisted the temptation to remind her father that her own media coverage would tell much the same story to an outsider. His words stung nevertheless. Perhaps she *was* the only one still hanging on to this dream.

There could be no disputing the evidence that the rock sensation was lavishing his considerable energy and attention upon his career, and harvesting all the trappings that came with it. Other lovers were being treated to his touch, gazing into those deep, dark pools of desire and listening to his expressive poetry, hypnotised as she had been, whether it meant anything to him or not.

'That's all well and good,' Bart continued. 'Has Diamond contacted you?'

The young woman groaned audibly, her head aching with the stress. 'No, Dad, he hasn't. You have to trust him, please. He's an honourable person, even if I'm not.'

Big D huffed at her willingness to defend someone so apparently undeserving, but admired the fact that she was prepared to admit her own shortcomings. It was clear that his daughter still felt an attachment to this headstrong and outspoken man, regardless of their time apart, which infuriated him more than the fact that such a large sum had been handed over. He had kept a keen eye on the emerging star and was beginning to concede that he might be dealing with a more formidable entity than he had initially reckoned.

'Lynn, I obviously can't stop you thinking about Jeff Diamond, but I must forbid you to do anything like this again. You are supposed to be moving on and leaving the past behind. You've made a commitment to us not to go backwards, and I think you know you've sailed very close to the wind on this one.'

'Yes, I do know,' the remorseful student answered. 'I'll apologise to Mum next time I talk to her. It won't happen again while I'm here, I promise. But, Dad, I can't hide the fact that I'm very happy that Jeff's living his dream. Doing these things has always been part of his plan, and I wanted to be part of that dream. Donating the money sort of makes up for that. I don't expect you to understand. Is there anything else you want to talk about?'

Father and daughter changed the subject and passed on various items of sporting news from their respective sides of the ocean. After she had put the telephone down, Lynn shouted out loud to expel the anger boiling away inside. She changed her clothes and went for a run out towards the bay to let off steam, just like her hot-headed black stallion would have done in the same situation. Her private outburst made her feel closer to him somehow. It appeared that her no-good tearaway of an ex-boyfriend was getting her into trouble all over again. She couldn't help it if she still cared about him. His memory wouldn't leave her alone, and that wasn't entirely his fault.

Her father's ire notwithstanding, there was another reason why the pretty celebrity now regretted being so spontaneous in authorising the sizeable transaction. She kicked herself, faced with her own short-sightedness. Now she couldn't be sure Jeff would figure out that the donation had come from her. What was it he always said? Hope for the best but expect the worst? With the end of May just around the corner, she had left herself with no means of acknowledging his twenty-first birthday. An anonymous gift on the second of

June would have been far better timing, with a much greater likelihood of the sexy philanthropist putting two and two together.

Lynn felt an acute loss; a hollow in the pit of her stomach which running did nothing to shift. Their mythical invisible elastic connection had snapped. Gravity had cut the cord with his nasty troll scissors, she rued, with tears rolling down her face. Lengthening her stride, she stared into the lifting fog and sprinted towards the sun.

***

Jeff's twenty-first birthday party was a blast, in the company of almost everyone he knew and with no expense spared by his faithful team. He was determined to enjoy the night, more for their sakes than his own, even though his mind had spent the day drifting back to his twentieth and to that first skiing trip; the mini holiday he had been gifted by someone who had really loved him. Thinking clearly for the first time in several months, no longer poisoning himself with hard drugs, he had begun to miss Lynn more and more all over again. It was the easy, mutual bond that he craved so much. Sure, he was surrounded by people who were falling over themselves to love him, but he needed someone he could love back. And still after all this time, it was simply inconceivable to love anyone else but his original, one-in-a-billion dream girl.

The despondent star hoped his former girlfriend might send him a Californian birthday card at least, but nothing arrived. She wasn't the type to forget the date, which led him to accept its nonappearance as a deliberate decision on her part not to send anything. He didn't blame her at all. If she were to suddenly make contact now, where could it go? It was far safer to leave things as arranged, but his ancient heart ached to hear from her all the same.

Celia Blake loved him too, in her motherly, almost smotherly way. Jeff knew this, but it was hardly what he was looking for. With the party in full swing, her eyes had followed him around all evening, painfully aware of the melancholy glossed over by his ebullient showbusiness persona. Eventually, she caught him standing alone on the balcony of the function room while his huge party carried on without its main attraction. He was smoking a quiet joint and made no attempt to hide it. He knew the conservative woman had detected it by smell, but she didn't seek to reprimand the birthday boy.

'You're thinking about Lynn, aren't you?' she asked instead.

Jeff nodded, taking another heavy drag. 'Yep.'

'Nearly halfway,' she added. 'It would've been nice to have her here with you, wouldn't it? I know that. You seem very lost, dear.'

'Yep, squared. Lost is a good word,' the handsome man agreed. 'It's a phrase I use all the time. For a bloke who professes to know exactly where I'm going, I am totally bloody lost.'

Gerry's mother linked arms with him, and they both leaned against the balcony wall. The star's first response was to recoil, the touch of the wrong woman on starving skin felt awkward and even slightly obscene. He valued the relationship which this woman in her mid-fifties insisted on maintaining with her adopted project, but his hormones were raging for a type of carnal satisfaction which he must not communicate.

'Don't worry,' Celia urged him kindly. 'You're very successful, Jeff. You'll find a way to win through it. You always have, darling.'

'Thanks,' he muttered, deciding to compromise with a hasty peck on the cheek, in the vain hope that he didn't seem too dismissive. 'Go and enjoy the party. And thanks for your help with arranging it. I'd have been sitting at home festering if you hadn't, so I'm very grateful.'

His joint finished and his friend's mother re-joining her husband, Jeff wandered back via the reception desk, where he booked himself into a room with a king-sized bed. He owed it to the Blakes to make the most of the extravaganza they had thrown for him. With assistance from the usual additives, he resigned himself to another transformation into Mister Life-and-Soul, celebrating on the dance floor with his many friends. As always, he quickly found himself encircled by enthusiastic female company, all flirtatiously competing with each other for his attention.

'Place your bets!' Gerry laughed to his parents from the edge of the dance floor, pointing towards the noisy spectacle. 'Who's tonight's lucky girl, d'you think?'

'Oh, leave him alone, dear,' Celia scolded her son. 'You're no different. Who are you going home with tonight?'

Feigning affront, Gerry shrugged. '*Moi?* Don't be ridiculous, Mother.'

True enough, as the evening wound up, Jeff made his choice and left a dozen disappointed young women either to pick from every other man in the room or to go home alone. Isabella Trimboli was a Melbourne University Commerce graduate who had recently started working at Stonebridge. She was smart, loud and pretty, and had flirted unashamedly with the handsome singer on the two occasions they had seen each other in the office. Conveniently for the birthday boy, she had also signed an employee confidentiality agreement which meant that any public confessions after the fact would cost the young woman her job. It was a callous world the celebrity now lived in, where he needed to protect himself from his own staff and in his home town.

The sexy *signorina* had brought a fellow university buddy as her guest to Jeff Diamond's twenty-first. In fact, as soon as the invitation was received, she had encouraged her friend to come down; a piece of news which hadn't escaped the horny man's notice. Amy was now based in Sydney, where she had joined an investment bank after graduation, and had at first shied away from him, overawed by the man in whose company Isabella was way too forward. However, as the abundant supply of alcohol freed her inhibitions, she had found it easier and easier to succumb to his many charms.

'So what are you doing after the party?' Isabella had quizzed the popular rock star over the music, stealing a kiss in front of her colleagues.

Playing his crowd as ever, Jeff reached into his pocket and brought out a room key, jangling it in front of the women's faces. He watched the throng swoon collectively, each turning to the other to whisper and giggle. He focussed back on the gregarious Isabella.

'You two care to join me?' he asked in return, stopping Amy from falling over as the surprise penetrated her drunkenness and caused her to catch her breath. 'Bottle of champagne, a smoke... Y'know...'

A hush descended over the scene, the collective swoon turning instantly into a wail of disappointment from the other women. The singer swang around to make sure they hadn't all been turned to stone, though not in the least bit surprised to have caused such a stir.

'Just us?' Isabella asked, looking at her classmate with wide eyes. 'Really? Are you sure?'

'Yeah! Don't look so surprised! Why not?' the confident man answered with a lascivious grin and held his arms out towards the pair of dark-haired Italians. 'It'll be fun.'

With little hesitation, the confident young woman grabbed her friend's arm and sidled closer to this irresistible man. Jeff took a few steps back, amused by their overtly territorial behaviour, and smiled as they followed his every move, trance-like and apparently submissive. The others had formed a semi-circle around him, eager not to miss out if his decision wasn't final. He sensed an aura of ill will radiating around the chosen ones, feeling a little guilty that this scenario was all of his doing.

However, once bored with the absurd mind-game he was directing for his spellbound audience, the rock star moved on to Stage Two of "Operation Enjoy Birthday". With a slim, high-heeled beauty on each arm and his room key in his teeth, the Latin lover nodded a brazen goodnight to Gerry.

'You're so fucking lucky, mate,' sneered Anthony, who was still propping up the bar, whence he hadn't moved all evening. 'That's every man's dream you've got there.'

'Not every man, Ant,' the star replied a little too bitterly. 'But you're right, I am bloody lucky. Perks of being the birthday boy, I guess! Have a good night.'

Jeff broke away from the two girls briefly to thank his manager once more for organising the ritzy *soirée*. He promised to ring the next day and swap their bawdy stories, while the three men watched lasciviously as the Mediterranean beauties linked arms and teetered on ahead. A brief sober thought rushed across the celebrity's mind about how ridiculous they looked and how stupid and shallow he was being. Yet the thought was fleeting, and the promises of illicit substances and some unconventional physical gratification motivated him to push through these reservations without too much trouble.

'Three's a crowd,' Isabella chuckled, turning round to confirm they were heading in the right direction. 'Isn't that what they say?'

'Why? Do you want to be part of a bigger crowd?' Jeff smiled. 'I'm sure we'll figure out what to do between us.'

Both girls nodded their inebriated, awestruck heads emphatically. Jeff Diamond all to themselves. Who wouldn't want that? Isabella leaned into his tall, athletic frame, and he twirled her around to the music, making her laugh when she nearly stumbled again. Gerald Blake Senior tutted to his wife as they watched the ugly scene unfold.

'You're just jealous,' Celia told her husband with a smile. 'He's lonely, and it's his twenty-first birthday. It's harmless.'

With the young women hanging on to his arms possessively, the guest of honour did the rounds to thank the Blakes for making sure his birthday was celebrated in good style and also the staff for taking such good care of everyone. Gerry slapped him hard on the back, as a sign of vicarious appreciation for what was to come. With all duties performed, Jeff steered his excited, chattering companions out of the function room and towards the lifts.

Outside his room, the birthday boy handed Amy his key. She giggled some more while letting them into the large suite, before screaming when she saw a bottle of champagne already sitting in an ice bucket on the chest of drawers. Sitting down heavily on the bed, both girls quickly flicked off their shoes and checked out their host unwinding the wire and foil from the top of the bottle.

Handing Isabella and Amy a long flute each, Jeff ceremoniously twisted the cork. The girls whooped at the loud popping sound, waving their empty glasses wildly in the air.

'Allow me,' the gallant birthday boy invited, taking back one glass at a time as the bubbles erupted from the neck of the bottle.

The trio toasted each other and drank their first glasses quickly, dancing to music from a late night radio station which had been left on for their arrival. Feeling warmly aroused, Jeff sat on the end of the bed and watched as the two girls moved together, more than happy to put on a show for the handsome entertainer, and before long, he was on his feet and dancing with them. The zip at the back of Isabella's dress slid down easily in his fingers, and he stroked her shoulders as he lifted the narrow straps. She shrieked in delight as she felt the blue satin slip down her body and end up in a heap around her feet.

Pleased with her reaction, the dark-souled, empty-hearted songwriter refilled their glasses and turned his attention to kissing Amy's neck and shoulders, while his employee unbuttoned his shirt and pulled him in closer to her.

'Isabella,' he beckoned to the taller girl, 'your friend seems to be wearing too many clothes. Why don't you help her?'

Both girls squealed with laughter at the series of naughty instructions they found themselves following. They were soon naked in front of their charming host, so he allowed them to start on him too. The lithe, muscular man closed his eyes as the latest dose of alcohol hit his brain and bumped into his fantasies of Lynn. These two inebriated young women would never know how much he was taking advantage of them, and all three would have a great time in the process.

Confident and animated in her excitement at spending a night with Australia's hottest property, Isabella pulled off each item of his clothing as slowly as she could bear, until they fell down onto the bed in a frenzy of sexual pleasure. Amy was more reserved, happy to have her hands and mouth placed exactly where her two playmates wanted them.

After a few minutes of laughter and feverish caresses, Jeff produced a condom from his wallet and began to open the packaging. The two girls began to finger each other at his suggestion, quietly at first but then less so, while he wound his tongue around Amy's nipples and fondled the jealous breasts of her friend. He then made sure a hand from each girl made its way onto his erection, and soon their vigorous stroking began to pump him way too quickly in their drunken efforts to please him. Breaking away, he handed the ripped condom packet to Isabella.

'We don't need that,' the extrovert whined, coaxing him back towards her. 'I'm on the pill. You are too, aren't you, Ames?'

'Oh, yes, we do,' the celebrity insisted, despite the shy girl's confirmation.

Kissing Amy's mouth hard while he rolled the condom on and lay between them, he took sustenance from both girls' writhing enthusiasm. No matter how turned on he felt, there was no way the wary lover was taking any risks, regardless of the confidentiality agreement and loyal employee-employer relations. He was not going to chance becoming the father of Isabella Trimboli's child, nor that of her university friend, should it turn out that their motives were less easy-going and unplanned than they seemed.

'I can't believe you're only just twenty-one,' Amy gasped, as Jeff pulled out and turned around to play with Isabella for a while.

'Why?' the birthday boy grinned. 'How old should I be?'

'Twenty-eight,' Isabella answered.

'¿Veintiocho? Tonight I can be twenty-eight, si te gusta,' he invited, thrusting inside her and feeling her arms grab around his waist in a mixture of surprise and pleasure. 'What else would you like me to be?'

'Nothing!' Isabella laughed. 'Fucking Jeff Diamond is amazing enough for me! What do you want me to be?'

The fingers of his left hand were busy massaging Amy's clitoris, and she moaned sweetly in pre-orgasmic delight. The expert lover kissed her while the woman underneath clenched her muscles around his penis, and he cursed the response which immediately triggered in his imagination. The man said nothing, feeling both women come simultaneously as he moved against them. Isabella screamed loudly, and her face flushed with the intense sensation.

'Jesus, I'm good!' he forced a laugh, amused by his own arrogance and giving in to his own climax.

'That was amazing!' she told him, after all three became still and caught their breath. 'You're the first man who's done that to me. I pretend to come to make them feel better normally.'

Amy laughed. 'You don't, do you?'

'Is that right?' Jeff smiled, sitting up and stroking her breasts. 'Glad I could make it real for you. Maybe you should try showing them what to do?'

Isabella was holding on far too tightly for her famous partner's liking. His eyes were burning with unspent emotion, and his jaw locked instinctively to retain control. Comically, the star backed away, pretending to be exhausted after their energetic half-hour. Both girls collapsed in a fit of giggles, and he was relieved not to have to stay in the intense moment too long.

Returning from the bathroom, Jeff lit three cigarettes and handed them round. When Amy refused, he sat down again with one in each hand, smoking them alternately. An expression somewhere between maternal scorn and unworldly surprise appeared on Isabella's face, probably wondering what sort of world she and her friend had literally stumbled into.

How often sex was full of pretence, the expert lover thought to himself, reaching for their champagne glasses and angling Amy's carefully towards her mouth as she propped herself up on her elbows. There was he enacting his fantasies of Lynn in duplicate, while these girls were enjoying being with someone famous, finding stimulation at his hand where normally they couldn't be bothered. Life was so strange sometimes.

'Do you think you'll ever get married?' Isabella asked the naked Adonis who was now searching in the mini-bar for the bottle of whisky he had ordered from Room Service earlier.

'No. Will you?'

His marketing assistant shrieked. 'Yes! Of course I will. I want the whole thing: kids, house, family holidays, et cetera. Doesn't everyone?'

Amy shot her friend a sideways glance, warning her against being so open and transparent. 'I guess you can just click your fingers and have a different girl every night,' she countered to their rock star companion.

'That's about right!'

Jeff had poured himself a large tumblerful of whisky and was now perched on the end of the bed, drinking in large gulps. The sexual interlude had sobered him up, and he was keen to reverse this process as soon as possible.

'Isn't that a bit empty?' Amy persisted.

The birthday boy nodded, cocking his head and shrugging. 'Sure is, baby. But empty's all I need right now. I like empty. It suits me.'

Re-anaesthetised after the latest top-up of stimulants, the celebrity quickly became aroused again, staring shamelessly at the two nubile playthings who adorned his room. He unwrapped another rubber and handed it to the woman from Sydney, who dutifully rolled it on to his huge penis. Moaning in pleasure, the lustful man lay down on his back with a girl on each side and rolled Isabella over on top of him.

'Do you want me to make you come again?' he asked, thrusting two fingers inside her and gripping her hips with his other hand.

'Yes,' Isabella shouted. 'Yes, I do.'

'OK,' he laughed. 'Let's come together then, like we really mean it.'

His sarcasm was completely lost on the intoxicated woman, who rode him hard as his fingers brought her close for a second time. Amy had disappeared into the shower, probably jealous that the twenty-one-year-old had picked her friend for a solo act. Feeling Isabella orgasm again, Jeff pushed himself to follow quickly, his mind calling someone else's name.

'Wish me happy birthday,' he teased, as his lover gave a contented sigh.

'Happy birthday!' she cried out. 'I can't believe I'm with you. Happy birthday, Jeff Diamond!'

'Cheers. I'm just another man, y'know,' he insisted, lifting her gently off him and heading towards the bathroom, from which Amy had emerged, wrapped in a thick, white towel.

'No, you're not!' Isabella shouted after him. 'You're amazing. Really amazing!'

Safely behind the closed door, Jeff splashed water on his face to hide the tears of longing which inevitably followed such physical fulfilment. His veneer was intact, his women were satisfied and his body had taken its just deserts from his birthday treat. He could hear Celia's words echoing in his mind. He *was* successful and he *would* win through, but at what price for his impatience and disenchantment at all these wasted nights?

Back in the bedroom, while Isabella took her turn to freshen up, Jeff emptied what remained of the champagne into the girls' glasses and helped himself to another generous glass of Scotch. He lay down on the bed, lit a cigarette, switched on the television and began to roll three joints. Handing one to Amy, who had spread out onto the bed still with the towel around her, he gave her another kiss.

'Thanks, gorgeous,' he murmured, fondling her breasts through the material. 'You were great. You wanna go again too?'

The dark-eyed beauty smiled, a glint in her eye. 'Do you? Can you?'

Her handsome bedfellow feigned offence, rolling to a sitting position and dragging long on the spliff. 'I can, but now I'm not sure I do. You're going to have to make up for that, lady.'

Amy giggled, picking up on his sarcasm. 'At least you get sex on your birthday.'

'It's not my birthday anymore.'

'Oh, yeah! Did you get it last year?' the young woman enquired, kneeling up and rubbing her hands over his muscular back.

Jeff inhaled sharply, memories immediately flooding back. It was all he could do not to stand up and walk away from the feel of someone else's contact on his skin at the same time. He gritted his teeth and leaned back into the massage, blocking out as much sensation as possible.

'Yeah,' he sighed. 'I got it last year.'

'On your actual birthday or on the night after?'

Isabella opened the door and came back to the bed, instantly joining her friend. The songwriter realised their intentions to be purely agreeable, giving him no civil choice but to allow them to continue. He twisted his body round and stretched out on his stomach, rapidly imploding.

'Both,' he answered.

Somehow the young man managed to trade on Lynn's memories long enough to provide him with the boost he needed to rekindle the flames for a third time, remembering his promise to Amy. He dismissed the pleasant thoughts from the past and focussed back on the present, just in time to notice Isabella's look of wonder.

'Is that dope?'

'Depends who's asking,' their famous host smiled wryly.

'Is one for me?' the outgoing woman asked, aghast.

'If you want,' he replied, holding out the third roll-up towards her nervous hand. 'It's not compulsory. Up to you. Our secret? Your future husband won't know.'

The late night entertainment programme showing on the television suddenly cut to a reporter who had attended the local star's birthday party earlier in the evening. Isabella shrieked as she saw her lover and Gerry on the screen. Jeff shrugged and stubbed out his cigarette, toasting her with his whisky.

'Sit down,' he requested, slapping the sheets next to him. 'Let's smoke these before they get cold.'

'Get cold?' the dumbstruck woman repeated, looking confused.

It's just an expression, Jeff thought to himself. *Just a joke.* She shouldn't worry her pretty little head. To his dismay, he seemed to be coming down fast, despite the new intake of cannabis. Amy laughed softly. Bitter thoughts gathered in a cloud above his head while he lit the remaining joint and offered it to Isabella. She accepted it gingerly. He took a long drag on his own, winking at Amy, who had obviously partaken of this type of activity before too.

The novice followed suit, coughing as the smoke curled into her mouth and down her throat. 'Oh, my God!' she exclaimed, quickly swallowing some champagne and coughing some more. 'That burns!'

'Good, huh?' the young man chuckled, closing his eyes and resting his head on the wooden headboard. 'I won't tell if you won't tell.'

Amy lay back on the bed, the towel open around her pale skin. She was slimmer than Isabella, quite boyish in a way. Jeff suspected her friend's breasts were not entirely her own, briefly wondering what led women to take such drastic action. He then stole a little more gratuitous pleasure watching Amy stroke herself all over, the weed having rendered her totally unaware of what she was doing. It turned him on instantly, finally feeling himself relax again too.

'So what's it like flying all over the world and being treated like royalty?' Isabella chuckled, the drug wending its way into her head.

'It's fantastic,' he replied. 'A whole bunch of meaningless connections made and broken in quick succession.'

Blank looks settled on both girls' faces, and the songwriter smiled. Long words were beyond these two, especially in their current condition. His fingers criss-crossed Amy's narrow hips and ventured down to the opening of her vagina, causing her legs to part instinctively. Jeff leaned over and retrieved his last condom from the bedside table, ripping open its packet and stretching it out over his hardness.

'I get sex from the glidesmaids,' he joked, turning his attention back to Isabella.

The woman laughed. 'Did you say glidesmaids? What are they? Hosties?'

'Yeah,' their lover nodded. 'We're not allowed to call them stewardesses anymore. Glidesmaids is what I call them. Fuck, I'm stoned! Come here...'

The threesome threaded their limbs around each other, Jeff again finding wandering hands evoking bittersweet but thankfully invigorating arousal.

'What about the money?' Amy asked between groans and sharp intakes of breath. 'What's it like to be making so much money? What have you bought?'

'Not much,' Jeff answered honestly. 'Heaps of bottles of champagne and marijuana. And a washing machine.'

'A washing machine?' his marketing assistant shrieked in disbelief. 'That's not very exciting!'

The rock star laughed. 'It was exciting for me.'

Flicking through the television channels, the young man eventually found a movie he didn't recognise and, feeling more mellow at last, he beckoned to Isabella to lay down beside Amy. The two girls obligingly caressed each others' bodies while they finished smoking. Before long, they were all entwined again, this time moving with much more determination.

'You're very good in bed,' Amy groaned. 'You make women scream on stage and in bed.'

'That's the general idea,' Jeff answered with typical arrogance. 'And in return they give me enough money to buy a washing machine and some drugs. Sounds fair to me.'

'That's funny,' his soporific companion laughed. 'What about a nice house?'

'Ha! What would I do with a nice house?' Jeff asked her, bringing Amy to orgasm suddenly and expertly.

His rhetorical question was lost in her pleasure. She screamed and kissed him passionately, letting him know how good it felt. Jeff closed his eyes and wished to any god who would listen to supplant his beloved Lynn into his arms right this minute, while he came into his proxy birthday present. What he would have given to celebrate his coming of age with the woman he loved more than life itself...

All three were thoroughly satisfied, breathless and overtired. Amy quickly became sleepy in the musician's arms. He stroked her hair and gently moved her head onto the pillow. In their drug-induced daze, neither girl objected when he told them of his plan to leave them to sleep peacefully in the sumptuous hotel room. He dressed quietly and picked up his wallet, kissing each forehead goodbye, and then scribbled a farewell note in case his parting message hadn't registered.

> "Thanks for a great night, 'bella. See you next time I'm in the office. And you too, Amy. Remember, I won't tell if you won't tell... Take care, JMD."

Walking home through the Botanic Gardens and along Alexandra Avenue, the drained man realised that, for the first time in more than six months, the old Jeff was back in town; the conscious, feet-on-ground student of the world whom he had come to quite like during the previous year. He found it mildly amusing, even frustrating, that no-one else could tell the difference between his spaced-out, party animal self and this more measured version. Or perhaps they were just too frightened to broach the subject? It had taken nearly six months for him to feel worthy of his new status, and ironically this admission had only come once he had reverted to his pre-rock-star lifestyle. The occasional relapse notwithstanding, of course!

Key in hand, the birthday boy approached the front door of his second-floor apartment in the inner eastern suburb, sweat forming on his brow and the hairs standing up on the back of his neck. His head ached from the many toxins which had been introduced into his lean body, and his stomach was nauseated by the thought of the difficult task ahead. As if surviving through to tomorrow's press conference to mark the release of his third album wasn't daunting enough, first the celebrity had to contend with the demons who guarded his door.

'Are you there, angel?' he whispered, gritting his teeth as bile inched its way up to his throat. 'Can you hear me? Feel me?'

The desperate songwriter's left hand shook uncontrollably as it attempted to slot the key into the lock. His legs felt like jelly, and anger seethed behind his eyes. To focus his mind, he fixed on the two new bottles of Glenfiddich which he had picked up from the bottle shop earlier that afternoon, guessing their help would be called upon after his party.

'I had another birthday, Lynn. Twenty-one! It wasn't like last year though. I wish it was. I really wish it was. Come and visit me. Remind me what love is, please? Just once. For my birthday, angel, please. Like last year.'

Regardless of how rich and famous he had become, how many new friends were hanging around and how marvellous his new life looked from the outside, the nocturnal Jeff Diamond was still another story; sorry, sordid and secret to the last. No attempts to fix the lost boy in him had had any effect whatsoever. If anything, the nightmares were worse, and he would see virtually no sleep for days on end. He had relented to another trial of sleeping pills, having been prescribed them years ago when Celia had checked him into the psychiatric hospital after he kicked the family's kitchen door down. The millionaire still felt ashamed when he remembered that night. The Blakes had long since forgiven him, but he remained racked with guilt nevertheless.

This time, his experience with sleeping pills was no better. They knocked him out for up to ten hours at a time, without returning to consciousness between nightmares, and then it would take him almost another full day to properly wake up. He described the feeling to the doctor as if his head was like a radio tuned slightly off-station. All five senses were ostensibly available to him, yet everything was distorted and fuzzy. No-one had a sensible solution for the unfortunate side-effect, nor any better suggestions, leaving him to persevere with the pills and suffer the consequences.

After a few weeks in this mode however, Jeff found himself unable to enjoy the full measure of any activity, be it through sleep deprivation or sleep medication. On top of this, the combination of sedatives and anti-depressants delivered violent hallucinations in addition to the nightmares. And as the icing on the cake for the frazzled jetsetter, even sex was turning into a chore.

With this final, insupportable straw, the successful student decided to abandon both sets of pills. He spent the light-time in his good life, day after day and with scarcely a moment to himself, making obscene amounts of money and relishing his ever-increasing acclaim. The night-time was ever his undoing, the hours between two and five in the morning left him weeping like a baby while everyone else slept peacefully. Irrational fears, dreams of dying quietly alone and the hollow loneliness of a heart that refused to heal, Australia's biggest star would often catch himself crying out for someone to take him away.

No, the handsome playboy reminded himself. *Be honest with yourself.* Left to its own devices, his heart could undoubtedly heal. It was he who was solely responsible for this obstinacy. The light of Lynn's return seemed like such a distant speck at the end of an inordinately long tunnel, stretching into a distance for which he no longer believed he had the patience. Life simply wasn't worth the pain at this time of the morning.

Jeff Diamond had so much to be thankful for and yet was unable to rid himself of the dark thoughts, regardless of how many external influences he applied. He likened his situation to being on death row, eking out an interminable existence between appeals and waiting for that elusive reprieve. At these times, his mind often turned to his father. The abandoned son had no real idea what life in prison might be like for a long-termer in an Australian jail, also having absolutely no inclination to find out. In his desperate pre-dawn state however, he found himself jealous of his old man's safe, secure, well-fed life, free from responsibility and with an army of wardens to ensure his day was occupied with constructive, character-rebuilding pursuits.

And neither could the Sydneysider help but ponder where the prisoner's thoughts turned at night. Did the bastard ever think about the family he left behind? Did he feel sorry for the violence and betrayal? Often overcome by a guilty empathy, Jeff would resolve to make contact and confess to his father that he still thought about him almost every day, even if he didn't love him. He didn't love him. He couldn't love him after what he put his mother and sister through. Could he? Did a blood relation ever really leave one's heart? Maybe he could love him, if he were to allow it. There was little difference from his coping mechanisms for living without his dream girl; he was such an all-or-nothing person, and therefore, by the time the morning came around again, his conciliatory resolve had frittered away until only the habitual bitterness and resentment survived.

During this brief pre-tour hiatus, the closet intellectual had also immersed himself in the latest research on the bipolar nature of manic depressives, with ample available hours ahead on aeroplanes and in hotel rooms. He regularly felt himself heading towards the extreme highs and lows of bipolar behaviour and knew he could only use his regular mix of recreational drugs to counteract the pendulum for a while before they would begin to destroy his faculties permanently. This was one boundary he would not cross. These razor-sharp faculties had served him well from a very young age. He had too much respect for the power in his own brain to see it go down in flames.

Rather, it was the machine behind the superstar which pushed him towards the North Pole, since his newfound celebrity status demanded that he be the life and soul of the party as soon as the cameras rolled or whenever a microphone appeared under his chin. And this was the second non-negotiable boundary. If his plethora of world-changing goals were to stand a chance of being accomplished, a new inspiration was essential to keep him interested in fending off Gravity's determined pull towards the South Pole. The single thing which could be relied upon for motivation during his teens was the dream of one day meeting Lynn Dyson. These days however, the prospect of regaining her attention was slipping further and further from his mental grasp.

Steeped in the fascinating coalescence of social medicine which his work with Professor Friedman had stirred, Jeff began to fool himself that there was a difference between reliance and dependence. If he could somehow learn to merely rely on what he needed to see him through, he could rid himself of the dependencies he had used as crutches over the last year. It worked for now, giving him enough willpower to carry on for the time being.

Another Tough Decision

The multi-millionnaire moved into his very own three-bedroomed apartment in September nineteen-seventy-three. It was in the perfect location for him, overlooking the Royal Exhibition Building and Carlton Gardens, where "I LOVE YOU" had been scrawled on the side of a dirty van on the night he and Lynn had found their fairground attraction. Melbourne's most eligible bachelor had been house-hunting for a long time, off and on, dismissing the usual celebrity enclaves: the ritzy suburbs of South Yarra, Toorak and St Kilda Road, preferring the hedonistic retreats of Fitzroy or North Carlton. He couldn't see himself living in the archetypal White Anglo-Saxon Protestant environment, opting to find somewhere with a diversity of life around him.

Jeff had seen this particular apartment while being ferried in a helicopter from the city to the airport one afternoon. It was a single-storey penthouse with uninterrupted views across the whole of northern Melbourne; close to the universities, the restaurant areas of Lygon and Brunswick Streets and right on the edge of the Central Business District. One problem though... It wasn't for sale!

But why should such a formality stop a persuasive superstar from getting what he wanted, especially when he had an army of financial consultants in his corner? He had Gerry make the owner an anonymous offer through an agent and was amazed to have it accepted second time around. One thing the astute player was quickly learning was that he always managed somehow to get his way, simply through honest, ethical perseverance and by making the right offer. It gave him hope that this luck might last for another year.

He certainly required more privacy than his current flat afforded. The tormented songwriter had already been caught once standing breathless on the landing by his neighbour, who probably assumed he was ill. Jeff played along. Fortunately, there was a steady turnover of tenants in the building, and they never saw each other again. From then on however, the desperate man decided he would rather leave the front door open and risk theft than have to battle the door demons in public.

The new property owner also hoped that the apartment and its bright, airy landing would bring some relief to the door phobia, but no. Even painting his front door an off-white colour made no difference. Same old story... He would reach the top floor, step out of the lift and then stand in the hallway, battling for ages and becoming progressively angrier with himself and his ridiculous plight. It was a farcical situation which frustrated him as much, and perhaps even more than his lack of sleep.

Despite a growing despondence about his future with Lynn, Jeff continued to hang on every piece of news of the blonde movie star. Hearing about her much-lauded achievements still pleased him enormously, and he wondered how closely she followed his career and his own successes. Neither could avoid hearing of the other, such was the media frenzy surrounding both stars. At first, he had cursed the sudden spike in his blood pressure whenever her name was mentioned or her picture graced the television or magazine stands, but after a while these accidental sightings no longer threw him such a curve ball. He took solace in talking to her in the middle of the night, or while standing on his apartment's doormat, just as he had done in his teens whenever life treated him poorly.

The playboy extraordinaire never went without female company, not that he took issue with this by-product of fame! The girls were absolutely everywhere; mostly screaming and always eager to please. Cathy had recruited three additional assistants to answer fan mail and to arrange the star's diary. She latched on to her boss' novel idea of employing bored housewives and mothers, intrigued and shocked by stories harking back to the days when he would accompany such women home from the supermarket.

The empathetic man knew these would make reliable staff members, often starved of interesting stimulation. Gerry, of course, was also at pains to admit they were a huge asset to his client's management company, purely for aesthetic purposes. These women would talk to callers and answer love-letters on the star's behalf, on the same wavelength as his fans and ready to share their excitement at being so close to the man himself.

Jeff's freshly re-cleansed brain cultivated a desire to write more serious music in addition to keeping the hits coming. On the way home from another European trip, he made an unscheduled trip to Africa at the behest of a music director in Mozambique whom he had met in Paris, and there he found significant inspiration in a type of music about which he had previously known so little. The result was one of the most experimental albums any Western rock artist had ever recorded, featuring prominent African sounds and instruments intertwined with sweeping strings and rock-influenced drum beats.

The album ended up being a huge commercial success, despite the obvious departure from his usual style, and yielded a string of Top Ten hits. It was one of the most ground-breaking recording projects of its time, and the artist's label initially had been unsure of its commercial viability. However, riding on his vibrant brand, it was snapped up as fast as any other of his albums, spawning yet more instant classics which were haunting and thought-provoking.

Travelling to Africa was also a tonic for the hard-working star, enlightening him with a new perspective on poverty and deprivation. He concluded that the western suburbs of Sydney needed to smarten themselves up, since in these third-world countries people quite literally had nothing, yet lived in tight family units and remained ever genuine and optimistic. There was little crime to speak of, and communities looked out for each other. These were huge lessons to be learned for Australia's diverse city populations, and Jeff vowed to incorporate similar messages to first-world society as part of his master plan.

The twenty-one-year-old introvert had completed the screenplay for his book and had paid the first of many visits to the film studios to begin work on the screenplay and the music score. The lofty themes woven through "The Runner", being the fight for survival, the meaninglessness of materialism and striving for perfection through higher knowledge, presented the production team with significant challenges for which they were delighted to include the likeable and inspiring author.

With the orchestral score and script reviews under his belt, the musician was pleased that he had been given the opportunity to nurture his intellectual self again. Perversely, he craved the pain and suffering of reliving old memories, because they culminated in such strong creative output. His fertile imagination was at its most potent when free of prescription medication and strung out on amphetamines or barbiturates. In any other state, he felt stifled and impatient, as if he were unable to express himself properly.

'What's life all about, angel?' he shouted into the air, anxious to come to terms with all these conflicting needs. 'What the fuck do I need to do?'

This Jeff Diamond asked of Lynn Dyson, as he often did, one cool, starry September night sitting alone on the balcony of his new apartment, smoking a joint and working his way through a bottle of mellow aged *Rioja*. His dream girl sent him no clues, so he plunged deep into his own thoughts again. He was becoming increasingly convinced that there were higher forces at play and that he was merely a pawn in a game the outcome of which he was currently powerless to influence. How could he turn the tables? Had he been anointed with pain in order that he might turn it into something positive for the human race?

He rebelled against the teachings of Buddha and Hinduism, which worried him too. Who was he to doubt so vehemently? Did he really possess the kind of wisdom that permitted such moralising? Was this some arrogant Christ complex or merely a way of renewing his determination to carry on? There was another alternative too, which may be the most likely of all... He was slowly descending into madness without his faithful *confidante* to set him straight.

One minute the distracted star was flying high, and the next minute he was tipped into a nosedive, unable to find a safe place to land. The months went slowly by, and he fought every day to convince himself that the light in his darkness was becoming brighter. He imagined himself drowning in those deep, blue eyes again, waiting for healing hands to run across his shoulders and feeling her slender body held tight against his. His guardian angel would pull him from the rubble of his destructive mind. She would. She had to.

Lynn Dyson turned eighteen on the twentieth day of the ninth month. The milestone was well reported around the world, and Jeff watched the Entertainment Tonight segment of the young woman in all her glory, attending a party in her own honour at a ritzy Beverley Hills hotel. He was in Perth, Western Australia, rehearsing for a concert to celebrate the opening of the city's new Concert Hall on Adelaide Terrace, feeling never more distant from his future.

His former schoolgirl girlfriend appeared radiant and happy, flanked by her parents and siblings and with a blond-haired man on her arm. Her former lover didn't recognise this man, who looked like a clean-cut college boy and just the sort of partner the Dysons would want for their highly eligible daughter. The sidelined no-good from Canley Vale allowed himself a wry smile when he picked up the slightest hint of an American twang to her accent, imagining how this must have annoyed the hell out of her father. Her demeanour reeked of a greater self-assurance and sophistication than he remembered, as befitting her new adult status, and starring in the latest James Bond movie had cemented her position as one of the world's highest-paid female actors once and for all.

Lynn's most recent album featured compositions which were equally self-assured and sophisticated. A raft of new band members had been recruited in this post-MAC, solo era, and their musical arrangements were slick and bluesy. The record took no time at all to find itself on the turntable at the renovated sixteenth-floor apartment in Melbourne, where her ex-boyfriend instantly fell in love with it.

Were the lyrics inspired from memories of their time together, or was a new *paramour* setting her imagination on fire these days? Jeff was genuinely pleased that his dream girl's career was going from strength to strength. His was too, leading him to wonder whether her outer happiness might bely a reciprocal inner anguish. Probably not, he decided. And he hoped not, for her sake. The beautiful songstress didn't deserve to feel miserable, whether she sang joyful, romantic songs or of lonely masquerades, all of which ignited his own flames of recognition to the point where he could believe her love for him still clung to life in the City of Angels. Could it be that their invisible elastic connection was tightening again? He hoped so, but expected not.

***

As if the hectic miscellany among which Jeff Diamond divided his tired brain wasn't enough, there was one last complication tossed into his life before the end of nineteen-seventy-three. His sister, who could scarcely believe the fact that her estranged brother had become such hot property, was filled with resentment at not being taken with him on his exciting, new journey. She joined the growing line of forgotten friends and relations and sent a letter to his recording company, which forwarded it to his management company, which duly passed it on to the man himself.

The poorly written letter took the young man back to their childhood. Madalena had never paid attention at school, barely literate and disinterested in anything outside her immediate sphere. She was demanding money, as were the others, on the pretext that she had suffered exactly as his songs described and that she considered herself somehow deserving of a share in the fruits of the rich celebrity's labour.

'*Lena, es Jeff,*' the twenty-one-year-old said, after the telephone number provided by his older sister connected. '*¿Que tal? Gracias por tu carta.*'

'English, *chico*. I can't speak to you in Spanish,' Madalena answered. 'Not now. I can't believe you're a big star now, eh? You still play guitar like when you were *chico*. Me and the cousins come to your show. For fuck's sake, you're sexy! All my friends want to screw you.'

The musician laughed sarcastically at her backhanded compliment. 'Cheers, I think! They're not the only ones trying to screw me. Can I come and see you?'

'Why? Here?' the defensive woman snapped. 'What for?'

'Because you wrote me a letter, and I want to talk about it face to face, not over the 'phone,' Jeff answered. 'Is that so bad?'

'*Abuela* says you don't exist anymore for her,' his sister changed the subject, referring to their maternal grandmother. 'They're all pretty fuckin' angry you're a big star. You can't come here.'

The tearaway from Sydney's run-down west couldn't give a damn what his grandparents might think. He hadn't seen them in several years, and their reaction was no surprise. Jealousy was a natural extension of the mutual rejection they had all experienced after his mother, their daughter, had met her doom.

The young man focussed back onto his sister and the letter of demand. 'So why did you write to me?'

There was a long silence down the line, broken only by what he discerned to be sucking air through a cigarette. His own cravings jumping at the association, he reached across the office desk for his lighter and open packet. Pulling the ashtray closer to him, he lit up and waited for his sister's response.

''Cause we deserve to share in your success,' came a hesitant reply.

Really? The songwriter was fairly sure those words had not emerged from his sister's mouth of their own accord. She must have sought some legal advice, or someone else had on her behalf; probably one of her clients, while paying a lunchtime visit to the seedy side of town before going home to his wife on the other.

'Who told you that?'

Madalena sniffed, her whining pitch ascending in defiance. 'No-one. You're sitting in a mansion drinking champagne and flying in private 'planes, and I'm still here on the Stones getting shafted. That's why.'

'Oh, yeah?' her angry brother objected. 'Who fed you all that crap? It's not my fault you're getting shafted. You should come down and visit, and then you'd see I don't live like that at all. I work hard and I'm getting well paid for what I do. Tell me when you want to come to Melbourne, and I'll send you a ticket. You been on a 'plane yet, Lena?'

'Na,' the woman snarled. 'But I wanna *mucho*. OK. Send me a ticket, *chico*, and I'll come see your rock star life.'

Madalena sounded suddenly excited, which was exactly the opposite to how her brother was feeling. Why had he made this offer? What would he do with her? He definitely couldn't introduce this small-minded suburban girl into his outlandish cosmopolitan lifestyle. Jesus! That had been a rash move on his part! Committed however, the pair discussed possible dates when the musician would be in town and picked the weekend between Christmas and New Year.

'*Bueno*,' Jeff sighed, ready to sign off. 'You let me know, Lena. OK? Then we can talk about the letter face to face.'

'No! Wait a minute,' Madalena interrupted. 'I got something else to tell you. Why I wrote the letter.'

The celebrity became nervous, his obsessive curiosity piqued by her change of tone. Perhaps there was news about their father? He didn't really want to know what was going on with the bastard but understood that for his own safety he should keep himself informed.

'*¿Que?*'

'Can you send me five hundred bucks? I need to get rid of this baby.'

Taken by surprise, her brother gasped, holding the receiver away from his mouth so that she wouldn't hear the extent of his frustration. He swore under his breath. This bombshell made everything crystal clear. News about the crime scene in western Sydney would have been preferable to this sordid topic.

'You're pregnant again?'

'*Sí,*' the working girl replied, obviously not happy about her situation either. 'I dunno who. I just know I need to get rid of it.'

Jeff steadied himself and adopted a compassionate tone. '*¿Saben los abuelos?* We talked through all this last time. I can't believe you let it happen again. It's a child, Lena. An actual person. Where are your good Catholic values now? Are you sure you want to do this?'

The previous time Madalena had found herself pregnant, she had barely turned twenty years old, and her mature younger sibling had been successful in convincing her to inform their very religious grandmother, in an effort to absolve himself of the responsibility of having to condemn someone else's human error to its death.

A few years older now, this time his sister was adamant. 'Ah, piss off, Jeff. I don't need no kid. It's not a child 'til it's born anyway. Stop putting guilt on me.'

'Stop putting guilt on you?' the celebrity echoed back in frustration, imagining his sister's huge, brown eyes staring into his. 'You write me a letter after not speaking to me for over two years, then ask me for five hundred bucks and say it's for another abortion? I think I'm entitled to put the guilt on you.'

'Fuck you, *chico*,' Madalena shouted and then began to whine. 'You gotta help me. I'm showing and I can't earn money looking like this.'

Her pleas were ragged, an awful rasping sound tearing through her brother's ears like a wounded animal. Fighting his conscience in the face of such a repellant noise, the self-made millionnaire was hit with an urge to suggest she choose a different career. He decided against it just in time, caving in to the disquieting images of his sister's abused childhood that travelled with him every day as they began to swirl in front of his eyes and dared him to leave her in the lurch. With everything they had been through in their young lives, he simply couldn't desert her. She had no-one else to turn to, and neither did he.

'Sure. Look,' he continued, sounding more conciliatory this time. 'I'll send you the money. Just be careful. Don't go to some butcher or you'll never be able to have kids when you really want them. *¿Me oyes?*'

'OK, *chico*,' Madalena responded with no trace of emotion. 'When can I come to Melbourne?'

Christ! What a pathetic situation. With no thanks whatsoever, the tearful damsel in distress had completely disappeared. His sister reminded him of Tamilla on the day he had turned down her romantic advances; thick-skinned, carefree and ready to move on. Why did people keep doing this to him?

Jeff sighed. 'Get yourself fixed up first, then we'll talk about you coming down. We'll have fun. Just take care. OK?'

'OK, *chico*. See ya.'

The line went dead. Bewildered and lonely, the Catholic Argentinean Polish Jew sat back on the couch with the top of the telephone receiver pressed against his lips. His sister was carrying another niece or nephew he would never see; a baby whom no-one would ever hold, not even its parents. Probably for the best, he rued, for it wasn't really a baby anyway, as his sister had informed him. It was just another mistake, and would most probably have a worse life than its uncle's. Christ Almighty! His world was totally out of control.

***

For his final semester at university, the diligent student had been required to complete a six-month placement with an organisation setting up a data processing department. Due to his gruelling tour schedule, RMIT's Science and Engineering faculty agreed to a reduced number of days spanning the same six months. Most of his fellow students were amazed that their famous classmate even felt compelled to complete his degree. However, this highly hands-on exercise had presented a welcome distraction for the intelligent celebrity, providing some much-needed contact with normal people with ordinary, nine-to-five lives, complete with bills, mortgages and car loans.

The internship was arranged with a construction firm of more than two thousand employees, running projects all over south-east Asia. Their new recruit quickly won the respect of the company's management team and worked every hour he could spare on this very practical application of his learnings. As expected though, he sometimes had the impression that his main function was to provide the novelty factor; eye-candy, as his manager would relentlessly remind him.

Already the subject of incessant office scuttlebutt, there always seemed to be a stream of passers-by intrigued by the environs of his desk. Occasionally, the good-looking worker would play with the attention, fixing them with a stare and embarrassing them into retreat. Mostly his time was spent very productively, and he formed a bunch of very solid friendships in this tiny enclave of normalcy.

So another year was coming to a close. And what a year! On one evening just before Christmas, when he had successfully completed his placement term and after the Managing Director's glowing reference secured the final component of his degree, Jeff sat on his balcony with a bottle of whisky, a packet of cigarettes and the photo which Lynn had given him for his twentieth birthday, revisiting some of the highlights of another stupendous twelve months.

Never had the twenty-one-year-old imagined such a wild ride! Going to the brink and back had helped the thoughtful superstar to crystallise what he wanted to do next with this bizarre life of his. Performing and recording were highly invigorating but they were only the foundation layer of his ambitious pyramid of goals. Touring the world was the easy part and a good way to reach a large number of people all at once, but it had no depth and made no permanent contribution to anything.

With Paragon Holdings raking in money hand over fist, the latent world-changer resolved to establish some sort of international development organisation for improving communication and collaboration, also planning to set up a children's welfare charity as an extension to The Fellowship. During the latter stages of his degree, the undergraduate had developed a strong working and personal relationship with a renowned Melbourne academic, another rising star in the world of international conflict resolution. Based on a common set of values and views, long discussions with John Francis had left the rock star resolved to focus his mind on this new pursuit as the end of the year rolled around, while he waited for the rest of his solitary sentence to run its course.

This was the only way his tortured soul would find the strength to move forward, now that the demands of his university studies were satisfied. He didn't want to escape back to the drug haze of a year ago, even though there were still many times when he hungered for and occasionally sought its complete abandon. About to turn the front page on another calendar, Jeff needed to be in a position to prove to Lynn and her parents that he had made himself worthy of her, once the opportunity arose again. Such opportunities would certainly not be on offer while his high-profile drug habit was in full view and he was regularly photographed drinking himself blind.

The prosperous loner saw off the final few days of nineteen-seventy-three in Sydney with the Blakes, having never heard from his sister again. The lovely Lynn Dyson and her fellow MAC favourites put on another Christmas television special, complete with handheld candles in the audience and a chill wind in the air. As was traditional, the whole family watched avidly from their luxurious drawing room. Jeff's dream girl looked hotter than ever, and Gerry's sisters continued to tease their brother's friend mercilessly. He kept telling himself it wasn't their intention to cause him such distress, but this mantra was hardly convincing.

At the Mosman mansion's annual, swanky New Year's Eve party, Celia again caught the superstar smoking and feeling sorry for himself.

'Another few months, Jeff,' she said, placing her hand on his forearm. 'Gradually ticking away, isn't it?'

'Celia, it's hell on Earth,' the young man confessed, caught unawares by the sympathetic gesture. 'The more I think I've learned how to deal with it, the more it hurts. It's almost as if something's testing me. The stronger I get, the harder it pushes back.'

The middle-aged, homely woman stood on her tiptoes to kiss his cheek. This boy whom her family had taken in almost ten years ago remained a complete mystery to her. Part misguided child and part sensitive intellectual, Jeff Diamond was about as different from her own son as anyone could be, and yet they had become the firmest of friends and were now also enormously successful business partners. Her husband was tacit in his admiration for the young man's achievements, and it was no secret to her that both daughters were in love with their extra family member.

And for her part, the devoted mother couldn't for the life of her understand how someone so blessed could remain so desperately unhappy.

'Darling, you're testing yourself. It's part of who you are,' she told him, rubbing his arm. 'You're going to keep pushing yourself until you get what you think you need. You just won't let yourself give up, will you? Like the day you fought me about seeing that doctor. And that's what makes you so special, dear. Lynn will absolutely love you when she finally gets home. You have to keep believing that. Why wouldn't she?'

'Thanks, Celia,' Jeff replied, feeling tears stinging the back of his eyes. 'Hope you're right.'

The celebrity excused himself and wandered off into the darkness of the Blakes' manicured garden, his tortured mind begging the ground to swallow him up and put him out of his misery. He rounded the corner to the wooden bench near the tennis court and slumped down onto it heavily, lit a cigarette and leaned back with tears streaming down his face.

'Do you hear that, angel?' he whispered up towards the stars which hung over the beaches of Sydney's north shore. 'You're going to absolutely love me. Is that true? For Christ's sake, I hope so. I love you, and I miss you so much. Give me something to believe in, will you? I need to feel you're still there.'

Celia could just about make out the shadowy figure sitting in among her prized roses. It broke her heart to think of him crying at this happy time of year. Somehow this immensely popular and successful man was still very much alone, and that seemed completely wrong to her. Although admittedly wild and outspoken at times, Jeff Diamond was a good man intent on doing good things. She said a prayer that Lynn would return to him when the time was right.

***

'There's no Statute of Limitations on this stuff, mate,' Jeff smiled.

He was watching Gerry's reaction to a difficult scene in Act Two. The corners of his eyes crinkled, and his mouth made a familiar ponderous, pouting shape which indicated great effort exerted towards keeping itself shut. The celebrity assumed his manager was of the opinion that he had been a little too honest for his own good. The older man sat back and crossed his arms across his chest, meeting his formidable *amigo*'s fiery gaze.

'It's up to me and the kids what I include in the book.'

Gerry nodded, looking up as the two Diamond children entered the room. 'And the Dysons?'

'Hey, guys. Sit down,' the father motioned. 'The thought police are onto me again. Pour yourselves some wine. We're well ahead of you.'

Ryan took the accountant's outstretched hand before standing back to enable the visitor to place a welcoming kiss on his sister's cheek. Two half-smoked cigars languished in the ashtray, still smouldering, and an empty wine bottle was acting as a paperweight to stop the autobiography's pages from being blown by the downdraught of the ceiling fan.

'Thanks, Dad. What was that about the Dysons? Which bit are you talking about?'

'The whole bloody thing!' Gerry exclaimed. 'They'd have every right to sue you over some of this stuff, I reckon. Have you read any of this, Kizzy?'

Kierney picked up the pile of loose leaves in front of the family's close friend and scanned a few paragraphs to re-familiarise herself with the contentious chapter. She leaned back against her father's stomach when she felt his hand grip her shoulder. They had missed each other while she had been overseas visiting the United Nations in New York and working with other songwriters. It was nice to be home.

'I'm sure Grandma and Grandpa are prepared,' she grinned. 'It's not like this'll be the first time it's been given air-time between Papá and them.'

'And with Mum too,' her brother added. 'If anything, I think Mum bore the bigger grudge, don't you, Dad?'

Jeff chuckled, picking up the dormant cigar and relighting it. '*Cierto*, mate. And no, Gez. I won't end up in court again. I have warned them they'll get a going-over. They expected it.'

'Right you are, boss,' the affable businessman cocked his head. 'I'm getting back to Fiona before she cashes in my conjugal chips for the night. Just don't come running to me when the shit hits the fan. Can I take the rest of this?'

'Absolutely,' the widower nodded, seeing his manager claim the second cigar. 'Say hi to Fiona for us. Is she panicking yet?'

'Panicking?' the seventeen-year-old piped up. 'About the wedding? That's ages away still.'

'Oh, she's panicking, Kizzo,' Gerry confessed. 'Probably realised she's made a big mistake. I'd be panicking if I'd agreed to marry me.'

They all laughed aloud, particularly at the alarmed expression on the bridegroom-to-be's face. At almost forty-seven years old, the Diamond family had never expected Jeff's oldest friend to succumb to monogamy after a lifetime of playing the field. Still a handsome man, save for a layer of high-living forming a paunch at his midriff, Gerry had made his own considerable fortune in parallel with guiding the megastars' financial interests for a whole generation.

Time had caught up with the indomitable one, first noticed by the superstar himself, ever perceptive when it came to subtle changes in behaviour and the odd throwaway one-liner. Both faced with entering their respective second half-century on their own, although for vastly different reasons, the grieving husband had called his mate's bluff by insinuating that his "hare to tortoise" transition coincided with finally leaving short trousers behind.

Ryan and Kierney waited for the older pair to say their goodbyes by the front door, idly sipping on fine *Tempranillo* and reading through some content which admittedly skated quite close to the edge of reason. It was true, they agreed, that their mother had been the one to retain the greater bitterness about those two years apart. Their dad had previously rationalised it as only one of many significant challenges to be faced in his early twenties, and thus he had learned to credit himself with weathering the storm in its entirety.

'So!' Jeff announced, clapping his hands as he re-joined his teenagers in the dimly-lit study. 'D'you think Gerry's got a point? Should I tone some of it down?'

Kierney shook her head emphatically. 'No, Papá. I think it's perfect the way it is. It's the truth.'

'The truth, but with a definite tilt towards the sensational,' her brother smirked. 'We all know how easy it is for this man to bend the truth to suit his own agenda. Just throw in a well-targeted metaphor or two... Come on!'

'Thanks for your support, mate,' the father jeered, digging his son under the ribcage and prompting a tirade of light-hearted verbal abuse.

'No worries,' the young man answered, bent double in a combination of laughter and pain.

'Don't you guys ever stop wanting to maim each other?' the dark-haired teenager wondered aloud. 'What's ready to read? Are you finished with the chapter when Mamá comes back to Melbourne? I can't wait to read that, after all this misery and substance abuse.'

Jeff smiled, turning his attention back to the pages in his daughter's hands. 'No, but I'm happy to start talking about it, if you want. The diary's sitting there, as yet unopened.'

The young woman followed her dad's eyes to a brown, leather-bound volume on the credenza, bundled with the type of stout rubber band used by the postman to group letters for the same address. There appeared to be envelopes full of photographs underneath the diary, and her heartbeat quickened at the thought of sorting through her mother's pictures and matching them to the relevant dates in nineteen-seventy-three or -four.

'Have you already sorted the photos?'

'Yeah, roughly. They're not indexed yet, so you can do that again. D'you want to?'

Excited eyes met her father's doleful ones, knowing this task would appeal to her and Ryan much more. Their grief had subsided these days, resigned to the situation and ready to move on with their lives. Not so for their dad, who was still see-sawing between good days and bad days.

'Yes, please. I love looking through them. When do you need them? I want to hear about you getting back together again. I so, so love that story.'

The widower issued a queasy half-smile. He so, so loved that story too, although telling it these days had somehow lost its magic. Her parents' romantic reunion had always been a bedtime staple for the young girl, no matter how many times she heard it. Ryan had little appetite to hear it again however, judging by the swift exit he had made from the study.

'What d'you wanna know?'

Kierney shrugged. 'I don't know. Something relevant to what you're going to write next. What was going through your mind in those last few weeks before she came back? How you kept hoping after so long?'

'Oh, I always kept hoping,' Jeff assured her. 'As I keep hoping now. It's the only thing that works, *pequeñita*. Hoping that all the twin souls crap is actually real. And even if it's not, why not, huh?'

The seventeen-year-old nodded. 'Guess so. You do know though, don't you? You're usually much more adamant than today. What's happened?'

'Nothing, baby. Nothing. I'm just pissed off with what Gerry was threatening, I s'pose. Ignore me. Of course I believe we'll be together again. What d'you wanna know?'

'About how it felt to see her again,' the teenager decided. 'A bit further on than you are, but that's the bit it's all working up to, isn't it?'

The songwriter sat down on the edge of the desk, savouring the way the warm, rich red stung the lining of his throat. Oh, yes. Every fibre of his being had been working up to this moment, there, back in nineteen-seventy-four: his chart-topping hits, one after the other; buying his penthouse apartment; the courageous media coverage; kicking off the Diamond Celebration Foundation and Teachers For Peace. It was all working up to that moment when he would be made worthy of the adult Lynn Dyson's affections.

'When I walked back into your mamá's arms after those years adrift, it was like our souls had united again,' he fixed his daughter's expectant stare. 'We were relinked. I felt some sort of inner peace engulf me. And Lynn did too, apparently.'

Kierney's eyes danced when her beloved papá's hand immediately reached up to rub the gratifying knot out of his pectoral muscle.

'Yes, she did,' he smiled, willing the sensation back again. 'It was as if her validation had suddenly given me permission to accept myself.'

'To accept yourself?' the young woman parroted. 'What do you mean?'

'As a "someone",' her father explained, painting quotation marks in the air. 'There were a whole heap of things I wasn't proud of during those months. All the drugs, the wild parties and dating all those gorgeously gruesome women. None of that was going to count in my favour, was it? I wasn't so far up myself not to see that.'

The dark-haired beauty giggled. 'No. Grandma told me a bit about that time. She used to follow you closely, I think. Did you know?'

Jeff sniffed. 'Ah, yeah. I didn't know for sure, but I was ninety-nine percent sure they'd be keeping tabs on me. I didn't know then that Big D knew

Lynn had made that donation though. She only told me afterwards, and at that stage I couldn't be certain it was her anyway.'

'You just hoped.'

The great man smiled. 'I just hoped. Jesus, it's a breath of fresh air, talking to you after that pompous prick's complaining.'

Kierney reached out her hand to the tearful man and watched him kiss it. '*Gracias, Papá. Digame para los* twin souls.'

'Sure thing,' her father grinned at his returning son, who was struggling to keep hold of two very chilled bottles of beer coated with a layer of condensation. 'If you'll indulge me. Cheers, mate. Mamá's soul, or the essence part at least, is still with me, and you guys too probably in some way, although her ego is gone.'

Ryan coughed as a laugh escaped mid-swallow. 'Did she have an ego?'

'Did she have an ego?' Jeff almost choked too, amused by his son's constancy, unfailingly coming to his mother's defence. 'I presume you're being facetious.'

The young man nodded, slumping down onto the armchair by the window. The lush trellises wore brighter colours today, after a morning drenching. He was getting used to this old house, and in fact quite liked it. It had an all-seeing air about it, complementing their dad's sombre countenance very well.

'She had one hell of an ego, mate. As competitive at its foundation as yours.'

'Really?' Kierney interjected. 'She didn't let it show.'

The widower raised the neck of his beer bottle to his gorgeous gipsy girl. 'You two weren't old enough to remember her on the tennis court in her absolute prime. She was as single-minded and determined to win as any of them. It wasn't like that later though. She lost the hunger to win for herself, and we benefitted from that. She sacrificed herself for us, guys.'

'Gladly though?' Ryan invited.

'Yeah, absolutely. No pressure. She'd had enough by then. It just wasn't her priority once you came along. *We* were. *La famille.*'

His son sniggered. '*La famiglia*. Sounds like the Mafia again. *Tito, capisce? La* famiglia è tutto.'

The dark-haired Diamonds smiled at the sportsman's overplayed impersonation of an Italian godfather. Ever the comedian, his influence never failed to brighten the others' mood. Kierney, on the other hand, liked nothing better than to wallow in the nether reaches of someone else's pain, compassionate to the core and filled with an eternal desire to soothe her father's troubles.

'What *are* essence and ego?' she asked.

'Mumbo jumbo,' her brother teased. 'Like communicating via a tattoo. The desperate grappling of a deranged mind.'

'Fuck you, Jetto,' Jeff snarled. 'Don't speak too soon. They're what the Buddhists talk about when they describe the two aspects of souls. Essence is the outward, connected-to-all-things half of a soul, whereas ego is inwardly focussed and directed towards finding one's own place in the connected world.'

'OK,' Kierney nodded. 'That makes sense.'

'Your mama taught me so much over the years, but there's one thing she definitely learned from me,' the intellectual continued. 'That it was OK to change our minds. When I first knew her, she used to carry on believing and doing things regardless of changes in her environment. Plato said, "Time will change and even reverse many of your present opinions. Refrain, therefore, a while from setting yourself up as a judge of the highest order."'

Ryan turned around from his view out into the garden. 'Bloody Plato! Always sticks his two florins in. So you convinced Mum that changing her mind was a sign that she was learning more?

'Spot on, mate. At first she thought not sticking things out was a sign of weakness. But she couldn't deny Plato, could she? Me, I could go to hell with my opinions, but Plato was a higher authority.'

Both children laughed at the effrontery in their father's sarcasm. Modesty had never been his strong suit, especially when it came to the esoteric and ethereal. For as long as they could remember, he had been at pains to push their entirely grounded mother into the other-worldly, while she had countered this with a liberal smattering of reality bites. A very rounded education had been had by all, forever in a state of vehement debate.

The seventeen-year-old stretched the elastic band from the diary and photograph wallets from nineteen-seventy-four. Leafing through the pages quickly, she searched for July and August, which were the last two months their parents had spent apart until that awful February morning earlier this year. A week after her birthday, the youngster recalled, with a shiver running up her spine. How she wished by opening the diary that somehow she could bring the absent fourth Diamond back to life…

'August thirty-one,' she announced. 'Here's a taste of what's to come, Papá. "Tomorrow I'm flying back to Melbourne. Home? Not sure anymore. I want going home to be like going back in time, but I already know it won't be. Damn the Dyson name! I wonder if Jeff will ring me? God, I hope so. But then, God, I hope not, because of what I'll have to say. What can be so bad in his past to make Dad so adamant that I have nothing to do with him?" See, Papá? She was looking forward to seeing you much more than Melbourne or Benloch. No mention of Junior, Sandy or Anna, or her friends. You're the only one mentioned by name.'

Jeff's face had turned deathly pale. His daughter was the first to read these auspicious words, and he was suddenly overcome with terror. Waving to assure the teenagers that he was alright, he ran out of the room and slammed the door of the downstairs cloakroom, whence they imagined him expelling much more than simply the contents of his stomach.

'Well, done, Kizzo,' Ryan teased. 'He needs to read these on his own. Too much of a shock, obviously.'

His sister raised her head, having lost herself in the ensuing daily entries. 'Hmm... S'pose so. He's OK. This is amazing, bro. You have to read it. She really missed him so much still, but at that stage she couldn't see a way to be together. Papá's right. Mamá didn't think she was able to change anything, even her mind. Grandpa had convinced her to give him up.'

The nineteen-year-old cricket star held his hand out for the diary, curious but nervous. He didn't normally enjoy invading his mother's privacy. Yet one false move in September nineteen-seventy-four would have had serious ramifications for his own existence. He felt strangely disconcerted by this prospect, without really understanding why.

'Which date?'

'Twenty-fifth. The night before she was due to meet him for breakfast.'

Ryan flicked over a few flimsy sheets until he found the entry Kierney referred to. The blonde singing sensation, who had only recently turned nineteen, described how conflicted she felt, how intriguing it was to be meeting her former lover again and how unwavering she would need to be when faced with the good-looking charmer who still dominated her memories. Unanswered questions flowed down the page. What would he expect of her? How would he behave? Jeff Diamond was verging on hard-core, while Lynn Dyson was ever the girl next door. Would he even be attracted to her these days, now that both lives had changed so much?

Publicly, Lynn Dyson had always feigned being putty in Jeff Diamond's hands, but the children knew otherwise. She had called the shots, from start to finish. None of them would be here had it not been for the one momentous, game-changing mind-shift awaiting its consignment to public record.

'Jeez! Did you read what she wrote for the twenty-seventh?' the young man asked his sister.

Kierney sprang to her feet with enthusiasm, ecstatic that she had a chance to discuss the diary's contents. 'Where?'

The law student followed Ryan's long, muscular finger as it traced the handwritten sentences. Lynn was hurting. The previous day, she had followed her father's instructions to the letter, and her outpouring of grief was no less heartrending than their other parent's extreme reaction to losing her twenty-two years later. According to the words they were reading, meeting each other again had left an even more indelible impression on the young movie star than she had feared, expressing a veritable diatribe of hateful thoughts about her overbearing parents and the constricting, precision-timed life over which she still lacked full control.

Jeff's first response was concern, walking back into the office and seeing tears in both teenagers' eyes. Kierney was hanging over her brother's left shoulder, and he knew they hadn't noticed his return. Years ago, he would have reacted with furious paranoia at the invasion of privacy. Now however, racked with shame and guilt for their sorrow, the silent moment was rendered yet more poignant when he realised his first response had been accurate. The man who had learned from an early age not to trust his instincts was today filled with bitter regret that it had taken the family's systematic and measured approach to recovering from Lynn's death to finally eradicate the few lingering symptoms of the Post-Traumatic Stress Disorder which had plagued him for so long.

Never before had the accomplished celebrity felt Miss Irony deal him such a kick in the guts. His greatest loss had not been his greatest trauma. Those violent and abusive events he had weathered as a child, wreaking havoc on the majority of his adult life, had gradually diminished to a level of insignificant undercurrent as a respected, affluent and contented middle-aged man. And the worst possible thing that could ever happen to him... to lose the love of his life... had left him in better shape mentally than ever. There was more than a certain injustice there, he admonished.

'Oh, Papá!' his daughter caught sight of a pair of bare feet on the floorboards and followed hairy legs upwards, past a pair of blue board-shorts and a shapeless, white t-shirt, until she made eye contact with the face she adored. 'You made me jump! How long have you been standing there?'

'A couple of minutes,' Jeff replied. 'I wanted to watch your unsullied reaction. Are those tears more happy than sad, or the other way round?'

Ryan slotted his middle finger like a bookmark between the pages they had been reading, folded the diary closed and held it out towards his father. 'More happy than sad. She loved you, old man. She really loved you. Can't think why, but you'd better believe it.'

Smiling, the forty-four-year-old shook his head. 'Thanks, mate, but no, thanks. Not now. I'll get stoned and read them tonight while you're out. We're going to have a hot date, just your mamá and me. No kids allowed, so don't come home early.'

Kierney grimaced. 'Ew! Gross, gross, gross! I wish you wouldn't tell me things like that. If I make dinner, can we talk more about what we think souls are? I have some questions, after reading that Buddhism book you lent me. Is that OK?'

The plan was confirmed, and the young woman disappeared to the kitchen to rustle up a hearty bowl of pasta. Their dad had definitely turned a corner of sorts, although neither child was totally comfortable with his new, rather unsettling direction. She had heard many stories of people turning to religion and thoughts of an afterlife as a result of losing a loved one, but in recent weeks the dedication demonstrated by the healing author in his quest to secure a double berth on the same cosmic train as their dearly departed had seen him plunge deeply into religious text of any and all varieties.

A fair degree of scepticism remained despite the passion and fervour, the young woman was thankful, and the passages she had read in the autobiography's recent chapters dissected the myriad theories in objective and judicious detail. Her doting dad had been at pains to put her mind at rest, assuring her that in order to gain perspective on the cliff of true madness he needed to drive to the very edge.

'My car goes in reverse as well, *pequeñita*,' he had smiled, kissing her on the forehead. 'There's no harm in looking. It doesn't mean I have to press the accelerator.'

The threesome ate dinner in the kitchen, with Indie circling the table in case tasty leftovers came his way. The golden retriever had quickly become part of the family, vying with the burly sportsman for second-in-command to Jeff's overriding authority as pack leader. Kierney was relegated to last place in the hierarchy, which was a position she was finally beginning to outgrow. With her brother away for most of the year in Cambridge, completing the final year of his degree, she had put her father's needs first and had been happy to do so. In the end, it had been the empath himself who had called her on it, these days regularly introducing her first in company and niggling her kindly whenever she pandered to him too much.

Tonight was no exception. As soon as the willowy nymph jumped up to clear the table, her father's index finger flicked downwards in protest, followed by a quick sideways glance at Ryan. Dutifully, the two men stacked their empty bowls into the dishwasher and cleared away the rest of the remains. Still savouring her glass of Shiraz, the inquisitive teenager gathered her thoughts.

'So, Papá-swami, do you think a spiritual source is the same as a god?'

Her brother laughed. 'OK! Let's start with an easy one, shall we?'

'That *is* an easy one,' Jeff countered. 'No.'

Youthful, dark eyes lit up. 'Thanks. That's what I think too, but I wanted to check. So it's just whatever inspires us as individuals?'

Jeff raised his eyebrows. 'According to me and you. Ry?'

'Depends how you define god,' the nineteen-year-old retorted. 'The equation could go either way, depending on what god means and what spiritual source means to each of our individuals. *La réponse est "Si ou non," à mon avis.*'

His sister sighed. 'Smart-arse. But you're right, isn't he, Papá?'

'*Si est non*,' the joker smiled. 'Yes *and* no. I think there's enough of a body of wisdom around the word "god" to be safe in likening it to some sort of divine being. A deity. Even if you believe you have your own personal god.

For me, a spiritual source could be a mantra, a text, a poem. Song? Or a saint? A living person even.'

'So your answer stands,' his daughter concluded. 'The man whose mind always changes is sticking. Good-oh.'

'Good-oh?' Jeff laughed. 'I've never heard you say that before. Is this new phrase something you learned horizontally?'

'Dad!'

'Shut up, Ry!' the young woman blushed. 'It must be. David does say "Good-oh" a lot. Shit! Caught in the act!'

The widower's long left arm swooped over the table and landed on the seventeen-year-old's wrist, squeezing it tightly. She was no longer his shadow, just like the hulking great meat-head beside her was barely recognisable as his tousle-headed little boy. They both oozed self-confidence and wielded their fine minds magnificently. As he had come to anticipate, Lynn echoed these very thoughts, dealing him a sharp serve via his "JL" tattoo.

'OK, old man,' his son brought them back on track. 'Why, if your answer is no, do you talk in such religious terms? Especially lately?'

'Hey! That's what I wanted to ask!'

Again two wise, grey-flecked eyebrows twitched, this time in jest. '*Religio*, the Latin and Italian word at religion's origin means linking back, hence I always think about it as like being saved from something harmful. Brought back from the brink.'

The two much younger souls opposite were immediately silent, again throwing their father back in time to when they were much smaller and only capable of forming their own opinions on topics of childish significance: how much chocolate they should be allowed to eat or whether their parents were unfair to deny them a late television show.

'Traditional religion,' he continued, 'as spread about by priests, imams, *et cetera*, seems to be all about re-linking... as in a shepherd reuniting his flock or a prison guard yelling drill instructions... a more coercive context of doctrine and conversion.'

'Whoa!' Ryan interjected. 'Priests, shepherds and prison guards in the same sentence? That's abstruse. Go on.'

'Jeff the Abstruse,' the father cocked his head. 'That I can live with. I refer to religion in a more constructive sense; when, in fact, if we believe in something within ourselves that wishes to be overwhelmingly good, then this re-linking should be more about resetting our own behaviour and attitude after we slipped off course for whatever reason. Relinking, or religion, should be an active thing, not a passive thing we have done to us.'

Again his words were met with a reverend silence, broken only by thoughtful sips from their wine glasses. How he wished their fourth Diamond was not elsewhere... How many of these life-affirming, challenging conversations had they undertaken, designed to shape characters and encourage enquiry from a very early age? The Grand Slam tennis champion had been as big a proponent of developing the muscle between their children's ears as she had of building strong limbs and stamina. Their lives had been endowed with constant exploration, privileged in many ways and yet sparse and simple in others.

Jeff rubbed his left pectoral muscle, hoping Lynn was on the same wavelength right now. Ryan and Kierney exhibited a solid sense of equilibrium which their parents had rarely seen in their school friends or teammates. The overwhelmingly positive attitude of their mother had counterbalanced her husband's scarred and engrained pessimistic streak, while neither sought to remove all risks or choices from their fledgling paths. The children were good to themselves in their quest to be good to others, community-minded and compassionate in the extreme.

And as for role models, who better than the world's greatest lovers? The bereft celebrity caught his breath, taken by surprise by a tingling signal from the other world while scoffing inwardly at his unswerving arrogance.

'What?' Ryan exclaimed.

'Nothing,' the great man grinned. 'Your mamá told me off for taking a self-congratulatory moment for your maturity. You can share the self-proclaimed super-parent label, angel. I'm not denying you any of the glory. Come back, and we'll reward each other.'

'*Papá*, carry on,' the caring seventeen-year-old urged. 'I'm glad *Mamá*'s here too. Hi, *Mamá*. What maturity anyway?'

The affable cricketer slapped his sister's arm, offended by her dismissal. 'Speak for yourself. I think super-parents are ones who joke with you. Allow you to send them up, and make sure no-one takes themselves too seriously. My friends' mums and dads are always trying to one-up their kids, so they never really get a chance to test their maturity. They're always just kids at home.'

'I like that, son,' Jeff nodded. 'Very nice. Your mamá believed in respecting your equality before I did, I think. She scolded me when I reacted to your lip, and I taught her to tolerate your stuff lying around everywhere. It was fascinating how we interacted on your behalves. Thanks, baby.'

The teenagers watched their father rub his chest again, his eyes watery and staring up to the ceiling. It was if he was trying to catch sight of her shifting soul, eager for any contact which might confirm their destiny.

'I think singing together helped us grow up too, in a weird way,' Kierney changed tack. 'Making music, writing songs, being brave enough to surface new ideas that weren't good enough yet. That's transferred into heaps of parts of my life. Don't you think, Ry?'

The intellectual waited for his fun-loving son's reply, which came in the form of a shrug and a grunt. 'That's interesting, pequeñita. A bit like eating together and all having chores to do. Just understanding that everything's easier and quicker with a bit of burden-sharing all round. But back to religion… People like Ralph Waldo Emerson, who said something like "We measure all religions by their civilising power," are in my opinion inciting all sorts of conflicting emotions. Don't you think? Like "We religious types are far superior to you heathens."'

This roused the surly, blond giant. 'Yeah! Like they believe in their divine right to fiddle with kiddles.'

'Jetto!' his sister yelped, screwing her face up in horror. 'Where did that come from?'

'Yeah, mate,' Jeff silenced the repulsed young woman. 'Absolutely. It's hard not to think that way, but that's precisely what I mean by inciting hatred. Thanks for being my stooge! Those who assume to represent religions don't mean you to react that way, but human nature and our sense of injustice put us straightaway on the defensive.'

The sportsman took a step back. 'What was that quote again?'

'"We measure all religions by their civilising power."'

'Civilising power,' the Cambridge undergraduate rolled the words around on his tongue.

Their father continued. 'Civility is of course basically laudable, but not necessarily with the connotation of power. Unless we think of power as a desire to care for others and make things better overall. Benevolence, if you like… then I'm happy with a sort of universal application of religion. Relinking ourselves and each other for the greater good.'

'The benevolent lion,' his daughter hesitated, recalling something Lynn had put in a letter to the man she had admired so much. 'The pantomime lion.'

Both men smiled. It had been a while since they had been reminded of the notes which had been instrumental in coping with their family tragedy. Life's pause button had long been deactivated, at least for the youngsters.

'You know…' the dreamy teenager said. 'I have to go to Sydney Uni' now, more than ever, because I need to show the people of Sydney that I don't blame them for what happened.'

'Sis!' Ryan impersonated his sibling. 'Where did *that* come from?'

Jeff lifted his hand again, encouraging his son's patience this time. 'Yeah, sis. You have to admit that came right out of the blue. *¿Estas OK?*'

'*Sí, estoy OK.* It's something I've been thinking about for a while. Just never aired it before. Do you blame Sydney in any way for what happened?'

The widower shook his head. 'No. I never blamed Sydney. I hate going there now, but then that's no loss really. I never felt a need to go there. Even though it's where my roots are, I feel like I go back further than that. I don't feel any less of an affinity for Sydney than I ever did. The word just turns my stomach because of what happened, as you so successfully euphemised.'

'D'you remember when Graham Winton asked you if you forgave García?' the ambitious lawyer-in-waiting dared again.

'Yeah…' Jeff spun the diphthong out in jest. My turn to say, "Where did that come from?"'

His son threw him glare of steel for yet another about-turn in favour of the prodigal daughter. 'Go ahead.'

'Cheers, mate. I owe you that one. Choose your punishment later. What did you want to know about Graham's question, Your Honour?'

'Why, when you're plundering the good bits of each religion, don't you ever talk about forgiveness? Isn't forgiveness one of the core tenets of most religions?'

'Christ, Kizzo! That's one hell of a question too. And you're right. I have been cogitating on the whole forgiveness thing in recent weeks, preparing to document the glorious homecoming and the months before we escaped to the UK. For the record, my most favoured conclusion so far is that the purpose of forgiveness is to give yourself and whomever you're forgiving peace of mind. Some level of security that there'll be no further retribution, I s'pose.'

'That I like,' his son teased, pouring another full glass of wine each. 'So?'

'Religions'll tell me I should do this both for García's and my own benefits. On one hand, I'm getting there… kicking and screaming, mind you… and this circumnavigates us beautifully back to essence and ego. My soul's ego will never forgive him, because he fucked up the perfect place in this world that the four of us created. However, the essence of my soul is erring on the side of granting us both peace of mind, since he played a part in steering us into the next life with a greater chance of finding each other than if neither of us had had time to work it out.'

Ryan piped up again. 'And when you write about you and Mum getting back together, are you going to forgive "G" and "G"?'

'No.'

His daughter couldn't help laughing. 'That was definitive. Why not? You got back together, so why not forgive them? Because you don't want them to forget the pain they caused you and Mamá?'

'Yeah, partly,' Jeff frowned, 'but I suspect it's for the opposite reason. Let's try and generate a hypothesis on the fly… If I look at it from an ego perspective, I can forgive them because they lost out to something more powerful anyway.'

'Love,' the romantic young woman insisted.

'Sure, pequeñita. More than love though. The pull of twin souls. We would've done anything in our power to be together, so I don't think they could've found a way to stop us. Fire, flood, pestilence or parents.'

'And from an essence perspective?' Ryan prompted.

'From an essence perspective, forgiveness isn't warranted either, in my opinion, because their stopping us being together and following through on all the plans we were making would've had a much greater negative impact than just stopping two ill-matched musicians from getting it on. At the end of the day, guys, as the next few chapters'll bear out, I choose not to be grateful for some of the things that happened to me, and to us. I have no doubt that I probably should, but I'll live and die choosing not to. I hope you can live with that. I hope Mamá can live with that, because I'm confident I can.'

LORRAINE PESTELL

Someone Worthy

By mid-June nineteen-seventy-four, Jeff had set out on his third road trip for the year, just days after his twenty-second birthday. Another twelve months into his massive career, he had celebrated with understated, stylish sophistication in one of a growing number of adopted home towns: Paris. Immersed in a Masters degree in International Relations and zealously plotting his new ambitions for social change, his name allowed him a certain flexibility while on tour to insert short diversions to Eastern Europe and Africa into his tight schedule.

Curious about goings-on behind the Iron Curtain, the songwriter also slotted in stops in Leningrad and Moscow, before landing in his paternal grandparents' home of Warsaw. The multi-linguist spoke virtually none of the highly complex language and was enthralled by a culture so unfamiliar, his childhood memories of Polish customs displaying a Jewish flavour which was no longer evident in the post-war, Communist stronghold.

In spite of this alien detachment, the esurient tourist saw his father in every Polish and Russian man he met: hot-headed, chauvinistic and bigoted; seemingly out to make a quick buck however they could. This parallel was peculiarly inexplicable to him since Pavel Diament had never set foot in Poland, and the estranged son didn't remember his grandfather ever demonstrating such aggressive characteristics. He concluded his father must have either inherited behaviour passed down through the generations or been heavily influenced by the underworld figures who had settled in Sydney since the nineteen-thirties and -forties, having emigrated from Poland directly to Australia.

Whether in the bleakest bars he had ever seen or on the grey streets of the Polish capital, the young man detected a deep-seated and hostile national pride which differed from anything else he had experienced on his travels. Nationalism with a chip on its shoulder, the empathetic songwriter decided.

Therefore it was with considerable joy that his appointed tour guide then took him to Krakow, wherein the starving poet found cultural sustenance not quite on a par with Paris or London, but sufficient to restore his faith in his Eastern European heritage. Cafés along the Vistula were perfect for reading in relative anonymity until the previous night's hangover wore off, or for engaging in stilted conversation with local academics and artists who took pleasure in extolling the virtues of Polish literature and enumerating the city's many Nobel Prize winners.

Back in London, Jeff was thrilled to discover that he had been invited to appear on the Michael Parkinson Show. This was an unmissable chance to get serious with a new audience, a large proportion of whom would be unlikely to ever attend a rock concert. He had been seated next to the *fêted* interviewer at an entertainment industry function shortly after New Year, while the chat show host had been visiting Sydney, as he often did, for the test match at the SCG. It transpired that Parkinson had been captivated by the young celebrity's fervent rhetoric, and the producers had reserved an entire, hour-long showcase for the British viewing public.

So, for his latest visit to the BBC's South London studios, the musician dressed in apparel appropriate for a scorching, purposeful intellectual, a black suit with a dark crimson, open-necked shirt, poised to make an impact. Michael Parkinson opened proceedings, after descending the steps of his familiar studio set.

'Welcome to the show! Tonight's guest burst onto the music scene in late nineteen-seventy-two with a string of hits all over the world. Since then, this young man has truly taken the world by storm, even being labelled "The Australian Elvis". I recently met him at a charity dinner in Sydney. I said I thought some of his lyrics were poetic, and he told me that where he comes from, in the western suburbs of Sydney, there's a fine line between poet and local idiot!'

The audience laughed politely, after which the host continued. 'I was so taken by what he had to say that we met for lunch the following day, and tonight I'm delighted to welcome him here to perform a couple of numbers and chat to us.'

A more generous round of applause rang out this time.

'Interviewing this man will be a pleasure because he has an opinion on everything,' Michael added, 'which you'll find out after he sings to us. Welcome, Jeff Diamond!'

The camera panned right until it fell on the band, fronted by the tall, good-looking star whose latest single was about to be given its first UK airing. After Jeff had virtually made love to his audience on stage and the screaming had died down, the two men met in front of the famous black leather interview chairs and shook hands warmly. Supremely confident and relaxed, the now well-established icon leaned back in his seat and exuded star quality from every pore.

'Good evening, Jeff,' the Yorkshireman began. 'Welcome back to London.'

'Thanks, Michael, and good evening,' the younger man replied and turned to the studio audience. 'Thanks to you too. By the way, before I let it go, I'm not at all comfortable with the Elvis comparison. I'm a huge Elvis Presley fan, and there can be only one.'

Receiving a respectful nod from his host, the natural showman carried on engaging directly with a hushed crowd which he could barely make out under the bright stage lighting. 'You know, I grew up thinking Michael Parkinson watched cricket for a living, because in Australia we only ever see him at the Boxing Day Test or in the SCG members' stand.'

The audience laughed again, warming to the swarthy, exotic-looking singer.

His interviewer smiled, ready to pose his first question. 'Sadly, no! You've earned quite a reputation as an electrifying stage performer. When solo, you come across as a sultry, troubled soul, but in person you're confident and outgoing. How do these three sides of your personality compete?'

Jeff laughed. 'Yeah. That new song's tough to do in a studio. I can usually sense the audience's feedback if I'm performing at a gig, but today there was nothing but a heavy sense of expectation until about a third of the way through. Singing without the full band is raw too, from the outside and from the inside. We have to make it sound lean and mean, and I don't need to wait for the band to catch up, so good and bad! And as for being a troubled soul? Yes, I'm always looking for answers. Life's not perfect, but who am I to complain after the ride I've had lately? Don't know why, but I've always been memorable. I was born with this knack of getting in people's faces. Love me or hate me, people tend to remember me. I try not to overanalyse it... Well, that's actually not true at all! But I have learned to use it to my advantage.'

'Being memorable must be a double-edged sword,' Parkinson smiled, drawing the audience's attention to his guest's appealing physical attributes. 'I could imagine there would be some people you'd rather didn't remember you.'

Again the young man chuckled generously. 'You may well be right, Michael. My upfront judgment is improving in that regard, thankfully. There have been some stalkers though and they're very tenacious. They just don't take no for an answer.'

'Mostly female, I'm guessing?'

Jeff shrugged. 'I don't want to come on your show and talk about my sex life. Other people are so much better at that than I am...'

The audience tittered with typical British reserve, and the musician smiled again. He already had them in the palm of his hand, which was exactly where he wanted them. He had spent several of the previous night's dark hours, stretched into the early morning, rehearsing the topics he sought to expound during this amazing opportunity, and his numerous and well-publicised romantic entanglements weren't among them.

'No disrespect to anyone involved, but it's really not that exciting to talk about after the fact,' he explained, receiving some more laughter in return. 'Well, I mean, it's exciting for me, but not for you; unless you're all a bunch of discontented voyeurs.'

Michael jumped in, directing everyone to the monitors around the studio, expertly cutting off the chatter and laughter. 'We've got some footage here of you giving an interview on Spanish television last year...'

A video clip ran, showing the superstar wooing another audience in his native Spanish, who were all applauding vociferously.

'Yep. Those crazy Spaniards!' Jeff nodded, recalling the occasion easily. 'That show was wild. We did shows all over Europe last year. I speak Spanish and passable French, so it's great to be able to talk directly with people. In other countries, I can get by or have to use an interpreter, but the nuances typically get lost in translation. I've only recently left Australia for the first time, so I'm still pretty wide-eyed and childlike about travelling the world. And performing to large audiences has taught me a lot about my own ability to communicate, because of the constant *yin* and *yang* of feedback. People want more, I give 'em more. They want to calm down, I'll calm down. It's easy once you learn how to read the signs, and the different cultures just add another dimension to that learning. It's fascinating, and I feel like I'm only getting started.'

The crowded television studio erupted with cheering and clapping, more closely resembling their less-reserved Spanish counterparts.

The guest continued. 'But performing, that's just the veneer; the outer shell. It's the semi-permeable membrane to absorb what's around me and the way my crazy thoughts get channelled outwards. I'm all about better communication. You know... I had a girlfriend a couple of years ago who used to tell me to talk to my car nicely because I was always swearing at it for not starting. I dismissed it initially as slushy, girly rubbish...'

Again the audience reacted with subdued amusement, which the young man acknowledged with a sly wink and a flash of his expressive eyebrows.

'"Cars don't have feelings," I said back. But then I thought about it... as I should have done in the first place, of course, ladies... and realised there was more to it. It's not about what we say, but how we say it and about which subliminal pieces of information are exchanged. If your car doesn't start, kicking it ain't going to do anyone any good! But if you open the bonnet and listen for the clues it's giving you, you'll stand more of a chance of figuring out what's wrong and fixing it. It's exactly the same with people. We think we can just nudge someone if they get out of line, but there might well be a perfectly good reason why they're not doing what you think they should do. Most of the time, we just don't care enough to find out.'

The interviewer nodded, waiting patiently for the charismatic guest to make his points.

'Now, I can talk a lot,' Jeff joked to the audience, pausing for a few seconds. 'Can you tell? But I also appreciate the value of listening before I get on my high horse about something. Yeah, I'm just a loudmouthed musician who's frustrated that governments and companies can't wait to tell people what they need. Do they actually know? People think because I've got a lot to say that I'm full of my own self-importance. I'm not.'

The young man motioned a theatrical aside. 'Honestly!'

His spellbound public clapped and cheered again, with a whistle blasting out from towards the back for good measure.

'I like to learn way more than I like to teach. It's just that I can't come on a show like this and sit here listening to you... ' the larrikin suddenly leaned forward, as if he were now the chat show host. 'Mister Parkinson, welcome to your show. It's great to be with you. I'm here to listen. So, tell me about yourself, Michael.'

The seasoned television personality smiled, obviously ensnared by the likeable company as well. His special guest continued, sitting back again and stretching his long legs. A cigarette would have gone down very nicely right about now, the addict mused.

'When I'm not working, I spend a lot of time talking with as many different types of people as possible. My favourite thing to do is to go to late night bars,' he stared suggestively at the individuals in the front row, who all laughed on cue. 'And supper venues are great places to catch businesspeople or politicians trying to sneak some bohemian pleasures back into their humdrum, process-oriented lives. At the moment, my most revered inspiration is John Francis, another Australian, a New South Wales policymaker and academic... backroom kind of guy... but with a fascinating view on life. His father was a leading light in the Uniting Church in Australia, but John reflects that there was very little actual religion in his dad's practice. His mission was more about social sustainability. John's now in here in Britain actually, at London University, and I was fortunate to be able to catch up with him when I arrived last week. My idea of a better future has been shaped and moulded a great deal by him, along with Gandhi and some French and Russian writers. Look him up: John Francis. It's good stuff, guys!'

The chat show's host appeared very pleased to take a back seat in the interview, considering his guest to be on a roll. As soon as the audience fell silent, he invited another opinion.

'Last time we met, you had some interesting things to say on independence. Were these thoughts also influenced by John Francis?'

'Independence?' Jeff responded, deliberately cementing the subject into the onlookers' consciousness like a true professional. 'Yeah, to a certain extent. John and I have discussed pretty much everything, but my views on all forms of dependence were more shaped from some psychiatric research my music's helping to fund in Canada. There's an professor at Toronto University whose research covers addiction, and it's no secret that I give refuge to a few addictions of my own...'

The twenty-two-year-old was not surprised to be met with a stony silence in response this confession. One day it would not be this way, he vowed. It would be possible to talk openly about such things. People had suffered addictions since time immemorial, and yet in this current era of free love and free-ish press, it appeared that these evergreen sins now bore a post-modern, rock'n'roll mantel.

'In my opinion, interdependence is where it's at. Interdependence,' he stressed, 'needs to replace independence as our byword, if we're to function better as a society that doesn't leave people behind. If I can get literary for a second, George Bernard Shaw was right to label independence as "middle-class blasphemy". As members of the human race, we are and should be all dependent on one another. This is what the world needs to sustain itself though growth and progress. Not everyone acting independently. That's like Extreme Capitalism, and will only ever favour the strong.'

Again, Michael gave the wilful campaigner his head. Jeff's eyes had by now adjusted to the studio lights, pleased to have a clear view of a swathe of facial expressions and body language from left to right. *So far, so good*, he reckoned.

'Here's something I've been playing with lately, both in songwriting and with the businesses and charities we've set up... Instead of wealth or fame, or even health and happiness, we should measure people by their humility-to-power ratio.'

The interviewer stopped in his tracks. 'Humility-to-power ratio?'

The handsome guest threw his head back, shaking his mane of black hair and relaxing further into his chair. 'Absolutely, Michael. Here's another weird quote I remember: Edmund Burke, the Irish author and philosopher, said, "The only thing necessary for evil to triumph is for good men to do nothing." And I trust he meant men and women, by the way... As much as I admire the sentiment, this sentence is inherently flawed, in its practical application, since the forces of evil are inevitably farther-reaching and more destructive than good people's ability to wield humility. To defeat evil, in my opinion, humility must be exercised as a pre-emptive strike against its power.'

For the first time, the previously-conservative crowd burst into an animated and prolonged round of applause, a few even shouting for more. Parkinson inserted a new question as soon as the orator took a breath and a large gulp from his glass of water.

'My researchers tell me that you recently completed a degree in Computer Science, with over two-thirds of last year on the road. How do you find the time?'

Jeff smiled, opting for modesty to diffuse the somewhat sermonic ambiance he had unwittingly created. 'Good question. I never sleep, that's how! It was bad timing on my part. I rushed headlong into my record deal and everything took off much faster than we'd expected, so I've found myself juggling my university studies with everything else. It's been great though. I'm doing a

Masters this year too, mostly by correspondence. Coming home to a pile of assignments is a good way to force myself back to reality.'

'My manager and I've set up a venture capital company in Melbourne and we've got a few really cool entrepreneurs brewing some excellent ideas. That's another fantastic outlet for my endless curiosity. We're looking to expand the holding company internationally too, but that's where I really do need to rein things in a bit. I'm running out of hours at the moment. My stupendously wise manager, the indomitable Gerry Blake, advises me that's what the next ten years are for, because he knows if it were just up to me, we'd be doing it all now and probably doing it all a whole lot more worsely than we could.'

The ardent campaigner caught his breath, side-tracked by his own use of the word with which Lynn had been keen to label his best mate. Her face flooded across his eyes, and he fought hard to dismiss his emotions. He was relieved to see the interviewer preparing to ask a new question.

'So I know from our previous meetings you have an interest in religion but no particular religious beliefs of your own. And yet a lot of your music has references to religion.'

'Yes, you're right,' Jeff affirmed. 'I think life hinges on making the right choices and I'm frequently amazed by stories of struggle between good and evil in religious texts. I appreciate the rallying power of religion, but it can just as easily rally for bad as it can for good. I'm fine with people having their own religious beliefs. I was born a Catholic Argentinean Polish Jew, so I'm a real ethnic and religious crossbreed.'

'Your own family background, you mean?' Michael interjected.

'Yeah. I didn't come about through any grand design, that's for sure... I always leave my girlfriends to find out whether I was baptised or circumcised.'

Another burst of furtive laughter emanated from the audience, and the guest fed off it to help him prevent the downward spiral which had taken hold.

'So which is it?' the veteran host enquired with a smile.

Saying nothing, the spirited playboy began to make moves to undo his belt, and the crowd whooped still louder.

'OK! Moving on...' he quipped, turning back to his host and resting anxious hands on his knees. 'You did ask the question, sir... Anyway, we somehow need to harness the fervour and passion that religion can deliver, but for secular change... Social change. For improving human rights.'

'Concerts at night, conversations by day,' the older man waxed lyrical. 'No wonder you keep your feet on the ground.'

Skilfully using the praise to his advantage, the songwriter maintained the momentum of the interview. 'Don't get me wrong, Michael,' he said. 'I enjoy myself in the more usual rock musician ways too... I've met so many of my idols in the last year or so that there's a danger of it becoming normal. I got here, to London, for the first time in November 'seventy-two, dazed and naïve, but I'll probably leave suspicious and paranoid like the rest of them after a while.'

The sexy intellectual crossed his legs, and felt a wave of appreciation from several metres in front of him. He could almost hear the females' heartbeats and lapped up the encouraging sensation, allowing his mind to wander to what might await him once they adjourned to the Green Room. Surely there was an evening of suitable entertainment somewhere in this respectful crowd?

'But I haven't seen the start of it yet,' he focussed back on the interviewer. 'I'm a graduate, yes, but Australian universities are small fry, so I'm really keen to work and study with people here and in America. There's a guy called Tim Berners-Lee studying at Oxford this year who has some fantastic ideas about using computers for better communication. I'm a trainspotter at my core, but being also the fool minstrel, as you alluded earlier, I tend to see it all as metaphors for life in general. Computer Science has adopted the term "communications" for moving data... bits and bytes, they call them... ones and zeros, from place to place. They call it traffic, and that's exactly what it is. If you're trying to send a whole swathe of information between two places, it has to go down a narrow cable.'

The young man made a circle by touching his thumb and fingertip together and lifting his hand to eye level and peering through at his inquisitive public. He mustn't go too far into the detail, or he else would lose their attention. It was Saturday night, after all; a fact that the horny artist's loins had readily endorsed only moments ago, and were now not going to let him forget.

'You've only got a thin pipe to get your messages down the 'phone lines. It's just like having a whole bunch of people travelling in high season between Italy and Switzerland through the San Bernardino Pass. You have to wait your turn. Communication between computers and between people is no different. The traffic has to be orderly and come out intact at the other end. You have to construct your message in the right sequence or it won't get through, i.e. there'll be a life or death situation. People only understand stuff properly when you give them the right information at the right time, and in the right order. When we're talking about politics or war or social justice, we're making judgment calls on people's lives, so it's important to get it right.'

The show's host swooned along with his audience. 'This is terrific stuff, Jeff. Tell us more about your views on politics versus government.'

'Well...' the songwriter obliged with a half-smile, 'that there's a topic we could debate all night. How long have we got? From my perspective, from the outside admittedly, politics in most democratic countries is basically flawed because the whole left and right thing is polarising. It's two-dimensional. Our lives aren't two-dimensional. Society isn't two-dimensional. Government run by politicians is doomed to failure because it's incomplete, short-sighted. It's designed only to appeal to the people who are on one end or the other of this continuum...'

He signalled left, then to the centre and finally to his right with a sweeping hand gesture. 'They're the ones who vote and who are actively engaged in the political process, but that doesn't represent all of us. What about those upstairs and those down below? Class... High or low income earners... However you like to describe the social divides... And what about in front or behind?' he pointed.

'You in the audience, and the crew behind us? In other words, how about doing things for the future while also learning from the past? We live on a sphere, in a sphere of at least three dimensions. Get used to it! In Australia, we have compulsory voting. Get real... It's not compulsory voting. It's compulsory rocking up to put an "X" in a box, when most voters have no idea what they're doing or they don't believe their vote has the power to change their life. Australia completely missed the point introducing compulsory voting. It doesn't engage any more people in our collective future. In fact, I think the opposite is true. People think, "Well, I vote, and my life's still not getting better, so why should I get involved?" It actually encourages the very apathy they were seeking to eradicate, in my view.'

Jeff paused to collect his thoughts, anxious not to lose his concentration against the intense feedback upon which his senses were feeding. This was a moment to be savoured, both the admiration from host and audience and for the testosterone boost he was embibing from his own self-satisfaction. His opinion wasn't humble at all, here on the grand stage of British prime-time television.

This was the famous songwriter's first real exposure as a thinker, to seriously air his pretentious ideas and to discover whether anyone might share his vision. Anyone other than his dream girl, his heart was quick to remind him. It appeared they were, rendering him still more determined to capitalise on his remaining minutes. Humble opinions were too weak under the circumstances. A compromise would sell everyone short.

The show's host took the rare break in the passionate monologue to jump in with another question. 'So, Jeff, now you're in the public eye and on the road a great deal of the time, how are you going to keep in touch with all these ambitions?'

The question reminded the twenty-two-year-old how tired he was feeling, and he let out an involuntary sigh. 'As I mentioned before, I don't sleep. I read as much as I can. I'm a very conceptual bloke, so my challenge is to muster enough practical, detail-oriented mates around me to make things happen. Great ideas are useless if they're impossible to implement. Take "Be nice to each other", for example. Now that's a great concept... Few people would turn away from it, would they? But how are you going to be nice to your neighbour who plays loud music at two a.m. or cooks strange smelling food, and how is he going to be nice to you when he has no idea why you mutter under your breath whenever you see him? We have to find practical, mutually-beneficial answers to these social problems to stop them escalating into hatred and discrimination.'

Again he paused, waiting for his followers to catch up. 'Life's all about appreciating and using our differences, not just tolerating them. Though that would be a good start... Take the difference between men and women: men see each individual episode of life as a discrete and distinct thing. Women, on the other hand, see everything as connected. Always have, always will. A woman'll think, "I spent four hours getting ready to go out last Friday, and he didn't even compliment me, and then he forgot my birthday yesterday, therefore he's going to leave me." Whereas men, when we're forgetting your birthday, we're not thinking about how great you looked last Friday.'

Laughter sprang from all corners of the studio, but the guest cut them off to continue to allegory. 'We did that on Friday, and most likely didn't tell you,' he raised his voice. 'Now we're thinking whether Arsenal's going to beat Spurs this weekend or which pub's serving the cheapest beer.'

Through the powerful overhead array of multi-coloured lights, both host and guest saw people nodding in agreement, smiles all around. They all laughed again, and still the rock star went on.

'But we men need to learn from you women because you've got it right.'

Several female audience members screamed. Turning his head to one side suggestively, looking for the origin of this hysteria, the star raised his expressive eyebrows but didn't pause.

'Everything *is* connected. To future-proof ourselves, men and women need to appreciate and use each others' differences as strengths. The whole "diversity in action" thing is so key to the human race's development, I believe, both in macro- and micro-communities. Race, age, level of education, introvert versus extrovert, doesn't matter... Everyone has something to bring to the table. White males have been dominant now for too long. Male supremacy was probably the best solution in the dark ages, since life was harsh and dangerous. Now our dangers manifest themselves in subtler, more insidious ways. Wars are a series of battles, and in the end it's whether we win the whole war or not that counts, which requires more than brute force.'

Parkinson interjected another angle, knowing he soon had to bring the show to a close. 'But you are fundamentally a pacifist, I read.'

Jeff nodded. 'Yes, inherently I'm a bleeding-heart liberal and a pacifist in theory. But in practice, once you make a commitment to go to war, I believe you're obliged to see it through. Everyone's screaming at politicians to take the troops out of East Asia, but people forget that soldiers are sent to war to fight. That's why we have soldiers, guys, whether right or wrong. So when they get killed, we can't ask the politicians to interfere and say, "Can't they fight somewhere less dangerous? Go and fight where our sons and daughters won't get killed." If armies bow to political pressure instead of getting the job done and out of there a-s-a-p, there's absolutely no point going to war in the first place. It's a hangover from the 'sixties. These objections would have never been voiced during the World Wars. Back then, they had strong leaders who told ordinary folks what the war was all about and justified the deaths. I still don't subscribe to it as a means of brokering peace, but at least they gave a clear message, and everyone could see who was running the show and what the point was. Communication again, y'see?'

The crowd screamed and shouted, clapping energetically, while the interviewer took another chance. 'Back to your music, if I may... I have to ask you, having now seen you perform... Are all your songs about your own experiences?'

'Most of them, yes,' the handsome man confirmed. 'It's called marketing, Michael. Blatant self-promotion, in fact. When I sing them live, it's to a captive audience, but the records are pure advertising. No, but seriously, the songs often spring from a deep empathy for a situation, and obviously I have the most empathy for myself! And then there are a whole bunch of songs about the fact that we're all in this together.'

The singer paused again, his heart suddenly caught in a strange, vicelike grip. Two months to go, it told him. Only two months, and this whole Mister Life-and-Soul charade would be over. *Hang on in there, mate.* Seeing Lynn's smiling face pass fleetingly across his mind's eye once more had inspired a final, parting notion.

'Often people with a lot to say are perceived as arrogant. And some *are* arrogant, granted. That's often because they forget they don't have the monopoly on opinion. But once we realise that other people can teach us with their opposing or tangential opinions, that's when we start to grow intellectually.'

'Indeed, I expect you're right. OK. Thank you, Jeff Diamond. You leave us with much to think about. There should be more like you, in my opinion,' the host began to wrap up, chuckling at his own attempt to play on his guest's eloquent style. 'A dose of reality once in a while does us all good. So before we finish, back to your upcoming schedule... You're on tour throughout Europe, starting here in London this week.'

'Yes. A few dates here, then around Europe and to the US. I think we're playing twenty-three or twenty-four nights in the month of August. My dad was born in New York, and I'm definitely gaining an affinity with America in general. There are a lot of parallels with Australia: new country, pioneering spirit, people whose ancestors made it on their own. It'll be a good experience, and I'll need some serious R'n'R afterwards! But I love London and Paris, and the older cultures of Europe in general.'

The audience reacted noisily, sensing the intimate encounter was about to come to an end and prompting Jeff to point a long index finger in the direction of a lone female voice, only to receive yet more screams. His level of power-induced arousal was already pushing the boundaries of self-control.

'OK! I'll see you later!'

'Your second song, I believe is from your "Higher Plains" album. What inspired this departure from your earlier rock'n'roll style?'

This was a last-minute, unscripted question, but one the musician was only too happy to answer, since it gave him another free hit into a crowd that was hanging on his every word. His mind briefly turned to the television audience, which until now had not figured in the showman's busy psyche. Finding the camera with the solid red light, he flicked a wry smile directly into its lens.

'Have you been to Africa?' he asked of his host and then of his audience. 'Well, it's an eye-opening place. Poverty like we in so-called developed countries have no idea. Talking to people in Mozambique, where I wrote most of the music for the album, it makes me feel so ungrateful. We complain about things they'd be glad to have. So "Higher Plains" is my attempt to adjust our expectations of life; not to take things so much for granted.'

Parkinson changed the subject again. 'Now when we met last time, in Sydney, you told me that being a songwriter is not what you consider your purpose in life to be...'

'True,' the young man agreed. 'I'm not a songwriter for the songwriting itself. Well, I am in some ways obviously, but I write songs because I want to be a changer of minds. Don't get me wrong... There's a long, long way to go, but it's got to start somewhere. I was never interested in any traditional careers as such. I'm your typical hippy. The nine-to-five rat race bores me stupid, and luckily for me, I've been put on this Earth to work with people to bring about social change, and that's not a nine-to-five job. It sounds pretentious, but that's what I believe I'm here for. Music's an excellent vehicle for initiating change, but it's not the end in itself for me.'

Out of the corner of his left eye, the aspiring leader saw his band returning to the stage. His sizeable spell on this high profile soapbox was almost up. What else had he planned to say?

'Taking a long-term view means we need to think more carefully about how everything is connected. Good government over a civil society should not be about politics. It's about integrity and respect. We have a diverse population with diverse needs and diverse opinions, whether you talk about a state, a country, a region or the whole world. Or even the universe, if we ever find any interplanetary neighbours... Government is not going to be fixed at the next election. It's going to take years of consistent communication, sending messages that people understand and know they need to listen to. It'll take generations to fix. We need good succession planning through our families, our schools and universities, *et cetera*, to make it happen. We have to instil good ideas and good behaviour into children so they grow up as respectful adults who want to do constructive things. And then most of all, we need to talk to each other. Or yourself, or your dog... Whomever! Discourse brings about a clarity of understanding that few of us will ever achieve in isolation.'

Liking what they had heard, the audience rose to its collective feet, and the studio erupted once more with cheers and enthusiastic applause.

'The rallying cry, ladies and gentlemen!' Michael declared, making eye contact with his producer, who was spinning his hands over and over each other from the sidelines.

Instinctively, Jeff took control of his final seconds. 'So would you like your world to change?' he asked the crowd. 'Say "Yes!"'

More chanting and clapping rang out. The fired-up orator cleared his throat and raised his hands, suddenly as exhausted as if he were signing off after a third encore.

'Well, do it then. It's up to us! Change starts in the mirror. Thank you, everyone. This has been a blast!'

Taking his cue from the man who had stolen the show, Michael Parkinson brought the metaphorical curtains down. 'Fantastic stuff! You're an inspiration, and I'm very pleased you were able to come on the show tonight. Watch this space, folks. We're going to hear a lot more from this man. You're now going to end the show with your latest single release, if I'm right.'

'Sure am,' Jeff replied, standing up and holding his arms out towards the generous audience. 'It's a song from "Higher Plains" called "We're All Brothers". Another late night composition after one of those in-depth conversations I mentioned earlier. Thanks again, Michael. Thanks.'

'Ladies and gentlemen, please thank Jeff Diamond!'

The confirmed celebrity shook his host's outstretched hand and made his way to the sound stage, where the band had already struck up the opening bars. Finding energy from deep within, their front man grabbed the microphone off its stand and launched into the rocking number.

***

While Lynn Dyson was putting the finishing touches to her last submission and preparing for her return to Australia, Jeff Diamond's quest for greatness developed as if it knew no bounds. In August nineteen-seventy-four, the acclaimed superstar played six nights straight at the Greek Theater in Los Angeles. He had been humbled by the invitation from a Hollywood impresario who was also busy making a name for himself, both men recognising the value in joining forces. Every single "someone" in the music business had played the Greek at some point in their careers. The hallowed, open-air venue, nestled in a picturesque, tree-lined canyon overlooking the city, had seen more than its fair share of memorable performances in its illustrious, seventy-year history, but Jeff's "Higher Plains" shows were reported as some of its finest.

These three-hour concerts were to capture a studious and dedicated artist at the pinnacle of his well-documented flight to superstardom, displaying his brilliance as an exhilarating live performer. The reputed emotion and intensity of a Jeff Diamond show drew in the hordes from all over America and far beyond. From the warm orchestral introduction of a hit ballad from nineteen-seventy-three to the raucous *encore* of African drums and gospel-flavoured *finalé*, the singer and his musical director cleverly balanced the evening's program with a sweet and edgy mixture of his instant classics while consistently maintaining an air of spontaneity through humorous banter and special guest appearances.

Each night in the southern Californian city, before the hyped-up songwriter went on stage, he would scour the audience for any sign of a certain sexy, blonde UCLA student. A week in the same town was almost more than he could bear, particularly when he knew the young lady's thoughts would by now be turning towards the future. He felt sure she would be out there one night, and it made him nervous but also extra-keen to put on the best shows of his life.

And as an additional surety, each night he would stop the band after one of the songs that Lynn and he had shaped together by the creek at Benloch to make the same speech, around about midway through the first half.

'OK! Thanks, everyone. I'm not sure if many of you know this, but I was privileged to become involved with a new charity organisation called "*Enseignants pour la Paix*". That's "Teachers for Peace" to you guys. Well, they're doing great work in Central America and in Vietnam. In fact, all over the world. Flying into remote places and setting up field schools in disaster zones or war zones where the displaced civilian population is huge. They set up classrooms so that the kids can get an education in spite of the horrific stuff going on around them. Those guys are doing amazing work in terrible conditions and they're making a huge difference.'

The audience gave an enthusiastic round of applause. Great! Another few thousand dollars, Jeff thought, but fundraising was only part of the basis for pausing the music and suspending their rapture.

'Now the reason I'm telling you all this, apart from convincing you to pledge money, is that not long ago we received a massive donation from someone who didn't care to leave a name. So now, whenever I do a show, I just like to say a sincere thanks to that person, just in case you're here tonight... Thanks from all my heart, and I love you.'

More screams and clapping would follow as the band struck up again, themselves unaware of the real importance of these interludes. Each night, Jeff hoped that one special person out there would know whom he meant and accept his thanks, yet sadly he felt no tightening of the invisible elastic connection onto which he clung perilously.

On his last night in Los Angeles, desperate for a sign from the woman he knew was not too far away, the exhausted star finally broke down during an empassioned rendition of "Can't Do No More". Twenty thousand adoring fans took the outpouring of emotion as all part of the act and devoured the raw, clamouring song in a state of heedless euphoria. Battling to regain his composure by sharing a joke with the band, inside Jeff was completely tied in knots, waiting for the smallest signal that his message had got through.

Gerry Blake had flown in from Melbourne for the final show at the Greek Theater, blown away by the reaction both inside the Californian amphitheatre and outside beyond the perimeter too. The "Higher Plains" season had brought the highest critical acclaim of the star's short career, and the bemused accountant watched his client accept the endless praise and adulation with consummate good grace. Secretly, he knew Jeff was extremely proud of his achievements both musically and otherwise. Nobody could say this man had wasted his life over the last two years, while he waited for the chance to be happy again.

There were also precious few moments the musician could call his own these days. Parties, television appearances and invitations to charity dinners dominated his evenings, always culminating in a depraved combination of sex, drugs and rock'n'roll, and the long, sleepless nights remained without respite from nightmares. Touring finally over, the superstar returned home with his manager in the first week of September, only to face another seething mass of screaming fans at the airport and then finally the solitude of his empty apartment.

Initially Jeff had difficulty settling back into a routine which didn't see him in a different city every day, and when he wasn't hurrying to complete his last, challenging Masters assignments, he eagerly accepted invitations from Gerry and other friends to home-cooked dinners and simple evenings in front of the television with relaxing company and no pressure to perform.

Women he had known at university or who had worked with him in the Richmond pub in those early days flocked around him, vivacious and dolled up to the nines, determined to renew their acquaintance with the handsome hot property. These so-called dates were cheap and unfulfilling for the lonely star, sick of talking about himself and listening to mindless flattery while he assuaged his carnal desires.

Then one Saturday night, the numb celebrity had been ambling home through Melbourne's CBD from a hotel whence he had left yet another sleeping stranger after far too much alcohol and speed, when his attention had been drawn to a billboard announcing an upcoming live television show. It was advertising Lynn Dyson's birthday and homecoming party on the twentieth of September.

Jeff stood for probably an hour in front of the laneway wall which was plastered eight-wide by three-high with copies of this one unassuming poster, practically hypnotised by its multiplicity. At first he didn't believe his eyes and assumed the drugs were playing a cruel joke on him. Over the next few days however, he read several newspaper articles corroborating the news of Australia's favourite daughter's repatriation, and eventually a television interview with the pretty woman herself confirmed it to be true.

Jesus! The day had finally arrived, the young man realised. The anniversary of their second year apart had ticked over during the previous week, and his dream girl was on the same continent at last. Against all the odds, he had made it. He was unable to sit still, and his mind was unable to focus on anything except securing time with the returning princess. He ran through the streets of the northern suburbs for two or three hours at a time, undetected under his baseball cap and the cover of darkness.

Could he claim her forever this time? Was she thinking about him? Did she still love him? Had she ever loved him? The lost boy from Canley Vale was once more all that remained of the multi-millionaire who had held court with his friends in the highest of places only weeks ago, his mind tortured by a guilty conscience and debilitating but wholly explicable feelings of inadequacy.

As always, still fighting his internal quandaries, the cool and confident public figure made a calculated attempt to control the situation by immediately releasing an album track which he had been saving for this express purpose and with the full intention that the beautiful superstar would hear it. He knew full well that Bart and Marianna Dyson would also get wind of this overt ploy and no doubt deduce that he was announcing his intentions.

Lynn was an adult now and free to make her own choices. If ever there had been a time for hoping for the best but expecting the worst, this was it. Twenty-five elapsed months had not dampened the intensity of Jeff's devotion one iota, gearing up for an almighty battle with Australia's well-connected establishment couple. He knew his face hadn't fit before she went away, and notwithstanding his success and newfound wealth, he was only marginally more assured that it would fit now. If anything, the publicity he attracted, intentionally or otherwise, probably increased the likelihood of his being misunderstood.

The unsolved element of this equation, of course, was whether the elder statesman's daughter would be on his side or theirs... What reception would her former lover receive on making that first telephone call? His heart jumped into his throat every time he envisaged picking up the receiver and dialling the number for Dyson Administration, assuming his dream girl would still call the building home.

***

Ellen Finley put down her tea towel and focussed back on Dannie's application. Her only child was hanging her hopes on securing a place at The Good School after she completed her Bachelor's degree, which would mean moving to Boston, Massachusetts. As much as she wanted her to achieve her dreams, she was not looking forward to being left alone in their pokey, two-bedroomed flat in Partick.

The daughter who had been through so much in her seventeen tender years was ready for much more though, the middle-aged woman confessed. Her twin brother's death after only two days in this world had wrecked their chances of a normal family, causing her husband to fly the coop, unable to deal with the situation for which no-one had asked. Dannie had tried her hardest to be everything a son should be: a high achiever at school, excelling at several sports and making a name for herself as a community leader in some of the more downtrodden neighbouring areas of Glasgow.

Her identity crisis at just two years of age had lived on inside the clever student's mind, resolved for the most part for Dannie, if not for her mother. The sensitive child had taken it upon herself to live her brother's life along with her own, in the hope that the family would reunite. Sadly however, apart from a chance meeting outside the County Court one snowy morning, her father had completely vanished from her life.

'There's a lot of pages,' her mum observed, watching the teenager fill in the first few sections of the form. 'Do you have to send money?'

'No,' the student replied. 'It's a scholarship, Ma. I wouldn't even need to find my fare over. Oh, God. I wish I knew what they're looking for.'

Ellen left to finish clearing away the dinner dishes. Her daughter would be heading out soon to teach her evening class. She had become a shining light in teen rehabilitation, sponsored by the National Society for the Prevention of Cruelty to Children, and had won a host of awards for designing a course for social workers and teachers. Ever since primary school, Dannie's sights had been set on running a home for disadvantaged teenagers estranged from their families. She was fantastic with the kids, her proud mother recalled, particularly the boys. Dannie had always had more of an affinity with boys than girls.

The deadline for application into The Good School's two-thousand-and-seventeen intake was the end of September, and Dannie's time was running out. She wondered if it would be better to submit early than at the last minute. Which strategy would yield best advantage? Would Ryan and Kierney be on the judges' panel? She already knew there was only a single sponsored place each year, so the chance of being selected was extremely slim.

'Oh, maybe I won't apply,' she said, half to herself. 'I know I won't win. They get entries from all over the world. I'm not doing anything that special.'

'You got to be in it to win it, hen,' her mother rattled off. 'Do you know anything about the other winners? Last year, like?'

"Aye, I do. I've been messaging last year's on Twitter. She's the first Australian to win since 'ninety-nine. It's part of the obligation, if you win, to help future applicants. She's nice. Freya's her name.'

'Freya? That's an unusual name,' Ellen nodded. 'Has she given y'any clues? What they're looking for, and all that? How did she win?'

The Scotswoman blanched. Dannie rarely spoke of anyone being nice, preferring to keep her opinions to herself. And certainly not with light in her eyes. It was a relief to hear, if she were honest. Her daughter had grown up a loner, treating most human contact as a business transaction; a service to be rendered.

'Aye,' the teenager answered. 'She's told me a wee bit. She's a painter, mostly. She's had loads of exhibitions. Beautiful. Landscapes, but with odd aspects, like stuff out of place. I can look them up on her website, if you want.'

'Sure. I don't want to hold y'up though.'

Dannie's fingers slipped like lightening over the keyboard of her tablet computer, and in only a few seconds, mother and daughter were scrolling through a series of images. Some of them were very appealing, the older woman acknowledged, but if painting was enough to win a scholarship to the most prestigious international youth leadership prize, then why shouldn't Dannie be in with a chance?

'They're nice, hen. Unusual,' Ellen gave a typically benign smile, pointing to a picture of a girl with long, dark wavy hair. 'She looks a bit like Kierney Diamond there. Perhaps that's why she won?'

'Ma! Don't be ridiculous,' the student scolded. 'She's a motivational speaker. I've seen all her stuff on YouTube. Her dad abused her. That's why she paints, and she teaches other kids to paint as therapy. You know, to release all that pent-up anger. I think she's amazing.'

'Ah, I see. That's great, love. You obviously hit it off with her. Can she help you with your application?'

Dannie shook her head. 'No. And I wouldn't ask her either. I know what I've got to put in. I just need to make it sound great, but without making me sound big-headed. Just concentrate on the facts and figures. Then I need three referees. Callum's agreed to do it, and Tam Needham. I just need one more.'

'How about that NSPCC director who rang here the other day? Stuart, wasn't it?'

'Hey!' the young woman exclaimed. 'That's a really good idea. I hadn't thought of him. Stuart McNally. He'd be awesome. Thanks, Ma. Freya did give me a quote I like. It's from "A Life Singular", of course. She adores that book too. She's read it more times than me, I think.'

In a couple of keystrokes, Dannie had opened a new browser window and brought up a search engine. Her mother marvelled at how well the kids all knew how to use computers, while she and her friends still struggled with e-mail. The name of John Wooden was typed into the box along with the words "quote" and "character".

'Here... See this? Don't you think it's great? "Be more concerned with your character than your reputation, because your character is what you really are, while your reputation is merely what others think you are." I love it.

Freya suggested repeating it to myself while I re-read my application. That's what she did, and she won. Seems easy enough!'

'Alright. That'great,' Ellen tried to sound encouraging. 'Who are you going to enter as?'

Her daughter's energy instantly faltered, not unexpectedly drawing a regretful sigh from her mother. 'I don't know. Haven't decided yet.'

***

'Listen to this, Ry,' Kierney begged her brother. 'This is beautiful. It captures them so perfectly.'

The Diamond children had finished sorting through over a hundred photographs of their parents' early showbusiness years; pictures taken by paparazzi in the street, at nightclubs, while they were on stage and even on aeroplanes. They had cringed at some of the more awkward or impromptu snaps, and then swooned at others where the stars had been given the time to compose themselves and present their best faces.

This absorbing exercise complete, the dark-haired teenager had sought out a new chapter to review while her brother checked his e-mails. Their father was out at a Diamond Celebration Foundation dinner, presenting cheques for large amounts of money to deserving individuals. It had given the youngsters a rare opportunity to delve into their parents' story without being disturbed.

'This is a good bit…

> "'Is it too bright with the curtains open?' Lynn asked. 'No, it's fine. It's your room.' I could sense Lynn felt comfortable for the first time that evening, left frazzled after the fraught family dinner.'"

Kierney paused to make sure Ryan was paying attention. 'It's interesting that Mamá was more nervous than Papá. Don't you think?'

'Guess so,' her brother answered flippantly. 'They're her parents. She was under pressure from all sides. Dad would've still put pressure on her, even though he didn't intend to. I can just imagine his eyes boring into her every time either "G" asked a question or made a comment. What's next?'

The young woman found her place again and read on. 'How about this?

> "It was before midnight, but we had stolen away to Lynn's childhood bedroom, thankful to have escaped the inquisition. I watched her scanning each wall, as if she hadn't recognised where she was.
>
> 'I have fond memories of this room,' she blurted out.

133

'So do I!' I replied, grabbing for her waist and pulling her into a kiss.

She relaxed onto me and smiled against my lips, drifting a hand down between our bodies.

'That's good. Are they with me?'

I feigned surprise. 'The memories? Of course! I hope yours are with me too.'

She nodded, her head resting against my chest, listening to my rapid heartbeat just like she had always done, as if it validated the way she felt.

Lynn laughed softly, and my insides caught fire. Again.

'You wanna make some more memories?'"

Oh, bro. You can just feel how in love they were. It paints such a beautiful picture.'

The cricketer couldn't disagree. The atmosphere their dad had conjured up more than twenty years after the event evoked the perfect mix of romance and lust. Even fun-loving, single men weren't immune to such stimulation. He was jealous of this closeness, if truth be told. His parents' marriage had been rock solid, and he often wondered if he would ever find a pairing that would live up to their idyllic family situation.

'Read some more,' Ryan murmured. 'Don't stop.'

His sister smiled. 'So you are human after all! OK. This is from later in the same chapter.

"Are your shoulders sore?"

"Mmm…" I replied, knowing full well what was likely to follow.

"Do you want a massage?"

"No. You're tired."

Lynn's eyes almost pleaded with me. "Are you tired too?"

"Yeah. You bet."

Her body couldn't be closer to me than it already was, but still I tried.

"That's good," she admitted.

I remember sighing deeply, fighting a raging erection and the all-consuming desire which festers between the ears in people like me. People with misaligned priorities.

"I just want to stay here for the next twenty-four hours," I said instead. "It's like a sanctuary. Away from all the attention and histrionics."

The most beautiful woman in the world simply smiled. My voice did that to her, for which I'll be eternally grateful.

"I love that word," she murmured against my skin. "Histrionics. Almost understates really, doesn't it?"

"Yeah," I agreed. "Gerry's dad uses it a lot."

How would she soothe my soul from this delectable torture?

"I like it too."'

Kierney looked up to make sure her audience was in attendance. It was. She smiled at the hypnotic effect their father's writing was having on them both.

'He's obviously really turned-on! It's torture just reading it, isn't it? I'll carry on.

""How about you, angel?" I hoped for a Get-Out-Of-Jail-Free card. "Have you got anything in need of soothing?"

"No," she laughed and grabbed me with a sly hand. "I'm lost in delirium."

"Delirium?" I gasped. "Sounds like something on the fourth row of the Periodic Table. Sounds like something they'll mine out of the Top End."

We connected. It was the best, and my shoulders weren't sore anymore."'

Such was the mesmeric effect of the erotic stanzas the teenagers were sharing, they hadn't noticed Jeff had crept back into the room. He had managed to walk between them and position himself almost close enough that he could read over his daughter's shoulder. His son nudged him playfully on his way out, now embarrassed to be indulging in such slushy fodder.

'Wow, Papá,' the dark-haired gipsy girl almost whispered when she realised he was there, scrolling further down the lines on the computer screen. 'This is brilliant. It's so evocative. What was it like to see Mamá for the first time again?'

'Scary,' the great man replied with a wry smile, massaging the youngster's strong, slender shoulders and picturing that same fateful moment in his dreamy mind's eye, 'and wonderful.'

Kierney slumped back into the big, leather office chair and sighed. 'That's a good combination. Scary and wonderful.'

'As in the true meaning of wonderful,' the poet added. 'I misuse the word wonderful all the time, as a synonym for fantastic, but that's not how I mean it now. Christ! Kiz, I was so full of wonder at what your mamá might've turned into, having left as a child and come back as an adult. As you're discovering, pequeñita, sixteen to nineteen is one hell of a ride.'

'S'pose so,' the dark-haired beauty nodded. 'It's hard to appreciate that when you're in the middle of it. So how was she?'

Jeff chuckled, leaning back onto the edge of the desk beside his casual editor and crossing his arms. He could almost feel the chill in the air on that Spring day in nineteen-seventy-four. He didn't remember ever having experienced greater confusion, neither before or since that meeting.

'Determined not to like me.'

'*Not* to like you?' Kierney shrieked. 'Why *not* to like you?'

'Ah, you know…' her dad smirked. 'Read on. You'll find out.'

The excited teenager pressed "Page Up" on the keyboard a couple of times and re-read a handful of preceding paragraphs, eager to discover how it was that her parents came to realise they were each others' soul-mates. She also hoped the next few chapters in her father's awe-inspiring and passionate autobiography would give her some clues as to how to find her own twin soul, while in the process of preparing to transport its readers from heart-wrenching separation to uplifting reunion, and then through the immutable partnership into which she and her older brother had been born.

The search for her own life partner must be up to no-one else but herself, Kierney concluded. That was the whole point of the book after all. Her parents, albeit through a single pair of hands, were creating the instruction book for her future. For anyone's future, in fact. The lessons contained therein would demonstrate the importance of understanding oneself and those around, so that one could make the right choices for the right reasons.

A gentle awakening made the young woman's insides churn. Even after they were gone, her parents would continue to change the world. This was entirely as it should be. Jeff glanced across to see tears running down the right-hand side of his daughter's blushing face, and she self-consciously brushed them aside when she found him spying on her.

'You must've been so nervous,' she smiled, approaching the end of another page. 'Was it wise, in hindsight, to release that song then?'

'I doubt it,' her father chuckled, inadvertently rubbing his chest. 'But I thought so at the time. I was young, arrogant and determined. How could I have done anything else? *Carpe diem* and all that…'

***

It was Wednesday the twenty-fifth of September nineteen-seventy-four, a date which signified the passing of two of the longest years ever known. Waking up on the couch in the half-light, Jeff could hardly believe he had served his sentence through to this day of reckoning. Was this really the day he would re-establish contact with the one and only Lynn Dyson. Both lives had changed immeasurably since his dream girl had left his bed silently and walked out of the old Richmond flat in the dead of night.

Out of his old life. His very old life.

During this protracted hiatus, the wild, ambitious twenty-year-old Computer Science student with whom Australia's darling had toyed briefly had become a instantly-recognised commodity on the global stage, with a rock'n'roll reputation to match. She too had made the smooth transition from child star to entertainment industry aristocracy exactly as her parents had foreseen. Everything, the boy from Canley Vale smiled grudgingly, had gone according to plan.

The stunning, blonde princess had been back in Melbourne for nearly a week, returning to a panorama of cameras and a fanfare of television appearances. Jeff battled with mixed emotions when he first saw her on home soil again. She looked and sounded different from the sweet, naïvely sexy schoolgirl he had farewelled two years ago. Her time in the United States had turned her from starlet to superstar, and her sporting successes had made her into a rolled gold Australian Olympic heroine. More mature by far, her media appearances revealed a confident air when dealing with reporters and interviewers which had been painstakingly polished, completely eradicating the cute, childlike responses with which she had wooed them in bygone days.

The young woman had returned just in time to turn nineteen years of age, and her former lover had spotted in the television coverage of Melbourne Academy's "Welcome Home" party a league of joyful family and friends all gathered around. He picked out Robert McLean, whose own twenty-first birthday party they had attended together when their relationship was virtually brand new. There was no sign of Natalie, however, who had been the young man's girlfriend at the time. He even spied Dean Keller, the footballer with whom he had sparred at the same party, and whom Bart Dyson had subsequently asked to leave.

Jealousy consumed him at the sight of the burly midfielder, furious that this brute who hadn't even been granted access to Lynn's virginal body, despite having pretended to all and sundry, would receive an invitation to her homecoming *soirée*. There were obviously still some circles the hot-headed songwriter's fame and wealth couldn't penetrate, and he wondered how much influence the birthday girl would have had on her own guest list. Perhaps it was like her stakeholder list, he gave her the benefit of the doubt, remembering one of their fraught final dates. Her first lover had been omitted from this artefact by design too.

Of course, Lynn had a man at her side in almost every shot. Jeff wasn't at all surprised and perversely less resentful. She was highly desirable these days, and he didn't assume for one minute that the bedroom skills he had imparted would have gone unpractised for the last two years. He cursed each bloke who reaped the benefits of all the good learnings he had passed on to his young muse. There had even been reports of a marriage proposal from the

Prince of Wales, which had apparently been turned down. The gods had been kind that day, the contemptuous musician concluded, imagining a Palace rife with scandal when the songstress from the colonies had declined the role of future Queen of the old country.

The current *beau* was an actor by the name of Peter Elswick, another Englishman who had co-starred in the accomplished Hollywood star's most recent movie. The Australian songwriter didn't like the look of him on principle. He had no issue with her well-publicised romances though, especially since he had been in the news almost constantly himself, linked with a number of notorious sex kittens and not to mention a few full-on, licentious lionesses.

However, all this bad behaviour was instantly relegated to the past tense now that Jeff was ready to reclaim his prize. If she would have him, that was... With his pulse coursing through his veins and his head aching madly, his fingers punched a number he hadn't dialled for a very long time into the telephone keypad.

'Hello. Could I speak to Lynn Dyson, please?' the deep voice asked the lady on the switchboard.

'Who shall I say is calling?' was the crisp response.

'Jeff Diamond.'

He heard whoops of unashamed excitement at the other end, which was nothing unusual these days. Not even the prim and proper staff at Dyson Administration were immune to his charms or his reputation.

'Hold on a moment, please. I'll try her line, sir.'

The air went dead for a few seconds, and then the nervous musician heard the call being answered.

'This is Lynn. Hello?'

'Hey, Lynn. It's Jeff,' he began, swallowing hard as his heart tried its best to exit via his mouth. 'Welcome back.'

The nineteen-year-old's voice was deeper too, more like her mother's. For a split-second, the dumbstruck caller hoped he hadn't been patched through to the wrong room. Thankfully, he hadn't.

'Jeff! It's been ages. How are you?'

The ice was broken to earth-shattering effect. His every sense sprang to life, followed in a split-second by his libido mounting into the danger zone. The ringing in his ears was almost as unbearable as the lustful pressure down below as he inhaled and collected himself to speak directly to his dream girl once again. A two-way conversation was long, long overdue.

'I'm fine, thanks,' Jeff replied to her perfectly rounded syllables and melodious tone of voice, which were at once electrifying and soothing; the proverbial manna from heaven. 'Is it good to be home?'

Lynn sighed and then let out a sunny laugh. 'It is, but it's been a whirlwind. But hey! What about you? You've become a huge rock star! I knew you would.'

'Yes, I damned well have,' the unassuming musician affirmed. 'Didn't you believe me?'

The line fell silent for a few seconds, causing his already anxious heartbeat to accelerate uncontrollably. Why had he given away his insecurity so readily? Evidently, Gravity the troll had also been waiting an eternity for this day of days, like a rotund country squire on a clay pigeon shoot, ready to shoot down any pleasant thoughts which might dare to take flight.

'Yes, of course I believed you,' the young woman answered. 'Your songs are amazing. And you've written some beautiful ones about us too. I love them all, even though some of them make me feel terrible.'

'Sorry,' the songwriter responded generously, although he wasn't. 'Congratulations on all your movies too, and the new albums. There's nothing you can't do now, Lynn. Nothing. You have the world at your feet. How does that feel?'

Another long pause ensued, before the American-tinged accent spoke again. 'Oh, but you know how that feels, don't you? Hey, Jeff, I'm really sorry, but I can't talk now. I have to go.'

Something was wrong, the nervous man thought. What a rapid rebound into rollercoaster territory! He tried to distract his building panic with sweet memories of their happiness chart discussions. Perhaps her boyfriend was in the room? He hadn't thought of that in his excitement to talk to her. Two years was a long time; far too big a gap to bridge with one telephone call.

'Wait a second. Can I buy you dinner?'

'That'd be nice, Jeff, but I can't,' she replied. 'I have no nights free for about three weeks.'

Initially, the twenty-two-year-old wasn't perturbed. He knew what it was like to be busy these days too. They could always manage to find time to see each other somehow.

'Sure. What about lunch?'

'Still no go, I'm afraid. Worse!' the smooth teenager answered.

'For Christ's sake! Breakfast then?' the comic quipped, his uncertainty increasing with her apparent avoidance, although definitely not prepared to give up.

'OK! Well, if you insist,' Lynn gave a subdued giggle, sounding a touch too dismissive to the man hanging on the other end of the line. 'I can do breakfast tomorrow morning, if you like. Say seven-thirty?'

'Yes. I'll take it. Fantastic, thanks. I'll come to Admin and pick you up. I'm guessing that's all still the same?'

'OK. Thank you. Yes, Admin's about the only thing that's still the same, actually. Gotta go, Jeff. Thanks for calling.'

The call was terminated abruptly, without even giving Jeff the time to say goodbye. Nonplussed and determined not to submit to disappointment, he sunk back into the luxurious black leather sofa and re-ran his mental tape of their brief conversation. He knew he shouldn't read anything into it, as a first awkward attempt to reignite the red-hot flame which had been reduced to low for so long. Yet it had definitely been odd. Lynn had started off friendly enough, but by the end of the call her tone had been verging on cold.

No matter, the twenty-two-year-old assured the persistent troll. He ought to reserve judgment until they were face-to-face. At least contact had been made, and the beautiful Lynn Dyson hadn't totally forgotten him. Breakfast date tomorrow or no breakfast date tomorrow, he felt a definite foreboding that the pair would not be picking up whence they had left off. Too much water had passed under the bridge for this to be a viable option, and he had been a fool to raise his hopes. Neither star in nineteen-seventy-four was the person the other remembered from two years earlier, and it would be interesting to see whether sufficient spark had survived to turn the flame back up.

Jesus, Jeff thought, his stomach knotting violently. What would his life become if the spark was no longer there? If their invisible elastic connection had really disintegrated? He hadn't allowed this idea to coalesce in him up until now, but if his beautiful best friend had changed so much during their time apart, perhaps it might be he who wouldn't want her anymore. Could that even be a possibility?

Thrown into a bout of disturbing confusion, the tortured soul allowed itself to conceive the inconceivable. If it were to transpire that he didn't love the latest model Lynn Dyson, where would he take his life next? The prospect wasn't worth thinking about. Not until he knew for sure, at any rate.

***

The foyer of the Dyson Administration building had been treated to a facelift since Jeff's last visit. He stood outside the revolving door for a minute or so, to soak in the occasion and to steady his nerves. If it were possible, he was more apprehensive this time than he had been back in February nineteen-seventy-two.

The security guard's display cabinet was gone. Michael was now sitting at a desk behind the barrier, no doubt equipped with a sophisticated alarm activator located under the desk. The two men smiled at each other.

'Mister Diamond, how are you?'

'I'm well, Michael, thanks. How are *you* going? Long time no see. Could you let Lynn know I'm here, please?'

'Certainly,' the man in uniform nodded, dialling the telephone. 'Congratulations on your success, Jeff. Your music's fantastic. Miss Lynn is very different these days, isn't she?'

'Thanks. Is she?' the younger man asked, caught by surprise. 'We haven't seen each other.'

The songwriter wondered what Michael had meant by this remark. Just how different? It was all too mysterious, and he was very keen to get the first few clumsy minutes out of the way. He stood nearby while one half of a very short exchange took place, unable to hear the female voice he craved through the updated telephone system.

'Miss Dyson's on her way,' the amiable doorman announced. 'So how have you been, Jeff? Making money, I see. And a good name for yourself.'

The friendly security guard was eager to discuss the visitor's albums and concerts. He was clearly a big fan, obliging the young star to humour him. Now into his third year as a recording artist, he was still in the process of mastering the skill of talking about his peculiar life with spontaneous graciousness. Whenever he listened to himself speaking, all he ever heard was arrogance.

Within a short space of time, a familiar tone sounded in the lobby, marking the arrival of a lift. Jeff looked up to find a vision of perfect beauty gliding towards him. The figure's grace took his breath away, and he fought to find a smile as dizziness temporarily overtook him. His eyes feasted on the heavenly being whose aura somehow appeared to radiate ahead of her. At first guess, Lynn seemed taller and more slender, now that her teenage years were almost behind her. She wore a tailored, mid-length jacket which swept out as she walked, high-heeled boots carrying her across the tiles with a regular rhythm.

Whoa! There was absolutely no point trying to curb his self-control. The hot-blooded male could feel his penis swelling quickly inside his pants, knowing that any attempt to dissuade it was only likely to make things worse. Instead, he planted his feet firmly on the ground and focussed on regaining his balance so that he might drink in two years' worth of inspiration as fast as he could.

Lynn's facial features had grown finer, as her former boyfriend had observed from the television news. There was no child left in her now. His jaw wanted to drop to the floor, and he wondered just how obvious his erection might be to the woman who owned it.

Slightly embarrassed, he turned back to Michael and nodded his appreciation. 'Miss Lynn *is* very different these days. You're right!'

The man with the job of protecting the famous family declined to comment. The Dyson security guards were pillars of discretion. He let the smiling celebrity through the turnstile and wished the pair a polite "Good morning."

Ushering her ahead of him, Jeff didn't dare touch his dazzling breakfast guest, although he badly wanted to. She was way too hot, and he was way too horny. Both observations led him to keep his distance. He didn't even move to kiss her cheek, and neither was it encouraged.

'Hello,' he said slowly, raising his eyebrows in an approving look. 'You are stunning. It's so good to see you.'

'Hi, Jeff,' Lynn replied. 'Thanks. It's nice to see you too. Where shall we go?'

Her impassive demeanour was fascinating, in a frightening sort of way, the young man acknowledged. There was no trace of the naïve, girlish enthusiasm he remembered. This woman was difficult to read. Not at all like the open book he had met at sixteen. Feeling both disconcerted and intrigued, he followed her elegant form through the revolving doors and down the steps towards the footpath which ran along the broad St Kilda Road boulevard.

The good-looking rock star hailed an approaching taxi, which immediately swerved on its brakes and screeched to a standstill. He struggled to take his eyes off his companion, whose golden hair was shorter than before, but not by much, and glistened in the morning sun. By the erratic driving display, it was clear he wasn't the only one to be spellbound by this gorgeous creature.

'Let's go somewhere along the edge of the park,' Jeff suggested, lasciviously watching her slim legs as they laced themselves into the rear seat footwell. 'We'll find somewhere quiet at this time, I expect.'

The taxi driver was full of questions for both musicians, requiring a chivalrous reminder from the young lady's chaperone to keep her movements confidential. The warning didn't deter the Eastern European man however, who seemed to know a great deal about the Australian music scene. Lynn nodded a brief thank-you to the smooth showbusiness heavyweight who had come to her defence, and the idle chatter during the five minutes it took to reach their destination gave him a chance to dampen his raging libido to a tolerable level.

While they drove, the returning local girl asked Melbourne's new favourite son about changes that had taken place in the city. She chuckled at the amount of information he was able to rattle off, especially when even the driver praised his memory. He shrugged, grateful for anything he might take as a compliment in her presence. They alighted outside a French-style café, seated themselves at the most secluded table and ordered two coffees. The waiter brought them a jug of water and some menus, fawning hopelessly over his celebrity patrons.

The gracious woman declined breakfast, much to her companion's *chagrin*, explaining that she could only stay for a short time. She placed her menu back onto the empty plate in front of her and folded her hands into her lap.

'Before anything, I'd like to say congratulations on your career, Jeff. You've had an amazing two years. Now you know exactly how I feel,' she laughed, relaxing a little. 'I expect you're mobbed wherever you go.'

The young man smiled and cocked his head slightly. 'I knew how you felt before. But yep, now I'm experiencing it on my own behalf. You taught me well.'

It was all the keyed up twenty-two-year-old could do to stop staring, almost salivating. The goddess on the other side of the table oozed confidence, dressed in a silk shirt open to reveal a tight, low-cut top, and a sparkling necklace which was intent on hypnotising his eager mind. Her blue eyes were trying hard not to engage with his, and for some reason Jeff found this incredibly tantalising too. It was fortuitous that he felt so nervous, because otherwise he would have been recklessly turned on. Or perhaps the nerves were fuelling it? *Lighten up*, he urged himself.

'So, tell me... What was it like being an American?'

'It was a blast,' Lynn laughed, putting on her best Californian accent. 'They're very conservative though. You were there. You know what it's like.'

'Yes. I was also in London at the same time as you at one point,' he added. 'It was unbearably difficult not to try and track you down.'

'I'm glad you didn't,' came a reply Jeff wasn't sure how to take. 'Thanks for resisting the temptation. I went to your concert, by the way, at the Greek Theater. It was amazing. You've got such great stage presence. They say those nights were the best ever at that venue. You created a legend!'

This time Lynn smiled without inhibition. For the first time, her former lover noted. Without question she was colder. Not superior, but aloof. She clearly wanted to remain distant.

'Really? I wondered if you would. Thanks,' his mind instantly flitted to the nightly plea he had made over that brief season.

The nineteen-year-old didn't mention a donation, and the novice philanthropist was sensitive enough to appreciate her silence on the topic. Assuming the quarter of a million dollars had come from her, he would have been disappointed to have such a vulgar admission divulged in a public place. Regardless, he so desperately needed to resolve this aching dilemma.

Putting his own menu down onto the table, Jeff shifted uncomfortably in his chair, drank down his coffee in a few large gulps and signalled to the watchful waiter for another round. How would he break this wholly respectable but tedious deadlock?

'I'm glad I didn't know you were there. It would've made me more nervous than I am now...'

Lynn looked up in surprise. Mission accomplished. *Man, I'm good*, the expert communicator smiled to himself.

'Why are you nervous?'

'Well, come on...' her companion responded, chiding her false modesty. 'You're not exactly the schoolkid you were when we last saw each other.'

'We've both changed,' the sophisticate agreed. 'That's true.'

The sportswoman exhaled, her body language conceding a certain unease of her own. This tall, incredibly handsome man was wearing the leather jacket she had bought him for his twentieth birthday, under which she also noticed the rather classy designer shirt he was wearing. Not to mention his stylish, polished Italian shoes. Even his haircut looked expensive. Jeff Diamond had learned how to behave like a millionnaire, she concluded. A far cry from the self-confessed nobody with whom she used to spend her spare time.

'You look great, by the way. Nice jacket. Did you buy an apartment?'

Jeff nodded and smiled, running the fingers of his left hand along the rough hide of his sleeve. The gentle sarcasm was welcome. At least she remembered him well enough not to assume he would have bought a mansion, as most people seemed to think.

'Yes, I did. Just on the edge of the CBD, almost in Carlton. It's got great views nôrth, from the airport on one side to the estuary on the other. And I bought my black Aston Martin too.'

An ostentatious waiter came back with a second cup of coffee each and placed them on the table with a flourish. Both guests looked up, smiled and thanked him politely. Seeing Lynn Dyson and Jeff Diamond together had sent the staff into a frenzy, and he returned their thanks before scurrying off, swooning madly.

'Good for you,' Lynn replied. 'Sounds perfect. So what's next for you? Did you finish your degree?'

Knowing he was on borrowed time once their second coffee had been consumed, the confused songwriter was growing tired of small talk. He wanted nothing more than to sweep this beautiful catch up in his arms and tell her how much he still loved her, before returning to her room on the top floor and spending all day in the bed he recalled most clearly. Yet Lynn was giving him nothing back whatsoever. Where was the telepathy they had fought so hard to tame in those fevered months? Was it really possible that she no longer had any feelings to reciprocate, or was she deliberately holding back?

Today's early date almost seemed like one of those puerile meetings which record companies insisted their contracted artists attend periodically with influential VIPs. Jeff had passed several boring but obligatory hours in such toil over the last couple of years; duty calls he had sought to finish as quickly as possible, which was precisely the signal he was receiving from his evasive dream girl right now.

On the positive side however, reluctant conviction that Lynn's attention was not wandering to the physical helped the keyed-up suitor to switch off his own rampant x-ray vision, leaving his fingertips fizzing with the anticipation of touching her cheek, her hand, anywhere... In fact, so light-headed was he with confused messages that it felt as if he were looking down in utter disbelief on a scene where he and his long-awaited lover shared nothing more than a table. How could she be so disinterested in him, when he quite plainly felt every bit as much for her as ever? Had the passion she had once shown for him and no-one else completely evaporated without a trace?

'I'd rather talk about what's next for us,' the determined man countered, staring into her blue eyes and making sure they didn't look away this time. 'It's me, Lynn. You're treating me like a stranger. I don't want to talk about my degree. It's like you don't want to be here.'

Lynn frowned. 'Sorry. It's nice to see you, Jeff. Really. I suppose we are strangers again, it's been such a long time.'

'No longer for you than for me,' the handsome man smiled and winked, not wishing to put her even further offside.

The blonde-haired beauty became immediately disconcerted. She finished her coffee and set the cup lightly back onto the saucer. There was an air of finality in the way she took a deep breath and began to speak, causing her breakfast partner to prepare himself for bad news.

'What we had was two years ago,' she responded, suddenly on edge. 'I was very young. I've changed a lot.'

'Yes, I know. I can see that. Heaps...' the Australian reminded his Americanised companion. 'A lot's happened to both of us since then, but I'd love to see you again. You know... Like we used to?'

Nausea washed through the twenty-two-year-old's insides like a tidal wave, and he felt a cold sweat gathering underneath the surface of his skin. It was a good idea, after all, that they hadn't ordered food, since even the second cup of coffee was a challenge to consume. It was he who had been naïve about this reunion. Just because he was beside himself with eagerness to pick up where the couple had left off, his misguided hopes for an automatic reciprocation were evidently a mistake. He wasn't yet ready to beg however. He had waited this long. He could wait some more if he had to.

Lynn continued, clearly also still nervous. 'I'm really busy. I don't have time for a boyfriend.'

Jeff shook his head slowly. 'You didn't last time either, but we managed to sneak a few hours here and there. At least have dinner with me next time you're free. Please?'

There, he did beg after all. Surely this gorgeous creature who had been so passionate and committed to their relationship two years ago must harbour some small amount of curiosity as to what might remain of their red-hot romance? There had to be some other reason for her resistance, but the empathetic man wasn't about to prise it out of her now. Lynn Dyson was no longer a dreamy, sixteen-year-old push-over, and clearly it would take some time to win her favour this time. She had the world at her feet and her former lover dangling on a string.

'In a few weeks, perhaps,' the popular returning celebrity held fast, clasping her handbag close to her chest as if looking for an opportunity to depart.

'OK. That's good. So what are you up to now you're back down under?' Jeff asked, accepting that small talk was the order of the day.

'I'm going to Sydney next week for the music awards. I'm doing the opening number,' she told him with some relief.

His heart skipped a beat at this news, instantly ready to pounce on another opportunity to get together, yet the intelligent songwriter's keen self-preservation instincts had second thoughts. No, he mustn't give everything away now. He changed the subject.

'How's Sandy?'

'Oh, he's OK,' Lynn answered, sighing a little. 'Thanks for asking. Dad's putting a lot of pressure on him. He's not Junior, but Dad's determined to make him into Junior if it's the last thing he does.'

One corner of the handsome rocker's mouth turned upwards, teasing her ever so slightly. 'That's a shame. He's got his own path to follow. Like you and me.'

Lynn took a deep breath, sat straighter and smiled back. Two years of additional maturity had made her more like her mother; courteous, diplomatic and publicly forgiving. How the puzzled reprobate opposite wished he could read her previously wide open mind. She had picked up on the involuntary irritation in his voice at the mention of her father and the power he held over his offspring, and yet he noticed she hadn't tried to defend him.

'Yes, that's true, but he'll be fine. When's your next album coming out?'

'Last week in November. I'll deliver one to you personally. Live, even better.'

'OK. Thanks,' Lynn nodded, not quite as coolly as earlier. 'I'd love a copy. That'd be great. Jeff, I need to get back soon. I have a meeting at nine o'clock with my management. It was nice to catch up again.'

Resigned to disappointment, the musician shrugged, fishing a pen out of his inside jacket pocket. He wrote the telephone number for his new apartment on an unused paper napkin and handed it to his date. How ordinary their encounter had turned out to be, after so long... Receiving the makeshift calling card graciously, the young woman folded the white serviette and slotted it into her handbag.

'Call me?' he asked, his eyes following her every move.

'OK. I will. I should be getting back now. Thanks for the coffees. I'm sorry to cut this short.'

Jeff stood up as the beautiful star rose to her feet. Was he imagining an air of resignation on her part too? He used to pride himself in knowing what his dream girl was thinking, but today she was utterly inscrutable. He held his arms out, inviting a hug and a better insight into her physical reaction. The gesture was brushed aside however, and she leaned forward for him to kiss her on the cheek, again remarkably like her mother.

The chivalrous celebrity did as he was asked, with the distinct impression that he was not required to accompany her back to Admin. The proximity drove him crazy, caught between the dignity demanded by the public situation and the private agony he was enduring. The young beauty smelled divine, and he felt a shard of electricity arc from her face to his. Apparently it had not travelled both ways. Well, not that she was going to let on at any rate.

'You're gorgeous,' he whispered, backing off and exhaling audibly. 'Welcome home.'

'Thank you. I'm really glad things have worked out so well for you,' Lynn replied, glancing around to make sure she was safe to leave the café alone. 'You must be proud of everything you've done. You really are someone now.'

Jeff shrugged, cut to the quick by her swift deflection. 'There's a whole lot more to do. I'm only just getting started. But thanks, Lynn. You too, of course. I'll ring you for that dinner. You won't escape, OK? And just so you know, you're even more irresistible than you used to be.'

The celebrity chose to reply with no more than a smile and a brief flash of her bright blue eyes. Jeff Diamond Mark II watched Lynn Dyson Mark II walk elegantly out of sight, high heels clicking sexily on the shiny tiled flooring, leaving her suitor feeling every bit like the nobody he had been as Mark I.

Whoa! That was weird in the extreme, the intellectual thought, slapping a few notes down on the table and waving his thanks to the waiter. The whole staff yelled out camp goodbyes, doubtless itching to huddle together or use the telephone to spread the juicy gossip they had just witnessed.

The regal blonde strode into the distance with great purpose, leaving her breakfast companion without so much as a second look. She half hoped he might follow her but knew he was too much of a gentleman to embarrass her in that way. Yes, he was still quite the handsomest man in the world. That much hadn't changed. And yes, her heart was racing a million miles an hour, longing for his heart-stopping kiss and to feel his arms draw her in as if he would never let her go.

Tears of regret started to flow from her eyes and down her cheeks, and the young woman steeled herself to stare through the concern of passers-by. Yes, yes, yes! Jeff Diamond was every bit as electrifying to her as a nineteen-year-old who considered herself beyond the starry-eyed stage. But no, Lynn rued. She couldn't. Things were too complicated to think they could simply release the Pause button. No matter how she felt upon seeing her beautiful black stallion again, it was simply impossible.

The musician walked back through the city to his apartment, crossing the Botanic Gardens and slipping on the dewy grass as he descended the steep hill onto St Kilda Road. Greeting fans to the left and right in the streets, which were now filled with commuters on their way to work, he was totally bewildered by the strange breakfast assignation. Once inside the penthouse, he took off his shoes and jacket and lay down on the bed, staring at the photograph of the two of them that the unfortunate Sandy had taken; the one he had received for his birthday a few weeks before Lynn had broken the news that she was leaving.

Two years apart, and the deepest thing the spellbinding superstar had said to him was, "You really are someone now." Was this the sum total of their relationship from her perspective? What had this parting phrase meant? Did she think he didn't need her anymore? Or was she hinting that he still wasn't good enough to be associated with her and her family?

His dream girl certainly had changed, and she was likely to be thinking exactly the same about him. Although now most definitely a someone, his behaviour while she had been away had hardly been exemplary. Perhaps Lynn Dyson had outgrown her stimulating sexual mercenary these days? Two years based in the United States of America and travelling the world as an adult had made her much worldlier now and less in need of an education from a passionate yet unconventional dissident.

Two coffees in a high-classed café with a rich man dressed in smart clothes and who had managed to abstain from his whisky chaser for an hour could not hope to cancel out his public record of debauchery and womanising. Shit! He had not done himself any favours in that regard. He had assumed his former caring schoolgirl would have afforded him some latitude, given the insights he had shared into his warped personality, but the downhearted young man was suddenly filled with regret at the reputation which must precede him.

Jeff's head and heart were heavy, but his body was bursting with an intense pressure for which there appeared to be no outlet. He was as horny as he could remember, spurred on further by his mind's conflict and confusion which in turn dealt him a heightened hunger for power. He masturbated half-heartedly, keen to rid himself of the tension that should have been ousted in a much different frame of mind. This mechanical activity brought some relief at least, yet he was far from flushed with the optimism he had anticipated at having finally seen Lynn again.

The frustrated man swore out loud, knowing he needed to come up with a new plan. Maybe it was too much to expect for things to ever be the way they were? Lynn Dyson had other priorities now. She had turned down a Prince. What chance did he have?

***

Dannie closed her notepad and inserted it into the heavy reference text from which she had been researching an assignment, flicking between Wikipedia and Google to make sure she had not missed any more up-to-date information. Her favourite book sat patiently on the shelf above the desk, next to her empty tea mug. That was enough work for tonight. She was tired but also dying to get back to the part of "A Life Singular" which never failed to send endless streams of excitement up and down her spine. She went into the bathroom and quickly brushed her teeth, before jumping under the quilt. She knew her mother was already asleep, since she could hear her snoring through the paper-thin wall which separated them.

In the soft light from the bedside lamp, the student switched on her iPad and opened the e-book at the start of a new chapter, eager to reactivate those latent memories once more. How must Jeff Diamond have been feeling that day in the mid-nineteen-seventies, knowing how much Lynn had grown up during their long period apart? And how would she, Dannie Finley, a latent world-changer in two-thousand-and-sixteen, find her own soul-mate? Was there even such a person for her? And how far from Glasgow would she be? Was she already thinking of her too, stuck in the cold, dank weather, so full of drive yet devoid of financial means? And would this mystery woman, like Lynn Dyson, be someone who would understand what to do with such a conundrum, when, or even if they ever met?

One thing was for certain... The seventeen-year-old Scot hoped she would never have to endure the type of heartache which had leached out of the pages she had read on the bus earlier that evening. She wondered whether she would find any extra pearls of wisdom this time that she may have glossed over last time, in her excitement to immerse himself in the physical passion of the famous couple's reunion.

Who was her Lynn Dyson? Her dream girl? Her beautiful best friend? What would she look like? Dannie could feel a stirring inside and reached under the quilt to stroke herself through her underwear while she read on. She knew exactly what she wanted her soul-mate to look like; the fantasy she had in mind right now. But how would she recognise her, whoever and wherever she was?

Her favourite book hadn't answered this question yet.

Sydney Showdown

Australia's newly-returned prodigal daughter was signed up as the Guest of Honour at the annual Australian Music Industry Awards to be held in Sydney the following Wednesday, at which she was to perform a song from her most recent album and present two of the awards. She had also been nominated for a couple herself: Best Single and Best Female Artist. Lynn and Peter Elswick, her partner for the function, had flown up that morning and were booked into the Intercontinental Hotel for two nights. The British actor was then due to fly directly back to the UK to film a television series the following day, making these their last nights together.

In the ten days since the nineteen-year-old had arrived back in Melbourne, Bart Dyson had passed on some more material to his daughter to substantiate why he was so against her meeting up with Jeff Diamond again. It had summoned to mind many of the long conversations she and her former lover had shared before they had parted, mysteriously foreshadowing the frightful events from his childhood.

The young woman didn't know what to make of this new batch of intelligence. On the face of it, there was indeed a great deal of circumstantial evidence to support her father's assertions, yet she found it incomprehensible that the tortured Sydney songwriter might be implicated. But then again, Jeff had been straight with her all along, saying there were certain things which he was unable to tell her. Were these the same certain things her dad wouldn't tell her either? She wished they wouldn't treat her like a child anymore. She was an adult and was being asked by both men to make a very adult decision.

For the awards dinner, Lynn dressed in a long, silver, tightly-fitting gown, with a low-cut neckline and a high split all the way up her right thigh. Her hair was put up beautifully by a stylist she had used several times before in Sydney. Peter whistled as she presented herself in the hotel bedroom, ready to wow the audience again tonight.

The glamorous pair took a limousine to the venue and paraded along the red carpet, amid cheering fans and flashing cameras. The smiling celebrity was pleased to be back on Australian soil, even though the level of hysteria generated by her homecoming was somewhat exhausting. The couple made its way into the reception area and was quickly ushered backstage to join the band and prepare for the evening's curtain-raiser.

Only a few minutes after the stunning blonde and her British *beau* had passed through, still more vociferous cheers and the occasional frenzied scream could be heard from outside the building. Australia's newest rock sensation had arrived, accompanied by the beautiful Gerry Blake. Jeff Diamond had been nominated for three awards, and the intrepid duo had flown up from Melbourne earlier that day. The older man had continued to do an outstanding job as the superstar's manager, and this gala evening was a small thank-you for all his hard work and sage advice.

Girls were shouting out all around them, leaning over the barricade and stretching frantic hands as far as they could to touch their idol, who planted kisses and signed autographs in the strangest of places. The fact that he had arrived stag had definitely not gone unnoticed.

'Jeff, can I be your date tonight?'

'Take me in with you!'

The handsome, dark-haired celebrity posed for the cameras, turned out smartly in a dark suit and sporting a gold earring which had been a spur of the moment decision that afternoon. He and Gerry made their way into the cocktail reception amid droves of other showbusiness guests, along the same red carpet that had recently cushioned Lynn Dyson's step.

The ebullient accountant was, as usual, taking the big occasion in his stride. 'So many beautiful women,' he shouted to his mate, casting his eyes over the assembled throng, 'and so little time...'

'Don't say I never take you anywhere,' Jeff quipped, slapping his mate on the back, largely for the benefit of the baying reporters and photographers. 'Just behave yourself while the cameras are out. You don't want your mum to see you in the papers tomorrow.'

'Yes, darling,' Gerry promised, threatening to peck his date on the cheek.

Still clowning around, the two friends climbed a sweeping staircase and helped themselves to a glass of whisky and soda each. Leaning on the upstairs banister to watch the glittering spectacle, they took position to eye up the ladies as they strutted around in their finery. The popular newcomer was not yet totally accustomed to being part of the sparkling set and was genuinely surprised when other famous people approached him as a peer and congratulated him on his success.

The men were still admiring the view when Lynn Dyson and her companion arrived back into the open area, sound-check completed. Jeff immediately froze to the spot. He had certainly not forgotten she would be here, but neither had he braced himself for such an early public encounter. Nevertheless, there she was, and more ravishing than ever. Far too good an opportunity to miss.

Gerry nudged his shoulder. 'Look, mate,' he hissed. 'Howzat? She looks fantastic. Oh, yes! Hot, hot, hot!'

'Yeah, OK,' the anxious man replied, urging his friend to keep his voice down.

Jeff hoped the loudmouth wouldn't do something rash, like call out or wave in his indomitable way. His mind was racing. Flagging down a passing drinks waiter, he pointed to a glass of champagne on the tray and asked him to take it to the shimmering silver goddess downstairs. His instructions were to tell the lady it was "shampoo" and to say it was from "a someone" upstairs. Thankfully, the excited young man was an extrovert and very keen to interact with any celebrity, particularly Lynn Dyson.

'Way to go, mate,' the equally famous messenger slapped his shoulder. 'Thanks a lot.'

Gerry and Jeff surveyed the scene while Lynn and Peter milled around arm in arm, chatting to the other special guests. Yesterday's man noticed that her broad smile never faltered and wondered how genuine her laughter was in the face of everyone's flattering attention. The drinks waiter didn't take long to reach the lower level, and the rock star aloft watched her reaction closely as the champagne and his coded message were delivered. Still leaning on the balcony railing, he coolly waited for the superstar to lift her eyes to where the animated employee was pointing.

When Lynn's sweeping gaze found the origin of her bubbling gift, the swarthy, dark-haired rocker raised his whisky tumbler in a subtle toast to the delicious vision. She reciprocated furtively but just as quickly looked away, returning her focus to the group with whom she had been speaking. Jeff feasted his eyes on how wonderful she looked. This was only the beginning of a very long, painful evening.

Surrounded by big names, Peter Elswick hadn't noticed his girlfriend's momentary lapse, and a few minutes later everyone was invited to file into the main *salon* and be seated at their allocated dinner table. The Australian Elvis was accosted by a swarm of eager females who were more than willing to swap places with his male partner. Politely turning them down one by one, the two *amigos* found themselves directed to the up-and-comers' table, sitting with the Amphlett sisters and Marcia Hines.

Gerry was enjoying himself immensely, both for his own sake but also through seeing his best mate in this now familiar environment of adulation and excess. Jeff Diamond had become a household name; worth millions and lauded by still more millions, all in a relatively short space of time. The handsome songwriter did his best to lavish the flood of females with the attention they expected from him, despite his own lustful thoughts being reserved for only one person present. His manager took his hat off to the famous client, knowing how hard these last two years had been to endure and marvelling at his ability to stay positive and driven to achieve his mind-boggling goals.

Lynn's polished performance opened the show, and she brought the house down. Her slender frame weaved its own magic in time to the music, and her mellow voice exuded self-possession and melodic quality. As the orchestral backing faded and her final note came to its end, Jeff applauded along with the rest. He could easily recognise now, from his inside knowledge, that she too had developed her artistic talent considerably since the private audience he had been privileged to receive in the ballroom at Dyson Administration. He whistled proudly, despite feeling his dream slipping away.

If he hadn't been encircled by adoring fans who kept him well occupied, the downhearted man with the fake smile would most likely have left for the night before the *entrée* had been served. He was unable to divert his eyes from the object of his obsession for more than the time it took to answer each inane question from his table-mates. Peter Elswick fitted the bill perfectly: a well-bred sophisticate of old English money who did as he was told and never challenged the *status quo*. From her seat in the established artists' *milieu*, Lynn seemed relaxed with her blond, Brylcreemed club-cut and completely oblivious to the newcomer's frequent attempts to divert her attention.

Dinner and the ceremony proceeded slowly, with speeches interspersed through each course and a liberal dispensation of wines and beers. Jeff Diamond and Lynn Dyson each won two awards, much to the delight of their fans. They were up and down, traversing the carpeted walkway to and from the stage, giving short speeches and posing with elegant hosts. Their paths never crossed however. The first award the outspoken rocker won was for Best Song, a popular vote for a number one in twenty-three countries earlier that year. He was presented with his award by Olivia Newton John, who kissed him with extreme enthusiasm, making the audience laugh and cheer loudly.

Before giving the acceptance speech he had rehearsed a few times in his mind, Jeff leaned into the microphone, pointing his crystal trophy out towards the table where his dream girl was seated. 'Thanks, Olivia and everyone. Hey! Isn't it great to have Lynn back in Australia?'

The audience clapped and whistled. The gracious man wanted the elegant star to interpret his gesture as meaning "This is for you", since he was unable yet to voice it openly. The beautiful teenager smiled her acknowledgement, though not particularly in the direction of the stage.

Dinner finally over, the tables were cleared and pushed back from the dance floor, and the party began in earnest. Jeff knew he needed to make his move on Lynn before she was whisked away by the boyfriend for whom she didn't have time. Neither celebrity was on home turf, and nor would she be able to use her family as an excuse. He couldn't let this torturous night end without finding out how she really felt.

The songwriter spotted the stunning silver figure dancing with her obedient partner near the main stage. He picked up an excited young professional dancer who had been flirting wildly with him throughout the meal and whisked her onto the floor, determined to get close enough to speak to his former girlfriend. Once in a while, the blonde beauty made eye contact and returned a slight smile. Just before the song drew to a close, Jeff twisted and turned his gleeful partner until he could lean over and almost whisper in Lynn's ear.

Then before the dignified star could move away, the handsome chart-topper placed a hand on her bare shoulder, causing her to jump at his touch. She gasped as the current sparked between them, seemingly even stronger than before.

Jeff was reeling too. 'Dance with me?' he breathed into her ear.

The sportswoman's statuesque body appeared to droop a little, as if she had been dreading such a proposition. 'I can't, Jeff. Not tonight.'

Attentive enough to his current partner to maintain some sort of slow rhythm as the music faded, the twenty-two-year-old brushed his fingers across the top of Lynn's arm again. 'Not even after that rush?'

Again the star shook her head. At the same time, Peter stepped forward to warn the bad-boy of Australian rock to watch his step.

'She said not tonight.'

'Who's *she*?' the dark-haired Adonis flashed his eyes. 'This is Lynn Dyson, mate, and Lynn Dyson's allowed to change her mind.'

Jeff backed away without waiting for a response, guiding his dumbfounded partner back to her friends. Checking quickly to see that Gerry was adequately occupied with his own string of females, he headed towards the *concièrge*'s desk and asked if he could use a function room for an hour. There was no way he could leave this event without obtaining an explanation for his former lover's cool reception.

The mature staff member behind the counter gave his famous guest a knowing look. 'We can give you a room upstairs, Mister Diamond.'

Jeff chuckled. 'No, thanks, mate. I already have a room upstairs.'

Absolutely not, he thought. That would send completely the wrong message. Obviously his reputation had preceded him again. Re-joining his business manager and accepting a glass of Scotch from a bottle which had been delivered to the table, Jeff surveyed the scene again. Lynn and Peter continued to dance, though scarcely touching each other.

There was no chemistry between these two, of that the ardent lover was positive. He recalled the many demonstrations of affection his dream girl was capable of communicating, and none was forthcoming for this colourless, conservative bore. Was this a subtle message? Was she trying to tell him there was nothing going on? Or had there never been any greater magic in their relationship? He understood this phenomenon only too well.

Another, slower number was coming to an end. The songwriter finished his cigarette while he waited, before striding purposefully through the crowd towards the fair-haired couple. He raised an unapologetic hand to the bemused and somewhat disgruntled actor, taking a deliberate stance with his back towards the Englishman. The beautiful singer stared at the new arrival in amazement, and the forceful interloper heard gasps of awestruck anticipation from all around.

'Jeff! What are you doing?'

'Come with me, Lynn, please,' he urged, taking hold of her left arm. 'I need to talk to you.'

'I can't!' she shouted above the music. 'I'm with someone. What do you want?'

'You. I want you. Please. Just a few minutes, I promise.'

The young lady followed, tugged off balance by the force of the tall man's grip, leaving Peter alone on the dance floor. Whatever happened, she certainly didn't wish to cause too much of a scene in front of the country's entire entertainment industry press corps, given her father's strict instructions before she had left for New South Wales.

With a lethal concoction of macho pride and blessed relief coursing through his veins, Jeff led his quarry out of the ballroom and towards a small meeting room off to the side, much to the astonishment of their fellow guests. His head began to pound on approaching a very solid wooden door. Fighting to catch his breath and with his brain jam-packed with the usual crazed images, he crashed straight through.

The anxious man slammed the door closed as soon as he had made sure Lynn was safely inside. While he struggled to regain his composure, he felt her hand on his shoulder, and a current pulsated from head to toe. It was all he could do not to spin around and grab hold of her shoulders to yank her into his starving body. He managed to stifle an almighty roar which was desperate to escape from his lungs.

'It's OK. Slow down,' the nervous woman smiled.

Stepping forward, Jeff deflected her conciliatory gesture by removing his suit jacket, tossing it onto the highly-polished, mahogany table. He was determined not to lose control in front of her; not after so long and with so much at stake. There was a familiar compassion in her voice that left him aching with desire. He did his best to block it out, unwilling to show weakness. He had waited two years for this moment.

'Please don't patronise me,' he warned through gritted teeth.

Lynn watched her former boyfriend pause, facing the wall with his eyes closed and head tipped back. His breathing was loud and laboured. Obviously nothing had improved for his scarred mind, regardless of the new star's successful career and considerable wealth. She dared to imagine what might be going through his head and considered the danger she might have brought upon herself by agreeing to leave the crowded dance floor unaccompanied. The recent commentary provided by her father's investigators spoke of violence of the highest order, and her mind flew back to the tennis skirt episode once again.

The nineteen-year-old's heart began to beat faster, the palms of her hands itching with perspiration. Was she about to fall victim to some horrendous act of jealous rage? Was the Jeff Diamond she remembered truly capable of such terrible acts? And was the shrouded history she had done her best to deny set to repeat itself right here in this Sydney hotel?

Suddenly and infused with high drama, the commanding man swung round on his heels and strode over to her.

'OK,' he sighed, rolling his shoulders. 'I'm sorry.'

The songwriter pointed to a chair and indicated for Lynn to sit down, which she did, a little more at ease now that his demeanour had lost its deranged edge. The atmosphere in the room remained turgid with anticipation, leaving both musicians breathing heavily and uncertain where their next move would take them.

Jeff inhaled deeply, his face breaking into a broad smile. 'By the way, for starters, you look absolutely, mind-blowingly gorgeous. You are the most beautiful woman in this whole fucking world. D'you know that?'

'Thank you,' the young woman responded. 'I'm sure that's not true.'

Her eyes darted downwards modestly, hoping her controlling captor would come to the point quickly. Having recovered from the effort required to enter the room, the lost boy felt a familiar anger welling up inside him. He had no choice but to confront this most irresistible of women and break the impasse that had robbed him of all rational thought. He needed to preserve his sanity and behave civilly towards the most important person in his life.

The rock star leaned back on the table, almost facing her, and stared at the delicious female form sitting in front of him. 'Lynn, I need to know what's going on. I need you to tell me why you're here with that bloody Englishman when you could be here with me. I love you so much. It's been a bloody long two years, and I've done everything you and your fucking family wanted me to. I've played by the rules, and then at breakfast the other day you were as cold as ice. Why, Lynn? Why? What more do you want from me?'

After courteously listening until his opening salvo had been released, the elegant celebrity took a very deep breath and attempted to provide answers to the many questions all of which were seeking the same answer. Everything her dejected former lover had said was perfectly true. He had stuck to his word, and she couldn't dispute that he was owed some sort of explanation.

'Jeff, I'm sorry I wasn't too friendly the other morning,' she began, with as much confidence as her nerves would grant. 'Your 'phone call came out of the blue, and I didn't know what to say. I shouldn't have agreed to meet you at all. You see, I can't go back. We're not the same people as we were two years ago, and I can't go backwards. It wouldn't be right.'

The intensity in those dark-ringed, bloodshot eyes sent a flood of sensuous memories through Lynn's body, and she fought the reaction they ignited in her core. Her explanation evidently hadn't made a positive impression on the disappointed man, judging by the steeling of his jaw and the familiar forced gulp of a tight throat. Still breathing heavily, she imagined him quickly replaying her response in his head to see if he could unravel it a second time around. After a long pause, he spoke.

'I have no fucking clue what you're talking about,' the angry man snarled. 'Back where? Who's asking you to go back anywhere? We *are* the same people. That's one of the few things that *are* still the same. We've just got older and done more things. We're no different to anyone else. No-one goes backwards, angel.'

Jeff thumped the table with his fist, and it startled the nineteen-year-old. She sat straighter in her chair. Angel. What a long time it had been since she had heard this endearing nickname. This man wouldn't hurt her, she worked hard to convince herself. He had never done her any harm; not even through those horrendous few weeks prior to their separation. Surely he hadn't brought her into this wood-panelled meeting room to unleash his wrath?

'I'm sorry,' he snapped, seeing her frightened eyes. 'Calm down. I know.'

'That's OK,' Lynn responded, scarcely remembering how to deal with the old mastery. 'It wasn't a very good explanation. I just can't think of anything else to tell you. I can't go out with you again, and you can't force me to give you all the reasons.'

'*All* the reasons? How many are there? Fucking hell!'

The sequined, silver-clad singer couldn't help but smile at the exaggerated tone of incredulity. 'That's not what I meant either,' she sighed.

'Yeah? Tell me something I can believe then. Don't you ever think about what we had at all?' the frustrated man implored, reducing the volume slightly. 'All those great times we had? Christ, Lynn! I know I do. I still think about you every minute of the day. Every woman I fuck, every time I go to bed and every bloody time I wake up screaming in the middle of the night. Is all that lost for you? Seven months of perfection... All that means nothing to you now?'

Lynn's heart was aching, drinking in the raw poetry of this quite majestic beast. Of course she had fond memories of their time together. She often thought about her mysterious Catholic Argentinean Polish Jew, and never more so than when she had arrived back at Benloch and was reminded of those heady weekends they had spent making love and writing music by the creek. Those seven passionate months most definitely meant something to her, yet her situation now dictated in no uncertain terms that those carefree days were over.

'No. It means a lot. But my father...' she started, catching her breath.

'Your father? Your bloody father.'

With his head bowed and muttering to himself, a pair of sunken eyes looked up at the fearless young woman from under his eyebrows. Her body language had relented somewhat, as had her strident gaze. Was that a chink in the stalwart's glamorous armour?

She continued. 'Dad told me I can't go back, that I must look forward and forget the past. You know how he is about drugs and partying and getting drunk. He doesn't want me to associate with you.'

Jeff thumped the table again, and this time there was no apology. 'Associate with me?' he echoed. 'I don't want your association, baby. I want you in my bed, as my soul-mate and my best friend. I want to become each others' forever again. Share all the plans we spoke about. All the things I've started in the hope we'd be able to finish them together. You used to want that too. Is your dad the only thing that's stopping you, or is there something else?'

'I can't live your kind of lifestyle, can I?' the aristocratic star reverted to her original argument. 'The parties, the alcohol. You know I can't. I still have to play tennis, *et cetera...*'

Her adversary stood up and began to pace the floor. Lynn allowed her eyes to follow him around the room. He wore a suit so well, and again she felt familiar *frissons* of arousal. He wore jeans and a t-shirt well too, she remembered. In fact, he wore nothing well! Her eyes darted back to the table-top, knowing he had noticed her dreamy expression. She blushed without warning. Nothing escaped this man's attention.

Despite the depth of her feelings, the strong-willed champion mustered a spirited objection. 'You're always making the news, and not always for the good things you do. I don't agree with my father on everything, but I do on that subject.'

He winked gamely at her disingenuous prudish excuse. 'Isn't it better to fear what comes out of people's mouths than what goes in them?' he deliberately sent her pulse rate into overdrive, determined to capitalise on his apparent hold over her senses.

Jeff walked over and pulled a chair up beside her, straddling it menacingly. He was staring straight into her eyes, but his gorgeous hostage didn't recoil. The Olympian hadn't forgotten how insistent he could be, and it unnerved her how readily she accepted his extreme behaviour. His special brand of persuasive poetry was drawing her in again. His every word caressed her, and she was only too aware of the lifeline she had inadvertently thrown her disconsolate suitor. The conflict burned inside her, knowing he was bound to pick up on this too.

What time was it? Lynn couldn't see a clock in the room, unless it was behind her. Her childhood self-defence classes had taught her never to turn her head away from an aggressor and risk missing a vital clue. She tried to read Jeff's watch, but half of its face was hidden in the sleeve of his white dress shirt. Her thoughts turned briefly to Peter, at the same time realising that she wasn't in much of a hurry to get back to him. Damn her father! And damn the promise she had made before leaving for the awards ceremony this morning.

'OK. I get it,' the young man repeated slowly, the veins on his forehead and neck pumping visibly. 'But what does your father have to do with us now? Didn't you just have another birthday? You're old enough to make your own decisions these days. You know that. Your parents shouldn't be running your life anymore. What do *you* want, Lynn? What do *you* want?'

With his patience smouldering under the surface, Jeff leaned over so that their heads were closer together. He could feel her breath on his face, and hoped she could do the same. He knew her responses well enough to be sure it would have the same effect. Each time he said the word "you", he gently pressed against her sternum with his index finger, just above the neckline of her dress, quite clearly aiming for her heart.

Lynn felt her pulse rate accelerating as he prodded her skin. 'I know, but it's not that simple.'

'Yes, it *is* that simple,' her former lover countered, more quietly this time. 'Christ! Do you know how much I want to touch you right now? It's exactly that simple. I'm sober, I'm clean and I love you. Plus together we generate enough electricity to power this whole damned hotel.'

The lady in the sleek ballgown raised a slight smile before smartly stifling it again, choosing not to reply. Her lips were full, red and so conspicuously kissable that the hot-blooded poet struggled to concentrate on what else he might say to convince her. In an effort to limit his distraction, he brought his mind back to the fact that she still hadn't explained why her relationship with Peter Elswick was sanctioned while he was out of bounds.

'So... You can go out with that pommy bloke, but you can't go out with me? Why is that? What does he have that I don't? Forget your dad for a minute. Am I not good enough for you either anymore? Even now, with everything that's happened?'

This awful home truth was far too difficult to explain away, Lynn realised, instantly driven to the verge of tears. She had prepared for this question before their awkward breakfast date, knowing that photographs of the blond pair had been plastered all over the television and magazines. She could only imagine how seeing them together must have made Jeff feel, having kept his promise to the letter. He hadn't asked the question that morning, and yet now here it was; front and centre, inescapable.

'It's nothing to do with whether you're good enough, or who's better than whom. I don't love Pete. In fact, he's leaving tomorrow, and we'll probably never see each other again. But that's the only kind of boyfriend I can have right now. It's a using relationship, Jeff. I remember what you used to say very well. I just need a using relationship at the moment and I've actually become quite good at them. Could you have one with me? I don't think so. What we had before is impossible now.'

No, absolutely not! A using relationship was definitely not what the devoted songwriter had in mind. This was something he understood, and he hung his head, feeling as if he had been punched in the stomach. Jesus! This smart woman had called his bluff, damn it. He cursed the alarming regularity with which his own words came back to haunt him. Those early, dangerous and intimate conversations with his naïve schoolgirl seemed a long, long time ago, and he was at least flattered to hear her quote him, even if it was to make the opposite point.

A wry grin spread across his face. 'Whoa! That's very good,' he sighed. 'You just shot me with my own gun.'

The physical attraction bleeding out of the millionnaire's every pore was beginning to overwhelm him. He watched as the superstar's supple, sexy shoulders with their shoestring straps sunk ever so slightly as his self-deprecating humour relaxed them both. He felt grateful when this tiny giveaway sign was followed by a shy smile from the tanned and radiant face.

'Listen to me, you gorgeous thing,' he requested, by now making no attempt to hide his lust. 'You can have whatever you want. Just don't tell me we're nothing without finding out for sure.'

Stroking Lynn's face and tracing his highly-sensitised fingers along her neck and then across her right collarbone, Jeff felt her muscles twitch at his touch. It had not been surprise which had made her jump so violently earlier. The spark was still there. No doubt about it.

'Tell me you don't feel anything,' his deep, sultry voice whispered in her ear. 'I dare you.'

The nineteen-year-old straightened up, gulped and breathed in sharply, as if trying not to cry. 'Jeff, don't. This isn't fair. I can't do this,' she blurted out. 'My father's told me he's found out some disturbing things about your past and he's forbidden me to see you. That's it. Plain and simple.'

Shocked by this sudden admission, the young Sydneysider backed away, a metaphorical dagger piercing his heart. Springing to his feet and causing the chair to rock a few times before righting itself, he threw his arms in the air and roared. Lynn thought his eyes were about to burst out of their sockets.

'Halleluja!' he shouted, spinning round to face her again. 'Finally we get to the real story!'

The young woman craned her neck to follow his imposing presence as he stormed around the end of the table. He looked magnificent in his anger. This was her beautiful black stallion, she was reminded; so wildly indignant at the stance her conservative parents had taken.

Again the staunch sportswoman stood her ground, needing to bring this clandestine standoff to a close. 'But what *is* the real story? Jeff, I don't know the real story. That's why I have to obey my father. I have no way of knowing whether what he knows is the truth or not. You didn't tell me, and now he won't tell me. I'm not a child anymore. You keep reminding me of that. I need to know what it is I'm being protected from by both of you. Can't you see?'

The tall man heaved his leaden frame onto the table and swang his legs to purge the cramp that was steadily sapping his strength. The conflicted celebrity had revealed the magic key to her heart, knowing it would be quite the hardest thing for him to grasp. Even though he had often contemplated disclosing his collection of immured secrets to his dream girl upon their reunion, he had not foreseen being pressured into doing so as a condition of their continuing friendship.

'Christ Almighty!' he exclaimed. 'The ultimate test! Is that it? You're fucking right you're not a child anymore, angel. You are truly formidable! I'll tell you everything, if that's what it takes. Is it? Would that make the difference? Would that make me better than that arsehole out there?'

Lynn was crying now, shaking her head. 'Jeff, please stop. You're too angry to talk about this sensibly now, and we have to go back to the party. This isn't getting us anywhere.'

The despondent man couldn't bear the thought of her returning to the clean-living, middle-classed actor, especially now they finally appeared to be making some progress, but the elegant beauty was right. He couldn't hold her hostage any longer. Her abandoned boyfriend would soon summon security, and then the rock star with the party reputation would be tossed unceremoniously out on his ear like a loutish troublemaker. Such a humiliating fate would worsen his position still further with Big D, not to mention the fun the paparazzi would have in documenting the spectacle.

Jeff calmly sat down opposite the stunning woman again and kissed her wet lips, wiping tears from her face. 'Alright. I'm sorry to kidnap you. Have dinner with me, and I'll tell you everything. Then you can make your choice. Is that fair?'

The graceful princess nodded, relieved that the hot-head had seen reason. The kiss tasted good. Really good. Another was therefore totally out of the question. Looking into his big, brown eyes, she smiled.

'Yes, OK. That sounds good, thanks. I will have dinner with you soon. I'll give you a ring on Friday when I get back to Melbourne. I still have your number on that napkin.'

'Great. Thank you.'

Her lowly serf pushed his chair back and let Lynn stand up in front of him. She adjusted the line of her dress, and he looked on in admiration while his libido had no trouble visualising the perfection hidden underneath. She turned the stiff door handle and exited calmly, with her fellow award-winner following at a respectable distance until she disappeared into the ladies' toilets. Pausing for a moment to take stock of his situation, he eventually turned and dragged himself back into the ballroom to locate his fun-loving guest.

'Where the fuck have you been? You look like shit!' Gerry shouted, as his famous friend approached him on the dance floor, only to be quickly engulfed by a surge of screaming admirers.

A skinny, half-naked brunette was hanging off the older man's shoulders, taking no time in transferring herself into the arms of Australia's hottest new star. Laughing at the pathetic sight, Jeff grabbed hold of flailing arms and re-hooked them over Gerry's shoulders, ignoring the incoherent bleating her mouth attempted to articulate.

'I'm getting out of here,' the dark-haired handsome man told his inebriated business manager. 'You seem to be in control of this situation, so I'll leave you to it. See you in the morning.'

Gerry wasn't at all bothered by his client's impending departure. He gave him a cheesy grin and a thumbs-up sign, and continued propping up his fickle dancing partner. The musician shrugged and walked away from a disappointed throng, shaking his head in a mixture of amusement and frustration. He recollected the sophistication oozing from the lovely Lynn Dyson, wondering how on Earth he could possibly consider himself deserving of her attention.

***

St James' Park was populated by the usual diverse set of nocturnal characters with whom the sleep-deprived rocker was disappointingly familiar; from homeless tramps to drug dealers, and from couples with nowhere else to go for privacy to small gangs of noisy but harmless youths. Too easily recognised, he skirted round the edge of the gardens looking for someone from whom he could score a mood-enhancing chemical or two.

The target of his illicit exchange duly located, Jeff lit a cigarette and began to wander the streets on the far side of the prestigious Sydney Grammar School, where as a teenager he had frequently hung around for the same purpose while waiting for Gerry after Saturday sports. Within fifteen minutes, he had struck a deal and made the transaction with the minimum of fuss, soon armed with a pocketful of amphetamines. He wandered around the park for a while longer, before heading back to the hotel to hook up with his manager's roving harem and indulge in yet another champagne high.

The philosopher's mind raced at a million miles an hour in a frantic effort to make sense of the brief encounter with his delightful dream girl. At least he could now be fairly sure that it was not the gorgeous beauty herself who objected to their reconciliation. The sweeping gaze which had chased him as he moved had been genuine, as had her carefully veiled enthusiasm for their new first kiss.

Rather, the songwriter deduced with a modicum of good cheer, it appeared that the young lady's omnipotent and overprotective father continued to dictate the course of her life. Or might she simply be using her family's embargo as a convenient excuse for rejecting him to save her own reputation? True, she had confessed to having no feelings for the English actor, and her reaction to his touch this evening had confirmed no less immunity to the strength of their physical connection. For both lovers, the spark had certainly endured over the last twenty-four months.

Could he dare believe his own hyperbole? The idea of the ravishing, silver-coated body melting against his hand sent the rock star's sex drive into red alert, and her understated but undeniable reflexes surely deserved the benefit of the doubt. Without this, there was nothing for him to hang on to until her verdict on his sordid past had been presented.

Except, the rueful man contradicted himself gladly, for the possibility that Australia's sweetheart had made that huge, anonymous donation to his charity last year. Had she done it to let him know she still cared? Unable to wait until he had re-joined the party, he lit another cigarette and popped a pill in a dark alley, gulping on his own saliva to ease it down a throat still constricted by lingering panic. So had she or hadn't she?

And now Jeff was doomed to wait until Friday for Lynn's call, or perhaps for longer. Jesus! The way he was feeling now, this might prove an insurmountable feat in itself, not to mention the preparation required to weave his unwholesome revelations into a palatable story. What disturbing facts or suppositions had Bart Dyson uncovered? The gorgeous woman had obviously been given very few clues, and the boy from Canley Vale wondered why her father had chosen not to pass them on. Was it simply overprotectiveness again, or had he come across something so sinister as to warrant keeping from his now adult daughter in perpetuity? The twenty-two-year-old shuddered as he attempted to piece together a version of the truth which wouldn't completely scupper his chances of winning her trust. This was definitely the more impossible task, he cursed.

After an hour or so circling around the emptying city streets in the damp night air, the crazy, mixed-up kid reached his hotel. It was well after midnight, and his instincts advised him to avoid being spotted alone and outside in Sydney this late. Without fail, being back in his home town always reduced him to a bundle of nerves. The lift opening on the eighth floor, he prepared for the next battle. After having crashed his way into the meeting room earlier, getting through his hotel room door ought to have been a breeze. Of course, it wasn't. Several minutes later, about to give up and go directly in search of the others, Jeff remained in the corridor, full of self-loathing and bitter disappointment at the way the evening had ended.

From the other side of the defiant, solid barrier, the dejected man heard the telephone begin to ring inside his room. Who would be calling him at this time? It was unlikely to be his manager, who would never think to check on his whereabouts. Perhaps it was one of those giggling groupies who had adopted him and Gerry after dinner... The entertaining prospect would undoubtedly help to push the night-time hours past. Of the many perks accompanying his newfound fame and fortune, the celebrity could certainly do with one of those convenient hormone release opportunities that invariably landed in his lap, so to speak. Christ, he could really do with someone paying him some undivided attention right now.

Pitting his raging carnal urges against the demons in his mind, the young man braced himself once more and pushed the key into the lock. The ringing started again, and he used its urgency to spur him on. Sweating and out of breath, he turned the key, flung himself inside and slammed the door just as the answering machine kicked in.

'Jeff, it's Lynn. Sorry to ring so late...'

The struggling superstar's heart leaped into his mouth in fear, his brain freezing in unbearable pain. Lynn? What had happened to her? His immediate conclusion was that she was in danger. Had the squeaky-clean English actor harmed her in some way, as punishment for leaving him alone at the party? If so, it would be his fault. Guilt on so many levels clanged in his ears, heightened by the barbiturates in his system. He lunged for the telephone, hoping to catch the call before she hung up.

'Lynn, are you still there?' he shouted, unable to hear anything clearly above the panic.

'Oh, Jeff! You're back.'

The normally self-assured voice sounded shaky and surprised to hear from him. Breathing deeply, the perplexed songwriter fought to slow his heart rate and stem the dizziness before it felled him to the floor.

'Are you OK? Where are you?'

'I'm in my hotel room. Yes, I'm OK, thanks. I didn't know if you'd be there.'

'What's happened?' Jeff continued. 'How did you know where I'm staying?'

Paranoia was rife, adding to the cocktail of emotions. He couldn't help but be wary, such was the state of his troubled mind. Further down, his sex drive ratcheted up higher and higher until it reached knife-edge proportions. If Peter Elswick had hurt his dream girl, there were soon to be a whole bunch more cardinal sins for him to atone.

Lynn became calmer and even seemed to be giggling a little. 'You're so sweet. I'm fine. You always think of everyone else before yourself.'

Nothing seemed clear any more. Jeff gripped his throbbing temples and pressed in hard to relieve the pressure. Had the sophisticated young lady been taking drugs too? She sounded a little high, especially compared to when he had left her less than two hours ago. Was it even Lynn Dyson on the line? He couldn't dismiss the possibility that a journalist or photographer hadn't witnessed their dance floor scene and was now attempting to steal a scoop.

'What's going on?' he asked again, more suspiciously this time. 'Lynn, are you OK? You don't sound OK.'

There was a long pause, punctuated by the echo of his rapid heartbeat, before the twenty-two-year-old heard what sounded like crying. He remained silent, waiting for the caller's reply.

At the other end of the line, Lynn couldn't contain her feelings any longer, sobbing into the mouthpiece. 'No, I'm not OK really. I'm sorry for what I said earlier, Jeff. Will you come to my room, please? I need to talk to you. I'm sorry about everything. You were right. I do love you. I love you *so* much.'

The disquieted man's head span. It certainly sounded like Lynn. And the old Lynn, at that. Not the polished and practised celebrity, but the honest and earthy teenager whom he had known before. *Cool it*, he urged his libido. It was he who was on drugs. Could he trust his own muddled senses? Maybe he had simply heard what he wanted to hear? The musician tried to figure out if he was hallucinating as a result of the stress.

'Lynn, are you sure you're OK? Where are you?'

'In the same hotel as you. We all are,' the showbusiness veteran told him, seeming to relax a little. 'Room five-one-six. Please could you come down? Or up? I don't know which floor you're on. I'd really like to talk to you.'

So Jeff had heard correctly. This was no crank call. He scratched the room number down on the notepad next to the telephone. At this point, he no longer cared what had happened. Whatever the reason for her call, he had no qualms about facing the consequences. All he cared about was that Lynn wanted to see him.

'Sure. Give me ten minutes, OK? I'll be right there,' he agreed and replaced the receiver.

The impatient rock star was still reeling in disbelief as he stripped off and prepared for the fastest shower of his life. He hurriedly squeezed out some toothpaste and began brushing his teeth with his left hand, while his right set about jerking off the overpowering tension in his balls which had been nagging at him since the award ceremony's opening act.

Jeff gasped involuntarily, lost in fantasies of blonde hair, long legs and pert breasts, when the tip of his penis bumped into the cold marble, and he shared a joke with his reflection at the bizarre circumstance. What a ridiculous scenario, but entirely warranted! The footsoldier had been summoned to the princess' chamber, but the last thing he ought to do when he arrived was bundle her straight into bed. The unexpected encounter about to unfold in the next hour needed to be one-thousand percent perfect. He couldn't afford to let his ragged and unquenched desire take control of what was shaping up as the most significant moment of his life.

The compulsive man knew his spaced-out brain would be hopelessly incapable of concentrating on Lynn's predicament, much less applying some intelligence to working out a strategy for being together, when his body's sole interest was in fucking her brains out. Moreover, if all the lady required from her peasant was for him to throw her down onto the sheets and take her to heaven, the chance of being unable to deliver the goods all over again was a big, fat zero! Stepping into the shower and flicking on the taps, Jeff stood with his back against the tiles and climaxed in less than twenty seconds of wild rush, calling her name into the strong jet of water. Lynn's needs must be his absolute priority. His future depended on it.

The good-looking musician dressed again in the same shirt and suit, towelled his hair dryish and combed it roughly, before splashing on some after-shave. He forced his brand new shoes back onto wet feet, knowing instantly that it was a mistake but without time to find clean socks. Neither was there time to order chilled champagne nor to purloin even a single red rose. He would rock up empty-handed, like in the old days. His charm alone had sufficed back then, when his dream girl had been but a susceptible sixteen-year-old schoolgirl. Would the same plan still work on the refined and worldly nineteen-seventy-four model? Simplicity, raw passion and old-fashioned *chutzpah* would have to do.

With only a smidgen less testosterone and probably a notch or two more adrenaline running through his veins than before his record-breaking ejaculation, Jeff hurriedly left a note for Gerry under the door of the next room. He scrambled three levels down the fire escape staircase, at least two steps at a time, not willing to waste time waiting for the lift and risk being caught for autographs and photographs again. He chose right over left by the sequence of the room numbers in the corridor which extended into the distance, where to his relief room five-one-six was the one with sufficient light shining into the corridor to let him know the door had been left slightly ajar.

Castigating his overly-suspicious mind for considering he might be about to fall into Bart Dyson's premeditated trap, in which his daughter was either willingly or unwillingly complicit, the lost boy was pleased not to have to fight with another solid door tonight. He almost broke into a run down the fifty metre stretch of hypnotic, patterned carpet, running a hand through wet hair and taking a deep breath.

This is it, mate. Don't fuck it up.

When Jeff reached the doorway, the room's sole occupant was already waiting like a marble statue in front of him, dressed in a short, silk nightdress and with her long, golden hair falling down over her shoulders. Framed by a subtle glow from the bedside light, Lynn Dyson looked more like an angel than ever to the ecstatic songwriter. It was a real-life portrait; an image that was to stay with him for the rest of his life.

Smiling, the handsome stranger held out his arms, and his dream girl walked into them. Her eyes were shining with unshed tears, and her hands caught hold under his ribcage. After a stealthy scan of the large room to dismiss the possibility of an ambush, he pushed the door closed behind him with his foot. The fated pair stood locked together for the longest time, breathing antagonistically against each others' desire.

'Jeff, I'm so sorry,' Lynn began, leaning back and staring up into his dark, searching eyes. 'I was...'

Her voice tailed off, at the behest of kind eyes. A quiet composure had already descended over the grateful romantic, who tenderly placed the fingers of his left hand over her pleading mouth and rested his lips on her forehead. He had been granted the single wish he had sought through the tumult of the preceding two years, and his reward was rendered yet sweeter by time standing still.

'Let's not talk about it,' he suggested, turning quickly to flick the deadlock on the door handle. 'I want to make love with you more than anything in the world. We can sift through the wreckage tomorrow.'

'Oh, I'd love that,' the young woman exhaled, smiling through her tears at the colourful language she had missed so much.

Still only having made it as far as the narrow hallway leading from the door to the bedroom, Jeff felt strong hands slip backwards inside his suit jacket and brush his sides, as they travelled round his body to take their long-awaited and deliciously familiar place over his kidneys. Her fingers tucked themselves in under his belt, and the couple kissed passionately, over and over again.

The rock star realised that his former schoolgirl must have grown quite a bit taller during their separation when she took hold of the lapels of his jacket and lifted it effortlessly off his shoulders. Not wanting to interrupt this exquisite dance, he shook its sleeves down off his arms and caught it before it fell to the floor. He then walked his partner backwards a few paces and, leaning her over to her left with a wink and a half-smile, threw the jacket over the back of a chair, never once breaking away from her mouth.

He discerned the tiniest sniff of appreciation and felt her lips smile against his. *No, I haven't lost my touch, lady,* his inner voice transmitted, as her body's total surrender let him know exactly how firmly his provocative moves had registered. No need to worry about winning *its* trust at least, regardless of the challenges that lay ahead... Jesus, it was good to be home!

Lynn held her long-lost lover so very close as she shed all the tears she had been storing up for the last few months. There were so many questions he wanted to ask, but the empathetic man decided simply to let her cry it out for now. Finally she turned her head to one side and leaned on his shoulder, leaving him to relish the feeling of his wet shirt sticking to the hairs on his chest.

'Do you want me to take this off?' she asked, deep blue eyes looking up into his, her fingers tugging at her nightdress.

A large, gentle hand slipped behind her blonde head and coaxed it back down against his clavicle. 'No. Not yet,' he whispered, savouring the warmth of her laboured breaths. 'I want to take as long as I can to reacquaint myself with you.'

Both charged with unspoken feelings, the two Australian superstars kissed again, their bodies pressed together to eliminate any last doubt in their intentions. Glancing down to the floor as he ran his hands down the slender frame and feeling the silk glide over her lean contours, Jeff caught site of Lynn's bare left foot with its painted toenails. It looked small and vulnerable next to the gleaming, black dress shoe which was pinching the back of his right heel spitefully.

'Look down,' he requested, drawing her attention to their feet. 'What does that picture say to you?'

The young woman's eyes darted downwards for a few moments and then up again to respond to his question, confident she knew the answer. She trembled a little, recalling the power this man had to draw her in.

'Control freak,' she replied with a grin, tears again welling into her eyes.

Elated, Jeff kissed her, this time with much more urgency. He recognised the small scar on her bare foot, having been told it was the result of an injury she had sustained as a child when a horse had trodden on her in the stables. The memory reminded him of the blissful times they had spent at the Benloch dam.

Lynn Dyson and Jeff Diamond were once again connected. His right hand slipped down her side to stroke the sensitive skin on her upper thigh, inching ever closer to paradise, while his left cupped her breast in its palm. Their tongues tasted each others' longing, and his erection stood engorged against her abdomen, fighting the urgency encouraged by her fingers.

'So have you found your freedom yet?' he ventured, guiding her chin upwards with both hands.

The nineteen-year-old paused for a second before responding. In truth, she wasn't quite sure.

'I'm getting there,' she answered with some reservation. 'I made a mistake a while ago. Pushed my luck with Dad. That set me back a bit.'

The philanthropist's insides were thrown into renewed turmoil, yearning to resolve this lingering unknown. 'Did it have anything to do with a donation?'

Lynn gave a subtle nod, joy flashing from her eyes, and the air in the room momentarily chilled. Message received and understood.

So the gesture had been made and accepted as originally intended, and its significance wholly appreciated by both. Jeff kissed her again and pulled her in as tightly as he possibly could, the depth of emotion rapidly overwhelming him.

'Thank you,' he replied, closing his eyes and feeling the sting of his own tears. 'Let's go to bed.'

Steering the slim sportswoman around to the right, her lover led her backwards and set her down gently on the covers. The events of the last weeks, days, hours had left him stressed to the max', and he barely had any sensation left in his shoulders and neck owing to the knotted muscles which were as solid as concrete under his skin. Every fibre in his body wanted her, and there was absolutely no doubt she wanted him too.

The musician winced as he prised the shoes off his sockless feet. Lynn frowned in sympathy at the ruddy blisters over his Achilles tendons, but any pain was soon forgotten once her nightdress lifted over her head. He feasted his eyes on the body about which he had been fantasising for so many months. It had transformed from adolescent into adult in all the right places.

Appreciating every sight, sound and touch now before him, Jeff moaned long and low with contentment. He brushed the underside of her breast before blowing on his fingers to tell this beautiful woman just how hot she was. Kneeling on the bed, he reached into his pants' pocket for the string of condoms snatched at the last minute from his hotel bathroom and raised it up to Lynn's eye level, twirling it triumphantly in his fingers.

'You look sensational,' he told her, turning off the bedside lamp. 'Shall we use one of these?'

'You don't have to,' the goddess replied, a little surprised but thankful for his concern. 'I'm still taking the pill.'

Her handsome peasant smiled a little shamefully. The adult Lynn Dyson spoke with the confidence of someone substantially more selective about her sexual partners than he had been.

'Just in case,' he grinned. 'And besides, it'll give us something to look forward to.'

The rock star unbuttoned his shirt and peeled it off, tossing it onto the floor behind him. Lynn immediately leaned forward to kiss an expanse of toned, hairy pectoral muscle, following this with a remarkably assertive left hand which drew his mouth to hers while her right began to undo his suit trousers. Her fingers ran tantalisingly along the length of his penis, gripping it through the silky fabric of his boxer shorts. Wrestling her hand away, Jeff slipped backwards off the mattress and discarded the rest of his clothes.

'You're what I'm looking forward to,' the blonde beauty claimed, a wide smile having replaced the tears.

'Steady,' Jeff warned her, rolling on the condom and desperately trying to keep his arousal in check. 'I'd like this to last more than thirty seconds, if you don't mind. Wouldn't you?'

The beautiful woman nodded childishly, making her man's heart sing. Nothing had been lost in the two long, intervening years since the duo had last been in this position. Their natural timing and sexual affinity were alive and well, and the lithe, tanned body he had dreamed of touching for so long was once again within his grasp. He lowered himself down onto his back, and

Lynn followed his cue, straddling his thighs and stroking him firmly. Hungry hands reached up to take hold of her shoulders, pulling her down to lay on top of him. Without another word, they were united.

The mood in this anonymous bedroom on the fifth floor of the Intercontinental Hotel was stifling with expectancy, broken only by the occasional light-hearted remark or excited utterance. Both were intent on making this renewal so very special, taking turns to pause and absorb its significance. On Lynn's face was that same speculative gaze which educed myriad more memories from their first tentative times together.

Its power took Jeff by surprise. 'What?' his eyes asked.

'Nothing!' the movie star replied out loud, sitting up again. 'I can't believe it's you. That's all.'

'*Soy yo,*' the boy in him smiled, beckoning her back down. 'It was a long, slow wait for this restless heart, angel, but we made it.'

Making love while wound so tightly was like driving with the handbrake on. The sounds of Lynn's pleasure flowed like warm, cleansing oil pouring into his brain, and those strong, coveted hands were soft yet purposeful as they helped the smooth liquid seep into the gaps between his tired bones. The fervent man didn't care if it took the rest of the night to bring this sublime act to its conclusion. A dose of suspended animation was just what they needed.

Both were exhausted but completely entranced at the climax, and the satisfied man collapsed onto the mattress heavily next to his golden-haired dream girl.

'Hey!' she cried out. 'Are you trying to bounce me off the ceiling?'

Jeff didn't even have the strength to laugh, barely managing a smile, but her levity was welcome. He reached for her hand in the dark.

'OK. So sex still works,' he quipped. 'I guess that was always going to be the easy part, but I'll take it anyway.'

Grateful to be back in the presence of this most exotic and electrifying of lovers, Lynn cuddled into the warmth of his skin and drank in the silence. She was convinced she had done the right thing, even though there would be hell to pay once her parents found out. How exhilarating it was to be once more in the company of this sensuous powerhouse of a man!

'I never stopped thinking about you,' she murmured out of the blue, her soft voice jolting her partner out of his drowsy contentment.

'Thanks. That's nice to know. Me neither. But you know that already.'

The young woman continued. 'I used to think about how I was becoming like you. You know... Living a lie, with a nice, polished veneer on life. I'd be doing all these exciting things, meeting interesting people and getting lots of praise, *et cetera*. And then I'd go home and wish I could swap it all for a night back at Admin with you. Trading songs and talking, talking, talking.'

Jeff squeezed her hand. It was all he was capable of contributing at this juncture. The latest model Lynn Dyson wasn't so different after all from the girl who had left him behind.

The effusive teenager continued. 'My friends all assumed you were well and truly over me, with all the publicity...'

'Hmm...' he moaned, unable to defend such an aspersion. 'Yep. I guess it'd look that way to the untrained eye.'

Lynn laughed. 'That's what I was going to say. I just held on to the hope that I knew you better.'

'You did. I love you, Lynn. I will always love you.'

'Are you OK?' the relaxed songstress sounded concerned. 'You're too quiet.'

'Sorry. Yeah,' he managed to cough his vocal chords awake. 'I'm spent. Totally, absolutely, utterly spent. I'll be back to my old self in a few minutes, I promise.'

The amphetamines were working their way out of his system, not helping his lacklustre mood. The musician remembered the small polythene sachet still secreted in the inside pocket of his jacket. He considered popping another pill to perk himself up, but knew this would take him to the opposite extreme, so decided against it. His virtuous companion was unlikely to tolerate such a ridiculous tactic, should she find out. He didn't even want to chance a bottle of beer, lest he unwound the magic spell which had ensnared them.

Lynn turned over to stroke the handsome face of Australia's hottest rock star. His jawline was tense, and his eyes were closed. Half a day's growth on his chin somehow made him look even more exhausted, but its coarseness was oh, so inviting to the touch. She too was overjoyed by the happy memories that she could finally allow back into her imagination and marvelled at how much she had underestimated her feelings for Jeff Diamond.

'So how old are you now?' she asked.

Another souvenir conversation revisited, and her bedfellow's weary soul warmed a few more degrees. One corner of his mouth curled upwards in a smirk, and he opened his right eye.

'You know... You're the same age now as I was when we met.'

'Yes, I do know,' the young woman affirmed, clearly waiting for a response to her question.

'How old am I now?' Jeff mused. 'Well... Before dinner, ninety-eight.'

'Ninety-eight?' she exclaimed, thrilled to have his peculiar sense of humour back.

'And right now, probably about fifteen,' he added, taking her by surprise by tickling her ribs with his left hand and laughing as she tried to wriggle away from his already refuelling engine.

'Hey!' she laughed. 'Stop it. I'm serious.'

Jeff stopped just as suddenly and lay motionless again. 'And most likely sometime during the night, I'll shoot up to about two-hundred-and-three.'

Lynn said nothing, her silence the only acknowledgement required. His melancholy would have affected her more if her attention hadn't been diverted to his growing erection. The many faces of her Catholic Argentinean Polish Jew were gradually revealing themselves once again, evoking a deep desire in her too. She suddenly realised he was staring at her while she stared at him. Again he winked, and again her heart melted.

'But by morning, hopefully back around the seventy-two mark,' the forthright man concluded.

'OK. Thanks,' Lynn sighed. 'That gives me a good idea of how you are. Things aren't getting any easier then, obviously. I hoped they would be. We should get some sleep.'

Jeff chuckled, watching her gaze alight on his turgid penis. Did she really want him to turn over and go to sleep? With any luck, this was the beginning of another long and fruitful relationship, but his wounded psyche was not about to surrender the present opportunity too easily.

'Sleep?' he challenged. 'Why? We've got a lot to catch up on.'

Lynn cuddled into her old friend's side and stroked the hairs on his torso, having forgotten how voracious his sexual appetite was. Every so often, she shivered as he kissed the delicate skin beneath her hairline, sending minuscule currents both up and down her spine. How delicious the sensation was, and so long overdue... Sex didn't feel like this with Peter, nor with anyone else she had known. It felt as though she belonged close to this man; almost as if they were occupying the same skin. Surely this was meant to be. She shifted her head sideways towards his, noticing deeper, slower breaths, and gently withdrew her fingers from his stomach.

'Where'd you go?' It was almost a threat.

The young woman gulped, swiftly returning her hand to its former location. She was suddenly overcome with emotion at his immediate repose as soon as her touch was reinstated, feeling her fingers encased in the warmth of his own. 'Oh, my God,' she whispered. 'Nowhere. I'm still here. Wow, sorry. I remember you. My heart remembers you so well.'

'*Gracias*, angel. I love you, and my heart remembers you too.'

'I tried not to think about you for so long.'

'Yeah, I bet. I gave that a go for a while as well,' the boy from Canley Vale whispered against her forehead, 'but I couldn't stop thinking about you.'

His compassionate *Regala* shuffled closer, crying softly. 'Oh, I love you. Thank you. Are you OK?'

'Yeah. Never better. Except my hand wants to crush your fingers.'

'What? Why?' she saw a mischievous expression on his face. 'No more piano-playing, no more tennis. Go right ahead!'

Jeff turned onto his right side so that he could look into her eyes. 'Great, thanks. Only sex from now on. Is that OK with you?'

Lynn stole a kiss. 'Of course! Not that you're selfish or anything?'

'Jeez, I love you so much,' her boyfriend chuckled. 'I just want to inhale you. I need all of you inside me again. Like it was before.'

'That's a lovely thing to say.'

'So have I changed?' he asked, once more serious.

'No, you haven't really changed. A bit bulkier and more stylish, but otherwise, no. Have I?'

A long, muscular arm winged its way overhead and wrapped itself behind her shoulders, pulling her mouth towards his. 'About the same, I'd say, except substitute bulkier with taller.'

His lover giggled. 'That's a relief! I love you. You're so gorgeous. Are you going home in the morning?'

Jeff nodded. 'Thanks. You are too. Gorgeous, I mean.'

The celebrity let out a sunny laugh. 'I was going to ask how you know when I'm going home!'

'My flight's at ten-thirty. Gerry's staying over the weekend, catching up with mates and family.'

Lynn patted his chest lightly, before being smothered into a fierce embrace. 'Oh, yes!' she gasped for air. 'I forgot Gerry was here. I saw him on the balcony with you. That was a nice touch, the shampoo. How is he? Still the same?'

The songwriter sniffed. 'Yeah. Still the same. I left him tonight with a very worse-for-wear-looking girl hanging round his neck on the dance floor. Did you know he's my manager?'

'Really? I think I did read that somewhere a while ago, yes. That's great. He'd be a good manager,' the singer answered with an approving grin.

The twenty-two-year-old was beginning to regain consciousness and found the young woman's gentle conversation energising. The aloof attitude from the other morning was nowhere to be seen, and two years had all but vanished in the time it had taken them to make love. Once more for luck, he thought, coaxing her hand downwards.

'He is,' Jeff confirmed. 'He's got an amazing business brain. I'll let you into a secret too...'

Lynn sat up onto her elbow. 'What?'

Her lover raised his left-hand index finger and touched her lips. His expression instantly heeded, the blonde beauty reached over to the bedside table and tore off another packet from the string of condoms. She grimaced as the nasty taste seeped out onto her lips when she tried to tear it open with her teeth.

'Give me that!' her partner shook his head. 'Don't you remember anything I taught you?'

The boy from Sydney's west knew only too well what a red rag this would be to the alpha female. Out of practice when it came to his mind games, Lynn rose to the bait and blushed as soon as she realised her mistake. He descended on her naked body, growling menacingly, and began to kiss and caress every available square inch of skin. Lynn moaned in pleasure, responding helplessly to his touch.

Hunger sprang from each one of the young woman's kisses. 'Oh, Jeff. I've missed this so much. I made myself forget how good you can make me feel. And I'm so comfortable around you too. Unbelievably so... I was relaxed with Peter, but this is so much easier.'

The man who had been such a thorough teacher suddenly put the brakes on, pulling out of her warm, moist vagina and flopping down onto the mattress by her side, breathing heavily. 'You cannot believe how good it is to hear you say that, angel. I hope you're more than just comfortable, but I know what you mean. It's natural.'

'Mmm,' the blonde beauty grabbed for his penis, steering it to where it belonged. 'That's a much better word. It is natural. Make love to me, Jeff. You're the only one who can make me feel this way.'

Fighting his emotions, the visitor did as she requested. 'D'you remember the time when I took you from special to normal in the space of a few hours?'

'Yes!' the smiling teenager exclaimed, hugging him with renewed energy.

'Well, I guess comfortable's on the same scale,' he grinned. 'Not exactly the greatest accolade, on the face of it, but under the circumstances, it's something to celebrate.'

His intractable tears brought on some of her own, and the reunited lovers rode each other as if nothing else was important in the whole world. How right did this feel? Whatever were to befall them in the days to come, neither cared to think beyond tonight, and the superstar's screams were only beaten in intensity by the satisfied roar of a man who was exactly where he wanted to be.

After the ardent lovers had transported themselves to heaven for the second time, the handsome stranger manœuvred his trembling body off the bed and slid the door to the tiny balcony across to enjoy a quick cigarette.

'You don't have to smoke outside,' came the sweet voice of his lover.

'Yeah, I do. Just give me a minute, angel.'

The night had chilled down, and the sky above Jeff's head was clear. Winter had been banished from Sydney, as always a few weeks earlier than his more southerly, adopted home. Lynn's room was on the other side of the hotel to his own, overlooking the very park where he had retreated during his prior confusion.

Back in the semi-darkness of the bedroom, Lynn smiled to herself. The wise man was right. They needed space. What a huge moment they had just shared! Watching him leaning over the railing and taking an opportunity to ogle the muscular shoulders, buttocks and legs of this intoxicating specimen, she waited for a few minutes before joining him in the not-so-fresh air. He laughed out loud when he saw the opened bottle of beer in her hand, covered in condensation due to the change in temperature between the mini-bar and the night air. His power over Lynn Dyson had certainly endured.

'OK, OK! I know what you're thinking,' the teenager put her hands on her hips. 'And I agree. I'm a sucker, I know. In exchange, tell me Gerry's news!'

'Thanks. Sure, but don't breathe a word,' the comic insisted, tipping the bottle to allow the cool liquid to run into his parched gullet. 'He's got a woman pregnant, and she wants to keep the baby.'

The society girl gasped. 'Oh, my God!' she cried with her new, almost-American accent. 'Really? And I suppose he doesn't want to be a father right now. That's awful. Is he going to marry her?'

'No. Can you imagine Gerry as a husband? Poor woman! Fate worse than death. Heather, her name is.'

Lynn's eyes were alive with wonder. This was obviously juicy gossip, and her exhausted entertainer was happy to indulge her whim. It would help him to keep the mood light while he navigated his latest bout of anxious unworthiness.

'So what are they going to do?'

'Don't know. He asked her to have an abortion at first, but she wouldn't. And now she's too far gone. I haven't seen her in weeks. Not sure Gerry has either, to be honest, but he's paying for the hospital and everything. I assume he'll pay maintenance. He's pretty honourable like that, but he won't want anything to do with the kid.'

'Sad for the baby,' the young woman offered.

'Yep,' Jeff nodded, knowing only too well what it was like to grow up without a father's love.

Lynn yawned. 'We should get some sleep. Are you coming back in soon? You've got a second wind now.'

'Yeah. I have, for the moment, but it's a good idea.'

Suddenly distracted, the last-minute guest pointed through the glass, towards the small wardrobe on the other side of the room. Stubbing his cigarette out in the ashtray on the balcony table, he ushered his beautiful conquest back inside. He also noticed that the clock-radio had vanished from the bedside table; another sign of a past revisited.

'Hey! What did you do with Pete? Is he in there? Tied up? Tell me he didn't hurt you after what I did.'

The sleepy woman climbed into bed. 'No! He moved to another room. I asked him to, but he'd already worked it out anyway. He was a bit pissed off at being embarrassed like that, but he was fine with it once I explained. He's a bit narcissistic, actually. Nothing shakes his self-confidence.'

'Thank Christ for that, huh? The man's cleverer than I gave him credit for,' Jeff gave a smirk, before kissing her squarely on the lips. 'You hid the clock. Thanks for remembering.'

His partner nodded coyly. 'I guess it doesn't matter so much when we don't have to get an early start.'

'No, but it's still fantastic that you care.'

'Oh, I care, Jeff.'

Moved by the singer's genuine response, the avid reader lifted a paperback which had been left beside the television. It was "Carrie" by Stephen King, a harrowing horror story from a new writer who had leaped into the bestsellers' lists on *début*.

'Are you enjoying this?' he asked, rousing her from a drowsy state. 'I wouldn't have expected you to buy it.'

'Yes, it's good. I didn't buy it for myself. A friend gave it to me for my birthday. It's a bit too creepy for reading on your own. You've read it, I'm assuming.'

Jeff laughed. 'Yeah. I know what you mean. I saw him interviewed while I was in New York. He wrote it because he was challenged about not understanding women.'

'Really?'

'Yes, really. You sound so American when you say that. I bet your mum doesn't like your new transpacific twang.'

It was Lynn's turn to chuckle, instantly self-conscious. 'Shut up. You're right. Neither does Dad, and Junior teases me too.'

The empathetic world traveller leaned across the mattress and kissed her forehead. 'Well, I think it's very sexy. It's the new you. You've left Melbourne behind and have taken on global citizenship. You've got every right to change the way you speak. It's individually you.'

Lynn shuffled across the bed until she had lined herself up with the dark-haired hunk of a man who now occupied the other half of her bed. He was still so warm, despite having stood outside for the last ten minutes.

'Have you read "Jaws" yet?' she asked.

'No. I want to. Have you?'

'Yes. A bunch of my girlfriends dared each other to read it on the beach in the summer. It was pretty scary.'

'I'm waiting for a library copy.'

The blonde superstar propped her head up on her bent arm and gaped in disbelief. 'You still go to the library?'

Amused by her consternation, Jeff did the same and with a similar level of indignance. 'Yeah. Why not?'

Lynn flopped down again, being immediately pounced upon and smothered with kisses.

'There's no point buying a copy if it's not something I want to keep. I go all the time. It's a sanctuary, to tell you the truth. People don't expect to see me in there and tend to leave me alone if they do see me, because they're not sure it's me. I used to go there and hope to find you, but you were never there.'

His gipsy eyes transmitted the pathos which his voice refused to acknowledge. His beautiful best friend caught her breath, bewitched by the brazen honesty she had all but forgotten.

'I'll go with you again, if you like,' the young woman promised, as if under his spell.

'You will,' he nodded, kissing her again. 'I'll make sure of it.'

'It'll give you closure.'

'It will. And perhaps you too.'

There was more truth in these last four words than the nineteen-year-old was prepared to admit just yet. The bond that had been neglected for so long had taken no time at all to reconstitute itself, which unnerved her somewhat.

Between them, the couple heaved the highly-starched sheet up over their tired bodies. Jeff lay on his back, staring at the ceiling, full of wonder at where he now found himself at the end of an eventful few days. He wondered what might happen next, once they left the confines of their anonymous hotel room.

'When do you get back to Melbourne?'

'I'm recording some television interviews tomorrow afternoon, and then my flight's at ten the next morning, I think.'

The beautiful celebrity was already sounding vague, as if she was on the verge of sleep. Her lover wondered if he should make himself scarce. He shouldn't push his luck too far too soon. However, before he could broach the subject, she turned and answered his prayers with another quiet request.

'Can you stay another night?'

Jeff's heart skipped a beat, a wave of ecstasy drowning him for a few seconds. Had this beautiful woman read his mind? Better words than these he could not have wished to hear. He racked his brain to think of any reason why he needed to return home tomorrow.

'Yes,' he replied. 'I'd love to.'

'Thanks,' Lynn smiled, rolling onto her back and yawning. 'I love you, Jeff Diamond. I love you, I love you, I love you...'

Chuckling at the sleepy woman's sudden exuberance, the humble manchild turned to face this angel whom he had waited so long to meet again. She had returned to her previous repose, as if bereft of all energy, and he gazed at her closed eyelids, scarcely able to believe the perfect way this night had concluded.

'I love you too, gorgeous,' he told her, kissing her unsuspecting lips once more. 'You wouldn't believe how much.'

A smile spread across the young woman's mouth, but her eyes didn't open. Almost asleep himself, Jeff lay on his side, instinctively gripping her biceps with his strong left hand and caressing the sensitive skin of her upper arm with the side of his thumb.

'Oh, that feels so good. Your touch is so wonderful,' the teenager murmured. 'Everyone else's is so wishy-washy compared to yours.'

Jeff chuckled gently and shook his head. '*Everyone* else's?'

Lynn gave a chaste laugh, embarrassed at what she had inadvertently inferred. Her former boyfriend wrapped her up in his arms, intent on never letting go. There was the smallest hint of innocence left, masterfully hidden beneath the refined exterior glaze.

'Miss Dyson, methinks you've been enjoying yourself way too much in California,' her former mentor scolded in amusement. 'I did teach you well...'

But his teenaged treasure was already asleep. On Cloud Nine, the songwriter lay awake for a while, overtired but glowing stupendously inside. How quickly things had turned around! From their tense conversation behind closed doors to the frantic shower after her telephone call, and from the vision waiting for him in the doorway to the angelic nymph who now slumbered peacefully beside him, here was motivation enough to languish on a bed of *cumulonimbus* all night long.

Hell, the dreamer was in a mind never to come down to Earth ever again. How he had missed sharing each and every snippet of information with someone who was on the same wavelength, back in the days when he was the only body she had shared too. The curtains hadn't been drawn to block out the night sky, bedecked with stars and a half-moon. There was nothing wrong about this relationship. Nothing whatsoever. They simply needed a plan to convince Lynn's parents of this fact, and the emotional investment the pair had consigned to their secret allegiance would pay off.

The boy from Sydney's west was only too aware that nothing came for free, but the soul-mates had already paid a high price for their portentous freedom. They had both wasted time living temporary lives, waiting for their destiny to catch them up. If they didn't take this chance, there may never be another during this lifetime. His beautiful best friend's will would soon be sorely tested, of that there was no doubt, but tonight had given her suitor a *soupçon* of the sportswoman's resolve.

Stretching his heavy limbs, Jeff had no desire to find out what time it was, reckoning it had taken about two-and-a-half hours for his fate to change from abject despair to blissful serenity.

Please let it be a one-way street this time, he begged.

Quest For Information

'How did you get in my fucking apartment?' he shouted, centimetres from the other man's face.

Jeff Diamond had Bart Dyson pinned against the wall. In his peripheral vision, he could make out two other men turning over his belongings, stumbling around his apartment aided only by torchlight. A woman was screaming in the background, but the lanky teenager was unable to get past the latest batch of intruders and reach her.

'What are you looking for? You won't find anything here. I'm fucking innocent. What have you done to her, you fucking bastards? Get the hell out of here.'

The angry adolescent let out a loud groan as his fist took aim at his girlfriend's father's All-Australian chin. Why was this hellhole of a flat continually invaded by men intent on doing his family harm? The agony emanating from the bedroom beyond was matched only by the despair in his heart as he embarked on yet another futile attempt to defend those who mattered.

'Leave her alone! Leave her alone!' he barked again.

Lynn woke with a start and grabbed a ghostly arm as it lifted beside her for the second time. It took only a few seconds for her to realise that she had landed right back in the thick of her lover's brutal nocturnal world, shocked by the heat radiating from his writhing body.

'Jeff, stop! You're dreaming! Wake up!' she yelled directly into his ear, shaking him hard.

Was this scene even more violent than the frequent noisy interruptions through which the teenager had lived before, or had her memory faded over time? She was sure that any peaceful slumber previously being enjoyed in the adjacent rooms would have now been shattered by such loud voices, briefly wondering if they might be disturbing people they knew from last night's awards function.

The mumbling, twitching mass which had transported her to heaven only a few hours ago suddenly coughed, and his head flicked sideways into the pillow. The king-sized bed shifted on its castors with the force of his movements, and Lynn could have sworn that someone had just punched him in his dream. She repeated her actions, and this time his eyes fluttered open briefly. One more time should be enough to bring him round.

'Wake up!' the frightened young woman cried directly into the sweat-drenched face. 'Jeff, wake up!'

Her sleeping giant sat bolt upright, drawing in air hard while still swearing at his dream's co-stars. The rasping sound was deafening in the silence of the night, and Lynn was sure he didn't yet know where he was. She lay still and waited for the nightmare to run its course, feeling helpless and desperately sorry for him. What had he been shouting? Something about being innocent and to "leave her alone"... The singer wondered who the woman in this dark dream might be. Her thoughts flew back to the afternoon before she had flown to Sydney and to her father's worrying message.

Sounds and images beginning to fade from his mind, Jeff gradually regained consciousness. He looked around, his eyes alighting on the beautiful woman's silhouette in the pre-dawn shadows. Cursing under his breath, he leaped up and crossed the room, still not totally awake. He leaned both hands on top of the television cabinet to stretch his taut hamstrings and loosen his back muscles. Two or three minutes would have passed before he spoke.

'I bet you missed this,' the furious man growled, without looking round.

'That was a bad one, wasn't it?' Lynn answered, almost asleep again. 'Are you OK?'

Sighing deeply, her tall, handsome lover sat down on the end of the bed, his naked torso still expanding and contracting visibly as he struggled to slow his heart rate. 'Yeah. Thanks. I'm really sorry.'

Jesus! What had he been dreaming about this time? There was no way he was prepared to tell his gorgeous angel about the latest twist to this familiar scenario. How wickedly his memory worked sometimes; melding the past and the present like that. And so soon after their reunion. Couldn't the bastards give him one night off to bathe in the rapture he had rediscovered?

The silk-clad angel stood up and disappeared briefly into the bathroom to refill their water glasses, returning to find her breathless boyfriend sprawled across the blankets at the foot of the bed. Leaving their drinks on the floor until he was ready, she sat down next to him and put her hand on his forehead.

'Wow! You're so hot. Come back to bed, and I'll turn the air-con' on for a while.'

Jeff hauled himself to a sitting position and put a heavy arm round her shoulders. 'You're so hot too,' he managed to smile, hugging her close. 'We make a good pair. If you can stand listening to all this shit again, that is.'

The exhausted songstress fell back to sleep within a few minutes of crawling back under the covers, lulled by the drone of the air-conditioning. Her simmering dreamer leaned against the headboard, desperate to know more about the information Bart Dyson had uncovered and what he might be planning to do with it. It wouldn't have surprised the Sydneysider if Big D's private detectives were more skilled than the New South Wales Police at piecing together evidence. There was a slim possibility that a more diligent level of scrutiny may even work in his favour rather than against him, and he welcomed the prospect of such a peculiar irony. Either way, Lynn would have to know his side of the story sooner or later.

Jeff spoke her precious name out loud to check that she was sleeping soundly. Good. No reaction. Looking around for the remote control, he slipped out of bed and retrieved it from the television cabinet. Purely out of habit, he also retrieved his watch from the dressing table, where it had been cast off hastily in the mad scramble for each others' bodies.

He smiled when he carefully eased his heavy weight back down onto the bed and went to put the watch down onto the glass-topped surface. Lynn's necklace, earrings and hair clips were lying there, sparkling in the shadowy half-light. Peter Elswick was obviously right-handed, and the swift suitor switch had left their common denominator displaced this morning from what must have latterly become her side of the bed.

Still far from drowsy, the anxious twenty-two-year-old turned on the television and hurried to click the volume down as low as it would go. He had become accustomed to using the television for entertainment during the nights' regular re-awakenings and had now become dependent on it. *Boy, it's just one screwed up trait after another with me,* he thought. He found a mindless comedy show re-run from the nineteen-sixties and distracted himself while the beauty beside him slept peacefully.

It had almost reached seven-thirty before Lynn awoke, by which time only a few pages of Stephen King's masterpiece remained for Jeff to re-read. She looked so tempting lying next to him, and the impatient songwriter was eagerly awaiting a third coming. The telephone rang on the bedside table, startling them both.

'Hello?' the nineteen-year-old answered, sitting up quickly and flashing her roommate a wide smile.

He leaned over and kissed her, but she pushed him away playfully. A man's voice could be heard through the tiny speaker.

'It's Pete!' the penitent celebrity mouthed.

Regrettably for the embarrassed woman, this impulsive utterance was her worst mistake. It only served to provoke the tall, dark stranger in her bed, who was feeling uncharacteristically refreshed and frisky for first thing in the morning. The more the she tried to fend him off, the harder he tried to distract her.

'Hi... Yes, thanks. You? Yes, OK. Safe trip back. You too. Good luck with the show. I'm sorry too. I'm sure! OK. Bye, Pete. Bye.'

Lynn pressed the button on the telephone to terminate the call and proceeded to whack her imbecile bedfellow from head to belly with the receiver. He slunk gradually further away, towards the edge of the bed, until the coiled wire connecting the receiver to the telephone was stretched to its limit, sending the base unit flying across the room as well.

'You're horrible,' the star complained, not sure if she should be cross with him or join in the laughter. 'Poor guy! I'm sure he could tell something was going on. How would you have liked it?'

Jeff held his hands up in guilty admission. 'OK. I know,' he agreed. 'It was mean. But funny though! Does it feel weird?'

'What do you mean? Does what feel weird?' she asked, following lively, hypnotic eyes until she found his fingers pointing to her jewellery on the bedside table to his left.

Instantly, the young woman's eyes filled with tears. Her visitor's man-sized watch had been placed around her much daintier ladies' version, with the smaller pieces of jewellery encased inside both circles. It was an emotive still-life image, and a perfect analogy for how she felt this morning; well-protected and part of something whole.

'Oh,' Lynn smiled, wiping her eyes. 'Yes, a little last night. I turned the wrong way a few times. But not this morning, strangely enough.'

'Right answer!' the musician proclaimed in mock arrogance, belying his own highly sentimental reaction. 'You didn't end up on the floor, so that's a bonus. They'd better be happy tears.'

Jeff made another playful grab for her waist, but the athlete was too quick for him, springing aside and heading into the bathroom. They certainly were happy tears, and she trusted his question had been rhetorical. When she returned, he was waiting for her with two cups of coffee made and a cigarette burning in his fingers.

Hiding nothing, he stubbed the last few centimetres out and swilled his mouth with the hot liquid. 'Come here,' he flinched at the broiling sensation, extending his right hand towards her. 'I need to be inside you.'

Lynn took his hand willingly, and they satisfied each other with extreme tenderness until the morning hours were almost into double digits. Even though they had both spent time with many other partners during their time apart, sex between them felt both familiar and exciting. Neither needed to concentrate on remembering what the other liked, and when he brought her to orgasm for the sixth or seventh time, the sportswoman was forced to scream for mercy. Her spontaneous outburst made them both laugh aloud, sending her expert lover immediately over the edge to complete satiation.

'I love you,' Jeff snarled in her ear, breathless and collapsing down onto the mattress. 'You make me feel so good. I'm now officially empty. Fucked to oblivion, baby.'

His partner was also breathing hard, and her face was flushed. 'I love you too. This is very special. I'm sorry it took me so long to realise.'

With their bodies cooling down, the alluring goddess lay on her back next to her very favourite man. His right hand idly traced a line from her thigh, past her hip and across the ticklish skin covering her ribcage, listening to her quiet laughter. Her hand chased his away, and he couldn't muster the energy to object. After a few minutes' silence, he rolled rightwards onto his side, leaning his head of dark, ruffled waves on a crooked arm.

'So... Are we a secret?' he asked, still preoccupied with her father's detective work.

The young woman sighed. Jeff looked utterly edible. He had put on a considerable amount of muscle since they had first known each other, no doubt taking advantage of a personal trainer these days. His skin smelled divine, even after their long lovemaking session. His black hair damp with sweat, those dark, expressive eyes and an unshaven jawline gave him a sultry, very clandestine air.

'Yes. We'll have to be. At least until we see how the land lies with Dad. I think it's sensible, don't you?'

The reprobate nodded, reaching for his cigarettes and lighter. 'Yeah, probably. There's a conversation we have to have. I haven't forgotten.'

'Shhh,' Lynn whispered. 'Not yet. I'd rather we were back in Melbourne with plenty of time to ourselves. Do you want some breakfast?'

'More breakfast?' the comic asked, his eyes widening. 'You're very demanding now you're a grown-up. Ease up on me, lady!'

The pretty celebrity cast him a frustrated glare. 'I forgot what a one-tracked mind you have,' she grinned. 'No. Breakfast of the eating kind. I need to check my diary. It's a bit weird that no-one's 'phoned me, because I've got appointments this afternoon. How's your screenplay, by the way? Aren't you starring in the movie?'

Jeff imagined the messages on his own vacant room's answering machine too. With any luck, the rest of the world had got the message that the reuniting soul-mates needed some privacy, he thought to himself. Lynn placed an order for Room Service, and they lay together for a while longer, watching television and swapping news about their various projects. The airline raised no objection to changing his flight, the clerk's screeching adulation from the other end of the telephone plainly audible to his partner. She rolled her eyes at his casual shrug of apology, realising the boot was well and truly on the other foot this time around.

After breakfast, the award-winning rocker left the star of the show in room five-one-six and ascended in the lift to collect the rest of his belongings and to see if he could track Gerry down. On his way out the door, he left his beautiful best friend with a kiss and a single sheet of hotel notepaper. She needed but a single guess as to what would be written on it, nonetheless thrilled to be right. Here was the first of many lyrics which she imagined already churning in her prolific poet's head. Tearful, she read the five-line stanza a second and then a third time, before folding the piece of paper and slotting it into the internal pocket of her suitcase for safekeeping.

Back on the eighth floor, Jeff braced himself for a reality check. To his amusement however, in his rush to get to Lynn's room last night, he realised he had left his manager's note under the wrong door. What must the people in that room have thought? He couldn't exactly remember the words he had used and hoped he hadn't incriminated anyone.

Getting through his door was surprisingly easy. The aftermath of the morning's nightmare was still fresh in his mind, so perhaps his brain didn't need a further reminder just yet. He dialled Gerry's room number and heard the telephone on the other side of the wall. It answered after several rings.

'Blake.'

'Gez, it's me,' Jeff replied. 'Yes, I'm fine... You? What did you do with that girl? What? Fuck! Are they still there? OK, listen... No, I'll tell you later. Listen, I've changed my flight. I'm not going home 'til tomorrow night... Don't think so... Who cares anyway? I'll be in touch Friday... Good luck with getting your harem out of there! See ya, mate. Enjoy the weekend, and say hi to the family from me. *Adios.*'

The habitual party boy shook his head. Typical, he thought. Left to his own devices, the fun-loving accountant had taken full advantage of his invitation as Jeff Diamond's guest and had ended up with no fewer than three drunken girls in his room, all of whom were currently comatose. He was preparing to check out, and was about to wake them and turf them out into the tail end of their morning after. Such a spectacle was almost worth sticking around for, Jeff smiled, tapping five, one and then six into the telephone's keypad.

'Hello?'

'*Sí. Buenos días. ¿Puedo hablar con la chica más hermosa del mondo, por favor?*' the clown asked in an extra-strong Spanish accent.

Lynn laughed. 'Jeff, is that you? Where are you?'

'*En mi camera,*' he told her, less gringoesque this time. 'Open the door in about ten minutes, please. I'm checking out now and will be up there soon. I've had an idea...'

'OK. That sounds interesting. See you in a few minutes,' the happy nineteen-year-old answered.

True to form, the handsome superstar found the door open when he returned to the fifth floor, having showered and changed into some very smart, tasteful clothes which immediately received the seal of approval from his discerning lady. Lynn herself was dressed in a deep crimson tailored skirt suit, with her hair sculpted and her eyes and lips made up. She looked as if she was bound for her office, like a true businesswoman.

'Jesus Christ! That's a side of you I haven't seen,' her lover gasped, looking her up and down and nodding his own adoring admiration. 'Very, very sexy. I want you to be my boss. I'd behave very badly around a boss like you.'

'Shut up,' the sophisticated woman scolded. 'When do you stop thinking about sex?'

His expression changed from appreciative of her attire to overtaxed by such an outlandish question. 'Mmm... Let me see... Last Sunday evening maybe, when I was choosing what I'd have for dinner. There might have been a few minutes' lapse then?'

Lynn stood on tiptoes to kiss him tenderly. 'Good. I'll remember that when I need to talk to you about something serious.'

'Right you are, ma'am,' the comic agreed. 'Now, d'you want to know what my idea is?'

The contented woman nodded. 'As long as I'm back here by two.'

'Sure. No worries. There's one person I'd really like to let in on our little secret,' he said, looking past her eyes and out of the window, as if collecting his thoughts.

'Gerry?'

'No, not Gerry. I'm not telling him yet. Hey! I'll have you know that there are three unconscious females in his room right this minute. Unbelievable! I don't know where he gets his ideas from.'

The well-bred young lady was a little shocked, although she realised this was foolhardy. She had read many stories of similar antics attributed by tabloid journalists to the man standing right in front of her, leaving no reason to expect that his loyal *amigo* had been excluded.

'Wow! That's very rock star. I've no idea where he'd get his ideas from either... Do you wish you were there?'

Jeff gave her a hurt look, wondering again where his adult dream girl's tolerance lay on such matters of vice. Of course he had enjoyed more than his fair share of drug binges, bedding multiple women at once and sharing the spoils of celebrity with his growing entourage. Would she ever believe he was ready to throw all that away for her? He damned well hoped so.

'What do you reckon? I've been doing that sort of fucked-up shit for two long years. I'm over it, baby.'

'Sorry,' Lynn frowned sweetly. 'Sorry to cast you in the same mould. I'm very glad you were here instead.'

The young man hugged her, filled with shame. How effortlessly he could persuade people of his supposed sainthood, when such depravity had been his *modus operandi* for so long. His worthiness was overinflated, and he wasn't so arrogant as to miss the hint of sarcasm in the Australian aristocrat's tone.

'It's OK. I have been just as bad... much worse, and way more often, in fact... of which you must already be well aware. Many, many times more. I'm not going to judge him. He's my mate and he works bloody hard for what we've built.'

Smiling, the young woman again raised up onto her toes to kiss his stubbly cheek, and he quickly gathered her body close. This man was so easy to forgive, particularly when he was trying so valiantly to hide his insecurities. He always had been easy to forgive, and didn't he know how to play on her sympathy! Regardless, she was curious to discover the identity of the mystery person Jeff wanted to tell about their getting back together.

'So who are we going to tell our secret to?'

'I'd like to see if we can have lunch with Gerry's mum, Celia,' he answered. 'She'll be totally trustworthy. She's kept some of my secrets for years. *¿Qué te parece?*'

The singing star liked the idea. She recalled Jeff speaking fondly of Celia Blake on several occasions, saying that she was the only significant female he had known in his formative years.

'That sounds fine. I'd like to meet her. Do you think it's too short notice?'

Jeff walked towards the telephone. 'Can I?'

The celebrity was not expecting him to ask, given his new, influential status. This man always had been unfailingly respectful, and after her *sojourn* in the assertive Californian culture, she wasn't used to such deference these days.

'Can you ring Celia or can you use the 'phone?'

'Both,' he replied with a coy grin.

Lynn nodded. 'Of course. You don't have to ask.'

'Oh, yes, I do,' he assured her, dialling a string of numbers from memory and waiting for the call to connect.

'Celia!' the sonorous voice greeted his best mate's mother. 'How the devil? I'm fine. What about you? And the old man? Good. Yeah, sorry, I know... I'm in Sydney... Yes. Well, that's why I'm ringing. Yeah. Did you see it? Your son was my date. He was radiant and so dignified... Ha! You're not wrong! Anyway, are you anywhere near the city today? Can I buy you lunch? There's somebody I'd like to introduce you to... Wait and see! Yes, but you'll have to keep it a secret. That's the one non-negotiable condition of this impulsive wave of generosity... Sure. We can get to Manly. OK... No, I don't know it, but we'll find it easily enough... Twelve noon is good... Thanks, Celia. See you then. *Adios.*'

Jeff turned to his dream girl with a triumphant look on his face, brandishing a leaf he had torn off the notepad, presumably where he had scribbled the name of Celia's restaurant choice. Listening to his sudden effusiveness, Lynn was also reminded of how wide his emotional spectrum spread, and how easy it was both to please him and to send him into a depressive spiral. None of these challenges frightened her this time around, and she wasn't entirely sure why.

'She'll have guessed it's you already,' he smiled, hugging the pensive woman close. 'They watched the awards, so she'll be able to work it out. We have to get to Manly by midday.'

The blonde beauty kissed him. 'We can do that. Do you fancy a coffee?'

'You bet! I don't feel dressed up enough to be having coffee with my boss. Do you want me to put a tie on?'

'No, you idiot! I'll change now that we're going to lunch first,' his lover laughed. 'I don't need to be your boss until two-thirty. Shall we rent a car? Then we don't have to worry about coming back here too early.'

'Great idea,' Jeff agreed, loving how naturally they had fallen back into their easy relationship, discounting the regrettable inevitability of nightmares.

Lynn telephoned the *concièrge* while in a state of undress, a sight which ignited her attendant lunch companion's sex drive yet again. He partook in some lewd and immature fun, wondering if the man on the other end could pick up the fact that he was speaking to the world's most beautiful woman while she was clothed only in *lingerie*. She was very cosmopolitan these days, he remarked to himself. There was still a lot for him to learn about life in among the rich and famous.

'No Aston Martins in stock,' the confident celebrity reported, fastening her blouse and frowning at his lecherous gaze.

'For Christ's sake!' her boyfriend exclaimed, reaching for her eagerly but being summarily pushed away. 'What sort of hotel is this? Everything about you turns me on. Let's get that coffee before you end up having to get changed again.'

Their *sojourn* in the hotel bar lasted for an hour, mainly because the carefree couple still had so much to catch up on. Lynn apologised again for being so unfriendly and for refusing to listen to her own heart. Jeff apologised in turn for his aggressive behaviour and language. She told him what it had been like to star in a James Bond film. He told her about his songwriting collaborations, how he had drunk and smoked his way through his various tours and how much he adored European cities.

'You really haven't changed at all,' his dream girl affirmed, her face bathed in the sunlight from an open window.

'Neither have you,' the nobody from the western suburbs replied with a grateful wink. 'Taller. Sexier. More of everything, in fact, but not changed.'

The modest young woman looked away, clearly flattered by his observations. Now wearing a classy flowing skirt, the colour on her lips had been toned down for their casual appointment, with only her eyes remaining shaded for sophistication. They made her man's whole body buzz with latent excitement, a condition he made no attempt to obscure. His fingers played incessantly with his cigarette lighter or the menu or the spoon resting on his coffee saucer, and the idea of this restlessness being in anticipation of their next encounter aroused Lynn too.

'Except I'm no longer a child,' she reminded him.

Jeff shook his head, throwing her a compassionate half-smile. 'Angel, you were never a child.'

'So we're the same then.'

'Yep.'

Lifting her coffee cup to her lips, the superstar sighed happily and reached her spare hand over to caress the stiff fabric of his shirt cuff. 'You dress differently. This is really nice.'

'*Les vêtements des nouveaux riches?*' he teased, nodding slowly. 'You're right. Guilty as charged. I have developed a taste for the finer things in life, but I hardly buy anything.'

'Don't have time?' Lynn offered with a lazy smile.

'*¡Justamente!*' the musician confirmed, muting his volume just in time. 'Nor the inclination! Christ, you're always so irresistibly on the money. I've missed you so much. What did your dad tell you about me then?'

Her enigmatic stranger's disposition switched at once to reflect the seriousness of the surprise question which had been casually thrown into the conversation. Aquamarine pools of light gazed upwards and blinked a few times while she reassembled the rather one-sided discussion she had shared with her father. She became a little nervous too, causing him to regret broaching the topic in such a public place.

The nineteen-year-old lowered her voice, scanning the coffee bar carefully. 'Just that your family was involved in a big criminal investigation about ten years ago, and that he believes you might've been part of it,' she tried to remember. 'I asked for more details, but he wouldn't tell me. I kept thinking you would've only been a boy, so how could you be involved? And then last night, while you were dreaming, you were shouting about being innocent, so I assume you do have a story to tell.'

Jeff looked down and inhaled deeply, cursing his nightmares again. 'Yeah, I do have a story to tell. You didn't tell me you'd heard anything intelligible through my thrashing. You never mentioned that before.'

Lynn put her fingers to her lips. It occurred to her that this new incarnation of their relationship was already heading down an altogether divergent track. In order to be honest with themselves and each other, they ought to acknowledge that they had only really known each other as adolescents before, especially in comparison with the complex world they now occupied, with new responsibilities that necessarily accompanied the rights of an adult. Life had been simple last time: hardly even formally dating; simply sneaking the occasional spare hours between school and training. Things were different now for them as a couple, despite their confident declaration that neither party had changed.

'Shhh... Let's not talk about this here. I'd rather wait 'til we get back to Melbourne, so we can talk freely and with no pressure. I want you to be comfortable telling me.'

Jeff levered himself up off the sofa and crouched next to his lover's chair, holding both her hands in his. He had picked up the gist of her concern too, and its power blew them both away. They shared a long, silent kiss, after checking again that no-one was looking.

'You'll know everything soon enough,' he promised. 'I'm determined to prove my innocence to your parents, and most of all to you. I love you.'

The stunning celebrity felt her heart rate accelerating and wondered how plausible it was for her persuasive Pied Piper to be telling lies while staring so deeply into her soul. She was so fearful for the outcome of this critical conversation that she didn't really mind how far in the future it happened.

'I love you too. Let's change the subject.'

Jeff checked his watch, leaning back on his haunches. 'Time to go to Manly,' he announced. 'And not a moment too soon!'

Their hire car was waiting outside the hotel's main entrance. It was a luxury, black Mercedes sedan, and Jeff whistled as the valet inched it up to the steps.

'That's a nice car. Thanks, boss!'

Lynn curtsied in front of the door the chivalrous chaperone had opened for her, before sliding gracefully into the leather passenger seat. She was glad he knew the streets of Sydney so well, because she soon found herself disoriented as they weaved the short distance between the hotel and Circular Quay, making their way towards the Harbour Bridge.

'I've never driven over the Coat Hanger before,' she admitted.

'Really? How come?' Jeff retorted. 'And I thought you'd done everything. And with everyone.'

The teenager giggled, slightly embarrassed again, and reached to touch his left hand, which was resting on the gear lever as they glided along. 'It's so good to be back with you. We can laugh at ourselves again.'

Her chauffeur smiled. 'Agreed, secret lover. I'm not going to let you get away again. No way, baby!'

They arrived at Manly's north beach with about two minutes to spare. The promenade was relatively quiet for a Friday lunchtime, with only a few hardy bathers brave enough for the autumn surf. After cruising the length of the shopping strip once and wheeling around for a second pass, the flamboyant driver located a suitable parking space and reversed the large vehicle into it with one finger.

'Show off!' his impressed companion teased. 'Which restaurant is it?'

'It's called "Felix",' Jeff replied, looking along the street until he spotted it. 'Up there.'

The good-looking pair briskly covered the seventy-five metres or so to the brightly-decorated seaside café. Several passers-by took second glances as they passed the celebrities, but the *duo incognito* refused to make eye contact with anyone. They remarked that it was going to be nigh on impossible to remain a secret if they were spied strolling together along city streets!

Entering through the restaurant's open door, the imposing figure of Jeff Diamond made straight for a well-dressed, middle-aged woman sitting at a table against the wall.

'Celia!' he called out, causing the lady to lift her eyes from a glossy magazine. 'Sorry we're late.'

He bent down to kiss Gerry's mother, who had removed her reading glasses and pushed her chair back to greet the youngsters. She was smiling broadly, charmed by her extra son's uncharacteristically high spirits.

'Hello, darling. You look well,' she said, giving him a hug. 'You're not late. I was early.'

Jeff turned around just in time to witness his next personal miracle. Celia's gaze alighted on the gorgeous creature behind him, not in the least bit surprised to see her.

'Miss Lynn Dyson! Lovely to meet you,' the lady's hand extended for the famous Melburnian to shake it, quickly clasping both hands around hers. 'I imagined the mystery guest to be you.'

True enough, Lynn did see her own mother in Celia Blake. And the look on her boyfriend's face was priceless. She wished someone would take a picture of the awe shining out of it. He caught her eye and was gripped by a sudden pleasurable awkwardness which could only be born out of true love, and his unmasked heart slipped a little further down the sleeve of his prized leather jacket.

'Thank you. It's lovely to meet you too, Missus Blake. Celia, if that's alright? Jeff's told me about some of the kind things you've done for him over the years. I'm so happy we could meet like this.'

The twenty-two-year-old millionnaire stood back and proudly watched the two elegant women interact. This was such a huge moment, and he fought the inevitable light-headedness that threatened to overtake him. His past and his present were fusing together right in front of his eyes. And his future too, hopefully. Celia was the closest thing he had to a parent. He was under no illusion that a long journey lay ahead of him before Lynn and he could properly be together, and it was by no means a done deal, but today he afforded himself some optimism. His ancient soul felt lighter and freer than he had known for a long, long while.

The trio sat down, Jeff's two most significant ladies opposite each other at the same table. Celia congratulated both artists on last night's awards and asked several innocuous questions about the ceremony and dinner. Lynn stole a glance at her man to let him know his dance floor invasion was off limits for discussion, which he acknowledged with equal telepathy. They ordered their lunch from a rather hysterical waitress, who scurried off after her manager was forced to intervene.

'So, Lynn, I suppose you've also met my actual son, rather than this imposter here,' Celia began. 'He's incorrigible, that one. I wish he'd settle down.'

This time it was Jeff's turn to issue a tacit warning, knowing what his girlfriend knew about Gerry's situation. Neither the pregnancy nor the post-awards gallivanting was suitable news to share with his manager's mother. As expected, his *confidante* was the perfect diplomat.

'I love Gerry,' she responded in all sincerity. 'He's so much fun. We had some great nights out before I went overseas, didn't we, Jeff? And by all accounts, he's a very good businessman too.'

Celia touched her hand. 'It's very kind of you to say so, dear. His father's very proud of him, work-wise. And I am too, but he needs to grow up a bit. Less of the playboy lifestyle's in order, I think. For both of you, I hope.'

Jeff nodded, smiling in response to the gentle maternal scolding. 'He'll have had a sore head this morning, that's for sure. So how are Gerald and the girls? I haven't spoken to Tammy for so long. Is she still with the horse trainer bloke?'

The farm girl hiding under a layer of tailored urbane fashion was interested to hear more. 'Horse trainer?'

'Yes,' Celia explained. 'Tamilla's boyfriend trains racehorses at Randwick. He's had a run of winners recently. He's divorced though, with a little boy.'

Lynn read the disapproval between the North Shore woman's polite lines but said nothing. The Blakes were obviously good Irish Catholics with traditional views evidently precluding divorced sons-in-law or stepchildren. Not so far from her own family's rigid values system, up against which she was about to pit her reinstated relationship. She imagined years' worth of hearty debates at the dinner table when no doubt the stately Sydney family would have collided with her passionate, left-winged boyfriend, also assuming a similar fate laying in store for her own parents.

The resplendent rock star answered Celia's questions about his itinerary for the rest of the year, which was useful information for his girlfriend too. She was not surprised to hear that the man-of-the-moment was greatly in demand and felt proud for him that he had achieved so much in a relatively short time. It made her wonder what his estranged family must think about the icon their black sheep had become.

Lynn excused herself to go to the ladies' room before their meals arrived. Jeff's eagle eyes followed her until she was out of sight, feeling immediately at sea. Celia reached across the table and took his hand.

'Congratulations, darling. You look very tired, but so happy too. I'm very pleased for you.'

Jeff felt the back of his eyes prickling and his throat tighten. 'Thanks. A whole different kind of tired. Self-inflicted, so deserving of no sympathy. But yeah... It's been a tough couple of years, and funnily enough, today it's all completely worth it! Gorgeous, isn't she? I love her so much, and already it's as if we've never been apart.'

A tear escaped and ran down the right-hand side of his face, and his friend's mother squeezed tighter. He pulled his hand free to dry his face, frightened that continuing down the same line of enquiry might release flood gates that were barely holding fast under the strain of two years of pent-up emotion.

Celia recognised the understatement which rendered his words so powerful. 'Oh, darling, that's wonderful. I can see how much she loves you too. She's very genuine. You've got to try to hang on to her this time.'

The fighter laughed, sniffing back the tears. 'I know. Tell me about it. You've got more chance of seeing Gerry settle down, I think.'

'Nonsense,' the older woman objected, clutching his hand again. 'Just be honest with her. Does she know about your troubles?'

By this time, Lynn had returned to the café and was walking towards them, causing Celia to slide her arm off the table. Jeff's mind was busy thinking of a new topic of conversation so as not to embarrass the singer with more of his mate's mother's slushy romance. Celia was also uncertain as to how open she could be in front of this beautiful teenager. She needn't have worried though, since the lonely man made a snap decision to stop pretending to be someone else, safe in the knowledge that his dream girl hadn't changed either.

'Some of them,' Jeff answered, smiling at his new, old girlfriend as she squeezed herself back into the booth.

'Some of what?'

Her enigmatic stranger winked at her. 'Celia was asking if you knew about my screwed-up head.'

The sophisticated young woman understood what he was saying perfectly. 'Oh, yes. But I wouldn't exactly call it screwed-up. It's an extraordinary head, in my opinion. You'd know, Celia, how many good ideas there are in here...'

Lynn touched her man's forehead lightly, as if it were the most natural gesture in the world. Shockwaves flew through his temple and zipped down his spine, ending predictably below the belt. He inhaled sharply, receiving a beaming smile from his blonde electrocutioner.

'Jesus! Lighten up, will you?' he teased, nudging her shoulder.

He planted a kiss on his fingertips and brushed them lovingly across her cheek. Very happy with the endearing spectacle, Gerry's mum turned to the stunning celebrity.

'Your parents must be very proud of you, dear.'

'Thank you,' the teenager acknowledged, as gracious as ever. 'We're all working very hard. I'm not sure I can take much credit because I'm part of such a big machine. I just turn up and do my thing, and luckily it seems to work.'

'And so modest too,' Celia said, glancing from one to the other. 'So what are you two kids up to for the rest of the day?'

Lynn answered without hesitation. 'Well, I have to do a couple of television interviews this afternoon...'

'And you should see what she's wearing!' her man interjected, waving his hand in the air as if it were on fire. 'Hot. Damned hot!'

'Shhh!' his girlfriend giggled. 'And then we're flying home tomorrow.'

We're flying home tomorrow. This new mode of "we" and "us" was only just beginning to sink into Jeff's addled psyche. He pushed his right foot sideways until it found hers, and she pressed back against his shoe. About to mention to their co-conspirator that her discretion was appreciated, his heart skipped several more beats when Lynn's left hand swept up his thigh and encased itself around his genitals. Her poker face gave nothing away, and a strained smile was all he could afford to transmit in return. This most adult of gestures was amply rewarded beneath the table however, instantly stiffened and with his attention scarcely extending to the conversation any longer.

'Celia, when I said on the 'phone that you had to keep us a secret, I meant it,' he said, breathing heavily.

The inquisitive woman listened with interest, discerning what she interpreted as serious overtones. She had suspected after his initial call that the couple may be operating somewhere under the radar at the moment. An ardent follower of all things Dyson, a plethora of recent magazine articles all told of the sporting ambitions and further musical engagements that were on the pretty nineteen-year-old's horizon. If she were honest, Jeff Diamond would not be her first choice of partner for a daughter either.

Rock music's walking headline continued. 'Our relationship needs to be kept under wraps, even from Jack and Tammy for now. Is that OK?'

Celia nodded. 'That's fine, dear. I have to ask why though. I noticed you weren't together at the awards dinner.'

In other words, the handsome man acknowledged, his friend's mother had noticed Lynn was with another man. 'Nope. And it's best we stay that way until we get a few things ironed out back in Melbourne. I'll tell Gerry later in the week, so it'll just be the two of you who know. There could be some serious implications if the wrong people were to find out, so I hope you understand.'

Celia couldn't hope to understand fully, yet she had learned to trust this troubled lad over the years. 'Very well. That's agreed. Your secret's safe with me, darlings.'

Lynn jumped in to thank the bemused woman too. 'It's my fault.'

Her boyfriend's head switched sideways, equally confused. Their telepathic powers had suffered a service interruption. What was she about to say? Why was she taking the blame when it was clearly his? For a second time, the expression on her radiant face didn't alter.

'My family's very protective of me,' she told their guest in a matter-of-fact way.

An all-knowing look spread across Celia's face. This must be some type of sophisticated women's code, Jeff resigned, because it appeared that a penny had dropped. Gerry's mother was being told in a roundabout way that the family didn't think he was good enough for their elder daughter.

'If only they knew,' the middle-aged woman rued, smiling at the youngsters and holding onto both of their hands.

In response to a flick of his girlfriend's eyebrows, Jeff decided to change the subject, far less sure of a successful outcome than Celia evidently was. 'We'd better go,' he announced. 'We've borrowed this swanky Merc', and it's liable to turn into a pumpkin if we don't get it back soon.'

Both women chuckled. All three got to their feet and prepared to leave. The charming millionnaire went to pay the bill, fishing his wallet out of the back pocket of his trousers. Hearing whoops of delight from the girls behind the counter, the Mosman resident turned to the young star and clasped their hands together again.

'Treat him gently, Lynn, please,' she almost whispered. 'I know you love him. I can tell you do. He's been through so much and he's held onto the dream of you returning so ferociously that I'd hate to see him let down. There's a lot of good in him, even though he might seem dangerous, and he's taught our family such a lot about compassion and tolerance. Let him fly. He won't hurt you.'

The two women kissed quickly, and the nineteen-year-old caught her breath. 'Thank you so much, Celia. I know what you mean. I don't want to lose him again either. You can trust me to look after him.'

Jeff returned to see the two ladies embracing, both with tears in their eyes. He felt slightly uncomfortable that they were already exchanging information behind his back, but realised it was to be expected in the new secret world order. After all, it had been his idea that the two of them meet, leaving him no choice but to face the consequences.

'Hey! What did I miss?'

'Nothing, dear,' Celia responded, picking up her handbag and magazine.

The blonde celebrity shrugged. 'Nothing, dear.'

Jeff frowned at the pair's innocent little joke at his expense. 'Where's your car?'

The threesome left the restaurant and paused on the footpath, ready to part company. The elegant lady pointed in the opposite direction to where the others had left the Mercedes. Ever the gentleman, Jeff asked if they could walk her there.

'No, that's not necessary, dears. It's only a few steps. You two had better run. The traffic sometimes backs up over the bridge. Thanks so much for inviting me. It's been lovely meeting you, Lynn. Really lovely. Safe flight home, and see you soon.'

They said their goodbyes, exchanging more kisses and hugs. Celia gave her favourite man an extra-special squeeze.

'Don't worry, darling. You're going to be fine.'

'Thanks,' Jeff nodded. 'It was nice seeing you too. I promise I'll ring more often.'

Heading in opposite directions and leaving a small crowd of onlookers gaping in awe in the street, Lynn Dyson and Jeff Diamond climbed into the big, black boat and sped off, tooting the horn at their guest as she reached her car. The Mercedes skimmed weightlessly over the Harbour Bridge. The early afternoon sun glinted on the water upriver and reflected its brilliance in the windows of the tall, harbourside buildings of Sydney's CBD. The celebrity had less than an hour to get back to the hotel, change back into her red power suit and slip across town to the television studios. Jeff was more nervous than she was about being late.

'We don't have to rush,' she reassured her sexy driver, needing to lean over at a pronounced angle to rub his shoulder in the capacious limousine. 'Do you want to keep the car for the afternoon?'

The Sydneysider considered his options for a moment, while also sneaking an appealing eyeful of cleavage. A plan was hatching behind his wide grin. He needed to head west to see if he could track down some people from his past. Since he was in Sydney and having heard the news that Big D was on his case, there was renewed urgency to discover who was still at large and who might still bear a grudge.

'No. It's OK, thanks. This baby's too conspicuous for where I'm going this arvo. I'll take the train.'

How strange, Lynn thought. In her opinion, being trapped on a train would present a greater risk for the man whose picture regularly graced the gossip columns. Pressing him for answers would do neither of them any good. He had promised to tell all, and she needed to exhibit patience and to be prepared to hear things she wasn't looking forward to hearing. Her father was a reasonable man, and the fact that Jeff was taking him seriously and not blowing off indignant steam in typical fashion made one thing very clear:

whatever was lurking in the shadows of her boyfriend's past must have the potential of disastrous repercussions for the present day.

'Celia's lovely,' the young woman began again, after a few minutes' silence. 'You're right. She is like my mum. She obviously cares a lot about you.'

Jeff smiled. 'Yeah, she does. Whenever I see her, it always reminds me how bad I am.'

'Bad? Why?'

'Ah, y'know… It's a sorry state of affairs when you think more of your best mate's mum than you do of your own...'

Lynn shot him a sympathetic smile. 'You must have your reasons.'

Her mystery man didn't respond, and their attention was soon diverted to crowds of commuters who were crossing the complex, multi-point intersections of the financial district with scant regard for traffic, all rushing to and fro on their lunchbreaks. The black sedan was soon pulling into the InterContinental's driveway, where the parking attendant was ready and waiting to claim back the keys. He couldn't believe his eyes when Lynn Dyson alighted through the opened door, followed by Jeff Diamond from the driver's seat.

'Cheers, mate,' the unassuming songwriter said in a friendly, most un-superstar-like tone and tossed the keys in his direction. 'It's a nice drive. No talking, by the way. You saw nothing.'

The expression on the valet's face was one of dumbstruck pride at having been taken into the confidence of a rock music idol. He mumbled his agreement and eagerly accepted the famous man's handshake. Inside the lobby, the chauffeur sent by the television studio was already waiting, pacing up and down. His blonde charge promised she would only be five minutes upstairs.

Jeff handed the young woman his leather jacket, since it too was inappropriate for where he was bound. 'You go on up. I don't need anything from the room. Please could you leave this up there for me? I'm going to head out. What time do you think you'll be back?'

Lynn nodded, looping the heavy coat over her arm obediently. 'OK. Probably about six, six-thirty. Thanks for a great morning, and lunch. I'll see you here when I get back.'

They kissed briefly, still wary of being caught on camera. It seemed somehow wrong to be parting company after the blissful time they had spent together since the early hours of the morning. Separately, both wondered what their new normal might look like, once they were back on home turf and going about their everyday lives. The anxious man gripped his beautiful partner's upper arm, squeezing so hard that she was forced to shake it free.

'I'll be somewhere around here,' he told her, pointing into the bar. 'I'll tell Reception where I am, so you don't have to go searching.'

The singer thanked him. How much she had missed his thoughtfulness too... In her determination to forget about loving him, she had also forgotten how much of a gentleman Jeff was compared to others she had met since. And so much more interesting in every single dimension.

'Hope you find what you're looking for.'

Receiving a sly wink in return, the intrigued but happy woman turned to towards the lifts, bound for power-dressing and the wooing of her adoring public. Jeff spread his feet firmly on the tiles in an effort to keep the onset of delirium from transporting him to the ceiling, willing himself to believe he was actually standing here. He was thankful that Lynn was respecting his privacy. What must she be thinking? And how would she react when she found out the truth?

***

Once more in the spring sunshine, Jeff lit a much-needed cigarette and strode down the hill towards Circular Quay. He bought a baseball cap and a can of Coca-Cola from a souvenir shop. Putting on the cap and his sunglasses, he made his way towards the train station.

Before he had even crossed the street however, four giggling British backpackers ran up to him, excited to have spotted their idol.

'Are you Jeff Diamond?' one asked, almost dancing around him.

The star stopped and sighed comically. 'I'm meant to be in disguise.'

All four girls whooped and clapped their hands. Even after this long in the limelight, the superstar still failed to understand the hysteria that so-called famous people generated in young women. And in older women too, for that matter. Yet these were very attractive holidaymakers, and he lapped up the attention, his covert intelligence-gathering mission momentarily taking a back seat.

'Can we get a photo' with you?' the bravest one asked. 'I'm Sally, by the way. And this is Janine, Mary and Donna.'

Sally had already flagged down another tourist to take their picture. Jeff obliged, compliantly posing with each girl. His mind wandered back to Gerry and his stuporous roommates. On any other day, he would have suggested these girls go for a drink with him, resulting necessarily in a guilt-free sex romp. But not today. Not only because his relationship with Lynn had been resuscitated, but also because this afternoon's free time must be directed to more productive pursuits.

Jeff signed autographs in the unlikeliest of places, and the girls went off happily, gushing and giggling. He continued on his way up to the station, bought a ticket and stood at the quieter end of the platform, hoping his identity would remain a little better hidden now he was off the main tourist drag. The train to Cabramatta pulled in a few minutes later, in which he took a window seat and instantly travelled back in time.

His overactive mind began to jumble as a wave of anxiety consumed his every rational thought. Struggling to retain control, the hometown boy focussed his attention on property values steadily decreasing as the train trundled westwards, and after a while he slowly regained his sanity. He rearranged the planned activities into their proper sequence and stared mindlessly at the rail network map on the train wall, knowing full well where he would alight. The first leg of his journey would take him to Fairfield and as far as his maternal grandparents' house. He needed to know what his sister knew.

Being now almost two-thirty, the Canley Vale native figured he had missed the opportunity to speak to Joe Cafici, the butcher whose shop was in the same strip where the Diamond family had lived. The portly Italian had given the youngster a part-time job when he was eleven, and had always seemed to know a fair bit about the comings and goings among the area's criminal element. His shop would be closed by now, and Joe would be at home working on his car or playing cards with his southern European cronies.

The celebrity managed to reach the modest house undetected, and he removed his cap and glasses as he rang the doorbell. He expected to feel more nervous than he did, standing in front of yet another door he had grown to despise, and he listened as shuffling footsteps came towards it. His grandmother opened the door.

'*¡Madre de Dios!*' she cried out, taking a few moments to place the tall, long-haired stranger darkening her door. 'What you doin' 'ere?'

There were no kisses or hugs. The pair faced off, both suspended in a sort of shock. The elderly woman would have been less than five feet tall, and Jeff felt like a giant next to her.

'*¿Como vas, Abuela?*' he started off politely, in as friendly a tone as he could muster. '*¿Puedo entrar?*'

'*No,*' she responded, making it perfectly obvious he wasn't welcome.

The diminutive lady leaned out, glancing up and down the street to make sure no-one had seen them. What a contrast, the arrogant young star mused. These days, most people wanted as many neighbours as possible to know Jeff Diamond was visiting!

'*Por favor, quiero hablar con Madalena,*' the estranged grandson explained. '*¿Sabe dónde está?*'

His grandmother shook her head in defiance, becoming more and more apprehensive. As far as she was concerned, her daughter's second-born was bad news, just as his father had been. Seeing him on her threshold after so long brought back too many sad memories. The door began to close.

'Espere, Abuela, p*or favor. Me ayude por una vez...*' he pleaded angrily, stepping forward and holding his hand out to prevent the woman from dismissing him so readily.

Images gathered around his head, crazed by the sight of another solid and impenetrable door about to be shut in his face. Just once the young man wished that somebody in his family would help him, or even acknowledge his existence outside the begging letters his management company received on a regular basis. The bitter, old lady had only to tell him where he could find his sister. Nothing else. It was a simple request, and then he would be gone. Most likely forever.

'*Chico, no está aquí.* You must go,' his grandmother turned to go back in to the house. 'Madalena, she forget you long time ago.'

'*Espero que Dios te olvida,*' Jeff muttered under his breath, while the door vibrated its frame with the force applied by such a tiny woman. '*Gracias, cula.*'

It was an evil thing to say to an old woman, that he hoped God would forget her, but what would it have cost her for one act of charity towards her own flesh and blood? The rejected visitor was annoyed at his reception but not really surprised, reinforcing his obstinacy at not pandering to the many requests his maternal relatives continued to make since he had come into serious money. He had hoped that time and absence would soften her reaction to him, but it wasn't to be. No great loss. He could live with that.

And neither had his sister forgotten him, despite the spiteful words which had been exchanged. She had only recently relieved him of five hundred dollars, to pay for her latest abortion. Where might she be on a Thursday afternoon? Jeff didn't know where she worked, or even if she was working at all. He remembered a pub where they had occasionally crossed paths before he moved to Melbourne. The landlord there would know if Madalena was still around. She was popular with the locals for all the wrong reasons.

No-one at the pub could help him. The famous musician sat with them and shared a beer, attracting more attention than was comfortable and many more customers than normally seen on a Thursday afternoon. They recognised him easily, calling him The Australian Elvis; high praise which Jeff suffered as reluctantly as ever. He omitted to alert them to the link between himself and the woman for whom he was searching, in case it triggered a slew of questions he had no intention of answering. If he headed down that path, sooner or later a public connection would be drawn between the chart-topping musician and the underworld of Sydney's western suburbs, which would be wholly counterproductive for his sister's safety, not to mention his own quest for exoneration.

The songwriter checked his watch and swore under his breath. Time was passing quickly, leaving him no further forward. He proceeded on foot to his old neighbourhood, jogging when no-one was around and slowing to a sedate walk on busy thoroughfares, in search of people he already knew as elusive by design. Finally standing outside the run-down Stones Road hardware shop, staring up at the windows on the second floor, he was thrown back to those bleak, hopeless days, long before he set off on the freedom trail to Melbourne. The smaller one on the left had once been his bedroom window. Who lived here these days? Was it still a shithole inside, or had the landlord eventually seen fit to remedy the many dilapidations?

His head felt dizzy remembering the countless hours he had whiled away in that pokey room, doing his best to study while his mother and sister were earning money for the people who "owned" his family. How hard he had fought to stop this never-ending humiliation, slowly strangling in the havoc it wreaked. It had been pointless for the youngest Diamond to interfere in the end, for this hustling constituted their only source of income, apart from the few meagre dollars he could earn from part-time jobs. Moreover, for the most part, this filthy money repaid a debt to the gang his father had betrayed. It was a vendetta too powerful for a thirteen-year-old boy to overturn.

Christ! Such gruesome events Jeff had heard and seen back then... They had given him an education of a whole different kind. There wasn't much he didn't know about the seedier side of life, and at least it had allowed him to sharpen his powers of concentration to their current magnitude. He smoked his last cigarette, throwing the empty packet into a nearby litter bin.

Suddenly, an idea occurred to him as clear as day. Of course! Alberto, the proprietor of a local boxing club, had helped the ambitious kid out once or twice. The old man knew everyone: who was inside, who had recently been released; who was selling what, and who was buying. A bus rounded the corner up ahead, splattered in paint and with several windows smashed. He couldn't be sure it would take him where he wanted to go, but he jumped on anyway and headed back to Fairfield again. The teenagers on the bus wore his old school uniform. They looked dirty and dishevelled, and their language was foul. Some things never changed, he smiled to himself, sinking into a seat towards the rear and staring blankly through the grime.

A bunch of girls began chattering and pointing in his direction. Jeff pulled the baseball cap down as far as he could and hid behind his dark glasses. In this forgotten land of low self-esteem, these schoolkids were nowhere near as forward as the backpackers on Circular Quay, probably never having been to the city centre and certainly not expecting to interact with anyone famous. He was right. They were content to worship from afar, if indeed they even believed it was him. He disembarked a few stops later and walked the rest of the way.

Very little had changed in these godforsaken suburbs, no matter where the star found himself this afternoon. No-one invested in Fairfield; neither governments nor private enterprise. A few shops were painted and well-maintained, but a far larger number were covered in *graffiti*, with their windows and doors roughly boarded up. There were homeless people propped up in draughty entrances, some with sleeping bags and others surrounded by flattened cardboard boxes, the empty bottles and food wrappers a Mecca for the flies buzzing around them.

Guilt percolated in the superstar's veins with each passing step. How far had the flamboyant millionnaire removed himself from these down-and-outs? He had likely been at school with half of them. Who did he think he was? His lofty goal of putting computers into everyone's hands was certainly a flight of fancy for these people. It was shelter, jobs and self-respect they needed, not substitute brains.

The reception area at Alberto's neglected and crumbling boxing club was unoccupied, but there were noises coming from downstairs. It was like stepping back in time for the former local. The equipment looked tired, and the punch-bags hanging from the low ceiling were held together by criss-crossed lines of silver or black duct tape. The wall mirrors were flecked and mottled where their reflective coating had worn away, and not a single ring sported a complete square of ropes.

Times had always been hard for the old Chilean immigrant and the small community he had fostered through the modest establishment. Protection rackets were rife in this neck of the woods, and victimised business owners rarely thought twice about paying. Jeff didn't relish venturing down into the basement without knowing who was there. He had been gone too long, and there was no guarantee he would be welcome or even remembered.

Hiding his face as best he could, the celebrity stopped to feed some coins into the cigarette machine in the entrance. In the old days, he had usually managed to lean on the cabinet just hard enough to trip the mechanism so that it returned his money along with the goods. He didn't try the old trick today, given the hardship the elderly man must be under. A young woman ran up the stairs, almost bumping into him.

'Eva!' the stranger greeted her at the top of the stairs, removing his cap and slotting his sunglasses into the breast pocket of his shirt. '*Es* Jeff Diamond.'

Alberto's daughter's eyes lit up. She let out a scream and gave him a vigorous hug.

'*¡Chico!* Oh, my God! It's been ages. You look great! You're a big star now. What the hell you doin' 'ere?'

Finally, Jeff thought, someone who was glad to see him. Eva and he had enjoyed each others' company countless times during their teenaged years. She was a year older than him, skinny and as rough as guts, but blessed with her father's heart of gold.

'You look great too. *¿Como vas? Buscando de su padre.* Is he here?'

'Aw, shame!' Eva pouted. 'I thought you come to sweep me off me feet and take me to your rock star mansion. He's not 'ere at the minute. He's gone with Mamá to the 'ospital. Stay and 'ave a drink. *Vuelva* pronto.'

The famous man laughed. This provincial girl was a breath of fresh air, possessing pretence and refinement in equal measure. Another kid who would never venture beyond the confines of the district, entirely ignorant about the wider world. Like his sister and most of their contemporaries, the prospect of a better future was unheard of.

'*Gracias*. I will,' he accepted. 'There is no mansion, by the way. Who's downstairs?'

'Ah... Just the usual,' Eva replied, starting down the steep steps.

Her old flame had no idea who "the usual" might be these days, so he followed the feisty woman down the dark stairwell with some trepidation. Threading their way through the gym' and into the tiny office confirmed that hardly anything had changed since Jeff had last caught up with Alberto. A small group of men were drinking in the far corner, sporting an assortment of tattoos and ostentatious jewellery.

'Boys! Look who I found,' Eva shouted over to them. 'It's Jeff Diamond! Jeff Diamond! Look!'

The swarthy quartet wheeled around to see what the excitement was about, and the new arrival recognised a couple of them without difficulty. Tony, a well-built, Greek plumber who had been training here for years, and Hassan, a Middle-Eastern man in his early thirties who was known to help illegal immigrants to secure poorly-paid jobs that required no official paperwork, while creaming off a percentage from both sides, naturally. He also dealt in a variety of drugs, and Jeff and his school friends had bought from Hassan many times.

These men were hard nuts, living from day to day and accustomed to watching their backs. Despite the other pair being unknowns, the celebrity with a similarly dubious past relaxed somewhat. His secret would be as safe with them as theirs were with him.

Eva thrust a bottle of cold beer into Jeff's hand. The reception he received was warm but guarded, reciprocated in kind. The two acquaintances broke away from the others to shake his hand, joking in true macho fashion about how uncool it would be to ask for his autograph.

'You're all grown up,' Tony remarked.

'It happens,' the twenty-two-year-old shrugged. 'It's good to see you again. What's going on? Club looks just the same.'

He offered his cigarettes around, which were accepted gladly. The respectful gesture was met with forthright nods, as if it were some secret code. Hassan brought out a lighter from his pocket to complete the ritual while the trio swapped trivial tales of the past and the present. The conversation meandered around the fortunes of their local football team, the Eels, and then onto the various disused buildings that ought to be demolished before too many more children died either of overdoses or jumping from roofs in their high-flying invincibility.

As the general neglect and apathy in this neighbourhood became further cemented in his mind, Jeff vowed to make amends for turning his back on his own kind. He was annoyed with himself for putting such a distance between gloomy past and glorious present, and nausea threatened to overtake him. He cursed the selfish objectives with which he had returned to these godforsaken parts, committed to creating the widest gulf possible between them and his new world.

Did his future with Lynn really depend on leaving the past behind entirely? These men were endeavouring to make the best of a bad deal. Alberto had helped him out when he was in need, and doubtless Tony and Hassan would have done the same for several other boys like him. How could he claim to be a man of conscience without deploying some of his newfound wealth and influence to give something back? It was yet another conundrum he couldn't wait to share with his beautiful best friend, once this clear and present obstacle were behind them.

Dragging hard, the visitor willed the nicotine into his bloodstream to calm his nerves. 'Gents, I'm looking for some information,' he said. 'I need to know if anyone's been sniffing around about my dad and the Jaworski brothers. Someone told me there are private investigators trying to dig up dirt that shouldn't be dug up. Have you heard anything?'

A pair of blank faces stared passively back for a few seconds, and Jeff read the awkwardness in their body language. Discomfort hung in the atmosphere between them until Hassan began to shake his head. Tony's eyes moved from the Arab to one of the training rings and back again, saying nothing. The good-looking star thought better of glancing over his shoulder to see if he recognised either sparring boxer, suspicious that the Greek's hesitance might be more than a convenient avoidance of eye contact. Finally, the drug dealer admitted to having heard something.

'Don't know the details, mate, but they say the cops are looking at new evidence. Only last week, so your timing's good. Alberto knows more. You should talk to him.'

The young man nodded. 'Thanks, mate. Appreciate it.'

Hassan continued, accepting another cigarette. 'Look, kid... Stay in pop star land. You got out, so stay out. D'y'understand? They don't need the evidence too strong these days to put us away. My brother's in the 'lea now; inside for robbery and GBH, and he didn't lay a hand on no-one.'

A shiver ran down Jeff's spine. He could picture Hassan's brother quite clearly. Imran used to carry a gun which was rarely loaded, yet he never shied away from using it to threaten people or even to beat them unconscious with it on the slightest provocation. The man was a coward with a mean temper, truth be told.

'Cheers, Hassan. Thanks for the warning. I'm sorry about your brother. Your mum OK?'

While the threesome conversed over her head, Eva had wrapped her arms and legs around her sexy childhood playmate and was now idly fingering his shirt buttons in an effort to attract his attention. To no avail, it appeared. Quite apart from the ominous preoccupation presently consuming his whole being, the momentous bouts of sexual gratification Jeff had enjoyed over the last twelve hours had rendered his skin immune to another's touch. He was disinclined to respond at all, hoping he wouldn't hurt her feelings. Eventually, he took hold of her hand and moved it gently away.

'¡*Culo!* You too good for us now!' the girl sneered, disappointed. 'You got rock star chicks all over the place?'

'Hundreds,' he nodded, grinning at her and then at the others. 'They're everywhere.'

Tony and Hassan gaped in curiosity at the incongruous pairing, most likely unaware of any history between them. They laughed at the musician's response, vicariously assimilating the fantasy of being surrounded by hundreds of girls. The image wasn't far from the truth, but the celebrity needed to move on.

'Listen… I can't stay, guys. I'm sorry I missed your dad, Eva. Can you tell him I came by, *por favor*?'

Jeff picked up a pen from the counter and wrote his telephone number on a beer mat. He gave it to the owner's daughter, who handed it straight back to him.

'Can you sign it?' she asked. 'I want your autograph, Jeff Diamond. And say something like I know you.'

The amused visitor obliged, placing a large X underneath his well-practised, flashman's signature. Passing the beer mat to his awestruck fan, he leaned forwards and gave her a real kiss. She swooned, immediately coming back for more and making the men laugh again. There was no more, however. He was prepared to play the part of a crowd-pleasing whore easily enough, but only up to a point.

'If either of you or *Señor* Alberto hears anything, I'd appreciate a call.'

Eva stared at the telephone number. 'Oh-three? Isn't that Victoria?'

'Yep,' Jeff replied. 'I live in Melbourne now.'

The plumber scoffed. 'Good thing, mate. Best place for ya. Anywhere away from 'ere gotta be good. We don't get many rich blokes down 'ere.'

The musician shook the others' hands again and wished them well. 'Money ain't everything,' he countered with a half-smile. 'Thanks heaps. Keep on fighting.'

Hassan waved casually, turning to leave his empty beer bottle on the bar. 'Stay away, mate. It's not safe. You weren't here, I swear.'

Eva followed her idol up the steep flight of stairs and out of the front door. 'Come back soon,' she urged, ever hopeful. 'You look good, Jeff Diamond. I wish you could stay.'

'*Gracias*,' the well-dressed man smiled, giving her another friendly kiss. 'Hey, d'you know where Lena is?'

'Na! She keeps away an' all. I ain't seen 'er in ages. Some bloke 'ere got her knocked up, so she split. Working the Stones again, I 'xpect.'

Working the Stones. The estranged brother contemplated these three sickening words. Only the seediest characters came looking for comfort on the Stones Road. Jesus! Perhaps there was a case for him to leave his past behind after all. How much could he do to help these people, when they seemed not to care enough to help themselves?

Jeff stepped onto the footpath, turned and raised his hand to farewell the dark-haired waif. 'It's good to see you, *chica. Toma el cuidado.*'

Back on the streets, the afternoon had turned cooler, and the lonely wanderer wished he had brought his jacket with him after all. It was now four-thirty, so he made his way back to the station and waited on the platform for the next city-bound train. The first few rivulets of afternoon commuters were drifting homewards, and still with his cap and sunglasses on, he buried his head in a copy of the Telegraph to avoid recognition.

The anxious man found it impossible to concentrate on the printed words. His mind was busy processing the sparse information he had gleaned from the boxing club, resolving to ring Alberto sometime in the coming week to see whether there was truth in Hassan's supposition. The local elder was not exactly a police informant, as far as Jeff knew, although he had earned a reputation for coming to the aid of young constables who had grown up in the area. These officers had probably risen through the ranks by now, and Alberto was wise enough to have kept them on-side. Were these Bart Dyson's men snooping around, or police officers? Or both, in cahoots? At least the boy with the memorable name could now be certain that it was more than just bluster on Lynn's father's part. He knew he had to take her warning seriously.

The songwriter looked at his watch again, seeing a train pulling into the station. So where was his damned sister? Shacked up with another pro'? Or maybe a pimp? He wondered what she would make of him going out with Lynn Dyson. Madalena had rarely commented on the many posters and magazine centrefolds pinned to his side of the bedroom wall. Hers had been covered with pictures of all the nineteen-sixties' pop stars too.

Sighing heavily, Jeff wished he could have saved his older sibling from the seedy life into which she had fallen. Returning to Fairfield had brought back so many unpleasant memories of how poorly the pair had been treated by their parents, not to mention the contempt with which the school system and neighbouring shopkeepers had viewed their kind. Yet, like Eva, the gritty young woman may not have wanted to be saved. This shabby lifestyle was all she had ever known, and as far as her brother was aware, she had never sought to break away.

'Fuck 'em,' the frustrated world-changer cursed under his breath, thinking of his grandparents, uncles and aunts, and how they had turned against him when he had most needed them.

Jeff couldn't help being Paul Diamond's son. His old soul hadn't asked to be born into that wretched excuse for a family, had it? He would much rather have been Gerry's brother than Madalena's. Celia was right. He had to hang on to Lynn this time. No matter what shady history or unlawful facts her father uncovered, he would stand his ground. He had nothing to hide and everything to prove.

The suburban train lost its anonymous millionnaire passenger at St James' station, and he jogged the final few hundred metres back to the Intercontinental, impatient to be reunited with his secret lover again. It was twenty minutes before six o'clock, and the last of the sun was slowly sinking below Sydney's skyline. The old-fashioned hotel bar was welcoming, with its leather Chesterfield sofas and shelves stocked with a wide variety of books and magazines. Jeff ordered himself a beer and scanned the rows of well-thumbed spines for interesting fodder to pass the time until Lynn's return. He selected one with a white cover, extracted it from the tightly-packed shelf and scanned the synopsis on the back cover. "Political Anthropology – A Collection of Essays". Perfect, he thought. It was hard to imagine a subject further removed from his recent circumstances and yet so apt for directing his own future!

The academic text was a fascinating read for the avid student, who had graduated from RMIT the previous year and was nowadays lacking intellectual stimulation. He had been toying with a Doctorate to top up the Masters degree he had hurriedly completed between tours, wild parties and solitary drug binges, but hadn't yet found a worthy thesis on which to base it. He had consumed most available knowledge on both Computer Science and International Relations, no longer inspired by either subject in its own right. He needed something to bring these fields together, as he had described to Michael Parkinson on his show, to develop a broad program of change to satisfy his social justice agenda.

Seeing the deprivation of the downtrodden, uninspired classes only a handful of kilometres away from the nation's largest and most booming CBD had reinvigorated Jeff's conviction. It had long been his view that modern politics were heading in the wrong direction, and not only in Australia. There was so much societal pressure for individuals to succeed, and yet societies the world over were desperately failing the individual.

The famous guest ordered a glass of cold beer from a passing waiter and settled down in the sumptuous sofa, leaning back and crossing his legs. He did his best to ignore the high-pitched chatter of two women who had spotted him from the far side of the bar. Out of the corner of his eye, he could tell they were plucking up the courage to approach him, so he shifted to the opposite corner of the couch and turned his back on them.

Soon lost in the thought-provoking prose, the closet scholar was oblivious to the tall, slender blonde sauntering towards him. She was almost able to touch him before he looked up.

'Anthropology and beer,' Lynn mused, her hips stopping directly behind his head, gazing down over his shoulder. 'That's a lethal cocktail.'

Smiling both at the powerful image and on hearing a voice he adored, Jeff closed the book with his finger holding his page and jumped to his feet. All ruminations summarily suspended, so ecstatic was he to see her that blessed relief and uncontrollable sexual urges immediately set themselves on a collision course, eager to make their presence felt.

'Hey, gorgeous! Welcome back. I was engrossed. I love this stuff,' he enthused, giving her a relatively chaste kiss on the cheek, so as not to encourage the nosy company, and keeping her crimson-clad body held at arms' length. 'Whoa! You look absolutely fantastic. Can I buy a drink for this random superstar I don't know?'

Lynn looked around, trying not to laugh at his absurd request. The after-work crowd had dispersed, and the bar was less than half full; mainly with tourists, judging by their casual attire. It would be particularly agreeable to sit and share an *apéritif* with her cultured mystery man after all this time. She had been able to think of little else during the afternoon, in fact. He looked relaxed and absorbed, and frankly rather delicious, and she could tell by the fact that his breathing had become audible that he was highly aroused by her return.

The idea of spending another night in his arms was turning her on too, much more than the dignified nineteen-year-old had expected. So what if someone spotted them together? They were only sharing a drink, and at least she was old enough to consume alcohol in public in this country.

'OK,' she agreed. 'It seems quite safe, I suppose. I'll have a vodka and tonic, please.'

Gesturing for his stunning lady to take a seat, Jeff nodded approvingly at her choice and made his way to the bar. It occurred to him that this was the first time he had legally bought Lynn Dyson a drink. When he returned to his seat, she was reclining in the armchair next to his, her long legs threaded around each other and shimmering in stockings. He felt a rush of pleasure to all extremities when he noticed her leafing through the book he had been reading, her finger now marking the page at which he had been interrupted.

There was something incredibly sexy about a short skirt on an intelligent woman, and it fired him up no end. Standing at her shoulder, he touched the cold glass on her cheek, and a drop of condensation clung to her tanned skin. Lynn smiled sweetly, almost as if she had expected him to do it, brushing the water off before accepting the drink. Life with this extraordinary man was just as she remembered; even the smallest act charged with sensual excitement.

'Thanks. This book sounds fascinating. You should borrow it and post it back when you've finished. How was your afternoon?'

Jeff hesitated a little, accepting the slim volume back and opening it face-down onto the table. 'Ah, not bad. What about yours? Did the red suit work? Did they crumble at your feet like I'm going to before too long?'

The teenaged beauty giggled. 'You're *still* thinking about sex!'

Her highly-strung paramour cocked his head in a mock apology. Little did she know that he could easily have spent the afternoon romping with backpackers or with Eva upstairs above the boxing club. He had actually shown considerable restraint today, all things considered. Altogether distracted once more, his guilty conscience forced a silent epiphany onto the self-styled sexual mercenary that such impromptu interludes must be henceforth declared out of bounds.

Lynn carried on, unaware of the fundamental seismic shift which had taken place inside the ever-changing mind of her most favourite rock god. 'My interviewers were actually both women, so no point in power-dressing. Not that I was intending to anyway.'

The couple maintained a discreet distance in the large bar, as they swapped tales of their respective afternoons. Sitting so near and yet so far was terribly tantalising for both lovers, although neither allowed it to show while they sipped their drinks. Every now and again, Lynn would flash her handsome companion a broad smile, and he would return the favour with one of his most disarming winks.

When the barman attended their table to alert his famous patrons to the fact that their glasses needed refilling, Lynn politely declined. Her answer was met with a sly thumbs-up sign, at which she rolled her eyes. She had a fair idea how her companion's libido would be faring, and had to admit to a strikingly similar level of anticipation.

Watching the stunning woman with inviting red lips sipping vodka with a slice, sitting elegantly upright and within touching distance was too much for Jeff to bear. In fact, it was likely to be a rather embarrassing ride to the fifth floor! Political anthropology wasn't all that absorbing, especially seated opposite the world's most beautiful woman... He steered his one-tracked mind back to the conversation he had shared with Hassan and Tony, thankfully achieving the desired effect after twenty seconds or so. He had bought himself some time to coax the gorgeous temptress upstairs.

'Where did you go?' Lynn asked, seeing a distant look on his face.

Jeff snapped himself back to the here and now. 'This afternoon?'

'No. Just then! You suddenly went a million miles away. Are you OK?'

'Yeah. Sorry,' the horny man replied, slapping both hands on his knees. 'Can we go up now? You are causing me a whole lot of angst, sitting there like that. I hope there's no-one else in the lift with us.'

The blonde celebrity laughed. 'You're incorrigible! What if I were to say no?'

'Simple! I'd have to jump you right here,' her biggest fan answered, ready to spring out of his chair.

How could a woman resist? Lynn was feeling exactly the same way, never before consumed by such irrepressible passion. One more shred of proof that she had made the right decision last night, regardless of the difficult situation in which she had landed them both. She placed her empty glass on the table and rose to her full, high-heeled height.

Jeff's puppy eyes followed her face upwards, levering himself out of his chair and then giving their surroundings a quick scan. The expression on his girlfriend's face was one of sympathy. Could she see the agony written on his? This delectable concept turned him on still further.

'Thank you, angel,' he sighed, downing what was left of his beer in one mouthful. 'And I really mean that.'

Welcome To Me

Fortunately the lift was empty, and the excited couple reached their room without encountering any prying eyes. Lynn let themselves in and quickly locked the door behind them. The bed had been made and was now festooned with all manner of decorative cushions and bolsters, as befitting Australia's Best Female Vocal, drawing jeers of derision from her beau. Both running hot and desperate to make love, the lovers laughed breathlessly while the ornate furnishings were quickly dispersed onto the floor in an energetic pillow fight.

'You can leave this on though,' Jeff urged, running rapacious hands over her tight-fitting, red outfit. 'I'll pay for the dry cleaning. You are completely irresistible, d'you know that?'

After the formality of her interviews and being on her best behaviour when so deliciously distracted, the elegant songstress was ready to play. She grabbed her man round the waist and dragged him down onto the bed with her. She could see the line of his erection through his pants and looked on acquisitively as he quickly disrobed.

'Take me then,' she teased, holding out her hands. 'I'm all yours. You are still that beautiful, black stallion, Jeff Diamond!'

'Sweet Jesus, woman,' he gasped, revelling in this new assertiveness. 'What are you trying to do to me? Help me break the land speed record? Couldn't you have said something just a little more off-putting?'

Who needed four British backpackers and little Eva when here was the one-and-only Lynn Dyson telling him she was all his? Jeff was very pleased he hadn't flown back to Melbourne this morning, and even more pleased he had behaved himself since. In fact, he couldn't remember ever feeling as happy. Had Gravity the troll finally admitted defeat? Surely it was too soon for that. Perhaps the bastard had packed his bags and taken a well-earned holiday, and the stresses of the afternoon had been sanctioned free rein to stir up such a storm of sexual tension.

With one hand sneaking under the hem of his angel's red pencil skirt, weaving his special brand of magic to bring his breathless lover to a pre-emptive orgasm, and with the other wrapped possessively around her neck, Don Juan, the master himself, moved a strong, determined thumb to and fro along her jaw bone and kissed her like there was no tomorrow. His onslaught met no resistance, fast sensing her body succumb. She let out a loud groan of satisfaction and weakened in his arms as her pleasure was unleashed.

Such was the sublime yearning in his own body, Jeff was in no doubt that should Lynn but touch him below the waist, he would immediately lose all semblance of control. He felt as if he had a ticking time bomb inside him. Wrestling to keep her hands away from his engorged penis, they laughed out loud at the intensity they had generated. His partner knew exactly what was going on, and realising this only made it more difficult for the raging bull to rein in his libido. He cried out in anguish for her to stop, and his wish was instantly her command, if only for a matter of seconds before she sought to bring him on again.

Their rapturous early-evening encounter was all too soon over in a vociferous rush. Only at the very last minute did the short skirt come off and their bodies join together in the most intimate ecstasy. They were both still emotionally and physically exhausted from the events of the last twenty-four hours, leaving their blood pressure for dust in its quest for speed.

Lynn stroked her lover's face while they floated back down to Earth. 'What do you want to do this evening? Are you hungry?'

'I want to tell you who I am,' Jeff replied flatly, turning over as if he had seen a ghost.

Not receiving the answer she had expected, Lynn didn't want to cause her enigmatic stranger any distress so soon. It had been a long time since she had seen such fear in a pair of eyes, and she recognised the familiar tension in his muscles which foreshadowed that her troubled boyfriend was indeed preparing to tell her something he needed her to know.

'I thought we were going to wait until we were back in Melbourne?'

'Yes, we were. And we still can, if you want,' he responded. 'But I'm ready to talk. I've been thinking about it all day, and the time's as right as it's ever going to be. I think... I'm not really hungry. Not with all this hanging over us. Are you?'

'No, I'm not,' the young woman agreed. 'And we can always order Room Service again if we get hungry later. Are you OK though? Are you sure you want to do this now?'

Jeff turned over and looked at his dream girl, naked, flushed and his for the taking. 'Jeez, I'm so fucking sure. I want to get everything out in the open. Even *I* underestimated how much I want to be with you, and I never thought I'd say that! This thing we have is way, way more powerful than I envisaged.'

'Oh, I'm so glad you said that,' the nineteen-year-old almost moaned, taking his hands and kissing both sets of knuckles in turn. 'Me too. I've been thinking that all afternoon too.'

The pair enjoyed a leisurely shower, content to clear their heads and delay the delivery of *les grandes nouvelles* for a few more minutes. Resigned against resorting to alcohol or the rest of the white tablets which were still inside the lining of his leather jacket, Jeff sat himself at the balcony table and smoked two cigarettes in quick succession. When his gorgeous lover returned from the bathroom, she found he had opened the curtains to reveal the lights of Sydney out of their fifth-floor window.

The singer laughed when she realised her rock star bedfellow had also lined up his two awards alongside hers on the desk. 'We'd better not get them mixed up. You don't want to go down in history as Best Female Vocal nineteen-seventy-four, do you?' she joked, wrapping a white, towelling bathrobe around her body once she saw the outside world looking in. 'Do you think anyone can see us?'

'No,' the nervous man answered with a kind smile. 'There's nothing to see anyway, with that on. Just two people in a hotel room. It's happening all around us. Come and sit here.'

He motioned to the expanse of the glass, sliding doors, against which he had moved the couch and one of the armchairs. His body seemed more relaxed, dressed only in boxer shorts, the room's second bathrobe having been spread out over the chair's coarse fabric covering. Lynn ran her hands all over his muscular chest, shoulders and arms, letting it be known how appealing a sight he was. Despite his determination to fill his system with poison over the last two years, the party boy remained a fine specimen of the male human species, lean and muscular all over, with long, wavy black hair and a countenance capable of stopping people in their tracks. A mix of brain and brawn in perfect proportion that was more appealing now to the beautiful blonde by his side than it had been to her naïve, sixteen-year-old antecedent self.

'This is like our first night together,' Lynn remarked, sitting herself down on command. 'It's beautiful. Thank you.'

Jeff's heart rate was already accelerating, and his head ached badly. Regardless, he was absolutely determined to go through with this. The reference to that first night on the windowsill in Richmond served to boost his confidence, and he leaned over and kissed her smiling mouth. This had been the night when he first realised that his teenaged crush never had been a teenaged crush in the first place, but more a destiny he was about to fulfil as they sat there together. Tonight would see history repeat itself, and the twenty-two-year-old shuddered.

His stunning roommate had brought them each a glass of water, from which they drank readily after their hot, steamy liaison. 'I've got a feeling we might be here for a while.'

The affectionate superstar nestled back into a pair of waiting arms, just like she had done on that first, uncertain night, when she had surrendered her virginity to a man who was nothing more than a handsome face with a cool name and an intoxicating turn of phrase.

For his part, Jeff remembered how delicately poised his sanity had been at that time, thanking his lucky stars that he had managed to hold it together and not scare her away before he could worm his way into her heart. And now, as they prepared to dive headfirst into the most sordid details of his past, the troubled soul was thrown back into that same maelstrom of emotions once more.

Lynn knew what she was in for this time. It was not so long ago that she didn't remember how this man's reactions could swing wildly along the arc between pain and pleasure with only a word or a touch. She was on edge too, understanding only too well that with smoke there usually came fire. Her father was not an unreasonable man, and the discoveries he had made into her boyfriend's past would not be petty nuisances.

'Just remember,' she opened, stroking his right knee absentmindedly, 'I love you for who you are now, and no matter what you're about to tell me, that won't change.'

Her boyfriend emitted a heavy sigh. 'Thanks, and I love you too. I hope you're right.'

The couple sat in silence for two or three minutes while the kid from the western suburbs gathered his thoughts, both staring at the Sydney skyline. The nineteen-year-old could feel the pounding of his heart against her back, and his body temperature was on the rise again.

'OK. Here goes,' he announced with an air of resignation. 'Once upon a time...'

Lynn couldn't help giggling. 'Hey! That's funny!'

The storyteller regrouped, hugging her tightly and drinking in her positive energy. 'Once upon a time there was a boy whom they imaginatively called Jeffrey Moreno Diamond. I say imaginatively because Jeffrey is a westernised version of my paternal grandfather's name, Moreno is my mum's maiden name and Diamond... Well, we'll get to that part later.'

Again his girlfriend laughed softly, passing no comment.

'This boy was a mistake, of course. His sister had also been a mistake, so at least he wasn't the reason his parents had to get married.'

'Oh. That's good, I suppose.'

Lynn's reaction was more subdued this time. How awful to go through life knowing you weren't wanted.

Jeff continued. 'Well, nothing remarkable happened during my early years. We didn't see my dad very often. He and my mum would only fight or fuck... or both... whenever he was over, so we kind of didn't miss him. No... Come to think of it, that's not completely true. I did miss him, but I used to want to see him without my mum and Lena being around. We never did manage to do the "happy families" thing very often.'

The young man paused, breathing deeply to steady his nerves. 'My mother never understood me. Sounds melodramatic, but it's true. Lena was the apple of her eye, but I only reminded her of my dad. There was never much of a bond between the two of us, and I swear she thought I was nuts.'

Shifting position, the privileged youngster spoke. 'That's terrible. I couldn't imagine not feeling close to my parents.'

'Mmm...' the man behind murmured in agreement. 'I suppose I didn't care at the time because it was all I knew. It was only when I was invited to friends' places after school and I could see how other kids' parents behaved that I started to get the message that our family wasn't too shit hot. Anyway, somehow I ended up with all the brains, which no-one understood, including me. Apparently, I used to drive them crazy with all the questions I asked. Neither of my parents was interested in school, so they never had any answers for me, and they got so frustrated. Or embarrassed, I guess. I stopped asking after a while because they'd end up shouting at me or hitting me with something to get rid of me.'

Lynn gasped. 'Now that's terribler. I'm going to run out of adjectives in this conversation, I think.'

'Then don't say anything,' the humble orator replied. 'I'm not looking for sympathy. Just understanding.'

The caring woman squeezed his arm, which was draped around her shoulders as heavily as a carthorse's yoke. She straightened herself up a bit taller, but the hairy limb didn't budge.

'How did you feel towards Madalena during all this?'

'Much the same as for my mother really. Protective towards them, but we just didn't like each other. We were blood relations, that's all. There was an unwritten rule that we stuck together, but it wasn't based on anything else. I liked my dad at that age. Idolised him, I s'pose, but wouldn't say I was close to him either. None of that stuff bothers me though. I'm long, long over it.'

Reaching back to the memories of old conversations, Lynn recalled more sentimental feelings towards the Jewish grandmother who had given the future rock star piano lessons. 'What about your grandma who gave you that *bar mitzvah*?'

'Ha!' Jeff exclaimed. 'So you *were* listening! That's right. What a joke that was. I hadn't been to any of those classes where you learn the scriptures and I hardly read any Hebrew, so we just ate cake and drank fizzy orange with brandy in it. I'm the only semi-Jew who became a man because of good cake.'

His attentive audience raised her water glass. 'Well, I drink to that cake!'

The grateful young man kissed his dream girl so hard on the back of the head that her teeth clinked on the sturdy hotel issue tumbler from which she was sipping. She voiced a futile objection, and his stressful soul fed off her laughter greedily.

'Sorry,' he smiled. 'That's not really what I meant, but I'll accept the compliment anyway.'

The story continued. 'Meanwhile, back at the ranch, I don't really remember the defining moment when I realised my dad was involved in criminal activity. I guess I just always knew. He stole stuff and got into a whole heap of fights; came home limping, swearing and sometimes with his face or arms cut. That was just him and his mates. It was like their job, and Lena and I would've considered it normal at that stage. There was an area in our lounge room full of piles of boxes and bags that we weren't allowed to go near. All sorts of stuff: televisions, booze, knives, drugs... You name it, we had it. I did help myself every so often too, when I knew there were too many of something for them to bother counting. My mother used to cry and shout and scream at my dad about all the shit lying around and the constant stream of dodgy visitors, but his helpful solution was to come around less and less often.'

'So did the stuff move somewhere else?' Lynn interjected.

'No. We were always the warehouse. I don't even know where he lived the rest of the time. With mates who had more respect for their families probably... My mum's parents always hated my dad, right from the beginning, which meant they hated me too, because I looked like him. And also because I wasn't given a Spanish name and wasn't being brought up as a real Catholic. All the usual pointless ructions that breed hatred in the unenlightened. So, in short, my dad's parents were the only real family I had.'

The amazed woman dared to ask another question, intrigued by how different and difficult his life had been compared to hers. 'Did your parents have siblings?'

'My dad didn't. They arrived by ship from New York when he was pretty young and never had any other children. My mum had two brothers, but they disowned her pretty quickly when she took up with my dad. I've actually got seven cousins, three of whom I've never even met. And... Get this! Two of the ones I haven't met are all over me since I've made some money. Funny that, huh?'

The young star didn't think so. 'Not at all. I can only say the same thing again. That's bloody terrible, Jeff. How can they? I hope you told them to go fuck themselves.'

'Hey! Excuse me,' her boyfriend laughed, tapping her on the head. 'I'm the one who's angry here. Not you.'

'Sorry, but please,' she almost snarled in disgust. 'Continue...'

'OK. So my dad was always in trouble with the police, always being arrested and disappearing, hiding either from the police or from other gangs. He did some short stints in prison for this and that; minor offences, burglary, *et cetera*. And when he wasn't banged up, I'd come home from school pretty regularly to find him at our flat, either beating up or being beaten up by rival gang members. That was likely the beginning of the door thing. My mum or dad would always yell at me to get lost, but all I wanted to do was join in and stop him from getting hurt. You think I'm pretty hot-headed now, but this is nothing compared to what I was like as a kid. I was a crazy, wild fucker.'

'But didn't your parents or teachers notice how angry and upset you were?'

'Yeah, some of my teachers did,' Jeff smiled and tucked his hand inside the collar of her bathrobe to stroke the back of her neck. 'I remember running back to school one afternoon after going home to some violent shit, and my science teacher caught me hyperventilating over a cigarette behind one of the school buildings. I was choking, and he made me stand up while he bashed my back to clear my lungs.'

Lynn turned her head to look into his eyes. 'And then did he do anything afterwards?'

Jeff shook his head. 'What could he do? I couldn't tell him anything, could I? I told him I'd been running, and he warned me to be careful smoking when out of breath. He was probably in a hurry to get to the pub. Anyway... My mum and Lena used to get caught up in the shit too. There was nothing I could do about it, and that only made me wilder. They didn't want my help, and no-one would talk to me about it, so I'd just storm out, sometimes for days at a time. Just me, my guitar and my school books. I hid in education, music and sports when I was a kid.'

The singing Olympian raised her glass again, this time more tentative. 'I'll drink to that too. Look at what it's made you into! I've never met anyone who knows as much as you do. And I don't just mean facts. I mean you even seem to understand the reason a fact is a fact. I'd love to be like you. It's as if you're perfectly in tune with why things are the way they are. That doesn't sound very eloquent, but I hope you know what I mean.'

The tired intellectual leaned his head back against the wall, letting her praise wash over him. It was wondrously heartening to hear his dream girl speak like this, so soon after finding each other again. It was as if they had spent the last two years frozen in time and were simply taking up where they had left off. He realised he felt strangely calm and content talking about the early days. He knew he was smart, but seldom gave himself credit for exactly how smart.

'Thanks, angel,' he responded, kissing her head more gently this time. 'It means such a lot to hear you say that. I get off on knowing things. Always have. No-one else around me in those days was interested in getting a good education; even most of the teachers. Schools like ours were just somewhere for parents to send their kids to get them out of the house, and the staff were so fucking disillusioned. It used to frustrate me to death. I would argue with them forever, because it was always crystal clear to me that knowledge was the key to getting out of a miserable existence, but the system had beaten their vocation out of them.'

Lynn nodded silently, thinking of the stark contrast with her own education. The teachers at Melbourne Academy would stop at nothing to get the most out of their students. Needing to move away from the easy topics, Jeff felt his heart rate increasing again.

'Anyway, back to the story. You keep leading me astray, you gorgeous woman. It won't do. We'll be here all night,' he said, feeling her body sink deeper into his with the gentle humour and taking another deep breath.

'When I turned eleven or so, I started to develop real anger issues. And I mean REAL ANGER ISSUES,' he hissed in his captive's right ear.

The slender superstar giggled nervously in his arms, the eerie tone in his voice sending tremors down her spine. 'Stop! I believe you.'

Jeff held her tight and kissed the soft skin on the side of her neck. There remained a lingering hint of this morning's perfume, infused with the intoxicating residual scent of their warm, recently united bodies. Breathing her in, his left hand returned inside the towelling robe and caressed the delicate skin along her collarbone and back towards her sternum. Tremors of a whole different nature resonated from her body back into his fingers.

'Christ, angel, I love talking to you. Can you feel it? I was so scared what we had before wouldn't exist anymore.'

The comfortable female form in his arms exhaled and twisted herself around until she could look into her lover's eyes. 'I'm so sorry I was such a cow to you the other day, and last night. I really didn't know if I had the guts to stand up to Dad, but since talking with you again and feeling your hands on my skin, I know you're everything I ever wanted. None of the men I was with made me feel the way you do. Not even close.'

'Baby, stop, will you?' the tormented storyteller begged, unable to control his emotions. 'I'm only just hanging on here. Can you believe it's been over two years since we sat like this and shared something this special? It feels like yesterday to me.'

'Me too,' Lynn agreed, turning round again, this time to kiss his lips. 'Although for me, the longer we'd been apart, the more convinced I was that I wanted to be with you. And that's the opposite of what was supposed to happen, I imagine.'

'Does your dad know that?'

'No,' she replied. 'I think Mum suspects, but Dad wouldn't have a clue. And my auntie… Mum's sister… had a real go at me the other day.'

'About me?'

'Yes,' the young woman laughed. 'Mum obviously told her that we used to go out together, because she gave me this "if you know what's good for you" lecture.'

The bad boy chuckled too. Whoever this auntie was, she had a point. Regardless, it was hard to envisage anyone lecturing someone so perfectly behaved, he lamented in silence, already fairly sure how the conversation would have gone. The beautiful face confirmed he was on the right track, but he asked anyway.

'So what was she saying?'

'Oh, the usual,' Lynn responded, stroking his face and putting on an upper-classed accent. 'Something like, "He might be ever so handsome, darling, but he's always drunk and he can't keep his trousers on." And to be honest, I couldn't argue with her. That's the only Jeff Diamond most people know, isn't it?'

The Australian Elvis scoffed at the irony of their situation but chose not to pursue the topic. He couldn't work out why he didn't feel at least a modicum of shame that people might characterise him in these terms. The sarcasm in Lynn's voice gave him confidence. He wasn't ashamed, so why should he fake it? He was who he was, inside and out. He was an adult, he made his own money, and no children or animals had been harmed in the process. If the amazing woman in his arms was prepared to accept him for who he was, who gave a damn about Marianna Dyson's sister's opinion?

'The only Jeff Diamond *anyone* knows,' he moved an amendment, 'until now.'

The lovers clung onto each other, hearts full with the release they both felt from being honest, and the amazing woman in his arms kissed him full on the lips.

'So carry on with the story, please.'

'OK,' Jeff sighed, sniffing back tears and relaxing a little. 'It's just so fantastic, that's all. I'd like to acknowledge the moment. Where was I? Ah, yeah. Anger issues. Probably from eleven to sixteen or thereabouts, I was constantly fighting and arguing. At thirteen, fourteen, I hated everyone, especially myself. At that stage, I hadn't learned to identify myself separately from my situation. I was full of blame and guilt. Still am, but I can rationalise it better now.'

'Did you know Gerry's family by then?' Lynn asked, trying to piece things together.

'Yes, but not that well. He and I were good mates, mainly from playing sports. We didn't hang out socially that much because of the distance between our homes. I didn't start spending time at their house until later, probably when I found out his sisters were good-looking. I hadn't formulated my using versus respecting relationships theory back then either, so I felt like a leech whenever I bummed someone else's hospitality. Quite apart from that, I was always in trouble, so the Blakes wouldn't have put up with me like that. My dad hung out with these other two Polish blokes, the Jaworski brothers. They dealt in everything: weapons, prostitutes from Eastern Europe and Asia, TVs, drugs, one hundred percent pure alcohol... Pretty much everything illegal. He tried to funnel it all through my mum's parents' business, but that was a no-go.

One of the Jawos had sons who were in on it, and my father always tried to get me involved, to fence stuff at school instead, *et cetera*.'

His girlfriend's weight shifted again, reaching for her half-empty glass. 'Fence? That's such a weird word, I've always thought. Why do they say fencing?'

'That's something I don't know,' the normally well-informed man admitted. 'I read somewhere that it was an abbreviation of "defence", but I don't see the association. It's pretty tenuous. Perhaps because the fence represents a boundary between the thief and everyone else, so you can't link seller to buyer? I prefer that theory, but it's probably crap.'

'Oh, OK,' his contented muse smiled. 'I prefer the crap version too.'

Lynn didn't really care. She was more interested in how the story was going to develop.

'So is this what Dad's so interested in?'

Jeff sighed again, knowing this piece was only part of a much bigger puzzle. 'I guess so. And I'm not blameless, angel. I can't hide the fact that I was involved. The police know who I am. I used to get hold of drugs for my own use, and for my mother, who by that time was totally addicted. Just imagine what life was like for her... She couldn't possibly have known that when she married my dad she'd end up a fucked-up whore. OK, I never loved her, but it was a shit-storm of a life for her all the same. She couldn't have survived on her own. She was clueless at the best of times.'

The angry twenty-two-year-old took a deep breath and banged his head against the wall behind him a couple of times in frustration. His audience said nothing, simply kissing the tense, muscular arm which continued to constrict her windpipe. He carried on, stroking her hair with his left hand to calm himself down.

'So if your dad wants to dig up stuff from back then, that's fine. I'm not going to deny anything, but it's not who I am now. Whatever I did as a juvenile, I was only doing it to survive. We never had any money, and my father never gave us any. Fuck knows what he did with any money he made.'

Jeff was beginning to feel quite dizzy. They should have had dinner first after all, he regretted, because they were barely past the start line in the long, drawn out life history of this nobody he would rather leave behind. His heart rate quickened still further, and his eyes stung. He leaned them both forward to give himself some space to breathe more deeply.

'Baby, do you mind if I have a cigarette?' he asked, slipping off the sofa and stretching his legs.

'No, of course not. What about a beer from the mini-bar?'

This was an excellent idea. The overwrought man crossed the room to the small refrigerator which was hidden behind a mahogany panel under the television.

'Do you want anything?' he asked, almost tipping backwards as he crouched down in front of the fridge.

'Is there any red wine? Are you OK?'

Jeff picked out a quarter bottle of *Cabernet Sauvignon*, a tin of beer and two miniatures of Scotch. He nodded and gave her the broadest grin he could.

'I'll pay you back for all this stuff.'

'No, you won't!' Lynn exclaimed.

Making his way back to the window, the tall superstar was amazed to see his goodie-two-shoes lover lighting two cigarettes from the packet on his bedside table. With both hands full, he bent down so that she could put one between his lips and watched in awe as she began to smoke the other herself.

He smiled. How sexy was that? Immediately, he felt his penis swell, pondering the rights and wrongs of taking a break from his harrowing story. No, he decided. They had plenty of time for such pleasures. His focus must be on ridding themselves of his secrets. He dropped the tiny whisky bottles onto the carpet and took the cigarette out of his mouth, tapping ash off the end and seeing his girlfriend's eyes alight on his full shorts.

'Leave it out, angel,' he teased. 'I can't control what you do to me. Get used to it, huh? I didn't know you smoked.'

'I hardly ever do,' Lynn replied, shrugging. 'I just feel like keeping you company today. I'll pay you back!'

'*Touché*,' her man whispered, leaning forward to share a sacred, smoky kiss.

The couple settled back down on the couch, this time facing each other with the undersides of their feet touching. There was an expectant look on the lady's face, so the *troubadour* continued. He knew he was nearing the dangerous part, not wholly sure he could go through with it while looking directly at her.

He took a deep breath. 'So... Where was I?'

'Your survival. And having no money.'

'Yeah. Thanks. Things just got worse and worse,' he nodded. 'Here, listening to my own words, I sound so sorry for myself. I don't mean to, but there's no other way to describe it without glossing over it. Lena spent a lot of time at my mum's parents' place, but I wouldn't go there. Christ, Lynn! I had so much hate in me. Still have, although I'm better at controlling that too. Slightly, anyway... You wouldn't believe how much I despised my family. I would've given anything to be adopted by Gerry's parents. I wished I'd been adopted out right from the beginning.'

'Do you still?' Lynn asked, before correcting herself. 'Well, no. I think I know the answer to that.'

Jeff's eyes invited her to offer her prognosis, looking provocatively downwards from under furrowed brows as he tipped his beer bottle almost vertical to empty it into his thirsty gullet.

'You wouldn't be who you are if you'd been adopted,' she confidently answered her own question.

'Correct,' her handsome stranger affirmed, toasting her words with a whisky chaser containing barely enough for a single mouthful. 'Jesus! That was ninety percent fumes.'

Lynn smiled as he drank the second amber dose wantonly along with the various other drugs.

Feeling anxiety mounting again, the twenty-two-year-old let out a long moan. 'Alright then... Because my dad was hardly ever there, the Jaworskis and some other men whom I didn't even know used to come around to our flat regularly and have sex with my mum and Lena.'

Hearing this latest nasty sentence, his squeaky-clean partner tensed up and inhaled sharply in shock. Jeff ignored her reaction to maintain his resolve.

'My dad knew about it but didn't do anything to stop it. Didn't or couldn't, I never knew which. That's when things really turned shithouse for the rest of us. I remember coming home from school one afternoon to find four blokes in the flat, taking turns at fucking them. They'd given 'em drugs, and they were all completely off their faces. High as fucking kites. I tried to rip the bastards off my mother, but she screamed and tried to stop me. I think she thought I was one of them. She had no idea what she was doing half the time.'

Lynn was aghast. 'My God. How awful. You must've felt so powerless.'

'You're not wrong there,' he scoffed.

Australia's darling could plainly see her man was struggling with his emotions. 'You can be angry if you want to,' she offered. 'No-one'll hear.'

Jeff stood up and turned out the lights, with the teenager following his movements carefully. It was as if he needed to rearrange his surroundings as a way to organise his thoughts. He lifted the upright chair away from the desk and sat on it, beside her but not facing her, then lit another cigarette and offered it her way.

The sportswoman refused, shaking her head and smiling. 'No, thanks. One's enough. Are you OK? Do you want to stop?'

'No and no. I'm not OK but there's no way I'm going to stop now,' the furious songwriter answered, leaning his head onto his hands. 'Give me a minute, please, angel. I just need to breathe without talking for a change.'

It was still possible for the pair to see each other reasonably clearly, courtesy of the city lights through their window. Lynn's beautiful, black stallion was wiping tears from his shining eyes, gazing out at the tall trees opposite and breathing deliberately. After an inordinately long pause, he eventually broke the silence.

'You know, angel,' he almost whispered, through gritted teeth, 'I honestly thought I'd carry this story to my grave. I'm just so sick of being blamed for everything. I think that's the crux of it all. I have so much anger and guilt and disgust at who I was and where I came from, but virtually none of it was my doing. I was back there today, actually. Tried to find my sister but failed. Then I went to a boxing club that these fuckers used to terrorise, to see if I can find out about anything your dad might be looking for.'

The awestruck woman felt guilty too. 'I'm really sorry you're having to go through this,' she lamented, leaning across and placing her hand on his knee. ''Specially when you should've been able to leave it all behind by now. You have every right to refuse and just leave me.'

Jeff let out a loud groan, slapping his thighs in frustration at the sheer inconceivability of this idea. 'Are you kidding? Leave you? Fuck, no! I've only just found you again. I'm not about to lose you over this. No way, baby. Not without one hell of a fight anyway. You're the only thing worth fighting for, as far as I'm concerned. You were the only thing that kept me going through all that shit back then, and the only thing that gave me hope after what I'm about to tell you. Jesus fucking Christ! Believe me, if you hadn't come into my life through the TV and radio and cast your spell over my soul, I would've checked out long ago.'

This almost throw-away comment rocked the compassionate star to the core. She presumed Jeff meant suicide and was beginning to appreciate the depths of despair that he had visited. Fancy being a boy with so much potential in such a damaging environment? She rose to her feet silently, walked round behind him and began to massage his shoulders and neck.

'I hope I deserve you.'

The old soul collapsed back onto her hands, unable to hold back the torrent of emotions any longer, his empathetic companion administering a catharsis beyond his wildest dreams after all these years of waiting. Breathing heavily, he lurched forwards again and held his head in his hands, while enormous teardrops began to land noisily on the carpet.

After a few minutes, the pressure behind his eyes lessened, and he sniffed back the tears and coughed. 'Sorry, angel. I'm not a very entertaining *raconteur*, am I?'

'Shut up. Do you want to stop?' Lynn asked. 'Even for half an hour or so?'

'No. But tell you what... Could we order a life-sized bottle of whisky?' he replied, holding up the two empty miniatures.

Lynn laughed aloud at the image his words conjured up, losing no time in crossing the room to dial Room Service and place an order. On her way back, she planted a kiss on the top of her lover's soaking wet head. His body was radiating heat, so she handed him a refilled glass of water, fearing he would dehydrate with all the alcohol he intended to consume.

'Thanks,' Jeff said, a little more collected. 'So... Where were we? *Yadda, yadda, yadda.* All this fucked-up shit went on for another couple of years. D'you remember, when we were going out last time, we went to the movies once with Michelle, and I was really edgy?'

'Yes,' the former schoolgirl affirmed. '"The Godfather." You told me to ignore you. I remember you kept looking around, and at the end you seemed very relieved to get out into the fresh air again.'

The young man laughed dryly. She remembered alright.

'Well, let me tell you where that particular endearing quality came from.'

His girlfriend nodded, inviting him to carry on. No longer inhibited, the scarred adolescent trapped inside roared again as the memories came rushing back, rocking on the chair's hind legs and shaking his dark mane as if to rid himself of some vile, ghostly noose.

'I was sitting in a movie theatre with some school mates, minding our own business, when my dad burst into the cinema. He was looking for me because he'd found out that my mum'd been raped and I hadn't been there to protect her. He'd snatched a torch from the staff and was shining it everywhere, shouting my name. It was so fucking embarrassing. All the girls were screaming. Anyway, he found me and dragged me out of my seat by the collar of my t-shirt. Then, in the foyer of the cinema, he laid into me... kicking me... and I was kicking and punching him back. What a fucking spectacle, huh?'

Jeff didn't wait for a comment, knowing there was little anyone could say. 'So ever since then, I've avoided going to the movies because my brain can't stop thinking of that time. Whenever I went again... and that was only once, I think, before our night out... I constantly felt him creeping up behind me, and all my mind could think about was is hand about to grab hold of my shirt and yank me backwards. All I wanted in those days was to be left alone. I didn't want to get involved, and he was determined to draw me into his seedy, no-hope world.'

Seeing her man was crying again, the apprehensive young woman moved nervously to sit on his lap. He wrapped her up in his arms hungrily, kissing her shoulder through the thick, towelling bathrobe.

'Jeff, I had no idea how bad things were. How you must have wished so hard for a normal life. I feel so sorry for you.'

Lynn kissed him long and tenderly on the lips. Never had a connection felt so deep between two people, as they shared these dark, unsavoury secrets in an anonymous hotel room. She vowed to see this relationship through to the bitter end, whatever that might mean, while her boyfriend's tortured mind independently concluded that if everything fell apart in the ensuing weeks, he would die a fulfilled man, knowing the depth of devotion his dream girl felt for him right at this moment.

There was a knock at the door, interrupting their private dedications. The famous blonde collected the drinks from the attendant and signed on the dotted line. She poured herself a glass of wine and half-filled a tumbler with ice and whisky for her secret guest. He gulped the whole lot down, crunching the ice blocks comically, and held the glass out towards her for a refill.

'Thanks. That's good. That night, the police arrested both of us and locked us in separate cells,' he continued. 'They thought I was sixteen, but I was only twelve, so they had to let me go.'

'Twelve? Wow!' Lynn asked, replenishing his glass without question. 'But not him?'

'Yeah, they let him go too,' Jeff answered. 'Later on. There was no way I was going to press charges on my own father, and they knew it wasn't worth holding him without that. They had much better things to do with their time than look after the dead-beat kid of a known offender.'

'But you weren't a dead-beat kid.'

'As far as they were concerned, I was.'

The privileged celebrity frowned and shook her head, astounded at how poorly a child could be treated by the law. 'I can't believe your dad punished you for not protecting your mum. Surely that was *his* job? Shouldn't he have been protecting her himself?'

'Well, you'd have bloody well hoped so, wouldn't you?' her rock star agreed bitterly. 'He was angry too. We were actually very alike, him and me, as you've no doubt guessed. Anyway... This is taking way too long. I've got to finish the story before we leave for the airport.'

Lynn allowed herself to laugh this time. 'Oh, my God! How much more is there?'

The exhausted man inhaled deeply. Oh, yes. There was plenty more.

'My dad went crazy after that. He always called the gang his friends. "*Kolega*", he used to say in Polish, which I think means "partner" as well as "mate", but there was never any friendship there. He turned on the Jaworskis. No, that's not accurate. They all turned on each other, more correctly. My dad was out to get revenge for what they did. My mum was completely hooked on LSD and amphetamines, and they were supplying her and then nicking his stock to pay for it. I'd long since stopped supplying her at that stage, wiser about drugs by then, and used to try and get doctors to come in and take her away. But no doctor would listen, or they just didn't want to get involved. Whatever... And there was no way I was going to contact Social Services because they would have taken me and Lena into care. Can I have a kiss?'

There was nothing Lynn would rather have given him right at that moment. Their lips found each others' in the semi-darkness, quickly followed by their tongues. This time, there was no sexual overtone. The two lovers tried their hardest to become one, both compelled to communicate their subliminal and unfailing commitment. When they finally pulled apart and took a breath, Jeff felt as if his heart was on the verge of splitting in two. Why was he so scared? He had been feeling fairly comfortable with spilling his guts up until the last few minutes. He was petrified of one thing, and one thing alone: the all-consuming childhood fear of abandonment, whirling like a Category Eight cyclone in his head. He couldn't face being freed from his moorings in such rough weather. There was no telling what he might do.

'Thanks for indulging me,' he said, fixing her blue eyes in his. 'Can I ask one more thing of you before we carry on?'

'Of course. What? God, you look so deadly serious all of a sudden.'

'Jeez, I am serious. I need to hear you say something, please. Look into your eyes when you say it...'

'Say what?'

The lost boy's eyes pleaded with hers. 'Whatever happens in the next few days and weeks, just don't throw me out tonight, please, angel.'

Horror spread across Lynn's face. 'Throw you out? Jeff, I love you. I most definitely will *not* throw you out tonight, nor any other night. I don't want to lose you again either. I want to be with you just as much as you want to be with me. Please believe me.'

'Even if you can't stomach what you hear, at least let me stay here until the morning. Please?'

The young woman blanched at the look of terror on her traumatised lover's face. This was one of the most influential men in Australian popular culture, with a reputation for electrifying concert performances and for his outspoken approach to social justice. It was almost impossible to accept that the quivering mess on whose lap she now sat was one and the same person.

Jeff appeared to relax a little, his eyes closed and his hands releasing her arms from the vice. Brushing his cheek on the way, Lynn interlaced the fingers of her right hand into his left and proceeded to kiss each hairy knuckle in turn, not forgetting the thumb. A smile spread over his face, and miraculously, the virile rock star made his latest comeback.

'OK! So one day, I'd been studying late at the library, not wanting to go home, as usual, when the librarian came looking for me, saying the police were there to see me. I was cornered, so I couldn't run, which was what my instincts told me to do. But that was a good thing, as it turned out. They took me to the police station. My sister was already there when I arrived, flanked by a female uniformed officer and a social worker, which I guessed could only mean bad news. They sat us in a grey, windowless room and told us that our dad had been arrested, suspected of murdering both Jaworski brothers. *Sang froid, comme on dit.*'

Lynn gasped, letting rip with her stateside drawl. 'Shit! Really? *Merde, je veux dire.* Oh, my God!'

This made Jeff laugh, jolting him back to the present. 'I love it when you swear, my gorgeous Yankee angel. It comes so out of the blue that it surprises me every time.'

'I'm glad you can still laugh. God, this is a terrible, terrible, terrible story,' she replied, holding her hands over her face momentarily.

The exhausted storyteller was grateful. It felt incredibly liberating to admit his beautiful best friend behind his thick, black clouds at last. He needed to be careful though, since it was way too soon to know what she really thought. This cataclysmic information couldn't possibly have sunk in yet, so he couldn't allow himself to trust her initial reaction.

'I remember asking the police where my mother was,' he carried on, kissing her temple. 'They either didn't know or weren't going to tell me. They wouldn't let me talk to my dad, so I got Lena out of there as quick as I could and convinced her to stay away from the flat until I could figure out what had happened. To this day, I've never figured out what happened. I wasn't allowed to go to the trial because I was too young. The lawyers gave me as much information as they felt like, which wasn't much, and I never got the chance to hear it from the horse's mouth.'

'Do you think he did it?' Lynn asked straight out. 'Your dad, I mean. Murder them?'

'For a long time I didn't,' Jeff replied. 'I guess that's how it is when you're a kid. You want to trust your parents instinctively because you're dependent on them. Kids don't see that parents can be bad people too. But in recent years, I've changed my mind. As I grew older and saw how my own anger was so hard to control, I believe he's guilty, yes.'

'So what happened to him?' the young woman hoped she wasn't pushing too hard.

On the contrary, her lover was grateful for her questions. It focussed his mind on the pieces of the puzzle which remained unexplained. He wanted to make sure he was giving her the truth, the whole truth and nothing but the truth. He was drinking steadily, directly from the whisky bottle, but wasn't feeling at all drunk, eventually letting out a bitter growl to signal he was about to speak the words he never imagined confessing openly.

'Paul Diamond's having a long stay at Parklea, one of the Queen's most salubrious holiday camps. Maximum security. He got two life sentences and will probably come up for parole in nineteen-eighty-five or somewhere around there. He won't get out. My grandparents'll never agree to it, let alone the Jaworski family.'

The rejected son's breaths were fast and erratic. He reached for his packet of cigarettes, but Lynn's swift reflexes beat him to it and pulled it smartly out of the way. Cocking his head to one side at her unexpected show of dominance, he acquiesced with a half-smile and a flash of his crazy-horse eyes. He wasn't sure what her game was, but felt so confused and lightheaded that he succumbed to what he hoped was a plan superior to feeding his brain with more drugs.

Now that she had a better idea of what she was dealing with, the patient, blonde celebrity elected to drive her boyfriend through this ordeal as quickly as possible. Everything was beginning to make perfect sense: the nightmares, the door phobia, his odd relationship with the rest of his family and his dedication to making himself into a someone... It was not a crime of Jeff's own doing that rendered him so unsuitable in her parents' eyes, but one he had been given no choice but to inherit.

With a considerable amount of relief, Lynn focussed on her stallion's dazed expression, smiled and spoke without a trace of sentimentality. 'Have you ever visited him?'

'No,' he shook his head. 'I just took the decision to walk away, rightly or wrongly.'

The young man caught his breath and fell silent for a while. His towelling-wrapped partner slid off his lap onto the floor, putting her hands on his knees and then laying her head on them. She felt his palm come to rest gently on the back of her neck, cold and clammy and really, really heavy. How this man could communicate so clearly without any sound at all never ceased to amaze her. His breathing was still laboured, and the muscles in his legs were twitching, yet a weird air of finality had begun to circulate in the darkening room.

'Wrongly,' Jeff corrected himself, suddenly shaking violently as the shock of putting these events into words after so long came to a head.

His voice cracking, the angry man continued. 'Then, about a year after my dad was put away, my mum took a fatal overdose. She was a full-time slag by then, feeding the addictions she'd cultivated to mask her depression. When she was lucid, she was really fucking lower than low, so she'd scrounge together enough money for another hit, and life would be good again for a few days. Lena'd all but vanished into my grandmother's clutches. She didn't care, and most of the time I reckoned that was a good thing best left as it was. My sister never learned to love anyone. I guess it must be pretty bloody impossible to love someone if you were raped repeatedly before puberty. Before you even know what love is... You know, in that respect, angel, I was the lucky one.'

Speechless, the empathetic beauty kissed her boyfriend's left knee. Signalling his heartfelt thanks, the twenty-two-year-old lifted her hands away and stood up. She watched from the floor as he struggled to control his temper, pacing around like a caged animal. Suddenly, he let out a loud cry and smacked the wall with the heels of his clenched fists.

'Lynn, I'm sorry. This is so fucking hard to talk about. I've hidden it away so deep, I never thought I'd get it out again. I'm just so sick of being alone in this secret, fucked-up world of mine. Help me. Please help me.'

The teenager was torn between the safety of the carpet and playing a part in this desperate scene. Never before had she been needed like this.

'Hey, you gorgeous man, come and sit down,' she invited. 'Just talk. You're almost done, aren't you? Surely there can't be much more. I don't care what words come out or how loud you shout. I want to be touching you.'

Feeling disoriented and completely unhinged, Jeff obeyed robotically. They resumed their former position, and he relented a little to the pressure behind his eyes. It was time to choose: surrender to his soul-mate once and for all or go over the edge into insanity, perhaps never to return. His macho pride was strong, but the desire for a better future was stronger.

Calling upon every ounce of fortitude, he continued. 'After my dad was put away, I stayed in the flat with my mum for about a year, I guess. Watching her slowly spiral downwards. I stopped trying to save her. She didn't want me to, and I didn't have any confidence that things'd ever get any better. I closed my mind to everything as best I could, but in reality it didn't work. I was only kidding myself.'

Lynn cupped his tear-stained face in her hand. 'I love you.'

'Fuck, I love you too. That was the final straw for my door phobia. It was always me who came home to those disgusting scenes, having to chuck out the pigs who enjoyed having sex with my spaced-out, semi-conscious mother. I don't know why, but that particular day Lena and I arrived at the flat at the same time. Psychic forces, maybe? Don't know if I believe in that stuff, but it was uncanny the way it turned out. I opened the bedroom door and saw my mum's body lying there, in a pool of blood and vomit, with pills and syringes everywhere. She'd tried to slash her wrists as well. Shit, Lynn, it was a real mess. I just froze. In disbelief, I suppose.'

Sensing they were reaching the end, the orator's shell-shocked audience looked up into his bloodshot eyes and urged him to go on. She guessed that too much sympathy at this late stage might give him licence to escape before he had fully exorcised his ghosts, and she owed it to him to make sure that absolutely everything was out in the open.

Jeff took another large swig of whisky from a glass his lover had poured and followed it with another deep breath, battling with the haunting pictures in his mind. 'I wasn't going to let Lena see, so I shut the door again and told her to go back to our grandparents. I must've had immense powers of influence over her at that moment because she didn't protest. She just disappeared. At least, that's how I remember it. So I phoned for an ambulance and tried to resuscitate my mum, but I knew she was already dead.'

The lost boy began to sob as he spoke, but he wasn't about to quit now. The end was in sight, and his *Regala* was behaving exactly as he had hoped she would. She was giving him all the space he needed while somehow not allowing him to wander off. She wasn't judging him and neither was she loading on the pathos. He crunched a large lump of ice, coughed and wiped his mouth. With angry resignation, he began to draw his story to a close.

'And I wasn't fucking there to stop it, was I? Again. My grandparents blamed me for leaving her on her own, and Lena immediately took their side. The police came and took statements from everybody. All the neighbours were there on our landing, peering into the flat. I went off at them. Really effing wild I was, apparently. I hardly have any memory of those few weeks. They took me into custody and ended up giving me a sedative injection. In case I killed someone too, probably...'

Chancing a sickly smile, Jeff paused to gauge the reaction of his subdued lady. Her chin still rested on his chest, gazing out of the window. Her eyes were shining, and she looked so incredibly exquisite. He felt her kiss his shoulder again and took it as another nudge to get this sorry tale over with.

'And do you know the part that pissed me off the most at the time?'

The spellbound woman shook her head. 'What was that?'

He let out a bitter chuckle. 'The next day, I was due to sit an early HSC exam. I didn't turn up. Surprise, surprise... And a few days later, when I went back to school, there was this sarky message for me to explain why I'd treated the school with such disrespect when they obtained special permission for me to take the exam.'

'HSC at fourteen?' Lynn checked, suddenly putting two and two together.

'Yep. Only three subjects,' the nonchalant reply came. 'Shows where my priorities were, doesn't it? And to tell you the truth, I'm not ashamed of it. Even now.'

The singer was dumbfounded. 'Wow. And what happened then?'

Her man laughed again, somewhat maniacally. 'You're probably expecting me to say I murdered the school principal, but I didn't...'

The nervous teenager raised her head to see if he was serious or not. There was only an impish smile on his face, but she decided to tread carefully nonetheless. Was there no end to the evening's twists and turns?

'No, I wasn't. I don't know what to expect,' she answered. 'The whole thing is just so horrible. What *did* you do?'

The young man regretted his last comment. He was asking a great deal for Lynn to take this all in at once. He definitely hadn't earned the right to any roguish arrogance, no matter how compassionate she was. He cursed the ease with which he had moved to take advantage of her open heart.

'Sorry,' he said. 'I didn't do anything. Didn't have to. Social Services rang the principal shortly after I'd found the message. They told him about my mum's violent end, and he and the teacher came crawling to apologise. I made 'em fucking pay, I can tell you.'

'Good!' Lynn smiled in wonderment.

She could just imagine the seething fourteen-year-old storming into the principal's office and laying it on the line. She was coming to understand what Celia must have meant when she described him as dangerous. Jeff Diamond had always fought hard to get what he wanted, the Olympic sportswoman concluded; just like Gerry and Suzanne had hinted when she had first met them, and not so unlike her own experience at the awards ceremony the previous night.

'Then, after the funeral,' her boyfriend's voice sounded much calmer now, 'Social Services were hounding me to stay at my grandparents' or they were going to make me a Ward of Court. I wasn't having any of that, so I disappeared. That's when I started spending the nights at school, or at Gerry's or with any girl who'd have me, or just outside somewhere. I got myself part-time jobs so I could keep paying the rent on the flat, and just eked out an existence as best I could.'

'And all through this, I kept on studying, socialising, putting on my game face every morning. And what makes me even more fuckin' angry is the fact that it's not just me. There's a whole heap of kids like me out there, being done over by all and sundry. I saw some of them on the bus today and tried to pick the ones who were going home to some substandard life or other. I should be able to stop it but I can't.'

Jeff's voice faltered again as he were finding it more and more difficult to breathe, causing Lynn to worry that he might be about to pass out. Thinking about coaxing him onto the bed, she made him drink some water, but he only chased this down with yet more whisky.

'Yet...' he added, summoning renewed determination. 'I can't stop it yet. But I will, if it's the last thing I bloody well do.'

'*We'll* stop it, Jeff. I'll help you. Come over here and lie down.'

The twenty-two-year-old didn't need to be asked twice. He picked up bottle and glass and made his way over to where paradise awaited him. Last night's silk nightdress had been hurriedly slipped over her head while he was looking the other way, the bathrobe now discarded on the floor. The vision was divine, all fear now having vanished from his angel's come-hither eyes. For his part, he felt remarkably calm and clear-headed, even though his heart felt as though it was about to implode and his head ached from the multitude of emotions which he was endeavouring to keep in check.

The final stretch, the relieved confessor thought to himself. 'So, there I was. Mister Wonderful, girlfriends chasing me everywhere, passing exams with flying colours, playing sport after school and going home at night as an utter fucking wreck. That's when the nightmares started with a vengeance too, on top of fighting with the door demons...'

Lynn interrupted. 'Who are the door demons exactly?'

'Anyone and everyone!' he laughed, astonished by how willing he was to answer the question which had previously been out of bounds. 'Different every time. Sometimes it's my dad, but mostly the Jaworskis or other gang members. Bosses, teachers, police... In fact, anyone whom I think has done me wrong. And I wasn't going to tell you this, but last night your father and I were punching each others' lights out.'

His lover smiled in recognition. 'I knew you'd been punched! Your face shot across to one side, and you rubbed your chin,' she mimicked his somnolent actions. 'I didn't know it was Dad though. I hope you didn't hurt him too much!'

Jeff felt guilty. 'No. He'll be OK. It's eating me up though, this whole investigation thing.'

'So when you were shouting, "Leave her alone" last night...' Lynn asked. 'That was your mum? Being raped?'

The exhausted man nodded, caught unawares by another wave of tears. 'Yep. Or my sister, or both,' he cried into his hands, sitting up and leaning his elbows on his knees. 'And the worst part is, even though in my dreams it feels like I care, when I'm awake I don't care. I can't care, and I hate that. The guilt strangles me.'

The beautiful woman, who had jumped out of bed and run round to sit at the distressed man's feet, moved his hand aside and rested her head on his thigh, rubbing it gently. At any other time, this would have made him instantly horny, but not now. Instead, he was overwhelmed by the amount of love his dream girl was channelling, with this new relationship of theirs not yet even twenty-four hours old. He thanked her by placing his trembling hand on top of her head and stroking her hair.

Lynn was pleased to finally have a clearer picture of what her boyfriend saw when faced with a closed door. All those mysterious snippets of information he had given her back in nineteen-seventy-two, when she was a virginal sixteen-year-old schoolgirl, were slotting gradually into place. On reflection, it had been judicious and thoughtful of the hot-headed student to have spared her naïve, under-aged sensibilities from such disturbing details, she realised. This wise and caring man had known then that she didn't yet possess the maturity to react properly. She scarcely did now. Most likely she would have seen it all as a heady, romantic adventure, thereby being keen to toss away her privileged, well-planned future for a good-for-nothing son of a murderer.

And no wonder Jeff had been so determined to succeed in his own right during their two-year separation. The aristocrat appreciated perfectly now why being a someone held such importance. He had built a rock solid name for himself which no-one could call into question, even if people were to find out where he came from. The issue remained whether these people included her father... Lynn wasn't sure, yet had no doubt in her mind as to where her loyalties would lie once the terrible story broke.

'So if you resolve a situation in everyday life, does that person cease to exist in your nightmares?'

Her boyfriend looked up and smiled. It was a question which demonstrated that this special woman understood perfectly how intertwined his subconscious was with his reality.

'Yeah, mostly,' he replied, reaching out for her hand for the first time in a while. 'I can't think of many things that've been resolved, to give you an example though. Actually, no... I can, and you're probably right. I don't see teachers these days, so I'd say they've gone to plague some other poor student.'

Lynn giggled. '¡Excelente! That gives us something to work with, at least. Didn't the doctors Celia sent you to offer anything to try?'

'Fuck. I didn't give a shit! I never listened to them in those days,' Jeff confessed in shame. 'I just went through with it to get the Blakes off my case. I was an ungrateful bastard back then. Even more than I am now. I really wanted so much for life to end, but forced myself to keep hopeful that I had a bright future. I knew there was a whole lot I could do to try and fix some of the problems around me; like those that had led to my parents being like they were. With a bit of education, most people's lives could be so much better.'

A huge, trembling hand hovered in front of the teenager's enchanted expression, and loving fingers began to stroke her cheek. Getting to her feet, her lips moved towards his and kissed them tenderly. She had already guessed what the intellectual was about to say, caught in another moment of unfathomable déjà-vu, and listened in wonderment, assuming she would never know how or why she had been selected so purposefully to walk this path with him.

Jeff exhaled, leaning forward and lifting the young woman up beside him on the mattress. 'And then there was Lynn Dyson. I had her records, posters and magazine cuttings stuck to every smooth surface in the flat. I used to play her music and talk to her like a madman when I was feeling like crap and wondering what else I could do to make sense of it all.'

The girl in his arms burst into tears and was quickly smothered in overdue sympathy. 'Can I ask you another question, please?' she gulped.

'Sure. Anything,' he nodded, putting on a frightened expression and making her giggle. 'Can't hide anything from you now. There ain't much left to tell, baby!'

Tentatively, the beautiful nineteen-year-old shifted away from his body, raised her hand and drew a line on his right side with her finger starting from his lower ribs to just above his hip, joining the three scars she had noticed a long time ago and had pondered ever since.

'How did you get these?'

At his request, both stood up, facing each other. His eyes bore into hers, nervous again, as she fully expected. There was no agitation this time however. He took hold of both of her hands and laid them on his chest, hugging her into him.

'You already know how I got those.'

'You told me they were from a fight at school,' Lynn recounted, 'but I'm not quite sure what that means anymore.'

Jeff kissed her full on the lips for a long time, evidently in no hurry to fill in the blanks. An odd serenity seemed to be floating in the atmosphere of their luxurious hotel room. As before, the depth of her comprehension took his breath away.

'It means a fight happened at school,' he repeated casually as she broke away, her eyes begging him for a straight answer, 'with someone carrying a knife.'

'Someone you knew?'

'Yes.'

The tone of his monosyllabic reply was reserved and ominous, leaving Lynn horrified that her suspicions were being confirmed.

'A gang member or your dad?'

The boy from Sydney's west let out a heavy sigh, knowing he had no right to obscure the truth any longer.

'It wasn't a gang member.'

An ominous stillness descended on the pair, more oppressive than the last, as they stood locked together. It was unthinkable for Lynn to gloss over this awful revelation without showing an appropriate amount of dismay and compassion. What kind of father stabbed his own son? And three times? This inexplicable act was more than her newfound maturity could cope with.

'They weren't meant to do me any real harm,' the distressed storyteller whispered into golden hair, his arms wrapped tightly around her sobbing, shaking frame, and feebly attempted to justify the actions of his own flesh and blood. 'He just wanted to warn me off.'

'Most dads would ground you,' the young beauty smiled, reaching up and kissing his mouth. 'You can't see your mates for two weeks, or something like that.'

Her boyfriend smiled back, tears running down his cheeks as well. Why couldn't he blame his arsehole of a father for hurting him? The man who had blamed his son for everything... Coming to terms with this conundrum would need to wait, and he was grateful to his saviour for interjecting a little humour to diffuse the situation.

'That wouldn't have worked for me,' he replied with a shrug. 'I had you. Impossible to ground a bloke from his fantasies.'

'Oh, Jeff. I'm so sorry,' Lynn cried into the hairs on his chest, feeling his arms gathering her in even closer. 'I so want to make you happy. Please will you let me?'

She looked into her man's shining eyes and encouraged him back down onto the bed. They lay down, bathed in the city lights, and she kissed his temples. She could feel his heart beating on the surface of his chest, and calm tears of relief continued to roll down his face and onto the pillow.

Still the story went on, at the stage now where its narrator simply needed to convert every last hidden memory into words. He had to thoroughly purge his soul of the shadows lurking in his past and to prove both to his guardian angel and to himself that he had nothing left to withhold.

'That's why I was so pissed off when Gerry and co' used to tease me about having a crush on you. They thought they were so damned funny, and of course I went along with the joke. It wasn't a crush. It was a fucking life preservation system. So that's why I jumped at the chance to move to Melbourne when I found out Gerry's dad was going to offer him the partnership. I'd been fighting to keep myself sane for so bloody long that I'd become so sick of the unrelenting effort it took. I couldn't see a way forward until that chance became real. It was my last shot. I just wanted to see if I could meet you, and then maybe my life would turn around.'

'And it did,' Lynn cried inconsolably, 'until *my* dad decided I had to go overseas for two years. Bloody fathers... Jeff, I'm really sorry to put you through so much pain. I wish I'd known all this back then. I would've refused to go. I had no idea. I'm so, so sorry.'

'Yeah, I know. And that's exactly why I didn't tell you,' the thankful man grinned, filled with an unexpected tranquillity. 'You know that, don't you? Angel, I blazed a trail of indifference away from my family as a result of what we put each other through, but I'm sure as hell not going to lose you through the same indifference. We value each other, and that's what makes this worth fighting for. I will fight for us until you tell me to stop, OK?'

His girlfriend kissed the bare flesh of an arm that showed no intention of letting her go. 'Thanks. That's so nice, but it shouldn't even have to be a fight.'

'Maybe. But if there's one thing I've learned through all this mess, it's that you can't put the genie back in the bottle. If you wish for something, and it comes true, you have no choice but to face the consequences. I said that to your mother, actually. Did you know she invited me for lunch just after you left?'

'What?' the cultivated daughter exclaimed in disbelief, sitting up smartly. 'My mum? No, I didn't know that. Why?'

It was a spirited reaction which heartened her lover no end, and he kissed her with an abject humility bordering on worship. 'Yeah. I still don't really know why. She rang me at uni' one morning. The call was put through to the computer room, and she asked to meet me at Georges' Food Hall.'

'And you agreed?' Lynn asked, sounding perturbed.

'Of course! I was starving for any damned connection with you I could get. I *had* to find out what she wanted to say. How could I not?'

The celebrity was curious. 'So what *did* she want to say?'

'Not much, as it turned out,' Jeff recalled with a chuckle. 'She said she was concerned for me. It was a bloody ridiculous conversation, to tell you the truth. I didn't get too obnoxious, but I certainly let her have it straight.'

Australia's sweetheart smiled, mindful of the distinct understatement. 'So what did you say about genies and bottles?'

'Oh, I don't remember precisely,' the amused man replied, pulling her down on top of him and running his hands over her body. 'Something about her having encouraged your dad to involve you in the arts, and that I suspected she shared some of your interest in social justice.'

The privileged youngster stared at her handsome stranger in admiration. 'Wow! That was brave. I couldn't have said that, but it's true. She does.'

He raised arrogant eyebrows, accepting her compliment and a kiss on the lips into the bargain. This honesty thing was hard to resist with a judge and jury every bit as supportive as she was.

'I love you for that,' his angel sighed. 'So how did Mum react?'

'She told me to stop, and I apologised.'

'I can't believe you chickened out!' Lynn teased.

'Shit, lady! I didn't chicken out, *s'il te plaît*,' the indignant world-changer replied, tapping his aroused audience on the nose in jest. 'I'd already said my piece by then. She knew exactly what I was trying to say. I told her that you would've grown up into the same person regardless of my influence, but it just might've taken a bit longer. I stopped short of suggesting it was unwise to think they could eradicate your every free thought...'

'Yes, I can see why that wouldn't have been such a good move,' the young woman laughed, before turning serious again. 'But Jeff, I don't want to distract you from the rest of what you were going to say. I'm just so sad that I never heard this story back then, because I promise you I would've stayed with you. I hate the thought of all the hardship I've put you through over the last two years.'

The rock star hugged her so tightly that she could barely breathe. 'Don't blame yourself, angel,' he urged. 'It's insidious. It'll eat you up. I heard you do it today with Celia. I deliberately didn't tell you this before you went away, because I wanted you to have those amazing opportunities. I couldn't have dared persuade you to change plans. I was a complete nobody back then, but I've turned into a somebody. Now I feel justified in persuading you to be with me because we could have such an amazing life together. I couldn't have done that before.'

Lynn squirmed enough for him to release his suffocating grip, feeling her emotions brimming inside her. She sat up, straddling his eager hips, and gazed lovingly at her gorgeous man. She remembered thinking how much of an enigma Jeff Diamond had seemed back in those early days, and finally today she knew why. The person into whom he had fashioned himself, hiding the boy from whom he was running away, was now a good deal more composed at least.

'Well, I'm here now. And it's only because of you that we're together again. If you hadn't marched me off the dance floor last night, I would've continued to miss you forever. You keep fighting until you get what you need, and I admire that so much. And so should my father. I love you more than anything, and I'm so glad you pushed me to admit it.'

Jeff opened his eyes after a few moments of indulgence, letting her words permeate his tired mind. Sweet vindication indeed. He reached to bring her down onto his torso again, enfolding his most precious gift in his arms. The lovers kissed passionately, his erection pressing against her abdomen and rendering her putty in his hands. He brought her swiftly to orgasm, assisted on its way by the sensation of silk between his fingers and her clitoris, in no hurry to climax himself in the wake of such tension.

'Jesus, that feels good! Never underestimate the power of intimacy, huh? I love you, Lynn. I guess we both needed that so badly.'

'I love you too,' she gasped. 'So glad it's all out in the open.'

Her boyfriend kissed her lips. 'Hmm... See what you think in the morning.'

'Same as I do now. I'll stand by you, Jeff. It's the very least I could do after everything that's happened.'

The last of the sunset had long since dipped below the horizon, leaving the park opposite in virtual darkness. Their eyes had become accustomed to the fading light, and they soon began to doze off in the comfort of their combined body heat. Jeff couldn't help but notice how his girlfriend's body was as limp and submissive as his was taut and defensive. He dragged himself out of his drowsy contentment and raised them both to a sitting position, wondering how to bring the extended scene to a satisfactory conclusion.

'So there you have it, baby,' he announced after a while, waving his hand in the air as if his story were winging its way around the room. 'Take it or leave it. I've given you my soul tonight. Lock, stock and barrel, *comme on dit*.'

Lynn grabbed at the air childishly, making her polyglot smile. 'Thanks! I'll take it.'

'Will you promise me one thing, angel?'

'Of course,' she agreed without hesitation. 'What?'

'That you'll never give it back.'

The young woman dissolved into tears for the umpteenth time that evening, falling under the spell of the handsome man's dark eyes and knowing how long he had waited to get these lifelong encumbrances off his chest. And how selfless he had been towards her two years ago... She had often accused him of being overly demanding and controlling, when all along he had put her ambitions before his own much greater needs. He waited patiently for Lynn to calm down from the same plaintive state as when he had found her in this very room after wandering around St James' Park, tears streaming down her face and shivering.

'I want to keep it, Jeff. So much. Please could we share it? And you can share mine too. You said I was your soul-mate ages ago. You're not the only one who wants this relationship to last, you know.'

'Then it's a deal,' the songwriter accepted, grabbing her right hand and shaking it in jest. 'And now you can stop crying, or I'll be forced to join you again. It's a waste of good Scotch.'

The songstress chuckled, wiping the tears off her face with the starched sheet, and slumped down heavily backwards onto the bed, sending out a long groan. Feeling drained but contented, Jeff reached for her hand. They had come through it. He hadn't ever dared to contemplate what this moment might be like. It felt mighty fine. He heaved himself to his feet and disappeared into the *en suite* so that they could give each other some time alone.

In the sanctuary behind the bathroom door, the boy from Canley Vale stood in the bright lights, gazing at the man in the mirror. *You did it, mate*, he transmitted silently to his reflection. *Thank Christ that's over.*

Who knew what tomorrow would bring? Only one thing was certain: there was no going back now. The eyes of the dashing hero's image staring back at him were bloodshot, with dark circles around them, and his hair was wet with perspiration and tears. The real thing turned on the shower full blast and stood under the strong spray which felt as if it might pierce the skin stretched tight across his aching shoulders. Internally however, his mind wasn't racing the way it normally did, and he was astonished that it hadn't played its usual tricks by re-running their conversation over and over again. In fact, he felt oddly serene and detached.

Lynn heard the sound of the shower and pivoted herself off the bed too. At first she hesitated, thinking her man might prefer to be on his own for a while, until an inquisitive urge got the better of her. She slowly turned the handle and entered through the steam.

Although Jeff followed the door as it swung inwards, he didn't see demons. Instead, a beholden hunger calmly consumed the moving picture through the frosted shower screen as the hypnotic female form approached. With neither saying a word, her translucent nightdress was dropped onto the floor, and his angel climbed into the bath. She took the soap out of his outstretched hand and began to lather him all over. He stood still and let it happen, already aroused and on fire. She kissed his soapy chest and then his lips, standing on tiptoes to reach them.

Feeling energised and all-powerful, Lynn's handsome lover hoisted her up without warning and whipped her round against the tiles. His cramped, aching legs would never have normally allowed him to do this, a fleeting thought occurred to him. The enchanted woman squealed as her skin touched the cold tiles, and then gasped when he penetrated her.

Bonded on every level, the couple closed their eyes and exchanged impassioned wordless messages to accompany their fevered hands. Pressing into her body as far as he could, they moved together until he threw back his head and gave into his orgasm, breathing hard and groaning loudly. He leaned against her while the sensation coursed through his body, his mouth eventually breaking away to speak.

'Sorry, gorgeous. That was pretty selfish of me,' he said, gathering his senses. 'I forgot how good it is to make love with heart, mind and body all at the same time. You OK? I need to warn you that gravity with a small G's about to take over.'

Lynn smiled and kissed his penitent lips, hanging on to his arms and with her ankles still linked behind him. The shower jet had only made half of her hair wet, and she tried to flick the soaking strands off her face. Balancing carefully, Jeff reached up and wove them behind her ear, and they kissed again.

'Fuck gravity. Both of them. It was perfect,' she whispered. 'I've missed you so much.'

The drained man lowered his girlfriend's trembling body down gently until her feet touched the enamel surface of the bath, and the warm water gushed around her. Replete, he crumbled into a heap at the end of the tub and looked on adoringly as she worked the shampoo through her hair and covered herself in soapsuds, before rinsing off the stress of the last few hours.

'What's so funny?' he asked, seeing her expression change.

The sly nymph directed the water jet onto him and doused him all over. 'Please wash me!' she responded, laughing openly. 'Do you remember that? When you wrote on that van?'

Jeff nodded. 'Yep. 'Course I do! That was a damned good night. You were so surprised when I stepped back from what I'd written. It was fantastic. No way I'm going to forget that, angel.'

The slender, nineteen-year-old beauty flicked the water higher, and her smiling boyfriend opened his mouth, trying to catch the streaming arc. After another minute, she shut off the flow and reached to grab two towels. Her hairy, muscular companion heaved himself to a standing position and accepted her kind gesture.

'So now I know what you mean by "Kill The Boy But Not The Man",' she told him, referring to one of the rock star's earliest hits, 'but who's "Carve It Out Forever" about?'

The lyricist smiled at her gentle but obvious opener for a new conversation. 'It's not really about anyone in particular. Maybe my dad's dad a little, but more about the plight of people who grow old alone. My Jewish grandfather made furniture. He tried to encourage his son onto the straight and narrow but never got his wish. My dad's mum died of a heart attack the year after my mum died. At the time, I convinced myself I didn't give a shit, but now I'm sure I did. I just didn't let myself feel anything, put it that way.'

Lynn nodded, wondering whether her man was about to slide back down from the happy place he had reached in the shower. It appeared not, she soon realised, as he made a playful grab for her towel and proceeded to truss her up in it, kissing her mouth with wild abandon. She laughed and screamed her lacklustre objections, vainly attempting to fight back but then surrendering into his arms.

Back in the bedroom, the athletic blonde hopped up onto the bed and rubbed Jeff's hair dry from her elevated vantage point. Standing naked in front of him, she used her hands to comb the long curls back off his face. He kissed her breasts and lifted her down to the floor.

'I'm hungry now,' he proclaimed. 'Are you? D'you fancy going for a walk to find food? I have no idea what time it is.'

'It's about ten,' she answered, pointing to the bedside clock. 'Where could we go?'

The Sydney native already had an idea. 'Are you up for some robust conversation? If you're not too tired, that is...'

'Conversation?' Lynn was intrigued. 'Aren't you sick of talking? What sort of robust conversation? Aren't *you* tired?'

Jeff grabbed her and drew her in close. 'Na! Not now. I feel great!'

'OK. So where'll we go?'

'The Supper Club,' her biggest fan announced with newfound enthusiasm. 'There are often politicians and parliamentary staff there after a late sitting. It's a great place to share opinions and test theories. I used to love turning up on spec' when I lived here. Have you been to the one on Spring Street in Melbourne? That's the same. And they wouldn't blab about us, because they're all probably there with their mistresses or gay lovers.'

'Wow! Really?'

Lynn agreed, keen to capitalise on such a positive mood at the end of their distressing evening. This suggestion of his was all very *gauche* and adult, even if she had no idea what she might talk about with such people. Jeff's world had always been much more interesting than any other she had known, and she was overjoyed to be invited back into it after her absence.

'Sounds fascinating,' she added. '*En-y va, comme on dit!*'

'*Bien sûr, mon amie,*' her partner chuckled and kissed her hard on the lips. '*Je t'adore.*'

Lynn ran the hairdryer quickly through her long, blonde locks, while the boy from Canley Vale worshipped her from the window, with a cigarette and the small quantity remaining in the bottom of the whisky bottle.

The delirious pair dressed quickly and headed out of the hotel, jumping into a waiting taxi. The driver couldn't believe his eyes when his rear seat was suddenly occupied by two of Australia's hottest celebrities, and he drove quickly around Hyde Park and eastwards onto Darlinghurst Road. Within five minutes, Jeff asked that they be dropped off on a corner and slipped a twenty dollar note into the man's outstretched hand, requesting and receiving assurance of the cabby's silence.

Outside in the cool, spring evening air, the adults-only tour guide pointed his gorgeous partner in a northerly direction and walked past the nightclubs, gay bars and knocking shops for which this district was famous. His ceaseless dialogue was lighter now, though no less animated, as he described some of the interesting discussions he had enjoyed at the underground venue a few years ago.

After a few minutes, the songwriter put his hand on the young woman's shoulder, pulling her back gently. 'Slow down, angel,' he requested, seeming to want to check out each shopfront window and inspect every alleyway.

Slow down? This was new, the sportswoman thought. Jeff Diamond always moved at breakneck speed. Whenever she had been out with him previously, he had never been one for taking time to smell the roses, forever impatient to advance to the next distraction. She glanced across at his face surreptitiously while they strolled along and wondered what he might be thinking. She hoped he didn't regret spilling his long-shrouded, metaphorical beans all over her hotel bedroom floor. He appeared relaxed, as far as she could discern, and now he was even asking her to slow down.

Had this overdue confession really changed The Australian Elvis' demeanour? Unbeknown to his curious girlfriend, the same questions were running through his own mind. Lynn felt sure his stride had lengthened, and he somehow walked taller. If it were true that beauty was in the eye of the beholder, perhaps it was no exaggeration after all to proclaim themselves as each other's most beautiful person in the world. Now that the evening's dark discoveries had begun to sink into her psyche, she resolved that the terrible story he had imparted had only increased her love for him, and hoped that her charming and humble enigma could take strength from having shared it with her.

As they walked and talked, the young woman found herself sorting through images of her distraught lover and filing them into her mental photograph album. How much would she commit to her diary's secret pages once she returned to Melbourne and some spare time? Care needed to be taken to reveal no specifics which might one day be presented as evidence, should she be called upon by her parents to answer for her defiant position. And yet she so needed to capture this moment; how differently she felt towards her beautiful, black stallion this time around, with added maturity in both lovers.

Jeff smiled, seeing her thoughtful gaze, and squeezed their joined hands. Lynn grinned back. A trace of sorrow remained behind his eyes, and maybe this would never change. Perhaps it should never change? She couldn't purge the sadness from his past, but would surely make it her life's work to give him a happy future, in whichever form they chose.

'I used to call you my mystery man,' Lynn blurted out, yanking his swinging arm and bringing them to a temporary standstill. 'Or my enigmatic stranger.'

'Did you? When?'

'In my diary. And to Michelle, probably. Now you're my perfect stranger. That's going to be my code name for you from now on.'

'Perfect stranger?' the twenty-two-year-old repeated, bemused. 'I'm neither of those things, but that's up to you. You're still my *Regala*. Always have been, always will be.'

'But what is a *regala*?'

He kissed his girlfriend's questioning lips. 'I'll tell you over the next few weeks. We've got so much more to talk about now, angel. So much more. Now that my history's out in the open, as you said. When my thoughts no longer get drowned out by the sound of you running away.'

Lynn frowned. 'I'm not going to run away. Never, Jeff. That's what I've been thinking about in the last few minutes. I promise I'll be on your side through everything Dad tries to prove.'

'*Gracias, Regala*. You need to make up your own mind at every step in the process. But thanks for the promise now. Let's leave this shit to one side for a while. Time to send our minds in a different direction, OK?'

Returning to the Intercontinental at two o'clock in the morning, after a few hours of suitably robust, after-dark discourse, the two stars lingered in the deserted gardens opposite for another half-hour before heading inside. The air was chilly but still, and they had both spent too many hours cooped up in air-conditioned aircraft or hotel rooms over the last few days, weeks and months. They wandered aimlessly, hand in hand, not concerned with re-treading each well-worn path.

'Don't you want to know how your dad got caught?' the inquisitive young woman asked.

'No. I'm past caring. He's inside, and there's nothing going to change that. I don't want him to get out, so what purpose would it serve to know how he got in?'

Lynn chuckled at his strange response. The teenager remained a little nervous about the incredible revelations, even though the storyteller seemed reasonably comfortable in talking now. Determined to press her point however, she wanted him to pay attention and changed tack, calling upon his competitive, control freak instincts to make it known.

'But do you want my dad to know more than you do? He'd probably find that sort of information out as part of his investigation, wouldn't he?'

'Hmm...' Jeff mused, coming to an abrupt halt and twirling his gorgeous girlfriend round by her shoulders. 'Excellent point, Miss Dyson. Never thought about it that way.'

'I'm sorry. I didn't mean to interfere.'

'Crap! You're not interfering. It's exactly what I need you to do,' the amorous intellectual reassured her. 'I'm too wrapped up in me. I need a fresh point of view. Let me think about it for a while, but you just might be right.'

'Perhaps you should hire your own private dicks?' she giggled, grabbing his hand and swinging it hard. 'And then I will too. Pretty soon every detective in the city will be following your family's trail.'

Jeff frowned, suddenly awash with fear again. 'Angel, can we stop talking about this now, please? I appreciate what you're trying to do, but I can't find that much humour in it yet. I will, I promise, but not yet. Is that OK?'

Feeling guilty, Lynn hugged him close. 'I apologise. I didn't mean to make light of it. We should get some sleep. We're both going to be so tired tomorrow.'

'Thanks, baby. Good idea. I love you so much, and I want you to keep challenging me, as long as you don't mind me pushing back every now and again.'

'*Yin* and *yang*. Definitely. I love you too.'

Face-off

Lynn knew there was a tough conversation to be had the moment she set eyes on her father. Junior and she had travelled back to Benloch together in the morning for a weekend of training and family time. Her brother's football team had suffered a rare loss the previous evening, and he had confided that he wasn't particularly looking forward to being in the country this weekend either.

The reunited lovers had gone their separate ways to Kingsford Smith Airport to avoid a press stampede, memories of their passionate tryst burning fiercely as each taxi left the Intercontinental in its rear-view mirror. They were flying on different airlines, Jeff in Economy and in the midst of excited fans, while the aristocrat took her seat near the pilots, anticipating flattery and fuss from the flight attendants, whether painted ladies or camp guys.

It had been a desolate feeling for the young woman to arrive back in Melbourne alone, yet this was easily offset by the thrilling prospect of what lay ahead. The former poor peasant with noble aims had transformed into her powerful black knight, and her inspired mind was reeling from the events of the last forty-eight hours. Not to mention her still-reverberating body, which craved his deep inside and would not let her forget it. First however, she needed to sort things out with her parents.

'Dad's putting so much pressure on all of us lately,' the driver had broken the silence, seeing a distant look in his sister's eyes. 'Have you noticed? I don't know if it's you coming home or what, but I'm really feeling it.'

Lynn agreed. 'I suppose it's hard for them to come to terms with their children growing up and becoming independent. But you're right. It's as if they've redoubled their efforts to make sure we live up to the old ideals.'

'Shit! Don't get me wrong,' Junior went on. 'I still believe in everything and I'm no less motivated. I could just do without the mounting expectations and constant watchfulness.'

The nineteen-year-old turned to him. 'Can I ask you something?'

'Sure. What?'

'Has Mum or Dad talked to you about Jeff?'

Her brother became slightly defensive. 'Jeff Diamond? Yes, they have.'

'Oh, I thought so. What have they been saying?'

Lynn looked nervous, despite her efforts to play it cool. The blond sportsman gave his passenger a frown, as if to say, "And I thought I had problems." Their father had shared some information in confidence with his elder son and had requested his assistance in ensuring that the successful and outspoken rock star was kept as far away from their family as possible. However, when the younger man had pressed for more details, none had been volunteered.

'Dad's got a private detective sniffing around apparently. What's he done? All the drugs, probably. I always thought he should be more careful. Are you seeing him again then?'

'Yes,' the singer admitted. 'I was planning to own up this weekend and see if I can stop whatever Dad's doing.'

Junior was intrigued. 'Is there anything juicy going on?' he asked. 'You're sailing close to the wind with this one. The big man's pretty keen on you not having him in your life. Have you seen him a lot? I mean, are you dating again behind their backs?'

'Stop it, June. You make it sound like I'm being unfaithful. Yes, we ended up together after the music awards' dinner last week. I love him. I always have.'

The footballer took pity on his melancholy passenger. He had guessed that their break-up two Septembers ago had been hard on both of them, having bought Jeff Diamond's albums and heard lyrics that were undoubtedly inspired by his popular sibling. He had always enjoyed the tall, dark-haired Sydneysider's company, not that he had really got to know him that well. On the few occasions when they had spent time together at Benloch or Admin, it appeared that he had been completely besotted with Lynn, and she with him.

'I know how you feel. I'm still pretty morose about splitting up with Astrid too, but Dad's adamant that Jeff's not the man he wants for you.'

'Argh!' the young woman replied, exasperated at that same tired expression. 'What about the man *I* want for me? I'm an adult now and legally able to get married or anything. I don't want to have to sneak around. It's not very workable for any of us, is it? We're bound to be spotted sooner or later.'

Realising that neither of them could influence the situation until they reached the homestead, driver and passenger agreed to change the subject and spent the rest of the journey discussing trivia from their busy schedules. They had hardly taken ten steps inside the house however, when Marianna accosted them.

'Lynn, you'd better go and see Dad as soon as you can,' she warned, almost whispering.

Their mother looked worried, making the teenager even more nervous. Perhaps her father's investigators had uncovered something that Jeff had omitted to tell her. She was determined to keep an open mind about the whole sordid business, but wasn't sure she would be able to mount as strong a defence against her parents as her courageous boyfriend would wish her to.

'About what?' she asked, feeling uncharacteristically defiant.

'I'm not going to pre-empt the discussion, darling,' the lady of the house replied, 'except to say that we're both very disappointed that your new Hometown Queen status seems to have gone to your head. You'd better go to the office. He's expecting you.'

The returning musician was shocked by her mother's choice of words and by the hushed tone in which they were expressed. Hometown Queen status? That was ridiculously dramatic, she thought. Was this really how she had been behaving? The only conclusion which sprang to mind was that her parents had been told something specific about the awards function, and it obviously hadn't been well received. Her conscience had been untroubled up until this point, safe in the knowledge that she had arrived intending to come clean with her secret this weekend anyway. Nevertheless, this strange ambush left her fearful of being gazumped by evidence impossible to deny.

Knocking on the door, the prodigal daughter waited for Big D's permission before entering. Any resolve she had brought with her was steadily trickling through her feet and into the gaps between the polished floorboards, having not even had the chance to put her bags down. Home for five minutes, and she already felt thirteen again! She dumped her belongings just inside the office door, looking up to see her father sitting at his huge, jarrah desk, staring at some photographs and papers on the worn, salmon-coloured blotter.

'Hi, Dad. You wanted to see me?'

'Morning, Lynn. How are you? Did Junior come home with you?'

'Yes, he's here too. I'm fine, thanks. How are you?'

The sight of the small pile of documents filled the young woman with foreboding, now certain that an awkward conversation was afoot. Her father was not in a friendly mood, and there was another bundle of paperwork to his right, topped by a manila folder with the word "DIAMOND" written diagonally in large capital letters across the cover. She scanned the surface of the desk as invisibly as she could. Her parents were keeping a file on her boyfriend, and it was giving out sinister vibes.

'Please sit down,' the terse statesman pointed to the chair opposite him at the desk. 'I've got some things to show you, and some interesting information too. But first I have a question.'

The courageous Olympic athlete tried not to gulp. This was already heading into unpleasant territory. Perhaps her mother was right to point out that she had been so caught up in the hype of her return that she had become too big for her boots. There was nothing like coming back to the family home for being cut down to size. Two years of virtual autonomy appeared to have shrivelled away to nought in the intervening weeks.

'Which question's that, Dad?'

'I want you to tell me whether you've been in the company of Jeff Diamond since you arrived back in Melbourne,' the imposing man enquired, looking the confident young woman in the eye.

Lynn refused to flinch. She had a good teacher. What would her strong-willed lover do in this situation? She was not accustomed to conflict with her parents and had never tested how far her freedom might stretch in expressing her opinions these days, notwithstanding that she was now technically independent.

'Yes, I have,' she answered, 'but mostly in Sydney.'

'Thank you,' Bart acknowledged. 'At least you're honest. I'm pleased about that.'

'Dad, I assume you have photos of us, so it would be pointless trying to pretend. What's the problem?'

It was a brave start, she dared to think, as an image flashed behind her eyes of an irate and grief-stricken youngster bursting into his principal's office and laying his outrage on the line. She had a lot to learn about direct communication, having always been taught to respect authority and to behave with polite reserve at all times.

'What's the problem?' her father exaggerated her insolent tone. 'Don't ask me what the problem is. You obviously think there is a problem then?'

Lynn hesitated. 'Sorry, Dad, but the fact that we're talking about this in here and not over dinner must mean there's a problem.'

'OK. You're very clever, my girl,' he acknowledged in frustration. 'You're correct. This is not a dinner conversation. There are pictures of you that were taken at the awards ceremony in Sydney last week, and they seem to indicate some fairly heavy-handed behaviour on Diamond's part. Lynn, I don't want to put you in any danger, and you also have a responsibility to protect yourself.'

Bart pushed the small pile of enlarged photographs towards his daughter. She looked at them and instantly remembered where they were taken. Wow! Jeff looked so good, with his white shirt unbuttoned halfway down his chest, showing off the type of tall, statuesque frame which men's suits were designed to show off. She hadn't had time to think about it when he had interrupted the dancing that night, but now gazing at the picture of him standing next to Peter, she wondered what she had ever seen in the suave, clean-cut Englishman. Or in anyone else, the woman realised, as her insides churned with longing.

'Yes. Well, it's definitely us,' she chuckled, trying not to seem too flippant. 'What were you expecting me to say? We were both award nominees, and I was performing. I didn't put two and two together when I went up to Sydney, but it was obvious that he'd be there. He's a big star now.'

Bravado quickly gave way to renewed nerves. Of course there was more to these photographs than the pop star wanted her parents to know. Big D picked one out from further down the pile and placed it on the top, smoothing his hands over it and grimacing. It showed Jeff's hand gripping the top of his daughter's arm and an alarmed expression on her face, while others around stood open-mouthed and bewildered.

'I'm told you were removed roughly from the dance floor, in full view of your guest, and forcibly taken to a hotel room by Diamond. Is this true?'

'Well, yes. In a way,' the celebrity answered. 'Not a hotel room though. More like a meeting room. There wasn't a bed in it, if that's what you're thinking. Jeff wanted to talk to me, and I'd been avoiding him because you had asked me not to go back and resume our relationship. He wanted to know why, and I did owe him an explanation. Dad, that's only fair, isn't it?'

Bart listened respectfully. He couldn't escape the fact that his dedicated and ambitious child was growing up very fast. She had matured considerably during her time away from the family, which had been the purpose of her sabbatical in the first place.

He continued. 'Has this man been violent towards you, Lynn? Please answer me honestly.'

'No, he hasn't. Never,' she replied, readily discounting the number of random blows she had received during nightmares. 'He just wanted to talk.'

On hearing this last sentence, the sportsman fixed her with an astonished stare. 'What? Are you still that naïve? Very few men only want to talk.'

'Dad!' Lynn exclaimed. 'We talked! He wanted to know why I'd been cold and dismissive when we met for breakfast the previous week.'

'I see,' her father murmured. 'So you *had* seen him in Melbourne before this?'

'Yes,' she confirmed with a sigh. 'We had coffee opposite the gardens, on Domain Road. Nothing violent happened then either, Dad. Why do you ask about violence?'

The young woman had a fair idea why, but wasn't yet going to let on to her father just how much she had been told. She needed to find out what the couple was up against before imparting too much of her own intelligence, as gathered from the key witness himself.

'Lynn, I need you to be aware of just what sort of man Jeff Diamond is and where he comes from. While you were in America, I watched carefully as he launched his music career. I was initially impressed with his determination to succeed, but then questions began to surface from reporters to which he was particularly avoidant. It started me wondering who he was, knowing how close you two had been.'

The nineteen-year-old sat back in the ornate office chair, leaning her arms on its rounded wooden frame. Again, her beautiful, black stallion's simmering temper presented itself as a sexy image in her mind, and her ears imagined they could hear the noisy, smoker's breathing which turned her on so much. She made up her mind to be patient, even if it took the last ounce of her resolve.

'I know who Jeff Diamond is, Dad.'

'Oh, I don't think you do,' Bart refuted. 'Beware of the wolf in sheep's clothing, my girl. I need to make you aware of some facts that I think will surprise you.'

'What are you saying?' a surprisingly worldly voice rose from nowhere. 'You think he's some sort of predator? Is that why you don't want me to see Jeff anymore?'

The dignified all-Australian hero nodded. 'Yes, that's exactly what I'm saying. I've always said that, and you know it. I've talked it over with your mother again, and we feel strongly enough about this to want to forbid you from seeing him. You have a lot of friends. There's no need for you to resume your relationship with Diamond. He's become a success, with all the trappings that go with it, and you have a great deal to do in the next few months. Including going to London next year...'

The nineteen-year-old was taken aback, instantly deflated at this news. 'London next year? When was that decided?'

'Nothing's been decided, as such, but the more we hear about your insistence on continuing to associate with this man, the keener we are for you to spend next year in London. He's bad news, Lynn. Very bad news. You have to know this about him. It's for your own good.'

The furious young woman felt indignance rising inside. For goodness' sake, hadn't her parents ever heard of aeroplanes? Did they think that by sending her to London as an adult they would be able to keep them apart, and that her tenacious and now wealthy boyfriend would be incapable of following her? Now it was her father who was being naïve.

'Jeff's not bad news,' Lynn riled against the damning indictment. 'He's ambitious, honourable and perfectly trustworthy. Didn't he keep his word while I was in the US? Tell me why you think I'm better off without him, please, because I don't see it, Dad. Give me specific evidence for why he's bad news, please.'

'Of course you don't see it,' Bart scoffed. 'You think you're in love. And as your father, I am not obliged to give you specific evidence, as you so discourteously suggest.'

The young woman saw red. 'Why not? I don't *think* I'm in love. I *am* in love. I'm *still* in love, even after two years in exile.'

'In exile?' the commanding man raised his booming voice too. 'Don't be so bloody rude! I can just imagine Diamond feeding you lines like that. Exile, for God's sake... You've had countless opportunities that very few people get to enjoy, and this is the treatment we're subjected to when we try and protect you? Lynn, this man you're in love with has a history of violence; drugs and weapons and all sorts. He's part of a crime family in Sydney's west. Your mother and I forbid you to have anything to do with him from now on. Do you understand?'

Lynn appreciated her father's directness, but he was telling her nothing new. She already had a well-fashioned mental picture of these drugs, weapons and all sorts, piled high in some tiny, second-floor flat where much nastier things had taken place than any investigation could uncover. She desperately hoped the police hadn't passed on every single case to be reported at that address over the years.

'No, Dad. I'm sorry, but I don't understand,' she replied quietly, feeling tears burning behind her eyes. 'Jeff's not part of that world. He left it behind ages ago. He's bought an apartment in Melbourne, and he's a hardworking, honest songwriter who wants to be successful on his own terms. And he is successful, isn't he? You *have* to give him that.'

'Yes, I do,' the stalwart acquiesced on this point, taking a deep breath as if about to deliver the final blow to seal her fate. 'But his criminal past is real, Lynn. He's known to the police. Well known. The detectives I hired have turned up plenty of evidence. He's had a record since he was a child. He's a dangerous, angry, aggressive young lout, Lynn. And what's even worse, his father's in prison serving a life sentence, no less! I'm sorry to have to tell you all this, but it should at least help you understand why we can't allow you to see him anymore.'

'Dad, please!' Lynn hissed through gritted teeth, trying to stay calm.

The way her father described her troubled boyfriend made the young woman uncomfortable. Hearing these disturbing words again, and in the absence of the raw emotion with which they had previously been delivered, it was no wonder that her parents were adamant she have nothing to do with him. She had to admit that the evil truth did strike her as compelling this time. If she had heard this clinical account without already knowing the other side of the story, she would most likely have sided with them instead.

She stood firm however. 'I know about Jeff's dad being in prison. He's serving two life sentences for murdering two other criminals called the Jaworski brothers. Polish gang members. He's told me all about it.'

Bart's eyes widened in surprise, clearly not expecting the Sydneysider to have been so open with his daughter. It was his turn to be caught off-guard. What was this man's game? He must still be tapped into the underworld to have been informed about any detective work underway. Perhaps his motive for forcibly removing Lynn from the dance floor was not solely driven from below the belt after all, rather seeking to pre-empt her reaction to the investigators' findings by spinning a yarn for which the compassionate singer would fall.

'Really? And what else do you know?'

'Heaps, Dad, but I'm not going to betray Jeff's confidence. He had an awful childhood. It's no wonder he's been in trouble. His whole life was wrapped up in crime, abuse and neglect. But that doesn't mean he's the same as they are. Not now, anyway.'

The straight-laced father was oddly pleased by his daughter's ability to argue with him, despite being less than comfortable with knowing she was already party to these horrific facts. 'So tell me when you were given this information, please. And also why it didn't make you behave differently. After all the attention we've asked you to pay to your safety, it's extremely negligent of you to blindly ignore such dangerous information and carry on as if he were the boy next door.'

Lynn hesitated a little. The truth in her father's words was painfully self-evident, and it was not as if it hadn't occurred to her at the time. She hadn't blindly ignored the danger. Much worse, in actuality: she had wilfully ignored it. How should she answer in the defence of such stupidity? She tried to put herself in her boyfriend's shoes. What would he want her to say?

'Dad, I'm going to be completely honest, because Jeff's completely honest with me.'

'That's good. I'm happy to hear that. From both of you. Go on.'

'After he and I met up at the awards dinner, we spent two nights together. It was my idea. I asked Pete to leave. Initially, I pushed Jeff away because you made me promise to, but then afterwards I changed my mind,' the brave woman explained. 'My feelings for him are just as strong as before. I tried to ignore them, Dad, to begin with, and to do as you asked. But then I realised that it's my choice whom I love.'

'Your choice?' the Olympian echoed. 'Or his choice on your behalf?'

The musician's patience was again running thin, and the sarcasm laced through her reply exposed her exasperation. 'My choice. Totally my choice. He wasn't with me when I changed my mind. I came up with it all on my own.'

Her father raised his right index finger, scolding her insolence, which only made matters worse.

She inhaled deeply. 'I told him you'd found out something suspicious about him, but that I didn't know what it was. I said that in order to make a choice, I needed one of you to stop keeping me in the dark. So he stopped keeping me in the dark.'

Bart had listened intently, his earlier hunch proving accurate. 'Very well. I suppose that's fair. But what I'm interested in, Lynn,' he probed further, 'is *how* he changed your mind and whether what he told you was the truth. With a history of coercion and violence, you have to allow me to be concerned that you've been railroaded into something. Has this man blackmailed you in any way?'

This question had come out of nowhere. Coercion? Blackmail? Lynn fought to maintain a neutral expression. Could it be that her cunning boyfriend had manufactured or embellished his story just to worm his way back into her life? Or merely to get her family off his back? Played on her sympathy? The accomplished showman *was* uncommonly convincing, and she had often been counselled about how seductive con' men could be. However, if her lover had wanted to confuse the issue, having his version of the truth tally with her father's didn't make any sense at all. Both men had given her the adult information she had been seeking in order to make her adult decision. Yet as with many adult decisions, the arguments were not necessarily cut and dried.

'Oh, for God's sake,' she began again, on the verge of walking out. 'Yes, OK. Jeff's an angry man. I agree. He's got a lot to be angry about though. While we were in Sydney, I heard some things that really shocked me. Truly horrible things that happened to his family. And I believe him when he tells me he wants no part of it. He's angry and bitter about the situation he was put in as a child and the legacy he's left with. The past that keeps haunting him, either in his own head or with his family demanding money now he's a famous performer. And then now there are these investigators of yours dredging up all the stuff that he's trying to put behind him. Jeff Diamond is kind, talented and very, very smart. He loves me and would never hurt me. Dad, you don't know him. He wants to make a difference to people's lives, and so do I. Together.'

Big D stood up and rested both hands on the desk, leaning over his daughter as she sank back into her chair. 'Well, I'm disappointed to hear you defend him so vehemently,' he said. 'Loyalty is an admirable quality, but your loyalty is misguided in this instance. Your mother and I are concerned for your safety and your future. We don't believe an association with Jeff Diamond is good for you.'

Lynn was growing impatient, her boyfriend's anger rubbing off on her too. 'Dad,' she stated, tossing her hair. 'It's not just any old association, as you seem to think. I've met the most amazing man; a truly beautiful person. You don't even know him. Why can't you give him the benefit of the doubt? Have you found out anything that implicates Jeff in any real crime? Is there any particular reason why he's a danger to me?'

In truth, the father was encouraged by the young woman's determination to champion a cause that had quite obviously had a significant impact on her. Yet still he could not bring himself to overlook the abhorrent gangland transgressions with which his sources had furnished him.

'Lynn, your words are well chosen, and I'm proud of your ability to mount a counter-argument,' he said, sitting down and inviting her to do the same.

'But?' she invited with renewed confidence.

Bart sighed at her impudence, shaking his head and unable to hide a smile. 'But I simply cannot allow you to have a relationship with Jeff Diamond, because he's not the material of your future. I understand why you couldn't accept Prince Charles' proposal. You would never have been happy with him, and believe it or not, your mother and I do want you to be happy. But Diamond comes from bad stock and he's not the right type of person for someone like you.'

The nineteen-year-old seethed inside. Someone like her? What kind of someone was she? Right now, her brain was dominated by a vision of her judicious but fiery world-changer thumping the wall with his fists and dearly wished she could do the same. Someone like her would never get away with that sort of behaviour though. She would have to make do with carrying on as calmly as possible until she could escape into his open arms.

'Well, I'm sorry,' she said. 'I don't agree with you. Jeff's a wonderful person. He's ambitious and intelligent and doesn't want anything to do with his family. He told me the other day that two cousins on his mother's side, who all disowned him as a kid because of his dad's criminal activity, have come out of the woodwork since he became a star and are demanding money from him.'

Bart's tolerance for this sudden tangent was non-existent. 'Really. I fail to see what this has to do with you.'

'Dad, please! It doesn't have anything to do with me. I was just trying to show you that people can change their opinions with the right motivation,' Lynn huffed, unable to keep the frustration out of her voice. 'I've never met anyone like Jeff. I want to be with him and see where our relationship might go. For all I know, it might not last long, so you may not need to worry. But for now I'm not going anywhere.'

The forty-six-year-old athlete stood to his full two metres, towering over his daughter. 'Young lady, I hear you but I cannot support you. You've been wowed by an extremely persuasive man. I remember his behaviour in this house. He knows what to say and how to please. That's all part of his plan. I don't doubt he's very clever. That's probably my main concern, actually. He *is* smart and he knows how to play the game. For the last time, I'm asking you, for your mother and for myself, to stop seeing Jeff Diamond.'

Lynn felt close to tears, desperate not to show her hand too early. It had been a long time since her father had seen her cry.

'I love him, Dad. I really love him. And he loves me. This is stupid. It's like Romeo and Juliet. Families feuding and forbidding their children to see each other. I never thought I would end up in such a silly situation. I'm over eighteen and in control of my own destiny.'

'Oh! So you think you can play the trump card of adulthood?' Bart challenged, using an unusually scathing tone.

'Yes, I can, Dad,' his daughter pleaded, 'but I don't want to. I don't want to fall out with you and Mum. I really don't. I'm extremely grateful for everything you've done and still do for me, but I love Jeff and would like to explore where our relationship's going. I'm careful and fully aware of who he's been, but I'm in love with who he is now and who he wants to be. If it means you strip me of the good things in life, then so be it. You know I can survive on my own, because you've made us all very self-sufficient.'

The musician heard the hinges of the office door squeak behind her as she was speaking and span around to see her mother standing in the doorway. 'How long have you been standing there?'

'Not long,' Marianna responded. 'I have been listening for a few minutes, dear. I'd be interested to know whether what Jeff has told you is the whole truth. I'm sure there must be a few stones left unturned in his version of the truth. Lynn, it's our duty to be suspicious of people like this. We have to be vigilant, don't we?'

'Yes, of course we do,' the teenager answered, annoyed at her mother's patronising tone, 'but I feel perfectly safe with him. You gave me enough training for recognising danger, and I don't recognise it with Jeff. Yes, sure, he could be the world's greatest con' man, but then so could the next guy. Just look at all the scandals that break out with people whom everyone thinks are pillars of the community...'

The head of the Dyson dynasty waded in again. 'Yes, you're right. You do never know. But if there's a precedent, you'd have to agree that it's a pretty solid indicator of what *may* happen in the future. Do you know, for example, that Jeff was seeing other women while you were going out last time? And he probably is now too. While you were in America, he was often in the 'papers associated with various movie stars and women who are definitely not of your ilk. Do you want that to continue? Are you prepared for that type of scandal?'

Hold on, the young star thought. Where did this come from? It was totally unlike her father to descend to tabloid news. He must be really desperate to get his way.

'Dad, that's not fair,' she objected. 'To be blunt, Jeff loves sex. I know you don't want to listen to your daughter talking this way, but it's true. Weren't you the same at his age?'

'Lynn! For heaven's sake, show some respect,' her mother shouted. 'Don't bring your father down to this level.'

But Bart silenced his wife. 'No, Marianna. The girl's entitled to her opinion. I want to hear how she can compare this man's cheating with my love life.'

'Argh!' Lynn shouted back in frustration. 'I can't believe we're having this conversation. Yes, I'm sure you think I'm naïve and starry-eyed about Jeff, and perhaps I am. I know he sees a lot of women. We talked about it at length when we were going out before. He gave me a good explanation, and even though I didn't like it, I understood. And as for what he did while I was away... We'd split up, hadn't we? *You* split us up! My God! I was in the papers too. I know I didn't make you too proud either, but it's normal for people our age and in our business. Even people of my ilk.'

The elegant lady sat down in the chair next to her distressed daughter, reaching out and holding her hand. 'Darling, please calm down. I'm sorry it's gone this far. Your father and I are concerned about your feelings and safety. We don't want to see you hurt.'

'But Mum,' the teenager replied, fighting with her emotions, 'you weren't concerned when you took me away from him two years ago. You knew I loved him then too. Jeff told me you met him for lunch and you talked about it afterwards.'

'That's true,' Marianna told her husband. 'The boy and I did meet for lunch shortly after Lynn left.'

Bart huffed and puffed, sensing that his daughter was intending to dig her heels in as hard as she could on this matter. He had completely underestimated the hold this charismatic man had on her.

The young woman carried on, determined to do her brave, black stallion proud. He had promised her he wouldn't give up without one hell of a fight, so why should she show any less commitment? Sitting in her father's office in their grand mansion and thinking of her luxurious bedroom upstairs and the enormous kitchen on the other side of the courtyard, it occurred to her that all this finery was wholly unimportant, especially when compared to the quest to eliminate hardship and suffering for which her boyfriend had sought to enlist her help.

Although Lynn knew she would hate to be estranged from her family and be required to walk away from her gold-plated Dyson heritage, the thought of never spending time with Jeff again tore her apart. If they broke up, she would never see him conquer his PTSD, or have the chance to work together and make a difference in ordinary people's lives. This, Lynn realised, was what she wanted most from her life. Their life, as her man had so romantically suggested.

'Please give him a chance, Dad, Mum,' the singer continued with renewed vigour. 'Jeff and I played the game last time, exactly as you wanted. He didn't make a scene, and it was horrible splitting up like that. He didn't run after me, and we didn't see each other even when he was touring in LA or when were both in Europe at the same time. I was lucky because I was going to a new, exciting life, but it still hurt heaps, and it took me a long time to get over him. In fact, I didn't get over him. I just learned to ignore it, like a torn ligament during a tennis tournament or period pains before a concert. But now he's back in my life, and I'm so happy.'

Neither parent spoke, simply staring at each other while their daughter made her case eloquently and with such fire in her eyes. She had definitely been inspired by something, they both recognised. The words coming out of her youthful mouth were not her own, or at least not the girl they knew. They had not raised their children to be so outspoken, and yet somehow it suited her, Marianna figured, smiling benevolently.

'And you can't say he's after me for my money or to get into the limelight anymore,' Lynn continued, sensing a change in the room's atmosphere and daring to give herself the credit. 'He was always so conscious of that. Before I went away, he vowed that by the time I came back, he would be a someone. And now he is. He doesn't need me to be rich and famous. He's great in his own right, isn't he? You have to admit that.'

'So what are you asking for?' her mother enquired, nodding. 'Are you asking for our blessing for you to date Jeff?'

Lynn gazed at her mother blankly, suddenly understanding perfectly how people could become uncontrollably angry at their own flesh and blood. 'Mum, I'm not asking for anything!' she replied, her voice higher pitched and urgent. 'It was Dad who wanted to see me! I was coming here this weekend to *tell* you that Jeff and I have started seeing each other again. I wasn't going to ask your permission, because I don't think I have to. I'm old enough to choose whom I spend my time with, am I not?'

'Right. That's enough,' Bart interjected. 'We get the picture. I'm sorry we've ended up in a shouting match. I thought we'd be able to convince you to concentrate on your goals, but obviously this man's power over you is greater than we thought.'

'His power over me?' his daughter challenged again, catching her breath. 'Please don't blame Jeff. He gets blamed for everything. It's totally my choice to be with him. I love him, and that's all there is to it.'

'Fair enough,' the elder statesman said, with atypical resignation. 'Here's what we're going to do, if you agree, ladies...'

Marianna nodded expectantly, and the nineteen-year-old followed suit, slumping back into her chair. Her father's change of tone was promising, but she didn't dare get her hopes up too soon. However this argument concluded, her loyalties seemed destined for ongoing conflict.

'Lynn, you are to allow me to conduct the enquiries I want to pursue into Diamond's past and present. I'll support you seeing him while this is going on... when you're free, that is... but there'll be no changing your plans for him. Your goals must remain your priority. Clear?'

'Yes. Thank you. Perfectly clear.'

'If, through this, it turns out that he has something to hide and the results of the investigation suggest he's not appropriate for you, I trust you'll accept your fate without a word. And otherwise, if I find no grounds against him, I promise I'll give my blessing to your relationship. Is that fair?'

The young woman nodded, desperately trying to cover up an overwhelming rush of triumph. 'Yes, thanks very much, Dad. But with one additional clause, if possible.'

'Very funny, Miss. Now you're talking like a barrister,' Bart chuckled, also more relaxed. 'What is your one additional clause, please?'

Lynn laughed too. 'I've got a good teacher.'

She knew her dad would think she was referring to him. She was partly, but by no means entirely.

'My condition is that if you find Jeff to be innocent, you apologise to him directly. He knows you're investigating him and he's understandably offended that you haven't discussed it with him face to face. I hope the two of you can have that conversation eventually.'

The great man signalled his approval of this condition, pushing a notepad and pen in his daughter's direction. 'That's a fair point you make. You're right. I'll give Jeff a call on Monday and I'll be up-front with him. Please write his 'phone number down here for me.'

Marianna breathed a sigh of relief. 'Are we done?'

'I hope so,' Lynn replied.

Bart raised both hands as if to declare the subject closed. The teenager wondered how her boyfriend would behave when Monday's call took place. Two alpha males going head to head would make an interesting "fly on the wall" scene. Neither man was egocentric enough not to see other points of view, yet neither man was too fond of backing down either. If only she wasn't stuck in the middle!

'Thanks, Dad, Mum. Please can I go now? I have to take my things upstairs and do some work. I've got so much stuff to catch up on.'

Still floating on air, the relieved romantic left the office, picking up her bags on the way out. Her parents stood looking at each other, wondering what had come over their good-natured offspring. This new, impetuous and grown-up version of their daughter could certainly put up a fight.

***

As soon as the confused nineteen-year-old reached her room, she flopped down onto the couch and picked up the telephone. She checked the time before dialling the number she had written down for her father just a few minutes ago. Twelve-thirty. Lunchtime. She wasn't aware of Jeff's plans for the weekend, so tried anyway. Her father's comments about his womanising had re-ignited old fears, and a vision entered her head of this call interrupting something about which she would rather remain in the dark.

'Hello?' her man's deep voice answered the telephone.

Lynn was quite nervous, still keyed up after the frenetic discussion with her parents. 'Hi, Jeff. It's me.'

'Hey, beautiful! How're you going?' the young man fairly shouted, ecstatic to hear from his dream girl out of the blue.

The caller was instantly cheered. 'I'm fine, thanks. What are you up to?'

'Jesus! I'm trying to work, but your face is obliterating the words on every page.'

The singer's heart skipped a beat, and she paused, unable to rattle off a suitable response. Another emotionally-charged reply to a relatively mundane question! She was relieved to find him at home at least, but couldn't help wondering if he had company. Judging by the sincerity in his voice and the desire laced through his words, the so-called bad boy was alone.

'Oh! Thanks.'

'Actually, that's not entirely true,' she heard him chuckle. 'It's not just your face.'

Sighing in a mixture of guilt and rapture, the young woman's smile illuminated her large, lonely Benloch bedroom. Her mind pictured Jeff leaning back in his chair, with the wide-eyed, glazed expression that often drifted across his face whenever he was thinking naughty thoughts. It turned her on too, imagining him stroking a growing erection as they spoke. The tense conversation with her parents had left her dying to run into her lover's welcoming arms and collapse onto the bed in the throes of passion.

'That's a nice thing to say. I was thinking about you too.'

'That's good,' the comic replied. 'I was hoping you hadn't dialled my number by accident.'

From his city apartment, the songwriter heard an uninhibited laugh following yet another quirky comment. This gorgeous creature never misconstrued his meaning. As usual, the dark-haired enigma presented an irresistible mix of confidence and insecurity to the returned celebrity, who swooned at the other end of the telephone line.

'So what are you going to do now you've distracted me?'

'I thought you were already distracted?' his lover flashed back in a teasing tone.

'Totally distracted, angel,' Jeff confirmed, reaching down and massaging his aching genitals. 'To distraction, in fact.'

Electricity buzzed through the telephone. How enticing it was to play sexual cat and mouse like this... They both knew what the other wanted, but neither was of a mind to capitulate and curtail their sweet, shared agony.

Lynn giggled again. 'So what would you like me to do about it?'

'Tell me where you'd like to put your hands.'

'But you're working,' the playful woman taunted.

He groaned. 'I *was* working. Are you working?'

'No, but I should be.'

'It's Saturday,' the breathless man offered idly. 'The Jew in me's telling me we shouldn't be working today.'

Lynn rolled her eyes and scoffed. 'That's convenient. And tomorrow will you be Catholic?'

'Depends, angel,' Jeff responded, as if her words had whipped his skin.

'On what?'

'On where you are.'

'Oh,' the nineteen-year-old gasped again, her stomach convulsing in pleasure.

The fifty kilometres between the Dyson homestead and the rock star's new *pied-à-terre* suddenly seemed almost as far as from Melbourne to Los Angeles, and tears pricked at Lynn's eyes. She missed her articulate, expressive perfect stranger dreadfully, and longed to give him exactly what he wanted. There was a serious message to deliver first however, and she forced herself to suspend their racy banter and concentrate back on the original reason for her call.

'Wait, Jeff! I have to tell you something first.'

'Oh, yeah? Is it quick?'

'Shut up, you sex maniac. You want to hear this, I promise. I rang to talk about my conversation with Mum and Dad about us,' the teenager redoubled, sitting up straight as if it would help her to concentrate. 'Is now alright?'

The telephone line fell silent for a second. 'Sure. Talk away,' her man replied, with a hint of disappointment in his voice. 'I was wondering when that lead balloon was going to drop. Are you OK? How did it go?'

'Well...' Lynn continued. 'It didn't quite go the way I'd intended.'

It was thus Jeff's turn to be nervous, and he felt Gravity immediately stand to attention. 'Shit! What does that mean?'

His girlfriend reassured him, and at the same time sought to reassure herself. 'It's OK. We're cool. Kind of... I was still planning to talk to them over the weekend about us seeing each other again, like I told you. Then as soon as I got in the house, Mum pounced on me and sent me to my dad's office.'

Her stranded lover said nothing. All she could hear were deep, irresistibly regular breaths, so she began to recap' the conversation. Her vision of him lighting a cigarette and crossing his long legs while he listened to her story gave her a tingling feeling all over.

'He started by showing me some photos of us taken at the music awards.'

'Oh, yeah? What sort of photos?'

'Of us going into the function room, with you grabbing my arm,' Lynn explained. 'But that wasn't really the issue. He's definitely running some sort of detective work and he knows about your dad. He was very surprised to hear that I already knew, so thanks for telling me when you did. That was my only trump card in the whole discussion.'

'Fuck. You're welcome, I guess. Are you OK?'

His girlfriend felt more relaxed. Jeff's supportive tone was exactly what she needed, and he certainly didn't seem to be hiding anyone else's presence. There was no hurry to get her off the telephone either. She shouldn't be so suspicious, she vowed. They were each others' centre of attention.

'Yes, I'm fine. Don't worry about me. I think you would've been proud of me. I managed to come up with an answer for everything.'

'Ha! *¡Excelente!*' the musician was glad to hear her sounding more confident again. 'So what was he saying?'

'Oh, all sorts... About your family, your police record, your girlfriends. All the predictable stuff. They think you're a criminal and a danger to my safety, but that's just code for they don't think you're right for me. He said, "someone of my ilk". I've never heard him say that before and almost burst out laughing. So what ilk are you, pray, kind sir?'

Her boyfriend sighed and chuckled half-heartedly. 'Your ilk? Bloody hell! That's fresh from the moors of Yorkshire. Where did he drag that one up from? I doubt if I even figure on the ilk scale, angel. Village idiot, maybe.'

'Village idiot?' Lynn echoed with a giggle. 'That's no better! Whatever, I don't care. I told him I was already fully across everything he was telling me and that it was my decision whether I see you or not.'

Sitting in his apartment, Jeff so desperately wanted to be with his beautiful best friend again. To hear her talk this way was gratifying, and he wished he could help break down this barrier to their future. His earlier arousal had subsided somewhat, given the serious tack their conversation had taken, but libido represented only one facet of his desire to be together. He had felt her loss acutely since their heavenly day in Sydney, compensated only by the promise in their secret affair.

'*Gracias*, angel. You're gorgeous,' he told her. 'They're probably right, but it is your decision. What else did they say? Was your mum there too?'

'She snuck in halfway through. Dad questioned my misguided loyalty. He's convinced you're a con' man and some sort of predator. And Mum really annoyed me, saying they were only acting for my safety and happiness. So I hit them with a good one...'

She heard a chuckle from the other end of the telephone.

'What's so funny?'

'You sound like me,' he encouraged. 'What did you hit them with?'

'I did sound like you!' the buoyed songstress agreed. 'I kept saying to myself, "How would Jeff answer this question?", and something would always come to me. I asked them whether they were acting for my happiness when they split us up two years ago.'

Her strident stranger whistled. 'Good work! So how did it end up? Are we history again?'

His voice pretended he was joking, but deep down neither lover took it that way.

'No. I've done a deal,' Lynn countered.

'Christ! You *do* sound like me! I'm feeling guilty now. Hope you didn't go further than you wanted to.'

'No, definitely not. I would've kept going,' she assured him. 'I have to agree to Dad finishing his investigations, and if he turns up something terrible, I'm to stop seeing you without making a scene.'

'OK,' the young man murmured.

'Jeff, is there anything terrible that I still don't know?'

'No, there isn't. Honestly, Lynn. I've told you everything he could possibly be interested in. But that's not to say there's nothing out there to incriminate me. In the wrong hands, it could still sound like the truth. It won't be the truth though, whatever it is.'

'Good,' his girlfriend muttered, more than a little disconcerted. 'So... Mum and Dad have agreed to let us see each other, but only if it doesn't interfere with anything. Reading between the lines, I'm sure that means that we stay a secret as far as possible.'

'That's fine. It's actually pretty on-turning to be clandestine for a while. There's something very sexy about sneaking around with you.'

'Oh, OK,' Lynn replied, bemused but happy that her headstrong partner was prepared to sign up to these terms. 'Then Dad said that if his detectives find nothing, he'll give us his blessing.'

This time, she heard a sharp intake of breath. This predictable turn of phrase had made the ambitious millionnaire angry. As if he needed Bart Dyson's blessing for anything...

'How bloody magnanimous of him.'

'Hey, wait!' his girlfriend stopped him. 'I know. It gave me the shits too, but that's just the way he is. I hit them with another condition though. Dad accused me of behaving like a barrister because I requested an additional clause.'

'Nice. You're more of a smart-arse than I am,' Jeff was impressed. 'What was your additional clause, my learned friend?'

'No, that's you. You're *my* learned friend,' the adoring woman laughed. 'I said he had to have a conversation with you, in person, because it was insulting to you for his people to snoop around in your life without talking to you about it. And also that if you're found to be innocent... which you will be... that he has to apologise to you directly.'

The tortured songwriter's insides dissolved as her words took his breath away. He did so want to be her learned friend, among other things. His hand reached back down the front of his pants and began to coax his latent erection back to life, instantly eliciting the anticipated result.

'Whoa! Thank you,' he gasped. 'That's awesome. I wish I'd been there to listen in. I'm stoked you stood your ground on my behalf.'

Lynn could feel his gratitude oozing through the telephone, mixed with more pronounced breathing once more. What was he doing? She had a pretty good idea, and felt her own urges stir too.

'You're welcome. *Our* behalf, Jeff. I kept thinking about how easy it would be to get really angry. I didn't though. I didn't want to give Dad the satisfaction of knowing he'd upset me. I did cry at the end, when Mum was putting on the agony about it all being in my best interests. I believe they're sincere in wanting the best for me, but it was a bit rich.'

The boy from Canley Vale agreed but didn't push his luck, knowing better than to criticise someone else's family too much. 'So where does that leave us?'

'What are you doing tonight?' his secret lover asked in return, allowing their earlier suggestive foreplay to run rampant in her mind again. 'I don't feel like staying here anymore. I'd much rather be with you.'

This was exactly what the anxious man needed to hear. The throbbing accelerated in his penis, now squeezed into the available space in his jeans. He undid his fly and began to stroke himself with more intent. An *entrée* before his dream girl arrived would certainly buy him time to show an unexpected visitor around his flat without overloading themselves with undue tension before she had even crossed the threshold.

'So come over then,' he leaped on the opportunity. 'That'd be fantastic. I could invite Gerry here, and we could have some takeaway and watch the footy. How does that sound?'

Lynn was slightly apprehensive about walking out on her parents so soon after securing her desired outcome, but she really wanted to see her beautiful, black stallion again. She also had a huge pile of correspondence to catch up on and some musical arrangements to review prior to her next set of tour dates. She could find time to do these things on the flight to Europe though, couldn't she? Having now obtained her father's approval to see her boyfriend as long as it didn't interfere with her hectic schedule, this afternoon would turn out to be one of the few opportunities at their disposal for quite a while. What the hell...

'That sounds great. Very normal. Do you mean come to your apartment?'

'Absolutely. If you want to,' Jeff affirmed. 'Or Admin. Anywhere's fine with me, but I really want you to see this place. Or I could drive out and pick you up, if you like. We could check into a hotel and go into hiding, like real fugitives.'

'Thanks, but no,' the adamant woman declined with a frustrated laugh. 'I'll borrow a car from here. I don't want to enflame the situation. I told Mum and Dad that I didn't want to fall out over this. Hopefully it won't come to that.'

The errant rock star read this as a signal for him to behave himself. He was struck by the notion that at this precise moment their invisible elastic connection was transmitting the same mental image in both directions. He recalled the desperately sad coaching session which Lynn had imparted just prior to her departure, and the plain-stated intention he gave to spirit her away while issuing his promised unsavoury hand gesture to her parents. This visualisation psychobabble really worked after all, he smiled to himself. It had taken a while, but his ill-conceived fairy tale was miraculously coming true.

'Sure. No worries, angel. Just let me know what you want me to do, and I'll do it,' he consented, closing in on his orgasm as their shared mood ebbed and flowed. 'I'd love to see you tonight; wherever, however, whenever. Who fucking cares? I hope you know that goes without saying. And I do want to play by the rules, as long as we know what they are and whose rules they are.'

Lynn laughed at his observation. 'Thanks. I knew you'd understand. I don't even know your address.'

No, she didn't, Jeff realised. No-one did. He rattled off the street number and gave her instructions on how to access the secure building.

'It's on the corner of Victoria and Spring Streets. Are you driving straight here?'

'No, I'll probably leave the car at Admin,' Lynn replied. 'I think I know where you are. Opposite the Exhibition Building?'

'*Exactamente.*'

'*¡Gracias!* Someone else'll want to take the car back before I come home again, especially after today's dodgy footing.'

'OK,' he muttered, his own all-consuming trip to fantasyland temporarily suspended until he was sure she was on her way. 'It'll be my honour to help you work up a head of steam here. Then you can tell me all the gory details. There's a spare parking space in the basement, but whatever works. Give me a ring when you get there, and I'll drive over and pick you up. I'm going to be here all afternoon. I'm just writing.'

'I'd rather turn up on your doorstep, if that's OK,' his excited girlfriend announced. 'I'll walk or get a taxi, depending on the rain.'

Jeff was bemused by the lady's desire for independence, but whatever Lynn Dyson wanted was absolutely fine with him. He had spent the last two days' worth of spare hours trying to form songs from the myriad lyrics and melodies playing tag with each other in his head, and he was chock full of pent-up energy. If he were honest, he was not yet fully comfortable with the new, mellow type of music, and he couldn't wait to share the fact that he was rebelling against it with someone who would understand. An impromptu *sojourn* with his *Regala* was like manna from heaven, so he was more than happy simply to go with the flow.

'What are you writing?' Lynn asked, hearing no response. 'Music or your novel?'

'Songs, mainly,' the artist answered. 'You know, I'm off in a dream world lately. I don't know what's wrong with me. You've made me all dozy.'

The teenager scoffed. '*I've* made you dozy? Might've known it'd be my fault. Is it good material though?'

'Wait and see,' Jeff told her. 'It's different. All laid back. I'll show you when you get here. Just turn up when you want. I'll be here.'

'*Bueno*,' the young woman replied in her best Argentinean accent. 'Probably around five or five-thirty then, by the time I've done what I need to do to smooth the waters.'

'Whenever, angel. Can't be too soon. Good luck with escaping. I love you.'

The superstar smiled. 'I love you too. See you later.'

She put the telephone receiver down on its cradle. Soon wasn't soon enough for her either. She had been collaborating with other songwriters for as long as she could remember, but she had extra special memories of sharing songs with the boy who became Jeff Diamond.

As Lynn re-packed her suitcase for the coming week, she shivered as she recalled also having to tell her tormented *amigo* about the plans for her to study in London, daring to dream that he might like to go too. That would be such a perfect solution. It would allow him a change of surroundings and maybe even help to lessen some of his residual symptoms, quite apart from giving the couple a chance to be together, far away from her family and all the do-gooders who thought they could run their lives.

At Home

True to her word, it was just after five o'clock when Lynn Dyson arrived at the front entrance of the tall apartment building. Looking quite new and relatively understated from the outside, she could see why the location would appeal to Jeff. He always liked to be close to the action, and it was within easy walking distance of the city, the university campuses in Carlton and all the interesting bars and restaurants on the northern fringe of the CBD.

She pressed the keypad numbers for apartment sixteen-oh-two and waited by the intercom. It clicked after a few seconds.

'Hey! You're punctual,' his deep voice sounded cheerful.

'How did you know it was me?'

The disembodied laugh was followed by a gulp and a short cough. Her mystery man's alcohol consumption was one thing the sportswoman needed to sort out, if he would let her, along with the various other substances which he tipped into his body on a regular basis. Indeed, she was surprised her father hadn't taken issue with this as well, because the new star's reckless party lifestyle had been well publicised.

'There are very few people who know where I live. Wait there, gorgeous. I'll come down.'

Lynn stood in the porch until the lift ejected the man she loved into the foyer, looking very relaxed in tracksuit pants and an old, light blue and very shapeless t-shirt. He opened the door with a bow, ushering her past him into the bright, open vestibule in front of the lifts and reaching to ease the strap of her overnight bag from her shoulder. She had come to stay, his heart alerted all related organs, which duly sprang to fevered attention.

'Where did you park?'

'On the street in Little Lonsdale. I've got one of the huge wagons from the farm, so if you need any bales of hay moved, now's your chance!'

The city boy smiled and kissed her flushed cheek. 'Hmm... Maybe later. I'll drive it into the car park for you in a while. Keep it out of sight.'

'Thanks.'

Predictably, as the lift doors closed on them, Jeff smothered his dream girl into a hungry but considerate embrace. Lynn wondered if his mind had turned to the tennis skirt episode, as hers had. Wow! This guilty memory stirred some strong emotions deep inside her, and she fought to keep them from transferring to her boyfriend's overly self-critical conscience.

She needn't have worried though. The handsome man's mind was, as he had mentioned on the telephone, totally distracted by her presence, as was his body. The strength in his arms and the heat radiating from his chest were very appealing, not to mention the feel of his already hard penis through the soft fabric of his tracksuit pants.

'Welcome to my new world,' he stated, with a huge grin on his face. 'This is a very happy day.'

The tall, slender beauty broke away for air, noticing that his kiss tasted only of coffee. 'Thanks! It's so good to see you press the top button,' she giggled. 'You've really made it. And thanks for dressing up.'

Looking down at his somewhat dishevelled appearance, Jeff shrugged an apology. Lynn kissed him again, tugging at the frayed hem of his t-shirt, and he wrapped his arms around her tightly.

The lift took them up to the top floor; the penthouse floor. There were only two apartments on this level. The celebrity guest imagined the one on the southern side to have good views over the city, whereas her boyfriend's would open out onto the flat northern suburbs and to the sun throughout the day. The smooth, brushed metal doors opened onto a light-filled lobby, with a glass ceiling and a staircase to the roof garden.

As if they had been transported back two years and into the old Richmond flat, the teenager held her hand out to receive the front door key.

'No need,' the grateful man smiled. 'It's open.'

The visitor looked along the landing. 'Is that safe?'

Her boyfriend shrugged. 'Yeah. Safe enough. Only my neighbour and I can get up this far, and he's overseas most of the time. He's an Aussie who runs a business in Singapore.'

'That's good,' Lynn said. 'Nice and quiet too. You can have wild parties, and no-one will care.'

'*Entrez-vous, s'il vous plaît, mademoiselle,*' Jeff invited with aplomb upon reaching his door, which was propped open by a set of telephone directories.

Through the doorway, the visitor could see a wide entrance hall. She walked ahead of her host and admired the distinguished, clean lines of the *décor*. The place reeked of class, and she was hit by a sublime sense of vicarious gratitude that the tortured and impoverished student she had known from before had managed to achieve so much so quickly. And so deservedly.

'Was it always like this or did you renovate? It's beautifully light and Mediterranean.'

The intellectual was pleased the apartment met with her approval, even though she had only made it as far as the hallway. 'I swapped carpet for tiles, so maybe that makes it more Mediterranean? I don't know. I just did what I wanted. No great design principles involved.'

Lynn smacked his arm. 'You're lying! I bet you researched it to death.'

Jeff feigned innocence and rubbed his arm, nudging his gorgeous guest steadily forwards. Had he really taken care of his sexual urges earlier? It didn't feel like it, standing so close to the most beautiful woman in the world. He dumped her bag on the floor next to an open door.

'I hope this is going in here.'

The young woman peeked inside the room and caught sight of the end of a large bed. She nodded.

'*Bueno.* And stop denuding me at every turn! It's exquisitely humiliating. You'll have to take the tour again, or I won't give you your security pass.'

Laughing aloud, the nineteen-year-old allowed herself to be steered around the spacious floor plan. Two spare bedrooms, only one furnished with a bed. A marble-tiled bathroom, a study or music room which had stuff strewn everywhere, and another room that was completely empty.

'What's this room supposed to be?' Lynn asked.

'Don't know yet. Probably a dining room, but I don't have cause to dine,' its owner answered, turning her towards the kitchen. 'Time to check out the extensive knife collection I have now.'

His favourite lady giggled again, sharing the memory of her original reaction to the deficiencies of his old flat and its limited amenities. Lynn dutifully opened the drawers one by one, expecting to see a large selection of utensils and gadgets.

'You idiot!' she exclaimed. 'You haven't bought anything new, have you?'

Jeff shrugged. 'Actually I have, but they're hard to find. Only furniture.'

'At least you've got much more space than in the last kitchen. But if you don't dine, I'm guessing you don't "kitch" much either…'

'Guilty!' he affirmed. 'But I do have my own washing machine, which is pure, unadulterated domestic bliss. First time in my life, and I'm still giving thanks to the gods of automatic laundrying. Oh, and a decent stereo.'

Seeing her boyfriend in his new, comfortable environment was so much fun for the privileged Victorian. It gave her goose-bumps to see him deriving such simple pleasure from things she had taken for granted all her life. How much his world had changed since she had last spent a night in his home, and yet how much hadn't changed also. Since his great confession in Sydney the previous week, each time they had spoken on the telephone she had noticed a gradual softening of his erstwhile unyielding, jagged edges. His voice was deeper and slower, and his eerie, protracted silences no longer threatened such foreboding.

'You're *molto legato* these days, *Signor* Diamond,' she smiled, planting a soft kiss on his cheek.

Jeff nodded. 'Absolutely. And it's all your fault, just as it was back then. You calm my troubled soul, angel, whether you're here or not. But no time for such nostalgic bullshit just now...'

Without hanging around, the host wheeled his perceptive guest out of the kitchen and directed her into an enormous lounge room. There was a baby grand piano next to a picture window which spanned the whole width of the room, and two sets of plate-glass, sliding doors gave onto a large balcony. He opened one of the doors, and the pair stepped outside into the warm afternoon sun.

'This is fantastic!' Lynn proclaimed expansively, walking to the balcony railing and leaning over the edge. 'And very private for something so open.'

The view was indeed magnificent, stretching all the way to the Macedon Ranges due north and as far as the hills east of the Yarra Valley in the distance. The enamoured songwriter stood behind her and enveloped her with his arms, kissing the side of her neck and pressing their bodies together. Leaning alluringly back into his embrace, his girlfriend pointed straight ahead, past the airport.

'You could probably see Benloch from here with a good telescope,' she guessed.

'Yep. I used to check if you'd snuck home.'

Lynn's head span round and her eyes looked at him quizzically. 'You didn't?'

Jeff smiled at her innocence while he drank in her beauty. Lynn Dyson was in his apartment again, and this time it really was his apartment. This achievement was one up on her, in fact, for which he dared to congratulate himself until his sex drive reclaimed his attention. With her long, golden hair being blown sideways from her face, occasionally assisted by a graceful hand movement, she looked so deliciously inaccessible to everyone but him. He almost didn't want to move away, in case she might disappear into his imagination, never to return.

'No, I didn't. Anyway, how do you like my new pad?'

The delectable female nodded childishly, accepting her host's invitation to return inside to continue the tour. He didn't attempt to touch her again, given the sublime agony he was now facing, yet it was abundantly clear that they were charged by each others' proximity.

Apart from the piano, the huge living space only accommodated three leather couches, a coffee table piled with books and papers, a television and a stereo. There were no bookshelves or pictures on the wall, and two guitars were leaning against one of the chairs. There were more piles of books spread along the wall and under the piano.

'It's sparse!'

The newly wealthy musician nodded and kissed her tenderly. This tour had already taken long enough, as far as his eager loins were concerned. However, like their heady re-acquaintance at the Sydney Intercontinental Hotel, the bedazzled suitor dearly wanted to linger in these precious moments for as long as possible.

'I've got everything I need. What more do you think should be in here?' he asked, his breath noisy in her ear.

The celebrity scanned the room again. 'This looks just like your old lounge room, only bigger. You haven't really bought anything, have you, you cheapskate?'

'I'm not a cheapskate. I'm a minimalist,' Jeff replied indignantly.

Lynn slapped him again, feeling her own heart rate quickening with each successive short and spicy physical interlude that punctuated her induction process. 'OK. You're a minimalist cheapskate! At least you should get some art to brighten up the walls.'

'I will eventually.'

Her eyes alighting on the piano, the singer noticed a familiar photograph. It was the one which had been taken at Robert McLean's twenty-first birthday party, after their slow dance to "Bridge Over Troubled Water". Her heart swelled again, remembering that momentous night so vividly.

'I still love that photo',' she said, pointing across the room.

Jeff nodded. 'Me too, although the one Sandy took's my favourite. It's in the bedroom. Speaking of which, there's still one room to go on the tour.'

'Saving the best for last?' the mischievous guest asked.

She knew full well what lay in store for her next. In fact, a certain part of her guide's anatomy had already gone ahead of them, judging by the state of his tracksuit pants. Seeing her eyes drift downwards, the sexy man winked unashamedly, inviting her to follow the rest of his hungry body back out into the hall and through the last, remaining doorway. Again, although its dimensions were substantial, there was nothing sumptuous about this room except that it boasted its own *en suite* bathroom. Another television and a bank of built-in wardrobes were the only items to set it apart from the bedroom in his previous home. Everything else was the same, even the bedclothes.

'Nothing's different about the way you live, is it?' his dream girl smiled, looking into his eyes as he drew her in.

'When I'm at home, not much, no,' Jeff replied, kissing her again, this time intensely. 'I've been waiting for you.'

So loving was his embrace that Lynn suddenly felt quite overwhelmed. 'Thanks,' she murmured, stroking the soft, taut skin of his upper arm beneath his sleeve.

'The whole place has been waiting for you,' he added. 'You're the only thing it lacks. It needs you to be here, like I do.'

There were tears in her eyes, and in his too. So Lynn's instincts had been right. It was evident that her prosperous boyfriend saw no value in material possessions without the significance of sharing them with her. To have sex in this bedroom would seal their allegiance, and momentarily her courage deserted her. Was she ready for this level of commitment, with London on the horizon and her parents' caveated endorsement hanging over them?

'I love you, Jeff,' she whispered. 'Thanks for inviting me here.'

The photograph that Sandy took looked on as they made love. With soft strings playing in the background from the expensive hi-fi system in the lounge room, the couple shed their clothing with complete abandon and fell onto the bed. While the patient man caressed her to a heavenly frenzy, Lynn permitted her senses to make friends with this room where it appeared she belonged. Already, the new apartment seemed strangely familiar, even though there was no wide bedroom windowsill at which to sit and dream, and its elevated position afforded it so much more light and fresh air than the old Richmond digs.

Perhaps it also felt familiar because it was so typical of this extraordinary man to do everything for a reason. He was always compelled to make a statement, whether with words or deeds. Both, most of the time, the young star mused. As he was touching her, Lynn lost herself in thoughts of love. Maybe this lost boy felt the need to make such bold statements to justify his existence, not only to others but even to himself. His unconventional childhood had forced him to build his own sense of self-worth, a gift which she had been handed on a plate and was never allowed to forget.

'You are the perfect man,' she whispered, as their lovemaking ended in a frantic rush of sensations.

Jeff kissed her forehead and slowly lowered himself down onto the bed beside her. 'Thanks. Not according to your parents, remember?' he smiled. 'How did it go? "Fuck my parents"?'

The young woman put on an exasperated air. 'Don't talk about that now,' she scolded. 'How to spoil a beautiful moment.'

The amused lover chuckled. 'Apologies. How about some tea? Would that prolong our beautiful moment?'

'What?' the dark-haired guitarist shot back, seeing a look of complete surprise cross his visitor's face.

She laughed, sitting up and kissing him passionately. 'A cup of tea's most definitely not what I expected you to offer me. Whatever happened to cigarettes, beer and loose women?'

'We don't have a licence here yet, ma'am,' the host quipped. 'It's tea or a glass of water. *Tómelo o déjelo.*'

'Pardon? What does that mean? I've never heard you use that expression before.'

'Take it or leave it. Or literally, pick it up or drop it,' the linguist explained, already floating on another metaphysical cloud coalescing out of their humorous banter.

The sophisticated lady chose the former, causing their magic carpet to fly a little higher still. The effect was greater than any drug. Her gentlemanly lover handed her his bathrobe and put on some shorts, and they adjourned to the kitchen. Lynn levered herself backwards athletically onto the kitchen bench as he made the tea.

'I have noticed something that's different,' she offered.

'What's that?'

'You haven't sworn once since I've been here.'

The rock star smiled. 'No. Well spotted. I'm giving up swearing, drinking, smoking and fucking around. I'm a clean-living boy now.'

The sophisticate's eyes gleamed, thrilled with what she was hearing. 'Really? Since when? Even socially?'

Jeff raised his self-assured eyebrows, grinning at her genuine amazement. 'Since last week. Although I don't think I ever fucked around socially... I'm serious though. I don't need any of that anymore, not with you back in my life and my new mellow self. I was doing way too much of the bad stuff. Now I have the good stuff, I don't need them substitutes no more.'

The genuinely clean-living sportswoman leaned over and hugged him, almost falling off the counter.

'Hey. Watch out!' her boyfriend gasped as he caught her. 'I don't want any injuries, thank you. And yes, I do still swear, smoke and drink socially, but much less.'

The curious woman dared to ask the burning question. 'Does this mean you're sleeping better now too?'

'*Tristamente, no*,' he answered in a rich Spanish accent. 'No change there, but I'm keeping positive.'

'You are amazing,' the blonde superstar told him, accepting her mug of strong, steaming tea. 'I can't believe how content you seem. You *are* mellow. Totally mellow. That's a good word. And it's a great apartment too. It's so you. I love it.'

Jeff paused with his own mug halfway to his lips, while Lynn's words seemed to hang in the air. Was it her imagination, or had the atmosphere become inexplicably laden with anticipation. She felt two dark eyes bore into hers.

'Do you love it enough to live here?'

It was as if her ears had received each word in slow motion. Love. Enough. Live. Here. Had she heard him correctly? The nineteen-year-old was totally blown away by the question. Was her new, old boyfriend really asking her to move in with him?

'Live here with you? Are you sure? I can't believe you'd ask me that. You've wanted to live on your own for all this time.'

'Yeah, I know,' her enigmatic stranger answered, with renewed anguish in his voice caused by Miss Irony's not unexpected kick in the balls. 'But I need you here, and we'd have fun. I've been on my own all my life and I've finally had enough. Please?'

The young woman looked nervous, dismounting from the kitchen worktop. 'Let's sit on the balcony and drink these.'

Obediently, the songwriter followed his visitor outside, and they stood together, surveying the northern suburbs. With the heightened state of suspense in which she had left him, Jeff experienced the strongest urge in a number of hours for the cigarette that Gravity was salaciously offering.

'What about my parents?' Lynn began, shielding her eyes from the descending sun, which shone bright orange between the city buildings. 'It'd be like rubbing their faces in the dirt.'

Jeff shrugged, pulling out a chair for her to sit down. 'Yeah. I see that. But you've told them we're going to keep seeing each other, haven't you?'

'Yes, definitely,' she replied, her mind harking back to their strained conversation earlier that day.

'So what difference does it make? Either I'd be at Admin with you, or you'd be here with me. I don't think they'd like either option too much right now.'

Australia's darling tossed the contentious notion from side to side in her head while she sipped her tea. The handsome man moved another chair out from the table and straddled it opposite his uncertain visitor, tipping forward on its front legs to plant a kiss on her warmed lips. His eyes were filled with insecure presumption, and her heart was filled with elated dread.

'I suppose not.'

'And with both our travel schedules, we'd be away more than we'd be here,' he persisted. 'So when we're both in Melbourne, it'd be fantastic to shack up here together, wouldn't it?'

The beautiful woman extended the fingers of her left hand and prodded his forehead to push him away. To no avail however, since the larrikin simply tilted his head back, releasing a series of audible crunches from sore neck muscles, and allowed all ninety-odd kilograms of his body weight to tip forwards. The chair slipped from under him on the glazed tiles, ending up caught between his bent knees.

'Careful!' the singer cried out.

Chuckling at the look of fright on Lynn's face, he kissed her own brow affectionately, rocking his chair back onto all four legs. 'Wouldn't it?' he urged.

'You are gorgeous and so bloody persuasive too!' his girlfriend laughed in exasperation. 'Of course I want to say yes, but I'm in such a difficult situation. You speak right to my heart. I can't believe how much I love you.'

'Then move in with me.'

The radiant superstar turned to face the view, locks of gleaming hair wafting lazily in the light breeze. Long, tanned legs stretched out in front of her, with their bare feet crossed over each other under the righted chair. At least she was considering his proposition, Jeff thought, marvelling at how sensational she looked. After a few seconds, her eyes turned back towards him.

'Does that mean my stuff too? Clothes and everything?'

Her anxious lover couldn't help laughing, forcing himself to lighten up. There was no need to put so much pressure on her. It wasn't fair. Lynn had chosen to be here now, and without the slightest cajoling. He ought to be satisfied enough with that. He wished his mind would stop demanding control of every situation and simply allow life to happen around him, just like the way today had unfolded. These lessons were so hard to learn, and he cursed his obsessive reflex actions.

'No. No clothes. You'd have to be naked the whole time. Sorry, I missed out that part.'

Her blue eyes dancing in amusement, the celebrity kissed her clown on the lips and then smacked his bare chest. 'Argh! You're too quick for me. You're supposed to be mellow, remember?'

Jeff took the empty mug out of her hand and led her back into the bedroom, his compulsion too strong to ignore. Gravity was busy flashing a slide show in the tortured man's mind of two years' worth of lonely pictures, while he walked his dream girl over to the far side of the room and opened the doors to the right-hand wardrobe. It was completely empty.

'This is yours. It says so,' he informed her.

Intrigued, she stepped forward and peered at a removal company's label which was stuck to the mirror inside the door.

'"Lynn's stuff goes here",' he read aloud, pointing to each word in turn. '¿Comprendes?'

Wow! The new arrival's heart leaped into her mouth at this statement to end all statements. Again she was floored.

'You had a plan all along, didn't you?' she said, sounding suspicious but blissfully amused.

Jeff smiled his most disarming of half-smiles. 'I cannot lie,' he replied. 'That sticker's been there since the day I unpacked. It's just taken a while to be able to show you.'

Tears welled up in the young woman's piercing, blue eyes, and she flung her arms around her handsome boyfriend. She wanted more than anything to share this quietly sophisticated apartment with the man who loved her so much and who had waited patiently for her to love him back. Why was she intent on playing hard to get? Why did people always feel the need to complicate things so much?

'Thank you. I don't know what to say. I can't think of anything more romantic you could've done to tempt me. I'd love to live here, Jeff. I'm a bit worried about Mum and Dad's reaction, but my answer's yes.'

The grateful rock star pulled her in close, and they kissed long and hard. 'Thank *you*. You won't regret it,' he told her, with a sincerity she could almost drink. 'And if your dad finds out I'm hiding something heinous, you can keep the apartment. I won't need it where I'd be going.'

Shuddering, Lynn understood exactly what was being inferred. It was too horrible to contemplate, but she didn't doubt his intent. How would she ever make up for the damage caused over the last twenty years and enable him to trust her implicitly.

'It won't happen. And even if it did, I wouldn't leave you.'

Looking into her shining eyes, he wanted so desperately to believe her. 'I'll help you talk to your folks, if you like. You're going to have to give them this 'phone number.'

'Thanks,' the sportswoman responded, 'but I really need to deal with this myself until Dad's fears and doubts are resolved. I could have a separate 'phone line put in. That way we can keep you guys apart.'

Jeff nodded slowly, chuckling at her apt expression. 'That's actually a bloody good idea. I might take you up on that.'

But the famous teenager's demeanour had altered again, and her eyes darted around the bedroom as if searching for something. He assumed she was ruminating on how to break the news to her parents. Was he being fair asking her to do this so soon? He should leave it up to her at this point and stop trying to dictate the play. There were already enough control freaks in this particular scenario.

'You OK?' he asked.

'Sorry,' Lynn brought her attention back into the moment, shaking her head and fixing him with worried eyes. 'But I've got one more question I have to ask you, if that's OK.'

The tormented boy was determined not to show how her change of tone had rocked his world so soon after agreeing to move in. Second thoughts already?

'*Digame.*'

The blonde beauty inhaled slowly, formulating a difficult question to put to him as tactfully as possible. 'Jeff, I know you saw other women while we were together before, and obviously you did while I was overseas…'

Where was this going? 'Yeah?'

278

'And I know my relationships have also been well publicised too,' she added.

'Yep,' he agreed again, allowing himself a wry smile, his telepathic powers having kicked in. 'And with everyone, I hear.'

Lynn continued, rolling her eyes. 'No, not with everyone. I wish I'd kept my damned mouth shut.'

The good-looking rogue in front of her scoffed, his kind eyes encouraging her to continue.

'Well, I'd absolutely love to move in here and sleep with you in your bed,' she hesitated, 'but I don't think I could do it if you've shared it with someone else. I just don't think I could feel comfortable. I know it sounds petty, but it's a big issue for me.'

'Come here,' he urged, exhaling slowly.

Jeff lifted her cold, uncertain hands and placed them onto his shoulders. The young lady stiffened. She was not going to be charmed out of this. His confidence duly restored, her resolute lover went to kiss her but then pulled back, having underestimated her reticence.

'OK. Sure. I understand, angel,' he said, holding his right hand over his heart and directing her eyes towards the bed next to where they were standing. 'I promise you, there has been no other woman in that bed. It's new since I moved in here. Until this afternoon, the only person who's either slept or shouted or screamed in this bed is me. Please believe me. I had a plan all along, as you said. You are only the second woman to set foot through the front door, and the first was the cleaner.'

Seeing his dream girl's expression soften a little, the empathetic man drew her in and kissed her waiting mouth. 'And I didn't have sex with her, in case you're wondering. I'll introduce you to her, if you like. Then you'll definitely believe me.'

Lynn's own fears and doubts were enormously pacified by his response, and she did believe him. This man had never deceived her before. She leaned her head onto his bare chest and kissed the hairy expanse of muscle.

'I do believe you,' she whispered, brushing a stray tear from the corner of her eye. 'Thanks. You care about me so much. I'm honoured that you'd do all this in the hope that I'd come back. I'm so glad we're back together. You're right. We're going to have heaps of fun living here. I'm sorry I even asked the question.'

The tall man kissed her again, with a tenderness that moved them both. 'Don't be. I was hoping you would. I know what's important to you, and I want to say a belated thank-you for the latitude you showed me before, when I managed to justify seeing other people when we couldn't be together. It was wrong of me to ask you to put up with that. That part of me's gone now. You're the only woman in my life, and that's the way it's going to stay.'

This was panning out as an afternoon of great revelations, and Lynn was particularly overjoyed to hear this one. Something in her expression made her partner do a double-take, suddenly hit by another bout of light-headedness, as if this elation might all come crashing down at any minute. He needed to relax, but why did he get the feeling there was more to her uncertainty than met the eye?

Lynn smiled, knowing it was she who withheld vital information now. She had the trifling subject of a year in London about which to come clean, thereby rendering moving into this apartment quite moot. She decided to wait until the morning to drop this residual bombshell on her unrelenting boyfriend.

'Even when one of us is travelling?' she asked, concentrating her attention back on the empty wardrobe.

'Absolutely,' he confirmed, again putting his hand on his heart. 'I promise. Do you want it in writing?'

'No! I believe you.'

'Thank you. That's the best thing you could've possibly said to me,' the young man sighed, feeling like another weight had been lifted off his shoulders.

'And I love you more than I can tell you,' his visitor added, hugging him tightly.

Jeff looked on in humble amusement. Despite his erratic and often untrustworthy instincts, this evening was surpassing even his wildest dreams.

'OK, so it was the second best thing you could've possibly said. Smart-arse! I love you too.'

'What time's Gerry arriving?' Lynn asked, a look of concern spreading across her face. 'It's six-thirty already.'

'Is it? Jesus! I didn't think we'd been talking that long. We're back!' the triumphant intellectual announced. 'I said any time after seven, so we haven't got long. Jump in the shower, and I'll tell you who's coming with him.'

'Oh. I thought it would be Suzanne, but obviously not.'

Her boyfriend shook his head and held out his hand. Lynn let the heavy satin robe slip off her shoulders and fall to the floor, and the pair climbed into a truly capacious shower in the rock star's luxurious *en suite* bathroom. Through the noise of the water gushing around them, he explained that his fellow southbound migrants hardly saw each other these days, both having moved on long ago.

'Suzie-Anna's got a man of her own now,' he updated her. 'He's a bit country but basically a good bloke. Name's Steve, and he's got a carpentry business out near the kennels. We'll have to invite them over too. She rang yesterday, desperate to find out if I'd seen you yet.'

The man of the house shut off the powerful jet and chivalrously invited his dream girl to exit ahead of him. Watching her lather her body with soap had re-awakened particularly lustful energy. There was no time for such indulgence now however, so he contented himself with towelling her dry instead.

'But wait, there's more…'

Lynn put on an impatient air. 'More? About Gerry and Suzanne? So tell me! Or *digame*, I should say.'

'No. Gerry's met and is going out with Junior's ex, Vanessa,' he divulged, smiling at her coy effort to speak to him in his native tongue.

'Vanessa Cooper-Brown?' the young woman yelled from the bedroom.

Jeff was right behind her and yelled right back. 'You don't have to shout! I'm right here. I don't know what her surnames are.'

Yet another degree of separation removed! The celebrity couldn't quite grasp the amazing coincidence that would see her at her new but former lover's for dinner, with his best mate and her brother's teenage girlfriend as a couple. How weird the way the world worked sometimes…

'And she's coming tonight?'

Her boyfriend nodded, slotting his arms into the sleeves of a crisp white shirt with the faintest silver thread striped through it. He acknowledged the appreciative nod for yet another classy piece of clothing, while a figure-hugging top made its way from her overnight bag and covered breasts encased in a lacy white bra. He struggled to bring his focus back to where it needed to be.

'Does she know I'm going to be here?' Lynn asked.

'Nope. And nor does Gerry,' he affirmed. 'It should be an interesting evening.'

The independent stars finished dressing and hurriedly made the bed, both feeling more than a little awkward about their new, more tightly-coupled status. They skirted round each other, passing from kitchen into lounge room and back again to prepare for their guests' imminent arrival, as if they hadn't quite earned the right to fully stake their claims yet. Neither had been in this situation before, and it had barely had a chance to sink in.

'Does this feel weird to you?' Lynn was the first to broach the subject.

Jeff's eyes flashed at her briefly, before being turned away on purpose. He began to walk towards the door.

'I'm going to have a social beer. Can I get you something?'

'Did you hear what I said?'

'Glass of wine?' her man responded with as straight a face as he could manage, much to the gorgeous woman's frustration.

'Are you deliberately ignoring me?'

'Yes, I am. And yes, it does,' he admitted, 'and we've only got ten minutes to get used to ourselves. I picked the wrong night to tell you I quit drinking.'

The young woman was glad she wasn't the only one who was feeling out of place, laughing at his response. 'OK. That makes me feel better. Yes, please. Wine would be great.'

They toasted each other with their respective drinks. No sooner had Jeff turned on the television to check the afternoon's football scores, than the buzzer sounded from downstairs. Lynn pulled a nervous face as he passed her on the way to the entry-phone. He patted her on the head like a little girl, provoking a barrage of half-hearted punches to his back.

'Good evening, Diamond residence,' he barked into the receiver, still fending off the blows.

'Hey, mate. It's me and the lovely Vanessa,' replied the familiar voice of Gerry Blake, followed by a female hello.

It was true. Jeff's indomitable friend and manager *was* seeing Junior's ex! Lynn let out a gasp.

'Shhh!' the apartment's owner hissed, putting his hand over the mouthpiece briefly. 'OK. Great. I'm on my way.'

The hyperactive musician propped the front door open with the weighty directories once again and descended to welcome his first ever dinner guests. Even if the extent of his domestication would only amount to ordering takeaway, this newfound desire to play host took him by surprise.

The lift ride afforded Jeff a few seconds' adjustment to the novel aspect his life had embraced over the preceding two hours. He gave thanks to the lift gods for making everything turn out so perfectly, soon finding himself on the ground floor. Opening the glass doors to the outside world, his shook his mate's hand warmly and bestowed a superstar's well-practised kiss on the dark-haired ballerina's cheek.

Still with beer bottle in hand, the handsome celebrity looked the picture of relaxation. 'Nice to see you again, Vanessa.'

Gerry's new girlfriend was shy towards their host, both because they shared a secret and because she was standing next to a famous and extremely handsome rock star. She had been eagerly anticipating this chance to have dinner with Australia's hottest male celebrity.

'G'day, mate!' Jeff slapped his fellow rugby fan on the back, knowing the accountant's team had suffered a big loss that afternoon. 'Bastard about those Dragons.'

'*C'est la vie*,' Gerry replied, handing his friend the two bottles of wine with which they had come armed. 'What are you looking so damned happy about?'

The younger man stood back and allowed Vanessa to enter the lift first. He turned his key in the special lock reserved for penthouse residents while Gerry pressed the button for the top floor, leaving lift doors to close obediently for its high-flyers.

'What sort of food do you want to get drunk with?' the no-nonsense Irishman asked his date.

The debate between Thai, Chinese and Indian cuisine had not concluded by the time the lift doors re-opened. Bantering back and forth, the trio made their way through the open front door, only to be met in the hallway by Jeff's very new flatmate.

'Lynn!' shrieked Vanessa. 'What are you doing here?'

Gerry also looked dumbfounded, turning back to his friend. 'What's going on, mate? You never informed me you two were an item again. That must be in breach of some doctor-patient code or other,' he said, seeing the tall, blonde singer walking gracefully forward to greet him and grabbing her outstretched hands *con gusto*. 'Such a pleasure, Miss Dyson. Ravishing, as ever.'

'You too, Gerry,' the teenager laughed. 'Nice to see you again, both of you. I need to hear the story of how you two got together.'

Jeff couldn't help but notice that his resident angel had dusted off her gracious crowd-pleasing diplomacy, which made him feel strangely proud. Did she realise how significant an event this was for him? He had expected their revitalised togetherness would simply turn back the clock and take up where they had left off, yet the dynamic between them was somehow different. With his hand possessively wrapped around her waist, he guided the others outside onto the balcony with their drinks.

While Vanessa and Lynn were sipping champagne and renewing an old friendship, Jeff and Gerry moved away to share a cigarette and the other secret. 'D'you know Vanessa used to be Junior Dyson's girlfriend?'

His mate was astounded. 'No, I did not! When?'

'Oh, since they were kids. Lynn used to call her her brother's fuck-buddy,' he confided under his breath. 'Not that I'm in any position to provide good counsel, but these two know each other pretty well, so better tread carefully.'

'Christ! Thanks for the warning. But look, mate, what's with the adorable Miss D being here? When did this happen? In Sydney? No wonder you're looking so bloody cat-with-the-cream chuffed.'

Jeff smiled a knowing, blokes-only smile. 'Good, isn't it?'

Introductions over, their host produced a few menus from local restaurants offering a takeaway service. They chose Indian, and the boys left to fetch it in Gerry's BMW while the girls swapped recent gossip. Over dinner, Lynn told the table about her experiences at UCLA and what it was like to make films with famous directors, including the highly prized Bond-girl appearance. Her rock star boyfriend then shared news concerning his own acting *début*, the starring role in the movie of his own book.

Since the young traveller had last seen her, Vanessa had been promoted to one of the principal dancers in the Australian Ballet, but had begun to think about moving overseas to gain international experience. She was full of questions about the various cities where the others had spent time.

And for the businessman's part, he had no hesitation in showing off how well his business was going and how many new employees he had taken on recently. The ladies groaned at hearing the crass chauvinist's selection criteria for female staff, but Blake & Partners' VIP client claimed he was all for it and requested a place on the interview panel. The evening flew by in happy chatter, and before long, they were stuffed with various curries and exotic breads, and lethargy had well and truly set in.

'Let's catch the end of the footy,' Jeff suggested. 'Leave this mess. Lynn'll do it in the morning.'

Vanessa instantly objected, not in tune with the rock star's wicked sense of humour. 'That's terrible! How dare you say that?'

Shrugging at each other, the two Aussie blokes slumped onto a couch each and settled down with the rest of the fourth bottle of wine. Lynn dutifully began to clear away the *débris*, making as much noise as she could by clattering the plates and cutlery together. Vanessa, still offended by the arrogant householder's apparently sexist attitude, pitched in to help her long-time friend, totally unaware of the joke.

'Keep the racket down over there, girls, please,' Gerry shouted. 'We can't hear the commentators' wisecracks.'

'You two are complete bastards!' cried the dancer. 'I can't believe you'd let Lynn do this by herself, Jeff. Get up here and help. Bloody football!'

The new flatmate carried on ferrying empty plates and glasses into the kitchen, having caught on to her boyfriend's nefarious plan. In truth, she didn't much care for such practical jokes, but having found herself slap bang in the middle of one, she could hardly spoil it now. Still the rock star's gaze didn't move from the television, infuriating the ballerina still further.

'Guys!' Vanessa shouted, holding her arms out in dismay. 'You're incredible!'

'She's enjoying herself,' the younger man shot back casually. 'Aren't you, angel?'

'Of course, dear,' Lynn affirmed, finding it hard to keep up the pretence for much longer. 'The quicker I get it done, the less the beating will hurt.'

Jeff rolled his eyes. 'Fuck, Lynn! That's taking it a bit far.'

Gerry guffawed with laughter, both at the look on his date's face and at witnessing his old friend squirm. 'She's better at this than you are, mate. Nice one, Miss Dyson.'

The seasoned entertainer curtsied, and Vanessa finally twigged that the whole scene had been played out at her expense. 'You guys are awful,' she whined. 'You too, Lynn! For a minute there, I thought you were really under the thumb.'

At three-quarter time, the contented host disposed of their food containers in the bin in the basement car park and managed to sneak a few minutes alone with a cigarette. He soaked up the solitude, leaning against his sleek, black sports car and wondering how on Earth he had got so lucky today. He was quite baffled by how naturally this unfamiliar blend of domesticity suited him, making plans for a return match with Suzanne and Steve after his upcoming Far East tour dates.

Meanwhile up on level sixteen, the two women loaded the apartment's virgin dishwasher, continuing to bemoan Gerry's laziness. While he lounged on his backside, steadily drinking his friend dry, Lynn and Vanessa installed themselves at the kitchen table, gazing out at the twinkling lights beyond the balcony. They had a lot to catch up on.

'This is really an odd co-incidence,' the brunette remarked, her hands wrapped around a steaming mug of tea.

'I'll say! It just proves how small Melbourne is. How long have you known Gerry?'

Vanessa's eyes looked to the ceiling as she tried to remember. 'I think we've been out four times altogether,' she answered, 'over a long stretch though. He's great company, but I don't trust him one bit. I knew he was Jeff Diamond's manager and had been trying to wangle some sort of meeting. I love his music, don't you? But then when tonight's invitation came out of the blue, and now here you are...'

Her childhood friend smiled. 'I know. I wasn't supposed to be here today really. June and I drove out to Benloch this morning, but I changed my mind about staying over. It's so weird... And I know what you mean about not trusting Gerry. We had lunch with his mum when we were in Sydney. She's tearing her hair out with him. Just wants him to settle down with a nice girl.'

'Well, he won't do that!' the ballerina scoffed. 'He's having way too much fun doing exactly what he wants. I'm not into that whole steady boyfriend thing either actually, but I'd rather not be one of quite so many. Hey, but what's the deal with you and Jeff? He's so absolutely, one-hundred percent spunk. I'm very jealous. I had no idea you'd got back together.'

'It's a highly confidential deal, actually,' the celebrity admitted. 'Mum and Dad know we're seeing each other again but they're not at all happy about it. They're against me spending time with him because they want me to find someone "more suitable", but Jeff suits me fine.'

'Ooh! You might be disinherited,' Vanessa jeered, open-mouthed.

'Who cares about that? I can make my own money. That's not a problem. It's more that I don't want to spoil my relationship with my family. I'm hoping we can work it out over time and we'll eventually be able to stop creeping around.'

Her friend giggled. 'I won't tell anyone. I haven't spoken to Junior for over a year. Is he seeing anyone?'

'I think so,' the nineteen-year-old replied. 'Julie McLaughlin. Do you remember her? She went to MLC; used to play netball against us. He's probably going to take over our farm in New South Wales soon, by the way.'

'Really? That'll be good for him. To be his own boss. But so far away…'

The women twisted round on their chairs towards the door to see the man of the house striding purposefully into the kitchen, heading for the fridge. A broad grin spread over his face on clapping eyes on two females in his kitchen, seeming to find their presence a surprise.

'Hey! This is where you guys are hiding. Is this girls-only corner? Don't you wanna watch the 'pies go down?'

He lifted out two beer bottles and came over to the table where the two friends were sitting. He bent down and kissed Lynn's hair, his spare hand caressing her neck fondly. He looked the picture of happiness in faded jeans and a striped shirt, with the sleeves folded over a few times and the neck open to reveal the hair on his broad, tanned chest. Lynn's fingers ran up his side, until they were caught by an avaricious hand and squeezed between a pair of velvet pincers.

'You guys OK?' Jeff's mouth attempted to articulate.

Vanessa stood up. 'I have to go to the loo. Be back in a minute.'

Conveniently left on their own, Lynn scrambled to her feet too and kissed her amiable drunk. 'I'm fine. It's good to see Vanessa again. That was such a mean joke we played on her though.'

'I am so off my face,' her co-conspirator apologised, trying his hardest not to slur his words.

'Yeah, I noticed,' his girlfriend replied with a smile. 'You've given up drinking, remember?'

The tall joker rocked backwards, steadying himself by grabbing onto the sportswoman's steadfast arm. 'Yeah. That's right, I have. I'll have some explaining to do tomorrow.'

'No,' Lynn shook her head. 'Don't you dare. It's so fantastic to see you relaxed and happy. Are you sure you want them to stay here tonight?'

Understanding her drift perfectly, Jeff rested his forehead on hers and nodded. 'Yes, I do. I want us to be normal, angel. Normal people doing normal things, like having our mates stay over. You're going to have to work your magic on me.'

'It'll be my pleasure,' the empathetic woman agreed.

She kissed him again, and he pulled her clumsily against his swaying body, hooking the two bottles over her shoulder for balance. The chilled glass was a shock against her skin, even through the fabric of her top. It was nice to know the dreamer felt secure enough to put his trust in her ability to silence his nocturnal rages before they woke the guests. She wasn't sure of being able to rise to the challenge, yet it made her feel very important and thoroughly wanted.

'Go and watch the end of the match.'

'No,' the amorous man refused, between tobacco-flavoured kisses.

Lynn pushed him gently, and he rocked again, this time genuinely in danger of falling. 'You idiot! Go and watch the footy. Gerry's beer'll be warming up.'

Shaking his head, the comic tried it on yet again.

'No, I don't want to,' he moaned like an eight-year-old. 'I don't care about that fucker. I only care about you.'

'Go and watch the football!' his determined partner commanded, rotating him by his hips.

Desisting after a second or two, Jeff obeyed and headed out of the kitchen, almost bumping into Vanessa, who was on her way back.

'Is he pissed?' she asked her friend. 'Boys!'

The women decided to join their partners in the lounge room, in spite of their intoxicated grunginess. Their attempts at humour were corny and crude, but they were in good spirits. Jeff beckoned for his dream girl to stretch out on the couch alongside him, prompting his drowsy mate to follow suit, and all four made themselves comfortable.

At one point, during the television coverage's post-match commentary, Vanessa caught her friend's attention, pointing from one inebriate to the other. They had both closed their eyes, with their beer bottles precariously balanced on an arm of each sofa. They were like two bookends; mirror images of each other. Lynn wished they had a camera handy.

Realising she shouldn't allow her man to nod off, the dutiful watchdog softly dug him in the ribs to rouse him. 'Don't fall asleep here,' she whispered.

'Thanks, angel. Who wants coffee?' the sluggish host sprang up off the couch, not yet drunk enough to miss her subtle message.

Gerry with a start. 'Coffee? Yes, mate. As long as you've got some brandy to go with it.'

With the late night sports shows over and several shots later, the quartet finally decided to call it a night.

'Thanks for a great time,' Vanessa said to her friend, while she steered Gerry's lumbering frame into the spare bedroom.

Lynn smiled, recalling that she had felt like an intruder earlier, ferreting around in her boyfriend's cupboards for sheets and pillowcases. She had to admit to a certain wariness at the control freak's level of comfort in letting her loose among his possessions, but was quite prepared to blame it on the amount of alcohol which had passed his most attractive lips. It would certainly never have crossed her wild boy's mind that sleepovers typically required beds to be made up, and she smiled on seeing the realisation hit him as he peered into the guest room.

'Good night and good luck,' the younger woman wished the other couple.

'You too!'

It was almost one o'clock, according to the video recorder's glowing digits. The teenager rustled up two glasses of water and dropped their coffee cups and liqueur glasses into a sink of bubbles. When she eventually found herself in the master bedroom, still a little disoriented, she spied her boyfriend already sprawled on top of the bed, fully clothed except for his bare feet and with his shirt completely unbuttoned.

'Come take me,' he moaned, sensing Lynn entering the room.

'Where are we going?' his girlfriend smirked. 'You're not capable of anything. Look at you!'

Jeff lifted his head up with great difficulty, scanning down the length of his long body. 'You might well be right, but it'll be fun trying,' he agreed. '¿D'acquerdo?'

The host's giddy head flopped back onto the mattress, and he grimaced as it bounced. Lynn undressed down to her underwear before tugging roughly at his jeans, glancing over her shoulder to make sure the door was shut. Then, sitting on top of his hips, she began to stroke his chest and stomach and watched his penis grow and straighten in front of her eyes. She might have known that this would be the only remaining functional organ.

All of a sudden, the room's serenity was shattered as Jeff let out a loud roar and threw his quarry sideways onto the mattress, pinning her down and covering her with ardent, slobbering kisses.

'Shhh! Remember we've got company.'

'Don't stress! They'll be doing the same thing. Forget about them.'

The enchanting temptress laughed at her man's ungainliness as he made love to her in his uncoordinated state. It wasn't long before they had worked themselves up into a fever, and he confessed that he lacked the control to hold on any longer. Lynn arched her back, aroused by the feeling of him expanding inside her as they moved.

'You're so funny! I'm so glad you're a clean-living boy now.'

Jeff climaxed with very little warning, smiling at her comment as the acute, blissful climax rushed through him. 'You bet!'

Both lovers collapsed into each others' arms and were soon drowsily exchanging reminiscences about their journey into love. Their two long years apart already seemed like a distant aberration, so naturally had they fitted back together.

'At the moment when our eyes first met, did you feel anything?' the dreamy singer whispered, kissing the stubbly skin on her favourite friend's cheek. 'They always talk about the dramatic feeling when you first clap eyes on "The One". Did you feel it?'

'When we saw each other through the door at the front of the lecture theatre, you mean?'

'Well, yes, I suppose so,' she murmured. 'I was thinking more when you asked me out, but you're right. That wasn't the first time.'

'Did you feel anything?' the romantic countered.

'I asked you first! I liked what I saw. That's why I was staring. Did you?'

Jeff nodded, hugging his dream girl closer. 'Same, I guess. I already knew I'd be hooked because I had been for years.'

'But how?'

'Who knows, angel? I just was. Am. Will always be.'

Lynn twisted free of his bear-like grip and propped herself up on her elbow. 'That's lovely. So will I. So did you feel something when you saw my face on TV or whatever?'

'Yeah, probably,' the satisfied drunk stifled a yawn that in turn masked a laugh, knowing full well that her face would most likely have been somewhere a little further down the list of body parts when it came to pure animal attraction.

'So you fell in love with eyes that weren't mine,' the nineteen-year-old teased. 'Weren't even eyes, really.'

'Now you're getting too surreal. Let's just go with the slow burn way to fall in love,' her boyfriend shifted onto his side too and kissed her smiling lips.

'OK,' Lynn acquiesced. 'And I hope it keeps burning hotter and hotter.'

'So do I, baby. *Certainement.*'

The pair fell silent for a few minutes, neither in much hurry to retreat into their slumberous worlds. Although she didn't admit it, the saviour-at-large was almost as nervous as the man himself to protect Jeff's right to dream aloud and in private. To divert his mind onto happier topics, the compassionate woman began questioning him about life as a rock star and the various media reports of his antics.

'Yeah, well. As you pointed out before, the lifestyle wasn't wholly unfamiliar to me,' he said without shame. 'Just the places were more exotic and the ready availability of mood-enhancing substances was new and therefore alluring. Everything else, to be perfectly truthful, was mind-numbingly the same.'

Lynn sighed. 'Sorry to hear that. It should've been so exciting to become who you always wanted to be. To finally have people appreciate your talent and ideas.'

'It was, angel,' the songwriter was at pains to assure. 'I'm just being my usual ungrateful self, I guess. It was exciting. Of course it was. Flying around the world and seeing these places that I'd only dreamed or read about. If you'd been there to share it with me though, the whole stardom thing would've been so much better.'

'I'm sorry, Jeff. I missed you too, so I know what that feels like. I used to go back to my hotel after filming, or sit in my college dorm room and write all the things I wanted to tell you in my diary instead. I didn't get over you either, not like everyone said I would.'

'No? That's good, I guess. For me anyway,' her lover's voice was laced with a sleepy, self-satisfied smile. 'I did that with the songs. Poured the contents of my shitfaced heart out and vented my frustration at the world.'

Australia's darling continued, hoping to lull her man to sleep on a positive note. 'I read *"Les Misérables"* while I was on tour last year, after I'd seen you in concert and wanted to get closer to you again. It was so long. I almost gave up a few times, but your face in my mind wouldn't let me.'

Jeff chuckled. 'Did you? Whoa. That is a big undertaking, I'll concede on Vic's behalf. Thanks. Did you like it?'

'Yes, heaps. And I couldn't believe how relevant it still is for today.'

'*Absoluement,*' he scoffed. 'Timeless. That's why they call them classics.'

Lynn removed her right hand from underneath the covers and smacked the side of her intellectual's head to punish his pomposity. 'Oh, thank you, professor! But listen… There was a line just before Marius and Cosette met for the first time properly; something like, "Neither was to blame for the way they felt, because Marius was someone who embraces sorrow and dwells in it, but Cosette felt it deeply but recovered." I thought that matched us perfectly.'

As she spoke, out of the corner of her eye, she caught sight of her handsome lover's mouth forming the words to reconstruct the exact quotation, as though the text were right in front of him.

'Hey! Do you remember it word for word?'

'Pretty much.'

'That's amazing.'

A shiver ran down Jeff's spine. 'Not really. I think I wrote it.'

'Oh,' Lynn inhaled. 'I wondered if you were going to talk to me about this again. I so want to hear more, but it's too late now.'

'Hmm… And I'm too wasted.'

There was no sound from the other bedroom as the delirious couple lay together in the dark, meditating on the implications of this impulsive comment. They were both reminded of that morning's fateful visit to the Abbotsford Convent, which had been deliberately cut short due to the singing tennis champion's tender, under-aged sensibilities. Was it time to continue this trip into the metaphysical? Not tonight, but soon.

'But we will, angel. *Ad nauseam*, I have no doubt. Just leaving it hanging tantalisingly in the air above our bed is good enough for now. Knowing there's something up there to not understand together.'

The star-struck soul-mate sighed, too tired to laugh. 'You say some very odd things.'

'Maybe so. Let's get some sleep. I'm tired. Are you?'

'Yes. Your breath's poisoning the atmosphere though.'

Lynn tossed her deep-breathing bedfellow out of bed after a few minutes' more easy contemplation, beginning to drift away into dreamland. With only a faint objection, he disappeared into the *en suite*, returning quickly and crawling back into bed.

'I'm going to feel like shit tomorrow,' Jeff moaned. 'But it was a great night. Did you enjoy it?'

His dream girl looked gorgeous, wrapped in his quilt, with her long blonde hair fanned out over the pillow. He leaned over and kissed her lips, commanding her not to move.

'Yes. Fantastic,' she murmured. 'I had a great time, thanks. Goodnight, flatmate.'

'G'night. Thanks for being my lodger.'

Exhausted and happy, they were both asleep within a few minutes. Peace descended on the north-facing penthouse apartment while the Saturday night traffic droned away on the busy streets below, and two-and-a-half hours went by in a flash before the young woman woke with a jump.

'Get the fuck out of here!' Jeff had yelled. 'Get out! Leave her alone! Fuck off!'

His arms and legs were wrestling with an invisible opponent under the covers. Despite her initial fright, everything made perfect sense to the young woman now. Breathing deeply to calm her nerves, she pushed back the bedclothes and grabbed his wrists as they flailed madly.

'Jeff, wake up. Wake up! You're dreaming. Be quiet. Gerry's here! Wake up. We're all safe.'

After a minute or so, the unconscious man calmed down and stopped shouting. He opened his eyes suddenly and heaved himself up, inhaling sharply. He felt Lynn's hand stroking the small of his back and reached rightwards to find her. She sat up and cuddled into him. His skin was wet all over, and his chest was heaving.

'It's OK,' she said. 'It's only me. We're safe.'

Saying nothing, the sweat-drenched man got up and vanished into the bathroom. From behind the closed door, Lynn could hear the taps go on and the sound of water splashing. She imagined him swearing at himself in the mirror. He returned after a few minutes and slumped down onto the mattress, his body temperature only slightly below boiling point.

'I'm sorry, angel. I'll go into the lounge room for a while.'

'Jeff, no,' she objected. 'Put the television on. We're in this together now. Didn't you want this to be *our* room? Come back to *our* bed.'

Appreciative of her compassion yet nonetheless crestfallen, the angry man accepted her offer humbly. What a vain hope it had been to think his *Regala*'s presence would provide an instant fix... He turned the volume down to the lowest setting and sat up in bed, while his gorgeous concubine settled back down under the quilt, leaving a reassuring hand at rest on his thigh. His head was confused. Bruised pride and a fair residue of alcohol were mixing with the joy of having his beautiful best friend right here, sharing every minute detail of his life. He knew this was destined to be an adjustment for them both, but hopefully an adjustment which would happen quickly and end happily.

About half an hour later, something made Lynn stir. She had fallen asleep within minutes to the background noise of whichever programme the night owl beside her was watching, but now it appeared as if his thoughts were drilling into her mind. Drifting in and out of her subconscious, she seemed drawn into every sip of water he took, every sigh from his overactive mind and every sly chuckle at something funny on the television.

'Hey,' she turned over slowly. 'You're still awake. Are you OK? What are you thinking so loudly that I'm overhearing it?'

The light was shining in her boyfriend's eyes, and there was a smile on his handsome face. His hand slid across and came to rest on her covered shoulder.

'What? Could you? Sorry. Just how amazing it is that we're going to be living together.'

'I know,' the smiling beauty nodded.

Jeff closed his eyes and exhaled. 'I don't think you realise how amazing it is for me.'

'I do. And for me.'

'But you're Lynn Dyson.'

'I'm aware of this,' she giggled. 'Go to sleep.'

'Lynn Dyson, angel,' he stressed again.

The modest star wondered if the man next to her was having some sort of withdrawal attack of humility. He pressed the Off button on the remote control and snuggled down beside her, dragging the covers on top of his recalibrated body. Her lover was always so gorgeously tender when he had had too much to drink.

'I know. I'm only Lynn Dyson, human female.'

'I know,' Jeff smiled. 'The one and only. Do you have any idea how amazing that is?'

'Not really,' his girlfriend replied. 'You're Jeff Diamond. The one and only. What's the difference?'

'The difference is you're here with me, in my home, with my best mate in the next room. It's fucking unbelievable, that's all.'

The smiling blonde sat up and leaned against the man she loved, nudging his head playfully. His left hand was unable to resist reaching up and cupping her breast to fondle it. She looked divine in the flickering light from the window.

'You invited me, so I came,' she reminded him. 'I practically invited myself.'

Jeff rested his head sideways onto hers, before turning his face to kiss her hair. 'Yeah. It's still amazing.'

Lynn's right arm reached around and took hold of his left elbow, hugging his shoulders tightly. She felt guilty at dismissing his genuine emotions, because if she were honest, she could feel exactly how amazing it was too. For them both.

'Yes, it is, although I think you're still drunk. This is very special, I agree.'

The exhausted man with the mixed-up brain cells grinned, his eyes staring up at the ceiling. 'Tell me about it.'

'Tomorrow. Goodnight,' his dream girl whispered, sliding herself down and leaving a kiss on his tense jaw.

Stretching and turning leftwards onto his side, the delirious songwriter sighed. 'Thanks. Ahh... Pure heaven. And you're not going anywhere in the morning either.'

'But what if I want to?'

'You won't want to.'

'Is that right?' she sniffed. 'Very arrogant, Mister D.'

'Very confident, Miss D.'

The one and only Lynn Dyson rolled over onto her side too, facing the wardrobes in which her belongings were soon to be stowed. Jeff was right. Only this afternoon, she had defied her parents and made a choice that two weeks ago she would never have dreamed she could make, and now she was facing the prospect of moving in with the reprobate dubbed "The Australian Elvis". This was indeed amazing.

'*Dors bien*, angel,' her boyfriend responded softly. 'I hope I don't wake you again.'

A slender hand reached backwards and brushed his hip. 'I hope you don't wake me at all,' she countered, with a smile she hoped he could hear.

The boy from Canley Vale sighed. 'One step at a time, *s'il te plaît*.'

'Sure. Of course. Goodnight. I love you. I hope you get back to sleep.'

'You too. Thanks again.'

***

Lynn could hear Vanessa and Gerry talking loudly from their room across the way. It sounded as if they were arguing. She climbed out of the bed where Jeff was still sleeping and pulled the curtains across the sundrenched window. She dressed and tied her hair into a ponytail before setting out to see what was going on with their guests.

'Men!' the dancer blurted out when she saw her childhood friend, hands waving in the air. 'I can't believe what pigs they can be.'

The nineteen-year-old laughed and cast her mind back to her own drunken and sullied bedroom companion. 'What's wrong?'

Vanessa was angry. 'I asked him if he'd give me a lift because I need to get home. I've got rehearsals in two hours. He said he was too tired, and could I get a taxi? Can you believe it? What a gentleman!'

The younger woman agreed with her. 'That *is* a bit unfair. I can give you a lift. When do you need to go?'

'Oh, yes. That'd be great. I need to go now really. Is that convenient?'

'Yes, it's fine. Jeff's still asleep too. I'll just get my shoes and some keys.'

Lynn disappeared into the bedroom. She found a notepad on Jeff's chest of drawers. The first few pages were covered in scribbled verses of different lengths. They must be lyrics, she thought. She wrote a short note on a blank sheet, tore it out and left it on her pillow. With any luck, he wouldn't even notice her absence. She picked up the bunch of keys next to her boyfriend's watch, trusting that one among them would enable her to get back into the building. She would also need to find her way unaided out of the building's underground car park for the first time.

'So will you be seeing Gerry again?' the Olympian asked, as they drove back towards Vanessa's apartment on St Kilda Road. 'Even Jeff thinks he's a bit of a sleaze, but his heart's in the right place. They're like brothers, those two.'

Her friend sighed. 'He is fun to be with but very selfish. It's all about his pleasure. He's a real hedonist. But Jeff's all over you. He really seems to care. Do you love him?'

The blonde nodded, looking straight ahead at the traffic. 'Yes, I love him heaps,' she opened up. 'I'm so rapt we're back together. Even more than I thought I'd be.'

'He's written so many sad songs,' Vanessa added dreamily. 'Do you think they're about you?'

Lynn nodded again. 'I'm afraid so. They're beautiful and they make me feel really guilty. That's why we need to stay under the radar. No press or undue attention. My parents need to get to know him. I hope they get used to the idea soon because I don't want to be sneaking around the whole time.'

Before too long, they were pulling into the driveway of a modest St Kilda apartment block. 'I hope you work it out,' the passenger wished, leaning over to kiss her famous friend.

'You too! It was nice seeing you again.'

'Say hi to Junior for me,' the ballerina called back to the car.

The celebrity waved through the window and drove off before she could be spotted. She toyed with the idea of dropping the car back at Admin but didn't want to be gone too long in case Jeff woke up in a panic. The traffic was busy on Sunday morning with shoppers making their way to the Victoria Market. Once she reached the northern fringe of the CBD, and without the wherewithal to re-enter the car park, she was forced to drive around the block twice before finding a space to leave the large, brown station wagon with the Dyson logo emblazoned on both sides.

Neither Jeff nor Gerry was up and about when she let herself back into the flat. The newcomer made herself some tea and sat down at the piano, where she found yet more scribbled lyrics on the music stand. She felt a little more guilty still in reading his heartfelt utterances uninvited, but hoped the songwriter wouldn't mind.

One in particular brought a lump to her throat, instantly dragging her back to their late-night conversation. It told of crowds being the same wherever he went and a surprising insecurity about how his fans might perceive him. As ever, poetic incarnations she recognised as in her own image came to his rescue, picking him up when he fell and bringing peace to his struggling consciousness. How draining it must be to fight with such conflicting perceptions of oneself, the young star pondered.

Wiping a tear from her left eye, Lynn sensed someone approaching from behind and quickly pulled herself together. She turned to see a bleary-eyed accountant dressed only in boxers and last night's crumpled shirt, down the front of which was a large, greenish-brown curry stain. He looked a sorry sight, far from the suave businessman she knew him to be.

'Hey! Who are you?' she asked, laughing. 'You look awful, Gerry.'

'Funny girl,' the re-arranged party animal sneered. 'Where's the lovely Vanessa?'

He was not a happy camper, clearly, but Lynn wasn't inclined to let him off the hook either. 'I gave her a lift home. She needed to get to rehearsals.'

The indomitable one snorted. 'Thanks for that. I expect that's the last I'll see of her.'

Gerry didn't seem too bothered, and nor did the young woman feel it her place to pass further comment. Slumping down onto the couch, he picked up a magazine half-heartedly and began to flick through it. Bloodshot eyes followed his mate's exquisite girlfriend across the room as she made for the door.

'Where's Romeo? Has he gone for a run?'

Shaking her head, Lynn pointed towards the bedroom. 'Still sleeping.'

'I don't think so! Are you sure?' the manager's face was a picture. 'You must've really worn him out last night. Well done!'

He stopped short of saying that nobody else had managed that, unusually thinking better of betraying his client's confidence. The singer shrugged. She was saying nothing.

'Do you want some tea or coffee?'

Gerry nodded. 'Yes, please. A medicinal coffee would be grand in my current state. I must take a look at Sleeping Ugly though. That's something I never thought I'd see. Plenty of sugar, please, sugar.'

The normally tireless artist's old friend padded off to peek inside the bedroom. Sure enough, there was Jeff, sparko, his head and naked torso above the top edge of the quilt. Returning to Lynn in the kitchen, the tall Irishman kissed her on the cheek and squeezed her round the waist, stealing a gratuitous grope while they were alone. Wriggling free of his rather too wandering hands, the young woman continued to make the coffee.

'That's quite an achievement, I believe. He'll thank you for it. He's always telling me how little sleep he gets. Do you know why he can't sleep?'

Lynn was pleased to hear some concern in the older man's voice, and for someone other than himself for a change. 'Yeah. Sort of. There's a lot going on in his head. He finds it difficult to shut off,' she answered benignly, giving nothing away except a steaming mug.

'Thanks for the coffee, Miss D.'

His concern quota spent, Gerry went off to take a shower, muttering something about headache pills, while the absent bedfellow crept stealthily back into the main bedroom. A second coffee mug clicked onto the bedside table next to Jeff's left ear. He opened one eye and smiled.

'You're already awake, aren't you?' she accused. 'Lazy sod!'

Both dark eyes confessed with a flick of their brows. 'Guilty, Your Honour,' his croaky voice answered. 'Enjoying the peace and quiet on the first day of the rest of our life. Are the others still here? I could hear Gerry just now.'

The nineteen-year-old sat beside her lover on the bed. He took hold of her hand and placed it strategically on the quilt to show her how much he had been anticipating her return. She rolled her eyes and abruptly drew her hand away, watching as his face changed from disappointment to smiling resignation. He never missed a trick to tug at her heartstrings, but she had also noticed his habitual dogged compulsion for instant gratification had waned a little, although this was more likely as a result of his hangover.

'Vanessa's gone. She had to go to rehearsals. Gerry wouldn't take her, and she's mightily pissed off at him.'

Jeff sniffed in amusement. 'Yep. That sounds like our Blake-san. What's in it for me? Where is he?'

'In the shower. Probably nearly finished by now. We don't have time for any playtime now.'

'Even a kiss?'

'Oh, alright then,' the blonde teenager giggled, leaning down to meet his lips, on which his seized wantonly.

'Still feel like home?'

Jeff's breath was grating and sexy, so close to her face. True to his resolution, he hadn't yet reached for his packet of cigarettes. Coming back to the present, the newcomer realised she hadn't considered her new circumstance so far that morning. She did indeed feel comfortable with the idea of living together. Predictably, hairy arms folded around her, and the embrace told her that he was relaxed about being denied sex, even though the insistence in his kisses said otherwise.

Lynn remembered their early conversations about addiction and wondered what level of pressure she might be subjected to while she lived in this apartment. Was the tortured boy in him still so insatiable and demanding when it came to meeting his basic needs? She smiled at the expectant look on his face. Oh, well… How bad could that be?

'Yes. It doesn't feel so weird this morning,' she gave him her answer. 'What about you?'

'I'm never going to let you go.'

Husky words sent tremors through the young woman's ear drums, while teeth grazed the delicate skin of her cheek. She knew her boyfriend could tell how much he was turning her on by the perfectly timed movement of his hand on her hip.

'You like that,' he smiled, kissing her mouth.

'No. I *love* that. You're driving me crazy,' she answered, out of breath.

'Good. Let's do it again then, and again and again and again.'

Lynn squealed as she found herself rocking from side to side, trapped inside a vice of ferocious arms and legs. 'Stop! Gerry'll hear us. Jeff!'

'OK. We'll hang five, whatever that means,' the horny man replied, bringing the beauty to rest with her head back on the pillow. 'I'm hungry though, and some arsehole drummer's beating the retreat behind my temples. D'you want to go somewhere for brekkie? There's *un bon café français* round the corner from here: The European. D'you know it?'

'Yes, I do. I've been there a few times but never for breakfast.'

The lazy musician propped himself up on his elbows. 'OK. So what are you waiting for?'

His girlfriend pushed him down again. 'You're gorgeous, and it's a great idea, but you seem to have overlooked the fact we're a secret,' she joined in with gentle pianist's fingertips on his forehead. 'How can we go out for breakfast?'

'Gerry and I can hide you, if he can be trusted with such a responsibility this morning. How does he look?'

'Pretty grim,' his girlfriend admitted. 'You've pulled up alright.'

Jeff frowned and started to get up. 'I'm not passing judgment until I start moving around. Get out of my way, pretty lady. Breakfast of the eating kind awaits.'

With her unusually languid flatmate in the shower, Lynn was free to leaf through the notepad of lyrics in the bedroom. He was truly prolific, she thought. So much he was trying to say. Where had he come from, this magic man? What was he here to do? And why had he chosen her? Sitting on the end of the bed, the golden-haired beauty considered what everyone had always told her as a child: that she would have the pick of all the boys. She did, of course, if she wanted it. Yet look how things had turned out... The picker had become the pickee, and most dramatically too.

The happy nineteen-year-old put the notepad back where she found it as soon as she heard the shower stop. She went to see what Gerry was up to and found him sitting on the balcony reading yesterday's copy of The Age, smoking and enjoying the morning sunshine.

'Hello,' she said. 'Are you feeling better?'

The visitor scoffed. 'Not really, but I'll live. Is the big man up and about?'

'Yes. He wants to go to The European for breakfast. Are you up for it?'

The hung-over accountant pulled a face but agreed that a square meal was a sensible idea nevertheless. 'Now?'

Lynn nodded and turned back to go inside. Her boyfriend's manager stubbed his cigarette out and clambered to his feet, putting his arm around her shoulder as they walked through the lounge.

'You've made my client a very happy man,' he said sincerely.

'Thanks,' she replied. 'I'm happy too, so it works out well. Are you happy?'

The affluent executive chuckled. 'Me? I'm always happy. You know me.'

His aforementioned client walked into the room just in time to hear the last couple of sentences. Lynn's words warmed his heart, although he was not going to say so in front of his macho buddy, who was well-known for his opinion that love was for girls, poofs and wusses. He had his limits too, after all. He had a reputation to uphold.

'That's good,' he gave her a wink, a possessive finger inviting his mate to remove his hand from the lady's person. 'Oy! None of that.'

***

The easily-recognisable sportswoman walked to the restaurant flanked by the tall men, smiling as the pair talked over the top of her head. She could sense their protectiveness as they all marched through the strolling public, and their shield felt welcoming. At one point, Jeff reached for her hand surreptitiously, so she reached for Gerry's too. If they had been her bodyguards, they would have been fired for such insubordination.

The trio consumed a slow and sophisticated cooked breakfast, reading the newspapers and discussing politics and sport. Jeff's hangover was beginning to deliver on its promise, and before he was halfway through his meal, his face had turned decidedly green. Gerry, on the other hand, was over the worst and began to behave more like his usual, animated self.

'You don't look well, mate,' the older man stated the obvious.

His friend nodded. 'Hmm... It'll pass. It's my punishment. I have to take it like a man.'

'Typical!' Lynn laughed. 'My dad says the same.'

'So what's the plan with your folks?' Jeff asked, shaking his head at the unpalatable parallel. 'What are you going to tell them?'

Gerry looked interested. 'Oh, yeah. The family feud. Very interesting.'

'Shut up, you,' the millionnaire warned, by this time feeling extremely queasy. 'It's no joke.'

Suitably contrite, his manager continued to read the newspaper, while Lynn blanched slightly. The new student year at the Royal College of Music would start in a few weeks, and she had already been granted dispensation to start the term late due to her concert commitments. Her enthusiasm for another year overseas was at an all-time low, and sinking further with each passing hour in her black stallion's company.

'I'd like to cross-check our diaries when we get back. I've got a plan.'

'Excuse me? I'm the one who has plans,' her control freak boyfriend countered.

'Point of order,' Gerry interrupted, gamely banging the table with his fingers. 'I have to counsel my client here. As your business manager, I advise you not to commit to anything without consulting me. I have your best interests at heart, my man.'

'Fuck off!' was Jeff's answer.

Lynn gave him a teacher's black look. 'Excuse me back! No swearing during the day, you said.'

The green man nodded an apology. 'Sorry, ma'am. Get lost, Gezza! You're just worried you won't get a cut.'

'Mortally wounded, mate. Mortally wounded,' his friend hammed it up. 'Perfectly true though. We need to talk tomorrow.'

Coughing, the younger man jumped up suddenly and left at the double. Scuttling a number of chairs which were sticking out too far in the narrow walkway, he smashed through the door of the Gents' toilets, much to the consternation of a few fellow diners.

'Good,' said Lynn, her eyes following her departing lover until he had disappeared into the back of the café. 'That needed to happen! Thanks for looking after him so well, Gerry. He's very grateful. He's always singing your praises. You have to get him to buy more stuff for the apartment though.'

The affable executive chuckled. 'Oh, no! That's your job now.'

After a few minutes, Jeff returned to the table and squeezed his dream girl's shoulder as he sat down. 'Shit! That's better. I knew there was a reason I stopped drinking.'

Lynn kissed his cheek. 'You're returning to a normal colour now. Shall we go?'

They all stood to leave. Gerry picked up the tab, and the threesome strolled along Spring Street, heading northwards in the direction of the apartment.

'I might as well hit the road,' the accountant announced, stopping next to a dark blue BMW which Lynn guessed must be his. 'Have fun with your respective calendars. Thanks for a great evening, and safe travels, Miss D.'

'You're welcome, mate. Thanks for joining us,' Jeff embraced his friend strongly. 'I'll ring you tomorrow.'

Gerry kissed Lynn under his friend's strict supervision. 'I'll ring *you* tomorrow,' he echoed suggestively to his mate's girlfriend.

The growling luxury sedan lurched into a u-turn over the tram tracks and sped off towards the railway and the river. Lynn and Jeff turned for home, knowing better than to join hands this time. The streets were busier by now, since the shops had opened, and the habitual whispering was already swirling around them.

'Are you feeling better now?' the kind teenager asked. 'It looked touch and go for a while there.'

Rounding the corner into Little Lonsdale Street, where there was a rear entrance to his building, Jeff put his arm around his dream girl. Instinctively, he went to open his cigarette packet with the other hand before remembering he no longer smoked during the day.

'Jesus! These old habits are hard to break,' he smiled, slotting his lighter back into his jeans pocket and handing the cigarettes to his girlfriend for safekeeping. 'Yes, thanks. I'm ready for another breakfast now. So... What's this plan of yours?'

'Oh, nothing yet,' the young woman stalled. 'I just want to see what our diaries look like, so I know what I'm talking to Mum and Dad about.'

Jeff didn't buy this superficial response. It didn't sound like much of a plan, but he resolved to wait until they were back inside the apartment. Lynn held her hand out for the front door key when they emerged from the lift. His face had paled again, and she wasn't sure if it was the hangover or the door which had caused it. She said nothing as she forged a path into the apartment ahead of him, dissipating any demons by her very presence. His sense of relief was palpable. The human mind was a very complex thing, she reflected.

'Thanks, angel,' he exhaled through pursed lips. 'Now... Where's this diary you're on about?'

Yesterday's visitor detoured into the bedroom and collected a folder of documents. Jeff did the same from his study, and then quickly buttered three slices of bread and cut off several large hunks of cheese. They sat down at the kitchen table with some coffee, looking every inch the normal couple.

'That breakfast doesn't look quite as appetising as the last one,' Lynn smiled in sympathy, seeing him tuck in to the austere spread.

'Real continental brekkie,' her recovering boyfriend grinned. 'None of this bacon, eggs and sausage stuff.'

'Not much of a rock star brekkie either.'

'Come on,' the impatient man implored, pointing at the open page in her diary. 'What's the real plan?'

'Well...' the tentative youngster answered. 'I heard you mention you'd be in Tokyo in November, and so will I. So I wanted to check the dates to see how far apart they are. I thought it might be good if we could combine the trips.'

Jeff looked interested. 'OK... Not sure how this fits with us being a secret, but go on.'

Lynn laughed and shrugged her innocence. Their tour dates were in fact only six days apart. The established artist was playing Tokyo first, and then while she was setting up again in Osaka, the newcomer would be on stage in Tokyo. In fact, their concerts in the capital city were booked in the same venue.

'Get this!' the rock star exclaimed, reading her itinerary. 'You're my warm-up act.'

The Australian aristocrat didn't really mind, but decided to complain anyway. 'A certain degree of arrogance you're displaying again, Mister Diamond?'

Jeff acknowledged her comment gladly, laughing at himself. 'Sorry, angel. I know I'm the new kid on the block. Feel free to put me in my place. I need it sometimes.'

He held his wrist out for her to slap it. Lynn obliged, and it stung sweetly. Their heads came together for a passionate kiss, followed by large, eager hands which promptly received another sharp rebuke. As he pulled away and looked into her eyes, he swore he saw fear again. Gravity sprang to attention in his queasy stomach as her nervous reaction put him off-guard too.

'What's wrong?'

'Wait. I'm not finished explaining my plan, Jeff,' she flashed back. 'I've got some suggestions that you must let me know if you don't like, but I'm hoping you will.'

'Oh, yeah? What are they?' he asked, now as cautious as he was curious. 'I can't imagine you'd suggest something I wouldn't like.'

She continued, breathing deeply. 'I was just thinking it'd be nice to appear on stage together, and overseas is perfect because it gives us some distance from the press. I know we need to keep our careers separate, but it would show Mum and Dad... and anyone else whom it may concern... that we're for real.'

Jeff nodded silently, contemplating the idea.

'And God knows, we've got enough material between us to be able to come up with some duets,' she finished. 'What do you think?'

The rocking chart-topper took a moment to weigh up the situation, being taunted by the troll inside that he should always search for the catch. 'I think it's a great idea. I'd love to do it, but what about all the people who wouldn't want us to do it? Your management, Sir Brad, your parents? My management'll be a push-over, but isn't it all too much hassle so soon?'

'Don't you want to?' Lynn asked, feeling a little disheartened.

The young man took her hand. 'Bloody oath, I do! It'd be fantastic. I'm just concerned about fall-out for you. Are you sure you're ready for the consequences?'

Thinking it over in her mind, the pretty blonde stared out of the window at the splendid view, never more certain of anything. 'Yes, I'm ready. You're the master of making statements,' she responded after a long silence. 'I want to make a statement of my own. I want to tell everyone I'm in love with you, because I am. It's not natural for me to pretend all the time.'

Jeff was fascinated by his girlfriend's observation, quite apart from being severely flattered by her adamant endorsement. He had never really thought about his own propensity for *largesse*, but she was right, as usual.

'Well... By November everything might be different anyway,' he suggested. 'I hope so, for Christ's sake. And if you've got something to say, you might as well tell it loud.'

'Exactly! We can't live in fear of the worst,' the young woman added, laughing and kissing him fondly. 'We have to behave like winners and believe we're winners. You know that anyway. I don't want to contemplate the alternative.'

Her boyfriend agreed, but silently claimed the right to some restraint until he knew what Bart Dyson had in mind for him. He flicked back through the pages of Lynn's crowded calendar and indicated a large block of time starting that very evening.

'We haven't even spoken about this yet,' he said, instantly overflowing with sorrow.

The celebrity saw where his finger was pointing and sighed. 'Yes, I know. I've been putting it off. It's almost a month. I'm in Europe for three weeks and then there's a tennis tournament in Singapore squeezed in before I go to Tokyo. I'm only home for half a week and then off again. It's hellish, I'm sorry. That's another reason why it'd be so good to meet up in Japan.'

Jeff hugged her, glad that he wasn't the only one who found the prospect of being apart downright miserable. 'It sure would. You're not wrong there. We'll survive, gorgeous. Now I'll show you mine...'

Lynn smiled at his provocative expression, surprised that she had been spared another sympathy drive. After making another round of strong coffee, the pair turned their attention to Jeff Diamond's own hectic schedule. A week in New York in October was followed by three nights in Los Angeles, and then nothing outside Australia until Japan. She wrote down her successful boyfriend's travel dates in her own calendar.

'I'm having another weird-out moment,' she confessed, leaning against his arm. 'It seems presumptuous to insert your stuff into my diary. Do you know what I mean?'

Jeff laughed. 'Yes, I bloody well do! I've felt like that ever since I met you. Go for your life. I love it, if you must know. Can't think of anything I'd like more than to only have one diary between us.'

After another long kiss, fast running out of time to communicate *la pièce de résistance* of her master plan, his dream girl suddenly became super-anxious again.

'What's wrong now?' her incredulous boyfriend cried out, sensing they hadn't yet dealt with whatever the burning issue was for his new flatmate. 'For Christ's sake, the suspense is killing me!'

'I've got something else to tell you, and ask you. It's big.'

'Big? Oh-oh,' he replied, trying a smile. 'Am I going to like this too?'

'Not sure,' Lynn confessed, unable to put off the inevitable any longer. 'When I spoke to Dad the other day, he casually mentioned that I'd been accepted into the Royal College of Music in London to do a composing and conducting post-grad' course. We'd spoken about it a few times while I was away, but I hadn't heard anything for months. And then, yesterday, he told me it was all happening.'

Jeff rocked on his chair with the force of instinctive rebellion, instantly feeling sick again. 'London? Fuck! Why? So you're going away for another year?'

The young woman realised from the ominous tone of his reply that she needed to work fast with Part Two of her bulletin before this quiet ire raised the stakes to the type of dangerous proportions he had described in Sydney and which she had witnessed first-hand in July nineteen-seventy-two. She pictured the shock of this news waking Gravity from his redundant slumber as she watched her previously calm and jovial boyfriend gripped by a customary and debilitating panic. Sure enough, he leaped up from the table and shoved open the sliding door onto the balcony, sucking in the fresh air in an attempt to combat the dizziness.

'Wait, Jeff!,' she shouted after him. 'That's the telling bit. Now I want to ask you something.'

Joining her raging, magnificent beast at the railing, on which he was tapping his cigarette-less hands in an effort to contain his emotions, Lynn saw tears in his eyes and hoped she knew him well enough to be able to extricate him from this downward-spiralling tornado. He crumpled onto the tiles on hearing her chase after him and leaned his head back on the balcony's glass panel, breathing heavily. She hurriedly sat down beside him, anxious to make him feel better.

'I can't believe you didn't tell me this before,' he hissed through gritted teeth, battling to curb his violent temper.

'I'm sorry,' she begged, hugging him and feeling how violently he was shaking. 'Wait a minute. Oh, God. I'm so sorry, Jeff. I didn't mean to make you so upset. I chose the wrong way to tell you.'

'What are you talking about? Is there a right way to tell me something like that?'

Confusion was written all over her dejected boyfriend's face.

'I hoped so, but I wasn't quick enough,' the patient woman replied as evenly as her nerves would allow. 'We haven't really had an opportunity until now, what with the guys coming over last night. I want to ask you if you'd come to London *with* me. After I spoke to Dad and he told me it was a done deal, I was going to put my foot down and say I wasn't going. But then I remembered seeing you so absorbed in that Political Anthropology book in the Intercontinental, and the idea came to me that you might like to study in London too.'

'Jesus, Lynn,' Jeff gasped, spinning around to face her. 'Enough with the bloody roller-coaster, OK? Are you trying to kill me off?'

The frightened teenager was relieved that her man appeared to be semi-joking, the flames having dispersed from his eyes as quickly as they took hold. Springing to her feet, she pulled him upright by tugging on his hands like a child, before leading him back inside and reaching into her handbag for the cigarette packet he had entrusted to her on the walk home. Almost snatching it, the addict's left hand fumbled in his jeans pocket and pulled out his lighter. His breath was erratic as he dragged the nicotine as fast as he could through his lungs and into his bloodstream, and finally stepping back from the precipice, the tormented man offered the cigarette to his apologetic girlfriend while lighting a second.

Such a desperate act of bonding from the seasoned self-healer brought tears to the singer's eyes, instantly reminded of their dark night in the hotel and realising that he must have latched onto this as a way of seeking her moral support. She accepted the first cigarette without hesitation, even though she really didn't feel like smoking at this time of day.

'I'm sorry. Really I am,' Lynn responded, grabbing her boyfriend's hand and blowing an unwanted plume of smoke into the air. 'I shouldn't have dropped it on you like that. I was trying to be clever and deliver a quick one-two, but it backfired. Are you OK now? What do you think about going to London together? We'd be in control of our own lives over there. We could get involved in the London music scene and continue our careers while studying. I think it would be awesome.'

Smiling at her impetuous determination to redress her inadvertent wrongdoing, Jeff collapsed down onto the kitchen chair and dragged the slender sportswoman onto his lap. His mouth locked on to hers with such pre-possession that it took them both by surprise, and his acquisitive grip dug into her flesh as if his hands were claws and she had become his prey.

'Hey! Be careful!' the young woman shrieked. 'Is that a yes?'

The black stallion's eyes were wider than ever, and he was shaking his head, pleading with her never to do that to him again. Meanwhile, a broad grin had spread across his face, even though his breathing remained laboured and his muscles twitched non-stop. How mentally strong he must need to be, the amazed celebrity wondered, to bring himself back from the brink so quickly...

'Abso-fucking-lutely it is!' he shouted directly into her face, kissing her again. 'I couldn't think of anything better. I love London, and to be there with you would be bloody paradise.'

The smoker's trembling hands had temporarily let go of her body so that he could stub out one cigarette and light another. So much for quitting! Declining a second, Lynn seized her chance to cuddle into him, feeling his heart still pounding under his shirt.

'Great! Me too. Let's do it then! And knowing it's coming in the New Year'll make this coming month apart heaps easier to bear, won't it?'

Oh, yeah, thought Jeff. It made everything easier. London for a year with the girl of his dreams, far away from his past and her family, enjoying the here and now and working on the future together. What could be more perfect? He stared at the vision in front of him, whose enquiring, blue eyes awaited his answer.

'You really know how to make me happy, don't you? Jesus! And horny. I feel like I'm on fire when I'm with you.'

'Oh, my God! That's such a relief,' the nineteen-year-old replied in a hushed voice. 'I'm sorry to hurt you. I won't do that again. Your happiness is my main concern from now on, I promise. I think that's what's called on-the-job training!'

The handsome man smiled, his heart soaring at the sound of this commitment. 'Well, I'm not sure I can promise not to fly off the handle again. I'll try not to be a burden to you in London. During the day I'm not usually so bad, providing you're not messing with my head like this.'

The celebrity continued, frowning. 'Jeff, I don't care about all that. I love all of you; the good bits and the not-so-good bits. I'll get better at dealing with all this, and we'll work through it. London may be the place to seek more specialist advice too. They have some of the best research hospitals in the world. And who knows? Maybe living in a new country will be different for you?'

'Get up a minute, please.'

Lynn slid off his thighs and onto another chair, watching her enigmatic stranger stand up and leave the room. He came back within a few minutes, brandishing a glossy coffee-table book on the British capital city. Excitedly gathering her onto his lap again, he opened the cover and began to turn the pages one by one.

'Let's have a look at us next year.'

The young musician was delighted that Jeff was enthusiastic for her plan, having learned a good lesson in the process. Her parents wouldn't be at all delighted, but they would have to make the necessary adjustments, just like their daughter. Whether they lived together in Melbourne or London, there was no turning back now. The couple happily leafed through the pictorial guided tour: Carnaby Street, Covent Garden, the parks, the West End theatre district... It would all be theirs.

Still sitting at the kitchen table as midday slipped by, the superstars discussed potential song-writing collaborations which would be more accessible in the northern hemisphere and found themselves caught up in spontaneous creative emotion. Jeff mentioned several French writers of interest, and he spoke of plans to record more music in his native Spanish, therefore having Europe on their doorstep would be a real bonus. London was also that much closer to New York, making US trips far more manageable too.

'Perhaps we'll never come back?' the devious Pied Piper suggested.

Lynn looked sceptical. 'I think I'll have to at some stage; for sport, *et cetera*,' she insisted, 'and you'd miss Gerry too much.'

'Would I? We'll survive.'

His girlfriend stood up suddenly, knowing that valuable time was passing and that they should make the best of it while it lasted. She was flying out that night to start filming for yet another movie, and there was packing and other

306

preparatory activities to fit in between now and then. They could hardly mooch around all afternoon waiting for the clock to tick round to airport time.

'Let's go and play tennis,' she announced, looking at Jeff's watch. 'I'll have to go back to Admin to get my stuff sorted out, but we've still got time.'

The elated songwriter embraced her with renewed intent, no doubt fending off projections of impending loss. 'As long as we've still got time to enjoy each others' bodies before you go. It's going to be a long, long, long, long wait. I couldn't possibly see you go without.'

Lynn slapped his shoulder. '*Me* go without?'

'When will you stop hitting me, woman?' the comedian yelped, rubbing his arm. 'Here I am, with the history of violence, and I don't lay a finger on you while you're constantly battering me.'

'Sorry,' the Olympian giggled. 'I'll stop.'

Her boyfriend shook his head. 'No, don't stop. I love it. It makes me feel alive. Now, I've only got one tennis racquet, so are we sharing or should we find another one from somewhere?'

'Aha!' the champion burst out laughing at the ridiculous vision that had been conjured up. 'I never thought of that. We'll have to go to Admin first then. That'll be better actually. I'll pack beforehand, and then we'll have the rest of the afternoon to ourselves.'

In the bedroom, under the guise of preparing to leave, the young woman found herself once more swept up into the hungry arms of her Catholic Argentinean Polish Jew. They kissed and sunk down onto the carpet, each thinking separate thoughts of their overseas sabbatical.

'You see this here?' Jeff asked, placing his girlfriend's hand on the front of his pants, so that she could feel his full-blown erection.

'Yes,' she replied, frowning in jest.

'I want you to know that I've changed, angel,' he looked into her eyes while pressing hard up against her. 'The old sexual mercenary's left town. You need to believe that the only thing that'll be wrapped around this thing over the next three-and-a-half weeks is my hand.'

Lynn smiled shyly as he kissed her again and began to remove her top. This was a change she could most definitely live with, and she thanked him by ceding her willing body to his touch, right then and there on the bedroom floor. Entranced and joyful, her lover couldn't believe his good fortune, immediately ripping off her remaining clothing and caressing her all over.

'Like this?' his playful partner laughed, gripping his penis strongly and staring into his eyes as the thrilling sensation reached them.

'Yep. Almost constantly, I'd imagine,' Jeff whispered.

Full of optimism and temporarily forgetting the spectre of Bart Dyson and his investigators, the couple headed out for the afternoon after their delicious, post-hangover interlude. Back at Admin, where the familiar surroundings brought back many happy memories, the boy from Canley Vale floated on cushions of air as he waited on Lynn's sofa, glued to finals football on television while she packed.

The soul-mates had come a long way from their romantic reunion in the Intercontinental, at which point neither had any idea what might befall them, all the way to supplementing yesterday's momentous decision to live together with an up-sticks relocation to the other side of the world. And the weirdest thing of all was the surreal sense of destiny being fulfilled, to which both had confessed midway through their furious love-making.

Every now and then, the idea of a month without sex crossed the red-blooded man's mind. How the hell was he going to cope with this unthinkable deprivation? Regardless, there was no way the former ladies' man would rescind on his promise; not now London was on the agenda and with Big D's spies hiding around every corner. He would be the picture of propriety and sobriety. His beautiful best friend had given her assurance that his happiness was at the top of her priority list. If there was anything worth a month of celibacy, this was it.

Background Checks

'Jeff? Bart Dyson. How are you?'

'Hello, sir,' the young man responded, not at all surprised to receive the call. 'I'm doing well, thanks. And you?'

'Well too, thank you,' came the stiff reply.

The Australian hero's authoritative voice was sombre and almost a little nervous. The young star looked around the open office of his publishing company, where he was busy trying to finalise material for his Masters dissertation. He didn't particularly want anyone to eavesdrop on this conversation, just in case it took a turn for the worst.

'Jeff, I wonder whether we could meet this evening to discuss a few things.'

'Yeah. Sure. No problem,' the famous rebel was intrigued. 'Can I ask what about?'

The longer the pretender had waited for this auspicious occasion, the more he was itching for battle to commence. He and Lynn had discussed how they would play the situation, with so much at stake, and he had promised to remain civil to the distinguished gentleman, whose response over the telephone was a little too evasive for the twenty-two-year-old's liking.

'Marianna and I have been talking over the possibility of Lynn wishing to continue a relationship with you, and now we hear she's planning to move into your home.'

'Correct. She is,' the proud man replied.

'Hmm... Well, there are a few things that we'd like to get clear and out in the open, if you don't mind. Nothing dramatic, hopefully. I trust you'll understand our perspective. Lynn's still very young and has a huge workload, and we'd hate to see her hurt.'

'Yes, OK. She's not going to get hurt, but I understand,' Jeff affirmed, hiding his scorn. 'That's fine. I can meet after five o'clock, if that works? Where?'

The songwriter was cynical about his girlfriend's father's underplayed opening gambit and found himself full of curiosity as to what exactly had fed their suspicions. Presumably, the Dysons didn't yet know about their daughter's plans for them both to go to London. To give them the benefit of the doubt, perhaps they were only being protective parents, bound to have questions after digesting any new information they might have received through their investigations.

He dared to probe a little further. 'Has Lynn mentioned anything that's worried you?'

'No,' the elder statesman was firm and business-like. 'This has come straight from us. Out of respect, we wanted to talk to you first and then perhaps to both of you somehow.'

'OK. I'll see you this evening. At your office at Admin?' the musician relented, recalling that the conservative couple had needed a nudge to treat him with respect.

There was no point forcing the issue over the telephone. Whether this was simply a typically sporting gesture to fulfil an obligation and pacify his daughter or if it was an invitation to appear in person to defend his past against the detectives' findings, the frustrated fighter would find out soon enough.

'Yes, thank you. That would be best,' Bart acknowledged before continuing. 'And Jeff, you might want to bring your solicitor along too.'

'My solicitor?' Jeff felt the hairs rise on the back of his neck. 'Why will I need a solicitor?'

'Do you have one?'

Annoyed by the superior tone from the other end of the line, the multi-millionnaire snapped back. 'Yes, sir. I have a small army of them, but I didn't think I'd be needing one to talk to you. What do I need a lawyer for?'

The veteran did his best to play down the seriousness of his intentions, but it was obvious to his younger opponent that this was going to be more than a fireside chat with a concerned father. Fear gripped him, wondering what damning misinformation might have been uncovered, and from which sources.

'I'll have a lawyer with me,' Bart pressed. 'It's just as a courtesy that I'm informing you, so you're not disadvantaged. Please don't be alarmed. I do it all the time. It's probably unnecessary, but... Just a precaution.'

As the stalwart of the Australian Olympic movement was speaking, the ambitious world-changer tried to comprehend why he was feeling so defensive. He should practise what he preached, shouldn't he, in an attempt to give Big D the benefit of an open mind and the respect the young pretender knew he deserved? Lynn would count on him to do this.

'OK, sir. I'll bring my manager, if he's available. His name's Gerry Blake. Don't think you've met him.'

The hot-headed tearaway was damned if he was going to engage a solicitor to talk to his girlfriend's father when he hadn't done anything wrong, even if he *was* the head of the Dyson dynasty. One thing was certain however: it was going to be especially difficult to concentrate on his university work between now and five o'clock with these shadows hanging over him.

'Thank you. I'm grateful for your co-operation,' Bart sounded relieved. 'I hope we're sharing a few beers later.'

'Right,' his adversary muttered, unable to envision such an outcome. 'I hope so too. See you at five-ish.'

'Good stuff. We'll see you then. Enjoy your afternoon,' the gruff voice signed off, and the line disconnected.

Jeff turned the telephone receiver towards his face and stared at it, stunned by what had taken place. He was still fuming inside and couldn't quite fathom why. After a second or so, he replaced the receiver and swallowed a gulp of cold coffee, before getting up from his desk for a cigarette break. He glanced around the office, but no-one seemed to have overheard the stilted discourse.

There was no opportunity to mull over the odd conversation outside either, as it turned out, since Andrew McMahon, the boss of an engineering consultancy with offices two floors below Stonebridge Music, joined the celebrity on the steps of the impressive Collins Street entrance. So rarely in Melbourne these days, the good-looking rock star and philanthropist was a veritable draw card among the smokers who gathered regularly to chat while they took their nicotine fixes and spent valuable time away from their desks.

'How's it going?' the friendly executive asked.

'G'day, Andrew,' the musician greeted the smartly-dressed man, offering him a cigarette. 'I've just had the strangest conversation with my girlfriend's dad actually. Bloody weird.'

The engineer laughed. 'Oh-oh! "I don't like you hanging around my daughter." I think I'm going to be the same when my two grow up. No man's going to be good enough for my little girls.'

'S'pose not,' the musician agreed politely, taking his medicine with reluctance. 'Especially someone like me, eh?'

Little did this well-to-do company director know!

'Yes, that might well have some bearing on things. I didn't even know you had a girlfriend,' Andrew remarked. 'She must have the patience of a saint, with everything the journoes print about you.'

'You could say that,' the cagy playboy smirked. 'It's kind of new. We'll soon see.'

'We all will,' the older man chuckled. 'The perils of stardom! Hence the 'phone call from Daddy? He'd be a brave man to call *you* up and complain. I expect your lass'd be pretty annoyed to have her parents ruin her chance of fifteen minutes of fame.'

The celebrity shook his head, dragging hard on his cigarette. Fifteen minutes of fame wasn't exactly Lynn's style, thankfully. This rambunctious Scotsman had no idea who he was dealing with, and there was no point in sharing his highly personal story with him, no matter how nice a guy he was and how discreet he would undoubtedly swear to be.

'Something like that. How's business, mate?'

The two smokers changed the subject and whiled away a few idle minutes in the morning sunshine, predicting the outcome of the following week's Grand Finals with supreme confidence. After his break, the bemused star returned to the seventh floor and dialled the oracle sitting in the corner office upstairs.

'Mister Diamond, sir!' exclaimed Gerry Blake, exuberant as always. 'What's up, old boy?'

Jeff looked at his watch, which reported the time as just after eleven-thirty. 'Are you free for lunch?'

'Not today, mate. One of the junior accountants is meeting an important client, and I'm supposed to be going with her.'

'Her?' his old friend quizzed. 'Might've known! I s'pose she can't cope with a knife and fork without your supervision.'

Soon to hit the quarter-century mark, Gerry remained as lecherous as ever and made no attempt to hide it. 'Well, you know how it is! I'd hate to have her spill wine over her blouse with me not being there to see it. She'd be so embarrassed, and it would be bloody hilarious,' the accountant joked. 'And I'd miss my opportunity to be the knight in shining armour she thinks I am. Now that wouldn't be funny, would it?'

Jeff muttered something inaudible.

'Anyway... Why do you ask? Work or pleasure?' his manager continued. 'By the way, are you paying?'

'Yes, you bastard,' the worried man answered, secretly glad of his friend's light-heartedness. 'I need to run something past you. No sweat if you can't. We can meet later for a coffee otherwise.'

The businessman sensed some urgency in his client's voice. The instinctive and intelligent artist hardly ever demanded his time on the spur of the moment, usually demonstrating a far greater self-sufficiency than advisable when it came to business acumen.

'What's up? This doesn't sound like a work thing? Nothing happened with the lovely Lynn, I hope? Are you OK?'

'Yes. No, we're fine. I just need to get your opinion on something.'

'Right you are, mate,' Gerry agreed. 'Come on over, and I'll get my assistant to order us a bite to eat. See you in half an hour or so?'

Jeff sighed. 'Cheers, Blake-san. I owe you one.'

An hour or so later, pushing open the heavy, glass door into the reception area, the popular chart-topper tensed up as he reached his manager's office.

This door was made of solid wood and it was closed. It looked too much like a front door for his heightened phobia to dismiss.

'Is His Majesty at home?' he asked Paula, the latest long-legged personal assistant.

The young woman smiled coyly. She had met her company's most famous client a few times and invariably went to pieces whenever he arrived for an appointment. Blushing deeply, she fumbled for the telephone, almost knocking a half-empty mug of tea over in the process.

'I'll see if he's available, Mister Diamond.'

'Jeff,' he corrected her, willing her to do it in person rather than by telephone.

Unfortunately, she picked up the handset and buzzed through to the corner office. 'Gerry, Jeff Diamond's here. Shall I send him in?'

The businessman's typically abusive retort was plainly audible through both the receiver and the door. The charismatic visitor put his hands over his ears in jest, making Paula giggle uncontrollably. This led to yet more embarrassment in front of the celebrity, for which she apologised to her boss, only to hear herself echoing back through his loudspeaker. Jeff took advantage of her plight and signalled that she ought to open the door for him. Anxious to restore her credibility in front of her idol, the tall figure of model proportions willingly obliged, rustling her short skirt further down her legs as she scrambled to her feet.

Excelente, the master manipulator was relieved. Disaster averted again.

The curly-haired joker of Irish descent stood up behind his big desk, looking every bit the executive, with his grey, shimmering designer suit and a colourful yet restrained tie. Blake & Partners' Melbourne branch was faring very well in its own right, not to mention the fact that his personal income had greatly increased since his childhood friend had hit the big-time. Several of Paragon Holdings' investment ventures were also attracting new clients to the accountancy and business consulting practices, cementing the songwriter's success as a definite win-win for him too.

The best mates shook hands warmly. Gerry pointed to a chair opposite, and they took their seats. There was a plate of sandwiches on the desk. The younger man wasn't especially hungry but helped himself to one anyway.

'So what's going on?' the businessman asked with his mouth full. 'You look stressed.'

Jeff gathered his thoughts. 'I've just got off the 'phone with Bart Dyson.'

'Oh, yes?' his manager acknowledged. 'That would've been tricky. Is Lynn still planning to move in? Does he know?'

'Yes, he knows. And he doesn't like it, obviously,' the superstar replied, lifting a second sandwich and dropping it onto the plate in front of him. 'But it's more serious than that.'

His manager was interested. '"Oh, yes?" I say again. How so?'

The boy from Canley Vale hesitated. He had managed to tell his story once but wasn't at all keen to divulge any aspect of it for a second time, particularly to a man who readily admitted having nary a compassionate bone in his body. It wasn't that he didn't trust his mate to keep his mouth shut; it was more that he wasn't ready to share his life's woes beyond his beautiful *confidante*.

'There's some shit he's found out about me and my past that he's not happy with,' the musician imparted somewhat defensively. 'And that's putting it mildly.'

'Does it have to do with all the women?' Gerry chuckled.

Flinching, Jeff hadn't thought of this angle. He had been so focussed on the issues with his family that he hadn't considered anything else. The likelihood was slim, given the fact that detectives had been sniffing around in western Sydney.

'That's a vague possibility,' he dismissed his friend's suggestion. 'I doubt it though, but can appreciate he wouldn't want his daughter being one of a long list.'

His childhood buddy threw his head back and laughed heartily. 'Long list? Fuck me! Between you and me, "long list" would qualify as the most outrageous understatement of all time! My mother gave me such a hard time the other day, and I blame you. She said she'd met you and Lynn for lunch in Manly, and what a nice couple you make. You're making life very difficult for me, mate.'

Jeff was a little perturbed but smiled sympathetically nonetheless. He had come here to seek his manager's judicious opinion, but instead his mate was dishing out blame for his own promiscuous behaviour.

'It's not about that, I'm positive,' he countered. 'It's about some dodgy stuff my family got involved with years ago. He thinks I was part of it. He's hired some private detectives and says he wants to talk to me this evening. I don't know what he thinks he's discovered, but I'm shit-scared.'

The older man leaned forward, his interest piqued further. 'So is this something to do with that episode when your mum died, and that time when you were kicking down doors and such?' he changed his tone, seeing his friend was concerned.

The songwriter shrugged. 'Yeah. Before that, even. Remember I used to do anything not to go home?'

'What, like sleep with my sisters?'

The millionnaire couldn't help but laugh. The gregarious accountant's delivery was dry and poker-faced. He would cop that one on the chin, for old times' sake.

'*Touché!* Very good,' he smiled, taking a packet of cigarettes out of his jacket pocket. 'Can we smoke in here?'

The executive nodded. 'I'm the boss! I try not to, but occasionally's not too bad. Just don't let the cleaners catch you.'

Gerry accepted a cigarette and fetched an ashtray and a chic, silver-plated lighter out of his top drawer, sleek and expensive-looking. His client regarded it covetously but didn't comment. This pretentious schoolboy from the North Shore had acquired superb taste, despite his sometimes crass manner, and the New South Wales nobody had learned many good lessons from him, recently serving him well since being catapulted into the moneyed classes.

'So what are you going to do?' the accountant asked.

Blowing a long cloud of smoke high into the air, Jeff explained. 'I've got to front up at his office at five tonight to face the music. But get this…'

The other man looked up. 'Get what?'

'He suggested I bring my lawyer. What do you reckon to that?'

'Your lawyer? Why?'

Jeff recounted Bart's words, his blood steadily returning to the boil. '"Just a precaution," he said. According to him, he often has his lawyer present and wanted to let me know as a courtesy. How the fuck should I know?'

'So are you going to do it?'

'No. I said I'd bring you,' Jeff scoffed, realising he ought to have mentioned this earlier. 'Sorry. I forgot to tell you that bit, mate.'

'Jeez! Thanks for that! I'm tempted to come along just so I can witness the showdown,' Gerry replied, becoming quite animated. 'I can't pass myself off as your lawyer in front of his though. This is a small town when it comes to that sort of thing.'

The celebrity put a hand up to acknowledge his friend's highly ethical reservations. 'I know, mate. Gallant offer, but not required. I told him I'd bring my manager.'

'Isn't that a bit of an admission of guilt though?' the older man strategised. 'A sign of weakness? If I were you, I'd go in there alone, like you've got nothing to hide. You know the law. You won't let yourself get sold down the river.'

Jeff contemplated this idea for a few moments. The affable businessman had made a valid point. He had everything to prove, but neither a manager nor a lawyer could help him with any of that, because they would neither be across the facts nor be able to anticipate how the story might be twisted.

'That's smart, mate,' he acknowledged after a short pause. 'Bloody smart. I knew you'd straighten me out.'

'All part of the service. Did you want a cuppa?'

The musician nodded, grateful for their close friendship. He leaned back in his swivel chair and finished the second sandwich, slightly more relaxed about this evening's appointment. He watched his friend gloat at the compliment and felt pleased he had been able to make him feel valued. Too often these days, the younger of the two would grab the limelight, or rather it grabbed him, leaving Gerry and his other loyal advisers to pick up the pieces.

The prodigious executive buzzed through to Paula for two coffees. 'That's the best option, mate,' he continued with confidence. 'Go and see what the big man has to say and what the likely outcome might be. Then you can decide if you need a lawyer or not. Even if his people were to issue you with some sort of subpoena today, you're not obliged to do anything without seeking counsel.'

'Cheers, mate,' the superstar agreed. 'I don't know if it'll be a showdown. I only know he's determined to find some way of turning Lynn against me.'

'Does she know?'

'Does she know about my past or does she know her dad wants to meet me tonight?' Jeff asked back. 'Or that her parents have hired a sheriff to chase me out of town?'

'Yes,' confirmed the accountant, sniggering. 'All of the above. Whatever!'

The celebrity sighed aloud at his friend's lack of empathy, assuming he was only bothering to ask so as not to miss out on any scandal. One of the secrets of their successful partnership was that the manager didn't feel compelled to mollycoddle his client, and in the vast majority of situations, this suited Jeff fine. It was just occasionally that he sought a little more than a slap on the back, a convivial beer and a dose of dutiful support.

'Lynn knows everything. I held off telling her for so long, but it was driving me crazy. You know all those anger issues you mentioned before? Well, she needed to understand where all that shit comes from.'

Gerry looked puzzled. 'But how does she know about all that anyhow?'

'Oh, I get pretty pissed off at life, mate. I try not to take it out on her, but sometimes it just happens,' the tormented soul explained, wracked with guilt again. 'And when we got back together, she told me her dad didn't want us to see each other because of something he'd found out, so I thought, "Jesus! I'd better come clean." I gave her a full confession up in Sydney. It was fucking cathartic, to be honest, mate. Highly recommended.'

The businessman raised his eyebrows but declined to comment, waiting for his friend to finish spilling the beans which were obviously weighing heavily on his mind.

'Lynn doesn't know that I've been summoned tonight though,' the rock star continued with a wry smile. 'She's in Germany. I'll ring her later, after I've been done over.'

'If you're still a free man,' Gerry joked.

The anxious man shook a long finger at his friend. 'That's not even remotely funny.'

Paula knocked on the door and entered with a tray, putting it down on the desk. The men thanked her, and she made a quick exit, Jeff's hungry eyes following her out.

'Mate,' her boss accused. 'She's too young, and you're spoken for. Or so I thought...'

'Shit, Gez,' the younger man replied, his mind awash with fantasies, frustrated at not being able to do anything about them. 'You can talk. I can still look. Do you mean to say you don't? How *is* Vanessa, by the way. And how's Heather? Oh, and the junior accountant you missed out on this lunchtime? Sorry about that...'

The gregarious party boy shifted in his chair, the reminder of his unwelcome situation a painful one. He had confided in Jeff that the mother of his unborn child continued to exert pressure regarding getting married, even though neither had feelings for the other. He knew full well that his friend's inclusion of Heather's name on his own long list was a loaded question.

'Yes, well... Vanessa? Not too happy. She left an obtuse message on my answerphone. And Heather... Well, let's just say we're working things through.'

The rock star grinned knowingly. 'I'd better get out of your way, Blake-san. Thanks for listening and for your wise words. It's all good. I'm ready now. Wish me luck!'

He emptied an entire cupful of coffee down his throat in one go and stood up to leave, threading his arms through the sleeves of his leather jacket. His manager circled the enormous desk and gave his most complicated and lucrative client a manly hug.

'You'll be right,' he said, slapping him on the back. 'Come back here after, if you want. We can go for a few beers.'

'Cheers, mate. I'll do that. Thanks again. You really helped me.'

'No worries,' his business manager waved him off.

'See ya, Paula,' the superstar called out casually, as he strode out of the office and towards the lift lobby. 'Thanks for the coffee.'

Paula blushed again. 'You're welcome, Mister Diamond.'

As he approached the lifts and leaned down to press the call button, the handsome, long-haired musician pointed to his chest and mouthed the name "Jeff" at the embarrassed secretary, grinning at her polite mistake. Christ, he was horny! How was this fidelity lark supposed to work? Still, he had more than enough fantasies of his dream girl to keep his right wrist supple again tonight.

***

Back at work on his dissertation, Jeff felt unbearably restless all afternoon. He was nervous and couldn't wait for the portentous meeting to be over. Continually glancing up at the clock, he was unable to apply himself to the dry topic without journeying back to the Stones Road and coming face to face with the criminal element who haunted him to this day. Conscripting his mind onto routine matters, he managed to spin out the day's tasks until a few minutes before five o'clock, when he put on his jacket and took the short walk over the Yarra River to Dyson Administration.

A familiar face was on duty again, and the two men exchanged greetings.

'Good afternoon, Jeff. I don't believe Miss Lynn's here. She's overseas.'

The young man put his hands up as if to say he was aware of this. 'Hi, Michael. I've got an appointment with Mister Dyson,' he told the security guard. 'Can you let him know I'm here, please?'

The uniformed man masked his surprise well and dialled Big D's number. The visitor imagined him drawing all manner of invisible conclusions as to the reason for this meeting.

'Good evening, sir. Mister Diamond's here to see you. Thank you, sir,' he responded to the big boss, before turning to Jeff. 'Please go up to Level Three. Mister Dyson will meet you at Reception.'

In no time, the lift doors opened on the third floor. His girlfriend's enormous father was standing waiting and held his hand out to greet the striking celebrity as he stepped out.

'Thanks for coming over, Jeff.'

'No worries, sir. Are you well?'

'Yes, thanks,' Bart replied. 'You?'

'So far,' the testosterone-charged musician answered wryly, by now spoiling for a fair contest.

The veteran sportsman took a good look at his elder daughter's suitor as he ushered him into a correspondingly enormous office. Diamond was fit, attractive and well-dressed, and apart from his hair being much longer than tolerable, his appearance met with Dyson's approval. Was that an earring though? Real men didn't wear earrings.

Despite his youth, there was a confident swagger about this successful recording artist, and the older man noticed that he didn't seem in the least bit afraid of confrontation. He also had to admit to being impressed by the upstart's rise to stardom. This pretender had been striking as a nineteen-year-old student, and had only grown in stature on his journey to fame and fortune.

'Please sit down,' Bart invited, pointing to a chair at the large meeting table.

There was a small, slightly-built man with a moustache sitting quietly on the other side. *Must be the lawyer*, the new arrival surmised, wondering when they would be introduced or if he wasn't supposed to notice the hired help. A small pile of paperwork was stacked in front of the observer, with a pair of wire-framed spectacles sitting on top.

'So is that my file?' Jeff opened, keen to get on the front foot with his opponents.

His host didn't take kindly to the boldness the Sydneysider was displaying, but his behaviour was to be expected under the circumstances. Reluctantly, he could see what his daughter might find so irresistible. There was a definite hypnotic quality about the way he communicated, and his movements were controlled and even somewhat graceful. Jeff Diamond had presence; the type of person to whom one couldn't help but pay attention. Much like himself, in fact... He had often heard that daughters were attracted to traits mirrored in their fathers, and this prospect stirred up some fairly base emotions in the middle-aged man. Obviously there also came a time when daughters forsook their fathers for potential husbands, and the possibility of Lynn forsaking him for this hot-headed womaniser with underworld connections filled him with dread.

The Olympian thought back to the athletic dance routines with which his daughter and her romantic partner had entertained the crowd at Robert McLean's twenty-first birthday party and conceded silently that it would be very hard for a hormonal, teenaged girl to resist such a well-architected package as the one now standing before him.

'Yes, it is. Jeff, I hope you understand the seriousness of why we're here.'

This was shaping up to be a battle of wills. The musician breathed deeply, knowing it was imperative that he keep his cool. There was no way he could squander this opportunity to prove himself to Lynn's father. He helped himself to a glass of water and drank most of it straightaway, not taking his eyes off the men on the other side of the table.

'Sir, I have a fair idea about what we're here to talk about, and yes, I'm taking it seriously. This is my reputation on the line here. My future with your daughter.'

'Good stuff,' Bart nodded, gesturing in the direction of his diminutive sidekick. 'This is Simon Steinmann. He's a solicitor who acts for me from time to time.'

Looking like a suited rodent straight out of "Toad of Toad Hall", the short man stood up and slid a business card across the table. He couldn't have been more than five-feet-six-inches tall, Jeff remarked as he circled the table to shake hands, suppressing the bizarre scene that pervaded his brain. Steinmann offered a weedy grip, and the statuesque celebrity shook it, frightened the bony hand would break off at the wrist.

'Simon,' the visitor said boldly.

'Good evening, Mister Diamond,' came a voice deeper and more confident than his body language implied.

'Jeff, please.'

Inviting the newcomer to take a seat, Bart sat down next to his solicitor and dwarfed him still further, pulling the pile of papers towards him. He opened a manila folder and placed a large, stubby index finger on the top page.

'Now, Jeff... You know already that I requested that Lynn not carry on her relationship with you after she returned to Australia, and also that she's informed me she loves you and wants to keep seeing you.'

Jeff nodded, making eye contact from under a furrowed brow, more interested in the contents of the folder. 'Yes, sir. That sounds familiar.'

'Good,' Big D continued, not knowing what to make of the star's somewhat flippant responses. 'Well, I hope you can appreciate that Marianna and I are concerned for Lynn's safety and happiness. She's not only very important to us but also to her country, her fans and to the teams she represents. We have an obligation to ensure any environment she's in... and the same for our other children, of course... is appropriate for someone in her position and with the future we have planned for her. Do you understand?'

Jeff paused, wondering what exactly he was being asked to understand. 'Yes, sir. I understand perfectly,' the young man hazarded, his anger growing inside but at the moment well under control. 'But I'd also ask *you* to understand that Lynn's very important to me too. I want the same things for her as you do. Well, mostly.'

'Mostly?'

'Yes,' his monosyllabic reply gave no more away.

While the elder statesman tried to decipher the cryptic answer, Simon shuffled a little, and his gaze fell on the pile of papers.

'Yes. Thank you,' Bart coughed and moved on. 'Jeff, to cut to the chase, Marianna and I decided that we needed to know more about you, if Lynn was going to continue to see you. She's over eighteen now, meaning we can no longer stop her from taking up with you again without a compelling reason. Therefore, we enlisted the help of a detective firm to do a bit of digging.'

The dignified man looked up from the files, and Jeff took his opportunity to counter. 'That's fine, sir,' he acquiesced. 'That's your prerogative. But can I ask why you didn't just ask me?'

The forthright youngster's calm intelligence took his adversary aback. It was a reasonable question. A more than reasonable question, in fact. His daughter's boyfriend was so far respectful enough but prepared to stand his ground. All the more reason to ascertain whether these traits were the characteristics of a good man or the mark of a seasoned criminal.

'We needed to get an independent view.'

Not in the least bit satisfied with this answer, Jeff sensed his blood pressure rising. He couldn't possibly let the big man away with such a lightweight justification.

'Have they been paid, your detectives?'

Simon intervened. 'We're not here to discuss the integrity of the agency concerned, Mister Diamond.'

'Jeff,' the young man reminded him. 'Oh, really? Thanks, but finding compelling reasons in return for large sums of money is hardly a hallmark of independence, I'd suggest.'

Nonplussed by this keen observation and receiving no support from the castigated lawyer, Bart decided to push on with the findings. He opened the manila folder again and flicked the top corners of the first few pages, appearing to be reminding himself of some details.

'Be that as it may, Jeff, what we found out was distressing, to say the least. Can you confirm that your father is Paul Diamond, or Pavel Diament by birth? I hope I'm pronouncing that correctly. Forgive me, if not. And he's currently serving a life sentence in a high security prison in New South Wales. Is that right?'

The young man's body language showed no distress, which was in fact a long way from the truth. He had been waiting for this moment yet felt all too ill-prepared, impulsively reminded of a favourite quote from another of his most revered authors, Honoré de Balzac. Drawing a distinct parallel with the anti-hero from *"La Rabouilleuse"*, he slowed his erratic brain by inwardly reciting the line describing Maxence Gilet as "never calmer in outward appearance than when his blood and ideas were in a ferment."

The slightest shiver ran down his spine, remembering his massive confession to the Olympian's daughter. 'Two concurrent life sentences, to be more accurate, sir.'

Dyson and Steinmann glanced at each other, but their facial expressions remained equally impassive. The fateful words had been spoken, which immediately released some of the tension in the room. All three took a few seconds to gather their thoughts.

'OK,' the confident showman broke the silence, casually leaning back into his chair. 'So the sins of the father are the sins of the son? That's a damned shame.'

'When it comes to the safety of my daughter, it's a serious concern, yes,' Bart stuck to his argument. 'This is not a petty criminal we're talking about here. Despite his being your father, you have to admit that.'

'Of course. That much I know already, sir,' the boy from Canley Vale shot back. 'There's nothing petty about any of this. I've lived with it for the last ten years, and I'm not going to try to belittle or condone what he's supposed to have done. I don't even know the truth myself. I was too young and wasn't allowed to see him at the time, so I've never heard his side of the story. I'll probably never find out the real truth, any more than you can.'

The rock star paused to gauge the others' reactions but continued almost immediately, not wishing to lose momentum. It felt good to have a platform to state his case, and he almost wished Lynn and Gerry were on hand to see it.

'My mother's family thinks he's as guilty as sin, as do the police. But they always hated him, so there's some more bias for you... They wanted him to go down, regardless of whether he committed the crimes or not. And as for the Jaworski family, they never avenged the deaths. Well, not so far anyway... So who knows what they think? They're hardly your squeaky clean, shining examples of community spirit either. And it's all hearsay. Circumstantial... There were no witnesses, or none who was prepared to come forward. In fact, on that score, I'd be as interested as you are to find out what your dicks have dug up. Even if a snitch were to suddenly open his mouth, I wouldn't want the verdict overturned. He was an arsehole, my old man. He's where he belongs.'

Jeff's rough eloquence was not lost on the great man. The ambitious star's reaction was objective and reasoned, and he certainly hadn't tried to deny anything. Simon coughed uncomfortably, probably not knowing how to direct his client next. Both father and boyfriend picked up on his professional hesitance and exchanged eye contact accidentally.

Bart inhaled. 'Tell me, Jeff... If you had a daughter, would your pedigree be what you'd be looking for in a partner for her?'

'My pedigree?' the wordsmith laughed a little unkindly. 'You make me sound like a bloody dog. I would've thought you'd have spoken more in terms of bloodlines.'

The mouse with a moustache raised a spindly finger, presumably to scold the young man for his insolence. Big D waved a slow hand to shut him down.

'Very amusing,' he replied. 'You've got guts, my man. I'll give you that.'

The twenty-two-year-old nodded a quiet acknowledgement, taking a deep breath to answer the big man's question properly. Hypotheticals were his thing, and this was the very topic for which he would go down fighting.

'So what would I want for my daughter?' he repeated, gulping another large swig of water, mostly for effect. 'Someone who makes her happy and who allows her to be herself now and in the future. Someone who'd help make a meaningful life together and who'd protect her with his life if he had to. The fact that I don't much care for the family of the man my daughter might choose is kind of irrelevant for me.'

'I see,' the sportsman nodded. 'So therefore, you think your father's extremely dangerous criminal conduct should be irrelevant for me and my wife too, I assume?'

'That's up to you, sir,' the resolute pretender shrugged. 'You asked me what I'd be looking for, not what I think *you* should be looking for. As I said before, it's your prerogative to do what you're doing. I don't doubt your best intentions for Lynn. Not for a minute. And neither does she, by the way. It's just that I only see the pile of "cons" you've assembled on me. Where's my "pro" file? Is there one?'

His girlfriend's father opened his mouth to speak, but Jeff cut him off. Seeing Steinmann raise an objecting hand out of the corner of his eye, he then turned his menacing eyes his way.

'This is Australia, isn't it? Not India?'

The young man was becoming increasingly angry but fought to remain courteous and confident, matching his experienced adversary as closely as he could. The last thing he wanted to do was lose the moral high ground and allow Dyson to gain total control.

'Surely you're not going to prescribe whom Lynn falls in love with? Are you?' the strident romantic suddenly felt a lump in his throat and chose to hold his tongue before he said too much.

Bart leaned forward after a long pause. Perhaps there was credit to be given to redress the balance somewhat.

'Now I will say, Jeff, that you behaved very maturely with that dickhead, Keller, at our place that evening. I was pleased with the way you handled yourself.'

'Thank you,' the visitor replied, staring the big man down. 'But?'

'There is no but,' the older man carried on, straight-faced. 'Only that I'm looking for the same maturity today. We also uncovered a string of lesser offences in the name of Jeffrey Moreno Diamond: drug possession, public disorder and drunkenness, fighting and handling stolen goods. Do you deny these?'

The swarthy, dark-haired musician leaned forward onto the table too, watching the lawyer's eyes following him intently while his tiny hands fished through the pile of paperwork to bring forth the substantiating evidence.

'Sir, I can't deny them, can I?' he answered, pointing to the papers which Simon was brandishing as "Exhibit A". 'There's a list on the piece of paper in front of you with my name on it. I'm not stupid. My record as a juvenile stands as it is. My record as an adult is completely clean. What danger does that put Lynn in?'

Simon piped up. 'This is a question of your character, Mister Diamond.'

The air in the Sydneysider's lungs exited in a rush, for this latest statement enraged him like a red rag to a bull. *Of course it is, you arsehole,* his inner child cried out. Didn't this puny solicitor reckon he might already know that? What did he think he had been doing for the last ten years, if it hadn't been to rebuild his fucking character?

'My character?' Jeff almost shouted. 'There's nothing wrong with my character. I'm not the one sneaking around prying into a bloke's life without telling him. I'm not the one trying to tell a grown woman whom she can or can't spend time with. Let me tell you I understand completely who Lynn is, who you are, sir, and who you are, Simon...'

The man from western Sydney's underclass sneered as he spoke the last five words. He had had just about enough of people in high places passing judgment on his character, forever branded with a handicap which was proving virtually impossible to shake off.

'I've spent a bloody long time figuring out how to live with the legacy my father so kindly bestowed upon me, and I've made a bloody good life for myself in that time too. I'm a law-abiding, tax-paying, university-educated working man, just like you and you.'

As he made his point, the index finger of Jeff's left hand prodded the air between himself and each man in turn. He was not about to lose his dream girl on the basis of his earned ability to stand among men like these.

'You want some character witnesses who'll testify that your daughter'll be safe and happy with me?' he taunted them arrogantly. 'Fine! I can line 'em up outside, no problem. How many would you like?'

Bart nodded, impressed once again by the slim layer of restraint over which this angry young man was hovering, and under that which he obviously perceived as considerable provocation. Was it any wonder that women fell at his feet? He was charismatic, passionate and articulate, and determined above all to get his own way.

He raised a hand slowly to silence him. 'That's enough, Jeff.'

'No, it's not enough, sir,' the celebrity continued, undeterred by the fact that a single hand's worth of fingers would suffice when tallying up his reliable character witnesses. 'You still haven't answered my question. What danger does my juvenile criminal record pose to Lynn?'

The All-Australian took a deep breath. 'Lynn is my daughter, and her mother and I love her dearly. She's enjoying great success at the beginning of a long career. She's young and still quite naïve to the world. Your lineage, your past and your string of high profile affairs over the last couple of years do not make you our favoured candidate to share her future.'

Jeff stood up, infuriated by the latest addition to his list of discredits, his left hand searching obsessively in his trouser pocket for his cigarettes. Thinking better of this however, he pulled it back out again and folded his arms emphatically.

'String of high profile affairs? That's rich!' he let out a bitter laugh. 'Sure, I've been with a lot of women, but there's no law against that. Lynn and I made each other no promises before she went overseas. And what about her own string of high profile affairs? I offer you the future King of England, no less...'

The furious man had dropped his hands again and was leaning on the table, but not enough to be threatening. Bart remained seated and signalled to his argumentative guest to do the same.

'We're not going to discuss Lynn's sex life here.'

Seething, the hot-headed celebrity compliantly sat down. 'Then we don't discuss mine either,' he returned, crossing his hands over each other to close the subject. 'Sir, will you please tell me what danger you envisage I am to your daughter? Has she complained about anything? Is she worried? Because if she is, I want to know about it.'

'No,' Bart closed the file which had been lying open in front of him. 'Quite the opposite. Lynn is over-the-moon in love with you and defends you to the hilt. She's of an age where she can't see past your looks and charms. And you are charming, and also very convincing. We don't want her to be taken advantage of. We don't want her to lose anything that's rightfully hers.'

Lose anything that was rightfully hers? This was the final straw. Jeff's resolve for conciliation was rapidly crumbling.

'So you think I'm out to fleece her... or even to fleece you... out of your fortune? Is that what this is about? You think I'm a con' artist waiting to charm my way into her bank account via her bed? Come on! Give me some effing credit, Mister Dyson. I earned just short of six million dollars last year. *After* tax. Christ! Do I need either of your money? I can't spend what I've got!'

'Please calm down, Mister Diamond,' came the comparably feeble voice of Simon Steinmann from across the table. 'Please remember who it is you're talking to.'

The big man raised another hand to request silence from his lawyer, who was clearly adding little value to this discussion. 'It's OK, Simon. I understand Jeff's upset.'

'Damned right, I'm upset,' the livid songwriter sniped. 'And I'm sure Lynn would be too, to hear you talking about us like this. What we have is worth more than money, than fast cars and country seats, or than rich man holidays in the Caribbean. Do you know how we spent last Saturday night, sir?'

'No, and I'm not sure I need to know,' the conservative man saw fit to rebuke, recognising the carefully-controlled aggression that his own daughter had exhibited only a few days ago.

'Yes, you do need to know,' Jeff was managing to maintain his cool better than he had expected a minute ago. 'You need to know. We spent the night in my apartment, with a friend of mine and his girlfriend. We had an Indian takeaway and a few drinks. We watched the bloody football. And in the morning, we walked to breakfast at The European, which I believe you know well. The whole weekend would've cost us less than a hundred and fifty bucks. Lynn wants to live a normal life, sir, that's all. And at least for the moment, she wants to live it with me.'

It was Bart Dyson's turn to rise to his feet, while his solicitor seemed to shrink down even further into the black, leather Boardroom chair. 'All very sweet, I'm sure,' he mocked. 'But the fact remains that you are the son of a convicted murderer. A double murderer, as you said yourself. You have your own criminal record, albeit expunged now. I would be derelict in my duty to my family to ignore these facts in the name of Lynn's romantic leanings. You have both proven that life can go on without each other. If I find any information that leads me to believe your intentions are dishonest, unlawful or violent, then I will have no hesitation in requesting the police issue you with a restraining order. I have no choice, Jeff.'

'Fine!' exclaimed the pretender, once his girlfriend's father had finished his own masterly oration. 'This is actually a fascinating situation. I'm really looking forward to how it works out. Though it'd be so much better if it wasn't all about me...'

Jeff laughed, somewhat too sarcastically, but he was not prepared to lie down and let this powerful symbol of Australian propriety and his squeaky, Jewish lawyer walk all over him. 'So there are two issues at play here,' he went on. 'First, there's my family background; whom I'm descended from, and the scourge it might bring upon the Dyson name, over which I have no control whatsoever. I'll just have to take my chances on that one, depending on what you uncover and what you believe the truth to be. Yes?'

Bart nodded. 'Yes.'

The younger man felt surprisingly calm all of a sudden. 'And second, there's me and my integrity. I need to prove my intentions are genuine, and you need to prove I'm a violent con' man. And whoever gets there first'll be the winner, I guess. That's a challenge I can accept. I need to have a good, hard think about how I can convince you, and I trust you'll let me know what a guilty verdict will be based on. Is that fair?'

'Yes, that's fair,' the sportsman agreed. 'Thank you, Jeff. I appreciate the way in which you've taken this news tonight.'

The Sydneysider exhaled sharply, shaking his head slowly, summoning one last ounce of civility from somewhere deep within. 'At the risk of plagiarising, I have no choice, Mister Dyson, do I? Do you know how often I've had to justify my own existence? Can you even begin to imagine how that feels, *sir*? Oh, yes, I'll shake your hand tonight and leave the building quietly, while you get on the 'phone to these private investigators of yours. I'll be waiting for their answer. Lynn's out of the country anyway, so she can't come to any harm of my doing, can she? You have no choice but to do what you're doing, and I have no choice but to face the consequences.'

Bart walked around the table and magnanimously shook the songwriter's hand while he was still speaking. Simon began to follow, but his client urged him to stay where he was. It was a wise move, the young man bristled.

'And one more thing...' Jeff turned to the two men. 'In case you're wondering, Lynn knows everything. She's not as starry-eyed as you might think. She knows how to handle me, believe me. She's made strong, like you, sir. But she loves me and she believes in me. Why don't you ask Lynn what she wants for a change?'

The father chose not to respond. The visitor turned and walked out of the office, down the wide, imposing corridor towards the lifts. The others didn't follow, and he left the building without speaking to the security guard.

The intellectual's mind was still spinning as he ran down the steps at the front of the Dyson headquarters and made his way towards Princes Bridge and the CBD. He could see people walking along the river, enjoying the spring evening air, and before too long he was fending off excited fans eager for his attention. Too busy signing autographs to look at his watch, he requested a time-check from one of the attractive females who asked him to pose for a picture. It was just after six o'clock, and he guessed Gerry would still be in the office. Not sure if he really wanted a *post mortem* of the heated exchange, he made his way over the bridge, past the ochre-coloured entrance to Flinders Street station and over the road to Flinders Lane.

When Jeff finally emerged from the lift, the head honcho of Blake & Partners' Melbourne branch was standing at the reception desk with two of his staff. One was a business consultant whom the VIP client recognised from office parties. The other, a ginger-haired woman in her early twenties, stood a good chance of being the accountant who had lost her lunchtime chaperone today. She looked perfectly at ease about it now, most likely on a new promise, the jealous man assumed.

'Evening! How did it go? I was wondering how long you'd be,' the firm's precocious director shook his friend warmly by the hand and slapped his right shoulder vigorously, nodding towards the consultant. 'You know Jonathan Ashwood? This is Jeff Diamond, in case you've been hiding under a rock for the last while.'

The celebrity smiled in acknowledgement and shook Jonathan's hand. 'Yes, we've met a few times. Jon, how're you going?'

Without allowing his colleague to reply, Gerry gestured towards their female colleague. 'And this is Natasha with the unpronounceable surname,' he laughed.

The red-head was very glamorous and just her boss' type; tall, outgoing and ambitious enough to do whatever it took to get ahead. The recent arrival smiled to himself. And why not? He had been known to do the same. Well, sort of...

'Hi, Jeff,' Natasha said without any qualms. 'It's great to meet you in person. In fact, I can't believe it! When I heard you were a client and a friend of Gerry's, I was so thrilled. I had to come and work here.'

She flirted so naturally. Born for the job!

'Thanks. Nice to meet you too, Natasha,' the superstar answered, absorbing the compliment with no visible trace of conceit. 'You guys on your way out?'

Gerry picked up his briefcase and the large bunch of keys that were sitting on the reception counter and set about closing the double doors on his growing enterprise. Jeff watched the others gather their belongings too, realising he would be expected to debrief in public if he were to join them. That was not going to happen if he could help it.

'Can we stay here, mate, please?'

'Yes, of course. OK,' his old friend answered, a little surprised. 'No beer? You two had better go on ahead. I might join you later, but don't wait for me.'

Natasha and Jonathan picked up their cases and coats and made their way to the lift lobby, cheerfully saying their goodbyes. The manager turned to his client, only to find him already slumped down into one of the sumptuous chesterfields.

'You look terrible,' he laughed, but not too much.

The businessman could see his client was full of anguish. For all his *bon viveur* and blokishness, he had a warm heart and was a true mate when it counted. He led the way behind the marble-topped reception desk and into the Boardroom, looking around to make sure Jeff was following him.

'Do you want a beer?' Gerry asked, fetching one for himself from the fridge discreetly disguised in wood and onyx.

'Yes, I fucking well do.'

The younger man exhaled, took the opened bottle gratefully and drank a mouthful, but then sat it down on the table. Tiredness had virtually overtaken him, and all he wanted to do was curl up with his favourite girl. As good a substitute as he were likely to meet tonight, his manager was anxious to hear what had transpired with Big D and the legal eagle.

'So, cough up, mate. How did it go with Daddy Dyson?'

'Christ Almighty! Where do I start?' Jeff looked towards the ceiling. 'He's completely right, you know, after all that. Perfectly justified in doing what he's doing. I don't like the way he's going about it, but he's protecting valuable property and he knows who I am. Stuff that no-one else except my family knows.'

'Was there any legal representation?'

'Simon Steinmann from Rosenberg and Partners,' Jeff tossed the solicitor's business card across the table to where his friend was sitting.

'Thanks.'

'He was the size of your old PA,' the musician laughed, remembering Belinda, who had been particularly short and rather incapable, and had ended up getting the boot after one too many stuff-ups.

'Queer?' Gerry asked.

'What?'

'Was he queer? Steinmann,' the businessman clarified.

The famous client stared across the table incredulously. 'Never gave it one thought. Why?'

Gerry laughed. 'I know him. Or know *of* him through a couple of the other partners. He's good, I hear, but smarmy. Small man syndrome, you know.'

Nodding in agreement, Jeff continued, anxious to get his friend's professional opinion. 'Anyway, he's uncovered stuff about my family and my rap-sheet as a juvie. He also accused me of too much sleeping around, which I didn't realise was a crime.'

'Maybe it is when you're in our league,' the older man scoffed, before becoming serious again. 'I didn't know you had a juvie record.'

The boy from Canley Vale smiled. 'There are a number of things you don't know, mate.'

'Apparently so,' Gerry responded, looking slightly concerned. 'Perhaps we need to have a longer conversation one day? As your business manager, I have to be prepared for anything that might come out in the press.'

The executive offered his strung-out buddy a cigarette. He was party to the self-imposed month-long stretch of celibacy which the lovesick man was undertaking, unable to come to terms with such a challenge himself. Jeff was definitely looking worse for wear, and this evening's battle of the Titans would hardly lend itself to his rest and relaxation.

'You're right,' the younger man acknowledged, accepting the cigarette and lighting it. 'But not now. I've only just found the courage to tell Lynn, and that was pretty horrific, let me tell you.'

'Was she shocked?'

The songwriter paused, thinking back on his gorgeous girlfriend's reaction to his long, drawn-out story. He had been so focussed on his own task that night that he struggled to recall any specific details.

'Yeah, a little,' he answered after a while. 'But according to Big D, Lynn can't see beyond my looks and charm. So she's spellbound, and obviously her opinion can't be trusted.'

Gerry shrugged. '*Is* there anything beyond your looks and charm, mate? Aren't you as superficial as me?'

The close friends both sniggered, the stresses of their respective days beginning to trickle away. The businessman swivelled his chair round to retrieve a couple more bottles of beer.

'Did you want to get some dinner?'

Jeff shook his head. 'D'you know what else he's worried about?'

'No, mate.'

'He reckons I'm a con' man who's going to cheat Lynn and his family out of their wealth and power. What the fuck is that all about? I couldn't believe it! I told him I'd made six mill' last year and I hardly needed their money, but he's still convinced I'm going to bring his empire down. It's like the fucking Gladiators.'

'Good on ya for standing up for yourself,' Gerry told him, stubbing out his cigarette. 'He's on a real power trip, by the sounds of it.'

Jeff was angry again, grateful for the chance to vent his frustrations. 'Mate, what's to stop me saying the same thing about Lynn?' he challenged. 'How do I know if she's genuine? She might be sleeping with a different bloke every night while she's out of town. I hope not, but how do I know? I could hire my own set of private dicks to follow her. Paranoia's a dangerous thing, but when you're Big D and your daughter's eligible enough to marry the future King of England, I guess he's entitled to be a bit paranoid.'

'That's ridiculous, mate,' his old friend objected.

'No, actually, it's not. He's protecting what's valuable to him. As he says, he has no choice. And much as I hate to admit it, I agree with him.'

The Irishman stared at his most important and influential client, astounded that he should accept his fate so philosophically. Although outwardly impulsive and single-minded, no-one could ever accuse Jeff Diamond of ignoring other people's points of view.

'So what are you going to do now?'

'Nothing,' the younger man replied, throwing his hands in the air in resignation. 'There's fuck all I *can* do. Carry on as normal and wait 'til his investigation concludes. Then I face whatever consequences come my way. I have no choice either. That's what we shook hands on.'

'I see. Bloody mess,' his friend sighed. 'Let me know if I can help.'

'Cheers, mate. That means a lot,' the twenty-two-year-old responded. 'And you do need to know some of this shit. I don't want to get you caught up in anything, so you need to make your own judgment about me too.'

Gerry looked at his watch. 'Are we done? We can catch Natasha and Jon in Rosati's if we're quick.'

'Yeah. I guess that's all there was to it. No, you go, mate. I'm not in the mood. I feel like going for a run, to blast all this angst out of me. And besides, I've given up drinking.'

'That's right,' the accountant chuckled, lifting the four empty beer bottles off the table. 'You have indeed.'

The pair left the offices of Blake & Partners and descended into Flinders Lane. They parted company outside the iconic establishment, and Jeff walked northwards up Exhibition Street, in the direction of his empty apartment. He felt a distinct urge to break his new rule and find some stringless female company, but dismissed the thought guiltily after indulging his fantasies for several minutes.

His sage manager was right. They had become accustomed to a very selfish, Machiavellian lifestyle which henceforth must stop. Time to grow up and face the music, he resolved. Besides, he also needed to march off a raging hard-on! How could he even think of betraying Lynn's trust after the confidence she had invested in him? If she was willing to go into battle for him against her formidable father, then he should be damned well prepared to take care of his own sexual urges until his beautiful best friend and he were once more in the same town.

'You still have a lot to learn, you greedy, egocentric arsehole,' he scolded himself, thinking aloud as he walked briskly up the hill. 'You are the luckiest man alive. Just fucking remember that.'

Since his mid-teens, the ambitious adolescent had measured his manhood by the number of female conquests he could notch up. Now however, those hedonistic days must be consigned to history. It was high time he began to measure the same instead by his ability to resist temptation. It was a question of character, wasn't it? He recalled Simon Steinmann's supercilious tone, and his stomach curdled. It appeared the odious little man had a point. How bloody self-satisfied would Dyson's lawyer be if he could read Jeff's mind now? People as unattractive as that slimy wimp would seldom be in the position of having temptation to resist, his cruel alter-ego presumed, but the observation held true regardless. Despite the arrogant and sex-starved star's initial protestations, there were still a few areas of his adult character in dire need of an overhaul.

Filled with renewed moral fortitude, Jeff decided to divert to Pellegrini's for a coffee and some benign conversation with its eclectic *clientèle* of elderly Italian men and discerning tourists. It was ten-thirty in the morning in Germany, where Lynn was, meaning he wouldn't be able to contact her for a few hours at least, and the idea of running had long since lost its appeal.

The smart and sophisticated celebrity with the bohemian looks ordered an espresso and a shot of Grappa, sat at the bar next to a dumbstruck American couple and lit a cigarette. Within a few minutes, a lively discourse had developed, taking his mind nicely off the events of the day. He looked around the bar at the happy, relaxed scene. Why would anyone think he needed Bart Dyson's money? This was the life he wanted: simple pleasures with someone special to share in them.

The last time he and his beautiful best friend had frequented this Melbourne institution, she had been about to fly away for two years. A pang of longing grabbed at his heart, wishing she was sitting next to him at the bar again. Soon, he vowed, and in London too... Old man Dyson evidently didn't know this small fact yet, the lost boy took pleasure in informing Miss Irony.

It was past ten o'clock when Jeff left Pellegrini's and arrived at his apartment building. He had eaten a cheap bowl of pasta and shared an expensive bottle of wine with the couple from Boston, Massachusetts, and on parting, they had swapped contact details. They had eventually confessed to being big fans who had attended one of his sell-out concerts the previous year.

Jeff had been interested in hearing about the old New England university town from a local perspective and promised to look them up when he was next there.

His new friends now long gone, the tired, dejected musician stared at his front door with defiance. He pictured Big D and the weasly solicitor mocking his inability to gain entry into his own apartment. They should write that down in his file too... Fucking hell! He was drunk and feeling sorry for himself again. Same, old spiral.

'OK, *Regala*, where are you?' he muttered under his breath.

Finally inside, Jeff threw his keys and wallet down on the coffee table, poured a large whisky into a tumbler and sat down at the piano with what remained of a five-star, aromatic Montecristo cigar he had bought from the bartender. He would give up drinking and smoking again tomorrow. Smiling ruefully, he lifted a photograph of himself and his stunning flatmate which had been taken the previous weekend by Vanessa using Lynn's Polaroid camera. It wasn't one for framing and had gathered a thin layer of dust over the last few days.

'Is this all worth it?' he spoke to the appealing image in the picture, while picking out some sombre minor chords with his left hand, almost like a funeral march.

Jeff laughed to himself, exhaled deeply and changed to a major key, playing louder for a few seconds in an attempt to disperse the melancholy death-wish which had descended over him yet again. 'Yes, it's definitely worth it, angel,' he projected into the room, as if on stage and in front of a huge crowd. 'You've always been worth it, and you're even more worth it now.'

His mind cast back to the previous weekend and to the romantic evening they had spent in this very room on the Sunday, before he had taken his dream girl to the airport. The lonely soul remembered her eyes glinting with gleeful excitement, and how relaxed and peaceful he had felt when all but one had gone home after Saturday's dinner party. *The* one. The only one. He also recalled their unbridled passion earlier that same afternoon, and the intensity of their togetherness, faced with nearly a month apart after such a momentous couple of days.

Even though he could feel a gnawing sense of urgency building up inside, Jeff breathed a sigh of relief that he hadn't stayed out and sought solace in pleasures of the flesh. No doubt in his mind whatsoever. She, Lynn Dyson, his Lynn Dyson was definitely worth it.

It was now twenty-two-fifty-five, Australian Eastern Standard Time. What time was it in Germany? Were they eight or nine hours behind? Nearly two o'clock in the afternoon? The touring celebrity was unlikely to be in her hotel room, but he would feel better for having left a message for her to pick up later. Her sex-starved boyfriend picked up the telephone, playing with his nagging testicles at the same time.

'*Hilton München, guten Tag. Wie ich kann, Ihren Anruf leiten?*' requested a brisk, feminine voice on a crackly line.

'*Guten Tag,*' replied the man in Melbourne. '*Das Fräulein Dyson, bitte.* Lynn Dyson. *Zimmer acht-Hundert-drei.*'

He wasn't absolutely sure of the room number. There were so many hotel rooms in so many cities. He hoped she hadn't flown on to Frankfurt already.

'Hello?'

Whoa! She was there... Was he dreaming? This single vivacious word drenched him like a cool shower on a humid summer evening. It was all Jeff could do not to cry with relief upon hearing it.

'Lynn, it's me. *Wie geht's?* Jesus, this is good! I was expecting to leave a message, but here you are.'

'Jeff, is that you? Oh, it's so good to hear your voice. I'm fine. What about you?' she replied, the American accent all but eradicated these days. 'I just called in here on my way back from lunch to grab some other clothes. Another minute, and I would've been gone.'

'Great! I don't want to hold you up. I just thought I'd ring to say hi. Christ, I miss you,' her boyfriend told her. 'I've had a tough day and really wanted to make contact, even with a machine.'

The young singer was quiet for a second before responding cheerfully, as if matching his mood in order to break him out of it. 'Thanks. I miss you too. So much. Are you OK? Why did you have such a tough day?'

Grateful for her sympathy, the tired man debated whether to worry her about the meeting with her dad. He decided to spare her. It could wait until she returned.

He lightened up and focussed instead on his fading erection. 'Oh, it doesn't really matter. It's just nice to talk to you and imagine you here in front of me. I feel better already.'

The inspired songwriter could feel his head clearing and Lynn's positive vibes quickly penetrating his soul. Visualising her naked body and her beautiful, smiling face was providing some positive vibes elsewhere too.

'What's going on over there?' he asked. 'Did you win any more awards?'

'Yes, two, thanks. They love you over here. Your posters are everywhere.'

'I love you over here,' Jeff stopped her. 'Tell me about you, not me. I know about me already.'

The young woman laughed at his turn of phrase. 'You're so funny. *I'm* interested in you. It gives me much more pleasure to see your posters than mine. Or isn't that allowed?'

'Thanks, angel. That's very kind, but no, it's absolutely *verboten*. Such selfless thoughts are only valid before lunch,' her boyfriend quipped. 'So what's on this afternoon?'

'Sound checks and a few interviews, and then on stage at eight. Did you want me to ring you in the middle of the night? I don't want to risk waking you up but I can't wait to talk to you for longer.'

Jeff leaned back in the chair, feeling his pants becoming tighter by the minute. This separate togetherness was sweet persecution indeed. He pictured Lynn's hands on his bulging organ, and then her mouth, running his fingers across the taut, sensitive skin of its tip and imagining her tongue in their place.

'You can wake me up any time, gorgeous,' he groaned in pleasure. 'I miss you so much.'

'I miss you too, very much, but I'm going to have to go soon. They'll be waiting for me downstairs. It's great that you rang at exactly the right time. Did you know I'd be here?'

'Of course I did,' the Pied Piper lied with a smile he hoped she could hear.

'Psychic powers?' his dream girl laughed again. 'Is there no end to your talents? Did you ring for any specific reason, or just that you'd had a tough day?'

'Hey, angel... I need your inspiration to take care of something that just won't go away,' he changed the subject. 'If you know what I mean...'

'Oh,' the naïve songstress replied, her distracted brain a little shocked to work out what the sex-mad caller was referring to, but also flattered to have this new topic of conversation on her agenda. 'Well, that's good from my perspective. I should be happy you have this problem, I suppose, but I'm not sure how I can help.'

Jeff chuckled at her response and at the embarrassed inflection in her voice. He tugged his pants and undies further down his legs and worked up a steady rhythm while listening to her voice. He was quite convinced he would be able to make himself come before the end of her next sentence, imagining how the image would be turning his lover on too.

'Believe me, you're already helping,' he told her, unsure how far to take her on this particular journey, especially when she ought to be on her way out of the room. 'Have you ever had 'phone sex before?'

'No!' Lynn exclaimed and then sighed, 'but I expect you have.'

'Actually, no, I haven't,' her lover reassured her, releasing his grip and redirecting his one-tracked mind where it ought rightly to be. 'You forget how new this monogamous status is for me, my gorgeous flatmate. Sex on its own is like milk or a loaf of bread. Nothing special, but it satisfies a basic need. Just one of life's necessities.'

His stunned girlfriend giggled. 'Really? It sounds like you're just off down the road for some fish'n'chips.'

'Exactly! Before, if I wanted sex, I used to go out hunting for it. But you... That's altogether different. Things've changed, Lynn. I mean it.'

'Oh, thank you. I love you,' the blonde beauty gasped, overcome by his unwavering resolve. 'I don't know what to say. I can hardly say "Congratulations." That'd be incredibly patronising, wouldn't it?'

Her boyfriend laughed out loud. 'Too right! Spooky as this may seem, I was thinking right at that moment how annoyed I'd be if you congratulated me, for that very reason. So thank you.'

He heard his long-distance girlfriend take a deep breath, and his desire welled up again.

'But I do want to acknowledge how much it means to me, and how much I know you've given up for us,' she added, slightly tentative now. 'Can I say that without sounding patronising?'

'Angel, you're perfect,' the aroused man moaned, more due to his own progress towards climax than because he was captivated by her words, but the response was appropriate for both purposes. 'You are really turning me on. I'm as hard as a rock sitting here, just in case you wanted to know.'

The woman in the northern hemisphere inhaled audibly. 'I like that idea, I have to admit, even if it is a little awkward hearing it on the other side of the world.'

'Sorry, gorgeous,' her lover responded, backing off a little again. 'Anyway, you have to go now, before we get you into a state that's too inconvenient for you to spend the afternoon in, and one which I can't do anything about from here either.'

'Jeff, that's disgusting!'

'No, it's not. It's perfectly normal. You're just not used to talking about it.'

'Damned right!' she exclaimed in a strong American accent. 'Are you?'

'No,' the amused man admitted. 'It is weird, I grant you. Anyway, get out of there and leave me alone. Enjoy yourself, but not too much until we get to try this again. OK?'

'OK! Thanks, I think,' the young celebrity replied. 'We're going to have to try again when I've got more time. I don't think I'm playing the game right.'

Jeff caught his breath, diverting his attention temporarily from the naked and writhing vision in his mind. 'That's priceless, Lynn,' he laughed. 'You know, once we get to London we should look at writing some comedy.'

'Hey, do you think these 'phone lines are tapped?'

'Christ! I hope not!' the obsessive man instantly picked up on his girlfriend's nerves.

'Dad wouldn't go to that length, would he? It's perfectly reasonable for us to talk while I'm away. Perhaps he thinks we're both hatching a plan?'

Her black stallion breathed deeply and forced his mind back below his belt. There could not be two more conflicting emotions...

'Hatching a plan? Us? That's a ridiculous suggestion,' he scoffed. 'You've thrown me completely off track now. Get out of that room this minute, and I'll wait for your call in the middle of the night. We can give each other what we need, slowly and sensuously, and if your dad wants a tape, he's welcome to it.'

'Oh, my God! I don't want to think about that,' Lynn complained. 'I love you, Jeff. Sleep well. Talk soon.'

'You too. Have a good show. *Ich liebe Dich, mein Schatz.*'

'*Ich liebe your Dich* too,' his lover sent back and immediately put the telephone down.

Left in such a sublime lurch, the young man grinned as he imagined his very proper girlfriend coyly regretting her naughty words. Life was very good, despite the spectre of Bart Dyson's investigation hovering over them. This heady process of getting to know each other for a second time was in some way extra compensation for the long, dark months now behind him.

Both Lynn and he were certainly leading very different lives compared to who they were two years ago. How on Earth could Bart Dyson accuse them of going backwards? They had been kids last time, just playing the dating game. This time it was for real, and there was no doubt that she felt it as much as he did. The adult incarnation of their relationship was already much deeper, and their forced separation appeared to be giving them both a much better understanding of what they wanted from it.

By rights, Jeff mused, stretching out on the couch, they should really have met now for the first time. It would have been so much more straightforward meeting an adult Lynn Dyson, but just think of the journey they had already been on... Perhaps this was why it wasn't possible to choose when two souls collide?

Game, Set And Match

'Papá!' Kierney gasped, jumping as her father's hands landed on her shoulders. 'It was so nice and peaceful in here with just me and Indie. Boys! Go and play somewhere else.'

Her brother and Gerry were wrestling each other for the patch of free cushion on the leather couch, having returned to the house through the study's French windows. All three men had been kicking the football outside on the lawn for the last hour or so of twilight, until it got too dark to see what they were doing. The family's rented golden retriever had seen sense early, deciding the calm indoor environment and the teenager's friendly female fingers would yield far more tender loving care.

'Get off!' Ryan yelped, losing out to the Irishman and being pushed onto the floor. 'This isn't even your house! Go home and torture Fiona instead.'

'Mate, you have a closer relationship with my kids than you do with your own,' the widower frowned.

'Yeah. S'pose I do. I know you guys better.'

The cricketer burst out laughing. 'No shit!'

'Right then! Respect your elders, Boy Wonder,' the Diamonds' longstanding manager teased. 'I know you guys much better.'

Jeff dealt his old friend a hard stare. 'And whose fault is that?'

'What about John and Alex?' Kierney piped up from the other side of the room, referring to Gerry's soon-to-be stepsons. 'Are you planning to get to know them?'

The accountant wasn't in the least offended by such a direct question, his aversion to children no secret. 'We go to the footy together.'

'Yeah. So do eighty thousand other people. Make us some coffee, please, Ry?' his dad requested, peering over his daughter's head at the computer monitor in an attempt to discover which part of his autobiography she was currently proofreading. 'How're you going, *pequeñita*? Easy or tough?'

'Easy. Very easy at the moment.'

A raucous ringtone they all instantly recognised disturbed the dark-haired pair's concentration, and Gerry fumbled in his pants pocket to retrieve his mobile telephone. Before he could accept the call, it had been knocked out of his hand by the mischievous nineteen-year-old.

'Oh, hi, Fiona,' he greeted their visitor's *fiancée*. 'Yes, he's here, but we've tied him up. We caught him stealing the silverware. Do you want him back? I'm willing to negotiate a handsome ransom.'

Jeff laughed at the oft-used phrase from his children's childhood, wagging a scolding finger. 'Silverware? Do we even have any of that? Give it over, son.'

The larrikin dutifully offered the handset to its rightful owner and exited the office, though not before he had needled the tapered toe of his shoe into the older man's shin. Gerry grimaced, leaning down and rubbing it through his drenched trouser leg. In truth, it hardly hurt, and the face he pulled was more because he was receiving a dressing down for not having left his favourite clients' Burnley South residence on time.

There followed a long pause during which it appeared the Blake & Partners Chief Executive was once again in the firing line at home. His old friend rolled the second office chair up close to his daughter's and kissed her cheek. They swapped enquiring and amused expressions as Gerry's story gradually unfolded. They soon discovered that the indomitable one was due at his partner's parents' for dinner, a social engagement which had quite clearly been overlooked.

'Yes, yes, yes,' tutted the refined but exasperated accent. 'I'm leaving now. Be there in ten, honey. Yes, with wine. Of course.'

'Dog house again?' the compassionate seventeen-year-old asked. 'Look at your pants! They're soaking, and yours, Papá!'

'Yes, boss,' Gerry and Jeff both answered at the same time and in the same bored tone, dissolving into a fit of drunken giggles at their identical retorts. 'Another suit for the dry cleaners.'

The young woman shook her head like a disappointed parent, not at all surprised to see her father rip his belt out of its loops and undo his fly, stripping down to his socks and shorts on the spot. Standards of behaviour were definitely slipping in the Diamond household with each month that went by without the oversight of their former resident etiquette officer.

'Can you take these too, please, mate?' Jeff tossed his wet suit trousers at his manager and lifted their matching jacket off the hook on the back of the study door.

'Yes, Your Lordship. It'll be my honour to take care of your laundry, sir,' the older man bowed and tugged his forelock graciously while unleashing a wild kick at his friend's nearby naked and hairy leg. 'Anything else for your pleasure this evening? And yes, Kizzo, dog house it is. No change there. I've told Fiona I want to move to the Sunshine Coast after the wedding. I'm putting my foot down.'

'Sunshine Coast?' Kierney cried. 'Why the Sunshine Coast?'

'Why not? It's warm, and I can moor the boat there,' Gerry shrugged. 'I've successfully avoided my own olds for so long, moving to Melbourne when I did. Now I'm stuck with hers, and to be brutally honest, I can't be effing bothered.'

The grieving husband lit two cigarettes and handed one to the youngster, before throwing the packet to his buddy. 'Watch out, mate. They'll move to Queensland after you. Besides, mums are wonderful things, aren't they, Kizzy?'

'Yes, they are,' his daughter agreed, leaning her head over until it touched her dad's arm. 'But what about John and Alex? Alex is going to uni' in Melbourne, isn't he? I saw him at a party recently.'

Gerry nodded. 'They're going to live with their dad. Already made that choice.'

'You or they, mate?' Jeff slapped his departing manager on the shoulder.

'Bit of both. Gotta go, you fucker,' he sneered, waving and heading for the door. 'And coming from a bloke who talks to an angel via his tattoo, I fail to see why I should pay any attention to your preaching on this occasion.'

His lonely mate sniffed. 'Fair enough. I'll cop that, even in front of these guys, and I'll continue to wallow in my delusion. Quite frankly, as the rest of my body insists on recovering faster than my heart, I probably continue to believe it just to have something to cling onto, since I have nothing physical to cling onto. Unlike you, mate, who should be gone now. It works for me, and everyone else can piss off.'

'They will if you keep talking to them like that!' was the accountant's parting shot.

'So be it. *Adios, mi amigo.*'

''Night, kids.'

Kierney and Ryan wished the eternal flyboy a goodnight too, helping themselves to coffee from the tray with which the young man had returned. The Diamonds teased Gerry regularly about the distance he insisted on keeping from his *fiancée*'s two sons, almost as if he were frightened that he might actually enjoy becoming their stepfather.

The teenagers were left on their own for several minutes while the two close friends departed, one to face the music and the other to put some dry clothes on. They were so deep in conversation about the chapters currently being proofread that they didn't notice Jeff sneak back in to overhear their divergent opinions.

'So what do you think of it?' the widower brought his children's attention back to the words on the screen. 'Where've you got to?'

The seventeen-year-old looked up into her beloved papá's eyes. 'The part where Mamá dropped the velvet London bomb on you.'

'Shit! Yeah, that was a good one,' he chuckled. 'She misjudged that one somewhat. Although I think it was Freud at work, in all honesty. I think subconsciously she was still testing me. But the look on her face when I flipped out was of utter horror.'

'I bet,' Ryan chimed in. 'She told us about it, didn't she, Kiz. I'm not even sure where you were. Away somewhere, and we were talking over dinner. In the kitchen at Escondido.'

Kierney's face lit up. 'Oh, yeah! I remember that too. Ages ago. She said she thought you were going to jump over the balcony.'

Jeff sunk down into the couch which Gerry had vacated, winded by the vivid suggestion. 'No, I wouldn't have done that. My thoughts weren't that organised, for starters. She told me later that day that it was like having to defuse a ticking bomb in record time, and describing it that way did us both a good turn. I never put her through that again. You know what? Don't focus on that stuff, guys. Does it read OK?'

'Oh, yes,' the youngster assured him, scrolling up to find a favourite passage in her parents' wondrous reunion. 'It's really beautiful. I cried at least ten times in the space of a few pages. I absolutely love this chapter. Your happiness really shines through. Such a contrast from the last few.'

'*Gracias, pequeñita*,' her father sighed. 'It was. "The greatest happiness of life is the conviction that we are loved; loved for ourselves, or rather, loved in spite of ourselves."'

'Let me guess,' Ryan chuckled at yet another literary quotation. '*Le vieux monsieur Hugo* again?'

'*Bien sûr, mes amis.* Nothing's ever dulled the memories of those last three months of 'seventy-four. We changed so much during that short time. Probably more than in the rest of our life.'

The young cricketer, regularly amazed at the depth of his parents' relationship at an age as tender as his own, approached the back of his sister's chair casually. The content of the upcoming autobiography fascinated him, although he did his best not to show it. He was in no hurry to broadcast his own romantic streak, with so much to achieve in sport and at university, and even within himself, he was struggling to admit to a secret hankering for the same type of fulfilment portrayed in his dad's idyllic prose.

'You were confident that Grandpa wouldn't find anything though, weren't you?' he turned to ask.

'No. Not really,' Jeff answered. 'Look back at Mamá's trial... Well-resourced prosecutors can make a case for any verdict, guys, with the right incentive. I thought I knew what my truth was during those Stones Road days, but had no idea how many people shared this version. I was prepared to defend all manner of lies about me and my family, some of which I couldn't be sure were actually lies.'

His sentimental daughter frowned, her left index finger pointing out a particular paragraph. 'But why did you think G and G had such strong feelings about you being together? To me, by the way you've written it, it almost seems like they hated the idea of Mamá being in love with you for itself, and the whole criminal background and Granddad being in prison was just a convenient bandwagon to jump on.'

The author smiled and sighed heavily. 'Interesting observation, gorgeous. If that's how you interpret it, I'd better tone it down, or they'll sue my estate.'

'Dad,' his son snarled.

'Yeah, mate. Sorry, but whatever... The hostility your grandpa felt towards me taking Lynn away from them came *verbatim* from her diary. I get the impression she wrote it straight afterwards, in the time between ringing me to say she was making a run for it and turning up on my doorstep looking like every Christmas and birthday present wrapped into one.'

The children watched their father wipe a rogue tear from his right eye, the image powerful in all three minds.

'What they'd said to her that morning was nothing compared with what was to come. He really stepped it up for the rest of the year. A three-way battle of wills, with your mamá stuck in the middle, right up until we left for the UK.'

'Then they admitted defeat?' Kierney asked.

'Sorta, kinda,' their dad shrugged. 'They couldn't stop me moving to London. I think he just conveniently gave the order to move on, so we all did.'

The blond sportsman, who idolised his grandfather as much as he did the swarthy, dark-hearted philosopher who had given him life, levered himself off the sofa and announced that he was going out. Jeff made no attempt to stop him, apart from a farewell squeeze of his muscular shoulder and a few shared crude comments about the night's promise. The virile pair had long since resolved this particular familial conflict, having thrashed more than the countryside a few months earlier, dressed in motorcycle leathers and battling the inhospitable weather on their manly Welsh odyssey.

In the time it took for his daughter to return with a fresh pot of coffee and a surprise dessert the men had brought home from the city after their drinking session, the widower had spread a dozen photographs out on the surface of the desk. He took a bowl of the sugary treat in return for a loving kiss on the youngster's forehead. She understood too. It was hard for all of them, but this protracted grieving process gave them no alternative but to navigate through its density in a whole host of weird and wonderful ways.

'Have you ever seen this one?' the forty-four-year-old spoke through a large mouthful.

He flicked a photograph towards Kierney as though he was skimming a stone across the surf, and she tapped it down onto her knee with her free hand. She turned it over to reveal a picture of a grinning Lynn Dyson having the wardrobe door shut on her in their city apartment, apparently being pushed

341

back into her hanging clothes and with something white stuck to her forehead. The dark-haired gipsy caught her breath, recognising this instantly as the remover's label which had reserved her future mother's space in her future father's life.

'No!' she gasped. 'What were you doing?'

Jeff had tears in his eyes again too, rejoicing in the teenager's genuine reaction. 'I found her camera after we moved her stuff in, so I thought I'd get me a souvenir of that incredible day.'

'She looks so happy.'

'Yep. We both were.'

'It must've been an amazing time,' Kierney whispered dreamily.

Her father tossed over another photograph from the assortment on the desk, this time with an impish flash of his eyes. 'How about this one?'

'What the hell is that? Is it rude?'

'No, but I'm getting to that part,' Jeff chuckled. 'It's a self-portrait.'

The young woman turned the old three-by-five-inch print over and over, trying on different angles to see if she could make sense of what she was looking at. After several attempts, she finally picked out two sets of interlocked lips taken very close up and from one side of their faces. She heard her father sniff as soon as her eyes must have signalled the association as forged in her mind. Both children appreciated their remaining parent's subtle efforts to shore up their mental resilience, and a rush of love surged through her impressionable body.

'It's beautiful, Papá,' she cried, sliding her empty bowl onto the desk and climbing onto his lap. 'Odd as anything, but beautiful.'

Jeff hugged her tightly. 'See Mamá's eyes are closed but mine are open? I always loved seeing her eyes closed when we kissed. Like she felt safe.'

'That's lovely. I'm sure she did feel safe. Did you ever talk about your Sydney conversation again?'

'Yeah, regularly,' the lonely man replied, hoping not to impart too many desolate feelings along with this subliminal transfer of happy memories. 'It ceased to be the elephant in the room pretty immediately. For both of us.'

'That's lovely,' Kierney repeated, laughing. 'Elephant in the room is so wanky. I'm surprised you used that expression. Don't you think?'

Her father rubbed his chest, actually feeling nothing but seeking to capitalise on the moment's therapeutic effects. '*Sí, pequeñita.* Although Mamá's scolding you for using such a bad word. As Celia would say, "Wanky is not a word we use in this house, young lady."'

'Sorry Celia,' the seventeen-year-old giggled, running her hands over her dad's shirt. 'And sorry, Mamá, but you would've laughed too.'

'Jesus! You saw through that?' Jeff cried out. 'That's not fair. You're too good, KLF. Too fucking good.'

'For my own fucking good,' the precocious student cocked her head to one side flirtatiously. 'So tell me what you talked about, once all that horrible stuff was no longer a secret.'

The forty-four-year-old couldn't help laughing. '*Attention, mademoiselle audacieuse!* Pride comes before a fall.'

A scream rang around the room, accompanied by a cacophony of disgruntled huffs and puffs with some reluctant laughter thrown in. Before Kierney had a chance to grab onto her father's neck, she had suddenly found herself falling through an unexpected gap between his long legs, ending up in an ungainly mess of skirt and feet on the floorboards. Indie thought this was the best game ever, joining in the humiliation and licking the teenager's face while she struggled to her feet.

'You gentleman not of illegitimate origins!' she yelped through gritted teeth, sitting herself down in the other office chair. 'Stop treating me like a child.'

'You are a child,' Jeff smiled. 'Like it or not, *pequeñita*. Just like your mamá was. You both hate it, and I understand. I'm sorry. You OK?'

Kierney nodded. 'Get on with the story, and I might forgive you.'

Coughing, the amused orator looked towards the ceiling for inspiration, this time receiving it by way of a sharp tingling sensation in his "JL" tattoo. 'Mamá did ask me if I'd ever killed anyone.'

'Wow! Did she? She didn't seriously think you did?'

'I don't know. Maybe she did!' Jeff shrugged, finishing his coffee and slamming the mug back down onto the tray. 'I remember wondering why I hadn't taken her question as offensive. As an insult, you know...'

'Yes. I can imagine,' the young woman exclaimed. 'Why did she ask? Did you find out?'

The grieving husband shook his head. 'Didn't have to. I suppose because it was a perfectly reasonable question, given the information I'd recently shared with her. Tell you one thing though... I'd have been ropable if anyone else had asked me the same question.'

'Grandpa, for example,' his daughter giggled.

'Yeah! Absolutely. I would've bawled him out; probably even hit him. But from Lynn it was a perfectly reasonable question.'

And the boy from Canley Vale answered again, for the sake of today's significant teenager. 'No, I haven't.'

'I know, Papá. Mamá did tell me one story a while ago...'

'What was that?' Jeff asked, bracing himself and making the big-hearted seventeen-year-old giggle once more.

'It's good,' she insisted. 'Well... It's good in the end.'

'Shit! That sounds ominous. Go on.'

'It's late. Anyway, it was about when you were both going on your separate tours...'

Kierney stretched and stifled a yawn, holding out her hand. She picked up the tray of empty crockery and led her obedient father out of the office, trying to avoid being tripped up by the excitable Labrador. The pair cleared away the remains of their takeaway dinner and adjourned to the patio before they and their trusty hound turned in, immersed in the detailed rendition of this latest episode.

'Mamá said you were trying so hard to control your emotions that evening, when you were down to your last hour before she was flying out again. You started to continually badger her, chanting, "Kiss me, kiss me, kiss me," over and over again and trying to cuddle her.'

She looked up to gauge the bereft man's appetite for these bare truths and met inviting eyes.

'She said she refused,' the young woman continued. 'At first, she was laughing, she said. Then, when it was starting to get really annoying, she began shaking her head and then even getting angry with you.'

'Yep. I remember.'

'Finally, Mamá said she just turned away, and you gave up. But then she saw such dread on your face when you figured you'd pushed her too far, and she immediately felt so guilty that she turned back and kissed you anyway.'

'Yep. I remember,' Jeff sighed again, his eyes wet with tears. 'I know where you're going with this. I haven't written about it. D'you think I should?'

Kierney frowned, leaning forwards to scratch the front of his shirt, as if trying to attract her mother's attention. 'That's up to you guys. It depends if it's too private, I suppose. She said you gave her a big grin, as if it was all part of an elaborate game. Deception, she said, I think...'

'Yep. Deception is exactly the word she used. She inhaled a whole lungful of air and shook her head,' the bereaved husband recounted, holding his daughter's hand over the breast pocket of his shirt, under which the skin was stinging sweetly. 'And did she tell you which word came out next, *pequeñita*?'

The teenager paused for a second or two, pulling her hand back and settling into the cushioned comfort of the outdoor furniture. 'Poisonous,' she whispered.

'Mamá was hurt and angry,' Jeff nodded. 'I told her I couldn't stop. "Can't you?" she asked. I was petrified. I thought I'd really fucked it all up again. I remember feeling like a five-year-old who'd broken something really expensive or precious that belonged to my grandparents.'

'Like when Ry was caught playing with the security grille at Escondido?'

'Yeah. Exactly like that.'

'Mamá told me that it looked like your eyes were shrinking into your head, and that your body language was full of remorse. She said she made a promise to herself then and there to fix such anti-social behaviour.'

'Jesus Christ! How long ago did she tell you this?'

'Not that long ago,' Kierney answered thoughtfully. 'After my sixteenth, I think. You were away somewhere, and it was the start of Year Twelve. Do you mind that I know?'

Her father shrugged. 'Kind of irrelevant now, that question... Back in those out-of-control days, I always thought too much still wasn't enough. In one fell swoop, at the end of that stupendous weekend, she taught me how too much was too much.'

'Wow!' the young woman's eyes widened. 'That's a great way to describe it.'

'When your mamá used the word poisonous, I knew she didn't mean me. But the word resonated so deeply within me. This thing was poisoning me, making me behave so badly... the PTSD... and I wasn't fighting back hard enough. That's what she taught me with that single word. And when I left her at Admin that night, knowing I had almost a month on my own, Mamá asked me if I wanted her to go to the airport from my apartment. I said no, but I still didn't intend going home. I just expected to go and get drunk.'

Kierney laughed kindly. 'Some things never change.'

The great man chuckled. 'Doing all that crazy shit was my messed-up way of playing down the alarm bells ringing in my brain. It just made things worse, but I didn't know how else to react. Then, over the next few hours, she stopped it dead in its tracks, *comme on dit*. She just kept up the positive reinforcement, just like a parent. Kept telling me she was looking forward to coming back and all the good things we'd get up to once she was back.'

'Like Celia again,' his daughter giggled, putting on a haughty accent. '"We don't do that in this house, darling, do we?"'

'*Exactamente, gorgeousita*. But I still went and got drunk. I didn't show you the rest of those pictures.'

'*Mañana, Papá*. It's too late. What are they?'

'More of our idiotic self-portraits. You know, some of them never came back from the developers.'

'I wonder why!' the mature teenager laughed. 'You must've hoped no-one would blackmail you with them, if they managed to identify your naked identities.'

Her father heaved his tall frame off the bench and reached his hands out to assist his loyal companion to do the same. Calling the dog inside and made their way through the house, he put his arm around the big-hearted teenager. He knew she was tired, but they both derived energy from these deep and

345

meaningful conversations. Thinking back to the compromising photographs the young couple had taken stirred feelings of a whole different nature inside the solitary soul, seeking to suppress the anger which invariably accompanied such carnal memories.

'I always knew when your mamá was in need of attention.'

'Attention?' Kierney repeated, eyes wide with amusement. 'You mean sex, I'm guessing. *Buenas noches, Papá.*'

'No. Listen,' he grinned, leaning against the wall at the top of the staircase. 'This is a good one. You'll like this. She used to scratch her fingernails along my thigh. You know, the sensitive area over your hammies, just under the bum cheeks.'

'Papá! Too much info'!'

'Jeez, it was instantaneous,' Jeff shoved both hands into his pants pockets, becoming quickly aroused and knowing he ought to tell his saucy tale and retire *pronto*. '"Yep, I'm ready, angel," I'd say. "Turn me over and do your damndest."'

The dark-haired romantic smiled patiently. 'Hmm... It does sound good. I'll have to try that! Goodnight.'

Jeff turned towards his bedroom. 'Sometimes I used to ignore her, to fire her up a bit more. She always saw through it though, reaching round and taking me in hand. Mamá'd whisper right close to my ear, "Are you keeping this all to yourself?" "Not if I can help it, woman." Sweet payback indeed, eh, baby?'

'Are you sure you're not ready for some real action?' Kierney asked, only half in jest. 'That's what Jetto'd say if he'd just had to listen to all that pornography.'

'Kiz, you can tell your brother I'm getting plenty of action. My *Regala* comes to visit me pretty much every night these days. It's an adjustment, but we've worked things out until there's a better alternative.'

'Good,' the young woman said, standing on tiptoes to kiss her horny father goodnight before crouching down and doing the same to the expectant dog. 'It's like 'phone sex all over again. Have fun, all three of you.'

'*Absoluement*. Sleep well, *pequeñita,*' Jeff waited while the willowy beauty let herself into her bedroom and closed the door firmly behind her. 'Except I can't hear her breathing.'

Inside the cavernous master bedroom which would never feel like home, the widower sat down on the bed and peeled off his clothes. Bundling them up into a ball, he launched them into the corner and watched as each individual item flung itself in a separate direction, set to commune with its crusty cousins until the room's occupant felt compelled to throw them all into the washing machine.

Indie had already settled himself down into his bed, pawing at the blanket until he was satisfied that three turns would yield the required level of comfort. Jeff leaned over and fondled his soft furry head on the way into the *en suite*. He hadn't expected to like sharing his nights with a dog, since he and Lynn had always closed their door to housemates of the canine variety. These days however, whenever he arrived back from a trip and found himself sleeping alone, whether in advance of collecting Indie from Suzanne's or if Kierney had stolen him for her own company, he found he missed his snoring and farting roomie.

'You here, angel?'

The hot jets showered the remnants of sweat from the tired man's body, aching after several hard tackles during the evening's football game. He did his best to conjure up the graphic details that he had recounted for his long-suffering daughter under the guise of happy memories. Happy memories they were indeed, but the moment had passed, and the only sensory subsistence to present itself tonight simply drove him to tears.

'No 'phone sex tonight, Lynn? Are you pissed off that I'm sharing so much?'

After a few minutes of spiritless masturbation, the world's greatest lover managed to coax some life into himself. He returned to the bedroom and selected an album of duets that he and his beautiful best friend had recorded when the children were toddlers, pressing the Play button and laying out on top of the covers. His penis responded to the caress of Lynn's velvet voice, as did his heart.

'Thanks, gorgeous. How're you going to get me out of bed tomorrow? I have to finalise the carve-up of the companies in the morning and talk to Gerry about retirement. He's threatening Queensland. Did you hear? Fiona's not going to like that!'

Bygone fantasies washed through the billionnaire's eyes on swollen teardrops. He imagined Lynn lying next to him, nude but for the brand new eternity ring he had given her as a birthday gift, her smile illuminating the room as she recited lines from a favourite song or a novel she was reading. Words of love blocked out all other sound, drowning him in their sensuous depth.

As the magic lifted his mood, Jeff began to hear the music again, coaxing himself steadily towards climax. Now the couple was making love in the shallow surf under the cliffs of Escondido, with the sun setting over their shoulders. Bitter themes from the present day dared to infiltrate his pleasure, causing his beautiful best friend to sing louder and more tenderly until the lyric's power overcame his sorrow.

Whoa! How this amazing woman could transport him away to places he had almost forgotten... Or perhaps they were places they had yet to visit? This thought did the trick, and he felt his balls constrict, sending stimulating currents through his whole body.

'I can see you, angel,' the passionate man spoke into the air, picturing themselves back at their hotel after a resplendent Mardi Gras in Brazil. 'How's that cocktail? Did you ever find out what was in it? Jesus, I love you so much. I want your wet lips over here, angel. Cold from the ice, wrapped around me to make me come. Will you do that? We'll be back together soon.'

Lynn's ghost obediently placed her martini glass on some ethereal side table out of her husband's field of vision and came to kneel on the bed by his side. He could feel her long hair brushing his skin and her teeth scrape lightly along his aching shaft, teasing him exquisitely. The soul-mates made love as though no barrier existed between her world and his, and together they soared to heaven again.

The damp spring night in Burnley South transformed into summer in Rio de Janiero, Lynn's smooth, tanned flesh entwined with his long, muscular limbs until he could imagine the sublimity of death finally upon him. His saviour was squeezing every last ounce of energy from him, ensuring he would sleep well for another night. Elation overtook him, injecting his system with much needed endorphins, and it somehow gave him strength to face tomorrow, knowing he would be one step closer to their destiny.

Jeff raised his left hand and placed it over his heart, where the skin was stinging merrily. 'D'you remember when you'd stick a bottle in one of my hands and a baby in the other and tell me to tell them everything I knew about landfill?'

His tattoo served another twinge, causing him to inhale sharply. There was no doubt his ghostly partner could hear him. He knew no-one else believed him, and why should they? How could it possibly happen? But who else but Lynn would respond to such a bizarre observation?

'Yeah, landfill. I knew you'd remember,' the grieving man cried, bringing himself slowly but surely towards the type of melancholy physical climax that served these days as sexual gratification. 'Or geography or party politics. I know you did it more to break me out of the doldrums and start my engines than to give our kids a subconscious head-start on their education.'

His breathing became erratic as orgasm rushed upon him. 'Head-start,' he chuckled, arching his back and coming by his own hand. 'Ah, yeah. That's good, angel. Thanks. It worked a treat back then, just like now.'

After a few minutes basking in spent rapture, Jeff swung his legs over the side of the bed and returned to the bathroom to rid himself of the evidence of this latest indecorous act. Indie raised his head briefly, following their routine and knowing it would be his turn for some tearful human affection in a few minutes' time.

'Fuck these one-way conversations, Lynn,' the desperate man shouted at the mirror. 'Fuck everything. Bring me home, baby. Just bring me fucking home.'

Sure enough, feeling calmer after having let loose yet another batch of tears, Jeff pulled his side of the quilt back and slapped the other half for his four-legged *confidant* to take his rightful place. This was Indie's very favourite part of the day, seeming more than content to sit through a regular nightly program comprising a male stripper's floorshow followed by a Greek tragedy, as long as he was granted ten minutes of his superstar master's undivided attention to bring the entertainment to a close.

'What do you know about weddings, boy?'

Man and his substitute best friend wrestled on top of the bedclothes for several minutes, paws flailing through the air in an effort to be caught, only then to squirm free from his opponent's strong grip. Careful jaws would close on Jeff's wrist, applying precisely the right amount of pressure to see Indie's pinned limbs released before too long. With Lynn's input channelling through the music, the forthcoming chapter's coverage of the Jeff Diamond Band's bass player's wedding was discussed at length, particularly the show put on by the Dysons in another peculiar attempt to turn their daughter away from her no-good lover.

'I hope you're coming to Gerry and Fiona's wedding, angel. It's in Byron Bay, so book your ticket soon. No need to worry about accommodation. I've got that covered. I don't even know if we'd get married if we were the kids' age now, heading into a new millennium? Would we, Lynn?'

To the best man's utter delight, an intense shiver shot through his chest, coupled with a vivid image of his departed wife in one of her most seductive poses. She wasn't wearing the wedding dress which had taken their breath away on New Year's Day nineteen-seventy-six. Instead, his dream girl was clad only in the lemon-coloured bikini to which his senses had been treated on the lovers' very first excursion to Coldwater Creek. One ornament was out of place however, Jeff noticed, as the golden-haired, tanned goddess turned her back and waited for him to kiss her left shoulder.

Yet how gloriously *in place…*

The dreamer ran his thumb over their shared symbol. '*D'accord*, angel. *Comme tu veux.*'

***

Taking advantage of an unusually sober and positive mood, Australia's bestselling recording artist had risen before the sun and hit the road, determined to run off the mounting animal energy which proved more stubborn to assuage with each passing day. Lynn and he had spent almost two hours on the telephone the previous night, rendered easier now she was in Singapore and with only two hours' time difference. Moreover, they were on the homeward leg of their mammoth three-and-a-half week vacuity.

Jeff knew his beautiful best friend was humouring him to a certain extent as they taught each other the dubious art of sexual intercourse via the telephone. Despite its sometimes amusing, sometimes self-conscious winding path and its extremely pleasurable rewards, both concluded that remote lovemaking was not a patch on the real thing.

Lynn had cried openly when her devoted lover renewed his promise to resist temptation, thereby fuelling his resolve yet further and carrying him all the way through the howling night to an early and enthusiastic awakening the next morning. He had sprung out of bed, donned his sports clothes and left the apartment within ten minutes, knowing he only had a short time in which to start the dopamine flowing before the great depression would set in again.

At first, the athlete hadn't noticed the flashing red light on his answering machine when he returned home, having crashed through the open front door and straight into the shower. It was only after he had dressed and made himself some coffee that he sat down on the couch to check his diary for the day and spied the message indicator blinking at him.

'Jeff, hi. Are you there?'

Shit! It was Lynn, and she sounded less than pleased. What had happened? Immediately, the young man was filled with shame and longing, regretting having been out for so long. It was clear by the tone in her voice that he should have been at home to take this call. What would she be thinking? Where was he first thing in the morning? And who was he with? He hoped the romance that had been infused into last night's long-distance antics had given the gorgeous creature sufficient cause to trust him.

'Oh, well... Guess what!' the message continued, his favourite female voice especially shrill and excited. 'You'll never believe what they've done now... Mum's turned up at the tennis tournament with a new boyfriend for me! Can you believe that?'

What? Jeff snapped out of his gloomy, self-deprecating disappointment and became instantly irate instead. The Dysons must be absolutely hell-bent on keeping their daughter away from him if they were now wheeling substitutes directly into overseas venues. Didn't this constitute interfering with her schedule, which was one of the criteria which her father had been so obdurate about preventing?

'Jesus fucking Christ,' the angry man in Melbourne swore under his breath, winding back the tape to replay the rest of Lynn's message, having lost all concentration.

'I just wanted to tell you as soon as possible, just in case some photographer snaps us together. Please don't be worried, because I don't want anything to do with him. I don't want to leave a long, drawn-out message about it either. I'll try and ring later on. I really want to talk to you. I love you, Jeff. Hope you're OK. Love you. Bye.'

So he wasn't to be worried. *Sure thing*, the tortured soul worked hard to steady his heart rate. That much was good, at least. Easier said than done. It seemed draconian in the extreme for his dream girl's parents to have lined up a suitable partner and chaperoned him to a sporting competition personally. How utterly bizarre, but how very par for the course! Lynn's message had said she didn't want anything to do with whoever this guy was, and therefore he must take her at her word. Funny how only minutes ago he had been hoping she would take him at his...

Without delay, the annoyed rock star dialled his girlfriend's hotel, just as he had done eight hours or so earlier. There was no answer from her room, and the receptionist happily informed him that Miss Dyson's key was safely stowed behind the counter. Damn! He had no way of contacting his dream girl, and now they were both left in limbo; a state in which people like him were doomed to failure. He felt the rumbling black clouds of all-too-familiar panic gathering in his chest, and engorged blood vessels began to throb behind his eyes.

The rock star opened his diary again to reveal a string of appointments taking him through to four o'clock that afternoon. Then, after these, he was due to fly to Los Angeles tomorrow morning for three more concerts at the Greek Theater, which had been sold out for months and were being hyped up wildly. Meanwhile, the Singapore Open tennis tournament would last the rest of the week, leaving four long days for Gravity the troll to taunt him about how close this mystery suitor might get to the love of his life. Jesus! He was only just beginning to master celibacy, and now he needed to add coping with jealousy to his list of skills to acquire.

But he wasn't to be worried. Lynn had said so, and this must be good enough.

Jeff snatched up his cigarettes and keys and crammed them into his trouser pockets, slinging his leather jacket over his shoulder. A violent slam of his front door helped to vent some aggression, and he was soon down at street level and bound for Stonebridge Music's offices in the middle of town. As he walked briskly through the rush-hour crowds, Lynn's peculiar message looped round and round in his mind.

The representatives of the recently-established Childlight charity were already seated in Reception when the prodigious venture capitalist arrived, being served coffee and generally fussed over. The celebrity immediately swung into charm offensive mode, managing to leave his new conundrum festering in the back of his head while he showed his guests into the meeting room.

On his way through the door, he pulled his office manager aside. 'Hey, Cath! Could you find out when the next 'plane to Singapore goes, please?'

'Singap...'

Jeff tapped his index finger on his lips to silence her questions. 'Please?'

The friendly employee's eyes widened. 'You *do* remember you're going to LA tomorrow?'

The millionnaire with money to burn glanced around at the roomful of good people waiting to spend it, before turning back to Cathy. 'Please just find out,' he urged. 'And let me know in the meeting?'

'OK!' the woman answered, frowning. 'As you wish.'

Jeff laughed at her superior sarcasm and closed the door after her. The proposal detailing new services planned for disadvantaged and abused children which his visitors had put together was professional and thorough, and the philanthropist fought with his overactive mind so as not to appear distracted. However, between each insightful and compassionate question he either asked or answered, visions of Lynn in someone else's arms and being kissed by another man continued to flash before his eyes.

Where had Cathy got to? Surely there was an aeroplane bound for Singapore at some point today? With any luck, he would be able to rebook his flight to the west coast of the USA in time for the sound check before his first gig. He and the band hardly needed to rehearse these days. A quick run-through would do, and they could easily scratch some of the less practised songs from their set without bothering the audience unduly.

Still the meeting dragged on, measured by the defiantly slow hands of the wall clock. Nine-forty-five and still no answer, and this presentation was supposed to go for another three quarters of an hour. Christ! Where was Cathy? The frantic obsessive was not prepared to lose his dream girl over this ridiculous stunt. He was not going to lose her.

By now, Jeff's anxiety was becoming almost impossible to hide, fidgeting in his chair and constantly looking towards the door. *Stop it*, he chastised himself. The people around his table deserved the respect of his sole focus. These were excellent goals they were intending for his money, and his accountants had already sequestrated the funds for them. His blood pressure was tracking so high that he could feel a pulse in his eardrums.

At last, one of the young administrative assistants whom Gerry had personally selected knocked on the door and excused herself, scanning the sea of faces until she found that of her boss. Jeff's eyes beckoned her over, and the junior scooted around the edge of the group almost as if her furtiveness might make her invisible to the others. She had a single, folded sheet of paper in her hand, which she handed to the handsome celebrity, smiling shyly.

I KNOW LYNN'S IN SINGAPORE, Cathy had written at the top, followed by four large exclamation marks.

'Thanks, Sam,' the young man whispered. 'Tell her I need it bad.'

Samantha gave a short shriek at his comment, the word "bad" elongated for particular emphasis. One of the charity workers could also be heard to titter beside the irresistible bad-boy. Both faces turned crimson as soon as Jeff made eye contact with them, and he dealt them a disarming wink to deepen their discomfort still further.

'OK,' the embarrassed office worker replied. 'Do you want me to go?'

Shaking his head and raising his hand to stop her, Jeff scanned the page quickly and then looked up at the clock. He would need to leave almost immediately if he was to stand any chance of making the flight, which the efficient Miss Patterson had also ascribed in her note, in the event that her boss were suddenly rendered incapable of telling the time.

'Ask her to book it now, please.'

Samantha nodded. 'I think she already did.'

The famous man smiled at the teenager. 'Perfect. Thanks. I'll be out shortly.'

Feeling calmer now that he knew he had a plan, Jeff turned his attention back to the presenters, who had trundled on undeterred while he had made these arrangements. They had reached the part where their cost calculations were under scrutiny, and one of Gerry's seconded hotshots was posing some clever hypotheticals to give the directors confidence that no stone was being left unturned. The numbers never excited the songwriter, except when they represented success indicators, so he gripped the edge of the table with both hands and prepared to interrupt the conversation.

'Guys, thanks,' he began, with all eyes instantly switching to the charismatic star. 'This is all great. I love what you want to do, but I have to get out of here. Can I leave you with Stuart to sort out whatever needs to be sorted out? We previously agreed three mill' now, and then we'll see what happens next year. Does that still work?'

There were a few relieved gasps and some muffled squeals of joy from around the room, and Jeff's gaze alighted on Fabienne, the chief proponent of this worthy and ground-breaking endeavour, who gave the impression she was about to pass out. She smiled and pulled herself together, watching the tall musician leave his chair and approach to offer his thanks.

As he did so, the rock star leaned over and kissed the startled woman on the cheek, causing most of the other females in the room to swoon visibly. Jeff then shook hands with two of the male representatives before turning to his loyal accountant and the other masterminds of the burgeoning Diamond Celebration Foundation.

'Sorry to cut this short, everyone,' he announced, making for the door. 'This is going to be really good. Let us know what you need, and we'll get it done. Thanks for putting all this together today.'

With a wave, the alluring celebrity left the room. Cathy was already stationed outside with a folder of information, which he guessed was originally scheduled to be passed to him at the end of the day, in preparation for flying to America again. He leafed through it idly, his mind already on its way to the airport. Hotel addresses and telephone numbers, his itinerary and an exhausting list of people he was due to meet over the coming three days of this stay.

'Thanks, Cath,' the young man said. 'You're fantastic.'

The office manager shrugged. 'Feeling randy, are we?'

Having lived through the star's dark rise over the last two years, Cathy had seen the best and worst of behaviour from the rebel with a cause: drugs hard and soft, drinks of every colour and an endless stream of young, nubile women had been freely laced through his colourful, fast-moving life. The star's skilled marketing specialist had only found out about her boss' previous relationship with Lynn Dyson after over a year in his service, having been overjoyed to hear that the couple was back together.

The discreet professional had also watched while in the space of the last few weeks the musical hotshot mutated into a model citizen; spending plenty of time in the office, lucid, serious and attentive to his many fans and to the companies' partner organisations. The return of Australia's darling had caused their wayward pin-up boy to straighten himself out and grow up, and she wondered whether such a high-profile relationship could possibly last. The two celebrities were like chalk and cheese on the surface, and as yet no-one in the office had met the stunning nineteen-year-old in person. Despite many conflicting rumours, the excited female contingent had no way of knowing the depth of reciprocal feeling Lynn Dyson might have for the lovesick puppy called Jeff Diamond.

It was also no secret that Cathy was very fond of the absolute hunk of a man standing next to her, smoking feverishly. She hoped he who had broken many, many hearts over recent months was not about to fall victim to his own heartbreak for a second time. Was this why he was changing his plans so impetuously and jetting off to Singapore for a matter of hours? The caring woman hoped not.

'You betcha,' her employer answered suggestively, fidgeting and looking at his watch. 'Can I go now, please, Miss?'

She laughed. 'Get out of here! Have a good time, and call me if you miss your flight to LA. There's only one other I could switch you to, but you'd be cutting things really fine.'

Jeff kissed the woman's cheek fondly and squeezed her shoulder, tucking the paperwork under his arm. 'I'm gone,' he announced. 'See you next week.'

***

The seven-hour flight from Tullamarine to Changi was tedious in the extreme for the twenty-two-year-old. He had jumped into a taxi on Collins Street, rushed up to his penthouse and hurriedly packed a small case. All his stage outfits and other touring paraphernalia were already making their way to

Los Angeles, along with his road crew, the larger musical instruments and their sound equipment. It took a lot of effort to move his show around these days, and thankfully little of his own.

Jeff hadn't had time to collect any reading material from the apartment, barely remembering his passport. He read the in-flight magazine and every broadsheet newspaper on board, and was currently making his way through Time magazine. Ironically, there was a feature article on Bart Dyson on page thirty-one, which the pretender at first flicked past in disdain before returning to it and taking his punishment like a man. Doing so kept Gravity at bay, appeased by the idea that life continued to throw curve balls at this good-for-nothing son of a murderer.

The aeroplane was not due to land until seven o'clock in the evening, and the young man knew that by then Lynn would already be at the National Stadium for the Women's Tennis Association championship and her second-round match. This much he had managed to glean yesterday, between batches of heavy breathing and attempts to visualise each others' stilted but tantalising sexual moves. The memory brought a smile to his face and a definite surge of energy below the safety belt.

Still preoccupied with this precipitous ring-in however, Jeff was plagued by a new set of demonic "suitable boyfriend" images every time he shut his eyes, desperate to reach his destination and bring matters to a head. He couldn't afford to fall asleep and risk drawing unwanted attention from his fellow passengers or from the cute, oriental flight attendants, so he resorted to flirting as his next pastime, unbuckling his seatbelt and making his way to the rear galley where he could find some company and smoke at the same time.

There could not have been a more relieved passenger on the half-full aircraft than the man sitting in seat 22C when an announcement came over the public address system to say they would be landing in forty minutes' time. Jeff's stomach churned, having not long ago picked at a serving of noodles and some pallid lumps that purported to be fried chicken. He was filled with excitement at the thought of setting eyes and hands on his dream girl again, albeit mixed with a definite fear of the reception he would receive from Ma and Pa Dyson. And the mystery drawcard as well... What did he look like? What did he do for a living? How had he been selected? And was there any danger that Lynn might find him attractive after all?

Snap out of it, Jeff scolded himself, as the twinkling lights of the Lion City loomed closer and closer. Soon they were on the ground and preparing to disembark, and his feet refused to keep still as they impatiently waited for the doors to open. Fellow passengers all around pestered him for autographs and photographs, and he obliged with a broad smile to while away the interminably long time it seemed to take to receive the "All Clear".

Eventually, the line of passengers began to file slowly up the aisle, grabbing at overhead baggage and moaning about the delay. The cattle-class millionnaire smiled at the futility of their complaints, thinking again about the plight of the Childlight children, who would think they had died and gone to heaven if they were offered the chance to fly in an aeroplane.

The superstar held his handsome head high as he strode through the airport, eyes turning towards him at every pace. Jesus, he was a mess, he thought, waving to his many admirers while inhaling deeply to counteract the dizziness. He vowed to shake off this compulsion, and not a moment too soon. One day, hopefully not too far into the future, these irrational fears would be eradicated by the enduring love of his *Regala*.

The relatively new world traveller had only ever transited through Singapore before, on his way to Paris, London or elsewhere in Europe. The small, south-east Asian country was not a popular stop on the rock concert circuit, and when he marched down the corridors lined with westernised advertising and designer label retailers, Jeff wondered why not. Balking at the stark change between the cool, air-conditioned terminal building and the sultry stickiness of the tropical climate outside, he joined the queue for taxis and debated whether to go to the hotel first and drop his bags off, or to ask to be taken directly to the National Stadium.

'Raffles Hotel, please,' the towering colossus requested of a typically pint-sized driver, slotting himself into the back seat of the small sedan, worn PVC upholstery squeaking as he made himself comfortable.

The Dysons always stayed at The Raffles, Lynn had told him, with its olde-worlde, colonial history. When the new arrival reached the prestigious, whitewashed building and caught sight of the doormen costumed in uniforms dating back to The British Empire, he couldn't help but chuckle at the hideous paternalism of it all. How typical of Bart Dyson to stay in such a die-hard conservative hotel.

Checking in amid squeals of delight from the multi-cultural cast of receptionists behind the counter, Jeff signed a few more autographs while his documents were processed and then almost ran to the lifts. Once inside his room, he quickly freshened up, changed his shirt and splashed on some after-shave. He had no idea what time Lynn's match would have started and how long it would take her to dispatch her opponent. This was such a bizarre situation to be in, when he should really be preparing for his next whistle-stop tour. And what if this trick from the tennis champion's mother were to disturb her concentration sufficiently as to make her lose? That would be retribution indeed.

With this in mind, the anxious man decided that in order to retain the moral high ground he would be best to keep well out of the way until the final score was announced. He couldn't afford to risk the same accusation. The next in the day's long series of taxi rides wound through the streets for no more than five minutes before a large stadium appeared up ahead. Jeff alighted at the main entrance, greeted by an eerie hush peppered by short bursts of applause which told him that the match was still in progress. He silently wished his dream girl luck and bought himself a beer from the deserted bar.

'Where do the players come out?' he asked the barman, a New Zealander on a working holiday.

'No idea, mate,' the young man answered with a cheery smile. 'Round the other side, there's an office and the pro' shop. Around there maybe, eh? Aren't you Jeff Diamond?'

The tired rock star nodded, pouring himself a glass of water and swallowing it quickly. It wouldn't do to drink too much in advance of his auspicious encounter either, and he certainly didn't want to wreak of stale cigarette smoke. Smiling wryly, he sniffed at the notion that every single one of his vices counted against him in his current predicament.

'I am, mate. Who are you?'

'Neil,' the New Zealander grinned. 'Great to meet you. My sister's in love with you, and my mum. And pretty much anyone else I know. Girls, that is!'

Jeff laughed. 'Not always, I assure you. Give me their numbers. I might be needing 'em soon.'

'Yeah, right!' Neil sniggered. 'How long are you in Singapore for?'

'Just tonight. Quick stopover. I'm *en route* to the US for a few days. Flying visit, literally.'

The bartender went to pour his special customer another beer, knowing his reputation for hard living, but pulled back when Jeff's hand hovered over the top of his glass. He offered the stunned fan a few lame excuses about being tired and needing to get up early, both of which were perfectly valid, even if they masked a significant omission.

A muffled cheer followed by a prolonged round of applause drew both men's attention. The match must be over, and the visitor's heart rate immediately shot through the roof. *Game on*, he vowed. He cast his mind back to the length of time it had taken Lynn to emerge after the first and only time he had attended one of her tennis matches, back in Melbourne and just before he had tried to rape her. A shiver ran down his spine, and Miss Irony took her opportunity to gleefully reinforce once again how very unsuitable a boyfriend he was for the lovely Miss Dyson.

Jeff sank the last mouthful of beer down his gullet and slapped a twenty dollar note on the bar. 'Cheers, mate,' he called out to Neil, who was busy stacking the glass-washing machine. 'I'll be back for those 'phone numbers later.'

The barman waved casually, not believing for a minute that the good-looking star would return and apparently not inclined to make any connection between his departure and the end of a certain blonde bombshell's work for the evening. The tired man was grateful. Their secret would be safe for a while longer.

It was almost ten o'clock by the time the impatient man had circled the auditorium and located the office which Neil had mentioned. He flagged down a uniformed employee and asked again about the location of the players' changing rooms. She didn't know. Or wouldn't tell? In either case, this setback frustrated Jeff further. He repeated the process with an older man wearing a suit and a badge with gold lettering, yet again drawing a blank.

Christ! Why did this have to be so hard? Anxiety was building fast, and the temptation to break down one of the doors marked "Staff Only" became virtually unbearable. The paranoid adolescent from western Sydney had reappeared with a vengeance, no less demanding and out of control as before, imagining the Dysons and their imported Valentino sneaking out through a back door and already on their way back to The Raffles.

Another thirty minutes went by with still no sign of anyone, and a highly disillusioned Jeff Diamond could finally stand it no longer. He wrenched the solid door open, sweating and tormented, and let himself into a labyrinth of corridors which extended under the arena's tiered seating blocks. A security guard of Indian origin rounded a corner, talking on a two-way radio, and made for the intruder at the double.

'Excuse me. This is a secure zone, sir.'

'I know,' the tall Australian replied. 'I'm looking for someone. Have the players left?'

The official was easily twenty centimetres shorter than Jeff and seemed somewhat intimidated by the large hulk which showed no sign of retreating. The citizens of Singapore were generally so law-abiding, the celebrity recognised, that this man had probably seldom needed to exercise his training drills for real, if indeed he had ever undertaken any. He raised both hands in front of his chest and smiled, attempting to calm down and behave himself.

'I'm looking for Lynn Dyson. Do you know if she's still here?'

A lecherous grin spread across the security guard's face. 'Oh, no, sir,' his head wobbled, perpetuating the intruder's confusion. 'Miss Lynn Dyson. Beautiful young lady. She is no longer here. All parties have now gone, sir. Only the tournament officials are remaining.'

The jetsetter sighed heavily, while Gravity bounced tennis balls against the inner walls of his temples. Jesus Christ. Fighting a dire urge to lash out at the nearest head, he thrust both hands into his trouser pockets and stared beyond the security guard. He had come all this way and hung around for over two hours, only to find said beautiful young lady had already left without him. She was most likely being spirited away by her new *beau* to a fancy restaurant somewhere for a candlelit dinner. Shit! What a bloody waste of time.

'Thank you,' Jeff did his best to smile. 'I'm sorry to bother you. Can I get a taxi from here back to the city?'

Looking at his watch, the young man cursed at now having to stand on the edge of the road and wait for another extended interval until a taxi happened along. His heart was heavy, and his head ached from a stressful and fruitless day, made worse by too little food and a self-inflicted withdrawal from nicotine. He spied a vending machine in the corridor, back towards the door through which he had entered, and dug his hand into his pocket to fish out some local coins. He had none. They were all annoyingly foreign, either from home or supplied from Cathy's stash for his next destination.

'You are welcome, sir,' the jovial Indian called after him. 'You will find many taxis outside. Enjoy your stay in Singapore, sir.'

The rock star shook his head in frustration and gave the uniformed man a glib flick of his hand in acknowledgement, hurriedly feeding a ten dollar note into the machine. The wire spirals curled around and released a can of Pepsi and a chocolate bar, both falling with a clatter into the tray at the bottom. Retrieving these and his change, the Australian took a deep breath and grabbed at the door handle again, steeling himself for the second encounter with his spiteful ghosts. He wondered what the cheery gentleman would make of his strange behaviour, not to mention the scorn that would be poured on him by his indomitable friend and manager if he ever were to get wind of this last-minute and so far pointless detour.

No matter, the young man thought. He would never see that guy again. Outside on the steps of the stadium, he chuckled to and at himself when his eyes fixed on the darkened road up ahead. There were still times when his greenness as a traveller shone through. He should have known better that Singapore was a place where virtually every car's roof was illuminated with a certain four-letter word!

In a matter of minutes, Jeff was back at the sprawling, old hotel, with its maze of white walls, russet red flagstone walkways and meticulously stained wooden door- and window-frames. His nerves were jangling, and his mind raced from an overdose of conflicting emotions: anger at being put in this situation in the first place, frustration at having missed his dream girl at the stadium, longing to see her smiling face and fear that they would fail to connect at all in the small number of hours left at his disposal. Approaching the *concièrge*'s desk, he requested his key and asked if a call could be put through to Lynn's room.

The noise level in the foyer rose steadily as the handsome celebrity began to attract a great deal of attention from the many westerners passing through. After stopping to have his picture taken with one couple and to sign autographs for a group of men on their way to the Long Bar, he ordered a beer and some coffee, sat down at a courtesy telephone and waited to be put through. All to no avail however.

Almost an hour went by, impatiently spent pretending to read and downing endless cups of coffee, until an appropriate amount of time had gone by to warrant another attempt at a person-to-person call. The Dyson party could easily have slipped past his watch, into any one of a dozen lifts around the hotel's tropical quadrangles, and he steeled himself against resorting to his considerable persuasive powers to cajole the awestruck staff into divulging the champion's room number. Very nearly giving into temptation a number of times, he settled for another telephone call instead. If they were to tell him how to find her, it would also freak him out to wonder how many other ferocious admirers might also gain access to the same information.

However, while his ears listened to the monotonous tones of yet another unanswered call, the tired musician became aware of a commotion from the main entrance and the sound of several sets of footsteps on marble tiles. Looking up, he could hardly believe his luck when he clapped eyes on the famous sporting parents and their precious daughter walking through the doors, laden with sports bags and flanked by both valets pushing trolleys holding yet more luggage. Alongside them was a slim, dark-haired and fresh-faced man who looked a little bewildered by all the attention.

Jeff immediately put the receiver back onto its cradle and stood up. All nerves had strangely vanished, and his sober mind was as clear as a bell. As yet, no-one in the good-looking group of new arrivals had noticed his interest in them, and he used the brief moment to take a few deep breaths in preparation for the overdue stand-off.

There she was, almost close enough to touch. And boy, did he want to touch her right now... His guardian angel was walking towards him, engaged in conversation with her mother and oblivious to his presence, while the two men fell into line behind. She looked happy enough, her boyfriend observed, as he paced purposefully in an intersecting line between the reception counter and the main lift lobby.

It was Big D who saw the familiar figure first, pulling up sharply and staring the tall Sydneysider down. The look of utter disbelief on his weathered face was gratifying, and Jeff continued on the same trajectory towards the small group. He was less than five metres from them when his beautiful best friend happened to glance to her right and came face to face with quite the most unexpected sight.

Instinctively, Lynn's left hand reached sideways in shock, and she grabbed hold of her mother's arm to steady herself. Marianna was equally startled by her daughter's impromptu reflex, and within a second or two, the entire surrounds of The Raffles Hotel seemed to grind to a halt.

'Jeff,' the young woman forced from vacated lungs.

The interloper smiled and stood his ground, this latest four-letter word clearly meant only for his ears. His libido instantly leaped into action, causing his heart to beat faster than he thought possible. Briefly, the blonde sportswoman looked to her left, to where her mother was also frozen to the spot, before dropping her bags onto the floor and running headlong into her secret lover's waiting arms.

'Oh, my God, Jeff!' she cried out, being smothered into a welcoming embrace and lifted off the floor so that his lips could lock onto hers. 'I can't believe you're here. Thank you! Oh, I love you so much!'

A thunderstorm had broken above their heads and heavy rain now fell on the rooftops and canopies beyond the lobby. With Lynn safely in his clutches, the passionate young man succumbed to the array of heavenly assaults on his senses.

The second dark-haired young man surveyed the scene, confounded and instantly recognising the world famous performer. It hadn't taken him long to work out exactly what had just occurred. His gracious date had been careful to inform him of an enduring love affair with a nameless man and that she was uninterested in pursuing the relationship her parents had engineered between them. However, he had not been made aware that his rival was none other than the great Jeff Diamond.

The uninvited guest said nothing, simply revelling in the intimacy which he had practically ruled out. In fact, he found himself unable to say anything, for some inexplicable reason. All he could do was hug the slender body more tightly, listening to an endless, tearful stream of endearing words.

There was something different about her steadfast lover though, the young woman observed. He smelled divine. It was as if this country's perfumed humidity had cleansed him, melting into her favourite of the millionnaire Bohemian's expensive colognes. Or perhaps it was the unusual absence of tobacco and whisky on his breath. Either way, she didn't want to let go.

When her mouth was eventually set free to take a breath, Lynn opened her eyes to find tears in his. 'I knew you were here,' she whispered, without a single care for the chaos she envisaged behind her. 'I felt something weird a while ago, while I was serving in the second set. I dared to think you were at the stadium.'

Still her beautiful, black stallion said nothing, totally overcome with emotion at the undiluted honesty of her reaction. After spending the last sixteen hours in suspense and trepidation, her uninhibited delight made everything worthwhile.

'I kept telling myself not to be so stupid,' Lynn continued, becoming more composed and raising her voice slightly. 'Hope for the best but expect the worst. You know... Are you alright?'

Jeff nodded, kissing her again with increased vigour. The young couple heard Bart Dyson cough loudly and very close to their entwined bodies. Raising his head and relaxing his grip on the tennis star, her boyfriend stared directly into the blue-grey eyes of the veteran Olympian.

'Lynn,' the father began. 'Would you please step aside? I'd like to talk to this man.'

Obediently, the nineteen-year-old slipped out of her lover's enticing embrace, standing down from her tiptoes. Marianna was quickly at her daughter's side, putting a hand on either shoulder and guiding her backwards and out of the way. Still the stunned suitor looked on in confusion.

'Sir, I have nothing to say to you,' came a particularly assertive deep voice, as the teenager's gaze was lured away from the encroaching duel.

'What do you think you're doing here, Diamond?'

The pretender's eyebrows flicked upwards, and his jaw tensed in anger, buying himself time to choose how to respond to the big man's question. It was none of his business what he was doing here.

'This is between Lynn and me, sir,' he replied calmly, raising his hand towards the substitute, 'and maybe this bloke, depending on what's happened so far...'

'Nothing's happened so far, Jeff,' the defiant woman interjected from the sidelines. 'Nothing was ever going to happen.'

'Lynn, enough,' Bart's gruff voice insisted, once more signalling for his daughter to retreat and remain silent.

Their raised voices had begun to draw a crowd, such drama a rarity in this society ruled by honourable forbearance. The show's protagonist saw red, sidestepping his adversary and extending his right hand towards the third party in this trite love triangle. His eyes shot daggers at his girlfriend's domineering father.

'The lady has a right to speak, sir,' he said, shaking the young man's hand firmly. 'Jeff Diamond.'

'As do I, Jeff,' the imposing figure retorted. 'And it's high time you weren't here. I don't want a scene, in full view of the public.'

'This is Jean-Charles Bouchard,' Lynn dared to help her gallant man out, leaving her mother's side and joining the pair of tall, dark, handsome strangers. 'He and I knew each other in LA. We were in some of the same classes. His father's a French diplomat who's been posted to Canberra. Mum and Dad invited him here to meet up with me again.'

Jealousy surged through the tormented soul's veins, reacting violently with the flames of uncontrollable lust which had already singed his insides. An ex-boyfriend, he concluded, and another new adult puppet still ruled by his parents. An eminently suitable ex-boyfriend, dredged up and probably jubilant at having been dropped into the beauty's life again. Who wouldn't be?

'Pleased to meet you,' the young Frenchman spoke with a heavy accent. 'Lynn has told me about her relationship. I admire your music and your charitable work very much.'

'Thanks,' Jeff almost laughed at the outlandishness of their circumstance. *'Merci, Jean-Charles. J'suis complètement désolé de cette situation gênante. J'espère que vous comprenez ce qui se passe. J'aime Lynn beaucoup, et nous nous appartenons ensembles. Ça'y-est.'*

The teenager's parents exchanged secret messages which the linguist caught out of the corner of his eye. Arrogantly, he tried to imagine what they might be thinking: "For goodness' sake, he speaks French too?" Yes, he sneered internally, there was a lot more to this no-good ratbag from the wrong side of town than they gave him credit for.

'Mister Diamond,' Bart Dyson's voice boomed across the three-metre gulf which separated them. 'I must ask you to leave. Mister Bouchard is our guest. Do not threaten him.'

'Dad!' the nineteen-year-old star called out, spinning on her heels and coming to Jeff's defence.

'It's OK, angel,' the musician gave a half-smile, before turning back to the hesitant challenger and smirking, lifting an idle left index finger. 'This man expects me, or probably even wants me to threaten to kill you or get into a fight, so he can prove his point. *Surtout, il ne faut pas vous méfier de ça, mais je vous jure que je ne vous laisserai jamais seuls, touts les deux.* Never. *Vous comprenez?*'

The European stepped backwards at the alarming tone in his idol's voice, especially when the message was delivered in his own language. As Jeff uttered his prophetic words, he felt awash with a mysteriously overwhelming sense of *déjà-vu* in facing off with this clean-cut version of himself. He clenched his teeth and prepared to finish exactly what Lynn's father had ordered him not to start. He knew by the blank looks on the others' faces that only he and the special guest had understood his intentions fully.

'Rest assured, I won't try to hurt you, Jean-Charles, but if you leave here tonight with Lynn, I'm telling you all that I will never, ever leave you two alone.'

Jeff heard both his dream girl and her mother draw breath upon hearing these words, but his wild glare didn't stray from the Frenchman's. He sensed movement beside him, followed by Lynn's hand alighting on his forearm. This simple gesture sent arcs of electricity zipping through his body and the blood rushing where he least needed it to go before he had established his precarious position. Whoa, that was some jolt! He flinched slightly, recovering before anyone had noticed.

Outwardly unperturbed and seeing no point in being concerned about the others' observations, he carried on. 'Unless Lynn asks me to, of course.'

The eminently suitable boyfriend's frightened stare shifted from the swarthy rock star to the young tennis player and then over to each of her parents, eventually returning to the nineteen-year-old superstar's concerned blue eyes.

'Which I'm not going to,' she appended, holding out her hand to her fiercely honest *paramour*.

'Jeff, please,' Marianna broke into the youngsters' heated discourse. 'We must ask you to go. Please leave us alone, or we'll have to call security.'

The angry twenty-two-year-old flashed a dark look at the elegant lady, whose expression was resolute yet as regally impotent as ever. He didn't need to answer to this woman either. Lynn was an adult now. He didn't have to curry favour from anyone but the irresistible creature herself. Again he turned away, ignoring the older woman's plea.

'I have nothing against you, Jean-Charles,' the intelligent songwriter continued in English, assuming the former UCLA student could understand him well enough. 'You seem like a nice guy. A perfect man for this most perfect of women. Doubtless. But Lynn chooses. Now, and in front of us all.'

Glancing leftwards to where his dream girl stood, close enough to feed his heart and stoke his inner fire, he watched her smile speak volumes and sighed involuntarily as another wave of emotion took him unawares.

'I'm walking away now, Missus Dyson, as you request, and I'll wait for Lynn to make her choice.'

The tall man in the smart designer jeans and black polo-shirt had turned his back on the others and had started walking at a steady pace towards the lifts. Four out of the five characters involved in this very public drama were oblivious of everyone else's lives continuing busily around them in the hotel lobby. After no more than a second's hesitation, looking first at her mother and father and then at the hapless Frenchman, the tennis player gritted her teeth and frowned. With a huge sigh and only the smallest pang of regret, she started after him.

'Wait, Jeff, please,' she called out, picking up her bags and heaving a strap onto each shoulder.

Her boyfriend stopped and turned sideways, momentarily unsure how to respond. Was his gamble about to pay off? No baggage was required for Lynn to condemn him to return to his room alone. He reached his hand out towards her, and the young woman readily offloaded the bulky grip of racquets as if it were the most natural thing in the world.

Nous nous appartenons ensembles, the *déjà-vu* struck again. *Please let this be Match Point...*

'I'll see you back here in the morning, Dad. I'm sorry. I choose Jeff. I've always chosen him, and you can't change my mind. Goodnight.'

The nobody from Canley Vale held out his hand for a second time and felt the luscious, tingling sensation of skin meeting skin. Marianna and Bart Dyson were left speechless, watching their elder daughter turn her back on them and her guest to follow this mesmeric Pied Piper. The relieved pair almost broke into a jog on their way to the other side of the foyer, and Jeff spied a broad grin affixed to his girlfriend's face. One to match his own, of course. This had not been a difficult choice for her after all, and he was so, so glad he had changed his plans this morning.

'You OK?' he asked, as the lift doors slid shut.

Alone in the brightly lit chamber, the couple embraced strongly, the young man's heightened state of arousal plainly evident to the object of his affections. She pressed herself against him eagerly, still reeling from the extravagant manner in which he had responded to her unspoken prayer.

'Yes. Are you?'

'I am now,' Jeff confirmed with a deep sigh, finally giving himself permission to feel the full effects of the last few hours. 'Thank you for choosing me. I love you so much. It's taken so long to get to you after that 'phone message. It was driving me crazy not being able to contact you.'

The doors opened on the third floor, and he led his willing co-conspirator to his room. Smiling, Lynn held her hand out for his key, which was eagerly slapped into her open palm. She let themselves inside and closed the door quickly, immediately being enveloped by ravenous arms.

'I love you too, Jeff,' the sportswoman assured him, leaning back so that she could see his handsome face. 'I can't believe you came all the way here. It would've been so expensive to book at the last minute. I got your message that you tried to call back. I rang the flat again, but you must've already left. I can't believe you're here. It's so amazing! Aren't you going to America tomorrow?'

'Yep,' her boyfriend nodded and smiled. 'Baby, I would've come here tonight even if I didn't have a few dollars in the bank. I'd have borrowed the money from Gerry or sweet-talked a granny out of her life savings to get to you after that bloody message.'

Glad of the light-hearted comment, the corners of Lynn's mouth turned downwards, a reaction that tugged agreeably at the charmer's heart strings. With all thoughts of the ugly scene downstairs behind them, both stifled a yawn and burst out laughing.

'Only temporarily,' he qualified with a guilty grin. 'I'd pay her back. You're worth it, Lynn. Way more than worth it.'

The beautiful athlete in her green and gold tracksuit, with hair that had been tossed roughly into a ponytail when it was still wet from the shower, smiled and hugged her favourite jetsetter like it was going out of fashion. The lovers stood locked together in silence, steeping in the happy ending to their respective stressful days.

Jeff realised that his girlfriend looked almost as tired as he felt, and while they were enjoying the closeness, the slender woman discerned a distinct change in her partner's deep breathing. Unbeknown to her, he had made a snap decision which was to surprise her even more than it surprised himself.

'I'm going back to the airport, angel,' he declared. 'You need to sleep. You're exhausted.'

The nineteen-year-old couldn't believe her ears. 'Back to the airport?' she echoed. 'Now?'

Her beautiful, black stallion kissed her again, letting go of one hand to retrieve his suitcase from the bed. He then let the other drop too, remembering that he had dumped his treasured leather jacket on the chair earlier. It had been everywhere with him over the last two years, becoming a sort of sick comfort blanket while he had lived out his lonely sentence.

Lynn smiled when she recognised the familiar item of clothing, totally inappropriate for both the Singaporean and southern Californian climates. She gulped on seeing this statuesque and important celebrity hug it to his body like a teddy bear. Here stood a man who was precariously balanced on the very edge of salvation. It would be wrong of her to convince him to stay, no matter how rebelliously sexy their situation felt. Blindly, she followed as he led the way out of his room and back down the corridor to the lifts again.

'Which floor's your room?' he asked with a heavy heart, beginning to regret his decision already.

'Second. Are you really leaving?'

'Shhh,' whispered the man with glistening eyes. 'D'you remember the last time I came to your room after you'd played tennis?'

The young star didn't know whether to laugh or cry, so she ended up doing both. 'Of course I do. That night's etched on my psyche.'

'Mine too, angel. I can atone for that sin tonight.'

The lift was almost full when it opened to receive its new passengers. Doing their best to act normally, the young couple travelled down one floor with their heavy burdens and walked almost the whole length of the passageway until they reached Lynn's room, protected from view by a wall of torrential rainfall pouring into the courtyard below. Jeff half expected to see Bart Dyson waiting outside, but thankfully he was not there.

'I wondered if Mum and Dad would be in the lift just now,' his girlfriend ventured, as she extracted her key from the pocket of her sports bag.

'Did you just read my mind?' the rock star asked in amazement, once more succumbing to a minor panic attack from yet another solid, wooden barrier. 'I was picturing your dad waiting outside this door.'

'Really?' Lynn replied, seeing him shudder and lose his balance a little. 'Are you OK? God, I wish this didn't happen to you.'

Jeff hugged his dream girl close, her compassion exactly the tonic he needed to boost his willpower. He assured her he was fine, stepping her backwards into the room until they were mere centimetres from the bed. Christ, how he wanted to lay down and share some long-awaited corporal paradise after so long! Why the hell had he made this ludicrous decision?

'Jesus, I want you so badly.'

Lynn stared deep into his dark eyes, which were pleading for her love. 'You can stay.'

Her highly principled lover shook his head, firing off another incandescent smile. 'No, angel. I'll get going. I didn't come here for sex. I came here to show you I care. I told you I could wait three-and-a-half weeks, so I will. I can. I think…'

'Oh,' the young woman melted into his arms, which wrapped her up again. 'That's the most beautiful thing I've ever heard. Are you sure? I feel bad that you came all this way and now you're just going to fly straight off again. Is this because Mum and Dad are here and you're not supposed to get in the way of the tournament? I love you for being so selfless. I really do.'

'Yeah, that too,' he sighed. 'But more because I love you more than I can tell you, and this is the best way I can think of to let you know.'

Tears welled up in both pairs of tired eyes, and they shared a last, long and lingering kiss. Jeff's erection was rigid against his lover's eager body, and her own insides were filled with a desire to feel it inside her. Regardless, the thought of him arriving and then leaving without demanding they tumble into bed and satisfy his obsessive, bestial needs was a commitment Lynn had no choice but to honour. It was the most romantic gesture and a greater gift than she had ever contemplated.

Jeff brushed her tears away with tingling fingers. 'This isn't about sex, angel,' he continued. 'It's about solidarity. I'm here for you.'

'We're here for each other,' his girlfriend corrected without hesitation.

'Even better,' the determined man nodded, lifting her chin gently with his fingertips and planting a tender goodbye kiss on her lips. '*Adios, Regala.* I'm going back to the airport. I have to fly to LA. I take it JC's got his own room...'

'I don't even know.'

Her lover smiled. 'Let them sort it out. He can roll a cot out beside your parents' bed.'

'Jeff!' the young star slapped his arm.

'Well, come on... You gotta see the funny side. Did you win, by the way?'

The young athlete laughed, before bursting into tears again. 'Who cares?'

'Not me,' Jeff shrugged. 'Except if it meant you could come home sooner. Just thought I'd better ask. Glorious victory and all that... Are you going to be OK?'

Lynn sat down heavily on the bed, unable to take her eyes off this fantastic friend of hers and almost wishing she had been knocked out in the second round. From his chiselled cheekbones and jawline, with a day's worth of stubble darkening his sultry complexion still further, to his long, wavy, black hair which glistened in the humid air; from broad shoulders that carried the leather jacket she had bought him so majestically, and then on past the flat, lean abdomen which disappeared temptingly inside his belt and down to the outline of an engorged penis stretching the zip of his jeans.

The champion wouldn't have been surprised if her flying visitor were about to blow a gasket, so fast was his breathing, and she felt much the same. 'I'm fine, Jeff. Are you?'

Bending long legs and crouching down in front of her, Jeff leaned forward and cupped her face in his hands. 'Sure. Just don't touch me, or I won't be able to go through with this. See you at Mark's wedding?' he whispered, kissing her lips once more for luck. 'After you win the final. *Te amo.* Lock me out, OK?'

'OK, thanks. *Te amo* too. I'll have to avoid you while the others are there, but hopefully we can escape later. I can't wait to get your clothes off, Mister Diamond.'

Exhaling until his lungs were nearly empty, her perfect stranger straightened himself up to his full height and grimaced in considerable discomfort. With a grin and a farewell wave of his left hand, he winked cheekily and turned on his heels. He waited outside until he heard the latch slide into place before continuing on his long and somewhat circuitous onward journey to Los Angeles.

The superstar could scarcely put one foot in front of the other, physically and emotionally drained. His testicles were throbbing with unspent passion, and the likelihood of the iron bar in his underwear softening any time soon seemed negligible. Nevertheless, another grand statement had been warranted and duly made. Thinking back to the altercation in the cavernous entrance lobby at ground level, he was sure the Dysons and the unfortunate French student had got the message loud and clear.

And more importantly, Jeff had done right by his beautiful best friend. True to his word, he would not be interfering with her schedule any longer, and moreover, he would be on time for rehearsals with his band at the Greek. And then, he and his dream girl would meet up in Japan for their first appearance on stage together, as a *prélude* to flying off to London for a year of freedom from these unwanted complications.

All was as right with the world as it could be under the circumstances, even though he was still outrageously aroused. The millionnaire rock star vowed to turn this sweet but crippling torture to good advantage and give his finest performances yet over the coming days. Cathy would laugh so hard if he ever dared tell of tonight's escapade, he smiled to himself.

Lynn Dyson's proud and contented boyfriend took the stairs down the two floors to ground level, astounded to find her parents and their guest still talking in the lobby. What perfect timing! They were equally disconcerted to see him, or probably much more so. As he passed by, taking deliberately languid strides, Jeff extended a long right arm and slapped Jean-Charles gently on the left shoulder.

'*Bonne chance*, mate,' he said, before turning to Big D. 'Lynn's fine, sir. Locked safely in her room. She's about to order Room Service and she needs to sleep.'

The young man paused to see if the stalwart had anything to say, but his words were met with perplexed reticence. He needed the stately couple to know he was not the type to give up. He would do whatever it took to secure the future he and Lynn were planning, which included neither a Gallic diplomat's son nor any overbearing family members.

He continued, reinforcing his point. 'I'm sure she'll ring you in the morning. I haven't killed her, in case you're wondering, and not even your beautiful daughter could make me come that fast.'

This last, point-winning volley of course was a lie, but for a very good cause, he rationalised with a smirk. A flicker of distaste washed across Bart's face, and looking across to his wife, the Olympian opened his mouth to speak.

Lifting his left hand to chest height, Jeff made it quite clear that he didn't care to listen to any more wise words, and to his astonishment, the influential man was silenced.

'*Adios.*'

The famous musician walked casually out of the hotel, past a lobby full of stunned onlookers, and hailed a waiting taxi. He slung his suitcase and jacket across the rear seat and climbed in, requesting the driver take him to Changi. He suddenly remembered that he hadn't even checked out, which would present a problem for Cathy in the morning. They wouldn't have to wait long for his money. He was good for it these days.

Meanwhile up on level two, as soon as she had pushed the door closed and flicked the deadbolt, Lynn had run to the telephone and dialled the empty penthouse apartment in Melbourne. She tapped her foot impatiently as she waited for the answering machine message to finish.

'Hello. It's me. You've just left my room, and I miss you so much. I'm the happiest girl in the world, and you are the most amazing man in the world. I love you more than I can say too. Thank you, Jeff. See you next Saturday.'

Open Verdict

It was Saturday morning, the last weekend in October. Lynn Dyson was due back on home turf today, and to say that her boyfriend was beside himself with joy would have been no exaggeration whatsoever. Having returned from his micro-tour to California, bathed in unprecedented acclaim, the part-time student had settled back to work on his Masters and count down the remaining few celibate days. He had survived the marathon abstention with flying colours.

Next stop the priesthood, the superstar joked to himself as the car sped in an easterly direction along Dandenong Road.

Jeff was on his way to the wedding of his bass player and good friend, Mark Davenport, and his *fiancée*, Shona. The ceremony and reception were being held at the famous Portsea Pub, right on the bay. It was a windy morning, precluding a topless journey in the Aston Martin. Gifted very few opportunities to drive his pride and joy these days, the superstar made sure he felt every ounce of power it willingly produced as he guided it around the streets and highways of greater Melbourne. As it happened, he was grateful for the swirling wind, since the traffic was slow through the towns and an open roof would have afforded its famous occupant far too much exposure.

Jeff Diamond's world had become even crazier over the last few weeks. Not only had he been around the world again and returned to Australia to see two of his albums vying with each other at the top of the charts, but he had also appeared on prime-time television several times. Editorials and opinion pieces lauded his work almost every day in at least one Australian newspaper, leading the ambitious world-changer to accept that he had indeed "made it". If anything, with Lynn overseas, he was beginning to capture more column space than she did.

In contrast, as if to bring him back to Earth with a bump, the young man had received another strange telephone call from Marianna Dyson the previous afternoon. She had opened the conversation amicably enough but had gone on to ask if he was attending Shona and Mark's wedding. Upon hearing him answer in the affirmative, she had become nervous and came to the point rapidly by warning him to stay away from Lynn during the function.

'Why?'

'No specific reason,' the sophisticated socialite had replied. 'We'd be grateful if you weren't seen together, that's all.'

Who was going to be there this time to tempt their daughter back to the straight and narrow? Not poor Jean-Charles again? Surely not, if the Frenchman knew what was good for him. To Jeff's knowledge, his pothead bass player certainly didn't hang out with anyone special, and the only facts the millionnaire rocker knew concerning Shona's background was that she had been born in Scotland and her research physicist father had moved his family to Melbourne while she was a teenager.

Jeff's mind wandered to other public identities in receipt of an invitation. Perhaps there was another perfect partner among the guests with whom the Dysons had done a deal; an arranged marriage for their elder daughter, designed to end her misguided flight of fancy with the riff-raff she had chosen to adopt. How proper! How very Victorian. How very, very infuriating...

The lovers had spoken almost every day while Lynn toured around Europe. After their lightning fast *rendezvous* in Singapore, they had managed to snatch several brief moments in wholly incompatible time zones. Their plans for the upcoming Japanese tour were progressing well, and they had already selected their set list. They had also decided not to push their luck by sharing accommodation, so the gallant gentleman selected a hotel not too far from where the MAC contingent was staying, to which he could retreat before the nocturnal horrors gave his presence away. Although Tokyo was a difficult city to find one's way around, especially from several thousand kilometres away, the resourceful artist had easily solved this problem by befriending a Japanese girl on the smokers' steps of 333 Collins Street. She had agreed only too willingly to help him in return for lunch. Only lunch.

In the meantime, the talented songstress had formally accepted her place at the Royal College of Music, exhilarated by the opportunity to develop her skills in composing, orchestration and arranging to round out her long-term career. Sir Bradley Morrison, MAC's Musical Director, was over the moon to think that another of his brightest *protégés* would be representing the Melbourne Academy in one of the finest capitals of the arts world.

The blonde nineteen-year-old also took great pleasure in her boyfriend's successful overture to his esteemed former supper partner, John Francis, who was these days lecturing at the University of London. There was a doctoral thesis topic burning in Jeff's overactive mind, and he was in danger of completing most of the thinking before he had even set foot in his future seat of learning. Despite their hectic timetables and rare snatches of free time to talk, the puzzle's many pieces were gradually being slotted into place by the songwriter's management company, right under the suspicious noses of Bart and Marianna Dyson.

Lynn regularly expressed guilt and regret for the underhandedness of her father's determination to discredit the ambitious rock star. The Sydneysider had heard nothing further from Big D or Simon Steinmann concerning the ongoing investigations, although he had been in regular contact with the men at the boxing club. Rumour had it that Diamond Senior had received a visitor in prison but that he had refused to talk to whomever it was.

Diamond Junior had no idea whether this rumour was true or otherwise, and ironically, Alberto had recently been caught harbouring some of Hassan and Imran Ali's illegal immigrants and was now facing charges of his own. These shady characters from his old world hadn't changed a bit, constantly dodging those above and below them in the moral food chain.

The lawn behind the Portsea Pub was set up for the wedding ceremony, with the placid waves of Port Phillip Bay sparkling in the background, perfect for photographs. Jeff parked the sleek, black monster in a secluded spot away from the main car park and strolled into the growing crowd of spruced-up guests. There were no Dysons to be seen, even though they had been invited as a result of their link with Shona's parents through their patronage of the Prince Alfred Hospital's cancer research fund.

The libidinous superstar had booked accommodation in a nearby Bed and Breakfast that had been recommended via Suzanne by her deceased aunt, and he had been careful not to tell anyone of its whereabouts. He had absolutely no hope of holding himself together long enough to transport his quarry back to Melbourne. One thing was for certain: nothing or no-one was going to rain on their parade tonight...

In the entrance of the iconic beachside hotel, the bridegroom was pacing around, looking apprehensive, and seemed very pleased to see his famous mate. 'Jeff! Glad you could make it. Did you bring the black beast?'

'Yep. Certainly did,' the smartly-dressed celebrity shook his friend's cold hand, indicating that the sports car was parked round the other side of the hotel. 'Nervous?'

'Shit, yeah!' Mark responded, holding out two trembling hands. 'Worse than my audition for you.'

Jeff modestly brushed off this unnecessary compliment. 'So where's the rest of your family? Let me get you something to calm your nerves. Then I can join you.'

Mark shrugged and smiled. 'The others are all still upstairs getting ready. Even my dad! That's why I was so glad to see you. Let's go get a beer.'

Feeling a good many pairs of eyes bearing down on him already, the songwriter thought better of this idea. 'No. Stay here, mate,' he advised. 'You shouldn't be seen propping up the bar before the wedding. Poor form, as Gerry'd say. I'll get 'em in.'

Inside the hotel, the kind-hearted front-man soon met up with his drummer and a couple of the band's regular Aussie roadies, who were looking lost and decidedly wasted after last night's pre-wedding party. 'Come out, guys. Porto needs some assistance. He's shitting himself out there.'

The musicians trooped into the garden to keep their mate company, unaccustomed to shirts and ties and daylight. Only one of the road crew had brought a partner, but Trish was a permanent fixture on tour these days and fitted in with the tight bunch easily. If anything, her habits were more hard-core than her masculine competition, and she would regularly be the last one standing at the end of long, licentious nights in foreign parts.

In dribs and drabs, the rest of the guests arrived, and the general level of noise and anticipation grew as it became clear that the ceremony preparations were in their final stages. The bridal party's cars pulled into the hooped driveway dead on time, immediately encircled by excited family members. With another round of encouraging handshakes and a few jokes at the minister's expense, the groom's jovial support crew left him to take their places in the congregation.

Still no sign of the Dysons though. All around him, Jeff could hear people whispering his name and pointing. It was disconcerting to say the least, especially when his role was as a mere bystander in today's intimate setting. Judging it best not even to make eye contact with his more vocal fans, he battled to control his rampant obsession with how unbelievably sexy Lynn's tanned body would look tonight, spread out over the king-sized bed. Imagining her smile in response to every touch and kiss, feeling her fingernails dig into his yearning skin and hearing her gasp and scream his name in the middle of nowhere all amounted to a most fitting prize for his recent sainthood.

Mark's sister sat down next to the attractive star as they waited for proceedings to commence, as brazen as ever. 'Can you hear all the chatter or do you tune out?'

'Yeah. I can hear it,' the dreamer nodded, lamenting the interruption. 'How're you going, Sophe? Sometimes I catch something so blatantly wrong and want to turn round and correct them. I can't though. Not here. What's new with you?'

'Oh, heaps. Are you here with someone? Weddings are awkward to go to as a single.'

Jeff smiled inwardly at such a transparent line. 'No, I'm here alone,' he told her, grateful that his erection had seen fit to wither away. 'As long as there's alcohol, I'm good.'

Sophie appeared slightly disappointed but chose to stick around anyway. Jeff Diamond was by far the best looking and most influential man to be seated next to while the photographer was snapping. She had asked Mark several times if he could arrange a date with her idol, but he had never come up with the goods.

'I can't believe my brother's getting married,' she said. 'Do you like her?'

'Shona? Yeah. She's great. They're happy enough, don't you think?'

What else could he say? This was not the place to air home truths of the road, and Jeff fully expected that his star-struck bass player was by no means ready to settle down, particularly now he and his buddies had experienced the best and worst of being at the top.

Mercifully, their conversation was cut short by music breaking through the loud speaker system. The tall celebrity glanced around to see not only the bridal party lined up at the back but also the Dyson clan filing in at the last minute. Perhaps Lynn's flight had been delayed? So near, yet so far! After almost a month, he was dying to see her yet also mindful of the effect her proximity would have on his frazzled self-control. He looked around again while Mark and his best man were receiving counsel from the celebrant, hoping to catch his angel's eye at least. He was disappointed to find that the family had taken their seats towards the rear of the bride's bank of guests.

The elaborate ceremony was beautiful, the wind having dropped on cue, and everything went according to plan. Mark and Shona were beaming, immediately more relaxed when pronounced husband and wife. The talented bassist was the first of Jeff's band members to get married since they had formed as a unit from the original motley selection of session musicians, and Sophie rambled inanely to anyone within earshot about how proud she was of her older brother.

The guests milled around with drinks while the wedding party were ferried all over the manicured grounds for endless photographs. The rock star became bored and impatient, lighting a cigarette and dutifully chatting to those around him. How he hated it when people insisted on turning the conversation back to him. He ought to be flattered, but it was so tiring balancing on the thin strip of land between the steep chasms of arrogance and ungratefulness.

All the while, the popular entertainer searched for an opportunity to speak to his dream girl. Even the sight of her eluded him. It was as if her parents had deliberately surrounded her with a force field of guests. Every now and again, he would catch a glimpse of the side or back of her head, and then she would vanish again.

All was soon revealed as soon as the wedding breakfast was served. The object of Jeff's desires was sandwiched between her father and another man whom he didn't recognise. They were deep in an animated conversation. Christ, not again! With the flashbacks to his Singapore stunt reminding him how well things had worked out, the red-blooded boyfriend was annoyed but not too bothered. He imagined Lynn sitting there, as bored as he was, being polite to this new candidate next to whom her parents had positioned her so conveniently.

The songwriter focussed his attention back on his own table's soporific talking points while the meal was served, locked in by a single school friend of Mark's on one side and some distant relative of Shona's who had flown in that morning from Edinburgh. The young woman to his right seemed only capable of grinning inanely at any wisecrack which emerged from his stellar mouth, evidently having scored highly enough on the ex-girlfriend stakes to secure the seat of her choice. Although conversation with the jetlagged, middle-aged lady on his left was actually much more interesting, the groom had almost begged him on several occasions to pay attention to Anne-Marie.

Jeff smiled at how peculiar these occasions full of pretence really were. Was this his destiny with Lynn too, whether they liked it or not? He wondered what incorruptible qualifications this latest ring-in might possess, reflecting on the squeaky-clean *Monsieur* Bouchard. The new bloke probably didn't have a father who was a double murderer either... This much was highly likely. And was he of good character? Or did he play around with sex kittens in drug dens when he wasn't off making the odd profit or loss on the Stock Exchange? Frustrated, the boy from Canley Vale amused himself by people-watching through both *entrée* and main course, before the first set of dancing began.

'You're not performing today!' Mark's mother exclaimed in front of her son's friends. 'We couldn't afford you, I'm afraid.'

The famous songwriter stood up and politely kissed the plump woman's cheek. 'You know I would've done this for free, Peggy,' he said, 'but I couldn't have done it without a bass player.'

'You smooth talker!' Missus Davenport cooed, counteracting the groans from the rest of the band at their leader's tongue-in-cheek reply.

Jeff shrugged as only he knew how, playing to the crowd instinctively. Not wishing to be rude, he urged the others to cool down and play nice, while continuing to scan the crowd for someone to free him from the puerile but unavoidable blandness of their surroundings.

'Ooh, if only I was twenty years younger!' Peggy shot an aside to her friends. 'Isn't he gorgeous?'

'Yes, you are,' answered a different female voice immediately behind the charmer's right shoulder.

The ecstatic musician had no need to turn his head in order to know who had spoken. Instead, he took a quick look around to find out where her parents were. Nowhere to be seen. The pair kissed quickly and as casually as they possibly could.

'How are you?' the delirious man asked, his heartbeat already well out of the starting blocks. 'You look amazing. Christ! It's good to see you finally. You've been gone so long.'

Lynn looked radiant despite a seven-hour flight on top of her week of competition. She was wearing a dark blue, mid-length satin dress, complimented by a fine silver necklace which sparkled on her tanned skin. Her breasts were full under the tastefully plunging neckline, and dark red lipstick intensified the arresting effect of her smile. The former schoolgirl was certainly all grown up today.

'It's so good to see you too,' the graceful woman agreed. 'I'm fine, thanks. Can't stay long this time either. They're watching me like hawks. Mum and Dad have gone inside to talk to people, so I ran over to say hello while I had the chance.'

Jeff lowered his mouth close to her ear. 'And to give me a hard-on.'

Blue eyes flashed, and his heart jumped into his mouth. Then his dream girl was gone as quickly as she had arrived.

'Gotta fly!'

Lynn's hypnotised lover grabbed her hand as she turned, squeezed it hard and then let go again, exhaling sharply as the passion engulfed him. All this sneaking around was very, very sexy, and it was fortunate indeed that he hadn't yet removed his suit jacket in preparation for gracing the dance floor. No-one around them appeared to suspect anything, but he was utterly convinced his carnal ambitions were by now advertised in neon lights above his head.

After another half-hour or so, during which the strung-out rock star vented his restless tension with a string of eager dancing partners, the Master of Ceremonies called the guests back to their seats to cut the cake. Jeff caught Mark's eye and gave him a thumbs-up. In fact, his bass player already looked rather glazed and enervated, his compassionate friend only too aware how daunting it must be for the shy groom to stand up in front of so many people. The speeches given by the bride's father and the best man were full of typical adolescent anecdotes and corny, family-rated jokes, at which the assembly laughed politely and applauded at the appropriate times.

Congratulatory toasts and dessert over, the tables were cleared, and the band began their second set. Jeff remained seated, lingering over coffee with the other band members and some Melbourne Academy alumni who were mutual music business acquaintances these days. He spotted Junior Dyson in his peripheral vision, talking to his father and looking in his direction. Their conversation seemed quite lively from this distance, continuing for some minutes while Marianna chatted with the mysterious extra gentleman.

The nervous *voyeur* could also see his dream girl sitting on a table on the far side of the function room with another group of former schoolmates. He dared to believe she had given her parents the flick again. Keeping tabs on the two Dyson men, the contemptuous songwriter couldn't care less for what they might be saying about him. He was doing nothing wrong, and quite deliberately so... He had toed the line all along, and it had been Lynn who had approached him earlier. He could hardly have spurned her in front of the groom's mother and her gaggle of high society onlookers, now could he? It was almost unbearable though, seeing the love of his life so seemingly accessible and yet totally out of his reach.

Suddenly, there was movement from the hotel entrance. Jeff saw Junior beckon to his sister, who obediently left her table and walked over to where the rest of her family was gathered. At first the mystified young man felt sure they were all about to depart. Shit! Surely she wouldn't leave without some sort of communication?

No. Wait. The Dyson party were saying their goodbyes, beginning to kiss and hug various other guests, including Shona's parents. As far as the rock star could make out, the scene suggested Bart and Marianna were leaving but that

Junior and Lynn may have been permitted to stay on. He breathed a huge sigh of relief. What a welcome sight!

Jeff hoped fervently that the silent movie he had witnessed from afar would have a happy ending. Before he could find out for sure however, his attention was smartly brought back to the present by one of the females at his table asking him to dance. *Why not?* He would be able to zero in on the action this way. His extrovert dance partner, Melanie, could hardly believe her good luck when the handsome idol accepted, and she squealed her way to the dance floor.

The blonde in the sexy, blue, strapless gown glanced around to see what the fuss was about. She had come to associate screaming girls with her boyfriend, and this time was no exception. The guilty playboy caught her eye, shrugging, and he saw her laugh out loud and wave. The evening was definitely improving at last.

The next thing the handsome rocker knew, the ever-attentive Nick Mason had asked Lynn to dance... or perhaps *vice versa*, he dared to dream... and he watched them winging their way gradually closer. The Dyson parents were long gone, and he assumed Junior could be trusted with his sister's confidences. Melanie wailed for him to hold her hands, desperately trying to claim her dark-haired idol, yet he was having none of it. He couldn't wait for the current song to finish so that he could engineer an exchange with his girlfriend's loyal minder. Soon enough, the band finished the last chorus, and the audience applauded.

The expert dancer made his move. 'Hey, Nick. Shall we swap?'

Without waiting for anyone to voice an objection, he took Melanie's hand and passed it to the burly giant, in return for Lynn's slender, piano-player's fingers. A sensual surge of energy flashed between them, causing both to lurch back from its power.

'I love you,' Jeff whispered.

'Thanks. I love you too. We have to be careful,' came his dream girl's rejoinder.

Giving into the infectious rhythm and following her gorgeous, athletic dance partner's lead, she scanned him up and down admiringly. He looked so good, with his tie loosened and his shirt's top button undone. Almost a month apart had been a test for her too, especially after their aborted reunion in Singapore.

'Junior's been told to keep us apart.'

Jeff pulled back from her body, as much to retain control as for their watchdog's sake. 'I thought as much,' he replied. 'I saw him and your dad having a conversation that involved a lot of pointing and staring at me. What's it all about this time?'

'Oh, my God! I can't believe their persistence,' his girlfriend sighed. 'Did you see the guy I was sitting next to?'

The bad boy nodded, kissing her surreptitiously on the cheek. After startling in pleasant surprise, she leaned into him a little closer, causing his pulse rate to change gear yet again. Without a word, he dipped his right hand and sent his partner spinning round. She gave an appreciative but subdued cry, and the couple found themselves thrown together again when she came full circle.

'He's some hotshot from an investment bank,' Lynn explained, grinning. 'They even switched his name on the seating plan. I'm so sick of them trying to match-make me.'

'*Intéressant, n'est-ce pas?*' her man teased, conveniently turning her round so she was hidden from Junior as they spied him walking back into the main room. 'At least he looked like a better conversationalist than Jean-Charles from where I was sitting.'

'Spying on me, were you? Don't joke about it,' the frustrated sportswoman smiled, feeling totally at home with being twisted and turned against his body. 'Dad's deadly serious still, and this guy came on really strong. It made me feel sick.'

Jeff gazed into her eyes, stoked at her girlish authenticity. 'Is there any wonder? You're dynamite! Who wouldn't want to come on to you?'

Once again, the electrical current running between the two stars suddenly coursed in an unforgiving arc, forcing their hands apart for a split second. Lynn blushed slightly at his compliments, and her seductive partner felt her body surrender yet further to him. How could they let anything come between a bond as powerful as this?

'So the idea is that I go to London and he flies back on business and we hook up. And where am I in all this?' she complained.

Australia's darling was fuming, and the rebel reprobate liked it immensely, opting to fan the flames a little more. 'Did your mum tell me she rang me to warn me off?' he asked, pulling her close into his body and kissing her collarbone.

Lynn stepped back in amazement, with a roll of her angry eyes. 'No! Not again. What for?'

The demonstrative couple had been rumbled however, unable to escape the stares of their fellow guests, and the young woman suddenly became distracted by someone approaching from over Jeff's shoulder. She warned her brother off with a flick of her hand, hoping he would stay away for a few minutes more. Thankfully, the footballer turned and headed back to the bar.

The Sydneysider continued, both hands cupping the highly expressive face he loved so much, and he kissed her hard on the lips. 'She was very cryptic. She told me they'd be grateful if we weren't seen together.'

'Oh, I've so had enough of this,' his girlfriend groaned. 'I'm going to have it out with Junior. This is completely nuts!'

Jeff smiled in agreement. 'Be careful, angel. I can wait. Don't do it for me, OK?'

Lynn kissed her *beau* quickly and marched off the worn parquetry, her stilettos carrying her with a tasteful, swinging gait that attracted the approving scrutiny of every man present. The ditched dancer returned to his table, sat down and lit a cigarette, his loins on high alert and his nerves buzzing. From a safe distance, he watched the irresistible young lady collar her big brother and begin to lecture him. They too were looking over in his direction, and she was not at all happy.

The suspense was too much for the notorious musician to wait on the sidelines. He knew he should be over there, helping to resolve this stoush with the unfortunate chaperone. The twenty-two-year-old stood up and wandered slowly across the room, giving his girlfriend plenty of opportunity to send him back if his assistance was surplus to requirements. His instincts were right, with no such objection raised. She casually took his hand once he was close enough.

'Are you alright?' he asked, squeezing her fingers in response to the subtle but friendly greeting.

Lynn nodded. 'Yes. I was just trying to explain to Junior that I'm not interested in anyone else and that I'm moving in with you. Our single-minded father hadn't seen fit to pass on that piece of information.'

'Hi. Good to see you again, big fella,' Jeff addressed his lover's patient brother, shaking his hand. 'I know what your dad's asked you to do, but Lynn and I are spending tonight together whatever happens. She'll be perfectly safe, and I'll make sure she's back in Melbourne before lunch tomorrow. Shouldn't it be Lynn's choice whom she goes home with, mate?'

The titanic sportsman shrugged and smiled. 'Sure, unless you're us. I know Lynn wants to be with you, and I've no idea what my parents have got against you. I like you a lot, Jeff, and I don't give a toss what the problem is, to be honest. But I'm under strict instructions. I'm going to get it from Dad when he finds out I failed to stop you spending time together, but hey... Go for your life. I'll just say I didn't see you leave, so do me a favour and don't make a big scene about it.'

His sister interrupted, scowling. 'June, I'll take the blame. I'll make sure he knows you tried to stop me.'

'OK,' the reluctant anti-hero agreed. 'Just play it cool, please. I don't want him to hear about some huge spectacle like at Rob's party. Are there any reporters here? Be discreet. You know that anyway...'

Jeff gripped Junior's outstretched hand again. 'Thanks, mate. Really. We need to be together. It's as simple as that. I don't expect your parents to understand, but that's the way it is for us.'

Lynn's enormous older brother walked away with an amicable wave. He had always been impressed by Jeff Diamond.

'You owe me!'

Alone at last, the stunning blonde sighed and pushed her triumphant man away. It was still too early to leave the reception, and she bargained with him to go back to the party for a while, for appearances' sake.

'Jeez, you're a sadist, angel,' he whispered in her ear. 'You're determined to cause me maximum harm tonight, aren't you? I hope you're going to make it worth my while.'

'I hope so too!' his playful woman retorted, brushing her fingers across the front of his pants. 'And a masochist, I assure you. Just my anguish doesn't show as much as yours.'

The evening continued uneventfully, each returning to their own cohorts. Jeff watched Lynn dance with hers, and she watched him talk with his. Every now and again, they would catch each other staring. He would wink, and she would look away.

After a slow-burning hour, the compulsive man lost patience with their provocative game. Standing at the bar, he sank his B and B room key into an ice bucket for several minutes, while he enjoyed a whisky with Mark's father and uncle. He then walked over to his girlfriend's table, where he pressed the flat side of the freezing key into the bare skin covering her left shoulder blade. She had seen him coming but had no clue as to his intentions. To her credit, she neither jumped nor uttered a sound, and yet the joker felt her squirm as the cold metal made its impression.

Still Lynn didn't move, leaving her clandestine infatuate to continue on by. She was playing with him now, and the result was exquisitely painful. The testosterone-charged man was ready to snap, but he could not bring himself to admit defeat in such a public arena. He loved how she teased him and yet hated it at the same time. After almost a month apart, there was little leeway left in the control freak's tolerance for power-plays tonight.

Then of course, at the point when he was about to throw in the towel, Jeff Diamond's dream girl stood up and strolled innocently towards him, wearing her finest "I'm yours" attitude. The trivia under discussion at the band's table stopped short, and time stood still while she accepted the rock star's silent invitation onto his most sought-after lap. With everyone still marvelling at what had just taken place, Jeff felt his whole self relax as soon as the pretty celebrity sat down, and he resumed the conversation exactly at the point where it had been paused. Life had righted itself of its ephemeral list, and everyone felt free to breathe once more.

The united couple saw no reason to move until the end of the evening, somehow able to halt their previously rapacious greed. They found themselves cemented to each other, laughing and joking with their friends. It was a complete mystery to the ardent young man why, with her presence secured, he had no difficulty in subduing his lustful urges into a mildly agonising preoccupation. The same phenomenon had evidently befallen his secret companion too, since he had teased her continually with tingling fingertips all over her back and arms and revelled in her quickening breaths and rising body temperature.

As the remaining family and guests were leaving the pub, the inseparable celebrities sauntered unnoticed back to his car hand in hand. Reward for their fortitude was upon them, with the car in sight and only a short drive to their private hideaway. He would see her horny as hell, and then raise her some...

'This is the first time I've met your Aston Martin,' Lynn reminded him, running her fingers lightly over the front passenger-side wing. 'It's sleek, and much bigger than I imagined.'

'Hold that thought,' Jeff chuckled, opening the door and kissing her so hard that they both had to draw a sharp breath.

The black beast sprang eagerly into action, its engine issuing an imposing roar as it stole through the car park and turned onto the bitumen. The successful rock star was not so naïve as to believe the other partygoers wouldn't guess the owner of such a virile, ostentatious machine from among their number. Sure enough, several heads strained to see who might be travelling with him, but the famous passenger remained perfectly anonymous.

Only a few minutes later, the purring vehicle turned a sharp right down a narrow lane and pulled up in a gravel car park, in front of a small group of chalets. The famous driver jumped out and ducked into a doorway marked "OFFICE", presumably to retrieve their key, before returning and brandishing a white envelope for Number Three. The pathway to the secluded cottage he had booked for their latest reunion was unlit and winding, and after fetching his belongings from the boot, the gallant gentleman made sure his maiden was following safely in his footsteps.

'Are you sure this is the right way?' the young woman asked. 'It's so dark.'

'Bloody well hope so,' her boyfriend answered, feeling excitement mounting again.

The couple rounded a corner to see a light shining ahead of them, and the secret celebrity in the satin dress and high heels held her hand out for the key. Once inside, the two lovers fell onto the bed without even pausing to take off their shoes.

'What were you trying to do to me in there?' Jeff asked, with a sudden desperation in his voice. 'I can't believe how hard you played.'

Lynn was stroking him in a regular motion through his suit trousers, and he knew he wouldn't have much time left if she were to persist. He rolled away and began to undress. She understood perfectly, switching off the main light and heading into the bathroom to fill some water glasses. Pulling the door half-closed on her return, the bedroom was bathed in a warm glow.

She grinned. 'Sorry about earlier. I wanted to push you to the limit; to see how far I could take you before you caved in. I wanted to turn you on so much.'

Standing naked in front of her, his penis at its full length and rock hard, Jeff pulled the vision towards him. He lowered the zip on the side of her dress and slipped his hand around her waist, delaying for a few seconds on her abdomen before sliding his fingers inside her undies. Lynn leaned into him willingly, moaning with pleasure.

'Well, congratulations, Madam Whiplash. It worked! I want you like you wouldn't believe,' he growled. 'I don't think I've ever been so keyed-up. I'm on a fucking knife-edge and I don't want to get off.'

'Good,' his tantalising temptress smiled. 'So now we have to slow down.'

The confident nineteen-year-old stepped away from his forceful, overheating body and began to remove her clothes agonisingly slowly. Blue eyes scolded him each time he tried to reach for her, and Jeff groaned so loud that they could probably have heard him back at the Portsea Pub.

'You sound like your car,' the enticing woman whispered, finally hugging his naked torso in close.

'No, it sounds like me,' the arrogant lover countered deep and low in her ear, nipping the sensitive skin underneath her right ear. 'I can't believe how good this feels. Don't you dare stop.'

'This is for my parents and the stupid matchmaking games they're playing,' Lynn cried out, wrapping her arms suddenly around his neck. 'Jeff Diamond, I love you. I don't want anyone else except you. Never, ever.'

She began to cry, pressing herself closer in response to his fingers on her clitoris. Her empathetic boyfriend pursued its goal relentlessly, knowing her distress needed it as much as he did, and he didn't refrain from stroking her until she overflowed in a ragged rush, sobbing into his chest. As he kissed her tear-drenched face, he wasted no time in entering her, the intensity generated by his size and roughness causing the dying orgasm to reignite instantly.

'Angel, it's OK,' Jeff placated, writhing in his own sweet agony. 'I know how you feel. But you're in control of your life now. We're just the same, you and me. Just from different sides of town.'

He came less than thirty seconds later, expelling another long, low Aston Martin snarl which rose from deep in his soul. The sapped tennis champion continued to weep softly, and he held her tight until she stopped. It was sweet to be able to return some of the compassion she had shown for him, and especially gratifying to be needed for something so basic and human.

The extreme high of Jeff's first penetrative orgasm for the best part of a month almost blew his red-blooded male mind, and his body shuddered violently as it reached a final, fading zenith. After about ten minutes lying together in idle contemplation, the handsome man slipped out of his woman's arms and soon returned from the bathroom, picking up the dishevelled bedclothes from the floor and draping them over his drowsy bedfellow.

The songwriter reached over and turned on the bedside light, stroked his lover's face and pushed a few damp strands of hair out of her eyes. 'You are so beautiful. I can't wait to be with you in London. I can't wait to have you back in Melbourne either. I'm just sick of waiting, full stop. Aren't you? You OK, angel?'

Lynn nodded, overtired from her long flight. 'I'm sorry. Thanks for being so patient. I don't know why I'm so upset. I'll be alright after a good night's sleep. And thanks for helping me talk to Junior. He didn't know what to do, poor guy. He's on our side but he's going to get such a hard time from Dad. It's unfair for him to be put in that position. And us, for that matter.'

Jeff propped himself up on his elbow and gazed into adoring eyes. 'Hmm... I owe your dad a 'phone call. I'm going to bring things to a head tomorrow, if that's OK with you. It's about time I took responsibility. After all, it's my fault we're in this ridiculous, fucked-up situation.'

'Yeah. That'd be good, I suppose,' his girlfriend didn't try to dissuade him. 'It would be good to clear the air and all be able to live happily. I'm sure they don't want me to be unhappy. Somehow we have to convince them that I'll only be happy with you.'

The young man's ego accepted this endorsement gladly, immediately channelling it lower down. He made no attempt to hide his re-arousal, only too aware that there was so much more stored in his tank for this long-anticipated tryst. Lynn's eyes widened and then closed briefly, and he wondered if her indulgence might already have been exhausted for tonight. She smiled, as if reading his mind, and rolled over onto his chest.

'Have you got the strength to go again?'

The blonde beauty giggled, grasping his penis gently and running her thumb across its turgid tip. 'You have, I see.'

'Goes without saying, gorgeous. You're here, and it's been a bloody long time. I'm ready to go all night, but there are two of us here.'

Lynn laughed. 'Yes, there are two of us. You're very clever. I'd never have worked that out.'

Her boyfriend smacked her tight buttocks, sending shockwaves through both sets of hips. To his delight, loving fingers began to trace a line from his temple, down the side of his face, past his jaw and ended up with its fingers drawing a heart shape on his hairy chest.

'I love you,' he murmured, pressing his lips on her forehead. 'And your touch turns me on everywhere. I'll be quick, I promise. I think I forgot how to be anything else, to tell you the truth.'

'Damn!' his dream girl chuckled, sitting up and straddling his throbbing body. 'You do feel like your motor's running really fast. I hope we can do slow and sensuous again once we get home too. I love it when you take your time with me.'

Jeff inhaled and almost toppled his partner to one side, suddenly in danger of losing his load then and there. 'Jesus! Don't talk like that!' he panted.

'You are not playing fair tonight, you minx. You have no idea how close I am to the point of no return.'

Lynn slunk backwards off the end of the bed. 'Come and get me then,' she taunted. 'In the shower, like in Sydney. I want to feel the tiles on my back again. Can we?'

'Can we?' her man grinned. 'Oh, I think we can. Just try and stop me!'

The excited duo rammed themselves through the bathroom door, almost tripping each other up in the process. Hot water spurted out of the jets, not having been used for several days, and the young man laughed at the corollary his girlfriend's lewd gestures were drawing.

Seizing Lynn's upper arms and lifting her championship weight into the bathtub with hidden force, Jeff leaned heavily on her body and worked his way down until he was kneeling on the slippery enamel surface. His tongue explored the heavenly folds of her vagina and quickly raised her heart rate until it almost rivalled his own.

'Come inside me,' the young woman urged. 'Please?'

Positioning two fingers to take over from his mouth, the expert lover straightened his legs just enough until he could insert his erection into the place it most wanted to be. Her warmth accepted him with a keen resistance that left him on the brink once again.

'You're the best, Lynn,' Jeff told her, locking his lips with hers and relishing her tongue filling his mouth to mirror his action down below. 'I love you so much. You're the only one I ever want to do this with.'

She moaned as he thrust into her, and he echoed the unspoken sentiment. 'Ever again.'

'Same,' the teenager murmured, feeling his penis prepare to unleash for a second time. '*Mismo.*'

'Oh, Jesus!' he laughed, letting go of both barrels on hearing her cute Spanish reply. '*Mismo, mismo,* baby.'

Smiling and crying together, Jeff turned the taps off, and the pair sank down into the bath and sat tangled up in long, wet limbs, kissing and holding each other close in the silence. The tensions and worries of the last few weeks had been ousted and washed down the plug hole, leaving them spent, purged and as one.

Lynn soon began to shiver, despite the heat still emanating from the human furnace beside her and the residual steam encircling their heads, so they towelled themselves dry and tumbled into the queen-sized bed. She willingly allowed herself to be smothered, amazed that her insatiable man was already hard again. He shrugged and apologised, promising that ignoring it was the only way to make it go away. They pulled apart and lay flat on their backs staring at the ceiling and waited for sleep to come.

'I bet your dad's never had a failed sexual experience.'

'Hmm?' the young woman responded, before opening her eyes. 'What? What are you talking about?'

Her boyfriend sniffed. 'I'd love to know what it's like to always think you're right.'

'From a mean perspective, or honestly?' Lynn teased, her tone telling him there was no point in defending himself.

'Both. Yeah, OK. Whatever... I'm not apologising,' he insisted.

'I don't want you to.'

'Thanks. But to be so single-minded that nothing distracts you. I could never be like that.'

The teenager turned back towards her prone lover and ran her hand across his chest, which felt divine under her tired fingertips. 'So when have you ever had failed sexual experiences? I thought you were the sexpert.'

Jeff chuckled, and a half-smile showed he remembered her made-up word from long ago. 'With you, yeah. But not always, and even with you sometimes.'

'Really? When?'

Lynn was genuinely interested, warming his heart, yet now was not the time to embark on another journey into vulnerability. 'Ah, hardly ever. You and I broadcast on the same channel, angel, but other women just used to go off their own way and leave me stranded sometimes. I learned to deal with it, cover it up with some bad joke or take a break until the panic passed.'

'With me too though? I always think you're totally in control.'

The handsome man kissed her concerned lips. 'You're welcome to think that! Anytime, baby. Occasionally, you throw me something I wasn't expecting. Just brief moments here and there. It's unavoidable, and I guess people who're not like me might not even notice it. Mostly they do me a favour. You know, slow me down a bit and take the focus away from my own self-serving mission. Like the troll-versus-angel moment at Suzanne's place that time. D'you remember that?'

The blonde sportswoman cast her mind back to the difficult, emotionally-charged night the pair had spent at the kennels, just before she had left for California. 'Oh yes. I do remember. That wasn't too bad though, was it?'

'No, not bad at all,' Jeff kissed her again. 'That's what I mean by us being on the same wavelength. Travelling the same path. But your dad, and Gerry... and you, to a certain extent too... We're all control freaks, but for different reasons. I'm one because I'm always petrified life won't go how I need it to go. I always wonder what it'd be like to be so sure of everything. I'm too busy worrying what it is about a situation that I don't yet know. What's going to fuck me over while I'm not concentrating. You guys are so damned confident in what you expect to happen.'

Lynn sighed. 'Like me teasing you tonight, you mean? Even though the others had gone?'

'*Sí. Exactamente.* You knew I'd keep tagging along forever, but Gravity had pretty much convinced me you were sending me an indirect message to piss off.'

'I wasn't,' the caring woman shook her head.

The dark-hearted songwriter stroked the flushed skin on the side of her face. 'I know, but that's how my mind works, angel.'

'I'm sorry.'

'Don't be sorry. It's me who has to learn.'

'No,' Lynn said, grabbing his hand and pushing herself up onto her elbow. 'I can learn too. I want to be more like you than Dad. Perhaps he needs a failed sexual experience or two?'

'Perhaps,' her amused boyfriend couldn't help but agree. 'But who's going to make it happen?'

'Don't look at me!' the teenager frowned, giggling.

'No, nor me! And I'm sure your mum's not up for that discussion.'

The pretty celebrity cringed at the very thought and snuggled down the bed again, chilled after being exposed to the elements. Her head felt a little dizzy, even after it had nestled into the softness of the pillow. The busy few weeks were obviously catching up with her.

'By the way, angel,' he said, warm lips meeting their cold counterparts. 'I know you only did that for me.'

Lynn's eyes opened. 'Sex in the shower?'

'Yep.'

'I wanted it too.'

Her lover smiled. 'Not sure about that.'

'I wanted to thank you,' the nineteen-year-old sighed, 'for waiting. And for putting up with my fucking family.'

'I know,' Jeff laughed. 'It's not necessary, but just so you know I feel thanked. And the favour will be returned.'

'Over and over, I imagine,' the young beauty giggled, feigning exhaustion.

'Whatever you want.'

'Whatever *we* want, Jeff.'

The satiated twenty-two-year-old kissed her swollen lips. 'Thanks, angel,' he whispered. 'You must be knackered. Let's get some sleep. It's great to have you back.'

'Goodnight, Jeff,' Lynn replied. 'I am really tired, but it's so good to be together.'

As soon as he began to hear the slow, rhythmic breathing of a sleeping princess, the young man gently released his grip on her hand and rolled over onto his back. A game plan was required to bring this preposterous stand-off with the Dysons to a swift conclusion. This primæval land-grab was clearly having an adverse effect on their daughter's state of mind, and he didn't want her to fall out with her family any more than she did. The potential for collateral damage was huge, and he could do without having to add that to his blame list.

***

Jeff fell asleep in the silence of the Mornington Peninsula. He didn't know how long he had been sleeping but found himself returning to consciousness in the midst of a nightmare with a different twist. It had started in the same way as ever, at the front door of his childhood flat, assaulted by the noise of shouting and screaming inside. The door swung away, and he could see Lynn ahead of him. She was beckoning to his dreaming, teenaged self, and his instincts told him he couldn't reach her. She was in trouble, and he would be powerless to save her.

'I'm so cold,' a weak, agitated voice murmured, her hand reaching out to touch his chest. 'I'm freezing. Are you awake?'

Coming to his senses, the boy from Canley Vale felt his pulse speed up. Somehow lifted out of his fitful slumber, he focussed his mind quickly away from the past and into the present.

'Cold?' the tormented man repeated, laying the palm of his hand on her forehead. 'You're not. You're boiling!'

'I don't feel well. I'm so cold.'

Jeff switched on the bedside light and found his girlfriend as white as a sheet and sweating profusely. Her whole body was shaking. His heart went out to her. Here was the explanation for her strange behaviour earlier, which had seemed so out of character. He slipped out of bed, closed the bathroom door to protect her eyes from the stark lighting and began to run a cool bath.

'You need to cool down. You've caught some foreign transit lurgy,' he smiled, gently peeling back the covers.

Even though cooling down was the last thing she wanted, Lynn didn't have the strength to resist. Shivering, she slid down into the freezing water and allowed her attentive lover to put an equally cold face flannel on her forehead. After a few minutes her temperature had dropped a little, and the worst of the fever seemed to be passing.

'Get out,' Jeff invited her, holding out his hand.

He wrapped a huge towel lovingly around her, drying droplets off her forlorn face with the corners. The siren temptress of a few hours ago had been transformed into a pathetic, quivering waif, and he loved her even more. Lynn saw him pull something out of his overnight bag and slumped back onto the mattress, completely devoid of energy. As she tucked the quilt around her shaking form, she fed her dull senses with the sight of her boyfriend's suit pants going back on and his arms slotting quickly into his shirt sleeves.

'Here's a spare t-shirt, angel. I'm sure you can put it on without even opening your eyes. I'm going out to the car. I think I've got some paracetamol. It'll help keep your temperature down.'

The automatic closer on the cottage door swung shut, and the sickly woman heard it click. She planned to get up and open it for her phobic carer as soon as she heard his footsteps on the gravel outside. However, when he approached, she found herself too nauseated to stand up straight. As she rested on the side of the bed, she heard the key in the lock. The door swung open almost immediately. Turning round, she saw him breathing hard but looking triumphant.

'Are you OK?' she checked.

'Yep. Don't worry about me.'

Shaking almost as violently has the patient had been earlier, Jeff sat down heavily on the bed and gave her two tablets. 'Fuck! It's pitch back out there. I could hardly find the car. The moral of the story is, "Don't buy a black car if you live in the middle of nowhere".'

Smiling, Lynn swallowed the tablets and a whole glass of water on strict instruction. 'You're a good doctor,' she said, leaning into him.

'*Muchas gracias, señorita.* Feel any better?'

The patient didn't look any better, shaking her head to confirm her boyfriend's diagnosis.

'Do you think you can sleep some more?'

Lynn looked at the clock: three-twenty.

She groaned. 'I've got to be at the Sportsdrome at ten o'clock for athletics training. I'll have to phone Dad first thing if I'm no better. He's going to be very suspicious.'

'Forget him for now,' Jeff encouraged, helping her back into bed and laying the quilt on top of her warm, shivering body. 'We'll deal with that in the morning.'

He switched the light off and waited for his beautiful best friend to fall back to sleep, allowing himself a small, optimistic peek into the future. His nightmare had turned into a dream instead of the usual full-on fury, and then he had been able to walk nearly straight in through the door just now, returning from the dark trip to the car. Had something really changed inside his head finally? Were the years of trauma being balanced by enough positive memories to rid himself of the symptoms of his illness? Christ, he hoped so.

Sleep overtook the hopeful young man fairly quickly, but there was little chance to put his new theory to the test, since his roommate was soon awake again, springing out of bed in her own urgent dismay. The wedding breakfast was on its way out, and her temperature was sky-high once more.

Jeff smiled at her, dejected and shivering in the bath for a second time. 'Having fun?' he teased, dispensing yet another glass of water and some more painkillers. 'Do you feel any better now?'

Lynn was unable to fight back. 'I feel terrible. I haven't been this ill for years.'

Doctor and patient returned to bed to make the best of the remaining night-time hours. Wrapped up in loving arms, the young woman did her best to apologise for ruining their night away and for potentially passing on whatever germs she had caught, but her man would hear nothing of it. This was reality, he insisted, and nothing gave him more pleasure than to look after her, regardless of the consequences. He reminded her that it was exactly what a respecting relationship demanded, and the droopy object in his arms was hardly in a position to disagree with her wise and irresistible adviser.

The invalid was still sleeping when Jeff awoke to slithers of daylight piercing his eyelids through the curtains. He felt strangely at peace and ready to continue taking care of someone who wouldn't push him away. It was eight o'clock. He needed to rouse her to contact her father with the news of missing their training session.

After making some hot tea, the rock star crouched down and stroked his dream girl's cheek, rearranging locks of hair which had become matted with the perspiration from last night's high temperature. She was still running a fever. Her eyes opened slightly, and the very smallest of smiles spread across her face.

'Hey, beautiful,' her boyfriend greeted her and planted a kiss on a burning forehead. 'You're damned hot!'

Lynn pulled a hand from under the quilt and held it against her right temple, groaning quietly. 'My head's thumping. What time is it?'

'Just after eight,' he answered. 'I'll get you some more paracetamol. Time to make that 'phone call.'

Lynn sat up slowly and groaned again. 'Oh, God. I feel awful. I'm so glad you're here.'

She looked up at Jeff and did her best to smile. He lifted the mug of tea into her hands.

'I'm glad I'm here too. Are you up to ringing, or do you want me to do it?'

The young woman shook her head. 'No, I have to do it. Not that I want to...'

The forbidden friends sat in silence while they drank, giving each other space while the sportswoman composed her rare excuse. Tea finished, she lifted the receiver and dialled the number for Dyson Administration. The line connected.

'Hello, Howard. It's Lynn. Please could you put me through to Dad?'

Jeff began to pack their things together. They would need to check out by ten o'clock. His stomach was baying for the cooked breakfast to which he had been looking forward, but it was patently obvious that he would not be proudly showing off his most prized award in the communal dining room this morning. He listened for Bart to come on the line.

'Morning, Dad,' the sportswoman began apprehensively, frowning at the pain behind her eyes. 'I'm really sorry, but I'm not going to be able to get to training this morning. I'm not well.'

There was a short pause, and her partner was unable to hear what was being said at the other end. Angrily, he considered how much of an understatement this was, watching Lynn cradling her aching head. There were beads of sweat on her brow, and her skin was very pale.

'But Dad, I can't. Really. I'm really sick... No, it's not a hangover... I've caught a bug or something. Drugs? No... Please, I...'

The young woman was doing her best to convince her father that she was telling the truth, but again the immovable patriarch appeared to know exactly what was going on a hundred kilometres south-east of the city. Jeff walked around to the other side of the bed and signalled for her to pass him the receiver.

'Let me talk to him,' he offered, his eyes filled with an urgent sympathy.

Reluctant but grateful, the patient agreed and allowed him to take over. This was not exactly how she had imagined her boyfriend bringing things to a head, as he had promised last night, and she was apprehensive about the lengths to which he might go to plead her case. She sighed and flopped back onto the pillow.

'Mister Dyson, good morning. It's Jeff,' the deep voice opened, not knowing what sort of reception he would get from Big D either. 'Lynn can't possibly train this morning. You should see her. She's got a high fever and she can't even stand up.'

Bart's curt tone portrayed his annoyance, laced with a good deal of suspicion, as his daughter had predicted, as he barked into the telephone. 'I might've known you'd have something to do with this, Diamond. Where are you?'

'Sir, we're still in Portsea, in a B and B. Lynn's perfectly safe but as sick as a dog,' he told his adversary, overlooking the accusation for the moment.

The young man listened while Bart informed his wife that their daughter hadn't returned to the city last night and that she was still with "that bloody Diamond man again". He smiled and shook his head, and Lynn gave him a questioning look.

'What's been going on to make my daughter unwell?' the authoritative voice demanded. 'What have you given her? I will not have her involved in your drug-riddled lifestyle, Jeff. I thought I'd made that perfectly clear when we met.'

Determined to keep calm in the face of this unwarranted onslaught, the rock star answered. 'Look, sir… Please don't blame me for everything bad that happens to your daughter. She's picked up the 'flu or some other airborne virus, probably from the 'plane or in transit.'

'Is that right?' the millionnaire heard from the other end of the line. 'Are you saying there weren't alcohol or drugs involved? You're seriously expecting me to believe you? I knew it was a bad idea to leave her at the wedding.'

'Mister Dyson,' he continued. 'Bart, thanks… You only have to look at Lynn to know she can't train today. Yes, I gave her painkillers. Four paracetamol, to be precise. There are no drugs here, and the bottle of Shiraz I had intended to open with her is still in the bottom of my bag. For Christ's sake, she can barely lift her eyelids.'

The father huffed, and Jeff could hear Marianna's voice in the background. Although the big man had given him permission to address him by his first name, he was not sounding conciliatory or the least bit sympathetic.

'So you think you're a doctor now?' he snapped.

The handsome musician watched Lynn's face as she listened to his half of the conversation, imagining what her father was saying at the other end. 'No, sir. I'm well aware I'm not a doctor, but even poor boys and sons of murderers get sick once in a while. It's not serious. Lynn just needs to stay in bed and sweat it out of her system. You can come and visit her if you like. Don't worry. I haven't kidnapped her. She's free to leave any time she wants, sir.'

The patient grimaced, burying her face in the other pillow, not knowing whether to laugh or cry. Her defiant black stallion was saying exactly what she hoped he would say, but she knew these fine words would only serve to aggravate matters further. She listened for his next salvo expectantly, and he didn't let her down.

'You've probably all caught it too by now anyway. She would've been extremely contagious yesterday, so we're all going down. The whole wedding crowd's probably got it, thanks to your gorgeous little walking, talking epidemic. Maybe she caught it from that banker you lined her up with at the wedding?'

Lynn rolled her eyes, as her man clenched his right fist and moved it suggestively up and down in front of his groin in the manner of something rhyming with banker. Jeff grinned at her reaction and blew her a kiss. He was beginning to enjoy himself now, which was slightly dangerous. The booming voice next asked him how he knew about the second suitor.

'Bart, it may surprise you, but your daughter and I do talk,' his terse opponent explained. 'We'll be back in Melbourne by mid-morning, and I'm sure Lynn'll ring you again as soon as she's feeling better.'

'Hello, Jeff. Is Lynn alright?'

Without warning, the irate father had transferred the telephone to his wife. The young man looked at the patient, pointing at the receiver.

'It's your mum,' he mouthed to the defenceless nineteen-year-old. 'Morning, Marianna. How're you going? Well, she's not too good at the moment, but it'll pass.'

Reaching forward to take his dream girl's outstretched hand, Jeff continued. 'Her face, although still very beautiful, is a delicate shade of green, and there's a vacant expression on it that leads me to believe someone's stolen her brain.'

Marianna laughed softly at the other end. Despite outwardly taking the same tough stance as her husband, she had always had a soft spot for the handsome maverick, even though she completely agreed that his underworld background made him totally unsuitable for their very special daughter.

'So how is she getting home?' the mother asked with renewed vigour, most likely prompted by Bart's anger.

Staring at the receiver and giving his dream girl a confused look, Jeff couldn't resist playing with this ridiculous question a little. 'Oh, I don't know. Haven't asked her yet. Walk, maybe? Marianna, she's being well looked after. Please don't worry. I'll make up a bed in the boot of the car,' he continued to ad-lib. 'A suitcase on either side, and she won't roll around too much.'

Lynn burst out laughing before feebly gripping her temples with both hands. At the other end of the line, Marianna couldn't help but chuckle too, prompting the charitable man to make the elder stateswoman an offer he never thought he would.

'Write down my 'phone number, Missus Dyson. You're both welcome to come over and check on the patient whenever you like. I'm sure she can have a roast dinner ready for you tonight, if you want to pop in.'

His girlfriend groaned, and he leaned forward to kiss her while rattling off the apartment's telephone number, waiting as it was repeated back to him. 'Correct. It's the taller of the two apartment buildings on the corner of Victoria Avenue and La Trobe Street, at the northern end of Spring Street. Does that make sense? *Bueno.* When you arrive, buzz the entry-phone downstairs, and I'll come down and let you into the car park.'

The tired traveller asked to speak to her mother, and her resident comic handed over the receiver, stroking her forehead.

'Mum, I just want to be with Jeff. He's being so nice to me. Please?'

Marianna took pity on her sick daughter. 'I know you do, darling. Here's your father again.'

'Dad, I'm really feeling bad,' she begged. 'I will ring tomorrow, I promise.'

The empathetic man watched Lynn stiffen in advance of the switch. Bart must have said goodbye fairly tersely because the young woman slumped back onto the pillow in disappointment and closed her eyes. Her boyfriend lifted the receiver out of her hand and checked that the line was dead.

'*Adios*,' he snarled into the mouthpiece before replacing it onto the base unit.

Jeff sat down on the side of the bed. He could see the situation was plainly vexing the gorgeous but ailing creature. 'You OK?'

Lynn shrugged. 'I don't know. I can't think straight. Mum seemed OK, but Dad's still angry that we're here together. I can't believe after two years of more-or-less total independence, I'm right back where I started all over again.'

'That's my fault,' the self-confessed blame consultant acknowledged sadly. 'Isn't it? Everything would be just fine if you'd got sick on your boring wanker, I'm guessing. Are you going to be alright if I drive us home, or shall I book in for another night?'

'Oh, I really want to go home,' the patient whimpered. 'I'll be OK. And don't blame yourself. It's not fair. You're not going to put me in the boot though, are you?'

'Too right, I am!' the comic ruffled her hair. 'You'll be fine. It's nice and dark. Good for your headache.'

***

Lynn was a picture walking to the car. Wearing the dress she had worn to Mark and Shona's wedding with Jeff's shirt and jacket over the top, she tiptoed barefoot to the waiting Aston Martin. She allowed him to fasten her seatbelt and steal a quick kiss, feeling a little better for having been out in the fresh air for a few moments.

'I'm glad I'm not on stage tonight,' she muttered, with a weak giggle.

The driver reached for her right hand and kissed it in sympathy. 'You don't look very superstarrish, I must admit. I'll drive home on all the straight roads. Tell me if you want me to stop.'

'Thanks, Jeff. I feel very loved. Sorry to ruin our weekend.'

'You are very loved,' he replied, 'and don't worry about it. I'm sure you're enjoying this far less than I am.'

After checking out and apologising to the staff for skipping breakfast, the contented driver jumped back into the sleek ambulance bearing an Aston Martin badge, amid a small crowd of admirers. The windows were tinted sufficiently that they couldn't discern more than an outline of the passenger, and Lynn deliberately kept her head low. The car prowled out of the grounds of the Bed and Breakfast, and they were soon speeding towards the city unhindered by the light Sunday traffic.

After a while, the exhausted invalid fell asleep to the drone of the engine, and Jeff switched on the radio to listen to some pre-match cricket commentary. Life was still good, his positive side persisted, glancing over at his pale but comfortable companion. Marianna was on-side, with just the big man left to work on. The soul-mates would get through this frustrating phase in their age-old relationship. He simply needed to trust in a future that for him remained somewhat indistinct, now buoyed by the fact that this fuzzy vision appeared also to have infiltrated Lynn's mind.

Before too long, the mean machine was pulling into the car park at the bottom of its owner's apartment building. The couple was fortunate not to meet anyone in the lift, reaching the top floor without stopping. Lynn was feeling queasy after the journey, but nevertheless held her hand out for the key as they approached the front door. Jeff didn't object. He was happy just to successfully secrete her inside. He would test for any change in his phobia later.

The young woman headed straight for the master bedroom, discarded Jeff's jacket on the chest of drawers and climbed into bed fully clothed. She was relieved not to have to go anywhere else. Her boyfriend followed her in, dumping their gear on the floor.

'Hey, before you get too comfortable, put these on. Then you won't have to move all day.'

He pulled out a pair of tracksuit pants and a t-shirt from a drawer. Lynn obliged, every movement an effort. Pulling the quilt up over her shoulders, she snuggled down into the warmth.

'This is so nice,' she murmured. 'I'm in your bed, wearing your clothes. And my mum and dad know I'm here.'

Yes, indeed, Jeff agreed. Actually far too nice for his own good. He had never been in this position before. There was a stunning, nubile blonde in his bed whom he couldn't touch, and his body struggled with the concept far more than it ought to.

'If you don't mind, I'll go for a run. I need to blow off some steam. Otherwise it's going to drive me crazy having you in my bed without being able to have my wicked way with you. Is that OK?'

Lynn nodded. 'I'm sorry. Sure. I'm not going anywhere.'

Her lover leaned over and kissed her. 'Thanks, angel. I'll only be an hour. Help yourself to anything you can find.'

Jeff closed the door behind him. His precious hostage's safety was paramount, so he would simply have to deal with whatever confronted him when he returned home. He took off at full pelt southwards down Spring Street and along Bridge Road, forcing the heaviness in his genitals to disperse along with the lactic acid in his thighs until he reached his old stomping ground of Richmond. How life had changed! His head was clear, and his legs felt super-strong as he passed the end of his old street.

While running and thinking, the superstar cursed Miss Irony again for visiting upon him a further dose of celibacy as a bonus for staying the course of Lynn's latest absence. A good hour had passed by the time he came full circle and arrived back at the sixteen-storey block, still with plenty of energy but feeling guilty for abandoning the patient in her hour of need. He confronted his solid front door head-on and pictured her in his bed, wearing his clothes, inside his apartment. The key turned, his head filled with the usual chaotic thoughts, and the runner found himself in the hallway. Oh, well... Still some work to do.

In the master bedroom, his flatmate was awake and looking a little healthier. She held her hands out to encourage him closer, as if encouragement were needed.

'How're you feeling?' he asked.

'Not too bad, thanks. Mum rang. They're coming over in about an hour. Sorry. They insisted.'

Jeff shrugged and smiled. He was ready. The lengthy burst of aerobic exercise had given him the opportunity to formulate a strategy, and it excited him to think he could put it into action so promptly.

'That's OK. It's all good. I really want to bring this thing to a conclusion.'

'I'm not going to be much help to you though,' the teenager mourned. 'Mum's bringing some clothes for me. She's being really nice, but I can't vouch for Dad.'

The athlete jumped into the shower, desperately needing to assume control of his nervous energy. After two years of waiting, the girl of his dreams was installed at long last in his apartment; and yet here he was, masturbating in the shower before her parents arrived. He felt like he was sixteen again. Now more than ever, he needed a clear head, uncomplicated by an excess of testosterone racing around his body.

'So... What *don't* you want me to say?' Jeff asked his beautiful girlfriend, who was trying her best to enjoy the mug of tea which he had made after his shower.

She frowned. 'I don't know. They know what we want, and we know what they want. I guess we just have to put our argument to them and see what happens. Dad's going to be tough on you. I can tell when he's going to give someone a hard time. He starts getting really sarcastic.'

'That's fine. I can do sarcastic too, as you may've noticed. I have to be able to convince him that I'm not what my past suggests,' the intelligent celebrity mused, glancing around. 'This place is civilised enough, isn't it? No evidence of sordid sex parties! Probably not in the right part of town for them, but it's secure. And I'll get them to park next to my Aston, which should make him realise that I'm not after you for your money. That just leaves my ability to stay above the law. That's harder to prove.'

'It depends if he's found out anything new. Have you spoken to Alberto lately?'

Jeff had to confess that the frail boxer was in his own trouble. 'He's not going to stack up too well as my character witness,' he relayed with a wry smile.

The buzzer sounded from the door downstairs, bringing their brainstorming session to a rapid close. In fact, this was as good a time as any to invite the Dysons into his home. He was stone cold sober, hadn't ingested anything adventurous for a few days, and although his dream girl was perking up a bit, she still had the unmistakable grey-green tinge of the unclean. They looked at each other with cartoon comic faces, and Jeff blew the patient a kiss.

'Hello?' he said into the entry-phone. 'Yep. I'll be right down. This is it, angel. Wish me luck!'

'Good luck! Leave the door open. They won't mind for such a short time.'

Her afflicted doctor put his hands together in a praying pose. 'Cheers. I'll take you up on that.'

When the young man reached the ground floor, Marianna was already standing in the interior lobby, elegantly dressed and dignified as usual. He put on a heart-warming smile as he stepped out and watched her pivot on her heels at the sound of the lift arriving.

'Someone let me in,' the sheepish woman admitted, looking out of place and slightly uncomfortable.

'Great,' Jeff replied, extending his hand. 'Welcome, Missus Dyson. Where are you parked?'

A graceful hand gestured directly outside, where the handsome man spied a burgundy red Jaguar stationary on the side of the road. Together they went down the steps towards it, and Marianna motioned to their host to climb into the back seat.

'Afternoon, Jeff,' Bart greeted him curtly. 'Where should I go?'

I can think of a few places, the successful, headstrong celebrity said to himself, before directing his girlfriend's father around the corner and down a narrow laneway. As they approached the entrance, he pressed a button on his remote control, and the garage door opened. He noticed the older man nodding in tacit approval. The Jaguar drove slowly towards the back of the car park and came to a stop next to the Aston Martin, which was flecked with wet sand from their recent journey back from the coast.

'Park to the right of the black beast, sir,' Jeff instructed. 'It's my second space.'

His visitor manœuvred their vehicle into the space, and the anxious songwriter pointed towards the door to the basement lift lobby. So far, so good, he thought, changing his mind about shoving his hands in the pockets of his tracksuit pants. Why did his body language always give the game away? One day he would succeed in aligning all his faculties towards the same objective. With Lynn's help.

'JMD,' Marianna read from the licence plate. 'Is this car yours?'

Jeff stroked the rear end of the sleek sports car, pleased that the plan he had thrown together at a moment's notice was working so nicely. 'Yes, ma'am! Cool, isn't she? Lynn did pretty well in the boot this morning. It's more spacious than you think.'

'Very nice,' Bart admitted, though refusing to see the funny side.

The young man ushered the couple out of the car park and into another lobby, inserted his security key into the lift lock and pressed the button for the top floor. Every movement was timed to perfection, cued by his Pied Piper eyes attracting the right amount of attention at the right time.

'How long have you been in this building?' the Olympian made polite conversation as they headed skyward. 'It wasn't new when you bought it, was it?'

'No, sir. I only moved in a year ago. Someone else lived in it from new but only for three years. I've only got one neighbour on my floor, and he's overseas on business most of the time. It's nice and quiet.'

Lynn was already standing in the hallway when the lift doors opened. She had changed out of her boyfriend's clothes in favour of a pair of her own pyjamas. No doubt as a symbol of their alliance, she had wrapped herself in his bathrobe however, a gesture which had far more than the desired effect on the man concerned. *Good on her*, Jeff thought, instantly wishing he had put on a pair of jeans instead. His flatmate was no less devious than her horny nurse! Plus, now her parents would think she had opened the door. She really was his *Regala*, in every possible way.

'Hi, Dad. Hi, Mum,' the young woman greeted the new arrivals, smiling through her headache. 'I don't want to kiss you in case I'm still contagious.'

'Go on in,' their host invited.

He motioned to Bart and Marianna to follow their daughter, glowing inside uncontrollably on discovering furthermore that she had donned a pair of socks so large and bunched-up on her smaller feet that her parents were bound to guess they belonged to the man of the house. The Dysons walked through the hallway and on into the lounge room, and the young man almost slammed the front door with pent-up contempt.

Gravity was limbering up, but Jeff was determined not to let that dastardly troll get the better of him today. 'Tea? Coffee?'

Lynn was the only one to decline. Her boyfriend went into the kitchen to make the drinks while she showed her parents around the apartment. Surprisingly, he wasn't even particularly nervous; more anxious to apply his considerable intellect to a good argument. He loved the fact that his gorgeous concubine felt comfortable enough to conduct the tour herself. Pouring boiling water out of the kettle, his heart began to beat a little faster. Perhaps he just wasn't nervous *yet*...

Everyone helped themselves to coffee. The devoted carer gave his charge a glass of iced water and a kiss.

'That's all you're getting, so be grateful,' he smiled, giving her the tiniest wink of approval.

The songwriter suspected the effort expended on welcoming her parents had left the patient feeling dizzy and weak all over again. Gazing upon her benevolently, he could also feel Marianna's eyes monitoring their every exchange, which was again all part of his master plan.

'Let's go outside, sir,' the humble foot soldier suggested to Lynn's imposing general of a father, pointing to the balcony and picking up his packet of cigarettes for something to occupy his restless hands.

'Good idea,' Bart agreed. 'The girls can chat in here. After you.'

Father and lover stood on the balcony together. While Bart was dressed smartly in sports jacket and tie, Jeff had hurriedly put on an old t-shirt and a pair of tracksuit trousers which had seen better days. The young man's hair was still damp after his shower, and his face hadn't seen a razor since before Mark's wedding. Lynn and her mother studied the two outwardly very different men from their vantage point on the lounge sofa, their respective body language fascinating. Both combatants had planted their feet firmly on the ground facing each other, about a metre apart. Jeff was smoking and had his right hand casually in his pocket. Every now again, he would reach up and scratch his head with his smoking hand, or stretch both arms into the air. Bart was clutching his coffee mug in one hand and making strong-armed, measured gestures with the other.

'What do you think they're talking about?' Marianna asked her subdued daughter.

Lynn sighed. 'Dad'll be trying to find a reason why Jeff's not good enough for me, and Jeff'll be trying to persuade Dad that he's not who he's supposed to be. They'll both say the same thing about ten times, waiting for number eleven to deal the killer punch. In that respect, they're quite alike, I think.'

The mother put her hand on her sickly girl's arm. She definitely didn't look well. The bad boy had told them the truth about her illness, and the older woman felt reassured that there had been no any illicit substances partaken to lay her so low.

'Well, darling, I can tell you he hasn't discovered anything new since they last met,' the elegant lady confided. 'Do *you* think there's anything else we need to know? You've heard his side of the story. Do you think he tells you the whole truth?'

'Yes! And no, Mum,' the teenager replied, instantly incensed. 'There isn't anything horrible to be worried about. Jeff's exactly who he says he is. He's had the worst life I can imagine and he's absolutely determined to be successful. His mother died of a drug overdose when he was fourteen, and he was the one who found her. Can you imagine anything so disgusting? Despite everything, he's so motivated to do good and he loves me more than you think. More than I think sometimes... Look how he takes care of me. I love him, Mum. I really do. I'd hate it if you and Dad told us we couldn't see each other anymore. Really hate it.'

Nodding, Marianna stood up and crossed the room to examine the various photographs scattered around the large room, giving her daughter the chance to compose herself. On the baby grand piano, she found the one she had given the dancing pair after Robert's twenty-first birthday party. She had to admit they made a great-looking couple. Next to this, there was one of the dark-haired rock star taken with Elvis Presley, superimposed against the lyrics to one of the American legend's big hits.

'Did Jeff write a song for Elvis?' she asked, scanning the verses carefully. 'These are very powerful lines. I can hear him saying them too.'

'Yes. Elvis has recorded three or four of his songs actually,' Lynn affirmed. 'He's a great songwriter too. He never stops. I don't understand where his inspiration comes from. He's an emotional powder keg...'

The teenager's voice tailed off, afraid that she might be giving away too much information. Her mother had moved on, now engrossed in a shelf of books which vaunted the successful musician's interest in a wide spectrum of the arts, from architecture to Dadaism and from Vivaldi to twentieth-century rock'n'roll. This boy from Sydney's downtrodden suburbs had certainly worked hard to cultivate his adult personage.

Meanwhile, outside in the balmy air, Bart reported to his adversary that his private investigators had failed to turn up any further evidence. Jeff received the news calmly, without displaying any hint of "I told you so", and his mind took pleasure in dealing Gravity a sharp slap.

'So no joy with Simon Scheisster either then?' the younger man enquired with a straight face.

'Steinmann,' Lynn's father corrected, before coming to the realisation that the smart alec had called his solicitor by this name on purpose.

The big man chuckled. He had fallen for that one. 'Very good.'

'So where does that leave us?'

Bart shuffled forwards a little in response to the challenge, while his opponent stood his ground, though more respectfully this time. Big D was only a few centimetres taller than the twenty-two-year-old, but much broader. In his mid-forties, he was still a very strong man, even by Olympic standards. He had not forgotten the young man's unflinching stance from the first time the two had met.

He addressed the young pretender, his blue-grey eyes drilling into him. 'Jeff, I'm holding you accountable from now on. Lynn's safety is your responsibility. Do you understand? I know she wants to be with you, and you certainly seem to have her best interests at heart at the moment. I only hope it's going to last.'

The Sydneysider nodded without changing his expression. Privately, he rejoiced at what appeared to be the beginnings of a truce, and he dared to raise a metaphorical middle finger to his spiteful inner demon. The subliminal act left him feeling strangely exposed, and he wished his dream girl was no longer separated from him by a sheet of bulletproof glass.

'Sure. You don't have to worry, Bart,' he found an equally stern voice. 'If anything happened to Lynn, I'd hold myself responsible anyway. Regardless of what you say or do now.'

'Good,' the father nodded. 'I hope you mean it. I don't want to hear anything scandalous in the press. No pregnancies... Lynn's or anyone else's. No playing around, no beating her up after a few drinks.'

Jeff took exception to these last few spiteful words, bile rising in his stomach at the hateful images. 'Look, sir... We've waited a long time to be together. Your daughter means the world to me, and if you think I'm going to mess her around like that, then you really don't know who I am. And that's not because I want to protect her reputation, your reputation or even my own fucking reputation. I love Lynn, and she's worth way more than that. Do *you* understand?'

Bart raised both hands, palms facing his opponent. 'Alright. Yes, I understand. I'm sorry. I overstepped the mark.'

The millionnaire musician acknowledged Big D's apology manfully. From the other side of the patio doors, mother and daughter were glued to the debate as it swang to and fro between their respective partners. They had witnessed the posturing back and forth and then the bigger man's apparent capitulation.

Lynn turned to her mum, wondering and hoping. 'Look how good he looks. They look the same, the two of them.'

'They're both fine men, darling,' Marianna agreed. 'Your father's only doing what fathers do. We want you to be safe and happy. When Jeff has a daughter, he'll be in Dad's shoes, and I wonder how different he'll be?'

'Yes, I suppose so,' the younger woman replied. 'But Jeff would always ask his daughter what she wants. I know he would.'

They glanced back just in time to see Bart extend his hand to the songwriter, and then her boyfriend's left hand clasp over it. The two men were actually shaking hands and smiling. The two ladies looked at each other, open-mouthed.

'Looks like they've struck a deal,' the nineteen-year-old hazarded. 'Oh, I really hope so.'

The temptation to run across the lounge room to the balcony windows to discover the outcome the men had reached was practically unbearable for the young star, but she knew she must exhibit an appropriate amount of adult decorum until the time was right. She also wanted to give her man every opportunity to dictate the play in his own home, having unwrapped another layer of his mysterious mind last night.

Eventually, the sliding door to the balcony moved silently on its runners, and the tall pair stepped back into the lounge room, even sharing a joke. Lynn noticed her boyfriend didn't make eye contact with her straightaway, which she took as a very good sign. If he had been floundering, he would most definitely have sent up a flare at his first opportunity.

'Can I get you a beer?' Jeff was asking.

Bart declined. 'No, thanks. We should be going. I need to do some work before the evening gets too late. And Lynn, Mum and I'll talk to you during the week. We'll choose a night for dinner, the three of us. Marianna?'

There were finer details to sort out, the youngsters transferred their thoughts telepathically, but a deal in principle had been struck. No objections would be raised in this case. The Dysons said their goodbyes to the grinning patient and wished her a speedy recovery. Jeff accompanied them down to the basement again, making sure they were able to drive out through the security gates. He lifted his hand politely as the horn beeped.

Mercifully, his poorly angel had redeployed the telephone directories to prop the front door open for her boyfriend's return. He didn't find her on the couch, so made his way back into the bedroom to see her curled up under the covers again.

'You OK? How do you think that went?' he asked, stroking her forehead.

'Well. Great, in fact. It's a huge relief. At least you didn't punch each other, like in your nightmare,' Lynn replied, smiling wanly. 'What did you talk about?'

'Do you really want me to dissect it now or would you rather get some sleep? You're not looking too flash.'

'Just the edited highlights, please,' she sighed. 'And no long words.'

Jeff kissed her. 'OK. I promise. Basically, he's passed all responsibility for your safety onto me, in an antiquated, women-can't-look-after-themselves kind of way.'

The blonde teenager huffed. 'Typical! So what does passing responsibility mean? What do you have to do for me, apart from wrap me up in cotton wool and keep me chained to the stove?'

'Now there's an idea!' her boyfriend chuckled, receiving a slap in return. 'Not get you pregnant, for starters. Or anyone else. He obviously doesn't believe I can last three weeks without you either.'

'Oh, my God! Not that again,' the perturbed woman moaned. 'I wonder if he even knows what the pill's all about?'

Her lover smiled. 'I doubt if he's that old-fashioned, angel. Next was no playing around, which is fair enough. I'll cop that one, and you have my word.'

Lynn kissed him. 'I trust you.'

'And lastly,' she sensed him tense up and stared into saddened dark eyes. 'And this is the one that pissed me off big-time. I'm not to beat you up, even after a few drinks.'

'He actually said that?'

Jeff nodded, with tears in his eyes. Looking away, he exhaled quickly through his nostrils. Lynn could see the anger brewing in his body and assumed his thoughts had turned to the horrific treatment his mother and sister had undergone at the hands of his father and the other gangland thugs.

'I'm sorry,' she said. 'I know that must be so hard for you to listen to. And now it makes me annoyed at myself at having joked about you giving me a beating if I didn't clear up the dinner things when Vanessa was here.'

The handsome rocker turned his gaze back, appeased to some extent that their minds were synchronised. He leaned forward to kiss her apologetic lips, further gratified to watch out of the corner of his eye as his cigarettes and lighter were being lifted towards him. Momentarily speechless, covetous fingers closed around the gift and transferred it to the mattress while he enveloped his favourite thing in all the world with appreciative arms.

'Jeff, I'm really sorry,' Lynn apologised again.

'It's OK,' he croaked. 'I'm just super-sensitive to that stuff, that's all. Anyway, that's everything. The sum total of my commitment to him, which is a tiny fraction of my commitment to you. Abridged version, of course.'

The relieved man lay down next to the patient, and she cuddled into him readily. He wondered if his sudden loss of energy was the result of the last stressful hour or whether his immune system was now under attack from his girlfriend's high-flying virus.

'Thank you,' she said, 'and also for sorting things out. I suppose that means we're not a secret anymore?'

'Guess not, no,' the songwriter frowned, beginning to feel more balanced at last. 'Shame, really. I was quite enjoying it.'

'Hope I'm not still contagious,' Lynn added, yawning.

'Too late for that,' Jeff smiled, catching her yawn instead. 'Hey! Maybe you are.'

'I'm going to try to sleep, if that's OK. I don't feel well again. Too much excitement.'

'Sure. That's fine. You need to. I'll concoct something suitably bland and unexciting for dinner, and then I might head over to Gerry's to see if he's got any urgent stuff for me to deal with.'

And to update him on my triumphant resolution of the Cold War, the cocky hero added silently. Lynn was already asleep. The contented superstar walked around to the other side of the bed and took her empty water glass to refill it, planting a soft kiss on her forehead as she lay there, gorgeously inanimate in his bed.

The Start Of Something Big

'Mate!' Gerry shouted, opening the front door of his salubrious Toorak bachelor pad. 'Just in time.'

'For what?' Jeff laughed, following his mate down the hallway and into the bright, shiny kitchen.

'To crack the top off a cold one. What else?'

The older man reached two beers out of the fridge. Accepting the bottle and taking a large swig, the visitor prepared to ask the burning question. His manager had endured a stressful week too, pacifying the mother of his unborn child and attempting to strike a balance between showing he cared and separating himself from the whole situation.

'How're things with Heather going?'

His old friend put his hands over his ears and groaned. 'Don't say that name to me, mate. I've had it with trying to be nice.'

'Why? What's happened? I thought things were settling down.'

'It's not so much Heather who's doing my head in, but her bloody mother,' Gerry moaned. 'She thinks she's got a hotline to my office and bails me up regularly to give me a hard time. I can't do any more than I'm doing, short of fucking marrying her, and neither of us wants that.'

'Doesn't she?' Jeff asked. 'Heather, I mean.'

'No!' the adamant accountant exclaimed in exasperation. 'At first she did, but that was just the shock of finding out she was pregnant. We hardly had a red-hot relationship going, did we? She told me the other day that she was glad I didn't agree to getting married.'

'OK,' the visitor acquiesced. 'That's good then, if you're both alright about it. What about the kid though?'

'There's a kid?' the Irishman feigned surprise.

The songwriter rolled his eyes and smiled. 'Nice one. Let's get our priorities right, shall we?'

'Yeah. You're probably right,' the self-centred executive replied, immediately changing the subject. 'How was Squire Davenport's wedding?'

'Fine. Subject closed. Posh and uptight, mostly. The speeches were lame, and the band misbehaved as usual,' his mate replied, shaking his head. 'And Lynn's probably infected everyone with some bug she picked up on the way home from Hong Kong.'

Gerry laughed heartily. 'Good for her. Did she go to Honkers after the tennis? Jesus! Between you, you're using up the world's oil reserves pretty damned fast. I thought you two weren't supposed to be seen together in public?'

Jeff leaned against the kitchen wall and prepared to tell Gerry the latest episode in his rollercoaster life. 'Right. We weren't,' he confirmed. 'It was a bit of a farce really. First of all, the Dysons were late and came screaming in at the last minute, just as the bride was about to march down the aisle. Then I saw they'd seated some poncy city git like you next door to Lynn, as an arranged dinner companion, and had to watch her make sweet, passionate small-talk with that bastard all afternoon. And *then* then, she snuck up on me and gave me an almighty stiff that was almost impossible to hide from Mark's mum.'

'Good grief!' his mate exclaimed. 'Poncy city git, you say? I love you too. Are you high on something?'

'No.'

'Well, you're very fucking excitable, for some reason. Must be getting your knob stuck in after so long. Was it worth it? I'm surprised you're still sane though, after all the drama. You mustn't know if you're coming or going these days either.'

'Literally,' the musician joked, pleased to be in the safe company of his frivolous friend. 'Things got much better after dinner though, when her parents pissed off home and left Junior in charge of keeping us apart. He was a soft touch. So I finally got her back to the B and B that I'd booked, bonked her stupid after a month at sea, only to find her spewing her guts up a few hours later.'

Gerry looked on in amusement as the story unfolded. 'What? Shit! This is a movie in the making, you know. Ker-ching, ker-ching!'

He drew dollar signs in the air before handing out another couple of beers and motioning for Jeff to adjourn to the lounge room. There was a box file on the coffee table, containing what was these days an endless stream of correspondence. The VIP client began to leaf through the pile absentmindedly.

'Does your lovemaking often induce vomiting?' his manager asked, as they dropped down onto leather sofas opposite each other.

'That's a trade secret,' the celebrity looked up and laughed. 'Who would you get to play us in the movie?'

'Steady on, old mate... Arrogance doesn't become you,' Gerry put his friend comprehensively in his place.

The superstar nodded, raising his hand in apology. 'Cheers. I deserved that. I think we've resolved the parental embargo, which is good.'

'Oh, yes? How?' the accountant was intrigued. 'What about the Dyson Detective Agency? Didn't they find anything?'

'Na! Not yet anyway. It's still going on, but the big man half-admitted defeat this afternoon. Mummy and Daddy came to visit the patient today.'

'To your apartment? Is Lynn really sick then? What's she got?'

'Yep. It was really bloody weird having them there, all dressed up like royalty, and with me just out of the shower,' Jeff affirmed. 'Some bacterial infection or other. 'Flu-like. Probably picked it up on the 'plane or in the terminal. It's no big deal. I've probably passed it onto you already, so sorry about that. But yes, to my apartment is correct. I took great pleasure in helping him park his Jag' next to my Aston. That was a savoursome moment.'

'Nice work, sir,' his old friend nodded. 'So did they approve of your digs?'

'Don't know. They didn't pass any comment. Well, Lynn's mum might've done, but I wasn't privy to their conversation. I was too busy out-posturing the big man on the balcony.'

The businessman laughed. 'You're so fucking complete, man. I envy your ability to tackle people on all fronts.'

'Why, thank you,' Jeff replied, raising his beer bottle to his mate. 'How am I supposed to answer that with arrogance not becoming me?'

'*Touché!*' the accountant nodded. 'So what's your security classification now?'

'OK,' the superstar took a deep breath. 'Yeah. Downgraded, I guess. It's still sinking in, to tell you the truth. Basically, it's alright for Lynn to move in, or rather they'll turn a blind eye to it. And OK for us to be seen together as long as I behave myself. But if they find something that they don't like and which I haven't already told Lynn about, I'm toast.'

The accountant looked confused. 'But that's a bit vague, isn't it? What does behave yourself mean? And what sort of something'll tip them over the edge again? Perhaps you do need legal advice.'

The musician closed the lid of the box file and sat it on the couch next to him, preparing to provide his manager with full disclosure. He leaned forward and tapped the table with his fingers in a drum roll.

'No surprise pregnancy. Sorry, mate. His words, not mine. No womanising, and no getting blind drunk and beating her up,' he listed, adding a flourish to the end of his drum roll. 'And as for the somethings, who knows? I can't think of anything I haven't already confessed to, but I can't trust my memory with all that shit from back then.'

'And what does Lynn have to do as her part of the bargain?'

'What d'you mean?' the younger man asked, suddenly defensive. 'Nothing. Not get pregnant, I guess. Don't bring her into this.'

Gerry persisted. 'Mate, I'm speaking as your manager now, as well as your buddy. Think about it... They're putting all this pressure on you, but their daughter can do anything she likes?'

'Bloody hell, mate. What the fuck are you talking about? Lynn's perfect. She doesn't need any conditions put on her. Leave her alone. This is between me and Big D. End of story.'

The older man recoiled dramatically. 'OK, OK! Fair enough, Mister Starry-eyed, but don't get walked over,' he warned, bemused by such an extreme level of protectiveness. 'When will you know you're completely off the hook?'

'The day I die, I expect,' the philosopher replied. 'Isn't that the way it's meant to be anyway? I made a promise to Lynn's dad to be responsible for her safety and happiness. I would've done that regardless of all this shit.'

'You're a better man than I, Gungadin,' his carefree friend scoffed. 'Far too principled for your own good.'

Jeff let out a cynical laugh. 'Probably. Anyway, all's well that ends well. At this very moment, Lynn's in my bed, wearing my trackies and about to eat a dinner that I'm going to cook, poor girl. Life's good, despite your valiant attempts to pour cold water on it.'

'Hey, wait a bottom-fuckin' minute... Don't get me wrong,' Gerry countered. 'Look, I'm glad you've got some level of approval. It's better for everyone. I just don't want you to get the raw end of the deal.'

'Raw end of the deal?' the younger man repeated, standing up to leave. 'Fuck off! You have obviously never been in love, mate. There ain't no raw end of the deal. Do you need any of this paperwork back tomorrow?'

'No, except if you want the cheque banked,' the executive focussed back on business. 'Most of it's already dealt with. Just FYI, mate.'

'OK. Thanks a lot, Gez,' his client responded with genuine gratitude. 'It's a pity I didn't have that cheque earlier. I could've waved it in front of Big D's face to prove I'm not going to rip Lynn off.'

The fun-loving accountant smiled. 'That's more like it. Way to go, money-bags. Where do you want it?'

'In a new account called "London",' the proud twenty-two-year-old answered on the spur of the moment. 'We're moving there.'

'Say what? Since when?'

'Since about a month ago. Sorry I didn't tell you sooner, but there's nothing organised yet. It'll be in the New Year. We're going to study and escape from everything.'

'Whose idea was that?' his mate asked, flabbergasted.

'Lynn's originally, but I love it,' the musician replied. 'It's going to be fantastic. Europe on our doorstep. Much closer to New York. I can't wait.'

'Wow!' Gerry exclaimed. 'That's a big move. And living together, presumably. Do the parentals know this yet?'

Jeff shrugged. 'I don't know what Lynn's told them. They wanted to send her overseas again because she refused to stay away from me. She called their bluff by saying she'd go, but that I'd be going too. Howzat for a metaphysical middle finger?'

'Mate, that's great,' his old friend told him, sensing the true romantic was becoming emotional. 'It must be good to know she feels the same way you do, especially after waiting so long.'

'You're not wrong. Fucking hell! Anyway, I'd better go and tend to the sick. Cheers for all this, mate, and for your dose of reality. It's good to get a going-over occasionally.'

The Irishman stood up and shook his client's hand. 'You're welcome, Florence Nightingale. Wish Lynn well for me. And congrats on brokering the deal with Daddy.'

'Cheers, mate,' Jeff waved. 'Thanks for the beers too. See you soon. Have a good week.'

The millionnaire let himself out of his manager's apartment, a little dazed after the harsh treatment he had received. Was Gerry jealous, or was he losing sight of reality, perched high on his new, heavenly vantage point? He couldn't wait to get back to Lynn and discuss it with her, mainly because he could.

Turning the car onto Church Road, Jeff stopped at a convenience store to pick up some treats for their evening alone together, daring to believe that his dream girl might have recovered sufficiently for him to redress his considerable sexual deficit.

***

Jeff returned to the apartment with supplies for the invalid, including ice cream. On the way up in the lift, he worked on convincing himself that the only thing behind his front door was the only thing he had ever wanted and that there were no threats lurking inside. He lifted the key to the lock, turned it and walked straight in.

The false sense of security was sadly short-lived, and a wave of anxiety rushed over him, causing him to drop the shopping bags onto the floor and spilling their contents. The young man swore under his breath. His *Regala* made the apartment a safe haven, didn't she? Somehow he had to condition his mind into believing this.

The sound of heavy objects hitting the tiles and rolling over the joins brought his girlfriend out from the lounge, where she had been curled up in front of the television.

'What happened?' she asked, picking up a tin which was trundling towards her. 'Are you alright?'

Her boyfriend laughed, embarrassed at his not-so-grand entrance. This evening had been a great leveller for him so far, leaving him feeling small after being on such a high from his heroic battle with Lynn's father.

'Sure. I'm fine,' he replied, walking over to greet her with a kiss. 'I thought I could get in with no drama, but it didn't quite happen the way I planned. How're you going?'

'Much better, thanks,' the patient answered, smiling in sympathy and helping to retrieve the scattered groceries. 'What've you been buying? There's all naughty things in here!'

'Yeah, absolutely. I don't get much chance to spoil you,' her lover confessed, nudging her sideways as they dumped everything on the kitchen bench. 'Thanks for getting changed again. I like seeing you in my clothes. For all the wrong reasons, of course.'

Lynn kissed his smiling lips. 'You're so sweet. How was Gerry?'

'Jeez! He gave me a keelhauling.'

'Keelhauling?' she echoed, laughing. 'I haven't heard that word for a long time, Captain Pegleg. What for?'

'For getting too up myself, I guess,' Jeff responded. 'I deserved it. I was on a real ego trip, telling him about your dad's deal. But he was acting generally weird also. I think he's jealous of us, and things are not too good re' the pregnancy situation.'

The nineteen-year-old frowned. 'Oh, no. Is Heather OK? Is there a problem with the baby?'

For the first time, Jeff saw a maternal look in his girlfriend's eyes, and it shocked him more than he expected. Her reaction was both frightening and attractive. Christ, she was growing up fast, which meant he ought to do the same. He was struck by a bizarre fear of the future closing in, not really knowing his own feelings on the subject.

'No. The problem's between Gerry and her mum,' he chuckled. 'Heather's resolved to the situation, but her mum isn't.'

'Ah, OK. That's not so bad. Complicated, though.'

'Sure is… Are you hungry?' the rock star moved to an early dismissal, deciding the ground was altogether too shaky.

'I think so. Not much though.'

'OK,' her boyfriend affirmed, wondering if the sportswoman felt as uncomfortable as he did. 'Good idea. Save room for ice cream.'

The patient giggled half-heartedly and clutched her head. 'Do you mind if I go back on the couch? I'm not too good again. Not ready to use up so much energy at once, obviously.'

The landlord placed his hands on her shoulders and steered his lodger into the lounge room, hugging her back tight against his body and kissing the side of her neck. Without speaking, his stomach flipped as he watched his dream girl make herself comfortable on his couch, under his quilt, in front of his television. It was pure magic, and he wondered why on Earth the churlish adolescent in him insisted on holding back.

Wheeling round, the man of the house assumed his position as cook for the evening, reflecting on another weird day in the life of Jeff Diamond. He thought back to the six-figure royalty cheque that he had seen in Gerry's box of tricks, and contrasted it with the simple meal he was endeavouring to rustle up in his apartment. The two were worlds apart, but he liked that just fine. He was still a novice rich boy, despite a comforting sense of security that he would be more than self-sufficient during their sabbatical in London.

What had Gerry meant by a raw deal? Mister Starry-eyed, he had labelled his client. The young man wondered if he might be missing something in the excitement of having his beautiful best friend back in his life. He didn't think so, but it was a timely reminder to be objective about everything. No matter how easily the boy from Canley Vale had dispatched the banker and the Frenchman, Bart Dyson remained a formidable force and could make short shrift of excommunicating anyone from his circles if he really put his mind to it.

'Grub up!' Jeff announced, walking into the lounge room with two bowls and two forks.

Lynn opened her eyes and pushed her hair away from her face, which was flushed from being tucked up in the duvet. She reached up and accepted her dinner from his outstretched hand, shuffling to a sitting position on the couch.

'Thanks,' she said, peering into the bowl. 'What is it?'

Her waiter looked aghast. '¿Perdóneme? You wouldn't say that in Florentino's.'

The patient laughed. 'Sorry! It smells great. Compliments to the chef. I didn't mean to offend you.'

'You didn't offend me,' her boyfriend bent over and kissed her. 'It was funny, that's all. It's a Jeff Diamond special. I used to make it for myself when I was feeling down or if I was sick. Comfort food. It's only chicken, some soup, baked beans and rice but with a lot of paprika and some chilli sauce to spice it up.'

Lynn took a steaming mouthful from her fork. 'Mmm... It's delicious. Thanks heaps. I didn't know you could cook.'

'I *can't* cook!'

'Yes, you can. What's this then?' his patient bleated, digging her fork into the steaming mound of food. 'It's giving me a facial at the same time.'

Jeff shook his head in blithe amusement. 'I know how to chop stuff and I'm aware of a variety of methods for warming things up, but I'd hardly count that as cooking.'

'Oh, well... In that case, neither can I. But I hope I get sick again soon. Is the paprika your grandmother's influence? I love that you made it so spicy.'

'*Smacznego,* as my grandmother was known to say. You're welcome. That's better,' he smirked. 'S'pose it probably is her influence. Don't really know. I'd like to say it was natural culinary flair, but that would be a blatant lie.'

Smiling, Lynn began to eat *con gusto,* and once again the confirmed loner marvelled at the conflict within. On the one hand, he was rapt that this co-existence was so easy, yet on the other, his rebellious streak taunted him mercilessly. The pair sat in silence in front of the television, lost in their own thoughts, until Lynn ran out of room just before her bowl was empty.

'Can you finish it?' she asked, holding the rest out towards her flatmate. 'It's beaten me. It was really tasty.'

Jeff willingly polished off the last few mouthfuls. 'Glad you liked it,' he said. 'That nice Mister Blake gave me my pocket money today.'

'Pocket money?' the invalid echoed, snuggling down again.

'I asked him to set up a London fund,' her boyfriend continued. 'We'll have to start planning who's going to pay for what. Do your parents know I'm going too?'

'Good idea. Royalties, you mean?'

'Yeah. A big one this month. Do they?'

'Mum and Dad?' she asked, looking confused.

The handsome man smiled. 'It's useless trying to talk to you today. You're a question behind all the time. I'll wait 'til you're feeling better. It's just so cool to have you here to share life's minutiæ. I want to monopolise your attention.'

Lynn raised her hands to her temples. 'Monopolise my attention?' she repeated. 'Long words hurt my head. You're right. I'm sorry. I'm sure I'll be fine tomorrow.'

Jeff hoped she would be too. Miss Irony was busy whispering in his ear, nagging him about the unfortunate timing of this mystery illness, just when he had surrendered the dubious entitlement of having his cake and eating it too. He ached inside whenever his mind wandered to the delicious body under the layers of warmth and wondered how long he could last in the vicinity of this untouchable woman. It was another good lesson, he concluded.

'OK,' he focussed his mind back on his nursing duties. 'Words of one syllable only from now on. Ice cream?'

'Yes, please!' the invalid giggled. 'But not yet. I need a break.'

'Right. You did well to keep it short.'

The blonde teenager slapped the cushion next to her on the sofa. 'Come and sit here, please,' she requested, maintaining their *staccato* vocabulary.

'No can do,' her horny lover declined, springing up and clearing away their dinner remains.

Despite the corners of Lynn's mouth turning downwards, the tall, handsome landlord left the room, shouting back from the kitchen.

'You're out of bounds.'

His impaired temptress hauled herself onto her feet and followed him, hitching up the long legs of his tracksuit pants to prevent herself from tripping over. 'Why?' she bleated. 'You won't catch any…'

Looking the picture of domesticity, Jeff turned around and flicked some suds in her face. 'Anything is not a one-syllable word,' he scolded.

'Argh! Neither is syllable. I don't want to play this game anymore.'

'Spoilsport,' her boyfriend shrugged. 'I'm glad you're feeling better.'

The patient pitched in to finish the dishes, and every time she came close, the comic would find some reason to cross the floor or to leave the room. But of course, avoiding her had completely the opposite effect on him to that which was originally intended. Fortunately however, their antics were doing the same to his flatmate.

Lynn broke the deadlock, much to her admirer's relief. 'I take it my germs are not what you're trying to skirt around.'

'Jesus Christ! Please don't say skirt,' he snapped back. 'That's just way too provocative.'

The young woman laughed. 'Is that why you dressed me up in this ridiculous outfit?'

'Absolutely!' the feisty twenty-two-year-old agreed, lying through his teeth. 'It's not working though.'

'So are you going to take me on the couch then?' Lynn teased, grabbing the man she loved round the waist from behind.

He span around and swallowed her up in his arms hungrily, before abruptly retreating. 'No, I'm not. I don't fancy you anymore.'

'Really?' the beautiful singer replied, making straight for his crotch before he could back away. 'That's a shame. Just when I moved in with you. What a boring time we're going to have.'

Jeff let out a huge roar and swept the bundle of clothing and female delectability off her feet, kissing her hard on the mouth. This latest game had gone on long enough, and his blood pressure was pounding from head to toe. His erection was full against her hips, his hand glancing across the rough but yielding fabric covering her vagina. Lynn gasped and pushed her pubic bone against his fingers wantonly, knowing it would drive him crazy too.

He groaned. 'Can I reconsider my options?'

'Oh, I'm not sure you can,' she shook her head, struggling down out of his arms and running into the lounge room. 'What makes you think you have options?'

The young singer's face was now far less pale, and they were both breathing heavily. The red-blooded man was enjoying their tussle, grateful to have his playmate back in the land of the living. Her body felt light and delicate through the layers of warm clothing, and he loosened his hold, scared his fervent strength might break her. It only made the sense of urgency more acute.

'Right now, my options are to take you forcibly on the couch or disappear for a wank in the shower,' he stated in no uncertain terms. 'Which would you prefer?'

The teenager looked shocked, leaning back in his arms. '¿Perdóneme?'

'You heard!'

The pair fell together onto the sofa, tangling themselves up in the quilt which the invalid had dragged there earlier. Jeff smiled at the vision of Lynn Dyson dressed in an old, floppy, oversized t-shirt and navy blue men's tracksuit bottoms. Never in his wildest dreams had he imagined seeing his dream girl in such a guise...

'I seem to remember there being several aesthetically pleasing places of interest underneath this manly attire,' he quipped, slipping his hand under the t-shirt and quickly finding her loose breasts. 'I'm sure you're under here somewhere.'

Lynn giggled. 'It was your idea.'

'Yep,' her boyfriend nodded, kissing in a line from her belly button downwards to below the waistband and feeling her hips rise up towards his mouth. He grabbed hold of the elasticated material and yanked the trousers down past her thighs and over her feet in one smooth movement, casting the offending item backwards across the floor. Watching him remove his own clothes, his partner peeled off her top and spread herself and the quilt out on the floor, beckoning her excited lover down on top of her.

'Jeez, it's so good to have you back!' he shouted, champing at the bit to take his place.

Sensing his gorgeous concubine lacked her normal quota of energy, having just eaten the first meal in a while and with her temperature still high, the twenty-two-year-old tenderly caressed her skin and took his time to satisfy her at her own pace. Twice, then three times she came, crying out and gripping him tightly. The sex was sublime as they continued to play with each other right up until the last minute, and his kindness was amply rewarded by the intensity of her responses and the heartfelt words of love that followed each time she climaxed.

'Christ Almighty! I can't wait any longer,' her lover hissed in her ear. 'You are way too good at this. You should make love for Australia.'

'I do,' she replied with a flirtatious smile.

The ecstatic man came into her, laughing hard and with rockets firing in his heart. Lynn's hand reached around the back of his head, exactly as he had yearned for so often during their long time apart. It was all he could do not to cry. She kissed his lips, feeling his chest rising and falling on top of her as his heavy frame pinned her to the floor.

'Perhaps we should tell Dad that?' she suggested. 'He'd look on us much more favourably if he knew there was patriotic glory available.'

Rolling off the couch and dropping down onto the floor, Jeff threw his arms back over his head and yelled into the air. 'For fuck's sake! Why didn't I think of that? Just think of the grief it would've spared us.'

Lynn turned around and placed both feet on her man's strong abdominal muscles, threatening to stand on him on her way to the bathroom. Laughing, he rolled over and let her by, still breathing hard and feeling so, so satisfied. By the time the blonde returned, clad in her own nightclothes again and with her tangled hair combed straight, the lounge room bore no evidence of their makeshift *boudoir*.

Her amorous carer was in the kitchen, busy filling two more bowls with ice cream. 'Congratulations!' he proclaimed, passing one over her head as she took her seat on the couch again. 'You've earned your gold medal dessert.'

'Why, thanks! So did you.'

Jeff could tell by the lacklustre tone in her voice that his exquisite concubine's spark was faltering again, still not out of the woods. He sat down next to her and relished the feeling of her leaning against him.

'You are gorgeous,' he whispered. 'You've gone downhill again, haven't you?'

The beauty nodded. 'A bit.'

'Sorry. I should've left you alone. You look beautiful, by the way. But fucked, in more ways than one.'

'No, you shouldn't,' she disagreed, giggling. 'You weren't the only one who wanted it. I couldn't bear to think of you in the shower. That would've made me feel terrible.'

Her boyfriend chuckled kindly, kissing her cheek. 'I was only joking.'

'Were you?'

'Probably not.'

***

Jeff and his band flew out to Tokyo on the twelfth of November, a week after Lynn had departed for Osaka. By the time he reached his destination, she would already have spent two nights in the country's capital. They had rehearsed their double act tirelessly both in the apartment and with the MAC crew, until they could have executed the dance routines with their eyes closed.

The same Japanese smoker who had helped the rock star to find accommodation in the confusing city had kindly translated the lyrics of two of his biggest hits for the show, and the couple was really looking forward to their official *début* as a duo on the world stage, fascinated to see how their respective sets of fans would accept the partnership.

Sir Bradley Morrison, MAC's musical director, had taken a good deal of persuading to allow the notorious party animal to be part of the tour's last concert. Initially, he had refused to allow the inclusion of the band's raunchy new arrangements, concerned that they didn't suit the style of the group and were not in keeping with the rest of the set.

The rocker had deliberately stayed away from the band's discussions with their boss, so as not to be seen to encourage any conflict. The last thing he wanted was for the distinguished servant of Melbourne's musical *élite* to make a telephone call to his good friend, Bart Dyson, who also happened to be the incumbent chairman of Melbourne Academy's Board of Governors, to inform him of the harm this swarthy reprobate was bringing to his daughter's professional prospects.

Checking into his hotel the day before the first gig, the much-adored celebrity was handed an envelope along with his room key. The sight of his name written in his beautiful best friend's handwriting was the perfect arrival gift, this recent phenomenon of being separated and together at the same time slowly changing from bearable to somewhat edifying. The musician opened the envelope to reveal a romantic, new lyric neatly set out on a card, which also wished him luck for his three upcoming shows.

In contrast, Mark Davenport's marriage was already in tatters after he had strayed once too often, having drunk and smoked to excess with some local girls who clung to the band like limpets on a breakwater. The other musicians rallied round him and poured heaps of scorn on their leader for bowing out well before the final curtain each night. They had difficulty coming to terms with his newfound abstinence, often begging him to stay on and enjoy the spoils which his fame never failed to attract for the whole crew.

More than happy to host the same lavish parties, the charismatic star held court with pretty girls dripping from his tall, muscular, leather-clad frame, only to retire alone at the end of the night. Instead, the superstar would spend hours on the telephone making out with Lynn or comforting a tearful Shona, feeling partly responsible for ruining his bass player's brief conventional endeavour.

In himself, Jeff had never known higher spirits. Even in his most manic moments up until now, high on whatever might have come his way, the eternal blackness had never been far behind his eyes. Yet, precisely how he had

416

envisaged it, his saviour's present influence exceeded every single angelic expectation. In the few days after recovering from her illness and leaving for Japan, Lynn had adapted well to her role of fly-in, fly-out housemate, and their original awkwardness had been replaced by a peaceful coexistence. On the few days which saw them both at home, neither put pressure on the other to stay in, both were decidedly reluctant to leave, and the right-hand wardrobe contained much more than a lonely remover's label.

Plans for their London sabbatical were also progressing nicely. The Dysons were initially furious to find out that the tenacious suitor was planning to study in the same city, but latterly the signs suggested they had resigned themselves to the fact that they could no longer direct their daughter's every move. Moreover, they had no choice but to admit that she too was deliriously happy and as highly motivated as ever.

Jeff Diamond and his cute Japanese public relations assistant took their seats in the crowd for the opening of MAC's final Tokyo show, surrounded by fans who could hardly believe their luck. He signed autographs and posed for pictures until the lights went down and the music began. Many of these Lynn Dyson devotees were coming back to the very same venue the following night to see his show too, as he found out through his able interpreter. His basic proficiency in such a truly foreign language was soon abandoned, yet the animated group managed to communicate nonetheless.

At the end of the first half of the set, the sexy performer introduced her new song to the audience via another translator. She spoke of being humbled by discovering someone special in her life and dedicated it to her favourite man by name. The lyric was the one written on his welcome card, figuratively describing her delight that he no longer needed to stand in the shadows and hide his strength from the world.

The object of Lynn Dyson's affections joined the tight-knit band of former school-friends on stage after the intermission, handsome, humble and bordering on heroic. He rode a motorcycle onto the set and swept his leading lady off her feet exactly as they had done in rehearsals. The band members were pleased that they had stuck to their guns with the arrangements, and even Sir Brad declared that the spectacle was marvellous. The audience loved the programme's additions, cheering and clapping in a standing ovation.

The show's absolute highlight was the stars' rendition of a song they had penned together in September called "Everlasting", which the stars performed as an *encore*. Their chemistry on stage matched its off-stage counterpart, adrenalin pumping wildly as their bodies flew around each other in carefully choreographed mutual provocation. The entire crowd was on its feet again, and the couple obliged by doing the whole routine for a second time, even though they were exhausted and their voices hoarse. The performance had been outstanding, and the following day's newspapers around the world reported the event feverishly.

Lynn Dyson and Jeff Diamond were now officially on the map as a showbusiness item. It had been a long road, but both musicians were overjoyed that their new united state had been well-received by their fans. Luckily, by the time the young man's return flight touched down in their home town, the latest celebrity romance was already old news, and all that remained was the endless round of media interviews begging for their secrets. His amused girlfriend let her wordsmith have his head while he toyed diabolically with journalists, running rings around them with his esoteric humour and wicked imagery. They had the press wrapped around their little fingers, and it was almost embarrassing to see their record sales dominating the music charts leading up to Christmas.

Australia's darling quickly released her first solo album, which included the songs the duo had featured in Tokyo, along with a new ballad written by her flatmate epitomising her silent anguish while following the dreams of others. The rest of the tracks were a selection of more upbeat and slightly *risqués* numbers to announce her arrival on the adult music scene.

Preparing to depart Melbourne for colder climes and consulting their various musical advisers, the two highly bankable celebrities made a decision to keep collaborative performances to a minimum. Jeff's idea of reserving such crowd-pleasing opportunities for the purpose of raising money for worthy causes immediately met with Lynn's approval, and hence the rock star also returned to his own hectic recording schedule when December rolled around.

The Diamond Celebration Foundation had achieved mainstream awareness quite miraculously, thanks to the likeable star's regular promotional work. The charity's management committee was unable to spend money fast enough. Its figurehead's second novel was to be published in time for the festive period, his partner finished the year at the top of the women's tennis rankings, and both stars had signed up to make films the following year.

It was as if they had developed the Midas touch, but through it all they and their friends managed to keep their feet planted firmly on the ground.

'Ker-ching, ker-ching!' chanted Gerry with alarming regularity.

The couple's first joint venture into the non-profit world, a children's welfare organisation, was established under the name of "Childlight". This had originally been Lynn's idea after another night hearing about the abuse and neglect that many kids faced in disadvantaged family situations. Her boyfriend had immediately seized on the concept, set his experienced Stonebridge resources to work and poured his boundless energy into spruiking it on television and radio leading up to the holiday season.

'We're too busy to go to London,' his partner had told him, as they fell into bed after another non-stop week.

'No, we're not,' Jeff responded. 'I'm just warming up. You ain't seen nothing yet, baby. *Digame...* Do you keep an up-to-date *résumé*?'

The young woman frowned, not expecting such a question at lights-out. '*Résumé?* A CV, you mean?'

'Either. Yes and no are your choices, in case you need some assistance.'

'Shut up!' the teenager smacked his bare midriff, trying not to direct her eyes to something growing lower down. 'Yes. Is it pretentious to have one?'

To the songwriter's surprise, his question had unlocked a genuine humility in the privileged society girl. 'What's wrong?'

'Nothing. It's just that with all the stuff we're involved with, our CVs would look a bit boastful. Don't you think?'

Lynn's hand sheepishly crept down her aroused man's side and slid around his hip until it found what it was looking for. These precious and fleeting moments of awkwardness between them sent his passion into overdrive, and he kissed her confused mouth hard.

'Angel, it's me. Only me, OK?'

The caring lover pushed himself inside her, feeling moist inner walls tighten around his erection. Whispering words of undying love, he waited for these spontaneous inhibitions to desert her, aided by the relentless pressure of his fingers. Moaning and writhing beside him, he knew his mission was accomplished once her strong Olympian's body flipped them both over and reversed roles to bring about his own satisfaction.

When their feverish lovemaking was at its end, Lynn placed a tender hand on her boyfriend's darkened chin. 'You're looking particularly smug tonight.'

'Could well be...'

'Why?'

Jeff flicked his head sideways, making her laugh by kissing the palm which hadn't been quick enough to escape his fast-moving lips. 'Not only have I got you in my bed, but I still can't believe I went a month without sex with a third party.'

'Third party? What about the second party?'

'You're the second party, you clown!' the voice of her handsome teacher was back, instantly turning her on again. 'I, you and she.'

'Oh, yeah!' his pupil watched his left hand point to each of them and to some imaginary guest in their bedroom.

'Except there weren't any shes.'

'Are you waiting for me to thank you again or something?' the sexy tease put her hands on her hips and crept forwards over his genitals. 'You're going to have to do it again next year, once the tennis season gets going.'

The young man sat up and wrapped one arm around her back, fondling her breasts and kissing her nipples. 'No sweat!'

'No sweat?' Lynn cautioned, pushing his hand away from her vagina, where it was doing its best to distract her. 'If it was no sweat, why are you so smug?'

'Yeah, well,' he sniggered, refusing to let up and allow her excited body to relax. 'It wasn't as sweat as when we were apart. Come for me, angel.'

His lover let out a long cry, pouring her regret into the earth-shattering sensation to which she simply had to succumb. Jeff rolled her over onto her back and covered her elongated body with his own, kissing her mouth hard as they both rode the pleasure until it subsided.

'But you'll never have to live through that again,' the beautiful blonde promised.

'Nor you with me.'

Lynn shook her head. 'Thanks, but you've hardly got anything to worry about. You haven't got anyone trying to clip your wings.'

'Oh, I think I do,' countered the lost boy who knew his own dictatorial influences still intervened in their relationship far too often. 'We're pretty much even.'

Again Lynn was surprised by the sanguine acts of her complex lover, who thrust inside her and instantly brought her to orgasm again. Another troll versus angel moment, and this time she had picked it. His half-smile told her she had been rumbled.

The young woman grinned. 'OK, by association.'

'I'll give you that,' Jeff panted, on the verge of ecstasy.

'Your demons are your association. That's what you mean, isn't it?'

Her boyfriend roared at the top of his voice. Whoa, this soul-mate thing was intoxicating! His dream girl had caught him on his way down and now had him dangling on the finest thread.

'OK. I'll buy it,' she laughed, pushing him as deep inside as he would go. 'Willingly. I love you, Jeff.'

A good many seconds of insurmountable nirvana engulfed the pair, collapsing together on the mattress in triumph. Jeff realised that relinquishing control was not the end of the world. *Regala* had his back, and he felt safe. The only forfeit was his authority to set the rules; not to break or even to bend them. He would meet this fantastic creature halfway from here on in.

'Jesus Christ!' the handsome man hissed. 'I win again! And I love you too. I'll love you forever, Lynn Dyson. For-fucking-EVER. You got it?'

Lynn slid across the bed a little, to put some distance between their sizzling bodies. The lovers lay in silence in the dark, gradually returning to Earth, and with only their fingertips touching. After a few minutes, her partner disappeared into the bathroom, returning quickly with fresh, minty breath and his skin cool and damp. She raised her water glass to her lips, sensing her black stallion was not yet ready for sleep.

'What?'

'It's just unfathomable,' Jeff said, his eyes shining.

'What is?'

'Getting it on with just any girl who came along,' he continued, taking hold of her hand and kissing it. 'I simply can't contemplate sex with anyone else anymore.'

'Me neither,' the young woman shrugged, settling down onto the pillow.

Her boyfriend laughed. 'But you never did.'

'No, but I still don't want anyone else.'

'I'm sorry I put you through that.'

'It's OK,' Lynn dismissed his apology magnanimously, stifling a yawn. 'It made us who we are.'

Jeff sighed, feeling tears stinging behind his eyes. 'Jeez, angel. I don't deserve that, but I like it. Longfellow once said, "All your strength is in your union." That's who we are.'

'My strength is in my onion?' his bedfellow giggled. 'Sorry, that's what Sandy used to say when I was teaching him to read. It's always stuck in my mind.'

The intellectual capitulated with a sigh, taking his cue to suspend all further poetic outpourings until the morning. 'Yeah, if you like. Soon it won't be all about me, I promise. I'll give you the best, angel. The very best.'

'*Ditto*, I promise,' his dream girl leaned across and left a long kiss on his lips. 'You already give me the best, and I try to do the same. Goodnight, Jeff. Sleep well.'

'Remember before, when I told you you feed me?'

'Yes.'

'Well, you do, but I think it's more than that now,' the contented man murmured. 'You balance me. You extract stuff from me too. Keep everything in equilibrium. And I hope I can do that to you too, if it's important to you.'

Lynn rubbed her favourite dreamer's shoulder gently. 'I've never thought about it, but I like the idea now you've put it out there.'

'Put it out there? I didn't put it out there, Miss California,' Jeff scoffed at the American idiom, his fingertips brushing the soft skin hiding her heart. 'I put it in here.'

***

Snuggling into his warm body and sensing his breathing quickening, the amazed young woman ran her fingers down his sternum and over his abs playfully, stopping just short of where her boyfriend wanted them to go.

Grabbing her hand and kissing it, Jeff rolled over and pinned her to the mattress.

The second nightmare of the night had woken the couple less than an hour after they had fallen back to sleep, wilder and with more urgency than the first. The romantic introspection which had sent them into their initial slumber had now been replaced with angry self-loathing on the dreamer's part and enervated compassion on his partner's. Determined to push him past his anguish, the young woman had taken him by the hand and dragged him comically into the shower, and then led him back again to the bed by his erect penis.

'What are you doing?' she smiled. 'You look as if you're about to launch into another big statement.'

A pair of insistent eyes drilled into hers, as his tongue found its way between her teeth. They kissed for a long time, their bodies moving to some inaudible rhythm concocted by their weary minds.

'Did you think it would be this good?' the breathless lover asked. 'Us, I mean. Sex, love. Nightmares notwithstanding, *évidemment*.'

'I hoped it would,' Lynn replied, smiling against his lips. 'I used to wonder if I'd ever see you again, let alone be living together or travelling overseas together.'

Her boyfriend levered his torso up until his arms were locked straight, staring into his dream girl's eyes, before dropping down beside her. Instinctively, her slender frame twisted round and a long leg looped itself over his hip.

'I used to run all our home movies in my head,' Jeff recalled, moaning and closing his eyes as Lynn's hand fondled him boldly. 'Exactly what you're doing now. I used to picture your face when you come. The way your hands used to be so tentative when we first met, and then now... They're all over me. Taking control.'

The beautiful blonde leaned forward and kissed him as he finished his sentence. 'My favourite was opening my eyes while we were kissing and seeing your eyes not quite shut and that typical, gorgeous lopsided smile on your face,' she added. 'And I love how you like everything I do.'

Jeff's left hand found its way between his lover's legs, and he sent one finger at a time inside, making her squirm in pleasure, while his thumb circled her clitoris steadily. 'I love everything you do,' he repeated. 'I love the unpredictability too. Where are your hands going to go next? The different responses I get when I change things around. And then I love the things I can rely on, like when your thumbs tuck themselves inside my belt as soon as we meet, and your hand clenched around the muscles in my neck as I tip over the edge.'

It was Lynn who tipped over the edge this time upon hearing his sensuous prose and realising the moment had been perfectly engineered by her sexpert.

Without delay, he pulled her leg further over his side, narrowing the gap which had opened up as her orgasm took hold. She cried out, gripping his ribcage and feeling him penetrate deep inside her.

'Oh, God. That was amazing.'

'Tell me what you love, angel,' he gasped, moving oh-so slowly. 'What movies do you play when you're travelling?'

The young lady smiled shyly, anxious to give him the stimulation he was looking for so deep in the night. 'I love the difference between the tenderness of being stroked and kissed, and then the slamming of my body against your shoulders and chest.'

'Like this?' the inspired man enacted her request, his left hand clamping down on her back and drawing her towards him roughly.

'Yes!' Lynn exclaimed. 'Exactly like that! You feel so strong. Powerful. And then you go and take my breath away with some expressive words that send me flying again.'

Jeff backed off slightly, not wanting his willing partner to come again too quickly. She whimpered, but the smile on her face told him his timing was perfect.

'Slamming makes it sound violent.'

'It is violent,' the desirous woman agreed, 'but good violent. You're so red-hot and burning. Controlled violent. Exhilarating violent.'

'Fine line between pleasure and pain,' her lover offered, his mouth finding hers once more.

Lynn kissed him back. 'Yes, because I know the pleasure's still to come. The pain is tantalising, until it's not really pain at all.'

'Jesus! That's such a turn-on. I'm going to give you more of that. Why didn't you ask?'

'Because I've only just figured it out,' the nineteen-year-old shrugged. 'Only now, I suppose. Oh, wow! Yes! That's amazing!'

The pace quickened, and their bodies moved in unison, both closing in. The lovers cried out in unison while their pleasure overtook them, and they exhaled together as their bodies finally let them drift back to reality. Every tired nerve-ending was ragged and on edge, and their eyes were closed in rapturous enjoyment. After a few minutes' silence, the teenager's hand reached up and stroked the stubble on her lover's face.

She adored this man so much and hoped he knew it. 'What do you need from me?'

'Just what I'm getting,' he sighed. 'Just your willingness to be loved and to love me back.'

The pretty athlete kissed him again, this time softly nipping the sensitive corner of his upper lip. He uttered a deep, dark moan.

'That's easy. It's unconditional, Jeff.'

The grateful man laughed. 'You sound like a puppy.'

'Thanks! I didn't know you were into bestiality too. That's cruel.'

The handsome face grimaced for second, before becoming serious. 'Don't let it be unconditional,' he urged. 'Make demands, angel. I'm here for you just as much as you're here for me. Two-way street, baby. OK? What do you want more of?'

Lynn's eyes glazed over, pensive for a couple of seconds. How could she ask for more from someone who was so unfailingly generous?

'I don't want less of this,' she whispered.

'Less of this?'

'Yes. Talking,' the beautiful woman nodded. 'And the times when we're connected and it's not only about sex.'

Jeff groaned, pulling himself clear of her body and kneeling up to drink in the view. The skin on her breasts was still pink from exertion, and her lips were swollen from their wanton kissing. She had crossed her legs over each other, so that only the last couple of centimetres of pubic hair above her vagina were visible. It was the most beautiful sight. He reached down and dragged his fingertips across her abdomen and down the centre, before diverting at the last minute to continue along her inner thigh, feeling her muscles contract in response to the gentle stimulation.

'Yeah. I'm still learning about that.'

'No, you're not,' Lynn objected. 'You're the best at it.'

He scoffed. 'Out of everyone?'

'Yes! You're never going to let me forget that, are you?'

'Nope,' her lover cocked his head to one side. 'But I am still learning though. I promise you'll get much more talk, because I'm coming to understand its force within our relationship. Soon you'll be begging me to shut up.'

Lynn exhaled through her nose, suddenly reliving the very force which Jeff continued to exert over her, as his left hand made contact with the flesh over her obliques and swept swiftly to the underside of her breast. He leaned down and kissed one nipple and then the other, before landing a third on her mouth.

'And what do *you* want more of?' she asked, watching him edge off the bed to retrieve the sheet that had slid onto the floor during their fevered activity.

'*Lingerie*,' came his curt answer, an impish grin on his face.

His beautiful best friend laughed in surprise at his simple request. 'That I can do. I expected something much more cerebral, but I should've known better. What colour?'

'Cerebral? Not me!' the Testosterone Kid responded with a vacant stare. 'Any colour. Who cares about the fucking colour?'

A long finger tipped with nail polish wagged at his bad language, as its owner sat up. Her partner twirled the sheet above her head like a cape and let it parachute down on top of her, before freeing her head and smothering her lovingly in the crisp cotton.

'*You* care about the fucking colour!' she reminded him. 'I want to appeal to your senses. That's what I love about you. It's about the whole experience, isn't it? You can't stand there and tell me you don't care about the colour. I'm not letting you away with that, Jeff Diamond.'

'Christ,' he muttered, dropping back onto the side of the mattress. 'London's going to be so utterly mind-blowing.'

'Anywhere's going to be mind-blowing. I'd like you to take me to Paris.'

The closet intellectual wrapped his arms around his accomplice. 'I'd love to take you to Paris,' Jeff told her, elongating the word "love" in order to tell her just how good an idea it was. 'And never come back, actually.'

'What is it about Paris and you? And why do you speak to me in French so often? I would've expected Spanish, but not French so much.'

'I don't know,' her lover replied. 'Paris has an understanding of what's important in life somehow. Through the ages. The theory that it's not only about the money. You know... The subtleties of life. But as far as speaking to you in French, that freaks me out too, frankly. It just feels natural, and you understand me. *Tu veux que je m'arrête?*'

'*Non! Pas du tout. Je l'aime beaucoup. C'est de nous.* Really special.'

'*Exactement, angel. C'est ça. De nous.*'

The relaxed couple pulled the quilt over their chilling bodies and commenced the process of falling asleep for a third time. Immediately tensing up, Jeff was soon on his feet again, having given into the temptation of another cigarette. It was impossible to climb back into bed without disturbing his ever patient girlfriend, who stirred and reached out for a cuddle.

'When did you realise you were addicted?' Lynn asked.

'To what? You don't want to talk about this now. Leave it, angel. I'm OK.'

'To anything? It's fine.'

'I don't know,' he sighed. 'I guess it sneaks up on you. At first you go for ages between hits, but always knowing you will again at some point.'

'Hmm,' his sleepy interviewer acknowledged. 'That makes sense.'

He kissed her forehead. 'It's different as a kid to an adult. There was certainly less expectation for me, in those days. I got it whenever I could. You have to be opportunistic as a kid, because you don't have your own resources. But as an adult, I was more driven to do stupid things to get shitfaced. The thing that screws me up the most is that I can't give you a decent explanation, baby. I just don't know. It's too complicated.'

Lynn's eyes didn't open. 'That doesn't matter. But how come you're not addicted to gambling?'

The twenty-two-year-old chuckled. 'Don't know that either. Maybe because I never had any money! You need money for gambling. For anything else, you can trade other things. I didn't have any money at the time when life turned me into an addict, so gambling was never on my list. Also maybe because I always considered gambling as dumb, whereas everything else was cool.'

His girlfriend squeezed his arm, right on the verge of sleep. 'I used dope to my advantage though. I was stoned off my face for a lot of my exams. Especially the ones that required any creativity. Not for maths or factual subjects. I was clean and sober for those.'

This last confession had been lost on the woman who cared about him the most. It didn't matter. They would talk about it again at some point. They had plenty of time to straighten every record.

* * *

So it appeared that nothing could go wrong for the devoted couple in the lead-up to the busy festive season. Each day saw new opportunities for the combined identity that was Lynn Dyson and Jeff Diamond, already superstars of the entertainment world in their own rights. With his dream girl's encouragement and his newfound inner peace, it was as if the dark-haired gipsy's veins were overflowing with potential energy.

Relations with Lynn's parents had thawed somewhat in the months following the fateful handshake on the balcony. Nevertheless, Jeff was still more than pleasantly surprised when she accepted an invitation from Celia to spend Christmas with the Blakes in Sydney. His Gerry's mother hadn't forgotten the promise she had coerced from him the previous year and had sealed the deal by telephoning their apartment at the beginning of December.

His gorgeous flatmate had answered the call and stood chatting for five minutes before her boyfriend realised who was at the other end. It was such a casual conversation that he had assumed she was talking to one of her many girlfriends, and only when the name "Jacinta" was mentioned did it sink in. Celia had then asked for a word with her pseudo-son, and suddenly the busy songwriter found the receiver in his hand.

'Darling!' the refined lady gushed. 'How are you?'

'I'm fine, thanks, Celia. And you?' the young man replied, grinning at Lynn as he moved the receiver away from his ear to protect it from the cultivated, high-pitched blast.

Already fully aware of the topic in question, the nineteen-year-old sat back and waited for her man's reaction, hoping she had done the right thing.

'Has she now?' Jeff asked the woman in Sydney. 'Is that what you two have been scheming up for the last few minutes? Yes, of course I remember. Sure was. No, we haven't talked about Christmas yet. We've been ridiculously busy. Thanks. Great, yes. I guess so. Celia, let me talk to Lynn some more, and we'll ring you back. Say hi to the others for me. Thanks, Celia. You too. *Adios.*'

No sooner had the call been terminated than the handsome stranger grabbed the goddess sitting next to him, lifted her off the couch and swang her round in a circle, just like he used to in the old days. She exhaled in relief, judging this exuberant response as sanction for her unilateral commitment.

'Darling!' she squealed in the manner of Missus Blake. 'Put me down, you brute!'

'Not likely... What have you done, you colluding minx?'

'Nothing!'

Bearing down upon the girl of his dreams, the animated musician took her hand and began to kiss from her fingers, past her wrist and on up her arm. 'Celia tells me otherwise.'

'What did she tell you?' his girlfriend asked, unworried by the dark frown on his face.

'That she invited us to their place for Christmas and that you said yes,' Jeff recounted. 'Is this true?'

Lynn smiled and shrugged. 'Might be.'

'And how do you account for this presumptive behaviour, Miss Dyson?' her lover requested, raising his hand as if he were preparing to unleash some tickling punishment.

'Well...' the young woman began and squirmed out of his grip. 'Celia told me you'd promised to bring me to Sydney for Christmas after I returned from the US, so how could I refuse?'

The young man chuckled, choosing to fondle her breasts instead. 'Right! That's not exactly how I remember it, but whatever... The end result's the same. Are you sure that'll work with your folks?'

'No, but I'm game to ask,' the teenager hesitated. 'I don't want to spend Christmas apart, do you?'

'Definitely not, but I assumed we'd have to. I must tell you, Christmas at Benloch doesn't fill me with joy, even now relations are more diplomatic. I just don't think I'm ready for that yet. Do you mind?'

The empathetic beauty kissed him. 'No. Neither am I. We'd all be stressed out, having to choose every word so carefully and listening to each other lying when answering *those* questions. That's what I thought when Celia asked me, so going to the Blakes' is perfect.'

Jeff stared at the ceiling, unable to believe his good fortune. 'Ah, yeah... *Those* questions,' he smiled. 'Jeez, my blood pressure's climbing just thinking about *those* questions! This is far more than perfect, angel. What'll your parents say though? Aren't they expecting you to be *en famille*?'

'Yes. Expect so, but tough shit, as you'd say,' Lynn feigned confidence. 'I'll ask them to excuse me this year because we've got another offer. I'd really love you to show me around the places where you spent your childhood. The ones I only know about through your songs. You know... The Stones Road, two floors closer to heaven, *et cetera*.'

As she feared, her boyfriend's mood instantly switched. Bringing his past and present together still required a delicate balance which the young woman had not yet perfected. She had made the assumption that catching him on a high would mean he wouldn't spiral so far down. The ominous shadow of their night-time tensions now gathering in broad daylight hinted at the error of her ways.

'That sounds good, but I need time to think about it,' he replied, turning pale and lighting a cigarette.

The sportswoman was disappointed that her man's reactions were still so involuntary and acute, angry at herself for having spoken of the dark times so casually and without warning. 'Jeff, I'm really sorry. I didn't think it through. I should have picked a better moment to talk about this.'

Being pulled into her contrite body, the angry adolescent shook his head. 'Baby, don't apologise. It's fine. It's just that I have no control over my responses to those days. The new me says it's a great idea. Another nail in the coffin of the nightmares and compulsions.'

'But the old you?'

'The old me woke Gravity up with a start, and he immediately began to kick me in the guts,' Jeff explained.

'I wish I could experience that feeling,' Lynn said, her voice wistful.

'Actually, you don't,' he snapped.

His girlfriend recoiled, momentarily stunned by the malice in his tone. Again, she had unwittingly peered through the thin veil between empathising and patronising; another salient lesson for them both, for as soon as his last retort had left his mouth, Jeff regretted his hasty words as well.

'Fuck, angel. I'm sorry too,' he said, reaching for her shoulder and squeezing it hard. 'I know you don't mean to hurt me, but I go to extremes so quickly that I can't catch myself.'

'It's OK,' the pretty teenager replied. 'Really.'

She was keen to dispel the mood of doom and gloom that had descended over them during what should have been excited discourse. She imagined her mystery man's happiness chart taking a nosedive below the line after luxuriating in the green zone for a fairly long, uninterrupted spell.

'It's not OK. It's bloody ungrateful. I can't promise it won't happen again, but I'll try.'

'Let's leave this to another day,' Lynn suggested brightly. 'I'll be in Sydney anyway in the week before Christmas, rehearsing "Carols in the Domain" and some other...'

'Angel, stop,' Jeff cut her sentence short. 'Don't let me off the hook like that. Look! I'm already over it, and showing you around that shithole's a fantastic idea. Wear your running shoes, so we can make a quick getaway.'

The confused sportswoman sat back on the couch and smiled, hoping that someday soon she would understand this complex beast a little better. 'Oh, good. You're the best. I know how hard you try. I can see it in your face. Thank you.'

'You're welcome,' he replied. 'Now I need a fucking drink, but I know you're going to stop me, so I won't. I'll be back in a few minutes. Is that OK?'

Lynn nodded, watching her boyfriend pick up his cigarettes and lighter and head for the balcony doors. He slid the glass pane closed behind him, and she was left on her own to wait for him to unwind. Not wishing to put any pressure on his already fragile state, she left the room to prepare for the following day's arduous training sessions.

At least these angry episodes were happening less frequently than they used to, and the young woman had no doubt in her mind that the scarred smoker was dedicated to smoothing out his peaks and troughs for the sake of their relationship. Unusually, she felt a flurry of words infiltrating her brain, almost as if they had aimed for Jeff but that their trajectory had been a little off-target.

When her enigmatic stranger returned from his cigarette break, he found his dream girl at the piano, playing and singing a new song which was already well formed.

'I think I've written your song,' she announced, with tears rolling down her face. 'It just came to me while I was watching you out there. Listen. I think I caught something that was meant for you.'

The two songwriters worked on the piece until they had added two more verses and a bridge, taking turns with the accompaniment. They were both crying as they sung it through a final time, sitting silently in each others' arms for several minutes and pondering this peculiar brand of esoteric collaborative telepathy that had gripped them.

'That's truly amazing,' Jeff admitted, breaking away from a long kiss. 'It sounds daft, but I know exactly what you mean. You don't write songs like this. I do. But this time you did. What's going on? It's spooky, but I love it.'

'I know. Weird, isn't it? I was just getting ready for tomorrow, daydreaming about you while you were outside, and something put words into my head and pushed me to start playing. That's never happened to me before.'

'Maybe I put them there,' the philosopher wondered out loud, stroking her forehead and kissing her again. 'Surreptitiously, from the balcony. Can I say surreptitiously to you these days? Can you cope with such long words?'

The feisty blonde whacked his arm. 'Yes, you bastard! Now who's being patronising?'

'You're right,' Jeff hugged her. 'I'm sorry. Feel free to abuse me. It's only fair.'

'I'll bank it for later,' Lynn teased.

'OK, boss. Are you sure it's wise to give your folks the flick for Christmas?'

'No, it's not wise, but it's what I'd like. Is it what you'd like?'

'Oh, yeah,' the happy man nodded. 'More than anything. And I'm even warming to you being able to visualise all the places where I grew up. I often picture you at Benloch when you tell me about stuff you did as a kid. And maybe it'll help me heal a bit faster too.'

The patient nineteen-year-old kissed his cheek. 'That's my plan,' she affirmed, with "I told you so" written all over her face. 'Trust me. I'll make sure everything's cool with Mum and Dad. They're much more accepting of things these days. Dad even asked after you the other day, so things are looking up.'

Her boyfriend scoffed. 'Unless he's hired a hit man and needs to check if I'm still alive, to know if he should settle their invoice or not.'

Slapping his arm again, Australia's darling objected. 'Don't be like that,' she whined. 'They're trying. You sound like Gerry. You're getting very businesslike and pompous in your old age.'

'Shit! Am I?' Jeff laughed. 'That's not good for my image. Gotta stop that right now. London'll sort me out.'

Normal, everyday activities were scarce in the young couple's action-packed lives, but still the pastimes that Jeff loved to share with Lynn the most. After all the showbusiness parties, glamorous record launches and cocktail receptions, he had never been prouder than to have her on his arm at the combined staff Christmas party of his and Gerry's growing empire. Sporadic dips into the corporate world afforded regular bouts of real life in among the adulation and hyperbole, and he had been very pleased to receive an invitation to the function without having to sing for his supper.

The gorgeous, blonde celebrity looked fantastic at the black tie dinner-dance, clad in a full-length, dark green evening dress. Every head turned, and compliments winged their way around, making her handsome partner dizzy with pride. Of course, they had been unable to resist cries for them to dance a few numbers, but for the most part they managed to keep a reasonably low profile, without the barrage of requests for "As and Ps", which had become the pair's shorthand expression for autographs and photographs.

Even better again though was an invitation to a barbecue hosted by a friend from Jeff's student days, to which the instantly-recognisable stars had rocked up in jeans. They had even brought their own beer, dumping it in the esky on the kitchen floor like everyone else. This was an entirely different kind of party for the well-bred sophisticate, where joints were passed around openly and alcohol mellowed out the guests to allow the famous couple to blend in without unnecessary attention.

The former nobody from New South Wales was in heaven; a beer in one hand, a spliff in the other, and his lover leaning back into him as he propped up the wall by the grill with a bunch of mates. Life's simple pleasures would always be the most enjoyable, he concluded, such as Lynn's hand resting in the small of his back while they talked to people, or stroking the sensitive skin of his inner thigh through his jeans or simply slotted into a convenient back pocket.

All these special messages he had refused to grant anyone else the right to convey during their time apart were now his and only his. Jeff knew he would never tire of them, and vowed to make it his life's work for this wonderful woman always to feel their magic too. The good-natured jealousy in his mates' eyes nourished his soul a little further, particularly when he received an unsolicited kiss for his trouble.

'Yes,' he had answered one of her questions, pressing his crotch into her backside to tell her just how sexy she was. 'Or no. Whatever the right answer is that you want, angel. Your wish is my command. Anything.'

And then, to cap it all off nicely, there was the barely discernible sound of his guardian angel's breath beside him on the couch when they returned home, his chest the perfect place to rest her head at the end of a very relaxing evening. If nothing else in the world were right except this, the lost boy would still be happy.

He was home.

And so, it seemed, was his dream girl.

Lynn Dyson's eyes loved him, her arms craved him, her lips relished the way they were kissed. This was the very time and place to which the dire struggles of the last twenty years had been leading.

Jeff Diamond had prevailed in spite of it all. Life could not be finer.

LORRAINE PESTELL

432

Every Christmas At Once

Gerry's mum's silver Mercedes station wagon brought Jeff's precious cargo safely to the door of the Blake residence. On Christmas Eve, a Tuesday, he had collected Lynn from the Channel Seven studios, where she had finished her last professional obligation for the festive season. The multi-millionnaire had flown up from Melbourne with his old friend the previous night, feeling like a giddy teenager, and the whole family had gathered round the television to watch his dream girl host the annual Christmas concert from The Domain, Sydney's famous park.

There was great excitement in the household, where catholic Christian observances coexisted inculpably with substantial material wealth. There was no such thing as a simple nativity in their affluent corner of Mosman, and Jacinta and Tamilla were beside themselves with anticipation to be welcoming such a famous guest to court. Of course, Jeff was famous, but Jeff was Jeff, and his adopted family now viewed his tumultuous success as old news. Lynn Dyson was a whole different matter. And she loved horses too, so the overgrown adolescents had planned to take their special guest out for morning gallops to make her feel at home.

The Blakes' extra brother was stoked at the fuss being made by the women of the house over his partner, not only because he was keen for Lynn to enjoy the holidays away from her family but also since it would afford him and Gerry some space to be mates again. The two men had spent so little downtime together over the last few months that he missed their blokish antics.

With Australia's homecoming princess having flown to Sydney a few days in advance for rehearsals, her boyfriend had invited his business manager and some key people in his ever-expanding management team to the most expensive restaurant in Melbourne for a slap-up meal. He had taken great pleasure in presenting them all with gifts and large cash bonuses. The accountant had continued to put a great deal of creative energy into the unforeseen arms of his business, namely managing a musician's career and setting up charities, and this year had also outshone all peers by helping his VIP client to assemble a squad of trusted advisers around Paragon Holdings' capital and research investments. The highly motivated team, all of whom understood the importance of the work Jeff was doing outside of being a rock star, were always professional, tight-lipped and unfailingly loyal in matters concerning his personal life.

For Christmas and as an additional thank-you for his stellar contribution, the grateful twenty-two-year-old had bought his manager a boat; a large, nearly-new ocean cruiser decked out with a flying bridge, a fully-equipped bar for hosting parties and several staterooms designed for other forms of entertainment. It was currently moored in Port Douglas in far north Queensland, where it had been undergoing a facelift, and the kind-hearted millionnaire had also included two air tickets for Gerry to take possession of his gift and sail her down the coast during January. He was really looking forward to seeing his friend's face once he opened the envelope the following morning.

By contrast however, Lynn and Jeff had decided not to buy each other extravagant Christmas gifts. They were poised on the cusp of their new life in London, which was all they needed, and they had planned an idyllic holiday in the Caribbean over the coming Easter instead. The busy celebrities had enlisted Michelle's help in purchasing suitable gifts for Celia and her daughters, and the songwriter already knew that Gerry's father would derive great pleasure from a case of carefully chosen wines.

The most important objective for this festive season, in the young man's mind, was that he would finally acquit himself with the Blake family. Now was his chance to give back and to acknowledge the love and support they had given him through the difficult years. He was not an official part of their clan and would certainly have rebelled against any attempt to draw him in. Nevertheless, he had been treated like a fourth child, which had also brought its challenges and was therefore all the more overwhelmingly generous.

Celia's blood pressure mounted suddenly when she heard the scrunch of tyres on the gravel driveway. 'They're here!' she called out to anyone within earshot.

By the time Jeff had reached the door and pressed the bell, a well-groomed welcoming committee had assembled in the large, open hallway of the Mosman mansion. Gerry opened the door and immediately closed it again.

'Jehovah's Witnesses,' he declared to his mother, who raised her hands to her head in anguish.

'Gerry, please! Let them in.'

'Mum, cool it,' her son whinged, reopening the door. 'It's only Lynn Dyson.'

On cue, the tall, blonde celebrity entered the house, carrying a large bouquet of flowers, and kissed the familiar face fondly. 'Hello,' she said, quickly scanning the row of faces. 'It's only me and him.'

'Come on in,' the joker replied, waving expansively towards the reception line, which now included the dog. 'It's all very low-key here.'

Jeff shook his head as he surveyed the scene from the doorstep, about to follow the elegant young woman over the threshold. However, before he had stepped onto the mat, his old friend shut the door again, making everyone laugh except Lynn.

'Hey!' she cried, with as much restraint as she could. 'Don't do that!'

Surprised by the urgency in their special guest's protestations, Gerry opened the door for a third time. It was as if the whole world had escalated to high alert, which disappointed the gregarious Irishman immensely. He had left his sticky situation with Heather and her mother back in Melbourne in the hope that Christmas with the folks would provide some highly sought-after merriment, but thus far the plague of worrying women had migrated northwards with him.

'Sorry, Your Highness. Didn't know it was you.'

'Very funny, mate,' his old friend jeered, frantically trying to maintain some semblance of composure.

Lynn shot a fleeting glance behind her to make sure her man was alright after Gerry's innocent but unwittingly cruel joke, before turning round to meet the people about whom she had heard so much. Celia rushed forward to greet their anticipated visitor and was duly presented with the bouquet.

The lady of the house swooned in awe. 'Welcome, Lynn. Thank you so much. These are beautiful. And welcome back, darling,' she enthused, moving along to hug the tall, handsome millionaire. 'I'm so glad you two could join us.'

'Thank you, Celia. It's lovely to be here. We're really looking forward to it.'

Yes, *we* are, Jeff agreed silently, watching his two significant females reacquaint themselves. His girlfriend's charming air and gracious words instantly turned him on. Most definitely looking forward to it, debilitating phobia notwithstanding.

'And Jeff,' the excited hostess gushed, planting an enthusiastic kiss on his cheek and hugging him tightly.

He smiled. 'For Christ's sake, I've been here for two days already. Leave me alone!'

Everyone laughed again. Celia was terribly excited, evidently. Undaunted, the elegant lady turned back to Lynn and caught hold of her arm.

'Let me introduce you around,' she began. 'This is my husband, Gerald Senior.'

Gracefully, the new arrival extended her hand, and Gerry's dad shook it, leaning forward to kiss her gingerly. Jeff's evil mind fought to rid his mind of the positively pornographic thoughts currently navigating downwards on the wings of pride, and dismissed the dreadful vision of the old man suffering a heart attack due to the stunning celebrity's close proximity. He assumed even creaky, conservative executives long in the tooth were still prone to undisciplined erections when under such severe stimulation.

'Pleased to meet you, Mister Blake.'

'You too, Miss Dyson,' he replied in a rare slip of gentle sarcasm. 'Please call me Gerald.'

'I will, thank you,' she promised, already being tugged towards the couple's two daughters.

Jacinta was the first to be introduced. The shorter of the two girls, she was glamorous and self-confident. Very like Celia in fact, Lynn thought, and equally excitable.

'Hi, Lynn! It's so good to have you here for Christmas. We hope you'll come out riding with us.'

'Thanks! Yes, I'd love to,' their guest readily accepted. 'Jeff told me it would be likely, so I've brought my gear.'

The twenty-seven-year-old would have clapped her hands and jumped up and down on the spot if her brother and his best mate hadn't been staring at her. She merely blushed.

'And this is Tamilla,' Celia continued. 'She's younger than Gerry. Jacinta's older.'

'Hi, Tamilla,' Lynn said, nodding. 'Nice to meet you too.'

The baby of the family leaned forwards, putting her hand on the younger woman's shoulder, and gave her a kiss, instantly receiving a stern look from her mother which told her she was being too forward.

'Hi! Thanks for coming,' the younger Blake sister gushed. 'We can't believe you're so keen on our Jeff.'

Celia tutted. 'Please.'

'Me neither,' Lynn heard a deep voice from behind her.

She turned round and smiled at her favourite man, who responded with one of his more disarming winks.

'And this is Monkey,' Tamilla brought the attention back to her welcoming committee.

Monkey was the family Labrador retriever who, at nearly thirteen years of age, no longer displayed the boisterousness that had earned him his name. The old dog immediately leaned against the newcomer's legs as she bent down and fondled his soft, floppy ears.

'We've got one of you at home,' she said. 'Hello, Monkey, old thing.'

'Have *you* got a dog?' Tamilla yelped excitedly at Jeff. 'You never told me.'

'That's because *you* hasn't got a dog,' the young man retorted.

'I mean at my family's farm,' Lynn clarified, picking up on the familiar way her boyfriend interacted with Gerry's sisters.

'Oh, I see. Sorry.'

The rock star raised a dismissive hand to the girl with whom he had shared many a secret liaison in this very house during his teenage years, all unbeknown to the Blake parents. It brought fresh feelings of guilt and shame as he watched the love of his life mixing with his former playmates. He hoped the situation didn't cause Lynn too much anguish.

The beautiful celebrity was then introduced to Gerald's elderly mother, who was wheelchair-bound and nearly blind, and finally to Celia's slightly younger and much more able parents. The family looked on as the consummate public appearer chatted comfortably with each person in line.

'And you must be Gerald Junior,' she teased Gerry, continuing around the circle unchaperoned. 'How are you? Enjoying being away from the office?'

'No, not really,' the businessman confessed, dusting an old-fashioned kiss on the back of her outstretched hand. 'I'm trapped in the conventional clutches of the olds. Get me out of here, you ravishing wench.'

'Steady,' warned the dark-haired visitor, seeing his mate attempt to grab his girlfriend's waist. 'And I'm Jeff.'

Lynn's eyes widened. 'Wow! Jeff Diamond?' she exclaimed. 'I've heard so much about you. I didn't know you'd be here. Can I have your autograph?'

'My autograph? Shit, yeah! You're gonna get far more than that, lady,' her lover joked, hamming it up for his surrogate family. 'Tough luck. I've been sent to haunt you. The ghost of Christmas future.'

'What?' the nineteen-year-old laughed, unable to fathom his strange comment.

Jeff shrugged too, realising he had made no sense whatsoever, relishing the sensation of her arm sliding round his back and sending him melting into the floor. The young woman leaned into his eager body. Perfectly understated choreography, he noted. He had come to expect nothing less.

'Is it time for a drink yet?' Gerald piped up, judging the pleasantries to be complete.

'Thought you'd never ask,' the extra son gasped in relief that the tension had been broken. 'This way, my dear.'

With a flamboyant sweep of his Musketeer arm, the boy from Canley Vale led his high society girlfriend into the drawing room, following their hosts and gripping her hand as if she were likely to run away. She nudged his arm playfully while wriggling her fingers free, gazing around the impressive home. They found themselves in a large room with period *décor* which was reminiscent of an English stately home, also now festooned with paper chains and other Christmas decorations. Lynn admired the scene, as a proper visitor ought.

'Miss Dyson, what would you like?' Gerald asked over the hubbub. 'Champagne?'

'Yes, thanks. That would be lovely.'

'And Jeff? Whiskey on the rocks?'

The young man nodded. 'Great, thanks, sir. Magnificent.'

'Yes, you are,' his dream girl whispered, cuddling into his rigid frame. 'Adorable, in fact. I hope this isn't too stressful.'

'As expected,' the songwriter replied, kissing her tenderly. 'You're awesome with them. Thanks for the door defence too.'

The host handed the couple their glasses, and everyone began to calm down a little at last. Celia and her mother disappeared to prepare dinner, and Jeff was disappointed but not at all surprised that the younger women didn't volunteer to help out. Champagne was the perfect tongue-loosener for Gerry's sisters, and they were soon talking freely with their special guest.

'Mate,' Jeff called across to his friend. 'Can you give me a hand to bring our stuff in from the car, before we get too pissed?'

'Can I do it?' Lynn interjected.

Gerry saw the tall blonde stand up instead and remained seated. 'Worthy substitute!' the indomitable son agreed.

'Yes, you can,' her boyfriend enunciated slowly, stoked that she should offer, not only from the perspective of helping him get back through those huge, glossy and very solid front doors, but also because it was a welcome opportunity to steal some precious moments alone in what threatened to be a frenetic evening. Outside, the cool summer breeze was refreshing, and the couple paused for a lingering kiss on their way to the car.

'Are you OK?' the nineteen-year-old asked, sensing the persistent troll was still on the warpath. 'What's wrong?'

Jeff smiled. 'Nothing's wrong. It's just bloody stressful, *comme t'as dit*. I'll get over it.'

'Good. That's alright then. It's a bit like the first time we went to Benloch together, isn't it? Everyone anxious to make a good impression.'

'S'pose so,' he agreed. 'Everything has to be such a big drama. Why couldn't you be someone ordinary whom no-one likes?'

The singer huffed. 'You can talk! I'll try harder.'

They gathered up the performer's luggage and some last minute shopping which the generous man had finished on his way into the city. The slender celebrity pushed the door open for him, and he followed her in as if nothing could possibly be bothering him. After dumping their belongings at the bottom of the stairs, he gave his companion a brief tour of the ground-floor rooms.

'We can take it all up later,' he murmured into her ear. 'If I get you in the bedroom now, I fear we won't get any dinner.'

'Me too,' Lynn agreed with a smile, sending Jeff's libido into overdrive. 'You're so sexy tonight. All on edge, like you're wide open. I love you so much.'

'Not fair, angel,' he moaned and pulled her hand down to the front of his pants. 'Not fair at all.'

Before too long, the family was summoned into the large dining room for dinner. Celia had put almost as much effort into Christmas Eve as she was planning for the holiday itself. Wine flowed like water, and after three courses and a selection of chocolates with coffee, everyone was replete and lethargic. It was quite like old times. Jeff sat back and took in the happy scene, appreciating the power of family occasions to unite people.

Jacinta and Tamilla were soon dispatched to assist their elderly grandmother with getting ready for bed, and having had their offer of assistance with the washing-up refused by Celia, the songwriter took his beautiful best friend on a more thorough tour of the house. They paused for a while in the den, where the visitor was keen to examine the many photographs on the wall, some of which dated back to when the Blake children were very small.

'Hey! Is that you?' she shrieked, thinking she had spotted a young Diamond in one of the pictures.

Jeff leaned over her shoulder and kissed her left cheek. 'You may be right. Is he devastatingly handsome?'

Lynn giggled. 'Of course. And look at that smile. It's definitely you. But so thin!'

'Yeah. Not much flesh on the old bones,' her boyfriend admitted. 'I hadn't started training at that point. I can't remember how old I would've been there. Can't even remember it being taken. But there was a year when I grew a foot in twelve months. It was a very costly time for clothes.'

'So you were just stretching,' the teenager grinned, her finger tracing along the lines of pictures. 'And that one... That's you too, isn't it?'

'Guilty,' he confirmed. 'That's Gerry's eighteenth birthday. We'd been to Bathurst. A particularly annoying day, actually. You'd relate to it, because Gerry and his two schoolmates all had their licences, but I didn't. So they got to drive these amazing sports sedans, and I just got to sit in the back.'

'Oh, that's terrible,' the young woman nodded, genuinely sad for him. 'I do know exactly how that feels. And there's you playing the piano.'

The aroused musician peered half-heartedly at the photograph while fondling Lynn's breasts, trying to divert her face sufficiently to kiss her mouth. 'Really?' he asked. 'Don't know why, but I can't seem to concentrate. I believe you.'

'Stop it!' Lynn hissed, moving his hands away. 'Someone'll spring us.'

'Jesus, I don't care!' Jeff replied. 'This is too on-turning for words; seeing you looking at photos of me when I was madly fantasising about you. And now I'm still madly fantasising about you, but with you right here.'

'This is more than a fantasy,' his dream girl giggled, leaning back against his body and threading her hand back behind her until she made contact with his excitement. 'I can feel it too.'

'So will you allow us to take your luggage upstairs?' he begged, turning her round to face him. 'Please?'

Lynn looked at her watch. 'What's going to happen now?'

'I'm going to jump you.'

'No!' she objected, hitting the mischievous man's chest. 'I mean what will the family do now?'

'Watch?' the comic suggested, his face alive with mock wonder. 'Learn? Applaud?'

The stunning celebrity gave her boyfriend an exasperated look. 'Come on then... No-one's going to get any peace unless I do. Let's get our stuff unpacked.'

Jeff dropped down onto his knees and thanked her profusely. The object of his manic affection extended her hand, seeing how grateful he was, and they left the haven of childhood memories to retrieve their pile of baggage. Lynn easily picked out their allocated room as soon as they reached the top landing, since its door was propped open with a chair. She didn't presume however, not wishing to seem patronising, and allowed him to invite her to enter once they arrived. Inside, there were clothes and other items spread out haphazardly all over the furniture.

'Oh, yes! This is definitely your room,' Lynn nodded, referring instead to the mess.

'It's not too bad,' her boyfriend defended himself, whining like an adolescent. 'It needs a woman's touch.'

The celebrity let out a caustic laugh. 'Oh, does it? I see... I think the appropriate response to that is "Fuck off."'

'Ouch! That's harsh,' Jeff objected, before pressing himself up against her attractive body and continuing impishly. 'Funny though! I didn't mean the room needed a woman's touch, by the way...'

Behind closed doors, pent-up passions took over, and the lovers were quickly naked and making love. Forgotten were the ghosts of Christmases passed lurking downstairs, and the couple hungrily satisfied each others' desires. Lynn loved the way her man was always so voracious around her, anxious to make this season as special for him as she could and to make up in some small part for the months he had spent pining for her company.

'I am forever in your debt,' the gallant suitor bowed, dressing again after a lightning-quick shower. 'Now I can look at you and still move about without hindrance over the next few hours.'

The beautiful blonde rolled her eyes. 'I need to slip some bromide in your tea or something. We're in polite company.'

'Are we?' the young man looked sceptical. 'Don't be so sure about that.'

The sated duo slipped back into the drawing room, trying to hide their furtive smiles but failing miserably. Fortunately, the television was droning in the background, and most family members were either reading or snoozing at the end of their day of suspense and excitement. To think they would have to go through the same thing again tomorrow and the next day, before the Christmas fairy could slink away for another year...

'Where have you two been?' Jacinta asked, with a glint in her eye.

Jeff shrugged and remained silent. Celia and Gerald looked up inquisitively at the sudden banter, both observing that their famous visitors seemed unable to disconnect from each other for a single minute. This tortured teenager whom they had helped raise was taking the recent vow he made in front of his best friend's mother very seriously indeed. He was making sure he didn't lose Lynn again if he could help it. Such compulsion wasn't entirely healthy, but the celebrities were both adults and hopefully it would pass.

'I've been on the tour,' the loyal beauty rescued her boyfriend, although hardly convincing.

'The tour, eh? So how long did you spend in each room?' Gerry probed, pointing to his watch in accusation.

'Oh, not long,' came Lynn's reply, as she shot a playful look back at her guide.

All five youngsters burst out laughing and cheered, causing Celia to wag a disappointed finger at her naughty offspring.

'Come on, give me a break! It's been more than forty-eight hours,' Jeff complained.

'My heart bleeds,' his mate interjected, throwing his packet of cigarettes at the latecomers.

'Cheers, everyone,' the younger man joked in a sarcastic tone, massaging his beloved's strong shoulders. 'I know I can always count on your support. Especially you, darling.'

'Ooh! Darling!' Tamilla teased. 'Jeff, you old romantic, you.'

Celia tutted and shook her head in frustration. Despite her concerns, the abject authenticity which surrounded their special guests was heart-warming. How lovely it was that the lost boy had been found again. Tears welled up in her eyes at the happy ending they were all witnessing.

No longer on red alert, the Blake children's kid brother didn't even try to retaliate. He was content to be at the mercy of these giggling girls now that his world had righted itself again. The family shared news and drank coffee until eleven o'clock, when Celia and Gerald announced that they were turning in.

And so with the parents and grandparents out of the way, the youngsters set about some serious drinking. The liqueur cabinet was raided, and the conversation became steadily riper.

'So will you come riding with us tomorrow morning?' Jacinta asked. 'Early?'

'Yes. Any time. I'm looking forward to it. I haven't ridden for a few weeks.'

'Are you coming too, Jeff?' Tamilla enquired. 'We know how you love riding.'

Their delectable dish failed to bite at the standing joke. 'No, thanks. I'm sure you girls'll have much more fun without me.'

'Good move, mate,' Gerry agreed. 'Those saddles'll entertain them nicely after a good night's sleep.'

Eyes lighting up, Lynn hadn't expected the conversation to go in this crude direction. 'Gerry! That's disgusting!' she exclaimed. 'Are you jealous? I never thought about it that way before.'

'What was that you were saying earlier about being in polite company?' her boyfriend asked, amused to bump into her *naïvetée* out of the blue.

'Darling...' Tamilla appended onto the end of Jeff's sentence. 'What's the matter? Don't you love her anymore?'

'You can goad me all you like, Tam. I'm not going to be lured into your trap tonight, spider-woman.'

'Ah, but do *we* have a lot of stories to tell, or what?' Jacinta added, with a certain menace in her voice. 'And there's all morning to tell them. Are you sure you won't come riding, to protect your reputation?'

'Cheers, Jack,' the young man chided. 'Do your worst. I'll take my chances with the consequences.'

Lynn moved closer on the couch and crossed her legs over his. Her boyfriend stared the older sister down, knowing she wouldn't miss a single move, and raised his eyebrows. *Where d'you think I'd rather be?* Jacinta scowled, and Tamilla stuck her tongue out. Message received and mission accomplished, he thought, though probably to his disadvantage come tomorrow morning.

Gerry sighed in frustration at the silly games the others were playing, being privy to certain information about his client's previous and not-so-platonic proclivities. Originally, this knowledge had given him a strange sense of pride: first, at having a mate who could seduce the good-looking siblings; second, that he had sisters attractive enough for a best mate who had spent his teenage years in huge demand from the opposite sex; and third, for the way it connected them all through this unspoken secret. Nowadays however, with his own domestic issues continuing to trouble him, their shared relations were all a little too cosy, and he had ended up the one left out in the cold.

Hearing a disgruntled snort from the other side of the room, Jeff sensed something was wrong in Gerryland. 'Cigarette, mate?' he suggested, extracting himself from Lynn's wholly irresistible, long limbs.

'Fantastic idea,' the grumpy accountant lifted his eyes from the car magazine he was reading.

The two childhood friends disappeared outside by the swimming pool, leaving the three girls alone in the drawing room. After an initial, slightly awkward lull in conversation, Jacinta felt guilty for the shameful taunting and took a unilateral decision to come clean with a history lesson, much to her sister's astonishment.

'Lynn, I feel bad,' she began.

The celebrity looked up. 'Why?'

'We're always teasing Jeff. You must've noticed.'

'No? I haven't noticed,' the newcomer laughed. 'Well, maybe just a little.'

Tamilla perked up. 'It's such fun, though.'

'Tammy, shut up,' Jacinta scolded. 'Lynn, do you know we've both been with Jeff over the years? Romantically, I mean.'

OK! In for a penny, in for a pound, as the saying went. Tamilla suddenly looked as though she were about to be sick, wondering what on Earth her elder sibling was playing at. Jacinta gazed back with wide eyes, equally uncertain of the damage she may be about to inflict on their old flame's burgeoning love affair.

The third party in these cameo interludes understood their predicament and bailed them out, hoping their choice of adverb had been a one-sided assessment. 'Yes, he told me. That's another hobby we have in common.'

Both girls' lungs emptied fully of air, giggling nervously.

'It's OK,' the famous visitor carried on. 'I was a bit unsure of how I'd fit in here, with everything that's gone on in the past, but I'm over it now. What's in the past is in the past.'

'Oh, thanks heaps. That's a huge relief,' Jacinta told her. 'We've been shitting ourselves in case you were pissed off about it. Or worse still, if you didn't know, and something slipped out over Christmas which you got upset about.'

The sophisticated star chuckled. 'It's fine. Jeff and I are as solid as a rock. Except if something were still going on, that is... I don't think I'd be too happy about that.'

Tamilla opened up. 'Don't stress. Our little get-togethers are nothing compared to what you have with him. He's unbelievably gorgeous with you, and I know he missed you so much while you were away in America. He's unbelievably into you. Always was.'

'Tammy, that's so obvious,' her sister teased. 'For God's sake!'

'No, but he is,' she insisted. 'I've never seen him into anyone, even temporarily. And even when he became famous and got hunted down by all those models and what have you...'

'Thanks,' the celebrity replied, slightly irked by the fuss they were making. 'I'm sure he enjoyed being hunted down on some level at least.'

'I've never seen him affectionate and using pet names before,' the younger sister carried on, determined to make her point. 'That's just not the Jeff we know, is it, Jack? We used to call him the "Love 'em and Leave 'em Kid".'

Lynn smiled, shrugging. 'That's funny. I expect he'd be proud of that. I don't know. He's always been the same way with me. I love the attention, so I'm not going to complain.'

The trio laughed at their vastly different impressions of their shared lover. Presuming the best way to dispel any lingering jealousy was to give the gossip princesses the scoop they were after, the celebrity upped the ante. So these two thought Jeff Diamond was into her? They didn't know the half of it!

'Even when we first met, my friends would moan about their boyfriends not showing affection or not talking to them, and I always wondered what they were on about. I can't stop Jeff talking!'

'Ahh, that's so nice. So did you have sex on your trip around the house?' Tamilla asked, feeling much more confident now.

'I'm not answering that!' Lynn teased. 'You'll have to ask him.'

Right on cue, the boys returned from their smoke to find all three women giggling, the liqueurs having a relaxing effect. Gerry was suspicious of their behaviour and deliberately stuck his nose into a newspaper to avoid being drawn into their *milieu*. Before joining them however, Jeff decided to divert upstairs, coming back clutching a book retrieved from his suitcase.

'What aren't you answering?' the older man asked. 'Have my sisters been giving you the Spanish Inquisition.'

'Gerry, shut up,' Jacinta moaned. 'This is between us girls.'

'Fucking hell!' his friend exclaimed, winking at the delectable blonde who was looking slightly off her stride. 'You've turned into those three bloody monkeys; see no evil, hear no evil, speak no evil. Who's who then? We'd better go for another ciggie, mate. Come and find us when you're done.'

Lynn held her hand out and encouraged her handsome partner to sit down. The empath realised she was asking for help and obediently reclaimed his place next to her, laying an enquiring hand on her knee. Still without speaking, he checked if she was alright. She nodded subtly, which he took to mean he would receive an update in due course.

'What's that?' his dream girl asked, pointing to the book beside him on the couch.

'Something I've been meaning to show you for a while,' Jeff replied. 'It's a sort of primer for tomorrow.'

'Pre-Christmas reading?' she guessed with a smile, chuffed that her plea had been understood and filed appropriately.

He shook his head. 'No. Pre-tour reading. For when we go out tomorrow morning, after your horse has satisfied you.'

The polite young lady screwed her face up in dismay. 'Which horse?'

'Moving right along...' the handsome man joked, basking in the veiled compliment in front of the Blake girls. 'It's something I wrote while you were off seeking your fortune and learning how to speak with an American accent.'

'Oh?' Lynn replied with renewed interest. 'Do I still speak with an American accent?'

'Gee whizz, Peggy-Sue!' Gerry piped up, putting on his best mid-western drawl. 'Ain't that quaint? Pass the grits'n'gravy.'

'Gerry, go and make some coffee,' Jacinta ordered her brother.

Jeff leaned in and kissed his Yankee princess hard on the mouth. 'Not much lately, angel. It comes out with certain words, like "Really?"'

Along with the others, the teenager laughed at an overly dramatic rendition of her oft-used exclamation. 'You're right! I do say that,' she agreed, slapping his thigh and focussing her eyes on the book. 'So show me then...'

'Come with me,' her perfect stranger requested, inviting her to stand up.

'Where are you going?' Tamilla enquired in a childish voice.

'Nowhere.'

Lynn obeyed, intrigued by his sense of purpose all of a sudden. The serious man took her hand, leading her through the house and outside to the swimming pool. He found the light switches and tried a few combinations until the desired mood was achieved.

'What are we going to do?'

'Sit down, please, Miss Dyson.'

Jeff pulled a couple of chairs out from under the long table on the deck, and his companion dutifully took her place. Nervous, he sat down beside her and set the book on the table. The inquisitive young woman examined it carefully. Was it a manuscript for another novel or screenplay? If so, why would he be so anxious? The single volume had a white cover of stiffened card and was about a centimetre thick, printed in full A4 size, like some sort of official report. She scanned the text on the front page. Its title was "Trauma, Mental Illness and Addiction – A Respecting Relationship".

Having got this far, the famous singer inhaled sharply and turned her head to search the eyes of the man sitting quietly to her left. They gave nothing away, so she refocussed on the words, feeling a lump rising in her throat. It was a University of Toronto publication, and its author was cited as Doctor

Sarah Friedman, Associate Professor of Clinical Psychiatry. Underneath this name however, was a co-author credit which blew the young star away.

'You wrote this?' her voice faltered as the emotion rushed through her veins, old memories flooding back. 'Diamond's Law of Compensatory Addictions. You did it.'

Jeff nodded, electing not to reply. His partner opened the book, and her eyes alighted on a hand-written inscription on the inside cover.

'Lynn, I'll love you forever and I'd love your help now. JMD'

The flabbergasted young woman read the Foreword, an executive summary from Doctor Friedman describing the reason this paper had been written and acknowledging the contribution of one Jeff Diamond, who had "opened his mind to her research in more ways than one".

'You don't have to read it now,' the handsome face smiled, 'or at all.'

'Are you kidding?' an unintentional American accent slipped out again. 'Of course I'm going to read it. You never told me about this before.'

'No. I was waiting for the right moment.'

Statements. So many statements. The amazed woman next read the section introducing his case study and digested the desperate man's explanation and heartfelt pledge with tears in her eyes. In true self-effacing fashion, the co-author's documented motives for funding and participating in this research project were not entirely altruistic. Sitting in the dark, both celebrities weighed up the portentous future benefit these words masked.

'Jeff, I'm so, so impressed. Everything's much clearer now. You express it so beautifully here, and it breaks my heart to think of all the damage that was done to you by your own family. Of course I'll help you, now and forever. What would you like me to do?'

Numbed by apprehension, the twenty-two-year-old who had been so full of fun earlier now sat mute, unusually incapable of translating his thoughts into words. Patiently, Lynn carried on reading.

'You're full of surprises,' she said, kissing his mouth and stroked his tense jaw. 'What happened after this was published?'

The intellectual songwriter leaned back in his chair and let out a long sigh. 'It received a lot of attention,' he responded, somewhat melancholy. 'It was presented to the Committee of Reactive Disorders and it's still under review by various Professors around the world, but it's broadly been accepted. There are some new treatment plans suggested in there, and I hear from Sarah that some university medical schools are beginning to trial them.'

'Wow, that's amazing!' Lynn praised, squeezing his hand. 'Congratulations. See? You *are* changing the world, and for people like you.'

'I know,' he admitted, still sounding downhearted. 'Thanks. It's a good feeling.'

'So what's wrong? You don't seem too happy about it. You should be so proud.'

Jeff ran his fingers through his long hair and stretched backwards on the wooden seat, clearly uncomfortable. 'Oh, I am,' he affirmed, taking an inordinately large intake of breath. 'Very happy about it. And I'm even happier that you now know about it, but I have to confess to one thing that I omitted during our long night in Sydney.'

The nineteen-year-old's eyes fixed on his in anticipation, detecting the tell-tale signs of dizziness and insecurity. She was convinced she could feel a change in his body temperature warming the night air surrounding her. What was the catch? Why had he used the word "confess"?

'What's that?'

'Before you find out from anyone else, I need to tell you that Doctor Friedman and I did not just have a professional relationship.'

His girlfriend chuckled bitterly. 'Oh, right. And that's supposed to surprise me?'

Jeff looked away.

'Sorry,' Lynn continued. 'I didn't mean that to sound quite as mean as it came out. It was my gut reaction, I suppose, like you.'

'Sure. I understand,' he told her, keen to get this episode over with so that he could concentrate on being fearful of the rest of their Christmas holiday plans. 'I deserve it. But the difference between this and other using relationships that happened while you and I were apart is that I'm likely to be working with Sarah again in the future, due to the success of this paper. I need to know whether you can be cool with it.'

The elegant beauty stood up and walked around behind her boyfriend's chair. He tensed up again, concerned she was about to disappear inside and go to bed without him. Gravity's trollish nails dug into his heart, and his thigh muscles became so unbearably tight that they twitched visibly through his trouser legs.

Then, just when the tormented man thought his chest would explode, and with an enormous dose of good cheer, he felt a sensorial pair of hands come to rest on his shoulders and gently begin to massage the knots.

'Jeff Diamond,' Lynn opened, bending down to kiss the top of his head. 'Doctor Diamond, I mean. I love you. You wouldn't be you if there wasn't an angle on everything you do. That's what makes it so exciting to be part of your life. I don't want to curb your passion for anything. And if this paper's going to change people's lives for the better, how can I possibly object to you continuing to work with this woman? Does she know about me?'

'Angel, you have every right to object,' her dark and dusky conundrum answered. 'And no, she knows nothing about you. Yet, that is. I will tell her...'

'Shhh!' his girlfriend cut him off, tapping his head with her fingertip. 'Hear me out, will you?'

Jeff laughed at her insistent tone. 'Sure. Pray continue.'

'I wonder what we'd have been like if we'd met when we were both virgins? Not half as interesting, I suspect.'

A few seconds of silence hung in the air, broken only by the sound of the occasional night bird. The couple stared out across the lawn and flowerbeds which were barely discernable in the dark, lost in their own thoughts. Lynn wondered how difficult it would be to live with her part-time research fellow, knowing his collaborator was also a former lover. This was quite another level of trust compared to sharing the holidays with Gerry's frivolous sisters.

'Am I allowed to speak?' the relieved star asked, with a smirk on his face invisible to his favourite lady.

'Yes, of course you are.'

'I don't know.'

There was another pause from over the author's head, broken in the end by a large hand squeezing hers onto his shoulder. Lynn was surprised how cold her boyfriend's fingers were, especially in contrast to the warmth emanating from his neck. This man's body could definitely do with a tune-up.

'You don't know what?'

'Nothing. Just I don't know,' Jeff repeated. 'You asked me what it would've been like both as virgins, and I said I didn't know.'

'Are you trying to be funny?' playful fingers swiped the side of his head.

'Yes, but clearly failing,' he laughed, grabbing her hand and bringing it to his mouth for a heart-restoring kiss. 'But you *were* a virgin, and I still found you interesting. About as interesting as humanly possible. Continue. Where were you going with this?'

'Argh!' she groaned. 'Where was I going? Oh, yes. I think if we'd both been virgins, one or other of us might have felt the need to experiment anyway, so the hurt would've happened in reverse and presumably after some sort of exclusivity promise rather than before.'

'True. I concur. So what's your point?'

The young woman sighed. 'Why is this so much hard work? My point is that you are who you are, with all the experiences that make you you. And I'm the same, just with less.'

'Are you sure? A few weeks ago you were boasting about everyone else,' the comic dared, more positive at last and drawing quotation marks in the air around the words "everyone else".

Lynn groaned anew. 'I know. I'm sorry about that. Again, OK? Anyway, while you and Gerry were off smoking just now, Jacinta came clean about she and Tammy having been with you. So I've already been subjected to something similar before you brought this topic up.'

'Shit!' Jeff was horrified to hear this latest complicated twist. 'Why did she do that? I can't believe she'd be so bloody heartless. I'm really sorry, angel.'

'But it's fine,' the nineteen-year-old reassured, shaking his shoulders. 'I'm OK with it. Am I not the winner? It's like you joking about Pete being tied up in the hotel closet... Wardrobe, I mean! We're the ones who arrived last and stayed. That's enough for me. Please believe me. I really mean it. I've come to terms with it all and I know I've got the most devoted, most intelligent, most caring and best looking sex machine on the planet. I'm not going to give that away because of someone whom you've been with and moved on from. Would you?'

The millionnaire rocker had tears in his eyes. He could hear Lynn's words and feel her touch, both heavy with pacifying intent. This was a speech he had been longing to hear ever since they made plans to spend their first shared Christmas in Sydney. Moreover, even more satisfying was the fact that the control freak in him had resisted his usual trick of putting words into her mouth, and his gamble had paid off. He hadn't tried to influence her response. This was the new, mature, worldly Lynn Dyson, who had grown into him. Or more accurately, they had grown into each other.

'No, I wouldn't,' he murmured, trying not to give away his precarious emotional state, for fear it would derail her train of thought. 'Thanks.'

'You're welcome,' the young celebrity said, leaning down and kissing the head of thick, black hair perfumed by his distinctive combination of smoke and shampoo. 'So now that we are each others' only one...'

'Which you are.'

'As are you,' she acknowledged, her lips sinking into the waves again. 'If either of us makes the decision to share ourselves around, then I think the other has the right to be upset and angry, and we'll need to face whatever fallout ends up being necessary.'

'Agreed,' the erstwhile sexual mercenary confirmed. 'One hundred percent agreed.'

'Great.'

The caring woman circled round from behind her pulsating human radiator, sitting up onto the table in order to gauge his state of mind. The wind had blown up off the coast, causing ripples to lap against the edge of the pool. Every now and then, a decking board or cross-member would creak or crack, but otherwise the humid stillness enfolded the earnest pair. Seeing his tear-streaked face in the light from the shimmering water, she leaned forward and stroked first his right cheek and then his left, smiling as his lips kissed her passing fingers.

'Now,' the guardian angel continued, 'you have to believe that I don't want that to happen, and I believe that you don't want it to happen either, so bugger everyone else. End of sermon.'

Australia's darling placed her hands behind her on the table and leaned back, having said what she wanted to say. Jeff smiled broadly at her definitive, most un-darling-like language.

'Perfect! Couldn't have said it better myself. Thank you.'

'So now can I read it?' Lynn asked, picking up the book.

'Now now?'

'Yes. Well, at least start it.'

'It's a good cure for insomnia, so go right ahead,' the modest academic chuckled.

'Let's go in and join the others. I'll read it over the next few days. They'll be accusing us of all sorts of nefarious behaviour again if we stay away too long.'

Jeff took the singing star's hands and slid her down from the table. After flicking off the light switches so that the pool area was once more plunged into darkness, each put an arm around the other and walked back into the house. Lynn had stowed his research paper carefully, intent on devouring it from cover to cover as soon as possible.

A few metres short of the drawing room doors, she tugged on the back of his shirt. 'So are you going to take me to the Stones Road tomorrow, if we can get away?'

'Sure am. I want to. I'm scared witless but I need to take you. Especially now.'

'¡Excelente!' the young woman responded, slotting her thumb deliciously inside his belt.

The Blake sisters were both still up, their eyes glued to the television. On the other side, Gerry was asleep in an armchair with the Sydney Morning Herald open on his lap. The women had become engrossed in an Alfred Hitchcock movie and hadn't even noticed their guests' return.

'Hey!' Jeff interrupted, making Tamilla jump out of her skin. 'This is "The Man Who Knew Too Much", isn't it?'

Jacinta nodded, stretching on the couch.

'I love this movie,' the happy man said, motioning for his lady to sit next to him.

The two musicians cuddled into each other, both yawning. The lost boy had relaxed considerably since coming inside, but in spite of having successfully negotiated this latest hurdle and being another step closer to tomorrow's crunch time, they both knew that the pressure of simply being in his home town would remain for a good while longer.

'Is it about you, this film?' the facetious nineteen-year-old flattered.

'Shut up, you hussy!' Jeff chided. 'Long eyelashes won't win me over. Much… Enough already. Just watch. It's great.'

Lynn declined any more to drink, feeling completely ready to climb into bed for to wake up on Christmas morn. Judging by the rings around her tenacious boyfriend's eyes, the colour of which rivalled the stubble on his face, he was equally tired. She assumed he was in no hurry to retire upstairs this time. They had already discussed the high probability of a disturbed night in advance of their proposed visit to the Stones Road, now fixed firmly into their itinerary on the promise of its curative power.

Although Jimmy Stewart and Doris Day turned in dazzling performances in the movie re-made in nineteen-fifty-six, and despite the scenes shot in London holding the young couple's attention for a while, some thirty minutes later, Jeff became aware of Lynn's fingernails scratching his thigh through his pants. It turned him on in his half-sleep, and instinctively he shifted around to pull her closer.

'That's nice.'

'I'm trying to keep you awake,' his girlfriend whispered, stifling a giggle on seeing his hand plunge into his lap to hide his growing erection.

The drowsy man nodded, rubbing his eyes and straightening up in the chair. 'Thanks. I love you. Do you still love me?'

Surprised at his sudden loss of confidence, his beautiful best friend played it safe. Was he awake or still on the verge of sleep?

'Errm…' she hesitated comically, aware of the sisters' eyes tracking their every move. 'Yes.'

'Are you sure?'

'Errm, yes. I'm sure. Shall we go up?'

The songwriter kissed the side of her head playfully, also watching Jacinta out of the corner of his eye.

'See? That's amazing.'

'No, it's not,' the blonde athlete disputed.

'Oh, yes, it is.'

***

Jeff remembered lying awake listening to Lynn's steady breathing beside him, worrying about the planned trip to his old neighbourhood. Part of him was optimistic that confronting the seedy locale again was bound to help, but as the hours passed, another, far darker part of him became increasingly neurotic about the potential of making matters worse. He had felt his heart rate quickening and sleepily trying to concentrate on slowing it down again.

What if he were to flip out? What if being there were to provoke something evil or deranged in him which he had managed to keep hidden until now? The terrified man didn't want his beautiful best friend to be placed in any danger, mindful of the commitment he had made to her father. Perhaps they oughtn't to tempt providence after all? Perhaps they should leave the past alone and make the best of what they had?

The anxious obsessive had obviously fallen asleep for a while, but right on the stroke of one o'clock, barely an hour after they had turned the light out, he was once again awake. And so was his beautiful best friend.

'Jeff!' she had shouted in his face. 'Wake up! Wake up! You can't disturb everyone this early on Christmas morning. Santa Claus hasn't even been yet.'

Angrily, the dreamer broke away from her grasp. 'OK. I hear you. Fuck, Lynn. Fuck! I'm sorry.'

'It's fine,' the sleepy voice refuted, kneeling up and reaching for some water from the bedside table.

'No, it's not. We're going to be wrecked tomorrow.'

'It *is* fine. It doesn't matter. Are you OK?'

'You're too good to me,' her disappointed boyfriend sighed and emptied the glass he had been given.

She blew him a kiss. 'That's because I love you. It won't always be like this. We'll sort everything out.'

Jeff lifted the sheet and invited his partner to cuddle into his aching body, desperate to make amends. Without hesitation, even though the night was really too warm for such close contact, she obeyed and draped her arm across his chest.

How could he possibly distract himself enough to fall asleep again? It wasn't long before this compassionate beauty would receive the wake-up call for her morning ride. The persecuted man's eyes darted around the bedroom which Celia always reserved for his visits, previously unnecessary of course. It was decorated in dated floral wallpaper that had probably cost an absolute fortune.

'Does this place remind you of Benloch?'

Lynn stirred from her drifting slumber. 'A little bit.'

Within a few seconds, the gorgeous woman beside him fell silent again, and her breathing became louder. Her boyfriend placed an apologetic hand on her forehead. He was keeping her from sleep she sorely needed after the last few hectic days of concerts and other public appearances. Lynn's smiling face turned to look at him, with that patient yet searching gaze that never failed to light his fire.

'I'm not homesick, Jeff, if that's what's worrying you.'

'Are you sure?'

'Yes. Go to sleep.'

The troubled man eased his body down the bed until he was lying flat, facing away from his *Regala* in an effort to leave her alone. Christ, he needed her help so much. What if his great confession had started something he couldn't finish? His mind tortured him relentlessly about the burden he had placed on her, his body responding in the only way it had ever learned. Sexual longing surged within him, knowing full well that he would be pushing his luck to wake his angel again for such a self-serving reason.

'Can't sleep?' she asked, sensing him restless beside her. 'Too stressed? Shall we go for a walk?'

'Walk? No,' he sniffed. 'Thanks, but that's absurd, angel. It's pitch black out there.'

Jeff's thoughts jumbled as he forced them to disconnect from the throbbing below the waist. Having pushed the sheet off her torso due to the heat, his dream girl looked unbelievably enticing in a silk nightdress with fine shoulder straps, and he wondered if it might not be too much after all just to roll on top of her and run his fingers along them to see if he could enliven her soft, tanned skin.

'Put the TV on,' came his partner's next, more predictable pitch.

'Yeah. OK,' the guilty man agreed, leaning over and picking up the remote control.

Celia didn't approve of electrical entertainment in bedrooms, he remembered with a start. There had never been any in this room before. He had better not let the Blake kids see how spoiled he was, recalling the fuss they used to make about their friends all having television sets and stereos in their rooms.

'Did you sort this out?' he asked in mock suspicion. 'The TV?'

His partner nodded.

'Thank you. You were captivating tonight.'

Her innocent face burst into a spontaneous smile, jolted out of her concern. 'Captivating?'

'Sure, angel,' her lover affirmed. 'They were eating out of your hand. We all are.'

Lynn kissed his upper arm, taut and muscular, and felt it tremble with unexpected pleasure. She knew he was trying so hard not to put a foot wrong. In the bluish light from the television, she could make out the shape of an erect penis beneath the sheet and realised the agony her compulsive boyfriend must be in. Today had been a big day for him, and tomorrow promised to be momentous by comparison. Even though she was so exhausted, she could hardly deny him the opportunity to relieve some of this pent-up tension, could she?

'The girls are in awe of you,' he continued. 'I've never seen them so simpering and attentive, running around after someone. Gerald's as spellbound as me, and Celia's just so happy for me. Every time I make eye contact with her, I think she's going to desiccate into a pile of caster sugar.'

'Well, in that case, you're mesmerising,' the thoroughly complimented young woman shot back. 'And Celia is very, very, very happy for you. She tells me every five minutes.'

'Captivating and mesmerising,' Jeff shrugged, his eyes scheming mischievously. 'That well-known double act. A fair amount of illusion suggested... Hypnotists and magicians. What are you doing?'

While her boyfriend distracted himself with poetry intended as subliminal seduction, Lynn had propped herself up to a sitting position and lifted the sheet up and down a few times so that the wafting fabric skimmed the tip of his manhood and then fell against the hairy skin of his testicles. His wild eyes flitted greedily between the tantalising sight and two impish, loving eyes.

Without a word, the slender woman turned from inanimate sleepyhead to lithe nymph, hitched her nightdress up around her hips and climbed astride her horny and incredibly sexy man. She took his erection in her hand and used it to moisten the lips of her vagina, listening to his moans of abject pleasure. Within a minute or two, he found himself inside her, and they began to move together slowly.

'You *are* captivating,' the bewitched lover whispered, his hands reaching up to her breasts and encouraging her to lean down against him. 'And I'm captured. Don't ever set me free, Lynn.'

'Shhh,' his girlfriend kissed the very corner of his mouth, sending shudders through both bodies. 'You make me so happy. I want to capture you. You're all mine. Come for me now.'

He did, and so did she, intense internal screams appropriately muted to protect the rest of the household from their impromptu nocturnal exploits. Laughing quietly, they eventually broke apart, and the young woman slid off the bed and headed for the *en suite* to shower off the shimmering layer of sweat from her skin. As she stood up, her nightdress fell silkily down her legs, sending yet more shivers of delight along her lustful partner's spine.

Jeff regained consciousness not long afterwards, feeling his upper arm being squeezed and his upper body shaking violently. It took a couple of minutes before he realised he was being woken by his dream girl again. His eyes refused to open.

'Hey! Are you awake?' Lynn was saying.

The horror-struck zombie was unable to respond. He couldn't remember how to make speech come out of his mouth. All he could do was bury his head in his hands, plunged back into despair yet again.

'Jeff, wake up,' his girlfriend urged again. 'Open your eyes. We're at the Blakes' house. Merry Christmas!'

The young woman repeated this process a few more times, gradually loosening his muscles. Finally, something clicked inside the young man's brain. Maybe it was the humour? A smile spread across his face, and he found his voice.

'Merry Christmas to you too,' he replied, slurring his words.

'Welcome back. Please open your eyes.'

'I can't,' he muttered. 'I really can't. I'm not joking.'

Sighing through her nostrils, the teenager prised open one eyelid and held it open. 'Can you see anything?'

'Yes,' he cursed under his breath. 'This is fucking ridiculous.'

Lynn let go of his eyelid, which slowly closed. Jeff shook his head violently, sending beads of sweat flying in all directions.

'What's going on?' she asked, starting to worry.

'I'll be OK in a minute. It happens occasionally. I forget how to work my body parts.'

'Seriously? You haven't told me that before.'

'No. It hasn't happened for six months or so. It's OK. No big deal.'

Relieved that her gorgeous, impaired man didn't seem too concerned about this latest debilitating development, the celebrity relaxed. 'All body parts?' she enquired, creeping her fingers along his leg from his knee upwards.

'Now who's obsessed with sex?' Jeff quipped. 'No, not all of them. Sometimes I can't speak. That's happened several times with you before, hasn't it?'

Lynn nodded. 'Oh, yes. I suppose so. When you take a while to register where you are. What do you want me to do?'

'Nothing. I'll just sit here for a while. Would you mind flicking the TV on again, please, angel?'

Lights of different colours danced around the room with the movement on the television screen, and the pair sat together, one watching and listening and the other just listening. Every now and then, the kind teenager would part her bedfellow's eyelids again to check if they could stay open of their own volition. At last, after fifteen minutes or so, when his heart rate had returned to normal, he turned around and stared at her, beaming.

'Ta-da!' he chimed. 'Told you they'd come back.'

'Fantastic! Shall we try getting back to sleep?'

The songwriter couldn't help laughing, even though Miss Irony had begun to dance the can-can in his churning belly. 'Jesus! Just when I've learned how to keep my eyes open, you're going to force me to close them again?'

'Yes. Otherwise we'll be useless in the morning.'

The lovers settled down to sleep again, and before long, the drama was once more upon them. After several more attempts at rousing her highly-strung stallion, Lynn finally managed to elicit a muffled response. This time however, for twenty minutes or so, the eyes were working but the mouth was not.

'I'm sorry,' the angry man blurted out once control was returned. 'I hate doing this to you. You must be as pissed off with this as I am. Thanks for helping me out.'

'Is it your brain or your body that's last to calm down?' the singer enquired in an effort to induce calm, recalling with a *frisson* of excitement the research paper which had been presented last night.

'Same,' he responded in gratitude. 'Both want to go to sleep but neither can. Adrenalin, excess testosterone... Fight or flight reflex, I guess. Takes a while to restore a balance. Your hand on my skin speeds up the process though. Knowing you're here.'

His beautiful best friend rubbed his chest vigorously in jest, before returning to the soothing strokes she had been administering while they spoke. 'Do you want me to stop asking questions?'

'Yeah, I think so,' Jeff sighed.

'Sorry.'

'That's OK. Here I am, trying to direct my last drops of energy towards calming down, and you're taking that energy elsewhere. It's fucking exhausting, but I haven't got a better idea. Who knows? I'm making it up as I go along. I'm sorry, angel.'

Lynn could hear the emotion overflowing in her man's voice. 'Don't keep saying you're sorry,' she replied. 'I know you are. Hopefully, things will be easier after tomorrow.'

'I like that hope,' the lost boy agreed, kissing her with lips that were still numb. 'Get some sleep, baby. I'll turn the volume down really low. I just don't want to risk it happening again.'

The blonde sportswoman agreed reluctantly, leaving her partner sitting up next to her in the flickering light of the screen. Oh, how she hoped tomorrow's daunting task would bring some sort of resolution for her irresistible troubled millionnaire philanthropist soul-mate...

Joy Triggers

Gravity had clearly enjoyed a good night's sleep and assembled in full battle-dress on Christmas morning, adamant that his host be prevented from basking in too much happiness. With the television still entertaining him when Lynn woke for her morning ride, Jeff did his best to lever himself out of the troll's gloomy grip to wish the girls a Merry Christmas. *Swear to God*, mornings were still so tough, and the depths of depression quite inexplicable for the man who now had everything he could ever wish for.

Downstairs, Christmas morning at the Blakes' was a jolly scene, almost as if the children hadn't grown up. Old family traditions endured, and everyone gathered in the drawing room to open their presents after breakfast. Jeff thought back to the previous holiday season, where he had sat in precisely the same spot and forced himself to enjoy the day even though his heart was swamped in Lynnlessness; back when his soul was lost, wandering somewhere along their invisible elastic connection.

Therefore, bizarrely, this year was the same but different, as the poet was at pains to let his beautiful best friend know. It was as if someone had turned his brightness knob to maximum at morning tea time, spiking high into the distortion zone on his happiness chart. After another wretched night that left him unrefreshed and infuriated, the welcome return of his lover from her ride, coupled with a hearty breakfast, had revitalised him no end. Lynn had enticed him into the shower for a festive blow job as his one and only Christmas present. This of course now placed him in gift deficit, and his imagination switched into overdrive to come up with a suitable reciprocation. A few ideas were drifting through his mind, but nothing inspired him as yet.

The family was due to depart for church after the customary present-opening ritual. Jeff had excused himself and his partner the day before with some trepidation, knowing full well that such a heathen lapse would not have been tolerated in earlier years. Certain standards needed to be upheld, Celia had always insisted, when her teenaged, atheist and unadopted son would voice his objection to being dragged to Mass. Yet this year, due in large part to the matriarch's vicarious glee, a leave pass had been granted to their special guests. They were now free to spin the wheels of Jacinta's little sports car before lunch, leaving the other youngsters once more jealous and fuming.

'You're my "Get out of jail free" card,' Jeff had whispered in his beautiful best friend's ear.

Gerry's face was a picture when he opened the gift from his biggest cash cow. The celebrity client had been deep in conversation with his mate's father about the following day's test match when he received a surreptitious tap on the knee from his girlfriend. She pointed to the accountant silently, and the big-hearted superstar watched with interest as his manager read through the paperwork inside the brightly-coloured Christmas envelope.

'Jeff, what's this?' he asked, his face becoming red and his breathing flustered.

'It's for your bathtub, mate,' the younger man answered, trying to maintain an authoritative air.

Jacinta and Tamilla were helping their grandparents to unwrap their presents, unaware of the fuss unfolding on the other side of the large room. Corny Christmas music played merrily and too loud in the background, while Celia bustled back and forth with mince pies and cups of tea.

Gerry finished scanning the pages, and the couple saw him gulp and heard a sniff. 'Diamond,' he ordered, making for the door. 'Outside.'

Beckoning for Lynn to follow him, the twenty-two-year-old stood up and left the room after his friend, leaving the others wondering what was going on. The couple found the surprised recipient sitting on the very table where they had been discussing books on addiction and their commitment to each other not half a day earlier. The executive had his head in his hands and was plainly sobbing.

The young woman had gleaned on their drive back to Mosman from the city the previous day that the indomitable playboy's normally well-engineered, carefree lifestyle had hit the skids when he tried to resolve the pregnancy issues with Heather and her interfering family. Seeing these complications catching up with him, she hung back while Jeff worked his magic, putting his arm around his mate and shaking him roughly.

'You absolute fucking bastard,' Gerry cursed, embarrassed.

'That's me!' laughed Jeff, stealing a secret glance back to his girlfriend. 'In an absolute fucking nutshell. It's from both of us, mate. Merry Christmas. Do you know how easy you've made things for me? This is for all that hard work, the good decisions, sound advice and mateship. I know you're bloody stressed at the moment, so hopefully this'll bring some fun into your life.'

The emotional accountant looked up and burst into tears again when his gaze alighted on the demure, golden-haired beauty who had stolen the collective hearts of his entire family. She was standing a few metres away, leaning against the pool fence, even more ravishing than usual.

'Merry Christmas, Gerry,' Lynn echoed.

'You must've seen me leafing through those boating magazines in Reception,' the off-guard Irishman mumbled, gradually regaining his composure. 'Did you? Jesus Christ!'

'A few times,' his client confirmed. 'Yeah.'

'This is bloody fantastic, mate. Thanks heaps,' the businessman gushed, looking again at the front page of the glossy brochure, which showed a picture of the cruiser and listed a few of its features. 'I could kiss you. Where did you find it?'

'You can kiss Lynn instead, if you have to. In Port Douglas,' Jeff told him, holding his hand out to encourage his girlfriend closer. 'You need to name her, then bring her down to the mooring in Brighton Marina, so either hire a sailor or become one. Your choice.'

'Fucking hell!' Gerry shouted at the top of his voice. 'I was having a shitty Christmas until now. I saw a large withdrawal go out the other day, but I assumed it was a present for this stunning creature here. This is the best thing anyone could buy me. Thanks so much, guys.'

He sprung up and planted a smacker directly onto the teenager's lips and hugged her close. She also had a tear in her eye, over the moon that both men had got what they wanted from the rather excessive gift.

An hour or so later, having locked an empty house and turned out of the driveway, Lynn could tell her handsome driver was supremely nervous because he barely uttered a word as they drove in the tiny MG Roadster, due west from the shore line. She had never known him so quiet, and the streets were almost deserted. The tinny car radio was tuned to a local station, and the mindless chatter of the presenter who had drawn the short straw to work on Christmas morning was blabbering away in the background, filling in between golden oldies and cheesy festive favourites.

'Change it, if you like,' Jeff offered, hearing his girlfriend groan at yet another stale *cliché*. 'Jack won't mind.'

'Are you OK? You're not sounding very Christmassy anymore. We should've waited until tomorrow.'

Jeff looked across at her and faked a grin. 'Nonsense,' he kidded. 'I'm extremely Christmassy. Would you like me to sing you a carol?'

The teenager groaned. 'No, thanks! Morose is preferable.'

'Ha! So you don't like me singing to you? It took you a while to own up to that one. Cheers, angel. You're cheering me up.'

'Where are we?' the young woman asked, not recognising any landmarks on the northern side of the Parramatta River.

'I have no idea,' the Sydneysider replied. 'All I know is we're moving from Nicetown to Boganville in a general south-westerly direction. About halfway.'

'So where was the football camp where you met Gerry?' came her next question, designed to focus her boyfriend's mind on some cold, hard facts.

Jeff was wise to her motives. 'You truly are the Christmas angel,' he told her, smiling and reaching for her hand. 'I know what you're up to, and it's working. The sports camp was in Ryde, not too far from here actually. We were in huge dorms rigged up in the school's classrooms during the holidays. Blake-san was a pompous prick back then too, and I couldn't understand why I liked him so much. He was so far removed from what I thought a man should be. I tapped him for a cigarette and then stole his girl after he was an arsehole on the footy park. I got my own back by getting my rocks off with her, and we've never looked back since!'

Lynn raised her hands aloft and lifted her eyes skyward. 'You really have been a sex-crazed bastard all your life, haven't you?'

'Yep,' he admitted. 'Sorry.'

'That's OK. I suppose it could be worse.'

'Like how?' the driver asked, staring beyond the road and far into the distance. 'Like I might be the sex-crazed son of a murderer and a drugged-up prostitute?'

'Yeah, something like that,' his kind passenger smiled. 'At least you're not technically a bastard.'

'Indeed. Not technically. Just in most other ways,' Jeff rued, immediately reminded of Gerry's situation. 'Though I think that would've been the least of my worries.'

The couple drove on for another ten kilometres, bumping along the uneven bitumen on dodgy suspension. Lynn prised memory after memory out of her guilt-ridden lover as they approached his former territory. He was glad to field her ceaseless barrage of questions, since it took his mind off the mounting fears.

Next, prompted by another innocent observation, the afflicted songwriter recounted a time at primary school after being invited to a friend's place for tea after school. When it had come time to go home, the boy's father had asked who would be picking him up, to which the youngster had informed them that he would be fine on the bus. Needless to say, his friend's parents had insisted on taking the nine-year-old home, not wishing to be responsible for leaving a child to walk the streets alone. That particular boy was never allowed to invite Jeff Diamond home for tea again.

'Did he wonder why?' his girlfriend asked, annoyed at the small-mindedness of some people. 'Did *you* ask why?'

'Angel, come on,' the tearaway replied in frustration, his head aching. 'Kids like us didn't need to ask why. It was clear as day. School was fine; a level playing field. But outside of school, you went your way, and I went mine. That's just how it was. It only served to make me more determined to break out. That kind of shit did me a favour, Lynn, if I'm honest.'

'I wonder what that boy's father thinks now?' his passenger asked rhetorically, staring out of the window. 'I bet that boy's girlfriends all buy your albums and go to your gigs, and I bet he's boasted any number of times that he went to school with you.'

'Yeah. Who cares, huh?' Jeff shrugged, grateful for her vote of confidence. 'It doesn't matter anymore, all that stuff.'

But the determined therapist wasn't finished with this particular planned step on her treatment plan. 'It's weird, isn't it, how our difference from everyone else makes us startlingly similar to each other.'

The boy from Canley Vale raised his eyebrows. 'How do you mean?'

'Well... Some of my friends' mums were too scared to invite me for tea. Most times, I was dropped off and collected by a driver rather than a parent, and I always noticed this odd look on their faces: a mix of pity, jealousy and a sort of pride that I had befriended their daughter. And neither of us could invite people back to our place, could we? Admin was a pretty boring place to bring friends to. As young girls anyway...'

'Yep. Guess so. So stop feeling sorry for me then!'

The privileged young woman laughed, slapping her hands on her legs. 'OK. I'll try. I had some pretty amazing weekend sleepovers at Benloch though.'

'I could say the same,' her boyfriend replied with a salacious smirk, 'but you'd accuse me of being a sex-crazed bastard again.'

Lynn smacked his left arm, and received a wink for her trouble. Their journey carried on for a few more kilometres in silence, until they began to see signs for Fairfield.

'Almost there,' Jeff told her, his stomach in knots.

He could feel his chest tightening, and the hairs were bristling on the back of his neck. The little car was too old to be fitted with air-conditioning, but driving with the roof down had kept them reasonably cool. Nevertheless, perspiration stuck the nervous man's t-shirt and skin together. He looked across to his left to see Lynn Dyson's smiling face, as fresh as a daisy, wearing a summer top over tanned skin and her hair thrown back into a ponytail.

Yes, it was official. The boy returning to Canley Vale was a mess. Familiar demons were already circling overhead, preparing to swoop down at any moment. His thorough research into Post-Traumatic Stress Disorder had convinced him that replacing old negative memories with new positive ones was bound to alleviate some symptoms, and he clung onto a slim vestige of excitement to think that he at last had the chance to experiment on himself.

Jeff's fingers drummed the steering wheel as they waited to turn right at a large intersection. His girlfriend figured they must be close to their destination, judging by the beads of sweat on his forehead and the shaking of his long legs. As she expected, the sports car leaned heavily as it screeched around the corner, making a sharp left turn and coming to a standstill in front of a parade of shops.

'This is a fantastic thing to do on Christmas Day,' the panic-stricken man asserted out loud, bending down to open the door of the red MG.

'Two floors closer to heaven,' Lynn recited from one of the rock star's earliest hits, looking around at the downtrodden neighbourhood. 'Is that it? The general store in the song? J Cafici and Sons?'

'That's it,' her tour guide confirmed. 'Up there. See? Those two windows?'

The graceful sportswoman let him lead her the fifty metres or so towards an antiquated hardware store, and they stood on the wide footpath looking up. A trembling finger pointed to the left-hand window, but his voice remained remarkably calm, as usual.

'The walls on one side of that room were covered with your pictures. And later on, once I had it to myself, pretty much the whole place was.'

Lynn marvelled at this parallel universe of which she had been completely unaware. Standing this close to the scene of her lover's tragic childhood struck a much deeper chord than she had anticipated, long knowing that her face adorned the walls of virtually every Australian boy's bedroom.

Jeff was jumpy and uncomfortable. She could tell he couldn't wait to leave.

'Not much to see here,' he declared, beginning to walk away. 'Move along, please.'

His singleton tour party giggled. 'OK. Where to next?'

The couple continued to drive around the district. The Fairfield native showed his charge his primary school, then his secondary school and some of the places where he had worked at part-time jobs. He took her past his maternal grandparents' home, and she had hurled some refined abuse at them on his behalf, making him chuckle. He presumed Madalena would be in the back yard with them at Christmas time, among the fruit trees and rose bushes he and his sister had pruned in the early days. He certainly wasn't prepared to knock on the door to find out, especially after the frosty reception he had received the last time.

After a while, the outing began to lose its appeal, which was oddly comforting to both of them. The rock star had difficulty finding his Polish grandparents' street, since many neighbourhood aspects had altered with the addition of several new buildings. Eventually he worked it out, and identifying the run-down block of flats caused his confusion to overflow into an angry outburst.

'Jesus! What a fucking dump,' Jeff yelled, hitting the gate post with his fist and fighting back tears. 'I hardly remember this place. How could a defenceless, old woman live here?'

Lynn rested her hand in the small of his back, allowing him to rant and rave beside the fence until he had banished the raw emotion from his system. Looking on in amazement, she suddenly caught on to how this tortured wreck had managed to develop into such a powerhouse of intellectual capacity. Absolutely everything he did was crammed full of passionate meaning and a spirited conviction.

A back-story, the fascinated teenager mused.   This was his secret ingredient.   It was as if the man had lived two lives, the public one running in parallel with the private one, even as a young child.   And what about all the other lives he claimed to have lived?   And would there be more in the future? Were there more than two in train right now?

The former schoolgirl fleetingly cast her mind back to their conversation about old souls.   She had never known a person to attach such significance to life; even more surprising for someone who didn't value his own.   Jeff's philosophical words were becoming clearer now.   It wasn't the life that was important, since each existence was transitory.   Perhaps more important were the things one accomplished in each life, and with whom?   If the vehemence her boyfriend applied to pursuing their relationship was anything to go by, hers may well be an old soul too.   But why didn't she possess an equally strong conviction, in that case?   Were the two soul-mates merely passing through, on some preordained mission to change the world?

The familiar spark and hiss of Jeff's cigarette lighter brought the young woman whizzing back to the present moment, feeling foolish for her flight of fancy.   She pictured the lost boy's peculiar *bar mitzvah* party taking place in the rooms on the first floor of this unassuming block, almost able to taste the endless bowls of borscht he had described so vividly.   And the piano lessons... Here had started The Australian Elvis' musical training, she reflected.   There ought to be a plaque on the wall!   It was probably more appropriate to commemorate this location than the miserable Stones Road flat, which had certainly lived up to the shabby image Lynn had built up in her mind.

The last scheduled stop on the tour was Fairfield Park, with its small hill at one end, stretching away from a patchwork of sports ovals and the children's playground.   The good-looking celebrities climbed to the top and sat down under a clump of ancient oaks, peering out over the sprawling suburbs in the bright sunlight and hoping to evade discovery.   Jeff's mood slowly relaxed as he smoked another cigarette and surveyed the kingdom of his bleak and complex adolescent years.

'This is where I used to come when I didn't want to go home,' he told his beautiful best friend, with his arm draped around her shoulder.   'This is where I'd do my homework, write songs and dream of you.'

Lynn kissed his cheek, feeling the stubborn stiffness in his jawline which hadn't yet dissipated.   She played with the hem of his t-shirt and made fun of the rip in the old pair of shorts he had chosen to pack for their short break. Neither showbusiness personality looked the part today, both sporting worn, comfortable thongs on their feet and not a scrap of jewellery apart from Jeff's watch. It was perfect, the matching millionnaires agreed, rolling backwards onto the grass and pretending to be horny teenagers with nowhere else to go.

'Thank you for bringing me to all these places,' the slender celebrity said. 'It's great to get a real idea of what they look like.'

'This is where "*Regala*" came from,' her boyfriend continued, oddly distracted by strong flashbacks being evoked around him. '"*Regalo*" means "gift" in Spanish, made famous in some ancient folklore. Sort of a cross between gospels and fairy tales, and sometimes even in religious teachings.'

The young woman giggled, lifting his hand and placing it on her breast. 'What's Spanish for sex?'

'Be quiet,' the authority retorted, nudging her sideways until she almost toppled down the hillside. 'Priests don't do that sort of things. Well, they do, but only with children, apparently. Rabbis don't do it either. We should respect the ancient texts. That's rabbits you're thinking of.'

'Oh, right!' she replied, behaving like a ditsy schoolgirl being berated by a teacher on whom she had an enormous crush. 'Terribly sorry, sir. Won't do it again, sir.'

For an agnostic and self-confessed naysayer on conventionality, her enigmatic stranger certainly was protective of certain sacred traditions, and again it made Lynn think of the sunny afternoon they had spent in the lush grounds of the Abbotsford Convent in their very early days, exchanging their respective beliefs.

Shivers ran down her spine when she recalled the heavy conversation about souls and mates, and also that Jeff had cut the discussion short, ostensibly due to her tender age. She hoped they would one day revisit this mysterious theme because it formed a significant part of their unfinished business, as far as she was concerned.

Today was not the day however. This much the inquisitive student understood. Meanwhile, her nostalgic man went on, hugging her tightly, his voice husky and deep. She snuggled into him, revelling in the one-on-one contact and eager to hear how she had become his gift.

'The word *regalo*'s used to refer to something or someone who's been sent to you for good purpose. That's what I wanted more than anything in the world. That you'd be sent here to me. I used to talk to you endlessly up here, but no-one ever sent you, thereby putting a fucking great question mark in my mind about the existence of God. So my only alternative was to come and get you.'

The couple kissed tenderly, while his dream girl searched in his dark eyes for more secrets.

'That's so beautiful. I still can't quite believe it, but it's so good to finally be here. You sent me to yourself.'

Her boyfriend chuckled, seeming initially stunned by this concept. 'I did. I guess you're right. You know, angel? I think that's exactly what happened.'

Although Lynn was overjoyed to have her assertion welcomed so gratuitously, she decided not to press the issue, and her black stallion voiced no objection either. Instead, they lay back on the grass and talked about London. Only the occasional group of people went by, either walking their dog or with their children, mostly trying out new bicycles or skateboards. Thankfully, nobody took the trouble to recognise the two off-duty performers, and the peaceful solitude was splendid after the frenzy which December had dealt the country's two biggest stars. Their respective, very successful years were drawing to a gentle close, and with so much promise in store.

Jeff drove back on the south side of the river, bringing them in a huge circle around Sydney. The hungry pair took a brief detour past Randwick Racecourse to the University of New South Wales, where the former student showed the Melburnian the location of the Computer Science faculty lecture theatres, and about two kilometres away, where the bar had propped him up on many an occasion at the Union. The buildings were deserted and locked up, and the tourists were soon in the car again.

'So I read the last few pages of your paper,' Lynn began a new line of questioning for their journey back to Christmas lunch in Nicetown. 'The part about looking after yourself.'

'Oh, yeah?' the driver raised an eyebrow in approval. 'Which part, specifically?'

'You know… Sleep, exercise, nutrition and all the other things that people can do to feel more positive,' the attentive pupil recounted.

'Yeah.'

'So have you got a plan for all these while we're in London? Because I'd like to help.'

'Not really,' the young man answered with interest. 'Not yet. The only one that'll be a real problem is sleep, which won't come as a surprise to you.'

Lynn smiled. 'No, but it's at the top of the list. For a reason?'

The intellectual glanced at his muse before focussing thoughtfully on the road ahead. She never failed to comprehend the core argument. His heart swelled with unspoken love, immediately receiving a torrent of romantic lyrics streaming into his consciousness. He shook his head, forcing himself back to this very practical of topics. The next hit song would have to wait. He shifted down a gear to overtake a particularly slow holiday driver, and the MG juddered as if it were about to break into little pieces.

'Jesus! I forgot I wasn't in the Aston,' the daydreamer cried out, ashamed of his negligence while conveying his Very Important Passenger. 'Right in one, angel. I can't remember the numbers off the top of my head. It makes sense. Along with positive attitude, sleep's the thing that can screw you up the most when you're in deficit.'

'So that's got to be my priority,' his girlfriend resolved. 'To help stop the nightmares and get you sleeping for long stretches. OK?'

'Yeah! Very OK,' Jeff grinned. 'Extremely OK.'

'And the other thing I want to help get rid of is all the guilt and shame,' she continued, knowing this would be much less enthusiastically received. 'There's no need for you to take the blame anymore. The things you've been blamed for are irrelevant to your life now, aren't they?'

'Largely, but I can't deny them.'

'Apart from Madalena, maybe,' observed the new clinical psychiatrist's assistant, much to his grateful amusement.

'Well, we can't do much about her while we're in London,' the scarred man scoffed, his anger immediately fired up again at the mention of his sister's name. 'Lena's OK. She asks me for money all the time but she's basically happy. I don't feel so guilty about her nowadays. She doesn't appear to bear any PTSD-type scars from back then, but I can't be sure they're not hidden away.'

Lynn persevered, sensing the surrounding air pressure climbing again, despite the cabin being open to the skies. Over the last few weeks, she had begun to notice her flatmate's anxieties were often magnified by a lack of food, so she relegated this battle for another day too.

'OK. Well, what about the addictions?' the nurse moved on. 'I have to read the detail yet, so I might be getting this wrong, but is the crux of your conclusion that you have to eliminate all three factors in order to recover completely?'

'It is,' Jeff confirmed, flattered that his dream girl was taking his work so seriously and without pathos. 'We don't have a dependency without a reason, and we don't have a reason without the memory of a cause.'

The clever woman took a few moments to work through this logic, imagining that conquering this level of complexity would be easier said than done. 'I get it,' she hesitated. 'I think.'

'We don't have to talk about this now. It's Christmas, and I'm fucked.'

His *Regala* reached out and touched the driver's left thigh. 'I know, but it's fascinating and it's my real chance to make you properly happy.'

'You already make me properly happy,' he smiled, placing his left hand on top of her right. 'But there is a way you can help more practically, angel.'

Lynn's eyes shifted sideways and were instantly trapped by those of her mystery man. They both smiled, hit by another rare moment of shared self-consciousness.

'How?'

His voice cracked again. 'I didn't tell you before, because I didn't know how I'd react to coming back to the Stones after escaping for so long, but I've bought the flat above Cafici's.'

'Really?' his girlfriend exclaimed in surprise. 'Your old home? Why?'

'Yeah, really,' Jeff mimicked the tell-tale Californian influence again. 'I need you to help me get inside. I don't know if it'll fix anything, but I absolutely need to try.'

Tears welling up, Lynn wanted to hug him so badly. She could almost feel the fear being transferred from driver to passenger. Pulling herself together, she did her best to feed positivity into her brave emotional baggage handler.

'That's fantastic. When did you buy it?'

'I tried shortly after we wrote the paper, but it didn't work out,' the millionnaire explained, slightly disturbed at hearing a level of enthusiasm he didn't entirely buy into. 'So I tried again when you and I got back together, and this time I got it.'

'Did the vendor know it was you?'

Jeff shook his head. 'No. It's all been done anonymously. You know how it goes... My people talked to their people. Very clandestine. I won't keep it, whether it serves its purpose or not. The Stones is hardly a long-term investment. You have to admit that, now you've seen it for yourself!'

'I suppose not. So when are we going to do this?' Lynn asked with a smile. 'This trip? Have you got the keys?'

Her direct head-on strike was challenged by wild eyes. Suddenly, the young man felt more than nervous. Terrified, even. His dream girl had brought the moment way too close, and he felt fury boiling over in an instant. He steered Jacinta's wobbly car to the side of the road and pulled the handbrake up, breathing deeply to stem the panic.

'No. I mean, yes, I have the keys, but no... Fucking hell, I need more notice of such questions! Christ, angel. I can't talk about this and drive at the same time. It wouldn't be safe. Let's go back and have lunch with everyone and maybe come back in the morning? Or after London. Shit! I'm sorry.'

'I'm sorry too,' his patient girlfriend agreed, staggered by the most severe loss of control she had witnessed since his confession. 'Are you OK? I didn't mean to put so much pressure on you. I'm in your hands. You tell me what you want to do, and I'll do it.'

They left the car and walked along the street in the warm, humid air. Jeff put his arms around the apologetic woman and pulled her in close to his agitated frame. He kissed her bare shoulder and then the side of her head as she leaned into him. The colour began to return to his face, and he managed a smile.

'Thanks for humouring my fucked-up-ness. We must do it. I'm putting my faith in you. You can help me with this because you can adjust to me quicker than I can adjust to myself. Look at you! You're a bloody lottery landslide, not just a gift. I just never thought I'd feel comfortable enough to do this with you. I've been thinking about it for years.'

The pretty blonde swung round to face him. 'I've got an idea!'

Her boyfriend still looked somewhat nauseated. 'Have you? Already?'

'Yes. Do you trust me?'

'Jesus, I don't know,' her troubled man replied. 'I'm shitting myself just putting it off 'til tomorrow. Look at me shaking like a leaf... You need to know, I might completely freak out. I was like a wild animal living in that flat, left to my own devices. Maybe we shouldn't do it on a whim.'

Wild animal was an accurate likeness. Lynn had seen this for herself, a few times now. Jeff was trembling, and beads of perspiration had appeared on his face. His beautiful best friend lovingly wiped his brow with her handkerchief and kissed his slimy, unshaven cheek. At this precise moment, it would have been hard for a man to feel more wanted.

'OK. That's fine. Think about it and let me know.'

'Great. I am grateful that you want to help,' he responded more calmly, as they ambled back towards the car. 'I just...'

'Don't,' his *Regala* scolded him. 'Leave it for now. It doesn't matter. I know this is an enormous step. Let's not talk about it anymore. What do you think's for Chrissy lunch?'

The hour's drive back to the genteel suburbs on the northern Sydney coastline gave the exhausted man a chance to steady his nerves and focus on the rest of the day. Lynn played him a tape of a song she had written for him, as a present for having survived this experience. It was called "No-one Else Like You", and he instantly fell in love with it.

'You flatter me way too much. It's beautiful. *Gracias.*'

The rock star was harbouring a bevy of songs for his soul-mate too, to be shared once they returned to Melbourne. In fact, he had hundreds of them. They wouldn't stop whipping themselves up in his head. Shaken or stirred, it didn't matter. In fact, another was already tapping him on the shoulder as they drove back over the Harbour Bridge, and he struggled to piece it together real-time and to sing through the wind.

Lunch preparations were in full swing when the young lovers finally returned to the household. Lynn apologised to Celia for staying out so long, but of course it was brushed off with good grace. She pitched in with Jacinta and Tamilla, while the men did what men tended do best on these occasions: drink.

'So where did you two go this morning?' Gerry's older sister asked their guest. 'What did you think of my little sports car?'

'Oh, it was fun! Thanks for the loan of it. Jeff calls it a "roller skate". I felt so low to the ground. We did the Jeff Diamond childhood tour. It's very popular, by all accounts. All the hotspots of the outer-west.'

'Ew!' Tamilla exclaimed. 'We've never had that tour. What's it like?'

The celebrity wasn't about to betray her man's confidences in front of these well-off young ladies who would probably never venture anywhere that didn't serve champagne. 'It's just like I expected. Like the songs. It was great to see them come to life.'

'So...' the elder Blake daughter was a little tipsy on lunchtime vodka and eager for some gossip. 'Did he tell you about his parents? He's never told us what happened. How he ended up living on his own over there. Did you know they tried to take him into State care?'

Celia interrupted. 'Jacinta, that's enough, please. That sort of thing might not be public knowledge.'

'It's OK,' Lynn waved the comment politely aside. 'I do know what happened but I can't be the one to tell you. It's up to Jeff whom he tells.'

'Did he also tell you he broke this kitchen door once?' Tamilla asked, pointing to her left. 'It was the weirdest night, wasn't it, Mum?'

The celebrity laughed along. 'Yes, he did. That should be part of the tour. You could charge people to have their photo' taken next to it. Jeff said he was too embarrassed to visit for a while after that.'

The sisters laughed too, but their mother had a pained expression on her face. The memory was evidently a bad one for her, and the visitor felt guilty at having made light of what must have been an awful time in their shared loved one's history.

'Yes. Poor boy,' Celia confirmed, her shoulders drooping a little as she recalled. 'He was in a bad way. Let's change the subject, ladies, if you please.'

Christmas lunch was a huge success; lively, tasty and never-ending. The farm-girl from Victoria fitted in perfectly with the Blakes, and her lowly city boy loved watching her interacting so naturally with his adopted family. It was a warm, sunny afternoon, and the pool beckoned. Celia dismissed the men from kitchen duties, much to Jacinta and Tamilla's disgust.

'Lynn,' the kindly woman urged. 'You go and enjoy yourself too. You're our guest. We'll see to all this.'

'No, I'm fine. I'd like to help out,' the well-mannered celebrity replied. 'It's a lot of work putting on a meal like this. I'd have to help if I were at home.'

Celia nodded, placing a manicured hand on the young woman's forearm. Lynn Dyson surely possessed the manners of an aristocrat, she mused, but the depth of someone destined for far greater things. For the first time, she understood perfectly what her errant and radical pseudo-son saw in this urbane sophisticate.

'Thank you. In that event, I'll make your mother happy by letting her think you didn't shirk your domestic duties, my love. Is this the first Christmas you've spent away from your family?'

Lynn shook her head and took her place at the sink, realising that Missus Blake was planning on going fishing for information on the last two years. The two grandmothers sat chatting at the kitchen table while the younger women fetched and carried, but she was left in no doubt that each pair of ears was trained on her.

'No,' she answered. 'Last year, I spent the holidays with college friends in Aspen, Colorado. We went skiing, and it was all very grand. The year before... my first year in the US... my family flew out for an LA Christmas. None of us enjoyed it, to tell you the truth. I wished they'd never bothered.'

'Oh, dear,' Celia frowned, walking back into the kitchen with an armful of crockery and cutlery. 'That was a shame. We didn't see Jeff the year before last either. I think he also stayed with uni' friends. You two have led a parallel existence for all this time. No wonder you managed to fall back together again so easily.'

The pretty celebrity smiled inwardly, remembering the stories of debauchery her misbehaving, black stallion had relayed about the haze of late December nineteen-seventy-two.

'Jeff was with you last Christmas though, wasn't he?' she deflected.

'Yes,' Jacinta piped up. 'And for New Year. It was amazing having a megastar attend our party. Twice as many people wanted to come as normal.'

The famous songstress knew exactly where this was heading, having often been in similar situations. She had a vision of the expert dancer listlessly winging countless high society friends and neighbours round the polished wooden flooring, in the marquee they had described over lunch. She hoped he had been thinking of her at the same time. She had certainly been thinking of him in Aspen, itching to find out what sort of person fame and fortune had turned him into.

'Your beautiful boy was extremely down in the dumps last New Year, Lynn, darling,' Gerry's mother's prim voice snapped the young woman out of her *rêverie*.

'Yes, I think I know,' she lamented. 'He told me about it after you asked us to come up this year. He said you caught him smoking dope and crying, and that he sent you away. He's very sorry he did that, Celia.'

The two sisters returned to the kitchen just in time to overhear these gloomy details, with which they were obviously *au fait*. The nineteen-year-old felt a pang of guilt, hoping the revelations wouldn't be used against her gorgeous man. These girls were brazen and knew him quite well enough to speak freely. She feared she may have gone too far with this latest snippet of information. *Too bad*, she sighed. It was done.

'Oh, I had assumed he was, dear,' the elegant lady dismissed the comments. 'He's always had a good heart, that boy. My reward is to see you here with him this year. I know how we all used to tease him, probably to the point of distraction, about his crush on you; wanting to know every last thing about you, always hungry for news. But goodness me! Here you are, my delightful young lady.'

Well beyond the point of distraction, Lynn now knew. Without warning, Gerry's mother launched herself at the unsuspecting visitor, hugging her tightly and crying. She hoped her fractious boyfriend wouldn't choose this particular moment to fetch some more beers from the fridge and attempted to break free from Missus Blake's overly zealous custody.

'Mum!' Tamilla shrieked. 'Poor Lynn! You're going to kill her. She can't breathe, for God's sake!'

Celia stepped back, suddenly embarrassed. 'Oh, my dear. I'm awfully sorry. It must be the wine on top of a day in the sun. Are you alright? For the love of Mary, I don't know what came over me. Forgive me, darling.'

Their guest smiled, outwardly unruffled by her host's boldness. She picked up the wine glasses one by one and washed them carefully in a sinkful of hot, soapy water while the others loaded the dishwasher. Soon it was only Lynn, the lady of the house and her elderly mother who hadn't found some excuse to shirk their domestic duties, and it became obvious by the increasingly trivial nature of the conversation that the middle-aged woman was bursting to ask another personal question.

'Celia, is there something wrong?' the teenaged stateswoman enquired, unable to stand the suspense any longer. 'You seem flustered about something.'

The Mosman socialite fanned her face with the damp tea towel, taking a seat at the kitchen table. She signalled to their guest to do the same.

'Lynn, dear,' she began. 'Are you coping?'

'Coping?' the young woman echoed. 'With Jeff, you mean?'

'Yes, and with your family's attitude to him.'

She smiled knowingly. 'Oh, yes, thank you. We've reached an understanding with Mum and Dad. They know we're going to London together. There's really nothing they can do, but we don't want to fall out over it.'

'Oh, that's lovely, darling. It's just that Jeff can be so...'

Gerry's mum had been rendered tongue-tied. What was she trying to say? Nothing to do with her parents, Lynn imagined. That was a red herring. What was eating her boyfriend's surrogate mother?

'Jeff can be so what?' the patient celebrity asked, maintaining a suitably diplomatic distance. 'He's so many things.'

'Goodness! I know, my dear,' the middle-aged woman chuckled. 'You're not wrong, as my son would say.'

The jaded guest laughed too. It was funny to hear an expression taken straight from popular culture emanating from such distinguished lips. She couldn't imagine her own mother using this phrase naturally either.

'No, I'm not wrong. I'm not sure what you're asking me though either.'

'Oh, yes. Of course. I mean can you cope with him when...' the woman blurted out. 'With his moods? Long term, darling?'

Lynn hesitated. Jeff's moods? Long term? How did Celia know about his moods? And what did she know? She must be better informed about his state of mind than he had let on. What should she tell his best friend's mother about her partner's moods?

'Yes, I'm sure I can,' the celebrity took the easy option and focussed only on generalities, as her schooling had taught her. 'Life's difficult for him sometimes, but I'm sure we'll work it out. He's so smart, Celia. And the main thing is that he wants things to be different in the future.'

The kettle appeared in need of boiling all of a sudden, which took the attention of her ruffled host temporarily, leaving Lynn stranded in conversational no-man's land. Should she keep talking?

'I love him, Celia. Is that what you mean? Do I *want* to cope with his moods?'

The older woman swung around, her eyes desperate for an answer. 'Ah, yes, dear. I suppose it is. Exactly so,' she sounded out of breath. 'I don't want to see him hurt again. He wouldn't survive, you see. He wouldn't. I'm quite sure of that.'

The devoted mother was clearly crying, leaning against the kitchen bench and peering into an empty teapot. Her hands were shaking when the guest arrived at her side. *Please don't let anyone come in now*, Lynn begged. Her heart was full of sympathy for this woman who cared so much for the wayward lad her son had brought home all those years ago, yet her head insisted on rebelling. She knew the same wayward lad would be angered that his special lady be put in this position. He would accuse their host of emotional blackmail, which of course was exactly what he himself resorted to on a regular basis.

'I love him, Celia,' the young woman repeated. 'We're very young, and who knows what the future holds, but I can't imagine being with anyone else except Jeff. I'd hate not having him in my life now. He's a challenge, I can't deny that... But he loves me so much too. We're not going to hurt each other. Make a cup of tea, please. I'd love one.'

These reassuring words returned some poise to the stately lady's demeanour, once she was refocussed on tending to the visitor's hurriedly-invented need. Her eyes were red, and she dabbed them with the corner of the tea towel, threading her finger behind her spectacles once the youngster's back was turned. Lynn poured milk into two china cups and rested them on their saucers.

'Come and sit down,' she urged Gerry's mother.

'Darling, I apologise for my histrionics,' the older woman said. 'I'm happy to hear you're not going to hurt each other. He's like our second son, dear.

472

We've grown to love him too, despite the darkness. He needs to get rid of the darkness, darling, if you get my drift.'

'The depression?' Lynn checked, dealt a new euphemism to decipher. 'Is that what you mean by the darkness?'

'Yes, dear,' Celia hesitated again. 'Does he still... Oh, my goodness. No. You might not know. I should be quiet.'

The celebrity frowned, wishing this conversation would come to a close. 'I probably do know. I think I know most things. Go ahead. Please ask me.'

'About his... I'm not sure I can say it. It's so awfully unnecessary. He used to have thoughts of ending it all. How silly is that, with all he's got going for him?'

'Yes, he does,' the empathetic beauty nodded, sounding as positive as possible. 'Suicidal thoughts, you mean? They're under control though.'

Tears appeared in the elderly lady's eyes again, and she suppressed a tiny cough. 'Oh. I was hoping that was a thing of the past.'

'Jeff's stronger than you think,' the famous visitor sighed. 'He doesn't think they'll ever go away. It's just part of who he is. He's got heaps of techniques to combat the waves of depression, and I'm learning to read the signs too. And you know what? We both think London's going to make a huge difference. We're so looking forward to it. I'm hoping he'll come back next year with virtually no symptoms.'

Celia stood up, busying herself by preparing a tray of juice and iced water to take out to the men by the pool. Lynn finished her tea and rinsed the cups and saucers quickly under the tap. Was that it? Cross-examination over? After a few seconds, she received her confirmation.

'Thank you, dear,' the Blake matriarch patted her arm again. 'I'm confident our amazing boy is in good hands. You are too, darling. If ever you need some help or some advice, please don't hesitate.'

The Olympic sportswoman fought to hide her defiant reaction to this latest offer, hearing her own mother's overbearing voice in the back of her head too. All the more reason to move to London, she smiled.

'Thanks to you too, Celia. Jeff thinks the world of you. We're all in good hands. Let's see what the others are doing.'

When the clean-up work and the emergency conference were finally done, the women got changed and went out to join the pool revellers, who were enjoying the sunshine. Jeff whistled as they arrived and lost no time in sweeping Lynn off her feet, deliberately tipping backwards into the water while kissing her. The pair lingered below the waterline for a number of seconds, before dramatically bursting through the surface and gasping for air.

'Now you have to get out,' Gerry shouted to his *amigo*, springing up from his lounger and extending his hands to help pull him out of the water.

'No way, mate,' the horny man declined, leaning against the pool wall and keenly watching his beautiful blonde stretch her slender body in a lazy front crawl. 'No effing way.'

Celia scolded the young men for their baseness, but everyone laughed anyway.

***

It was after midnight when Jeff and Lynn finally got to bed on Christmas night, once the happy family had exhausted their collection of board games and eaten enough mince pies to last a lifetime. The couple was keen to be alone after the evening's frivolity, and they made love as slowly as they could.

'Merry Christmas!' the teenager cheered, as her mystery man orgasmed inside her.

Groaning with pleasure, her boyfriend laughed and smothered her with kisses to silence her. 'Again? Same to you. This is the best ever Christmas. It's so good to see you here with these guys. Are you sorry you're not with your family?'

'No, not at all. I've had plenty of Christmases with them. I'm having a great time and I'm glad you are too. I just could've done without Celia's "You don't know how to look after him like I do" lecture.'

Jeff sighed. 'Yeah. Sorry about that. Just think what she'd be like if she really *was* my mother... Christ! I'd never be able to bring you here.'

His tired lover kissed him tenderly, knowing he had no real idea what sort of information had been demanded and supplied during their host's intense suitability interview. Now wasn't the time to open up either. The poor man had enough worrying to do about tomorrow, without becoming further antagonised by Celia's interference. This was the least of his problems.

Lynn turned out the light, and the pair settled down to sleep, lying on their backs in the dark. They were too warm from an evening of non-stop eating and drinking, not to mention their recent exertion, to bear the sheet on top of them. Their sleepy brains independently processed the morning's events and projected forward to the huge milestone that lay ahead of them.

'I trust you.'

Jolted from her drowsiness, his dream girl turned over and tried to focus on the dark shadow to her left. 'Are you sure?'

'Yep,' he replied. 'I'm freaked out but I'm sure.'

'Do you know what state the apartment's in? I mean, clean or whatever?'

'Don't know,' the bemused man replied. 'Haven't even thought about it. Why?'

Lynn was tentative in her response. 'We should take a picnic lunch and some coffee. I'll go in first and be inside, and then you'll be able to trigger a positive experience as soon as you open the door.'

A thick silence hung in the air for a while, as Jeff lay in the dark and shook. The subject was so confronting. Just considering the options was hard enough; far less picking one. Whatever had gone on between the two most important women in his life had certainly fired the teenager up. Her indignance had been amusing up until this point, but now there was fervour and purpose in her voice for which he had no appetite.

'As soon as I open the door? You mean *if* I can open the door.'

The singer continued, sensing his reticence. 'OK. True. But stay positive. We should set a time limit. If you're not able to get in within half an hour or an hour, I'll just come out. We can do it another time. How does that sound?'

Her man's nervous fingers reached across and found her hipbone. His palm was sweating when it made contact, and his breathing had accelerated again. She lifted his hand to her lips and kissed the thin, sensitive skin just below the knuckles.

'I like it, in principle,' he told her. 'Just don't expect too much, angel, please. I don't have much confidence that I can go through with it.'

The caring nineteen-year-old squeezed her tortured man's several-hundred-year-old hand, her initial optimism being sapped by the reality of his naked fear. They would get through this impediment somehow. She leaned over and planted a kiss on the beaded forehead. He smelled sexy, freshly loved and wound up.

'That's absolutely fine. As long as it takes.'

The couple fell asleep soon afterwards, keeping their distance from each other due to the heat. The peace was short-lived however, with Lynn waking to the sound of her bedfellow arguing with someone. She quickly tried to calm him down in case he disturbed the others. He didn't return fully to consciousness though, and a few minutes later, his struggles became more violent and the usual shouting match ensued.

'Jeff, wake up!' Lynn spoke close to his face, shaking his torso. 'Wake up! You're dreaming. Wake up!'

Feeling her hand tighten around his biceps, the fighter gradually came to. He sat up and tried to steady his breathing, while his guardian angel leaned back onto her haunches to give him some space.

'Bloody hell. I'm so fucking sick of this. I'm sorry. Thanks for waking me yet again.'

'You're bound to be uneasy about tomorrow,' his girlfriend reassured, switching on the light. 'Why don't you read for a while? I don't have to ride in the morning, if you'd rather.'

At his wits' end, the tormented soul heeded the good advice and watched the gorgeous creature drift back to sleep within a couple of minutes. What a perfect sight! And what an imperfect day tomorrow would turn out to be if he were unable to execute the grand plan. He could accept her every offer of help, yet at the end of the day, his actions alone would count for or against the solution to these testing afflictions. He vowed to go through with her well-meaning scheme, lock, stock and barrel, and placed his hand gently on her hair.

'Thank you, but no. You should go. I'll be fine. *Te amo.*'

After surrendering for an hour or so to the plot of Gabriel García Márquez's "One Hundred Years of Solitude", which he had tossed into his bag for the flight to Sydney, Jeff felt sufficiently relaxed to try his luck with some more sleep. However, within half an hour, the whole infuriating rigmarole had begun again, until, with his customary cruel dawn approaching at a sprint, he finally succumbed to peaceful slumber despite the persistent trepidation for what was to come.

At first light, Lynn heard a gentle but persistent knock at their bedroom door. It was both Blake sisters coming to collect the famous guest for their second daybreak ride on the beach.

'Morning!' whispered Jacinta. 'Is Jeff still asleep?'

'Yes.'

'Can we take a peep?' Tamilla added, not waiting for an answer.

All three girls, one from today and two from yesterday, stood watching the gentle rise and fall of the handsome man's chest, completely mesmerised, as Lynn had described. To her surprise, she didn't feel in the least bit jealous. This Mediterranean sex-god had chosen her over these two and over all others, and would continue to do so, she didn't doubt.

'I've never seen him sleep,' Jacinta admitted gingerly. 'He used to be so full of nervous energy all the time.'

The celebrity kept quiet. She was not ready to tell tales about their fitful night and disclose the fact that the sight the sisters were witnessing remained relatively rare.

'Let's go,' she suggested, pulling the door closed on the dormant dreamboat.

While walking their horses out onto the road and towards the bridle path, Lynn told her companions about the couple's London plans. This was exciting news for the sisters, and they immediately invited themselves over for a holiday. The celebrity was happy to accept their invitation, since she knew their childhood playmate would revel in entertaining them in his prospective home, once it had been established.

With their mounts rubbed down and fed after a fast gallop along the sand, the three girls sauntered back to the house, still immersed in talk of travel, relationships and shopping. The Blake daughters were off to the Boxing Day sales in the city that morning and were anxious to get on the road to make sure of securing the best bargains. There was no sign of Jeff downstairs this time, so the teenager made her way back to their bedroom and found him emerging from the *en suite*, his wet hair combed back off his face and with a towel wrapped around his waist. Despite his outward delectability, his face was as white as a sheet, and his breathing clearly distressed.

Something was obviously very wrong, and once again the young woman regretted her actions. She dropped her riding helmet and sunglasses onto the bed and met her boyfriend in the middle of the room, where he hugged her even more tightly than usual. Although the window was wide open, there was a strange smell in the air which at first she refused to identify as alcohol.

'You look awful,' Lynn declared, kissing him and confirming her suspicions through the minty taste of toothpaste. 'What's the matter?'

The pale man sank down onto the end of the bed and held his head in his hands, his body immediately beginning to shake violently. 'Christ! I'm a total, fucking wreck. I must've heard you go, in my half-sleep, and went into a bloody tailspin.'

'Oh, no. I knew I shouldn't have gone. I'm really sorry to abandon you.'

Jeff stood up and hugged her again. 'It's not your fault. I told you to go. Anyway, you're back now, and everything's fine.'

The sportswoman could plainly see this wasn't true, but went along with the concept anyway. Sure enough, on the floor beside the bedside table was a half-empty bottle of brandy which she recognised from the drinks tray downstairs. She pointed to it, eliciting a shrug and a defeatist sigh.

'That tells me how you're feeling about this morning. We don't have to go. How are you now?'

'Fucked,' he answered, chuckling almost hysterically. 'But we do have to go, angel. I need to do it, but I don't want to do it. In fact, I really, really, really don't want to do it. Can we go right now, before I chicken out altogether? Christ, I need you.'

The young woman felt desperately sorry for him, being scooped up into trembling arms again. The self-made millionaire detested not being in control, especially of his own faculties. She smiled and kissed his pouting, oh-so tempting mouth and dragged him down onto the bed on top of her, loosening the towel and pulling it clear of his omnipresent erection.

'We can't go right now. I have to shower and get changed,' she countered. 'Come here.'

Immediately pounced upon by her frantic lover, Lynn was perplexed and a little scared by the strength of her unbroken stallion's obsession. Almost as soon as these two words had left her mouth, he seemed to engage a sort of auto-pilot, to which she judged best to give in and let him have his head. The fact that he needed her to this extent was also powerfully erotic, although her mind struggled to come to terms with this sudden and acute level of dependence.

'Hey! Calm down,' the slender woman urged, as he pushed himself into her as far as he would go. 'You're hurting me.'

'Sorry, angel,' Jeff groaned. 'I've got to have you. You feed me courage. I don't want to hurt you. I want to hear you scream because you love me.'

'It's OK. I do love you, but I can't scream here. Not in this house. You'll have to imagine it, and I'll owe you one,' his sexy lover smiled, running her hands down his back and feeling it arch in pleasure. 'You're making me as nervous as you. Is that deliberate?'

'Fuck knows,' the desperate man hissed. 'I can't stop.'

They moved together at a tempestuous pace, hurtling towards urgent satisfaction. Lynn sensed his anxiety rising still further, unsure of how close he was to his climax. She couldn't let him panic again, she understood. This was therapy she was administering right now. They were not making love. They were compensating via an addiction.

Physical fulfilment rushed through the disturbed young man without a shred of emotion, and his shocked partner was driven to kiss him hard on the mouth simply to remind him of her presence. Immediately racked with guilt, he became full of apology, which only served to escalate the intensity of their situation.

Although not an observation for airing in their current situation, this morning was actually a frightening glimpse into the future the sportswoman would face if they chose not to go to the Canley Vale flat today and begin to unwind his damaged psyche. Celia was closer to the mark than the infatuated celebrity had credited earlier, she realised. *Ceteris paribus*, the famous couple's life would unfold blithely in public and yet conflicted and destructive in private, which was something neither of them wanted.

'Wow, that was a wild ride! How are you doing? The fear might be worse than the real thing,' the nineteen-year-old offered, as her boyfriend's tense body finally dropped down beside her onto the mattress. 'Next year you can start forgetting all this.'

The songwriter didn't respond. His eyes were closed, squeezing her hand to the point of numbness. Babysitting such a hyperactive child was exhausting, Lynn rued. She squirmed round to see the clock next to her pillow and found herself struck by a bright idea. Rolling over and off the bed, she opened her suitcase to retrieve a notepad and a pen.

'Let's shower quickly, and then you've got homework,' she announced with a grin on her face.

Jeff's eyes opened and raised himself up onto his elbows, only to have the notepad land on his belly. He could sense a special dose of Dyson mind-over-matter treatment coming on and was atypically enthusiastic in the face of such profound fear.

'Homework? What kind of homework?'

'While I'm drying my hair and getting ready, you need to write down exactly how you're going to feel after we've been to the flat and got through the day. Can you do that?'

The tired man summoned up a half-smile and exhaled deeply. 'Of course I can.'

'*¡Excelente!*' his girlfriend responded, holding out her hand. 'Come on then.'

The pair disappeared into the *en suite* and showered quickly, before the amateur psychologist sent her student away to complete his assignment. She then took advantage of a few moments' peace to mentally complete the same task herself while she dressed and stood at the vanity with the hair dryer.

When the singer returned to the bedroom, Jeff stood up to cuddle her again and brandished three pieces of paper which he had torn out of the notebook, completely covered in stream of consciousness writing on front and back.

'Thank you,' he whispered, seeing the approving look on his dream girl's face.

'Shhh... That's great, but thank me afterwards.'

'You hope.'

'Be positive,' his coach pushed him a little. 'You were positive yesterday, so read it again and picture yourself there. You know we have to do this, and you'll soon be able to throw these three sheets away and rewrite the story from real experience.'

'Yes, ma'am,' Jeff agreed with artificial enthusiasm, releasing her from his clinch and crossing the room to locate his thongs. 'How are we going to escape from here?'

The young woman gave him a quick thumbs-up sign and collected the brandy from the floor for his next assignment. 'I expect they'll be planning a big breakfast, but let's see if we can get out of it. Do you want me to talk to Celia?' she replied, holding the bottle out. 'And while I'm doing that, you can take this down and put it back where you found it.'

The songwriter looked grateful. 'Could you? That'd be great. I just don't think I could find the words to explain. There's no way I could eat anything anyway.'

'Leave it to me,' Lynn declared, hugging his rigid body. 'How much did you drink, by the way? Do I need to drive?'

'No,' the guilty man shook his head. 'Not much. Not enough. Jeez, you're hard on me.'

'For a reason!' she teased and took him at his word. 'OK. I'll make an excuse for us and say we'll see them this afternoon. That'll give us plenty of time.'

'You're an angel,' her boyfriend told her, slumping back down onto the mattress. 'We'll probably be back within the hour, the way I feel now.'

The *élite* sportswoman shook her head. It was time for more mind games and to make her father proud, hoping that at some point they would all be able to share the success of his teachings outside of the sports coaching field. She looked into her favourite rock star's dark-ringed eyes and forced them to engage with hers.

'You don't chicken out, Jeff Diamond. You know you don't. I know you'll go through with this.'

The couple descended, going their separate ways in the hallway. Leaving her lover to mull over his fate, Lynn arrived in the kitchen to find Gerry and both his parents. They were preparing to serve breakfast, looking round inquisitively as their famous guest launched into the speech she was hurriedly assembling on the fly.

'Good morning, everyone.'

'Good morning, dear,' Celia responded. 'Did you sleep well? Good ride?'

'Yes, thanks,' the cheerful celebrity replied. 'Lovely, thanks. Bess was still tired after yesterday.'

Gerry stole a kiss on her cheek, having enjoyed sweet dreams about the profusion of entertainment opportunities his new craft would avail him. His mate's girlfriend was looking particularly attractive this morning, dressed for warm weather and somehow more strong-willed than usual.

'Was that Bess or Jeff you were referring to? So is he up yet? You're spoiling him with all this R'n'R. Get him down here to help, or I'll boot him out of bed myself.'

Lynn laughed. 'You don't have to. He's up and showered. We have a favour to ask though, please.'

Gerald looked up from the paper. 'Is there something wrong?'

Their guest decided she had better tell the truth, or at least an abridged version thereof. She was a hopeless liar, and if they were successful in their quest, she knew Jeff would want to come home and tell everyone. This would surely be the statement to end all statements, she thought with renewed optimism.

'There's something we really need to do this morning, so do you mind if we skip breakfast, please? Jeff wants to go back to his old apartment and exorcise a few ghosts. Is that OK?'

The younger accountant's expression altered, as if a light bulb had illuminated above his head. 'I wondered why he bought that old place. We had to do it all cloak and dagger.'

The Blake parents looked at each other knowingly. 'The poor boy,' Celia whispered. 'Of course, dear. You go with him. It'll make it a lot easier if you're there.'

For the first time since Lynn had met him, the henpecked husband volunteered an opinion, such an exercise habitually redundant when living in a house full of extrovert women. He coughed twice, letting his newspaper drop onto his knees and fixing the earnest teenager with a stare.

'Yes, indeed. By all means. Sometimes life is so unfair, for some more than others. If I could get my hands on that boy's father and mother, I'd wring their bloody necks.'

'Gerald!' Celia exclaimed, surprised at the spontaneous, vehement commentary.

'No, my dear. Let me have my say,' the man of the house continued. 'The young lady should know. Over the years, as you know, we've treated Jeff like another son. As much has he'd let us anyway... I've had more conversations with the police and Social Services than I'd care to remember about all the violence and the mistreatment of that boy, and still he fights on with the effects of his trauma. I even had to make a statement for a detective hired by your father, Lynn. I take my hat off to him, I really do. There are not many to have made such a success of life from such dreadfully humble beginnings.'

The polite superstar walked over and gave the scrupulous man a kiss. 'Thanks for everything, Gerald. I'm not sure Jeff even knows about half of that. Does he? He'd be very grateful these days, now he's not so hot-headed and proud. You should have the conversation with him, but maybe not this morning.'

Gerald Junior looked shell-shocked. 'So what's all this about? He's my best mate and my biggest client by a mile, and everyone else has been running around after him. No-one thinks to tell me what's going on. Is there something I should know?'

'Yes, there probably is,' the celebrity replied with a smile, 'but it's up to Jeff to tell you. I think he's getting closer to being able to talk openly about things. It's been a tough road for him, and you've been an amazing friend, Gerry. He couldn't have done half the things he has without you around, so I hope you know that.'

'Well, that's at least good to hear. I'm glad about that,' the businessman replied, though no less confused. 'Hey, whatever! I'm happy just to be the Good Time Guy.'

Celia laughed in exasperation. 'Yes, darling. You're very good at that. In fact, the both of you are very good at that.'

Frowning, Lynn turned to Gerry's mother. 'Celia, do you have a cassette player I could borrow, please? And could I take a flask of coffee and some water with us too?'

The housewife straightaway began bustling around, preparing a small basket of comestibles for the special pair, before disappearing to the den to retrieve a radio cassette recorder that belonged to her children. The refined singer-songwriter voiced her thankful goodbyes and headed back to the bedroom, where she found Jeff sprawled on top of the bed, no less pale and dazed than he had been earlier.

'All sorted,' she announced, sitting down beside him. 'You still look terrible. Let's go for a walk first or something to ease you into things. Where are the car keys?'

At first, there was no sign of movement. The rock star's eyes were closed, and his face had tension written all over it. His girlfriend resisted the temptation to kiss or caress him, concerned that it might induce yet another sexual diversion. She wondered whether her man was engaging in his own brand of mind games by refusing to move until she touched him, but she held fast to her resolve. Two could play at that game.

The distressed man dragged himself to his feet in the end, pointing to a set of keys on the chest of drawers. 'OK! *Vamanos*. Thanks, angel. What did you tell them?'

'The truth.'

Jeff didn't know whether to be alarmed or resigned. 'The truth? What does that mean? I can't think straight, so I don't know if that's good or bad.'

'It's good,' his dream girl insisted. 'They understand. Come on. Let's go.'

She picked up the guitar and the picnic basket, ushering her quivering mess out into the corridor. They sneaked down the stairs and out of the front door without being seen. Once behind the wheel of Gerry's mum's Mercedes and with his no-nonsense accomplice and her deliciously short skirt next to him, he began to relax a little.

'Thanks for helping out this morning. I wouldn't have known how to escape properly. I'd have just disappeared. I'm feeling a bit more human now.'

Lynn reached over and held his left hand. Her touch felt like velvet on his hypersensitive skin, almost bringing tears to his eyes. Not wanting to incessantly remind her of how out of kilter he was, the nervous man turned to his right to wind down his window and adjust the wing mirror.

'You're welcome,' she mouthed over the engine noise. 'I love you.'

As they drove fast along the empty roads, unimpeded by the need to dodge other traffic, the young man's mood began to slowly lighten. 'It's weird. I feel strangely excited now. I can't wait to get there but I know it's going to be bloody tough. What's in the basket?'

'Breakfast,' his dream girl replied. 'Celia packed it. I don't know what's in there. It'll be a surprise.'

They listened to a sports radio station which was eagerly anticipating the opening innings of the Boxing Day Test from the Melbourne Cricket Ground. It was just after nine o'clock, and the stores and offices were closed for business as the station wagon crossed the top of the city and sped towards Parramatta, taking the same route as had the little MG yesterday. It was a warm, sunny day, and the water glinted brightly whenever they caught sight of the dirty river through the buildings.

Predictably, Jeff began to tense up again as they approached and continued on through Fairfield. He fumbled in his pocket for his lighter and lit a cigarette. Taking a long drag, Lynn watched his pupils dilate as the nicotine hit his nervous system. Finally reaching Canley Vale, he pulled the car into a service lane in front of a row of shops.

'Let's walk from here,' he declared authoritatively, switching off the ignition. 'I don't want to leave this car outside the flat. I don't trust the neighbours.'

The couple walked hand in hand in the general direction of the Stones Road. The haunted man jumped at every sound and stared down each side street as if someone were about to leap out and attack them at any moment. His girlfriend did her best to keep the conversation going, despite receiving only testy, monosyllabic responses.

'Jeff, even though this is so incredibly tough for you, I'm so glad you've chosen me to help you. It's nice to be needed for something really meaningful for a change. I hope you get what I'm trying to say... Representing your country or performing in front of a crowd is big, but it's not meaningful, if you know what I mean. Those things don't change lives.'

The tall songwriter kissed her fingers, not really concentrating. 'Thanks. I understand what you're saying and I agree. I just wish it wasn't me, right at this point. I promise you, after today, I'll never be selfish again.'

Lynn let go of his hand and slapped his back playfully, startling him again. 'For God's sake, you're the least selfish person I know. Shut up.'

Rounding a corner, they reached the run-down European delicatessen next door to Cafici's and came to an abrupt halt. Jeff stood gazing up at the two front windows of the second-floor flat, in the exact same spot as they had stood the day before. It was as if nothing had moved during the time they had been gone. He lit another cigarette and closed his eyes, lost in thought, with his blonde companion patiently waiting for him to initiate the next step.

When he was ready, the apprehensive landlord walked over to a nearby litter bin and stubbed out his cigarette. The confusion inside was fast dissolving any courage which had brewed during their journey, and the wanton adolescent suddenly realised he had hardly looked at his dream girl this morning. He hoped it was the nerves, rather than a sign that he was beginning to take her for granted.

Smiling sheepishly, he turned to see the beautiful poster girl and the old guitar propping each other up. She looked divine; her hair wrapped up in a loose bun, with wispy strands falling around her face, and a feminine, floral skirt which every now and then would need smoothing down against her legs to stop it from blowing up in the wind and revealing the tops of those eye-popping, long, tanned thighs. His *Regala* was so perfectly formed, and also so utterly his.

'Sorry. Change of plan,' he announced. 'I've changed my mind about you going in first.'

'OK,' Lynn shrugged to let him know it didn't matter. 'What do you want to do instead?'

Jeff hesitated, sweating and shaking visibly, with his left hand holding his head and its fingers pressing into his aching eyes. 'I'd prefer if we both went in at the same time. I need to see what it's like inside. Last night I was dreaming about leaving you there and someone else was already up there. If anything happened to you up there... Christ! I can't knowingly put you in that sort of fucked-up, risky situation.'

The pretty nineteen-year-old watched her boyfriend struggling with so many conflicting emotions but didn't approach him. It would be wrong to help him too much, she concluded.

'Thanks. It'll be fine. There won't be anyone in there. We'll go in, let you get the lay of the land and get over the initial shock. Then you could go downstairs and come back in with me still inside. Does that sound better?'

'Yeah, it does,' the relieved man agreed, steeling himself to go through the glass door between the shops.

Was his memory cheating him? No, there hadn't been a door in this opening when he had lived here. The corridor used to be filthy and smelly, he remembered, full of household refuse which residents couldn't be bothered to dispose of responsibly. With a loud inward breath, the tortured musician picked up the Blakes' old guitar and strode towards the door.

'Shall we go?'

Lynn followed dutifully. All the words she could think of to say at this point had already been spoken yesterday, so she remained mute and allowed him to take the initiative. Jeff pulled the glass door towards him, and they entered the stairwell.

'Fucking hell!' he grimaced, turning to check the well-bred woman's reaction to the stench of stale urine and festering rubbish. 'The smell's even worse now the door stops the air going through. What do people do in here?'

His girlfriend crinkled her nose and nodded. 'It is pretty foul.'

The former tenant looked upwards at the four flights of stairs, nothing but bad memories filling his head. Who shared this staircase these days? Much the same mix of life's cast-offs as before, he imagined. And what would they think of him having bought the place? Did anyone ever make the connection between the Polish scumbag who once ran his dubious business from the top floor and the chart-topping musician now standing at the bottom?

'Onwards and upwards,' he proclaimed, sounding neither convinced nor convincing.

His twenty-two-year-old legs were like jelly and seemed to weaken with each step. On the first turn, he stopped and leaned against the wall. His face was flushed, and he was starting to breathe heavily again. Lynn looked up at the next landing, and Jeff's eyes followed hers.

'I wonder who lives here now?' she mused, in an attempt to reduce the stress just a little.

But her companion was no longer interested in this question. He started to climb the second flight, and then continued past two front doors towards the next set of stairs. The teenager shivered in the cool air flow that seemed to bounce off the concrete walls, picked up the picnic basket and followed, anxious not to cause him to lose this momentum.

Reaching the third landing was much harder however. The colour had by now drained out of Jeff's face altogether, and he could barely catch his breath. He crouched down, leaning against the wall. It looked as if he was praying.

Lynn put her hand on his shoulder. 'It doesn't matter how long it takes.'

The terrified man gave no response for a good few seconds. The sportswoman wondered which thoughts were racing through his head, searching for something inspirational to say. The return to his former home was literally his waking nightmare, and she imagined all those horrible childhood recollections jockeying for position in his mind and feeding his panic. She sank down beside him and tried to see his face, which was buried in his hands.

'Are you OK?' she asked, running her fingers through his damp, wavy hair.

After a while, Jeff removed his hands and stared straight into his beautiful best friend's deep blue eyes. It crossed his mind how trusting he had become in the short time since the lovers had reunited. He never could have been this open with her two years ago. He had grown up too, he realised, and had learned to acknowledge his weaknesses with far less shame.

'Yes, I'm OK. Thanks for being so lenient. I'm all over the place,' he said, getting to his feet and pointing with the neck of the guitar, which flopped around in its olive-green *faux* leather carrycase until it settled on a black door marked with the number four. 'That's it. The door of doors.'

The singer smiled. 'I'm glad you can still find some shred of humour. That's a good sign.'

They reached the top landing and walked past the door marked with a wonky, plastic figure three. The air, trapped under the roof frame and parboiled through a broken skylight, had become still, stale-smelling and sweltering, lending yet more credence to the corruption and immorality wrapped up in the building's history.

'I expect the old woman who lived there's long gone,' the wayward son gasped, scarcely able to find enough oxygen to speak. 'Her husband died when I was seven or eight. She was nice enough to me and Lena but she must have wondered what the fuck crazy kind of people she lived next to. D'you see these marks?'

The attentive celebrity searched the railing where Jeff was pointing, but there was nothing to be seen. She gulped as her mind flew back to the expression she had used in Singapore about memories being etched on her psyche. The marks to which her lover now referred were no less real for being only in his mind's eye.

He continued, watching the silent beauty drag her fingertips over the smooth paintwork. 'I made a pulley for her shopping trolley once. She used to have to climb these stairs almost every day because she could only carry a small amount at a time. So I rigged up a bunch of ropes so she could hook her trolley on at the bottom, then climb the stairs and winch it up. It worked bloody well.'

Lynn hugged her nostalgic mystery man. 'You're always looking out for everyone. I love you for that.'

Resting the guitar against the wall to the left of the front door, the flat's new owner produced a set of keys from the pocket of his shorts, the real estate agent's label still attached. He picked out one of the keys and held it up as if it were about to burst into flames.

'This is the one, I think.'

Out of habit, Lynn went to offer her hand and ask if he wanted her to open it, resisting the reflex just in time. She was torn between allowing him to work through the ordeal at his own pace and helping to force the issue. They must have already been in the stairwell for about twenty minutes. She mustn't rush him, she told herself, even though the atmosphere was stifling.

Jeff stood back from the wall, leaning on the railings. Facing the all-too-familiar front door, he felt somehow too big for the stairwell. It was a weird feeling that made nauseated him. His girlfriend stood next to him, gazing over and down whence they had climbed. Luckily, there was no activity from any of the other apartments. Her handsome stranger was welded to the spot, motionless and transfixed by the solid, painted surface.

'Another cigarette, and then we go in,' he decided, lighting up and sucking the smoke in madly.

His head swam, and the tall man had to hang on tightly to the banister to stop himself from falling.

Lynn caught him and laughed. 'Perhaps you shouldn't have any more nicotine?'

'You're right,' he replied in a gruff voice and dropped the half-smoked cigarette onto the floor, squashing it out with his right foot and kicking it through the railings into the stinking chasm below. 'That's what everyone else seems to do. It must be the custom around here.'

His girlfriend chuckled softly to humour him, knowing full well that the world-changer would never normally condone such an anti-social act.

'OK. Here goes,' he stated with renewed intent. 'Let's open it together.'

The pretty, all-Australian superstar stood at her boyfriend's side, with his left arm resting on her right shoulder. She could feel the body heat radiating out. He had the key in his left hand, and she put her hand over his. The key slipped into the lock easily, where his hand froze. They stood silently in this position for two or three minutes, his breathing loud and laboured.

'I hope you're not going to have a heart attack,' Lynn said in jest.

The young man's head teamed with images and noises from his past, and the pressure in his eardrums told him that his blood pressure was at the max'. Screaming rang in his ears, doors slamming, little girl's cries and men shouting. The sights, sounds and smells of his childhood were as vivid and real today as they had ever been. Why the hell had he come here?

'Angel, help me,' he begged in desperation. 'I've got to do this or I'm going to go fucking crazy.'

Their hands gripped the key once more. Lynn waited for him to turn it, but still nothing happened. He had asked for her help. She had no choice.

Without warning, the teenager's strong hand flicked the key a quarter turn to the right, and the door unlocked. A chink of light broke through from inside the flat, momentarily blinding them.

At her side, Jeff let out a blood-curdling growl, cupped his hand in front of his mouth and ran. The bewildered woman watched him leap four or five steps at a time, bounding round the corners of each landing until he was back at ground level. She then heard the door to the street being wrenched open and then swinging shut, the hinges squealing their displeasure.

Downstairs in the fresh air, Lynn Dyson's millionnaire boyfriend was bent over the litter bin vomiting. The pain in his head was unbearable, and the well-worn footage of his past played loud and frenzied behind his eyes. Jesus! What had she done that for? He had hurtled down those steps as a twelve-year-old, like he had done countless times back then, fleeing the Hell on Earth which had once been real.

Jeff trudged off down the street, dejected and embarrassed, to collect his thoughts as best he could. He wondered if Lynn had gone inside without him. What would she make of him running away? He hated himself for having trusted her, yelling out at the top of his voice. A man walking his dog across the street turned to discover the origin of the racket, before quickly turning away again as the famous face stared back at him menacingly.

Self-loathing filled the angry man's brain. Yes, this was who he really was. He was playing with the genteel set these days, sitting at their tables, buying them expensive gifts and drinking their fine wine, but this was where people like him belonged. He began to walk more quickly, turning corners at random, not knowing where he was going or why.

Back on the top-floor landing, Lynn had closed Door Number Four straightaway. *Back to square one*, she rued. She sat on the top step, from which she could see directly down to the glass door, and the concrete roasted her flesh through the fabric of her summer skirt. Where was her mysterious and irresistible Catholic Argentinean Polish Jew? Should she go down and make sure he was alright? He probably wanted to be alone for a while, and the young woman imagined him cursing under his breath.

Ten minutes went by. The recording star began strumming the guitar softly, playing and singing along with the tape she had brought to play inside the flat. It was another new song she had written for Jeff and had planned to unveil on this special occasion.

Another ten or fifteen minutes passed. The musician felt sure her protective lover wouldn't leave her here. If he wished to call it quits and drive back to Mosman, he would easily be able to shout up from the ground. Mustering enough patience to wait for his next move, she amused herself by looking through the picnic basket which Celia had packed for them, and it immediately made her very hungry. It contained cheese, bread, some cold meats and olives. There was also a Thermos of coffee and a water bottle; everything she needed, apart from someone to share it with.

At long last, the blonde singer heard the door downstairs creak open. Leaning over, she noticed the silent entrant didn't look up to check where she was. Instead, he walked slowly to the back of the building, and his feet started to climb the stairs for a second time. Poor man, she thought, having to go through all this again. She regretted turning the key.

Jeff reached the third landing to find his beautiful best friend sitting on the top step, the guitar resting strings-down across her knees. She was holding out a bottle of water, her smile never more inviting. This was the very vision he had hoped to see after having found the mettle to ascend a second time. She hadn't ventured into the flat without him. He felt buoyed to think she understood him that well, even if she had pushed him too far.

'Thanks,' he gasped, taking the water bottle from her.

The taste of bile and tar was fresh in his mouth, and his throat burned with acid from his empty stomach. The thirsty man tipped his head back and drank steadily, sloshing the cool liquid around his teeth. He peered at his gorgeous companion out of the corner of his eye, hoping to read her mind.

Discouraged in the extreme, the twenty-two-year-old sat down next to his empathetic angel, long legs extending a step further than hers. He angled his knee out to the side until it touched hers, and she applied an equal and opposing force, along with the sweetest of forgive-me nudges. They kissed long and passionately, ignoring the revolting taste on his tongue.

'I'm sorry,' Lynn admitted. 'I shouldn't have turned the key.'

'No. That's OK. Something had to happen. I know I asked for help, but that wasn't exactly the help I was expecting.'

The exhausted man's face was drawn and gaunt. His girlfriend put her hand on his back and felt the soaking t-shirt, as wet as the hair on his forehead and neck.

'So what *were* you expecting?' she asked, holding the water bottle out again to encourage him to rehydrate.

Taking another large gulp, Jeff shrugged and smiled. 'I don't know. Nothing specific. Just a miracle, that's all.'

The kind woman laughed. 'Perhaps that was your miracle in disguise.'

'Most likely,' her forlorn boyfriend nodded. 'And now I've missed it, so we might as well go home.'

Tired and utterly fed up, he leaned over and felt his beautiful best friend do the same. He was heartened that she wasn't giving him the full-on Dyson treatment in order to speed things along, and gave thanks for her unspoken understanding. It was beyond his wildest dreams that this girl who had been born to succeed also possessed such innate compassion for failure. His suffering soul had been drawn to her strength, and her soul's strength substantiated his suffering in perfect counterbalance.

'Happy Boxing Day! Christmas is fun with me, isn't it?' the nobody from right here chided, before spying the cassette player. 'What were you playing? What's that for?'

'Oh, it's another one of the joy triggers,' Lynn owned up, hoping to spur him on a little. 'Another song I've written for you, and I thought it'd be nice to give it its *début* inside the flat. It's kind of appropriate, lyrics-wise.'

'Can I hear it here?' he asked, turning on the charm.

'No, you can't. The batteries aren't working. We need to plug it in.'

True enough, the teenager was a poor liar. Jeff didn't believe her for a minute, appreciating the incentive being offered nonetheless. He felt guilty for passing up her miracle. This amazing woman would never spare him his tribulations, he realised. This was another reason why she was so good for him. Perhaps the time had come to let her take control after all?

Muffled voices drifted up from downstairs. A door had opened on the floor below, and a Middle-Eastern couple and three children emerged onto the landing. The surf of superstars perched on the top step fell silent and watched them leave, thankfully undetected. Lynn grinned as their minds both acknowledged the bizarre situation in which they now found themselves; two internationally-acclaimed celebrities hiding out in a squalid tenement in Sydney's western suburbs.

'OK,' the former resident sighed. 'Let's try again.'

They both stood up, and the young woman closed the picnic basket and carried it back towards the door. The guitar was put back in the same place also, and with a comedic flourish, Jeff presented the key again.

'Do you want me to turn it or not?' the Olympian asked.

'No,' her boyfriend's heart rate was accelerating again, and the same invisible vice began to tighten around his heart, dragging it upwards towards his mouth. 'I'm ready.'

Jeff slid the key into the lock and glanced sideways at his partner-in-crime, cocking his head. 'Come on then!' he urged her to put her hand over his, like before, and she obliged. 'On three…'

Standing on tiptoes, his dream girl kissed him quickly on the lips. 'Good luck!'

He took a deep breath in. 'One… Two…'

Again dizziness overtook him, and the nervous woman sensed he was about to fall down. What could she do?

'Lean on me,' she suggested.

Grimacing, he regrouped.

'*Uno… Dos… Tres…*'

Lynn gasped when the key turned in their joined hands. The lovers lurched forwards as the door opened and found themselves finally inside. An initial spray of loud expletives gave way to a long, low groaning noise as the time-travelling tearaway battled to stay in the here and now. His summer-clad beauty moved further into the hallway to give her struggling man some space and a pleasant outlook for his rabid eyes.

Jeff gradually calmed down. The small apartment was bright with sunlight, beaming in from a back window. The teenager turned round to see her boyfriend close the door behind him. His brow was soaking wet, and his body was shaking from head to foot, but there was now a huge smile on his face. She ran forward and enveloped him in a hug, at the same time as his legs gave way. He crumbled to the floor, taking her with him.

'You did it!' the elated woman cried out, slapping him on the shoulder.

'We did it,' he corrected. '*We* did it.'

The exhausted pair sat on the floor in each others' arms, waiting for his racing heartbeat to return to somewhere near normal. Delayed shock gripped him suddenly, fed by the fears of the boy inside, while the man outside desperately took in air. His face was deathly pale, and his eyes were bloodshot, pupils fully dilated.

'My beautiful black stallion's all crazed,' Lynn whispered, kissing his forehead. 'Your eyes are amazing. Can you see anything?'

Jeff sniffed and flicked the sweat from his face. 'Yes, I can see but I can't focus yet,' he reported. 'It's so quiet in here. And it smells weird. Not like I remember.'

'That's because there's only us here. I can hear "Roads of Stones" in my head.'

The athlete levered herself gracefully up from the floor and walked into the kitchen area, anxious not to halt progress in her attempt to provide the joy triggers prescribed by Doctors Friedman and Diamond's Post-Traumatic Stress Disorder treatment plan.

'This looks quite new.'

The anxious man lifted his head and dared himself to take a look around the place he had called home for sixteen years. The usual images continued to fade and reappear in his mind, becoming a little less lifelike each time he concentrated on something else. It had been almost three years to the day since he had slammed that accursed front door shut for the final time, climbed into his old, blue Ford Fairlane and driven to Melbourne to seek his fortune.

The nineteen-year-old university student who had left town that day had naïvely hoped his southward journey might bring closure, and of course he soon found out that he had been sorely mistaken. Yet now, back again after his life had changed so much, somehow this place still felt exactly the same to him, despite the new cupboards and appliances in the kitchen and the unfamiliar aroma in the air. The sink was in the same place, under the window, but with this new fit-out there was no longer room for the table at which he and his sister used to sit and eat as young children.

Jeff felt a sudden wave of nausea roll up from his stomach. He hurriedly stumbled to his feet and raced towards where he remembered the bathroom to be. Lynn could hear him throwing up again. How on Earth could his body still think there was anything left to purge?

The bathroom had also been given a facelift since his time. The tiles were no longer mouldy and falling off, like the former occupant remembered, and new plumbing gave the songwriter the impression that water might actually come out of the shower head these days, rather than from the connection between the hose and the wall. He remembered the regularity with which he had resorted to taping it up, unable to ask the landlord to fix it because he wasn't supposed to be living there on his own.

His internal turmoil stabilising a little, the millionnaire rock star collapsed onto the tiled floor, which was baking hot from hours of direct sunlight pouring in through the frosted window. It was also new, he concluded. He leaned against the bath and folded his hands around his head in an effort to stop it spinning. His emotions were still completely at odds with one another, despite Gravity and Miss Irony being strangely conspicuous in their absence. He didn't know whether to laugh or cry.

Lynn Dyson was here though, the former teenaged tenant reminded himself in a moment of abject wonder. She had always been here in spirit, but now she really *was* here... It was clear she didn't feel any link to this place, which was perfectly fine. He would much rather she didn't, in fact. But how exactly had it come about that one of Australia's most loved and most successful personalities had sat patiently in the blistering heat, on the top step of this odorous, neglected tenement and waited while some no-good boy from the western suburbs had got his act together?

The philosophical rock star on the bathroom tiles shook the reprobate's head and forced them both back to the present. Had he really this gift to himself, or was this simply a fellow empath responding to the story she had been spun the day before? What did it matter? Lynn Dyson was here with him to face his darkest fears. Who cared why? He had simply to be thankful and move on.

Closure

Music drifted down the corridor from the kitchen. The real Lynn Dyson in his childhood home must have found a radio station, and the stunned Jeff Diamond had found his senses again. He hauled himself onto his feet by grabbing hold of the lip of the washbasin, then quickly swallowed a few mouthfuls of water while splashing some on his face.

'Hey, angel! Come over here, please,' he called out. 'Let me show you something.'

Still a bundle of nerves, the boy with the survival crush watched his beautiful best friend come towards him down the dimly-lit passageway. He took in the vision in front of him. His beloved *Regala* had helped him conquer his phobia, and they were now both inside the home whence he had first begun his long distance relationship with her, all those years ago.

He waved towards the room at the front of the flat, facing the street. 'This was our bedroom. Madalena's and mine. My bed was under the window, and hers was over there.'

Lynn walked in at his request, her heart soaring to see a broad grin on her man's face. The room had been freshly painted, and the shade was lowered to shut out the summer heat. She looked first at the window and then at Jeff, seeking permission to open the blind. He nodded. The room instantly filled with light, causing him to take a couple of steps backwards.

Looking around, the young man remembered where the beds had been, the tiny wardrobe with doors hanging off their hinges, and the bare floorboards stained by a variety of juvenile disasters over the years. His caring girlfriend could see him beginning to shake again. She went over and took his hand, guiding him to find a wall to lean on.

'Are you OK?'

The twenty-two-year-old exhaled. 'Yeah, thanks. Whoa! This is a trip.'

His eyes focussed on the doorframe, and the couple walked over to it hand in hand. Jeff ran his fingernails across several notches which had been painted over many times, etched both on psyche and in wood this time.

'Here's my growth chart.'

Smiling, Lynn studied the faint marks. There was a malice in his voice the like of which she hadn't been expecting, and it gave her hope. Even after a long morning of heartache and humiliation, this beautiful, black stallion of hers remained vital and uncompromising. She had been right to tell Celia that they could conquer the darkness together.

'You started out pretty tall,' she quipped, observing that the first notch was well over a metre off the ground.

Sadly, her boyfriend didn't take it as the joke she had intended. He lit a cigarette and dragged on it noisily, once more dejected, as if painful memories had been conjured up.

'I started this myself,' he explained through gritted teeth. 'I went to friends' houses and saw they had growth charts that their parents had created. So one day I came home and took a knife from the kitchen and deliberately cut into the paintwork above my head.'

The young woman sat down on the floor, leaning against the fresh, off-white wall. Her eyes willed him to continue, the smile gone from her face, and he duly pointed to the other side of the doorframe.

'That side was Lena's,' he added. 'It didn't bother me that much at the time, but it began to later. I just felt so cheated. My dad smacked me around for gouging out the cuts though. I remember that.'

Tainted animation slowly returned to the handsome star's face. He wandered back down the passage towards the living area, which stretched from back to front of the building. Springing to her feet, Lynn followed him into the lounge room again, which was also freshly painted, making it doubly difficult to imagine how it must have looked in the late nineteen-fifties.

Jeff pointed at the wall, as far as the back window, drawing an imaginary rectangle in the air. 'That whole area there, to about halfway down... maybe more... was where all our stock used to be.'

The celebrity chuckled at his use of the word "stock".

'Piled to the ceiling it was, sometimes,' he continued. 'Then we had the other end to sit in.'

'Pretty small space for a family,' the teenager remarked, her words eliciting no response.

Her boyfriend had begun to gaze nervously back down the corridor, towards the one door through which they hadn't yet ventured. His sensitive lover watched him tense up again, amazed at how quickly his mind could alter his body. She presumed this to be the room in which he had witnessed his mother having sex with multiple men, either voluntarily or otherwise, and where he had ultimately found her dead.

The intelligent woman thought back to the summary of causes and symptoms of Post-Traumatic Stress Disorder which she had read in Sarah Friedman's publication just the day before. In the last ten minutes, her troubled soul-mate had described being deprived of something that other children had, being demeaned by a person in a position of trust and being corporally punished, then even physically abused by a family member. And now here, behind the remaining closed door, was the legacy of his having witnessed the abuse of others and some extremely unhealthy adult behaviour, on top of suffering his own emotional abuse.

Moreover, if that hadn't already been a long enough list, the caring celebrity remembered something else from an old conversation. Hadn't there been an occasion when, as a thirteen-year-old, Jeff had been sexually assaulted by his own mother after she mistook him for one of her attackers while drugged to the eyeballs? How absolutely awful...

'The last door?' she asked, engaging directly with a pair of frightened eyes.

A small boy's soul silently beseeched her from within a grown man's body. For the first time that day, real tears were flowing. Despite the fact that her boyfriend claimed to have no feelings for his mother, the young woman could see this wasn't true. Children could never really hate their parents, she assumed. Even through all the hardship and neglect, there must have been some inherent bond between Jeff and his mother, notwithstanding the despicable acts their situation had prevailed upon him and his sister.

'I don't think I can go in there,' his voice was weak and cracked again.

Lynn took his hand. 'You have to. This won't be complete unless you do.'

The handsome man pulled her in close, also for the first time since they had been in the flat. 'But that's my parents' bedroom, angel. That's where I found...'

He began to sob, shaking in her embrace. The louder he cried, the tighter his saviour held him, rhythmically stroking his back and repeating how much she loved him. Bulbous, raindrop-sized tears rolled down his cheeks, one by one landing on her arms, her face, her chest. She kissed him, knowing it was her job to force him to be strong and carry on. She told him so. He had sent her to himself to fulfil a purpose. She told him so. She was his *Regala*. She told him this too, over and over.

'I know how horrible this is, Jeff. I know what happened in there. It's why we're here. Let's get it over with, shall we?'

Lynn broke away from her man's overpowering grasp and fetched the packet of cigarettes he had deposited on the kitchen worktop along with Celia's car keys. Jeff took one gratefully and allowed her to light it for him. The confident woman knew he found this small act a turn-on and was instantly rewarded with a sly wink, freeing butterflies to take flight inside. The lovers were making progress; slow but steady progress.

'That's why I love you,' she smiled.

'Thanks. *Ditto*,' he replied, running the back of his middle finger down her bare arm and gripping her hand as it came up to reach his. 'You're so good to me, you exquisite creation. Don't ever leave me.'

The young woman assured him that she wouldn't, instantly sealing it with a long, searching kiss. The loving pair stood staring out of the front window onto the street down below. It was already nearly midday.

'Where's Madalena living?' Lynn asked, directing her boyfriend's busy mind to a different subject for a few minutes' rest.

'Who knows?' he answered. 'It won't be too far from here though. This is her patch. I couldn't envisage her moving anywhere else.'

'I'd like to meet her one day.'

The anxious man nodded, but only half-heartedly. 'One day.'

Another obstacle to scale in the weird race that was his life, the old soul acknowledged, walking over to the sink to stub out his cigarette before returning to his guardian angel and holding out his hand.

'Shall we do this thing?'

Facing the one rear-facing door that remained resolutely shut, Jeff rapidly began to lose control once again, as they both anticipated. The disgusting images of his mother and sister's agonies were now also invading Lynn's mind, as she grappled with how she might be able to help him with this final piece in the puzzle.

'Christ Almighty! I can't do this,' he shouted, clenching his fists. 'Fuck!'

Panic-stricken and angry, the deranged man delivered a swift left hook into the wall to the right of the door handle, its impact so hard that it left an impression in the plasterboard.

'Hey!' Lynn yelped, grabbing his fist and flicking it downwards, in the way she had been taught in self-defence classes. 'Careful! You'll hurt yourself.'

'Fuck that!' he raised his voice still further. 'I love it. Being hurt. It's great. You know how it is. I'm hooked on it. It's what I deserve.'

Almost maniacally, the tormented adolescent laid into the wall with both fists this time, one after the other like a boxer. His girlfriend stood back and let her magnificent, crazed steed let loose again. It was imperative that he expel the fire from his system, and she didn't feel in any danger. He would never touch her, even in this sort of temper.

'Why don't you kick the door in?' she proposed, ad-libbing fast. 'It'll make you feel better.'

Somehow, this unexpected suggestion broke the twenty-two-year-old out of his furious rage. He looked at the gorgeous woman beside him and laughed out loud. He knew how ridiculous the idea was, but also that it might just work. Turning round, he put his back to the closed door and held his hands out towards her.

'Why not? I keep forgetting this place is mine now. And this door sounds pretty hollow,' he responded, leaning his head back against the door and knocking hard on it. 'I'm sorry for getting so unhinged.'

Lynn shrugged, standing her ground. 'It doesn't matter. Come on. Do it!'

She beckoned for her rock star seductively to come towards her into his old bedroom, pointing at his feet one at a time while playing with the hem of her skirt. Her spent supplicant duly indulged her flirtatious antics, pretending to fall under her spell, his breath rasping. Then, on her cue and yelling at the top of his voice, he took two steps forwards, span around and delivered a well-judged *karate* kick just to the left of the metal handle. The door flexed and shot open, revealing to the young woman another empty, half-lit room.

Not so for Jeff though. Dumbstruck, he dropped to his knees in the doorway, staring straight ahead. Lynn held her breath, initially fearful of the cataclysm that might manifest in her complex beast. Yet as uneasy seconds ticked loudly in her mind, her doubts began to recede. There was no angry outburst this time, nor even his trademarked roar of lament. She advanced a few short steps behind him and stood with her hands gently massaging his aching, concrete shoulders while he came to terms with what he had done and where he was.

It was as if her boyfriend had been turned to stone. Save the rise and fall of his chest, his knees supported him stock still. Scenes from the past were mirrored in his mind like frame negatives burned into a television screen. The tortured soul pictured his mother's inanimate body curled up on a blood-spattered mattress, an empty syringe dangling from the vein in her ankle. He visualised the broken glass around her right hand, where she had been clawing madly at her left wrist. One after another, he imagined the men on top of a deranged female, hitting her, teasing her. Some she knew, some she didn't know and some she didn't even know were there.

Overlaid on this ghastly home movie was the soundtrack... The neglected son could never forget the screaming and yelling which had come from this room over the years; first from his parents' own volatile relationship, and later from the endless round of visitors his mother entertained. Then there was the ear-splitting sound of a little girl being grabbed by a grown man, and the hysterical objections of a spaced-out woman watching acts of cruelty unfold and being unable to do anything to stop them.

And superimposed on top of the video and audio tapes running simultaneously in Jeff's head was the sense of utter helplessness felt by a lost boy, unwanted and misunderstood behind a closed door, desperate to drown out the sounds of his mother and sister and their so-called guests. The rejection felt by a teenager full of hatred, who would attack these unwanted strangers and who wouldn't give up until they left the building, only then to be chastised for getting rid of them. Chastised by his mother for letting good money walk out the door, and chastised by his fly-by-night father for not protecting their women.

Kneeling in his deceased mother's bedroom, it slowly dawned on the twenty-two-year-old that time had indeed been healing him. Granted, his nightmares kept the vivid, painful memories well and truly alive, but being here now, seven years after his mother's fatal overdose, Jeff realised that he had become somewhat anaesthetised to the worst of his grief.

The ambitious and intelligent man who had been so afflicted for so many years sensed a sort of welcome disassociation taking place. A definite decoupling encouraged by the feeling of his dream girl's loving hands on his tired shoulders and from hearing her soothing, unpatronising words of love; a separation that he had long hoped for but had never expected to achieve. He felt the distance winding back off his odometer, bringing him slowly closer to his real age.

The lost boy reached his left hand up towards the gift he had found, and his *Regala* held it tightly.

'I love you,' she reprised, leaning down to kiss the top of his head. 'It's over. The worst is over.'

Lynn sat on the floor beside the trembling body and turned Jeff's face round towards hers. They kissed for a long, long time. She posed question after question. What had he seen when the door had first opened? What had been going through his head as he knelt in silence? How did it feel to see the room as it was now: clean and bare, with no trace of the horrors that had taken place? Patiently and without once losing physical contact with each other, every angle of the disgusting memory was dissected, never to be reconstituted again.

As the day's stresses began to melt away, the young man's watch informed him it was one-fifteen. 'Jesus! It's late!' he exclaimed, finally breaking the pattern. 'I can't believe where the time's gone.'

His girlfriend could. The morning had taken its toll on her too, but it was totally worth it just to feel his slow, regular breathing return and to see a hint of a smile on his face.

'Are you OK now?' she asked. 'Being in here? What does it feel like?'

'Not so bad, if you force me to admit it.'

'It's up to you,' the nineteen-year-old replied, releasing herself from his grasp.

The statuesque rock star clambered to his feet and went over to the window, which overlooked an industrial warehouse behind the row of shops. The view was very different from the one he remembered, and he didn't understand why. The buildings outside weren't new, so his only conclusion was that he had not seen the view from either back window for a good many years. Or maybe he had simply blocked everything out.

'Uncomfortable,' he continued, staring through the glass. 'I feel like a fraud. It's just an empty room, angel.'

'Don't be ridiculous!' Lynn yelped, following him over to the window. 'It's just an empty room now, but you can't call yourself a fraud when you reacted the way you did. I'm sure you'd much rather have walked in and seen an ordinary, empty room.'

To her dismay, Jeff began to shake all over again, gripped by another panic attack as he leaned his back against the window and took a further look around the room. The gruesome scene rapidly rebuilt itself in his mind's eye while the man turned back into the boy, raising his hands to his face and groaned. He slid down the wall, crouching under the window as if he were hiding from the outside world. His girlfriend moved to assume her rightful place beside him again, repeating the steps of her delicate reparation for a second time. She waited for him to speak, wondering what he was thinking.

After a minute or so, he too descended onto the floorboards and stretched out his arm to invite her to cuddle into his side. 'Thanks,' he sniffed. 'Your support is gratefully received, Miss Dyson, but what took you so long?'

Ecstatic, the pretty star feigned offence, wilfully refusing his advances for all but an instant. She thought back to the cool, lanky teenager whom she had spied in the photographs on the wall in the Blakes' den and tried to picture him in the bedroom opposite, doing his homework surrounded by posters of herself.

As if reading her mind, he carried on. 'It's impossible to believe I'm here, sitting in this room with you. Now that I have some clear space in my head, I guess it's all pretty overwhelming. It's as if I'm detaching from all those memories and supplanting myself in the present tense with you, but part of me doesn't want to let go of what's familiar, even though it's revolting and painful.'

'That's no surprise,' Lynn kissed his cheek. 'It's all you've ever known. Let it take as long as it needs to take. It's just great for me to hear you're detaching. It means the joy trigger thing's working, doesn't it?'

Jeff nodded. 'Yeah, I guess so. Thanks.'

'You're welcome. Did you doubt it? You wrote it, Professor.'

'Of course I doubted it,' he smirked.

'Hope for the best but expect the worst,' the star-crossed couple chanted in unison, laughing and staring in amazement at their synchronicity.

'Coffee?' Lynn asked.

Her boyfriend stood up, flexing his stiff, cramping legs, and offered a hand to his beautiful best friend. 'Yes, I think so.'

Before returning to the kitchen area, the deserted son turned around once more to look at his parents' old bedroom. It had been several other people's bedroom since that time, and would be again soon. Nonetheless, one last shiver insisted on running down his spine, so he focussed on the corridor outside, keen to arrest his involuntary reaction. On his way out, he examined the split wood on the door frame, where the strike plate had been forced away from the jamb by his own act of violence.

'Damned tenants! I'm not giving them their bond back now.'

***

Back in the kitchen, the young celebrity opened the picnic basket to reveal the selection of goodies which had been provided by their considerate host. She spread various items on the kitchen workbench.

'Help yourself,' she invited, as her dishevelled brunch partner returned. 'Celia didn't put any plates in, but there are plastic cups for coffee.'

'Yeah. Coffee, please,' Jeff selected, lighting a cigarette and picking up a chunk of crusty bread. 'I'm starving.'

'Me too,' Lynn replied, frowning at his odd digestive combination. 'We haven't eaten anything since last night's dinner, and you threw up what was left of yours. It's no wonder you're starving.'

The pair feasted on their make-shift meal, the determined *Regala* insisting her boyfriend walk around the apartment again with his coffee and a sandwich, demanding he articulate a happy memory in each room. She then asked him to take her photograph, standing in the corner of his childhood bedroom, under the window that figured in one of the songwriter's most popular hits. Eager to create as many joy triggers as possible, the sexy woman struck pose after suggestive pose, making him laugh and cry at the same time.

When the dazzled man became fed up with this game, they discussed their flight home over another cup of coffee, followed by planning how their respective schedules were counting down to New Year. Gerry had invited his sisters and their boyfriends to Melbourne for a swish party he was throwing for his friends and special clients, and the musical couple took guesses at who else might attend and the format of the evening. In a weak moment, they had agreed to be the night's cabaret act, which of course meant more rehearsals over the next few days.

All of a sudden, the young man remembered something. 'Hey! What was it you were going to play with that tape player?'

'Oh, yeah!' Lynn exclaimed. 'I totally forgot about that. It's a new song I wrote for you. I'm going to release it as a single next month, if you like it.'

The appreciative fan grabbed the dated radio-cassette from where it had been discarded on the floor earlier and pressed the Rewind button. The tape clicked when it reached the beginning. The singer invited him to push Play, and the complex production did its best to render itself through the unit's tiny loudspeaker. Her voice was unmistakeable however, and when the song finished, the besotted musician immediately rewound it and played it again.

'That's fantastic, angel. I love it,' he praised her, kissing her smiling mouth. 'And you're right. It's just perfect for this moment. Thank you. Thank you for everything, in fact. You are the absolute best.'

'No, Jeff. I should thank you,' the privileged teenager countered, prising her lips away from his. 'I want to thank you for putting your trust in me and for letting me share this intense time. I've learned such a lot by going through this experience with you.'

Hungrily, the young man tried to wrap his vociferous lover into his arms, but she had more to say.

'Wait a minute! Listen... I realise now that what I used to think of as difficult just requires application and practice. The truly difficult things are the ones you have to fight yourself over; the things we can't control but still need to manage. I hope you know just how much I admire you, and how strong you are. Do you?'

Replaying the song for the second time, Jeff focussed on something unseen through the window, beyond the rows of rooftops behind the flat, making sure he acknowledged her kind words and the sincerity with which they had been delivered.

'Yes, I do. Thanks, Lynn. And it means a lot to hear you say that. I will admit, secretly I sometimes congratulate myself for hanging in there. I know I've kept going when many people would've given up or gone completely whacko. And Christ knows how many times I wanted to give up. Right up until half an hour ago.'

The blonde superstar poured out another cup each of coffee, draining the last drops from the Thermos. 'There's one more thing we have to do while we're here.'

The tall, handsome stranger took a step back. 'If you're suggesting having sex here, I'm not going to do that.'

His girlfriend laughed in surprise. 'No! That's not what I meant at all. I'm glad you're at least thinking straight again though.'

'Thank Christ for that! You had that mischievous look on your face.'

His girlfriend wiped the smile from her mouth with her hand like a circus clown. Truth be told, she could hardly wait to get her man home and naked, which may have led him to this conclusion. Perhaps she was giving off all sorts of inappropriate vibes. Now was definitely not the time, and even the sexual mercenary himself recognised this.

His *Regala* had a much more important task to oversee first. 'Sorry. I didn't mean to. I was actually going to say something serious.'

'Hmm... That's probably worse,' her gorgeous companion reasoned. 'What were you going to say? Suddenly, the sex option seems stupid to pass up.'

Shaking her head at the rapid return of her boyfriend's one-tracked mind, Lynn pointed back towards the front door. Brightly, she described the rest of her plan.

'You have to go downstairs again, shutting the door behind you. Then I'll go into your parents' old room and wait for you to come and find me. And if it doesn't feel right the first time, we do it again and again until it does.'

Another bout of anxiety involuntarily bubbled up inside the handsome superstar. This woman was a hard taskmaster, but he owed her too much not to follow this plan. Immediately, he felt his stomach churning and counted the seconds before Gravity cottoned on.

'Yeah, OK,' he reluctantly agreed. 'That was supposed to be the main point of coming here in the first place, I guess. To get over the whole doors thing. Shit, Lynn! I thought you were going to let me go home for a shag and a relaxing swim.'

The young woman felt sorry for him, watching this stoic man's fight-or-flight instincts kick in again. Perhaps they didn't have to do everything today? He had been perfectly compliant so far, and she was looking forward to sharing in the reward as well.

'We could come back another time.'

Jeff rested his hands on her smooth, sculpted shoulders. 'No,' he countered. 'I never want to see this place again.'

With renewed resolve, he sexily swallowed down the rest of his coffee and grabbed his cigarettes, lighter and the jangling set of keys. Lynn smiled in admiration for his newfound sense of purpose.

'I'm off then. Have a nice day, dear.'

The pale-faced man pecked his partner abruptly on the cheek and left the flat without ceremony. She checked the door was closed properly before running to look out of the front window. Within a few seconds, she spotted him walking briskly along the footpath, chased by a plume of smoke. His body language was much more purposeful and positive than earlier, but she doubted he was out of the woods just yet. The mere fact that he hadn't turned around straightaway and loped back up the stairs was a sign that his comic exit line was only *bravado*.

Lynn cleared away the remains of their picnic and made her way into the back bedroom. Knowing what had gone on in this nondescript room gave her the creeps too. She left the door open so that she could hear Jeff's footsteps on the landing, wondering how long it would be before he came back. This was certainly a novel way to spend the Christmas holidays!

Five minutes or so later, the young woman thought she could hear something. She went back to the front door and put her ear up against his own compositions. Yes. She could hear heavy breathing and footsteps coming nearer.

'Showtime!' she whispered to herself.

Back in the bedroom, with the door pushed back into the broken latch, the blonde musician waited patiently for the click of the front door opening. She felt nervous but optimistic.

And there it was. Amazing! It might even have been less than a minute. The door creaked on its hinges, and Lynn heard a familiar cough inside the flat. She took a couple of paces backwards to give the door enough space to open into the room.

'Hi, Jeff!' the cheerful nineteen-year-old called out, sensing her boyfriend's presence on the other side of the door. 'Are you OK?'

'Yeah, I guess so,' came his deep voice, faltering but surprisingly strong.

The door slowly swung towards her until it was fully open to reveal a much-anticipated and boundless human compensation stepping forwards into her lover's arms. In his left hand he was holding a single red rose. His skin was fevered and clammy, and his face looked haggard, but he was here and relatively collected. No angry swearing, no frustration and no interminable waiting in front of the barrier whose density was its least significant property.

'You did it!' Lynn told him again, inching backwards while they kissed. 'And you seem like you're alright. Are you?'

Jeff embraced her passionately, even swinging her round in a circle inside the fateful room. His face remained slightly green, belying his apparent ease, but his triumph had now rapidly translated into a much more common physiological reaction. Being set back onto her feet, the blissful woman couldn't resist pressing herself up against his arousal, meeting no resistance.

'Thank you. *Muchas gracias, mi amor.* You are the best. I couldn't have done it without you, but you're right, I did it. *We* did it.'

Ecstasy consumed his beautiful best friend, who accepted the rose with delight and kissed his hungry lips over and over. 'Where did you go?' she asked. 'I saw you walking off down the street. And what did it feel like, coming in from the landing?'

The contented man stood back until the pretty face was at arms' length. The corners of her mouth turned momentarily into a smile, especially when she saw him adjust himself to relieve his embarrassing profile. Board-shorts didn't leave much to the imagination. He grinned at her salacious look, wagging a threatening index finger.

'Ignore it. Now's not the time. I didn't know what to do at first, when I got out onto the street. But then I thought of the servo round the corner and wondered if they'd have flowers on sale today, being Boxing Day. You know... So I walked over there, saying to myself, "Look, I don't want to come back here, so let's do this properly. There's nothing going on in there anymore except *mi Regala*, my guardian angel." And when I got back, I kept that mindset right up until I got to the door.'

'That's great,' Lynn responded. 'Then what happened?'

Jeff continued, the magnitude of his achievement beginning to sink in. Jesus Christ, he did feel good! And so annoyingly horny to boot.

'On the top floor, I felt everything coming back to haunt me, but less intense than before. Well, I think it was. Who knows? I just put the key in the door and in I came. The best part was hearing your voice when I couldn't see you. That was a big help.'

'Good. I'm glad.'

'The hardest part was opening this bloody thing,' her boyfriend recounted, pointing over his shoulder at the offending bedroom door. 'But that wasn't half as hard as I thought it'd be either. And I'll never have to open this fucking door again, so who gives a shit?'

Jeff was truly elated. Lynn could tell he was about to burst with happiness but was also equally determined to keep a lid on his emotions.

'Thanks for the rose,' she attempted to remain casual too, reaching for his hand. 'It's a beautiful thought. No thorns this time. And you are an amazing man. A really great man. One more photo' in here, then we should get out of here. Unless you want to do it again to reinforce things?'

The grateful man allowed himself to be led further into his parents' room, now with the young woman's camera in his hand. Lynn broke free of his instinctive grasp, took a few steps towards the window and turned around. She kissed the tight petals of the young red rose and clutched it to her breast, smiling broadly. Blown away by the perfect *vista* in front of him, Jeff snapped two or three more pictures without a single demon floating around his tired head. Even Gravity appeared to have taken a cigarette break.

The pair embraced again, on Cloud Nine and laughing as he guessed how to angle the camera to include both their heads in the frame. At this precise moment in time, they ceased to be Lynn Dyson and Jeff Diamond. In this stark, inauspicious room were two ordinary people who had come through something extraordinary together. Their accomplishment hadn't called for money or fame, nor the highest score or the biggest hit. It had simply taken a whole lot of belief and patience; qualities which these special people possessed in abundance. And of course, right up there at the top of the list of required resources sat love.

'No. I'm done. Let's get out of here,' the grateful twenty-two-year-old suggested. 'We've been gone way too long. The Blakes'll be wondering what's happened to us.'

Lynn gathered up their stuff and handed her man the guitar to carry downstairs. 'Any last requests?'

The handsome face gave her a quizzical look. 'That sounds a bit terminal. Nope. I'm sick of this place already. It's going on the market next week. What a lot of effort to go to just to make a bloody tax loss.'

Once back on the street, the local boy turned and kissed his dream girl again, relieved to be back in the open air. After one final photograph outside the dilapidated block, they walked the half-kilometre or so to where they had left Celia's station wagon. It was still there and untouched, they were relieved to note. Jeff drove back through the suburbs like a madman, weaving in and out of the traffic. Lynn Dyson had labelled him a great man, an accreditation for which he would spend the rest of his life striving. He felt unassailable in fact, and all without a drug or a drink in his system.

'You're going to get a speeding ticket,' his passenger warned.

'No, I'm not. Not today. The gods wouldn't be so mean.'

'OK,' she eyed him suspiciously. 'So it'll be interesting to see how you go getting into your apartment tomorrow.'

The driver returned the favour, feigning fresh fright. 'Yeah, I know. I've been thinking about that too. I'm sure you'll come up with a strategy.'

'And guess what I found out this morning?'

'What?'

'Did you know that Gerry's dad was asked to provide you a character reference for my dad's investigators?'

'Really? Fuck! How?' the former bad boy was surprised. 'How did they link him to me?'

Lynn shrugged. 'Probably because he's provided the police and Social Services with sureties before. He was telling me this morning. Poor Gerry was very confused.'

'Whoa. Hang on... I'm not too happy to hear this,' Jeff said, looking worried. 'What did you tell them that brought all this to the surface?'

The pretty nineteen-year-old knew her man would be supersensitive on this topic, but their successful morning now gave her the courage to stand her ground. She was learning quickly how to cope with this complex and afflicted genius, as Celia had put it yesterday. He was accustomed to demanding his own way, and for the most part this was just fine. Once in a while however, it was important for him to let someone else take a turn at being in charge.

'I had to tell them something plausible,' she explained. 'I couldn't just say we felt like a morning on our own. That would've been pretty rude. So I said you wanted to visit your old home to exorcise some ghosts. That's all.'

After doing his best to dismiss the default onslaught of fury and forcing his mind to spend a few mature seconds cogitating over her answer, the young buck nodded approvingly. 'Actually, I like that. Thanks.'

'They know more than you think,' Lynn continued with a wry smile. 'Except Gerry, who's obviously still kept completely in the dark by everybody. But he said he was happy to be the Good Time Guy, so no harm done.'

'Ha! That'd be right,' Jeff laughed. 'That sounds like Blake-san. But so what were Gerald and Celia talking about? What exactly did they say?'

'Oh, I can't remember exactly,' his girlfriend sighed. 'But suffice to say that they've a good idea of what you've been through and how it's affected you. They're smart people, and Gerald called you their second son. Perhaps you should open up to them a bit. It'll probably help the healing process too. They really care about you, you know.'

The driver exhaled, more than a little unsure about this new advice. He had lived in silence for so long. It was convenient and easy just to skirt around these issues. Yet perhaps Lynn was right. It did feel good to talk to people who cared.

'I guess I'm not used to having people around me I can trust.'

'Maybe it'll help Gerry grow up a bit too?' the brave sportswoman added.

'Ouch!' younger half of Melbourne's notorious duo smirked. 'I wouldn't say that to his face, if you value your life. You might be the one getting any last requests...'

The millionnaire turned the Mercedes into the Blakes' driveway and crawled along the gravel carefully. Lynn had fallen asleep beside him and was now stirring with the change in sound and vibration under the tyres. His lustful eyes drank in the view, her short skirt shifting on her thighs as she sat up straight and stretched. He winked, smiling at her drowsy, heart-stopping countenance.

'Not quite the same as being in the old Fairlane, is it?' he observed, gripping her right hand tightly. 'Those were good days. But what's to come'll be way better, I promise.'

'I know,' his beautiful best friend agreed, opening the passenger door and being assaulted by the scorching heat.

Celia was already at the door as they pulled up. 'There you are! We were beginning to get worried. Where on Earth have you been? Is everything alright?'

Jeff ran up to Celia and gave her a bear hug, while Lynn began to unload their belongings from the back seat of the car. 'Oh, yeah!' the re-energised man shouted. 'Everything's very alright, thanks. Sorry we were so long. It's all her fault.'

He pointed to the tall, slim blonde coming away from the vehicle with her hands full. The patient young woman attempted to plead her innocence, but found herself playing along as usual, while her boyfriend and their host rushed to help her.

'I'm the blame consultant for today obviously,' she conceded with a mock sigh.

Celia took the picnic basket from her guest's hand, and they all went inside. The air-conditioning was working hard, and the house felt cold after their brief blast of mid-afternoon sunshine. Lynn smiled as she watched her macho boyfriend disguise a shiver and wondered how the rest of the day would unfold.

'We've just finished lunch,' said the elegant lady. 'Did you want anything?'

'No, thanks, Celia. Our picnic was great, thank you.'

The pair made a sly detour to the den, on the pretext of returning the guitar and cassette player to their rightful places. To the young woman's surprise and even a little disappointment, her boyfriend didn't pounce upon their solitude in the usual fashion. After a tender kiss and another heartfelt thank-you, he backed off, complaining that any semblance of self-control would surely evaporate if they were to go any further at this precise moment.

As the young lovers reached the back doors, Gerry was coming in from the pool with a pile of empty dishes. 'Mate! What time do you call this? I haven't had anyone to play with all day. Did you get plenty of ex*orc*ise?' the wicked man hinted.

'Hysterical, mate,' his friend quipped. 'I could murder a beer.'

After depositing the lunch remains on the kitchen bench-top, the bored executive collected three bottles from the laundry refrigerator and handed one to Jeff. 'Mum's been worried sick. There's something going on that I don't know about, isn't there? Last I knew, I was still your manager. You have to tell me everything.'

'Cheers, mate. You're right,' the younger man slapped his buddy on the back. 'I will, but just not this minute. Right now, I need some ex*erc*ise...'

His dream girl was out of earshot and missed the overt sexual innuendo. Celia was anxious to know that things had gone well and had pulled the patient celebrity into the laundry for another emergency update. This time, Lynn knew exactly which juicy morsels of information she was prepared to pass on and which she would choose to keep to herself.

'Yes, comparatively speaking, it went very well,' the dignified youngster confirmed. 'It was very stressful for him, but he stuck it out. He has amazing endurance. My dad'd be proud.'

'Is he getting any professional treatment these days?' Celia asked, furtively checking that the others couldn't hear their conversation.

Lynn shook her head. 'He *wrote* the professional treatment,' she explained with a smile. 'He co-wrote a book on mental illness, trauma and addiction while he was in North America. Did you know? I only found out yesterday.'

The older woman's mouth was open. 'No, dear. I didn't know. He's such a dark horse, isn't he?'

The man in question entered the room in time to hear the last few words, keen to round up his exercise partner. His eyes questioned hers to make sure she was alright and received a quick flash in the affirmative. He hoped it wouldn't take too long to extract his lover from this discussion because, as he had found out earlier, board-shorts didn't leave much to the imagination.

'Dark horse? Please don't be talking about me again. Enough with the horse references already!'

The Victorian beauty put her arm around her excitable *beau*, and they kissed. She felt a *frisson* of guilty embarrassment when she noticed him turn sideways and slip behind her, away from Celia's prying eyes. He shot her a warning glare, but it was way too late.

'I call him my beautiful, black stallion,' the coy teenager told their host, turning round and patting his chest. 'Today, with your eyes huge and dilated, you looked just like a colt that didn't want to be broken in.'

Jeff was far too aroused to take advantage of the compliment. 'That's quite enough. Can we talk about something other than me for a change? Unless you were going to say, "Hung like..."'

'Shall we go for a swim?' the polite guest suggested, putting her hand over his mouth. 'You need to relax a bit. You're getting hyper. Off the top of your scale.'

'Would everyone please stop focussing on me? It's Christmas,' the songwriter moaned, grabbing Lynn's shoulders from behind, still clutching his beer bottle, and steered her towards the stairs. 'Let's just enjoy ourselves, huh? Come on, gorgeous. Time to go. Wave bye-bye.'

Obediently, his girlfriend gave Celia a childish wave and complied with her stallion's irresistible wishes. Smoothing his happiness curve would involve a much longer treatment program than one successful afternoon of joy triggers.

Once upstairs and back in their chintzy surroundings, the petulant rock star threw himself backwards onto the bed. 'Bloody hell! Will you please stop this merry-go-round? I've had enough now.'

His sympathetic playmate jumped on top of him, only to be immediately drawn in by strong, possessive arms. His penis was turgid and felt enormous against her abdomen, turning her on in an instant. She ran her hand down his chest and stomach, then inside his shorts to take him forcefully in hand.

'I'll try, but you'll have to put up with it as long as people are worried about you. I'm afraid it goes with the territory. If you calm down, so will everyone else. You're leading *us* along your wavy line, Jeff. Not the other way round.'

Duly put in his place, the young man apologised. 'You're right. I promised I wouldn't be selfish anymore and I've blown that already.'

Lynn undid the button on the waistband of his shorts, and he dispatched the very feminine top with its narrow, lacy straps which had been teasing him all morning. His erection bounced free, eliciting groans from both lovers.

'Be quiet and take your medicine like a man,' the insistent woman instructed, kissing him all over his chest and abdomen. 'We care about you and want to make you happy. Get used to it.'

'You are so good to me. And for me. Come here. I have less than thirty seconds before I not-so-spontaneously combust.'

The sex was especially sweet since they were both riding high on the day's achievements while still rather bewildered by the whole ordeal. Slowing things down to the best of his ability, the overwrought sexpert used the welcome one-on-one time with his dream girl to really thank her for what she had done for him. Words of love tumbled from his eloquent mouth between passionate kisses and breathless gasps of pleasure. After what seemed like ages, to him at least, the red-blooded superstar could hold on no longer. Their combined orgasm rushed so fast through their bodies that it purged the morning's stresses from their souls completely, leaving them feeling refreshed and so, so alive.

***

'Mate, I'm fried,' Jeff told Gerry, midway through a chess game later that afternoon. 'I can't concentrate on this anymore. You win.'

In response to this uncharacteristic declaration of defeat, the businessman whipped his opponent's king and queen off the board triumphantly. The family, minus the sisters, who were still shopping, had enjoyed a relaxing Boxing Day afternoon by the pool. After their mammoth conquest of the door of doors and its exquisite aftermath, the rock star and his pop idol partner were at pains to pay due attention to their hosts.

Jeff had been on his best behaviour, drinking far less than Lynn had feared he might, and had provided his bored friend with some much-anticipated quality male bonding time. However, recent events had worn him out, and several yawns later, he decided to quit while he was ahead. Over on the other side of the shimmering water, his dream girl was reading peacefully and hardly needed the pressure of any more of his assiduous ardour. She had been more than generous and forgiving already.

'Don't mind if I do!' Gerry whooped. 'Anyone for another drink?'

The answer was a resounding no from the others, leaving Blake Junior firmly seated. His friend with the heavy eyes and the Cheshire cat grin stood up and walked over to the ladies.

'Excuse me, Celia,' he said, putting his hand on Lynn's left shoulder.

Both women looked up from their magazines.

'Hey, baby. Watch this...'

The handsome performer proceeded to screw his pool towel into a ball and toss it the three or so metres into the laundry bin. It hit the side and unravelled a little before dropping in. Looking up from the copy of "Horse and Hound" she had borrowed from the girls, Lynn giggled as her washed-out man chalked up a slam-dunk on his imaginary scoreboard.

'You're going to bed? Good idea.'

'Yep,' Jeff affirmed, stroking her sun-kissed cheek. 'I can't keep my eyes open.'

The celebrity began to stand up. 'Did you want me to come with you?'

'No. You stay here. Will you wake me before dinner, please?' her respectful boyfriend requested, crouching down beside her sun-lounger and kissing her lips tenderly.

'Of course I will!' she replied with a sunny laugh at his tired, doleful puppy-dog expression.

Her overgrown toddler must truly be spent if he was voluntarily putting himself to bed alone, the sportswoman figured. What a very good sign this was! Quietly, Jeff took her right hand in his left and pushed it quite hard against her heart. There was more then, obviously.

Helping him along, the celebrity made sure she exhibited a sympathetic sign of her own exhaustion, which was read and acknowledged with humility. Of course there was more. It had been a big day, and again the lost boy knew he was forgiven.

'D'you remember how you told the story of those Greek farmers?'

Lynn nodded, wondering where this was leading. His eyes transmitted a deep sincerity. He was about to ask her something significant. She could sense his foreboding.

'Yes, I do.'

He moved their clasped hands from her chest to his own, pointing his index finger back towards her. 'I trust you with my story.'

The nineteen-year-old kissed him again, fully comprehending the delegated task. Her heart filled with happiness and promise for the future, overjoyed that their hastily-concocted treatment plan had yielded such excellent results. She was staring into the eyes of a changed man.

'Go to bed,' she whispered.

'Thank you,' Jeff mouthed back, standing to his full height and puffing out his tired, thankful but utterly Titanic chest.

His long fingers brushed across her back as he turned to make his way into the house. Celia looked from one lover to the other, having witnessed their poignant but mysterious exchange. After a minute or so, the tall, slim athlete stood up and slipped her sundress over her head, instantly attracting the attention of both Blake men, who chuckled at each other in embarrassment.

'Who'd like some tea or coffee? No, Celia, I'll make it.'

In the kitchen, Australia's darling collected her thoughts. A huge responsibility had been vested in her by her healing soul-mate. In reality, it was too much to ask, and one almighty cop-out too, but she would comply with his wishes to help him get the most out of this stupendous day. The reliance would stop tomorrow, she resolved. She returned to the pool with a tray of hot beverages and a jug of iced water.

Placing the drinks on the table, Lynn made her announcement. 'So, everyone... I don't know if you heard what Jeff was saying before he went upstairs, but he'd like me to explain a bit about what happened today and why we went back to his old flat.'

Celia and Gerald looked up at the same time, obviously eager to find out more. Gerry, on the other hand, seemed a little perturbed.

'D'you know, Lynn?' he started. 'You're going to have to stop doing everything for him. You know what he's like. He'll keep on taking as long as you're giving. He has all you women under his spell, the bastard. Isn't this something he should do himself?'

The young woman nodded in agreement. 'Yes, it is really. I agree. I was thinking the same thing while I was inside just now. Don't worry, Gerry. Things are about to change, I assure you.'

Celia came to the young woman's rescue. 'Leave well alone, dear. It's their business. Lynn, please begin.'

'Hmm...' the celebrity mumbled as she thought about how to open. 'Where should I start? Oh, I know... Have any of you ever seen Jeff open a solid door? Like your front door, for example?'

The puzzled family members looked at each other and then back to the stunning orator, all shaking their heads.

She continued. 'Well, he can't. He can't open a locked or closed door, especially his own, without having an extreme panic attack. It's a phobia of sorts that comes from what happened in the flat he grew up in, where we went this morning. He witnessed some pretty disgusting things, coming home from school, *et cetera*, over the years, and it's left him in mortal fear of closed doors and what lies behind them.'

The audience around her were instantly hooked, open-mouthed and waiting for more details of the boy who had grown up in their midst but about whom they had discovered so little.

'And do you know his father's in prison?' she added, hoping she was introducing topics slowly enough not to confuse the story.

Celia nodded, and Gerald said, "Yes" firmly, which left only the incredulous Gerry behind.

'What? Jesus! No way. What for?'

His father answered on the champion's behalf. 'Son, we never told you at the time. You were sitting your HSC exams, and we didn't want to upset the apple cart. We only found out because Mum had sought psychiatric help for Jeff after the incident with our kitchen door, which is now beginning to make sense for the first time.'

'So what's he in prison for?' Gerry asked again. 'I always thought he'd done a runner. Something serious, obviously. And he's still in there?'

'He's serving a double life sentence,' Lynn revealed. 'He killed two Polish brothers, supposedly. They were involved in all sorts of criminal activity: drugs, stolen goods, weapons, booze. You name it, by the sounds of it. So was Jeff's dad and most of his circle. They dealt in anything and were pretty violent.'

This was news even to Celia and Gerald. 'When was this, dear?' the older woman enquired.

'Oh, I'm not sure. For as long as Jeff can remember, I think,' she recounted, totting up the years on her fingers. 'The murders happened when Jeff was twelve or thirteen, so nine years ago or thereabouts.'

'No wonder your father doesn't want him involved with you!' Gerry scoffed at the blonde storyteller, scarcely believing what he was hearing. 'And no wonder there've been private detectives crawling around everywhere. Wow! The Fairfield Mafiowski. That's amazing.'

The patient beauty smiled. 'And that's not the half of it.'

'But what does that have to do with opening doors, my dear?' Gerald interjected.

'Oh, sorry! We've wandered off track a bit already,' Lynn apologised. 'Well, the reason Jeff thinks his dad murdered these two brothers was because they had been using his mother and sister as prostitutes, in a way to get payment for deals that didn't go well, or something. I'm not sure of the details. Suffice to say that Jeff witnessed his mum and sister being drugged and raped violently many, many times. He used to come home to the flat and open the door to see all this going on, and gradually it just built up to a real phobia because he never knew what he'd see next. He still sees and hears it in his mind, even after all this time.'

'My Goodness! That's awful. Poor, poor Jeff,' Celia squealed, with tears in her eyes. 'I knew there were serious issues going on but I'd honestly never noticed he had a problem with opening doors. That must've been why he ended up bashing ours down. That's right... Because we locked it, not knowing that he'd made an arrangement with the kids to let himself in.'

The Melburnian nodded and continued. 'There's a whole lot more to tell than I'm going to today, because I don't know how far he wants me to go. As you said this morning, Gerald, Jeff's parents didn't have a clue how to be proper parents. They had to get married when his sister came along, and then by the time their son was born they were already in all sorts of trouble. He wasn't wanted, and they never gave him much love or attention, from what I can gather.'

The pretty teenager was also fighting back the tears by this time. Celia moved her chair closer and took her hand, which was accepted gratefully.

'You're doing very well, dear. Stop if you want. We can find all this out some other time.'

'No. It's fine, thanks,' the teenager declined, composing herself like the stalwart she had been groomed to be. 'Anyway, despite being a real outcast in his own family, Jeff always tried to pull these men off his mum and Madalena, his sister. But then his mum or dad would hit him and tell him off for stopping them from earning money. And now he has violent nightmares every night, where he opens the front door of his flat to find blokes in their bedroom, on top of the women, and then fighting them off. Sometimes you can see his head shake after someone has punched him, and the language is pretty graphic.'

Celia gripped their guest's hand more tightly. 'Every night?'

'Yes, every night,' Lynn confirmed. 'Last night three times! If I'm there, I try and wake him as soon as I hear one start, but it takes him ages to wake up properly and calm down enough to go back to sleep. That's why he would never sleep here before. Or anywhere for that matter... He can only ever get an hour or two's sleep at a time before a nightmare starts. Sometimes the shouting and swearing's really loud. Did it disturb you last night?'

Everyone shook their head, stunned by the string of revelations.

'That's good,' the young woman sounded happier. 'He'll be relieved to know that. That's why he hardly ever goes to bed, because he's so sick of waking up in a cold sweat with his heart in his mouth, reliving those horrible memories.'

'And this still goes on after all these years?' asked Gerald.

She nodded. 'The psychiatric hospital that you took him to diagnosed him with something they're calling Compound Depersonalisation Disorder, and Jeff's been working ever since to figure out what his condition really is and trying to find some relief from the symptoms. He's quite an expert in his field, which I knew from before I went away. And he's ploughing heaps of money into research too.'

The rock star's manager coughed. 'That I can vouch for,' he agreed. 'The man's got to be mad, the way he gives so much money away. One day he's going to leave himself short.'

'He won't care if he leaves himself short,' the empathetic celebrity challenged. 'He's really committed to helping these people out, especially the social workers, because they helped him a lot when he was younger.'

Emotion ran ragged when the devoted youngster recalled their first visit to The Fellowship, learning about happiness charts and watching her first love interact with Brian, the man who was recovering from a suicide attempt. Tears welled up in her eyes, picturing the night she abandoned her selfless soul-mate in the old Richmond apartment, on her way to California and to great acclaim. Today's crowd was gaping at her expectantly for the next tranche of the story, and she gladly left her own painful reminiscences behind.

'That's why Jeff decided to buy the Stones Road flat. After he worked with Sarah Friedman in Canada on their paper... She's a doctor of psychiatry in Toronto, by the way... he wanted to see if associating the scene of the nightmares and the door problem with something joyous would help. That's what we were doing this morning. I hope it works, because it's a really, really desperate situation for him.'

Gerry had turned pale. 'And for you too. No wonder he's always out chasing the action in the middle of the night.'

The young star smiled sweetly at her boyfriend's drinking buddy. 'Yes! It's tough sometimes, especially when I can't wake him up. Although I really want to help. I'm pleased to be needed. All my life, people have looked after me, so now it's my turn. That's why I'm prepared to do this for him. He's really grateful for the help, so I don't feel at all used.'

'You're a good girl, Lynn,' Gerald praised.

The youngster carried on. 'Thank you. I just feel so sorry for the way he's had to bring himself up from nothing. It's amazing how he did so well at school and how he's taught himself how to be successful, putting himself in positions where he'll learn how to get where he wants to go. I admire him so much. He really inspires me.'

'Is he ever violent towards you?' Celia had finally found the courage to ask the question she had been dying to ask all along, now searching youthful, blue eyes. 'You must tell us if he is.'

'No. Absolutely not!' Lynn answered without hesitation. 'Occasionally he hits out when he's dreaming, and I get a fist in the back or something, but it's not intentional. He hates himself for it too, which only fuels his desperation. Anyway, after his dad went to prison, his mum was already completely addicted to all sorts of drugs and alcohol. Their flat was always full of illegal contraband, so there was a good supply of things to space herself out on, even when the male visitors weren't feeding her.'

Gerry interrupted this time, his face ashen. 'What about his sister? Where is she now? I've heard him mention her a few times, but it doesn't seem like they're very close. Didn't he have to pay for her to have an abortion not so long ago?'

Lynn smiled. 'Yes. It's funny how he always passes on pieces of information that don't give the true extent of his situation away too much. Madalena's on the game, and Jeff doesn't seem to want to have much to do with her. Nor she with him, I suppose. They were a really dysfunctional family right from the beginning, and it just got worse and worse. People like us, we can't imagine what it's like not to be loved and protected by our family. It's so alien. That's why Jeff loves you guys so much. It's a kind of adoption in reverse.'

'Jeez!' exclaimed the younger accountant, punch-drunk after an afternoon consuming beer in the sun and now facing this startling news about his long-time friend. 'I don't know how to take that, honestly. It's hard not to feel just a wee bit used, isn't it?'

He glanced around the room for agreement from his family, but there was none.

The celebrity storyteller supported him however. 'Yes, it is, and he'd agree with you. You should ask him to explain his relationships theory to you. It's interesting and very convincing, but still wrong on so many levels. But it worked for him during these dark times, which is why I forgive it. You need to work out if you do too.'

Gerry turned unusually serious. 'So do you mean to tell me that he singled me out to help him become who he wanted to become?'

'Yes. And me too. All of us, in fact.'

Blake Senior laughed at his son's annoyance. 'He's selected his disciples very carefully, has our Jeff. You should be flattered, son. Perhaps he's the new Messiah? What about that? Half Jew, half Catholic. It's perfect, to be sure!'

The devout Missus Blake didn't appreciate the direction in which her husband was directing the conversation. It was Christmas after all, and blasphemy wasn't tolerated in their household.

'Gentlemen, please. That's not appropriate. Lynn's right. We shouldn't be damning Jeff while he's not here to answer for himself. Whatever his motives are, or were, he's still had a terrible childhood, and there are obviously a lot of scars he has to live with.'

'Thanks, Celia,' the younger woman replied. 'Jeff's desperate to move on from all that, and I believe him. He didn't have anyone in his family whom he could trust and he'd tried everything. He hoped moving to Melbourne would help, but it didn't. He was born with all this super-intelligence and so many ideas and ambitions, so he set about finding people he could learn from. He saw the pursuit of knowledge as his only way out of the doldrums and into a position where he could start doing what he really wants to do.'

Gerald nodded to his wife, pouting. 'I rest my case, Your Honour.'

'Who knows?' the pretty blonde carried on, keen to complete her task. 'Whatever happens, please know that Jeff hates himself for the burden he's been on us. He really does. That's why he wants to take every possible step to solve the problem. I should finish the story, I suppose.'

'Didn't his mother die when he was fourteen?' Celia interrupted, helping their special guest to retrace her steps. 'I know we didn't find out for a couple of months.'

'Something about doing the washing, wasn't it?' Lynn smiled. 'He told me that it all came out one day because you made a comment about him wearing the same clothes.'

The older woman didn't know whether to laugh or cry. 'Goodness. Yes. That's right,' she confirmed, reaching for her towel to dab away tears. 'I joked with him that I didn't think his mother had been doing a good job with the laundry, thinking he was just the typical teenager who never saw the need to change his clothes without being prompted. He laughed too at first, but then his expression turned thunderous, and he shouted at me full in the face, "Don't bring my mum into this!" I told him off for raising his voice to me, and he apologised, and then I noticed his eyes were red and watery. It turned out that his mother had passed away a few weeks earlier, and he hadn't told any of us.'

'That sounds right,' the nineteen-year-old had become serious again. 'By all accounts, it was terrible. She overdosed on something, and Jeff found her, again after opening the bedroom door, in a pool of blood and vomit. She'd broken a glass and had been trying to slash her wrists at the same time. Can you imagine finding your mum in that state? And too late to do anything about it?'

Lynn continued to a row of horrified faces, fighting back her own tears. 'He refused to let his sister into the flat, sending her to their grandparents' house. So this poor, unloved, fourteen-year-old had to call the emergency services and have them take his own mum away, and then he had to clean up the flat before the police arrived. His mum's parents were supposed to look after him as well, but they didn't have any time for Jeff because he reminded them of his dad.'

'Apparently, they still blame the Diamond men for what happened to their daughter, which I suppose is justified from their perspective. And for that reason, Jeff never liked them either, so he spent the next few years sneaking around, avoiding Social Services and the school and anyone else who was likely to stop him being allowed to live on his own. Oh, I can't imagine going through life like that... And doing exams at school at the same time, *et cetera*. That's why I'm happy to help, because he's certainly done everything he could do to help himself every step of the way.'

Gerald came over to Lynn's chair and gave her shoulders a rough hug. She was grateful for the awkward display of affection, and tears began to roll down her cheeks. She felt a little ashamed, quickly pulling herself together.

'So I assume Jeff's father is aware that his wife passed away?' the shy man asked.

The young woman shook her head, unable to answer this question. 'I don't know. We haven't tackled that side of the story yet,' she replied. 'Jeff told me he just walked away from his dad when he was sent to prison. I think he should get in contact, if only to hear his version of the truth. But I'll wait to let all this settle down first before I make that suggestion.'

Celia nodded. 'I think that's very sensible, my dear. He's still young. There's plenty of time. No point in risking pushing him down again if today was a success.'

Her son had fallen silent during the last few minutes. 'I think I need to make a 'phone call,' he said, looking directly at his mother.

The elegant woman startled. 'What do you mean, darling? Are you alright? You're looking a bit off-colour.'

'Well...' Uncomfortable, Gerry was preparing to make his own confession. 'While we're all laying our cards on the table, there is something I have to tell you, parents of mine.'

His father stiffened up. 'What's that, son?'

The successful businessman gave an embarrassed chortle. 'All this terribly moral behaviour has made me feel somewhat rat-like.'

His parents were confused and anxious to hear what their high-flying heir had to say. It was a rare sight to see the indomitable one looking so queasy and timorous. Lynn leaned back in her chair and let Jeff's manager have the floor.

'I'm going to be a father,' Gerry blurted out. 'I managed to get a girl pregnant, after all these years of being bloody lucky. She, Heather, wants to keep the baby, but we're not together. In fact, we were never together, which won't come as a shock to either of you.'

Too late! Celia was already decidedly in shock. She was to become a grandmother. As Boxing Day nineteen-seventy-four took another confounding twist, it was Lynn's turn to hold the older woman's hand while her husband poured a glass of water.

'Well, that's a big surprise too, darling?' she stuttered. 'When were you going to tell us?'

The Melbourne playboy moved to sit next to his mother and held her other hand. 'I'm really sorry, Mum. I don't know when I was going to tell you. Probably never. I will help her out financially. That's already arranged. But we're not going to get married or anything. I never intended to have much to do with the kid...'

The haughty parent shot him a dark look. 'Kid? Please don't refer to my grandchild as a *kid.*'

'Sorry, Mater,' Gerry responded sheepishly. 'The child. But what I was going to say is, after all these stories about tough lives for children, I think perhaps I ought to get more involved. I know this'll be hard for you to believe, but I need to have a think about it. Jeff's been lecturing me about it too. He's not happy about his sister having had two abortions, even though he concedes that it's probably best because the kids... children, I mean... would have a terrible life with a mother on the game. But I can give a child a good life, can't I?'

'You all can,' Lynn joined in. 'It'd be nice for your baby to know both sets of grandparents.'

'Right-oh! It's after six o'clock,' Gerald announced to everyone, bashing the arms of his chair to bring them back to reality after their highly eventful afternoon. 'I think it's time for an *apéritif*.'

Celia nodded, her face still flushed after her son's revelation. 'Good idea. Make mine a large one!'

'That's no way for a grandmother to behave,' teased Gerry, glad to have got his news out of the way. 'Lynn, what would you like?'

Before their guest could answer, Celia beckoned for her to stand up, and the two women hugged each other. 'Darling, thank you for telling our Jeff's story for him. It all makes perfect sense to me. I had no idea it was so horrific, but it certainly does put everything into perspective. You are the perfect girl for him, dear, and he's very lucky to have you. Let us know if we can help with anything.'

'Thank you. I will. It'll take a few days to find out if we made some progress today, but judging by his reaction, Jeff's confident.'

'And you...' the perturbed mother turned to her son, who was in the process of slinking away from the verandah. 'We'll deal with you later. I have to get the dinner ready.'

Lynn sprang to her feet again. 'I'll help you.'

'No, dear. You go and give your young man a dig in the ribs. He's missing all the fun.'

'Alright, if you're sure,' she answered happily, for this was exactly what she couldn't wait to do. 'Thank you again.'

The dignified teenager realised that their host was anxious to bring her household to order after such a tumultuous few hours. Her daughters would be returning any moment from their hard day's shopping, and she most likely didn't want them to come home to a family in chaos, or else the drama would start all over again.

As she climbed the stairs, Lynn congratulated herself for imparting a steady and fairly objective account of her mystery man's complicated life story. Twisting the door handle, she wondered what tomorrow might bring, when they returned to their Melbourne apartment. Would Jeff be able to turn that key more easily, or might they need to work on a whole new treatment plan?

Gerald's new Messiah was still peacefully sleeping, and the caring woman bent over to kiss his forehead.

'Jeff, it's six-thirty.'

Dark, gipsy eyes flickered under closed lids, and the fingers of his left hand flexed. Lynn loved to watch her perfect stranger awaken normally. It was so much better than the noisy, nocturnal wake-up calls she had become accustomed to giving him. She sat down on the edge of the bed and lifted his left hand into hers.

'Wake up, gorgeous. It's dinner time soon.'

One eye opened slightly, and a smile spread across the young man's face. 'Hey! Thanks.'

'You look very relaxed,' his girlfriend said, seeing both eyes now open and noticing that his right hand had hold of something. 'What's this?'

She lifted his fingers to reveal the tape she had been playing earlier. He must have retrieved it from the cassette player before it was returned to its dusty corner. Jeff twisted the plastic object through his fingers and flamboyantly presented it to his *Regala*.

'It's "It Feels Like Yesterday",' he crooned, laying the cassette down onto the bedside table. 'I meant to stick it in your case. Didn't get very far, did it?'

Lynn hugged him. 'How do you feel?'

'Fantastic!' the dark-haired dreamer replied, before blanching when he remembered the assignment with which he had charged her. 'Shit! Is it done?'

'Yes,' the blonde beauty sat up again and nodded solemnly. 'It's done. I outed you.'

Her boyfriend gave a nervous smile. 'Great. Thanks. I owe you. Yet again.'

'You're welcome. I hope I did the story justice.'

'I'm sure you were word perfect,' Jeff assured his beautiful best friend, sensing she had other news to tell. 'What are you looking so excited about?'

'Gerry's done a *mea culpa*,' she responded, wide-eyed. 'He told his parents he's going to be a daddy.'

'Whoa!' the young man gasped, sitting up quickly. 'I asked him if he was intending to, and he said, "No way." He's always maintained he's not going to be a dad. Only a bank.'

'Well, I think your story shamed him into it,' Lynn recounted. 'He went quiet for a long time, and I thought he was taking in what we'd just been talking about. But then he came out with everything and apologised.'

Jeff was astonished. 'OK! I s'pose that's good. What was their reaction?'

'Celia was shaken, obviously. Huge understatement. She still is and went into full-on Good Housekeeping mode straightaway. Gerald was typically stiff-upper-lipped about it though. He just asked if anyone wanted a drink.'

The sleepyhead burst out laughing mid-stretch. 'Damn! I'm annoyed I missed all that. Are the girls back? Do they know?'

His girlfriend shook her head. 'No. Well, they might be back by now, but they've missed it all too. Gerry's a bit pissed off with you, by the way, about being used to get to the top.'

Jeff's smile vanished. 'Yeah. That's fair enough. I expected that, and I deserve it. What about Celia and Gerald?'

The celebrity sighed, knowing she needed to put her foot down at some point. 'You're going to have to find out for yourself. They seem fine, but you owe them an explanation.'

Her boyfriend got the message and took her hands in his. 'Jesus! I'm a lucky bloke. Thanks heaps. I know I was out of order asking you to deliver my message. I'm sorry, and it shouldn't have happened. I'll repay you a thousand times.'

'Shhh... I know you will,' she acknowledged, feeling him tense up again. 'You're not allowed to get stressed anymore. It's fine. I understand why you did it and I'm honoured to be trusted with something so personal and so sensitive. Truly I am. Let's not talk about it today. We'd better go down soon and help with dinner.'

Lynn stood up and allowed her man to climb out of bed. He wrapped her up in his arms and held her tight.

'Thanks again.'

'Get dressed,' she commanded, pointing to his erect penis, 'and get rid of that.'

The young man gave her a salute and obliged, quickly donning a pair of boxer shorts. Running his fingers quickly through his hair, he looked at himself in the mirror and spoke to his reflection.

'Well... You're public knowledge now. No more hiding in dark corners, mate.'

His dream girl walked up behind him and cuddled against a warm, inviting back, smiling into the mirror. 'It'll be OK. They're your friends.'

After a sublime *sojourn* in the shower, the couple descended towards the kitchen and could hear Jacinta and Tamilla shrieking in excitement.

The extra brother looked at his girlfriend and grinned. 'Either they had a really successful day at the sales or they've found out Gerry's news... Place your bets!'

The well-bred Melburnian put her fingers to her mouth. 'Better not say anything, in case it's the former.'

The rock star nodded. 'Sure. If they do know, good old Gerry, huh? He's successfully deflected the attention away from me. He'll be sick to know that, especially after what you were saying.'

Gerald met the good-looking pair as they approached the dining room door, carrying a crate of empty beer bottles in from the pool. 'Welcome back, you two! Could you please go out and collect the rest of the *débris*?'

Jeff was glad to help, immediately heading outside. The sportswoman carried on into the kitchen, keen to discover what was behind the hullabaloo.

'Lynn!' both sisters yelled at once.

Jacinta hugged her enthusiastically. Their shopping trip had been punctuated by several glasses of champagne, the celebrity assumed.

'Mum's just told us that you demystified our mystery man this afternoon. We're really miffed that we missed it.'

The pretty blonde laughed. 'Sorry! Did you have a successful day otherwise?'

The younger sister pointed to a colourful stack of shopping bags in the hallway, waiting to be taken upstairs. 'Not too bad, thanks!'

'Celia, what can I do to help?' Lynn asked.

'Nothing, darling,' the lady of the house answered, her face pink from alcohol and cooking, but beaming with happiness nonetheless. 'In case you're wondering, I have told the girls about their naughty brother.'

'Good. Thanks! We didn't want to let any cats out of bags. What do you think?'

Tamilla threw her hands in the air. 'I can't believe I'm going to be an auntie. I hope she doesn't mind us being on the scene. Heather, I mean,' she corrected herself, catching her mother's prompt for more respect. 'Do you know her?'

Despite Lynn shaking her head, Jacinta was anxious for more information. 'Is she nice though? Do you think Gerry should marry her?'

As discreet as ever, the society favourite wouldn't be drawn on this subject. 'I've met Heather but I wouldn't say I know her. She's a doctor, I think. A GP.'

Celia scolded her daughters again for asking such questions of their famous guest. A mother's work was never done, the teenager realised, reminded of her own. Gerald and Jeff returned from the patio with the last of the glasses and cups to a chorus of shrill whoops.

'Ladies!' the handsome musician exclaimed, raising his arms to protect himself from their enthusiasm. 'Had a good day on the town, have we?'

Gerald issued firm instructions to his daughters to take their purchases upstairs and ready themselves for their meal. Quiet descended again on the kitchen, and the seasoned host took orders for another round of pre-dinner drinks. His wife sensibly refused, and Lynn did the same.

'Scotch and dry, Jeff?' the senior partner asked, heading off to the dining room.

'Perfect. Thanks, sir,' the songwriter replied, sidling up to his beautiful best friend and whispering in her ear. 'I've just had this weird scene come into my head of Cinderella.'

His dream girl smiled. 'That's mean! Who's the fairy godmother?'

'What's the secret?' Celia asked, seeing their heads together. 'How are you now? Did you get some sleep?'

Jeff kissed his friend's mother on the cheek. 'Congratulations, Nana! I'm greatly rested, thanks. In very good hands. How are you feeling?'

'Oh, my goodness! I don't know how I'm feeling, to be honest,' the older woman cried, clutching on to his arm. 'It's not exactly the circumstances I'd hoped to hear about becoming a grandmother, but it is exciting to think there will be another generation of Blakes. I take it you two knew about the pregnancy?'

Both stars nodded, feeling slightly guilty. The errant musician took the lead manfully.

'Yes. I've known for a few months and told Lynn when she came back from the US. Gerry's been pretty honourable about it. He wants to do the right thing by Heather and the baby.'

The lady of the house seemed consoled by her pseudo-son's words and brushed his cheek with a varnished fingernail. A good sleep and the evening's first beer had brought colour back to his face, and she was happy to see the brightness in his eyes. What a memorable day they had all had!

'Let's eat, shall we? Can you grab those jugs of water, please?'

Everyone was seated for another extravagant meal. Having ferried the grandparents to other siblings, only the immediate family and their two Victorian visitors graced the table tonight. Gerald and Celia positioned themselves at each head, with Gerry and Jacinta on one side and the others opposite.

'I'd like to propose a toast,' their normally reserved host announced before they all began eating. 'This has been a fairly eventful Boxing Day, to say the least. I'd just like to raise our glasses to all of us, for sticking together as a family and as an extended family. Jeff and Lynn, it's been wonderful to share in your quest for rehabilitation, and long may your partnership continue. And Gerry, your mother and I are keen to extend our support for whatever choices you make. Just one wish though...'

The prodigal son looked slightly concerned at what his father was about to say. Everyone was poised with their glasses raised and sighed as one at the delay.

The older man lifted his wine glass again. 'Our one wish is that you don't name the baby Gerald, because there are too many of us already. Here's to the next generation of Blakes.'

Relief all round. Everyone toasted each other, and dinner officially commenced. The sisters recounted the highlights of their shopping expedition, and the celebrities spoke about their plans for London and new record deals they were both negotiating.

'So how's the horse trainer, Tammy?' Jeff asked, tucking into his second helping of roast lamb with all the trimmings. 'Has he got you under control yet?'

Tamilla kicked her former playmate hard on the left ankle. Years of practice had taught them all to expect such a response to having secrets exposed, and his expression barely altered as his ankle bone absorbed the point of her shoe.

'Bastard!' she exclaimed.

The songwriter didn't need to feign innocence in front of the Blake parents for a change, having no idea that his mate's kid sister would be upset. 'Why? What did I say?'

Lynn piped up. 'Sorry, that's my fault. I was supposed to tell you something and I forgot.'

The comic swung his head between the girls on either side of him, as if he were following a tennis match. 'Then you deserve the bruise that's now stinging nicely on my shin.'

Choosing to ignore the childish shenanigans, Celia turned to her son. 'So, darling, when are you going back to Melbourne?'

'Tomorrow morning. Same as these guys. I'm hosting a New Year's Eve party, which means I've got to be back for the prep'. There are over a hundred clients coming, Dad.'

'All female,' Jeff interjected, much to everyone's amusement.

The main course over, Celia and Jacinta carried the empty plates back into the kitchen and returned laden with various desserts. Gerald recharged everyone's glasses yet again, as delicate china bowls were filled and placed in front of each person.

'Thanks, sir,' the confident young man said, clearing his throat and turning to each host in turn. 'Can I say something before we start, please?'

Celia looked round expectantly. 'Of course, dear.'

The table fell silent, and for someone at ease performing in front of tens of thousands of people, Jeff was instantly reduced to a bundle of nerves. He was about to close the door once and for all on his past, but not without some reluctance and trepidation.

'Everyone, I'd just like to say thanks for an awesome Christmas. It's been amazing for Lynn and me to be together for our first festive season, and I can't think of anyone better to share it with.'

His partner nodded. 'Agreed.'

The orator continued. 'First, I need to apologise to Lynn for leaving her in the lurch this afternoon, and also to you guys for sending in a substitute to do my work for me. A very worthy substitute though, I hope you found.'

'Agreed,' the young woman repeated.

The Blakes all laughed, assenting readily.

'Hear, hear!' Gerald added, raising his glass to the beautiful woman on his left.

'As you found out earlier,' Jeff carried on, 'I've had an interesting life so far. There's much to forget about it, but I also acknowledge that it's been responsible for bringing me wisdom and wealth, and it's taught me to derive strength from all sorts of weird and wonderful sources. Today, we went to open some doors with a view to closing some too.'

Seeing nothing but friendly faces, the boy from Canley Vale cleared his throat again. His heart was calm, but his head was swimming.

'Henceforth, I need to discover a new source of inspiration, and I've got the distinct impression it's sitting here to my immediate right.'

'Hear, hear!' their tipsy host chanted again. 'Indubitably.'

Lynn smiled and raised her glass to thank her charitable boyfriend, who had now relaxed. He was indeed a great man, and destined to be even greater. Thoughts of the boutique London apartment she had rented, close to the West End and its wealth of historic and artistic institutions, she couldn't wait to see her ambitious partner immersed in intellectual pursuits of social justice and other world-changing activities. These were ventures she was itching to sink her teeth into as well.

'As you guys know and never let me forget, Lynn's been my inspiration throughout anyway, so the only real change'll be in working out what our life together's going to be like going forward, rather than just wishing for it.'

'Fantasising, more like,' Gerry's elder sister jeered, making a rather obscene gesture with one hand.

'Jacinta!' Celia pounced. 'That's enough.'

'Thanks for that, Jack,' the speaker scoffed. 'I just want to say thanks to all of you for keeping me alive. It sounds dramatic, but it's the truth. Yes, I am guilty of using you all, as I believe Gez pointed out earlier. I've used a lot of people in my life and I'm not proud of it, but I had to do everything in my power to break out of where I was. A few months ago, when we were at the music awards, I took an afternoon's train ride back to the neighbourhood I grew up in and saw some people I was at school with. Most of them are still stuck in the same place, with no future and a bloody shitty present.'

Jeff raised his hand to Gerry's mother, to apologise for his language. 'Sorry Celia.'

This time however, the spellbound woman offered no reproach.

'But as I got to know you guys,' the superstar's voice became croaky with emotion, looking around at each Blake in turn, 'I hope I've managed to gain your respect too, somehow, along the way. Except for the kitchen door episode, which still makes my skin crawl every time I think about it.'

'Actually,' Celia piped up, in an attempt to save the young man's unease, 'we could do with another new kitchen door, dear.'

Lynn caught her boyfriend's eye, and he nodded. He knew exactly what she was going to say.

'I witnessed a door being kicked in today. It was very dramatic!'

The assembled party looked bemused and more than a little concerned. Jeff steered clear of the detail, continuing with his speech.

'We'll tell you about that later. Now, I know there are many people who are at least as badly off as I was. Some a hell of a lot worse. Many people have serious mental disturbance going on from stuff that happened in their lives. I'm not special, but we all have to fight our own battles. Today I fought the hardest battle yet. I probably won't know whether it was worth it for a few days, but I'm very optimistic. And I couldn't have done it without you, angel.'

The romantic storyteller took his dream girl's left hand in his right and lifted it to his lips. 'It's all Lynn's fault, what happened today. And I've used her too, repeatedly, obsessively and wantonly...'

The Olympian shook her head and urged him to continue, tears of pride shining in her eyes.

'I saw something in her back when she was only eight or so that told me she would understand this godforsaken waster. Who knows why, eh? But I saw it. So when you guys used to tease me about my unhealthy infatuation with Lynn Dyson, it used to kill me because it was never like you thought.'

The songwriter paused, not wishing to go so far as to alienate them all.

'I'm very sorry, Jeff,' Tamilla interrupted. 'I remember how hurt you were on that skiing trip, when I was cruel, laughing at you for thinking you needed Lynn to help you when you'd become the biggest star on Earth.'

'Yeah,' he agreed with a half-smile, his chest constricting painfully. 'You got me at a very weak moment that night, Tam. Anyway, Lynn did understand, luckily, didn't you?'

His beautiful best friend nodded, gripping his forearm in moral support. 'Yes. We understand each other,' she corrected. 'You make it sound like such a one-way street. I love you too, remember?'

'Thanks, angel,' Jeff's voice cracked. 'This stunning woman, who's actually even more beautiful on the inside, listened to all my ranting and raving in the middle of the night, then reached inside my soul and located all the loose ends; the raw nerves that had been hanging there neglected for so long. She worked out how to tie them all together, and now I feel all connected again.'

The analogy was perfect. To his delight, Lynn levered herself out of her chair to kiss her man full on the lips.

'I hope so,' she replied.

The dark-haired superstar looked around the table at five other pairs of eyes that were fixed on him. 'You know the saying "Physician, heal thyself"?'

They all answered in the affirmative.

'Well, it's crap,' the knowledgeable man laughed, as did everyone else, grateful for some levity. 'I learned so much about myself but still couldn't do anything to cure myself. It's not 'til someone loves you enough to help you learn how to love yourself, and respect yourself, that this type of healing can happen. I studied it, wrote about it, sang about it, but couldn't actually change it without Lynn's understanding and figuring out how to fix me. She also told me to open up to you guys, and I'm really glad everything's out in the fresh air now.'

Jacinta gave a frustrated groan. 'I can't believe we missed all this today, Tammy. Now we've got absolutely no idea what you're talking about.'

'Well, I'm not going to do it all again, I'm sorry,' Lynn chuckled at their frustration. 'I hope it can be delivered second-hand without many Chinese whispers.'

Jeff sniffed. 'Yeah. Christ! You'll end up thinking I'm having a sex change and my dad's been nominated for the Nobel Peace prize.'

The sisters looked thoroughly confused, and Celia came to their rescue.

'I'll do my best to pass on the salient facts tomorrow.'

'Thanks, Mum,' Jacinta replied.

Suddenly, Gerry scraped his chair backwards and got to his feet. 'Fearing our puddings'll dry out if we wait any longer, I'd like to bring this fascinating soliloquy to a close by wishing Jeff and Lynn good luck in London, and for the forward-facing half of your life. I'm still insanely jealous of you, mate, but this pain's been eased somewhat by the prospect of my new toy. Ever since we embarked on our friendship and endless forays into the female population...'

'Steady, mate,' Jeff advised, knowing his warning would go unheeded.

True to form, the junior partner ignored his VIP client. 'We've had a lot of fun, you and me. I was only following his lead, Mum, honestly. He started it, and then I got to like it. And today I find out he was only doing it because he couldn't sleep and Lynn wasn't there to tie his loose ends together! There was me, forcing myself to stay awake during school and work after endless nights on the town, and he had exactly the reverse problem.'

'No, I didn't,' the twenty-two-year-old corrected him. 'I was always dead tired too.'

'God knows,' Gerry continued, sighing, 'I'm making a shitload of money from you these days, so I hope *our* partnership continues too. You're bloody brave, that's all I have to say, mate. And the lovely Lynn, you're equally courageous to take him on.'

The Australian aristocrat objected. 'No, I'm not! I've learned such a lot about humanity and humility since I've known Jeff. Every day's an adventure, and I love it. I wouldn't swap it for anything. But thanks for your good wishes, Gerry, and thanks to all of you for allowing me to share your Christmas. Hopefully, next Christmas will be more humdrum and peaceful.'

'I'll drink to that!' Gerald declared, once more raising his glass. 'Let's eat.'

Reborn

After the dinner feast had been cleared away, the Blake parents sent the others away into the den for some "youngster time". After an appropriate amount of protestation, their Melbourne guests accepted their fate and made their way down the tastefully decorated corridor. The lid of the piano had already been opened, in advance of the accomplished musicians in the family's environs.

'This is more like a normal Christmas,' Tamilla stated, primarily for their visitor's benefit. 'We always used to come down here after Sunday dinner and play the piano, sing and smoke pot. Has anyone got any?'

Gerry grinned, urging his little sister to keep her voice down. 'Yes. There's some in my room. You guys get the coffee and liqueurs, and I'll fetch the weed. Lynn and Jeff, you're the entertainment, OK?'

The younger man sniggered at his old friend. 'You want a floorshow?'

'No, mate,' his manager laughed, screwing his face up. 'Not even you could be that much of an exhibitionist. Just tickle the fucking ivories or something.'

Much to Lynn's relief, the Blake kids disappeared to find their various secret ingredients, leaving the two *artistes invités* temporarily alone in the family room.

'Well done,' the young woman praised her favourite after-dinner speaker as soon as she was let loose from a very long kiss. 'That was a great speech. I think you're giving me too much credit though. You've done most of this yourself.'

The serene twenty-two-year-old closed his eyes. 'On the surface, I agree, but it's only because of you.'

'OK. Let's just agree we're a good team.'

'I just hope that someday,' the handsome stranger told her, his eyes drilling into hers, 'I get the chance to help you... or maybe someone else, if not you... so I can repay this huge debt I now carry.'

'Shut up,' his girlfriend covered his mouth, wagging an accusing finger and smiling. 'There's no debt, Jeff. No debt. Get it?'

'We'll see…' he answered, unwilling to relent.

Lynn sat at the piano and began to pick out some random tunes. Her partner did the same with the old guitar that travelled west with them earlier. He laboured over a chorus hook which had been nagging him throughout dinner, but as yet it lacked a good strong melody to carry it, so the collaborators set to work.

'That's great,' the pianist said, listening to her intense poet gradually craft the song. 'Sing it again.'

'It needs a classical piano background like the swell of the ocean,' he expounded, repeating the chorus and adding a verse which had just that minute come to him. '"Born Again" sounds too corny, too Christian, Bible-bashing shit. It needs to hit me harder.'

'Recreated?' his beautiful sidekick offered a tongue-in-cheek contribution. 'Reprogrammed?'

'Reprogrammed? You think I'm a robot? Thanks a lot, angel. What about just "Reborn"?'

Their soft banter was definitely reprogramming the young man's soul this evening, after the madness of the day. Sitting with the love of his life in a room that reeked of friendly familiarity, the theme of being reborn refused to leave him. He felt safe, which was new, and loved, which was not so new but no less valued. Overwhelmingly, he felt vindicated, as though all the rejections and rebuttals he had received through his early years had now been redressed.

'Yeah. Go with "Reborn",' Lynn agreed. 'Or redefine "Born Again". It doesn't have to be a religious experience.'

While the imaginative lyricist played with the lines of a verse, she conjured up a piano accompaniment fitting his description, and the song took shape very quickly. By the time the girls returned with the drinks tray and glasses, it had become a well-formed duet. Having abandoned the guitar, Jeff moved to sit beside his accompanist at the bass end of the piano, marvelling at her fingers gliding effortlessly over the keys.

'What's that song?' Tamilla asked, excited. 'Is it new?'

'Brand spanking,' the proud man replied, looking up. 'D'you like it?'

'It sounded very impressive. You play really well, Lynn,' the younger sister gushed, more than a little awestruck.

'Thanks,' the celebrity responded, seasoned at receiving compliments. 'That's kind of you, Tammy.'

The blonde entertainer nudged her reluctant co-writer again playfully and started to sing the next verse. He joined in, soon switching the words to a much dirtier version and causing everyone to laugh. Gerry returned to hear his sisters in their new posts as background vocalists.

'Excuse me! You can't use my client without a signed contract.'

'Piss off, Gerry,' the millionnaire told him, pouring the coffee for everyone. 'Sit down and roll us a joint.'

'Can you guys do "Everlasting" for us?' Jacinta requested. 'I love that song so much. It'd be amazing for you to sing it right here in our house.'

Ever the comic, the rock star searched through his pockets. 'Angel, did you bring the band? We must've left them in Tokyo.'

Shaking her head at his antics, his girlfriend attempted to pick out a piano line that would work, groaning each time it fell apart. 'We could try, but it'll be weird.'

The couple hammed their way through the hit song, much to Jacinta's disgust. She protested and begged them to sing it properly, but they insisted the mood wasn't right and that it didn't work with the piano. To save the day, Tamilla found the seven-inch single she had bought when the song had been released and put it on the record player.

'Shut up, guys. Let's hear the real version.'

'Good idea. Leave it to the professionals,' Jeff agreed, smiling and kissing the top of his lover's head.

While the track was playing, the happy songwriter excused himself to visit the bathroom and to avoid the inevitable heaping of praise. This family stuff was fun, he thought, making his way down the hall. Just like the old days, except way, way better with the addition of the most special guest of all.

Lynn took advantage of the modest star's absence and asked the others if they knew "Light My Fire" by The Doors. She struck up a suitably flammable accompaniment and ran through the lyric with her confused chorus line, suggesting they sing it when Jeff came back. The sisters were suitably puzzled once more, especially at the glint in her eye.

'The Doors is Jeff's favourite band.'

Gerry burst out laughing. 'Good one, Miss D! Very clever.'

The piano rang out until even the tone-deaf accountant joined in. During this rather raucous rehearsal, Celia and Gerald appeared at the door, pausing for their children to finish their particularly rough rendition of the classic hit.

'Do you mind if we join you? It sounds as if you're having a lot of fun down here.'

'Come on in, both,' their son invited, opening the window to flush out some of the smoke and heat they were generating. 'The more the merrier.'

His father spied the clear plastic bag of dope on the side table, next to a lighter and some Rizlas. He had never known his children to roll their own cigarettes.

'Is that what I think it is?' he asked around the room.

'I'm afraid it is, Dad. Do you want one?' Gerry responded, audaciously holding the bag out.

He picked up two joints from the arm of the chair and came clean with only a trace of guilt. His father shook his head disapprovingly. Celia had had more than her fair share of surprises today, valiantly opting to go with the flow.

'Goodness! We're learning much more about our children than we really need to know today.'

Lynn empathised with the confused woman. 'Don't worry, Celia. It's everywhere. My friend, Michelle, told her parents it was dried spinach, and they fell for it.'

Jacinta had disappeared a few moments prior to go in search of her former lover. She located him having a quiet cigarette in the garden, seizing a few moments alone to take stock of the day.

'What are you doing out here?'

'Hey. Just thinking,' the tired man replied. 'It's been a big day, and I had to escape for a while. My brain needs clearing out. What about you?'

The brazen twenty-seven-year-old put her arms around the sexy superstar, pouting her lips to tempt him. 'I came to steal a last kiss.'

'Oh, no you don't,' Jeff mocked, pushing her away. 'I'm off the market.'

'Just a kiss,' Jacinta insisted, full of a touch too much wine. 'Only one little kiss.'

'There's no such thing as one little kiss with you, Jack,' her old friend chuckled. 'Let's go back to the party.'

His mate's elder sister reluctantly gave in, respecting the good-looking man's wishes. There had been a time when he wouldn't have hesitated. She remembered how insatiable he used to be, not to mention how amazing he could make her feel. These days, all that pure carnality and sexual prowess was being devoted to just one woman. To Lynn Dyson, no less.

'You're so boring now,' she whined.

'Maybe so,' the millionnaire admitted with no sign of regret, opening the French doors for the elder sister to pass through into the hallway.

The pair arrived back at the den in the middle of a bout of cacophonous laughter. Jacinta was astonished to see her mum and dad had chosen to join them, and Lynn glanced up from the piano to see the old flames returning together, which flashed a pang of guilt through Jeff's heart. He earnestly hoped his dream girl wouldn't think he had been renewing their alliance, because nothing could have been further from his mind.

'Tickets, please,' the star requested casually, holding his hand out to each parent.

Everyone laughed, and the classically-trained musician began to wind her fingers around the opening bars of "Light My Fire". On their cue, the others joined in, without exception having trouble keeping straight faces. It took no more than a few seconds for her boyfriend to realise the joke was at his expense.

'Very funny,' he sneered.

In truth, he was none too amused, though man enough to know he should get over himself. 'Did you put them up to this?' he waved a scolding finger at Lynn, who shrugged back innocently.

There was nothing Jeff's wounded ego could have done about it anyway, since the Blakes were off and running. They each sang over each other with different verses, with their bandleader doing her best to keep the rabble together from the piano. His humiliation dissipating, he joined in, still propping up the doorframe. Once they were finished, he made his way back through the crowded room, climbing over several pairs of legs, and sat back down next to his dream girl.

'You'll pay for that,' he whispered in her ear and then kissed her smiling lips. 'I love you.'

'I love you too.'

'Can you read my mind?'

The young woman shook her head, wondering why he had tensed up again. 'No. What's wrong?'

'Nothing, I hope. Tell you later.'

Lynn leaned against him, drawing a smiley face in the air with her index finger. After a few seconds, the songwriter's anxiety subsided, and he kissed the back of her hand like a true gentleman.

'Next!' he proclaimed.

Winking impishly and sliding the young beauty's hips along the piano stool until she almost tipped off the end, the songwriter began playing the riff of "Love Me Till Tomorrow", another monster hit which had been recorded by several artists in the US and Great Britain since its release.

'Get up there, girls. Time to dance. And you, Celia!'

After some resistance, the grandmother-to-be was permitted to stay seated. Nevertheless, she joined in with the vocals, and the performer was stoked to see that even Gerald knew the words. Watching Lynn Dyson sing his songs would never lose its spine-tingling appeal, and his fears began to retreat into the nether reaches of his brain. When this song came to an end, the humble rocker felt it was time to dish out some of his famed reciprocity, striking up a busker's interpretation of "Guilty Pleasure", which had been a huge Number One for his beautiful best friend only a few months earlier.

'Christ!' Jeff laughed, as he attempted to keep pace with the enthusiastic females belting out the chorus. 'I'm ashamed to admit I don't know how to play half of this.'

Lynn left their makeshift stage and sat back down at the piano. 'You play the guitar,' the diva instructed, flicking a melodramatic hand.

The rocker was indeed more comfortable augmenting his girlfriend's dextrous keyboard flair with guitar-based percussion, and it also afforded him the opportunity to survey the scene. He was the common denominator between these people who were all enjoying themselves, some more harmoniously than others. This was what life ought to be about, he concluded. This was what was important.

By now, Gerry had lit both joints and passed one to his sisters to share. The guitarist signalled for a puff, and the older man obliged, feeding it to his friend like a baby while he strummed out the rhythm. Sensing the smoke curl through his lungs and up into his brain, the flamboyant musician tossed his head back, shaking his long, black mane and rolling his eyes like a wild animal, causing the girls to swoon, including Celia.

'God, you are so sexy!' Tamilla shouted. 'Do that again!'

Jacinta scolded her sister. 'Tammy, shut up. He's off the market!'

Flattered by their reaction, Jeff looked sideways at Lynn and hoped she wasn't too offended. He dared to presume she understood that whatever had happened between him and Gerry's sisters was well and truly in the past, despite their continuing devillish behaviour. He needn't have worried. A wide smile soon put his mind at rest.

The night rolled on, and seeing the marijuana being freely passed around, the Blake parents concluded that discretion was in order and took their leave.

'Thanks for entertaining us old folks so well,' Gerald said, his eyes focussing on the fresh-faced blonde who had so far abstained from the illicit substance. 'It's quite like the olden days, but much higher quality this time.'

Celia made her way around the room, kissing everyone in turn. 'Goodnight, darlings. Have fun, and we'll see you in the morning. A last breakfast together before you go.'

The friendly group took a rest from the music and poured themselves a selection of liqueurs from the tray. The joints continued to circulate, and everyone began to feel very mellow indeed. Jeff moved the piano stool closer to the wall, leaned back and invited Lynn to sit on his lap. He wrapped his arms around her, offering her a drag. She declined again but sniffed in the residual smoke anyway.

'D'you want anything else?' he asked, strangely proud of the young woman's abstemiousness.

He knew the tennis champion had a big New Year's Day assessment ahead of her and had already fallen behind in her preparation on account of their getaway Christmas. They also had a great deal to do before departing for London, and the songwriter recognised that the majority of this organisation would be undertaken by someone other than him. The changed man made a silent resolution to correct this imbalance tomorrow.

'No, thanks,' the gorgeous bundle in his arms replied, leaning back into the warm, welcoming body. 'I'm fine, and this is so much fun. I'm perfectly happy watching you all descend into oblivion.'

'You outbraved me today, mate,' Jeff teased his old friend, relaxing into Lynn's softness. 'Thanks for taking the heat off.'

'Yeah. Bloody stupid timing, wasn't it?' Gerry replied, remembering his confession through the haze. 'I thought about that afterwards. I knew you'd notice too, you bastard!'

'So are you going to get married?' Tamilla asked her brother. 'Would she have you?'

Gerry issued a somewhat lame laugh. 'Negatory! I can't get married. It'd last six months, tops. Can you honestly imagine me married?'

'Jack, put some music on, please,' the younger man asked, in an attempt to change the subject for their unfortunate brother.

And as much for himself, in the event that the question were to move around the room. He was only too aware of how things must look to Gerry's sisters and how easily their tongues loosened after a few drinks. Despite his blissful satisfaction, he was not yet ready for their conversation to travel to such a scary, grown-up place.

'Cheers, mate!' Mister Indomitable raised his brandy glass. 'Nicely done.'

Jacinta had chosen an album for reasons of pure nostalgia, given that it was Christmas and they had a real, live star of stage and screen in their midst. It was the soundtrack to the film "South Pacific", which the sisters had performed endlessly as teenagers. In fact, it had been during one of these raucous rehearsals that they had first stumbled upon their extra brother's supreme musical abilities. She moved the needle across to "I'm Gonna Wash That Man Right Outta My Hair", causing both men to groan aloud.

'Fucking "South Pacific"!' Gerry exclaimed. 'I thought I'd heard the last of this crap years ago.'

'Must be a girl thing,' Lynn laughed. 'It's great, Jack. Leave it on.'

'See?' Jacinta sneered at her brother. 'The discerning amongst us appreciate it.'

The decidedly unappreciative accountant stood up. 'Jeff, ciggie?'

'Awesome idea. Do you mind?' the younger man asked his girlfriend, already extracting himself from the leather-topped bench which was squashed into the corner of the room.

'Of course not. Go!' she urged. 'I'm sure you do a great "Some Enchanted Evening" though.'

'He does!' shrieked Tamilla. 'Boys, please stay?'

But Jeff was already halfway out the door, having deftly picked up the bottle of whisky and two glasses on his way through. Old habits die hard, he thought shamefully, wondering just how many bottles of spirits he had pilfered from this generous family's drinks cabinet over the years. Another wrong to be righted in years to come.

'Nope. It's definitely a girl thing! See ya later.'

The two men let themselves outside, taking care not to leave a gap between flyscreens for the many moths and mosquitoes that would be keen to swap places. They followed the whitewashed walls of the large house until they reached the swimming pool and settled in for the more peaceful concert of cicadas and bullfrogs. It was a warm, balmy night, and the sing-along in the den was barely audible. The businessman produced another joint from his pocket and lit it, while his millionnaire client poured the whisky.

'Fuck!' Gerry cursed, sounding tired. 'What a God-awful day!'

'Yep. Agreed. You OK with all the baby talk?'

The older man took a long drag on the roll-up and passed it over, considering his response carefully. 'I don't know what to do, to tell you the truth, mate,' he confessed in a serious tone. 'I spoke to Heather before dinner. She was glad to hear from me, but also told me she's going out with someone else now who knows she's pregnant. She doesn't know if it's going to last, but she's got used to the idea of not getting married. Now I'm fucking jealous. Can you believe that?'

'Shit! Nothing's ever simple, is it?' Jeff replied, feeling sorry for his usually happy-go-lucky business partner. 'If she were pining after you, would you have stayed with her after today?'

'I doubt it, but it might've been worthy of consideration. I can see how happy you and Lynn are, and it looks inviting, but then I know I'd get pissed off with all the expectation it generates. Do you really want the whole package now? You know, living together twenty-four by seven?'

The twenty-two-year-old nodded, slurping a large mouthful of whisky. 'Yep. Twenty-five by eight, if I could get it. It is an adjustment though,' he admitted. 'You remember that night when you and Vanessa came round for our curry night?'

'Yes?'

'That was only a matter of minutes after Lynn agreed to move in, and we both felt really weird skating round each other in the apartment. I was ridiculously territorial for quite a while. We were both walking on eggshells the whole time. But then after a few days, the strangeness just dissipated, and everything became pretty natural.'

'OK,' the accountant frowned.

His old friend continued. 'Of course, it helps cushion the blow when we're not at home constantly. It'll be a bit different for us in London, and it'd be even more different with a mum and baby in the house. You'd have to move to a child-friendly environment too. Could you do that?'

'Me in the 'burbs?' Gerry shook his head defiantly. 'I like having South Yarra and the city on my doorstep.'

Through their smoky haze, the two men could now hear the strains of "The Sound of Music" wafting through the air. The affable executive raised his glass to his mate, thanking their lucky stars that they had escaped when they did.

'Jesus!' the musician groaned, shaking the fast emptying whisky bottle. 'We'll have to get another one of these. There's no way I'm going back in there with that racket going on.'

'So, mate... Do you think you've kicked this Post-Traumatic whatever thingo?' his friend asked. 'I had no idea about all this, you know. You did a pretty good job of disguising it for all that time. Did Lynn find out, or did you tell her?'

'I told her,' Jeff answered. 'I'd never stayed the whole night with a woman before, so never had to explain myself to anyone else. She just understands me so well. Fucking hell! I only have to tell her one little piece of information, and she puts the rest together herself. It's bloody amazing. I never used to think there was really such a thing as a soul-mate, but now I'm convinced of it.'

'And the weirdest thing is that you knew in advance. That's what I can't get over,' Gerry chuckled. 'Perhaps it'll happen to me too, one day? Or maybe I'm too insensitive to notice? But what about the Post-Trauma stuff?'

'Who knows?' the younger man replied with a shrug. 'The true test'll be going back to Melbourne. If I can get into my apartment within two minutes, I'll be happy. One step at a time, mate.'

'So you mean to tell me that for as long as I've known you, you haven't been able to get through closed doors?' the company director looked incredulous.

Jeff frowned. 'Yep. God's honest truth. Since I was fourteen or so. If someone else opens them I can, but not opening them myself. What kind of daft, fucked-up thing is that? I developed some pretty ingenious ways of circumventing the problem though.'

'What? Like kicking people's doors down?'

'Yeah. Something like that,' the guest replied, still a little ashamed. 'The doors thing's a problem, but it's the never-ending bloody nightmares that kill me. Going week after week with only a few hours' sleep is fucking exhausting, let me tell you.'

Gerry shook his head. 'So you'll definitely wake up kicking and screaming tonight?'

'Well, it'd be nice to think not, after today,' his mate crossed his fingers. 'But probably, yes. I don't expect they'll go away immediately, but I'm hoping, over time, if I can replace enough shit images with positive ones, they'll gradually fade. Even if it's once a week, it's a hell of a lot better than it is now. And much better for Lynn too. If anything, that's more important for me, to be honest. Now that we're an item officially.'

'Does she get pissed off with you?'

'Not yet,' the melancholy romantic answered, 'but I'm prepared for it.'

With the exception of their business affairs, Jeff had never had such a sensible conversation with his long-time friend. It felt good, so he carried on.

'She has no problem getting back to sleep, which is the saving grace. Sometimes I'm still waiting for my pulse rate to return to normal, and she's already sparko again.'

The accountant fixed his client with a stare. 'Do you think *you'll* get married?'

'Don't you start!' the twenty-two-year-old shouted into the night air. 'For Christ's sake, I thought it was only girls who were obsessed with getting married.'

'I'm not obsessed with it, mate,' the defensive Irishman retorted. 'I just want to know that if I do it, you might join me?'

Jeff felt guilty for his outburst. 'Sorry, mate. I was out of order. But you just said you weren't going to.'

Gerry looked expectant. 'Well?'

'Ask me when I'm sober,' the millionnaire alcoholic dodged. 'I'm too stoned and drunk to give you a reliable answer.'

'Arsehole! You fucking fence-sitter. I'll ring you tomorrow for your considered opinion.'

The celebrity extended his right hand, and the two men shook on it. The music from the den had become much softer, and there was no sign of the girls singing. Paranoia suddenly breaking out, nerves began to jangle around the younger man's head, knowing that his beautiful best friend was once again at the mercy of two former partners whose propensity towards vindictiveness might escalate in inverse proportion to their sobriety.

Jeff raised himself to a standing position with some difficulty, the alcohol driving upwards and the blood draining from his head. 'Should we go back in?'

'S'pose so,' Gerry replied. 'I'm pretty whacked. Time for bed, methinks.'

'Not a bad idea,' the rock star smiled, making a lewd gesture.

His manager winced. 'I walked into that one. Christ! I'm slipping. It's alright for you, Romeo. I've just got a magazine and my left hand.'

Jeff chuckled. 'Shame, mate. Yes. I'll come off better...'

Without warning, the envious man punched his good friend quite hard in the stomach, just underneath his ribcage. 'That's right. Rub it in, why don't you?'

'Mate!' the superstar cried, winded. 'That was uncalled for. I can't take body blows when I'm this tanked.'

'I'm surprised I even made contact,' Gerry sniggered, staggering along the path. 'Apologies, me old cobber!'

The two men wandered back into the house to find the females engrossed in conversation. A stunned silence greeted them at the door however, the topic evidently not for sharing. Gerry bid his sisters and their captivating companion goodnight and slapped Jeff's back on his way out.

'Don't stop on our account,' the dark-haired charmer invited, crouching down in front of his most prized possession. 'Bed?'

The Blake sisters giggled, reminded perhaps of their abandoned story. Their childhood plaything refused to bite, and they soon fell under another princely spell as Lynn extended a graceful hand for him to pull her out of the chair.

'Yes. I'm finished. Can we help with all this mess?'

'No,' Jacinta replied. 'We'll do it in the morning. I'm going up too.'

The piano lid was closed, and the lights in the den flicked off. The four remaining revellers wended their way upstairs and issued their hushed farewells on the landing since the Melburnians were due to leave earlier than the others expected to rise. Lynn moved swiftly to open their bedroom door, not wishing to put her intoxicated but placid bedfellow under any additional pressure after such a long day.

'Cheers,' the grateful man said, closing the door behind them. 'You're too good to me. Way too good.'

'Tomorrow is another day,' his girlfriend smiled, pulling him towards her and kissing him tenderly. 'Are you OK? What was wrong earlier? You looked like you'd seen a ghost.'

The inebriated romantic closed his eyes, feeling the room swinging from side to side. A wave of pure joy washed through his addled mind as he felt confident hands begin to caress him in all the best places. Doing the right thing definitely had its benefits, and he couldn't wait to claim his bounty.

'Oh, don't worry about that. I got over it, and now I'm so OK that I can hardly describe it. I'm stoned, drunk and in the loving arms of the world's most beautiful woman. It'd be impossible for me not to be OK.'

The young woman frowned at the double negative. She was already heading for the bathroom when Jeff took off his shirt to reveal a red mark on his skin where his mate had landed the unexpected but surprisingly coordinated fist, causing her eyebrows to raise.

'Look what Gerry did to me...'

'Gerry? Why? What happened?' Lynn asked, obligingly returning to rub the sore spot.

'He punched me,' her boyfriend moaned like a six-year-old.

'You poor thing! Did you deserve it?'

Laughing, Jeff grabbed her and lifted her onto the bed. 'You don't really care about me, do you? You even made a joke about The Doors...'

'Let me go! Yes, I did. Can I go now, please? Didn't you appreciate it?'

'Yes, I did,' he admitted, allowing his prisoner to jump back onto the floor. 'After I got over the initial sting, that is. Jesus, you're gorgeous! Get out of here. I love it that you're able to play with me like that. I need to be brought down to Earth every now and again.'

The lovers undressed each other and took a cool but steamy shower, tenderly egging each other on until passion won out over comedy for the rest of the night's entertainment. They lay on top of the bed with the window open to the warm summer's night, reliving the events of the day. Lynn switched off the lamp after a while, allowing soft moonlight to stream into the room without its dominant competition. Mellow with the effects of cannabis, red wine and whisky, Jeff took his time to please her in as many ways as his inspired imagination endowed.

'I can't believe how good this feels, considering the day we've had,' he murmured, sensing the inevitable climax. 'I want to go on forever, but I know you must be so tired.'

Lynn nodded and kissed his chest. 'It's perfect. I love you and I want you to be happy.'

Her hot-blooded stallion arched his back and thrust into her in orgasm. He hardly made a sound, but the feeling was so intense that his partner couldn't help but do the same, for the fifth time at least. After freezing in suspension for a couple of seconds, he lowered himself down on top of her, kissing the blushing skin at the base of her neck while the aftershocks from down below continued to ripple through their conjoined bodies.

'Whoa, that was one hell of a ride! Can I say it again? You are so good to me, Lynn Dyson. So bloody good to me.'

'You're worth it, Jeff, but I'm really zonked,' his lover bleated, after a few moments of silence in each others' arms. 'Can we go to sleep now? What a day! It seems like several days rolled into one.'

'You're right. The old flat seems like ages ago already.'

The sportswoman shoved the heavy weight to one side, squeezing a yelp from his sleepy mouth, and retired to the bathroom again. Her spent *paramour* stretched out on top of the bedclothes, slightly sickened by the ceiling fan which appeared to be spinning in the opposite direction to his head. He wondered what sort of night lay ahead of them. *Just one night without a nightmare*, he begged. One whole, peaceful night's sleep for his beautiful best friend, as thanks for her matchless contribution to the day.

'It's only midnight,' Lynn sounded surprised, climbing onto the mattress. 'Feels like three o'clock or something.'

Jeff was unable to respond, staying still with his eyes closed. Tears were clinging to their corners, waiting to roll down his face onto the pillowcase. His compassionate girlfriend kissed first one side and then the other, but still he didn't move.

'Thanks,' he whispered. 'You're fantastic. I love you.'

'I love you too. Are you alright?'

'Yeah. I'm absolutely fine. Just tired and emotional,' a croaky voice answered. 'I just want us to have a good night. I hope I can give you that for once.'

The sincerity of her lover's words hung in the air above them, melting his *Regala*'s heart. 'Don't put pressure on yourself. If it happens, it happens. We'll deal with it.'

Turning over onto his right side to face her, the overwhelmed millionnaire thanked her again for everything she had done. His pulse echoed in his ears. Why did such a simple thing as preparing for sleep put him so on edge?

It was as if Lynn could hear the stress too, consoling him gently. 'You know, we don't have to test the door tomorrow when we get home. We could leave it until we go to London. Then, by the time we set foot in your apartment again, you might be completely OK.'

Jeff smiled. 'I like your optimism, angel, but no. I have to try it. I'm excited about it and scared at the same time, just like this morning. I'll be pretty disappointed if there's no change.'

The teenager kissed the bridge of her courageous boyfriend's nose, where a tear sat poised to cross over from his eye, making a break for the pillow. 'That's why it might be best to leave it,' she argued. 'You don't want to go backwards from today, do you?'

Her lover sighed. 'There you go again with the whole backwards thing. There is no backwards, Miss Dyson. I have to accept whatever I get. No point avoiding it.'

'OK. I'm sorry.'

Exhaustion was stirring up the many substances in his bloodstream, and the caring young woman sensed the lost boy's return, slipping into a self-destructive spiral with the pressure he was heaping on himself. Keen to keep his heart from being kidnapped by Gravity at the end of such an amazing day, Lynn assumed control and decided to call it a night.

'Let's go to sleep now. I'm whacked, as Gerry would say.'

The young man sniffed, rubbing his bruised stomach and oozing with gratitude for the sweet loving to which he had recently been party. 'I'm sure he has by now.'

The refined teenager smacked his arm. 'That's disgusting. Go to sleep!'

'I love you, Lynn,' he added, rolling onto his back and pulling the sheet on top of them.

'I love you too. *Dors bien, mon ami. Je t'adore beaucoup.*'

These simple Gallic phrases put the finishing touch to the polyglot's night, and the playful singer was very happy to hear his breathing slowing within a few minutes until she knew he was almost asleep. Just one more joy trigger would do...

'Jeff?' Lynn whispered. 'Will you sing "Some Enchanted Evening" for me one day, please?'

The drowsy rocker chuckled softly. 'What did they tell you?'

'That you sang it once to my picture, and they were all crying their eyes out at the end.'

Sheepishly, her enigmatic stranger nodded. 'Yep. That's about right. I was extremely drunk that night and very unhappy at the time, but as usual pretending to be happy. Jack and Tammy'd been on at me to sing it for hours. I'd been helping them practise for some school concert or other, but I kept on refusing their request. So in the end, Jack went to get a centrefold picture they had of you in a magazine and held it up in front of me. Jeez, I was so sick of their constant goading that I knew there was only one way to make them stop, so I just let you have it with both barrels.'

The celebrity sighed before giggling in empathetic amusement. 'No wonder you made a hasty exit tonight.'

'You got it! G'night, angel.'

''Night.'

***

Lynn reached her hand across and tipped the clock up to read the time, before replacing it face-down beside her bed. Just after two o'clock. She had woken to the muffled sound of Jeff talking to someone in his sleep. It didn't sound like the normal frenzied shouting match, but he was definitely dreaming. She lay still in the dark and waited in case a nightmare developed in its usual way, her heart cautiously optimistic.

The next thing the young woman knew, it was six-thirty in the morning. The sun was up and cool air was blowing in through the open window. Stealthily, she slipped out of bed to draw the curtains. No nocturnal action whatsoever, she celebrated in silence. Amazing! She was filled with an urge to rouse her bedfellow and tell him, such were her relief and joy.

Did she dare go for a run? After a series of delicious festive meals and the unusual activities of the last few days, the sportswoman was beginning to feel lethargic and ill-prepared for the strenuous tests she was about to undergo on New Year's Day, when her family had their annual appraisals and goal-setting meetings. It would be highly beneficial for her to get out on the open road this morning before flying back to Melbourne, but what might it do to Jeff's mood if he were to wake up alone?

Her handsome stranger's slumber continued peacefully, and no new confrontational spectre lay in waiting for today, save for arriving back home in Melbourne. Had their painful trip back to his childhood home really done the trick? Or perhaps his extended restful period was due to the cocktail of drugs he had taken after dinner? So many questions still to answer!

The young woman decided to take a chance, wrote a note and left it on her pillow with yesterday's red rose. Grabbing her toiletry bag and a towel from the *en suite*, she left the room and deposited them in the downstairs cloakroom, where she would be able to shower quickly upon her return.

The local roads were quiet, and the exclusive Mosman air was especially fresh. Lynn ran quickly towards the beach, following the road which ran parallel with the bridle path they had taken the two previous mornings. As the lactic acid in her legs broke down and the endorphins began to flow, she found herself replete with happiness at the prospect of taking her changed man home and then away to foreign lands.

After half an hour of running northwards, weaving around the coast where the path diverted, the athlete turned around and powered back up the hill. Within no time, she was back at the house and showered, creeping as quietly as she could back up the stairs and into the bedroom. It was with considerable satisfaction that her eyes alighted on the rose still languishing across the torn piece of paper.

Lynn slipped under the sheet and pulled it up over her shoulders, feeling the mattress move as the hulk next to her stirred briefly. Wonderful, she thought. How happy he would be when he finally woke up! She lay on her back and smiled to herself, feeling her muscles buzzing and listening to light snoring coming from her left. She must have drifted back to sleep quite soon because she awoke again to gentle fingers stroking her face.

'Hey, angel. Wake up. It's nearly nine o'clock. We have to get going.'

'Good morning,' she replied cheerfully, still marvelling at the long stretch of sleep her bedfellow had enjoyed. 'Nine o'clock? Wow! How do you feel?'

'Physically, like shit. But mentally, a million dollars,' Jeff reported. 'Please tell me you didn't have to wake me.'

'I didn't have to wake you,' she crossed her heart with the absolute truth. 'I did hear you mumbling at one point, but it was like you were having a normal conversation. I couldn't understand any of it, and then I fell asleep again. I've been for a run and everything. You hardly moved.'

Lynn could see the sheer elation brimming from her man's eyes, receiving an enthusiastic kiss into the bargain. 'Jesus Christ! Thank you. This is all your fault.'

'It's *our* fault. You taught me the treatment plan, and we made it happen. Don't blame me!' she insisted, laughing. 'I was so excited that you were still asleep that I wanted to wake you up to tell you that you were still asleep.'

'You could've done,' the amused man replied, grimacing in jest at her convoluted explanation. 'If a nightmare was going to happen, it would've been over by then. This is bloody fantastic! I can't really believe it. Are you sure you're not lying to me?'

His girlfriend shook her head and put her right hand on her heart. 'The truth, the whole truth and nothing but the truth. I promise.'

Jeff was already on his feet and raring to go, despite a hangover and a queasy stomach. 'We have to get moving,' he reminded her, before gripping his head.

'Oops,' his dream girl couldn't help but smirk at his misfortune. 'Not good?'

'Shit, no! My head's agony. Don't let me drink or smoke tonight, please?'

'You're a grown-up now. You're in charge of your own destiny.'

The handsome man pointed a long index finger at his spirited partner. 'I can see you're going to be trouble today,' he frowned, trying to smile but only managing a groan before sinking down onto the bed. 'Have we got any painkillers with us?'

Lynn took pity on him, and genuinely this time. She fetched some tablets from the bathroom and offered him a glass of water.

'Drink all of it,' she insisted, 'and then I'll get you another one. You don't want to feel like this on the 'plane.'

Jeff groaned again and lay down flat. 'You're right. I'll be OK in a minute. I need some breakfast, woman. And fast.'

Sniffing haughtily, the nineteen-year-old returned and supervised his consumption of the second glass of water, before getting dressed. 'Your move,' she teased. 'I'm not stopping you!'

The blonde sportswoman grabbed a limp hand and tried to lever the heavyweight to a standing position. There was a sharp knock at the door, at which they glanced down at the invalid's naked body and laughed. He made as quick a bee-line into the bathroom as he could muster, and Lynn reached the door just as it swang open.

Jacinta let herself in. 'So... Did he have nightmares last night?'

'No!' the celebrity crossed her fingers on both hands and lifted them triumphantly in the air. 'He slept the whole night.'

'Yay!' the brunette yelled, hugging their very special guest and gesturing towards the bathroom. 'Is he in there?'

The celebrity nodded.

'Great news, Jeff!'

No response was forthcoming, except for the sound of gushing water.

'Don't shout too loud,' his minder warned with a smile. 'He's not feeling too well...'

Jacinta put her hand on her own head. 'Eugh! Me neither. You're OK though?'

'Yes,' the singer replied, grateful that she had abstained for most of the evening. 'I took it pretty easily, and now I know why.'

Not before time, the inquisitive intruder turned to go. 'Breakfast's nearly ready, by the way.'

All eyes... all bleary eyes, as it happened... were on Jeff Diamond as he walked into the kitchen. Self-consciously, he gave a thumbs-up sign with his left hand and clutched at his temple with the other, engendering a suitable ratio of sympathy and congratulation. Celia administered a hearty, motherly hug to her adopted son and then did the same to Lynn.

'Well done, you two,' she said. 'That's such good news. Now sit down, and let's eat. It's a real shame you all have to go today.'

After a quick and fairly subdued round of bacon and eggs with all the *accoûtrements*, those southbound gathered their belongings together and waited in the hallway for Gerald to drive the Melburnians to the airport. Jacinta had already departed to see her boyfriend, who was a chef and had been working over the festive period, while Tamilla had returned to bed, nursing her own headache.

'Thanks for everything, Celia,' Jeff insisted, giving the lady of the house a goodbye kiss. 'You guys are amazing. I've had the best Christmas ever.'

'Me too,' Lynn echoed. 'You've given us wonderful hospitality, and I'm sorry we disrupted your family celebrations so much.'

Gerry's mother dismissed the young couple's apologies. 'Nonsense, dears. We're glad we were able to share in everything. And in your news too, my incorrigible boy,' she gushed, turning to hug her son afterwards.

Jeff's manager was feeling as unwell as his client. Gerald suggested the two sorry sights travel in the back seat, giving him the perfect excuse to engage in sensible conversation with someone who was *compos mentis* and particularly attractive. The young men gladly obliged, and everyone wished Celia as cheerful a farewell as their constitutions permitted.

'What a couple of bloody idiots you are,' Blake Senior scoffed. 'You'd think you'd never had a drink before in your life. I bet your brother doesn't do this, eh, Lynn?'

The sophisticated young lady smiled. 'Oh, I'm sure he has, a few times. Just not in front of our dad.'

Gerald tutted. 'So you're all the same then. Fine examples of modern Australian manhood.'

Their trip to the airport and journey home were uneventful. The TAA flight staff were excited to have their famous passengers on board, quickly surmising that they were better off left well alone. With both men sleeping off their pain, the famous musician ignored the fact that she was the centre of everyone's attention and took refuge in the newspaper for a while, before she too fell asleep.

Rain was lashing the aeroplane's fuselage when it made a bumpy landing in Melbourne. Jeff was beginning to feel a little better and pacified the nearby rows of fans with his own inimitable brand of humorous "As and Ps". His manager, however, was still very much under the weather. The taxi dropped him off at his South Yarra apartment first, where the two men clung onto each other for moral support for several seconds, much to the driver's amusement.

'They had a good Christmas,' Lynn told the plump, good-natured Turk, as she coaxed her boyfriend back into the cab. 'You'll see each other again in two days' time, boys.'

'You owe me a phone call,' Gerry sneered at his old friend, as the taxi's wheels began to turn.

The younger man waved in acknowledgement, sinking back into the seat. Sighing contentedly, he slipped his hand onto his girlfriend's thigh and squeezed it affectionately. The phrase "Countdown to London" looped endlessly around his lethargic brain, generating anticipation galore.

'Now here's the plan,' the patient woman explained, as they headed north on Chapel Street towards the river. 'I'll go up first and let myself in, then you follow whenever you're ready. OK?'

'Aye, aye, captain. Whatever you say.'

The pair rehearsed some stage banter for the Blake & Partners' New Year's Eve *cabaret* to prevent the nerves from taking hold. Before long, they were within a kilometre of the multi-point intersection. His apartment block came into view, and Jeff predictably began to feel his heart rate climbing again. It wasn't quite the usual panic this time. Rather, he hoped his reaction was more due to excitement than to anxiety.

Once out of the taxi and inside the ground-floor lobby, the pair followed the plan to the letter. The songwriter waited downstairs with the suitcases, his heart bursting with emotional lyrics which were in danger of spilling out onto the floor if he didn't write them down soon. He applied the brakes by visualising the next few minutes, when he would once again walk into the arms of his dream girl. It had been a truly amazing Christmas.

Checking his watch, Jeff delved into his jeans' pocket for his keys, staring moronically at them for a few moments. *This had better work*, he thought, pressing the lift call button. Placing the three large pieces of luggage inside, he stepped in just as the doors closed. At least that would have been funny, his warped mind teased. Fancy Lynn meeting only a set of suitcases on the penthouse floor! He shook his head, anxiety increasing as the floors went by. At the top, he was pleased not to hear anything from the apartment across the hall.

This was it. The man who had everything had sobered up for his big test; the moment when he would discover if he was living in the past or in the future. He felt suddenly sick again. Thinking of his perfect flatmate inside, most likely putting on a pot of coffee primarily for his benefit, he inserted the key into the front door lock. Familiar voices and images began to approach at the periphery of his consciousness, but he kept them at bay simply by concentrating on the vision of loveliness he knew to be inside. Bizarrely,

"Some Enchanted Evening" drifted into his mind. It made him smile, and the key turned without any further drama.

There was but a brief rush of panic as he crossed the threshold, lasting only until he saw Lynn standing in front of him.

And then it was gone. His heart pounded behind his ribs, and his hands were sweating, but Gravity and his cronies had left and taken his miserable angst with them.

'Honey, I'm home!'

The young celebrity lunged towards the loudmouth and hugged him tightly, being instantly propelled into the air and rotated at great speed. After a few turns, Jeff became so giddy that the helicoptering pair nearly ended up on the floor. Thudding his shoulder against the wall to right themselves, he locked his saviour in a long, passionate kiss.

'Welcome to your apartment,' she panted, revelling in the thrilled expression on her lover's face. 'How was it for you?'

'The best,' he replied, holding her at arms' length to take issue with her greeting. 'Welcome to *our* apartment.'

The pair walked into the bedroom with their suitcases, and Jeff paused, silent and motionless for several minutes, as if taunting the demons to reappear. Lynn left him plunging the depths of his own mind, hoping a strong cup of coffee would seal his positive fate. Not seeking to count their chickens too early, she wanted to find a special way to celebrate a successful homecoming and set about leafing through the Arts and Entertainment section of the newspaper.

Anything but a movie, the teenager remembered. The cinema presented another hurdle they would need to cross at some stage, particularly as many *premières* were to figure in their lives over the coming years. She turned the pages and read through the many sporting and cultural events that their home town was putting on to serve the peak holiday tourist season. The funfair in Alexandra Gardens might be worth a visit, providing her man's hangover was under control by then.

Her flatmate, meanwhile, had completed his research project, even having let himself out and back in through the front door a couple of times. The ill effects were minimal, and he was filled with a lazy equanimity which he didn't quite recognise as his own. Deciding to search for another, much more appealing presence in his apartment, Jeff entered the kitchen and looped his arms around the beautiful blonde.

Kissing her neck sensually, he peered over her shoulder. 'What are you looking for?'

His *Regala* didn't turn around or even attempt to hand him his coffee. It felt so good to have him hold her, knowing how peaceful he must feel. Against her back, his heart rate seemed reasonably high, but his breathing was no heavier than normal. Barely discernible, in fact.

'Just wondering if there was anything on in town that we could do tonight.'

'Good idea.'

The sexy, masculine voice which the young singer had grown to love was laden with a different sonority today, deeper and somehow more prepossessing. It educed an acute physical response deep within the sensitive woman, almost primæval and most definitely carnal. The tall frame behind her shifted ever so slightly, registering her reaction also.

Lynn carried on reading, enjoying the warmth of her boyfriend's body and pointing out the odd advertisement here and there, to see if any met with his approval. On any other day, he would have demanded she pass him his coffee and lavish him with her affection, yet this morning he did neither. With a shivery brush of his lips on the side of her neck, he simply sat down at the kitchen table, picked up his mug and began to read another section of The Age.

The nineteen-year-old could almost feel the undercurrent of happy turmoil floating through the air as their eyes met. Anticipating that the confused songwriter was about to relent and launch into another apology or expression of gratitude, his determined therapist locked eyes with him.

'That's it now,' she asserted. 'I know you're going to thank me again, but don't. It's over. No more thank-yous or sorries. I understand and I'm so, so, so happy for you.'

Jeff raised his hand in acknowledgement and remained quiet, merely shaking his head at his own transparency. How did this woman understand him so well? After thirty seconds or so, he drained his drink, left the table and exited the kitchen with nothing more than a friendly squeeze of her shoulder. Lynn soon heard strains of piano music filling the lounge room and took them as her cue to stay exactly where she was.

If this was the work of an obsessive autocrat who was trying to manipulate her into joining him, from now on his concubine would refuse to comply. And if it was not, it didn't matter, because this was the clearest indication yet that all was already right in their world. No doubt about it, things were going to be very different from now on.

With her New Year's resolution firming in her mind, the confident superstar was suddenly hit with a slight panic attack herself. What if losing his compulsive edge were to turn Jeff into someone a little too normal? What if the devotion she felt from a man so desperate to have her share his life were to subside and be replaced by the type of behaviour about which her girlfriends often complained? Broken promises and being taken for granted had never factored in this re-instigated coupling, but perhaps these all-too-common traits in her friends' partners might now start to manifest in hers too.

No, the optimist convinced herself vehemently. That wasn't this gorgeous man's style. For those who most mattered, he was unfailingly honourable. Plus, she didn't take Jeff for granted, so why should she expect it from him? Theirs was a relationship based on a solid set of shared ideals. It was bound to work. They meant too much to each other to throw their happiness away for a casual betrayal.

After about ten minutes of uncharacteristic solitude, Lynn's curiosity got the better of her. The piano was no longer playing, and not a single sound ran through the apartment. It was eerie, in fact. She wandered into the living room, only to find it empty. To her delight, Jeff was outside on the balcony with a cigarette and a new book on contemporary philosophers which she had bestowed on him before they had flown to Sydney.

Perfect, the happy woman smiled at the tranquil sight. No big statements. No clamouring for attention. Just the calm intellectual she knew her man desperately wanted to be. A wide smile met her gaze as she stepped through the glass door onto the balcony, and then followed her in admiration until she stood close enough to touch.

'This is great,' she said, sitting down on the chair opposite and stroking his outstretched palm. 'How are you?'

'Well, thanks.'

Marking his page with the glossy sleeve, her man closed the book and stubbed out his cigarette. He expelled the last of its smoke sexily out of his mouth, and turned his hand over to clasp hers before it retreated. Tears filled Lynn's eyes, and she tried valiantly to quell them. This was hardly the time for *her* to start making big statements.

The majestic and heart-stoppingly handsome rock star nodded and squeezed her hand. 'What's up?'

'Nothing,' she flicked her long hair over her shoulder. 'It's just that you've never said "well" before. Only "fine". Was that deliberate?'

Empathetic eyes reassured her. 'It's OK for you to cry, angel. It's your turn.'

'No. I'm not going to,' the young woman refuted, hurriedly wiping her self-conscious cheeks. 'I've had a fantastic Christmas, and it's time to get moving on other things. I need to go to the Sportsdrome to get some serious training in for Wednesday. I just know Dad'll have some extra-special treats waiting for me! Do we need to do anything to help Gerry for the party?'

Jeff looked at his watch. 'I need to ring him but won't do it 'til later. He'll have gone to bed, I reckon. I'll find out what the go is by the time you get back. Exercise is a bloody good idea, I have to say... to blast out all these toxins... but I can't be bothered.'

His beautiful best friend stood up and came round the table towards him, fully expecting to be pulled down onto his lap. Instead, her ennobled intellectual did the same, meeting her halfway. The lovers lingered together momentarily in the bright midday sunshine, engrossed in unspoken dreams.

'So this is really it, angel,' he whispered, kissing her and holding her close. 'This is our future. *Notre vie singulière. Nuestra vida singular.* Our life singular.'

The assorted translations of the celebrities' coined catchphrase rolled off his tongue, their prophesy pendulous in the air until it fully absorbed itself into their souls through a strange, ethereal osmosis. Then, floating on air, the couple sauntered back into the apartment hand in hand. Dark clouds were rolling in from the west, prompting Jeff to slide the door closed in order to prevent the wind from sending his overabundance of disorganised lyric sheets flying around the lounge room.

Lynn danced round in a circle, as if caught up in the heady romance of her poet's words. 'Might be a storm. It's still so humid,' she glanced back over her shoulder to see where Jeff was. '*Una vida singular*. Oh, I so love that expression. Almost sounds like a magic spell. Singular meaning only one and singular meaning unique. Very clever.'

'Glad you like it,' her partner nodded. 'You can add extraordinary to that list of synonyms too. That's what I want for us. Two people, one life. And one unique and extraordinary life. Perfect, you gorgeous genius.'

Filled with fanciful notions of their life singular, both set about unpacking their suitcases and figuring out what they needed to prepare for Gerry's New Year extravaganza. Most of Jeff's clothes ended up on the floor, as usual.

'Is that all for the wash?' Lynn asked.

He looked up at his flatmate from the other side of the bed and unleashed a mischievous grin. 'OK, OK! I'll sort it out. I'm just a man, remember?'

His dream girl shot him a killer look before disappearing without comment into the bathroom to change into sports clothes. Chuckling to himself, Jeff set about transforming his bomb site, and she emerged a few minutes later to find everything in its rightful place.

'¡*Excelente!*'

'I'm going to bed for a while,' her mystery man announced, to her further surprise. 'I'll get some supplies in later, while you're gone.'

Lynn kissed him, rubbing his back and feeling him scrunch his shoulder blades in pleasure. 'Sounds great. Sleep well. See you in about four hours or so. I love you.'

'I love you too. Take it easy, angel.'

Seeing sheets being peeled back without recourse to sex, the speechless woman closed the door on the darkened room and left the apartment. Take it easy? "Take it easy" had never made its way into the Jeff Diamond songbook before! She was extremely content with how their return to Melbourne had panned out so far. Her complicated lover seemed well in control, and they been granted a calm, shared certainty which set her heart aglow.

***

It was after six o'clock in the evening when Lynn finally left the Sportsdrome. Her brothers and father had also been there, and the athletic family had endured and enjoyed a productive training session. Bart had not passed comment on his elder daughter's absence from the family Christmas celebrations and had even asked after Jeff's wellbeing. Sandy had performed much better than expected, with his dad making a special effort to congratulate him in front of his elder brother.

Turning the car she had borrowed from Dyson Administration into the space next to the secure steel container that housed Jeff's already moth-balled Aston Martin, for the first time since she had moved in, Lynn felt as if she was coming home. Typical, she thought. Just when they were moving overseas...

Everything was quiet when the sportswoman entered the apartment. Was Jeff out buying groceries at this hour? Dumping her bag inside the door, she noticed the main bedroom was still darkened. Her man was sleeping soundly, and there was no sign of him having moved since she left. Ecstatic, she picked up the laundry basket and busied herself with getting some washing done.

The refrigerator was indeed virtually empty after their trip to Sydney. Famished from her long training session, Lynn realised that she would have to sharpen up her act too with regard to division of labour in their new life singular. She and Jeff were equally recognisable, and therefore just as easily impeded in everyday pursuits, so she could hardly expect him to continue to run the supermarket gauntlet on her behalf.

Scribbling a quick note and leaving it on his bedside table, the young woman headed back out and down to street level again. Luckily, the city was emptying out after a slow post-Christmas working day. She was very much the amateur shopper when it came to food and household items, since such necessities had always had a habit of arriving by magical means in her privileged life. She decided to make for a Chinese-run supermarket a few streets away, which was likely to be the only place still open at this time. Its shelves displayed so many tasty items left over from the festive feasting season that she felt like a child in a lolly shop. Not very grown-up, she scolded herself.

The shopping bags weighed heavier and heavier as the blonde star walked back unobstructed to the north-eastern corner of the city grid. She successfully fended off some excited tourists on the edge of the Greek precinct and managed the rest of the journey unscathed. Stepping out of the lift on level sixteen, she came face to face with a man whom she assumed was Jeff's neighbour. And her neighbour too, these days.

'Good evening,' the man greeted her politely, after a distinct double-take. 'Excuse me, but aren't you Lynn Dyson?'

The sophisticated young lady put down her bags and extended her hand. 'Yes, I am.'

'Wow!' the man exclaimed. 'Are you with Jeff? His girlfriend, I mean?'

Lynn nodded. 'We try to keep a low profile, but yes. You're back for Christmas then? Jeff told me you live in Singapore most of the time.'

'That's right, I do. I'm only here until Tuesday, then it's back up there for New Year's. I'm Pete, by the way. Peter Bourke. I run a small investment firm in Singapore, trading Aussie securities mainly.'

'Hi, Pete. Nice to meet you. A very Melbourne name you have,' the celebrity diplomat chatted. 'We were in Sydney over Christmas. You must come over for a drink before you go. Don't know if Jeff already told you, but we're moving to London next week for a year. I'll have a word with him and see what we can arrange.'

The man next door was stoked. 'Excellent! Wow! Lynn Dyson living next door! Thanks. I'd love that. Jeff's a good bloke, but we've only met a couple of times since he's lived here. Just give me a knock whenever.'

'We will. Maybe tomorrow?'

Pete handed the attractive woman his business card, still unable to believe his luck. 'Fantastic to meet you,' he gushed. 'Just wait till I tell my mates!'

Lynn let herself into a silent apartment for the second time that day. Incredible! Her dormant flatmate was stretched out in exactly the same position as when she had left. He would never sleep tonight, she thought, although it was actually very handy to have some time to herself after such a hectic few days. She put away the groceries and made herself something quick to eat, ravenous after four hours of strenuous exercise.

Settling down in front of the television, she began to sift through the bundle of post which had been left for her at Admin. At nine o'clock, she checked in on Jeff again. Dead to the world. It was lucky she hadn't invited Pete in for a drink this evening after all! At ten-thirty, bored with the holiday season television programming, the teenager decided to join Sleeping Beauty, who didn't so much as stir while she brushed her teeth, undressed and slipped under the sheet beside him. The experience felt more than a little odd, given his normal relentless exuberance around her, but being accepted into his bed with this new level of surety uplifted her spirits at the same time.

Saturday morning was the same story. The nineteen-year-old woke at seven o'clock and lay listening to the sound of regular breathing. It lulled her back to sleep again for another half-hour, but by then she was wide awake. She rang Michelle and arranged to meet for a run and breakfast. Happily, she replaced yesterday's groceries note with today's running note and left the apartment again.

Her childhood friend was already on the corner by the gate to the Botanic Gardens when Lynn arrived. 'Merry Christmas! How was Sydney?'

'Thanks. Merry Christmas to you too,' the celebrity replied, as the two girls exchanged air kisses in true Toorak fashion. 'Sydney was great, thanks. We had a fantastic time. Gerry's family's lovely. How was yours?'

The pair stretched for a few minutes before commencing their run along the gravel track known as "The Tan". It seemed like the whole population of Melbourne was out for its morning exercise; some with dogs, some with children. All were pointing, shouting, whispering and waving at Lynn, as per usual. At least when moving at a healthy lick, there was no obligation to give more than a fleeting acknowledgement to her many admirers.

'Where's Jeff now?' Michelle asked.

'Sleeping!' the blonde athlete exclaimed. 'He's been asleep for nearly a whole day! It's beginning to get lonely in the apartment. It's so quiet.'

The two young women chatted about their lives, running fluidly along the track's two kilometre incline. Only when scaling Anderson's Hill for the third time did they pause from babbling and slow up a little, focussing their motivation on breakfast. They succeeded in finding a table for two in the corner of a crowded café, and the red-haired law student helped her famous friend to remain as anonymous as possible by shielding her from view.

'I can't believe we're leaving in a week's time,' Lynn said dreamily. 'I'm going to miss you for a second time. You must come over when you can.'

Michelle laughed. 'Just try and stop me! I can't wait to come over, but not 'til the spring. I don't want to freeze. Maybe May or June? What about for Wimbledon? Do you know what you're doing yet, sports calendar and gigs, *et cetera*?'

'No. Not too much anyway,' her friend admitted. 'Wimbledon would be great. We're trying not to make too many plans for the first few months, while we settle in and start our courses. I don't know how busy I'll be with music, but tennis is scary huge this year.'

It was decided over their meal that both would return to the apartment after breakfast, with a view to braving the shopping crowds on Chapel Street. The telephone rang while Michelle was in the shower, and Lynn ran quickly to answer it.

'Hello?'

'Lynn, hi! It's Gerry,' came a familiar voice from the other end. 'How're you going?'

'Fine, Gerry, thanks. And you?'

'Great. Better than this time yesterday. Is my client available?'

The singer laughed. 'Well, he's here. But no, he's unavailable at the moment, sir. He's sleeping.'

'Oh, for God's sake! It's after eleven,' the accountant sounded perturbed. 'What've you done to him? He's becoming a right lazy oaf.'

Lynn chose to overlook the accusation. 'He's been asleep since yesterday lunchtime, if you must know,' she teased her boyfriend's manager. 'I'm going out with a friend now, so I'll leave him another note to ring you. Are you at home or at the office? Can we help with anything for the party?'

'Thanks, but no. I'm at home. All under control, methinks. Come early though. By seven-ish, so you can help me greet everyone.'

'OK. No problem. See you then. Let us know if anything changes. Bye, Gerry.'

With all the noise having suddenly broken out in the apartment, of showering and telephone calls and such, the nineteen-year-old felt sure that her sleeping giant would have woken by now. She checked in on him before leaving for their shopping trip. He had turned over but was still sound asleep, looking unusually at peace, and she hoped at last he was dreaming happy dreams. He had many years' worth of catching up to do.

'Looks like he's going to sleep for a year,' the superstar told her friend as they travelled down to the basement car park. 'I'm going to have to wake him soon, or he'll miss the flight to London.'

The blonde and the redhead made their way through hoards of excited onlookers, bound for the upmarket stores which provided safe haven for famous shoppers. Within an hour or two, they had uncovered a number of bargains. The morning had been a good chance for them to catch up with each other after the chaos of the last few months. Lynn had been away more than she had been at home since her official return from the US, and the two women had plenty of gossip to share.

By four-thirty, sufficient retail therapy had been applied to last for a couple of months. The celebrity drove Michelle home and stayed for a cup of tea to bid another goodbye to her father and brother. Once back at the apartment building, she grabbed her purchases out of the boot and ascended once more to the penthouse floor. Surely Jeff would be awake by now? Solitude in his presence would soon verge on tedium if not.

The bedroom and its eternal denizen remained in the same state. His girlfriend suspected there may have been some movement, given the fact that her notes were lying on the carpet. The wind from the open window could just as easily have blown them there, leaving her unconvinced either way. There was certainly no evidence of any consciousness, but at least the human being in the bed was still breathing. Was there such a thing as too much sleep?

Sunday evening alone. Lynn left yet another note and headed to Admin to make use of the office facilities. She would take advantage of this unexpected hiatus to ensure their travel plans and her other correspondence were completely up-to-date. With any luck, the gregarious star might even run into someone she could talk to. She never knew that moving in with Jeff would be so exciting!

She was in luck. Her mother and sister were in residence, having also been shopping that day. They decided to head out to Lygon Street for a pizza. Lynn made excuses for her boyfriend's extended rest period without giving away the whole story, leading Marianna to express a wistful desire to sleep for thirty-six hours herself.

Safely returned to the apartment by nine-thirty, the young woman finished her planning checklists and watched some television before crawling into bed at around eleven. Jeff stirred a little as she pulled the sheet over her, and she thought he was about to wake up. She lay staring at his eyelids for a while, waiting for them to open. But no.

Fondly, the pretty teenager stroked his bare shoulder and whispered a brief message of love that she hoped would reach his slumbering soul. She must have fallen asleep fairly quickly, and in the morning woke gently to music playing and the smell of fresh coffee brewing. Looking across to her left, the other side of the bed was empty. Halleluja!

'Good morning!' Lynn cheered when she found her boyfriend in the kitchen reading the newspaper. 'What time did you wake up?'

Pleased to see his dream girl up and about, the handsome man stood up and gave her a powerful bear hug. Her long, blonde hair was delightfully ruffled, and her silk bathrobe revealed just enough to fire his imagination.

And her touch...

'Whoa, hands off! You set me alight, lady. *Buenos días*. Not long ago. Probably twenty minutes, max'. Sorry I slept so long.'

Lynn laughed. 'That's OK. It gave me heaps of time to meet up with everyone, and I'm super-organised for our departure. How are you feeling?'

'Why? Where've you been?'

'You haven't seen the pile of notes I've left you, have you?'

His girlfriend had a smile on her face, realising that Jeff obviously had no idea how long he had been out for the count. She glanced at the clock on the oven, which told her it was just after eight o'clock. He shook his head, confused by her demeanour, returning to read the date on the newspaper.

'*Digame...* We came home on Friday, right?'

Lynn nodded. '*Sí.*'

The intrigued lover watched another smile spread over his flatmate's face. 'And this is Sunday's paper, and you haven't been out anywhere this morning?'

'No.'

Wonderstruck, Jeff ran his left hand through his hair. 'Which means this is Monday morning.'

'It does indeed,' the young woman confirmed, putting her arms around him. 'You've been asleep for forty-three hours straight.'

'Christ Almighty! No way!' her boyfriend whooped, now with both hands on his disbelieving head. 'Forty-three hours? I must've been knackered.'

'No shit!' his dream girl impersonated him lovingly. 'You've got a pretty big overdraft to pay off, remember? It's going to take a while to discover what normal sleep pattern you actually need, I suppose. For the first time in so long, your body's been able to decide for itself when to wake you up.'

Jeff poured out two mugs of coffee, still dumbfounded by the news and deep in reflection. 'S'pose so. Sounds logical.'

The excited teenager continued, accepting an invitation to sit on a lap incapable of betraying its owner's innermost thoughts. 'Gerry phoned, saying he was waiting for a call from you. He didn't say what about. Yeah, and I met Pete Bourke from next door. I sort of invited him in for a drink, so we'll have to decide when. Tonight?'

'Sure! Why not? Lucky you didn't arrange something for last night,' he replied, eyes wide with amazement.

'How do you know I didn't?'

'Because you wouldn't,' her relaxed lover answered.

Lynn took both his hands in hers, shuffling against a full erection. 'No, I wouldn't. We should knock on his door today though. He's leaving for Singapore again tomorrow. What do you want to do today?'

Jeff hugged her close, relishing the silk as it slithered against her breasts and moaning when her fingers brushed the tip of his penis through his shorts. 'What do you think? Jeez, I'm still reeling, angel. We should get out of here anyway. Brekkie somewhere? How about meeting Suzanne and Steve? They'll be up by now. Shall I give her a ring?'

'Perfect,' the happy musician agreed.

Her formerly enigmatic stranger went into the lounge room and dialled Suzanne's number. Lynn followed and stood behind him as he sat on the couch, waiting for the call to connect. She began to run her fingers through his long, unwashed hair, coaxing his head back until it rested on her abdomen.

'Suzie-Anna. Merry Christmas! Yep. Good, thanks. You? Oh, yeah. They spoiled us rotten, as usual. Hey, listen... D'you guys want to have brekkie with us this morning? Anywhere. Ten's good. Let me check... Ten o'clock in St Kilda?'

Jeff craned his neck round, nestling into the soft material of Lynn's robe and registering her agreement, endeavouring to resist the sensuous movement of her hands down the back of his neck and on round his shoulders to his chest.

'Yeah, Suzie. We'll see you on Acland Street somewhere. Pick a place, and we'll find you. Great! *Adios, amiga.*'

The amorous young man put the telephone down and turned to kneel against the back of the couch. 'You're driving me effing crazy, doing that while I'm trying to have a sensible conversation. It was so good though. Look what you've done.'

Jeff grinned, pointing to where the fabric of his boxers was at full stretch, leaning over so far in his attempt to kiss his evasive girlfriend that the couch nearly tipped over. 'Come back to bed,' he begged. 'I miss it already and I've definitely missed you.'

Lynn beckoned suggestively for him to follow her. Hungry to play, the eager man stepped onto the back of the couch with one foot, causing it to pivot on its rear castors. He tipped backwards and forwards before jumping off and giving chase. The leather sofa rocked back into position, echoing its indignance on the floorboards.

'Take that, downstairs neighbours, whoever you are!' Jeff yelled at the top of his voice.

Back in the bedroom once again, the energetic lover snared his beautiful best friend and flopped backwards onto the bed. 'You are fabulous,' he crooned, soft and low.

Lynn kissed him. 'So are you. You're like a different person,' she said directly into his ear. 'The frantic edge has gone, and your voice is much, much lower. It's as if the real you has finally arrived.'

Her boyfriend caught his breath and paused to absorb her appraisal. 'Is that really what it's like to you?'

'Absolutely! I can't explain it any other way. The you who's been waiting in the wings for the right time to come on stage.'

'I do feel different,' Jeff was clearly ecstatic. 'Can't put my finger on how, but I feel weirdly jubilant. Did you spike my coffee?'

'No! You made it! Natural high, *mon ami*. Isn't that what you wanted?'

Undressing in a hurry and caressing each other all over, Lynn gazed into dancing eyes. 'Before, you would've asked me if I still loved you after a comment like that.'

'Would I?'

'Yes, I'm sure,' she affirmed. 'So hopefully the insecurity's gone too. I do still love you and I *will* always love you, and now you somehow accept it.'

Jeff thrust his aching organ inside her when the time was exactly right and stroked with such purpose that the young woman cried out. She knew he was trying to distract himself from the raw emotion, waiting patiently for whatever comic prevarication he might dole out instead. He almost made it too, but lapsed at the last minute.

'That's good, because I'm not letting you go. Not ever.'

The nineteen-year-old came quickly, grabbing his hips. Her gorgeous partner let slip that he felt so clear-headed and was experiencing everything in finer detail than before. True enough, every tiny shudder she issued aroused him rampantly, each sharp breath and gentle moan like sweet music. He fought the urge to immediately follow her orgasm, bringing himself deftly back from the brink. Fleetingly suspended in exquisite symmetry, he turned her stunning body over in one slow, smooth move.

'This is like a ballet,' Lynn sighed, looking down on this new man of hers. 'You've gone from sexual mercenary to sexual poet. I don't know what it is you're doing differently, but it's really, really fantastic.'

Jeff couldn't speak. He pulled her warm, slender body down on top of him and kissed her smiling lips as he came, switching to slow motion until they had almost come to a complete stop. The enamoured woman felt his climax burst through him, sparing none of the tankful of love which had amassed during his mammoth hibernation.

A low roar and wild, penetrating eyes flaunted the violent sensation that could no longer wait to saturate this woman who had performed a miracle. So this was what it was like to feel properly alive, the old soul realised. He had been living under a shroud of weary gloom which had taken the edge off every single experience.

The young man grown old before his time sensed customary anger rise up inside him for a brief moment, while Gravity the troll enumerated the years he had wasted in half-life. It soon subsided however. Lynn's positive words were already penetrating his psyche, persuading him to leave the past behind and capitalise on their current nirvana.

His *Regala* raised herself to sit across his hips and embibed the welcome sight of his senses latching onto the orgasmic pleasure and gradually let it go. 'That was good, wasn't it?'

'Oh, yeah,' Jeff smiled. 'Sexual poet, huh? I like that! I'll have that on my epitaph, please.'

A shiver ran down the sportswoman's spine while he spoke. She wondered whether deeper sexual fulfilment might fuel his addiction or tame it, slightly disturbed that the topic might be tackled with Doctor Friedman in due course. *Don't be stupid*, she read in his eyes. She only had to draw the line. Their life singular would not be sublet to anyone else. That was the whole point.

'Oh, my God!' Lynn shrieked, looking at the clock. 'We're going to be really late.'

'Don't panic!' her black stallion baulked at the consternation in her voice, still meandering his way back from paradise. 'They'll be OK. They can read the 'papers and drink coffee. They won't mind. Come here and be mine for a while longer. I love you so much.'

***

Driving back from St Kilda towards the city, Jeff took an impromptu left turn. It was a beautiful, bright sunny day, and he was feeling on top of the world. He and his dream girl had spent two carefree hours in the company of old friends who had allowed him *carte blanche* to wax lyrical about spending a year in London with his favourite friend.

'Where are we going?' Lynn asked.

'Albert Park Lake,' the driver answered. 'I thought we'd take a walk in the sunshine before we head off into the cold, grey, rainy winter, if that's OK?'

'Yeah. Very OK. We'll probably feel cheated after a few weeks, knowing we're missing the best of the summer.'

The couple parked their borrowed sedan near a children's playground and ambled towards the water. Black swans, a variety of ducks and the odd squawking seagull gathered in their droves, being fed by families on the jetty. Attention on the famous duo quickly gathered momentum as people recognised them and started the usual routine of pointing and then waving, before finally plucking up the courage to express their fanaticism by regurgitating every single useless fact that had escaped into the public domain about the two stars. The good-looking youngsters conversed with the crowd for a few minutes, answering polite questions about Christmas and their plans for the New Year.

After the overt joint appearance on stage in Tokyo and a series of carefully proofed festive edition magazine articles, the news that Lynn Dyson was dating Jeff Diamond had been granted tacit acceptance at home and abroad. By all accounts, their respective Melbourne fan-bases generally approved of the match, in spite of a few professional busybodies who frequently made a meal of the perceived incompatibility between the squeaky clean beauty and the outspoken party boy. Both particularly photogenic however, being pictured together made a striking subject for glossy front pages, and a glamorous love story at Christmas time never failed to hit the mark.

Finally free of their admirers, the lovers strolled on, taking a clockwise route around the lake to a stretch where only the occasional dog-walker or jogger crossed their path. Hand in hand, they took in the warm, clean air, and Lynn could almost feel the energy sparking between them.

'So, new man... How are you feeling now you've been awake for a few hours?'

Jeff laughed. 'Great, thanks! But we don't have to talk about this. You need a break from all my shit.'

'No way!' the nineteen-year-old objected. 'I'm dying to know what's going on in your head. Please don't keep quiet just for me.'

The grateful man gestured to a bench a few metres up ahead, and they sat down facing the lake. The sun shone on their backs, and its reflection on the water shimmered brightly in their eyes. He wrapped his arms around his prize while they gazed at the well-known local cityscape.

'It's hard to describe, angel,' he began, his voice deep and resonant behind her head. 'I do feel different, but it's subtle.'

His girlfriend squeezed his hands. 'How so?'

Kissing her fresh-smelling hair, Jeff attempted to put his feelings into words. 'The image that comes to mind is a big pan of hot liquid.'

'Soul soup?' the young woman suggested.

'Yeah! Exactly! Perfect. Soup of the soul. *Sopa del alma*. Well... For as long as I can remember, it's been like this boiling cauldron of thoughts and ideas and songs, hate and anger and bitterness all bubbling around, being stirred up by all the nasty events that went on. And now it feels as though the temperature's dropped down to a simmer.'

Lynn twisted around to smile at the imagery.

'But definitely not cold,' the orator continued. 'It's no less full now either, but whereas before I was constantly fighting to keep the lid on and stop it boiling over... and many times didn't manage to keep the lid on, as you well know... now I just feel in total control. Calm, clear water instead of murky, lumpy, boiling soup.'

'That's another great analogy,' his biggest fan responded. 'I understand perfectly. You've gone from stew to *consommé*.'

'Yeah. Guess so,' Jeff became more subdued. 'Looking back from this new position of stability, I must've been so volatile all the time; always on a tightrope, trying not to fall off. And I think, because I had so many bloody issues to fix, when you came along, you only added to the volatility, so I ended up being even less stable.'

'Oh,' the teenager sounded disappointed.

He hugged her tightly, anxious to finish his explanation. 'No, listen... What I was always looking for from us was stability, and it was my fault that we couldn't have it. And now we *can* have it, thanks to your patience and understanding, and because you didn't let me give up until we found a solution.'

'You're welcome,' the relieved celebrity was pleased to hear her lost boy express himself so lucidly and objectively.

'My music's going to change too, I can tell,' he continued. 'Already, the ideas that are wandering around my head are mellow, more positive, less chip-on-the-shoulder types of themes. It freaks me out a little because I don't identify with that stuff yet.'

Lynn pressed back into her boyfriend's chest and rested her head on his chin. 'It'll come. Don't worry about it. I'm sure you'll work yourself out soon enough. The timing's perfect really, isn't it? We've already blocked out some time to adjust to the London lifestyle, so now we just need to factor in our adjustment to your new self too.'

Jeff chuckled again. 'It's so easy, isn't it?'

'What's easy?'

'Adjusting. That's what I need to learn from you now, angel. All I know is how to blow a fuse when things challenge me, like the world's going to end. But now I need to learn how to react like you do.'

'I think you just will,' the supportive young woman assured him. 'I don't think you'll have to learn from me. You'll just start doing it subconsciously one day, and before too long, the old reactions'll be few and far between.'

'D'ya reckon? Hope so.'

Again, Lynn turned around as far as she could stretch. 'I forgot to tell you,' she said with renewed excitement. 'Our new flat came through. Three bedrooms, so a nice amount of space for all our junk. About a hundred metres from Warwick Avenue tube station. There are some photos at home. It looks great.'

'*Magnifico*,' the Bohemian-in-waiting replied. 'Does it have heating?'

His partner laughed. 'Yes, of course it does. Shall we go? Then I can show you the pictures. We also need to start thinking about what we're taking on the 'plane.'

The pair lifted themselves off the creaky wooden bench and began the trek back to the car. Jeff put his arm over Lynn's shoulder.

'This is all I need to take.'

'Well, you're going to be mighty chilly then,' the singer joked, 'with just one t-shirt and a pair of shorts. Better make sure we pay the heating bill on time.'

Inching through the lunchtime traffic towards their apartment, the young star remembered something else she had thought to ask her boyfriend while he had been off in the land of nod. She turned to look at the handsome man in the driver's seat, feeling more than a little nervous.

'Can I ask you two serious questions, please?'

'Sure,' Jeff replied, glancing quickly sideways.

'Next time we're in Sydney...'

'Which'll be when, d'you think?' he interrupted, chuckling.

'Good question. Probably next Christmas. I'd like to see where your mum's buried.'

The songwriter tensed up at the mention of his mother, but made a conscious effort to dismiss the negativity which instantly filled his mind. Lynn's intentions were noble. He must do his best to run with this.

'OK,' came the hesitant reply. 'And you want to meet my sister.'

'Oh, yes. If that's alright? Only if you're comfortable though.'

Jeff smiled. 'Well, I can pretty much guarantee I wouldn't be comfortable with either, but at some point it's got to happen. I can't be selective about which parts of my life I include you in any more. That's another thing I'm going to have to get used to. If I say I want you in my life... which I absolutely do... I have to let you in completely.'

'Thanks,' the passenger reached over and touched his left arm, which was jiggling the gearstick as they waited for some traffic lights to change. 'Do you think Madalena would want to come to London for a holiday?'

'Hmm...' the young man paused. 'Not sure I'd want that, to be honest. She's never even been to Melbourne, so overseas travel'd be one hell of a deal for her. And even honester, I'm not sure I'd do a good job entertaining her. If she came that far, she'd have to stay for a few weeks to make it worthwhile, if only to get over the jet-lag. So we'd have to be prepared to take her everywhere. Practically speaking, I think it'd be too hard. And that's not an excuse, by the way.'

His dream girl was satisfied with this answer. 'OK. I agree. It's probably not a good idea. And the other question is what was your mum's name?'

Even though the second of her questions had been slipped in with such sleight of hand, Jeff's instincts reverted to abject panic, since the only picture his mind made available for viewing was the one of his mother lying dead on the blood-stained mattress. Feeling exposed and outraged, he couldn't stop himself freefalling out of control once more, desperately trying to take something positive out of his determined girlfriend's torment.

No, mate, he countered the anguish in his head. *Don't go down.* It was good that she wanted to know. It personalised things. He had written about it, he forced himself to remember.

'I'm sorry, Jeff,' Lynn groaned, feeling really guilty.

By the look of his thunderous expression and from the way the car jerked as his foot tapped the accelerator impatiently, it was far too soon to ask this question. She regretted it wholeheartedly, watching the tortured man's eyes sinking back into their sockets, his jaw muscles clenched and his brow becoming instantly furrowed and bathed in sweat.

'I shouldn't have asked you,' she added, sensing him spiralling into Gravity's eager grasp.

Yet after a few turgid seconds, his pained expression began to lighten. The passenger noticed her boyfriend struggling admirably with the quest she had set him, taking heart again. She knew that answering this question while driving would prevent him from completely losing control, simply because he was too responsible an individual not to reserve some brainpower for their physical safety. His jawline gradually softened, which she hoped signified a troll conquest in the offing.

Jeff breathed in deeply and shot a fleeting glance to his left, eyes wide with dismay. His attention reverted to the road and to absorb his next conditioned reaction: that of denial. Why was such a simple request so difficult to grant? He could tell his inquisitor that he didn't remember his mother's name, but Lynn would see through this straightaway. He could kid her that he didn't believe one should speak the names of the dead, but that would be a blatant lie too. It occurred to him that his mind was much more devious than he realised, and wondered just how many white lies he had told over the years of self-preservation.

The boy from Sydney's west fought to picture his mother's face when she was younger, prettier and alive. Hadn't he ever thought of doing this before? To his amazement, there *were* some images which came back of happier times. He had simply never tried. He saw his mother's unruly mop of dark hair, her girlish face with bright red lipstick and her rather too skinny frame. When he was small, Jeff recalled, she had often worn a heavy gold crucifix pendant around her neck that would knock against his forehead when she bent over him, on the few occasions when he had stood close enough.

'Are you OK?' his passenger was asking from the real world.

'Sorry. Yes,' the confused man answered, focussing back into the moment and feeling surprisingly at peace. 'I went time travelling.'

'Was it to a nice place?' she checked, immediately cursing the patronising tone she had used.

'Luciana,' he blurted out. 'Her name was Lucy Moreno. I forgot what she looked like before. I had to go to the archives.'

'Thanks,' his girlfriend replied, appeased by his good humour. 'Luciana Moreno Diamond. Another "L"...'

Jeff closed his eyes and inhaled quickly through his nose, as another sticky silence forced its way inside the car. '*Madre de Dios,*' he whispered.

Then without warning, the vehicle veered across to the kerb, and its driver scraped the handbrake up roughly. Thrown forwards by the sudden change in direction, Lynn was frightened that she had pushed her boyfriend too far by enunciating a string of names that had gone unspoken for a very long time. She tugged at the seatbelt to release its tension from her neck and watched him jump out of the car into the busy road.

Oh, God, the celebrity thought. What had she done? It looked as if her crazed stallion was about to bolt. Or worse...

However, before she could blink, the handsome stranger appeared at the passenger door, which opened next to her and admitted some scorching air along with the noise of the city.

'Get out,' he requested, holding out his hand. 'Please?'

With some trepidation, Lynn clambered out onto the footpath, surrounded by astonished office workers scurrying past on their lunchbreak. Jeff took her in his arms and planted a huge kiss on her lips.

'Another "L",' his eyes were full of tears but the manic intensity had vanished. 'Say it again. *Diga su nombre, mi Regala.*'

In the excitement which consumed them both, his thrilled girlfriend could scarcely remember the three names. 'Luciana Moreno Diamond,' she chanted, staring at the broadest smile she had ever seen.

The emotional man kissed her again, and then signalled for her to get back in the car, holding the door open and doling out menacing stares to any fans who dared approach them.

'*Gracias*,' he mouthed, and slammed the door.

Without further words, his tall frame dropped back into the driver's seat, and they drove the last few minutes back to their car park in silence. Ascending to the top, Lynn couldn't wait any longer.

'You have to tell me what happened back there,' she implored. 'You scared me.'

With a dramatic sweep of his arm, Jeff invited his beautiful companion to exit in front of him from the lift. 'One thing at a time, if you don't mind,' the comic replied, clearly tense again. 'I've got to get in here first.'

His flatmate nodded apologetically. She was getting carried away. It was appropriate to let Jeff set the pace right now. She had been in and out of the apartment several times while her lover had spent nearly two days asleep, and she had temporarily overlooked the fact that this was the first time he had faced his front door since they had arrived back from Sydney. Moreover, she wasn't already inside to greet him and let him successfully protect her from the images in his head.

Nevertheless, his left hand was rapidly making its way towards the keyhole. Lynn hung back and watched his reactions carefully. This man was very determined. She had to give him credit for that.

'What are you waiting for?' the boisterous songwriter quipped, turning round to see where she was. 'Aren't you coming in?'

Was she patronising him again? Is that what he was hinting at? Yes. Maybe she was.

'Sorry,' the nineteen-year-old responded, walking towards him and offering no explanation.

Jeff used the momentum of his approaching dream girl to marshal his forces, galvanising his mind for key-turning. He so wanted there to be a smooth transition from two people outside to two people inside. Was that so much to ask?

'OK. Here we go.'

The key turned, and the door opened away from the couple. The apartment's owner paused chivalrously to allow his companion to pass in front of him. Deliberately taking things slowly, he waited until she turned to offer reinforcement before he crossed the threshold and closed the door behind them. Beautifully done, he congratulated himself. Virtually no interference from the old enemies this time.

'*Ven' aquí*,' the young man invited, realising Lynn was feeling awkward. 'It's fine. I'm sorry too. I know you were only trying to help.'

The pair kissed in the hallway, her heart beating faster than his. 'I was too keen to see what would happen.'

Her lover put a finger to his mouth to stop her. 'It doesn't matter. I just want life to be as normal as possible from now on. OK?'

Feeling humbled by this new sense of contentment which seemed to be following him everywhere, Jeff walked through to the lounge room and flopped down onto the couch. He pulled his cigarettes and lighter from his shorts pocket and sat them on the coffee table, surprised by how easy it was to resist the craving. Monday lunchtime, he thought, surveying his surroundings with a curious smile. What did normal people do at lunchtime on the last Monday of the year?

'Hey, gorgeous,' he shouted. 'Where are those photos?'

Lynn entered the room and pulled out an envelope from a pile of papers on the piano, handing her boyfriend the information about their new, English home. 'There's a map there too,' she said, standing behind him and stroking his hair. 'It's very close to everything. We definitely won't need a car, although there is a parking space in the garage at the back.'

The excited migrant leafed through the photographs one by one, examining every last detail in the background. He couldn't wait to be there. He glanced up and patted the cushion next to him.

'Please sit down, angel,' he asked. 'I'd like to feel you next to me.'

His girlfriend glowed inside. He would like to... Not *need to*, but *like to*. This was already much better. Apart from those moments when his insecurities were most challenged, the change in his disposition evoked feelings of pure joy from the blonde superstar. Their short Christmas break was all that stood between last week's impetuous and prurient adolescent and today's languid, mature master of his own destiny.

Lynn obeyed gladly. Inspired by the prospect of their new life far away, they laid the selection of pictures out on the coffee table and pored over the map. The former nobody looped his arm around his favourite treasure, and she cuddled into him. Notwithstanding the apparent release from an obsessive sexual appetite, their common desire for closeness was palpable.

'I owe you an answer,' he began, feeling her head nod against the side of his neck. 'I had to think pretty quickly, you know, when you asked for my mum's name. My first thought was, "Holy crap! Not now."'

The caring woman chanced a soft chuckle, staring at the London pictures while her mind flashed back to the frightening juncture and waiting for the storyteller to continue.

'But I caught myself sliding down and said, "No, you've got to take your own medicine." If I wrote the words, I have to sing the song. Ain't that how it goes? So I forced myself to think of an image of Mum that was more pleasant than the one I've been living with. The only one I thought existed.'

'Great,' the therapist kissed his cheek, leaving her guilt behind. 'And there's another difference there...'

Jeff paused. 'What?'

'I can't be a hundred percent sure,' Lynn answered, 'but I think that's the first time I've heard you say "Mum" and not "my mum". D'you know what I mean? The distance is shorter between "Mum", with a capital "M", and "my mum".'

Her boyfriend considered her observation for a second and tried to remember exactly which words had come out of his mouth. 'You could well be right,' he reflected. 'Well... That's something else to add to the list of December nineteen-seventy-four achievements.'

The nineteen-year-old wondered if her boyfriend was being sarcastic, but her fears were soon allayed by a red-hot kiss.

'I know what you're thinking. You can take it at face value, angel. No hidden meaning.'

Sighing, she kissed him again. 'Tough, isn't it?'

'Yep. You're not wrong,' he replied. 'But we'll get there.'

'So you found a good image?'

The recovering soul gave a hesitant nod. 'Yeah, eventually. It took a while. I had to go back a long way. She was only eighteen when Lena was born, and I don't think she grew up much after that either. The earliest memory I have is when I was about three, so she would've been twenty-four or -five. The same age as my sister is now, in fact. She had hair about the same length as yours, but as dark as mine.'

'Does Madalena look like your mum?'

Lynn chose not to use his mother's name. She didn't consider she had earned this privilege yet.

'Ah, yeah. I think so,' Jeff answered, exhaling sharply and shaking his head. 'A lot.'

His guardian angel gripped his trembling hand. 'So meanwhile, back in the car... What happened after you found the happier memory?'

The millionnaire songwriter took a long inward breath and expelled it through his nostrils, staring at his cigarettes as if willing them across the table. 'I remembered one day... a rare friendly day... when we'd all been out together. Can't remember where. I can remember her smiling, eating an ice cream. And lipstick on her ice cream. It's weird what you remember as a kid, isn't it? I wondered what ice cream would taste like with lipstick in it.'

Lynn grimaced and kissed him. 'Horrible, I'd expect. That's lovely though. What else?'

'Nothing else. Until you got really smart, my angel of mercy...' Jeff's tone changed, fixing her with another intense stare. 'You linked Mum and you together with the two "L"s, didn't you? At first I recoiled from it. Pretty violently, as you saw. But you're too smart. You know better than me how to fix this, and I love you for that.'

'I'm glad,' the young woman sighed. 'I thought you were going to run off into the traffic. I was really scared until you asked me to say her name. Then I realised you were alright.'

He nodded. 'I needed to reinforce the link. I had to hear you say it. Can you say it again?'

'Definitely! When you asked me on the side of the road, I was so shocked that I almost forgot. It's Luciana Moreno Diamond. Am I pronouncing it right?'

'¡Perfecto!' Jeff affirmed, kissing her again. 'Hablado como una verdadera argentina.'

'¿Qué?' Lynn giggled. 'That was way too fast.'

The linguist repeated the Spanish phrase word by word. 'Hablado, spoken... como, like... una verdadera argentina, a true Argentinean of the female variety.'

'Aha! Gracias,' his girlfriend replied, grateful for his appreciation.

'My dad called her Lucy though, or just Luce, which my grandparents hated,' he explained. 'She was more than loose by the end of it, so he was obviously a pretty prophetic bastard.'

'Shhh,' the nineteen-year-old brushed a lone tear from her man's cheek. 'Don't say things like that.'

The musician forced a smile, staring into the distance. 'OK. Thanks. Madalena's named after my grandmother, which is kind of ironic too really, when you think about it. I'm sure my parents wouldn't have done it on purpose. I have difficulty crediting them with a single intelligent decision, which is most likely another sin I'll pay for someday. But it must've been a slap in the face for mi abuela to have her name given to the bastard child of a bloke she couldn't stand the sight of.'

Lynn was captivated by the way her man was now able to calmly relay this information to her. There was a fondness for the past which had never been intimated before; nostalgic and reminiscent, despite the occasional acerbic barb.

'How's your soup?' she asked.

Jeff laughed out loud at her latest unexpected question. 'Simmering nicely, thanks. And yours? Sorry to stir it up earlier.'

'That's OK. I deserved it. I love you, and don't you forget. It's you and me now, baby. Una vida singular.'

Her boyfriend nodded slowly, with a wry smile on his swarthy, unshaven face. 'Very good! Te amo también. Anyway, that's enough about me. Look at the bloody time! Do you mind if I watch some of the cricket before the day's over?'

'Good idea. Can I get you a beer?'

Her boyfriend's eyes widened in delight. 'You absolutely can!'

Lynn was walking on air as she went to the fridge to collect their drinks. This gorgeous, erstwhile troubled enigma of hers was steadying at last; a few wrinkles still to iron out, but basically in good shape. And being in London could only help the healing process. She imagined him sitting in the cafés of Covent Garden or Soho, chatting with the locals and his fellow imported, intellectual Bohemians, or solving the world's problems over endless glasses of *Côtes de Rhône* and *Cálvados*. There would be boxes of Cuban cigars and copies of the New Yorker and the New Statesman strewn around their apartment, not to mention piles of books and the new grudge-free music to which he had alluded earlier.

The young woman couldn't wait to see how their life singular would unfold. Not exactly what her father had in mind when he first agreed to her enrolment at the Royal College of Music, she chuckled to herself. Her parents would much prefer to see her living in Knightsbridge or South Kensington, within a stone's throw of Harrod's and Sloane Square. Regardless of *locale*, she was no less committed to the studies that lay ahead of her than they would wish, and Jeff's vision of their future together was precisely what she wanted too.

Lynn caught her breath as she remembered the stilted, rushed breakfast conversation they had shared on Southbank shortly after her return to Australia. She had all but pushed her former boyfriend away. Oh, how heartbroken she would have been if he hadn't persisted, and what a wealth of experiences she would have missed out on...

The sporting celebrity cringed at the thought of that son-of-a-French-politician with whom her parents had tried to set her up. He had been nice enough. Nothing at all wrong with him, in fact. Yet she couldn't help but project forward to the boredom and predictability of life if stuck with a partner like him, in comparison to someone as physically and intellectually stimulating as Jeff Diamond.

And for all the turmoil they were facing together, he couldn't love her more. Nor she him.

Bring It On!

Later that afternoon, Lynn returned from an arduous training session at the Sportsdrome. The songwriter heard the apartment door open, rising from the piano to meet her in the hallway. She looked flushed and pumped up from hours of Olympian exertion, which turned him on no end.

'You look hot,' he said, pulling her in close. 'Can I make you hotter?'

The athlete opened her mouth to object, but his kiss took her breath away. They made love in the sweltering heat without bothering to turn on the air-conditioning. It was deliberate on Jeff's part, because he had a burning topic to discuss and needed to set the scene.

'Angel, I've been thinking over your comment about stew versus *consommé*,' he opened, rolling onto his back and staring at the ceiling.

'Oh, yes?' the lethargic woman responded, disappointed by the re-emergence of his worried tone. 'What about it?'

'It scares me, you know. *Consommé*'s too insipid. Stew is a hell of a lot tastier than *consommé*, and I'm not sure I want to lose that edge. That fire. D'you know what I mean?'

Lynn sat up and wrapped the sheet around her naked body. 'Mmm... I'm getting a flavour of it.'

'Ha! *¡Muy buen!* Thanks,' her boyfriend chuckled, deducing the humour in her retort belied the concern on her face. 'It's not that I want to stop what we've started. I don't at all.'

'How did you go getting back in on your own, by the way?' his flatmate interrupted, having forgotten that he had opted to abandon the televised cricket for the pub while she trained.

The young man smiled, but without opening his eyes. 'I'd be lying if I said it was easy.'

'Oh,' his lover sighed. 'Why? What was it like?'

Jeff sat up, took her hand and looked into the patient, empathetic eyes. 'It was much tougher on my own. Not that bad though. Nowhere near as bad as before, but it was a bit of a step in the wrong direction. Seems like I'm destined to be dependent on something, and right now it's you.'

The beauty leaned over to plant a kiss on his lips. 'And is that a problem?'

'I don't know. Is it? It feels like it should be.'

'Not from my perspective,' the athlete reassured him. 'Isn't that what partners are supposed to do? Depend on each other? Anyway, carry on about the soup. Sorry to digress.'

'OK,' the philosopher continued, collecting his thoughts. 'It's just that I'm scared I'll get so calm and mellow that I won't have the same desire to fix stuff, to work on social justice issues and get people mobilised. I'll just become a self-satisfied fat cat who sails through life without leaving an impression.'

Lynn laughed out loud at the image forming in her mind. 'You are awesome!' she declared, shaking his chest and rocking him from side to side. 'I love you so much. You're not going to become a self-satisfied fat cat.'

Amused by such a vehement validation, the ambitious man watched his beautiful best friend counting on her fingers.

'One, because you're too passionate about these issues to let them go; two, because you already recognise the difference in yourself; and three, I won't let you!'

'Good,' he replied, grateful but a little cynical too. 'Well, that's settled then! I'm glad you're so convinced I'll prevail. I'll stop worrying forthwith. But what makes you believe in me so strongly?'

His beautiful best friend grinned in affirmation. 'Come on! I believe in you because I know, deep down, that you believe in you. This *consommé* business is all new at the moment, and it's only natural that you're off-kilter. Hey, I'm nervous too! You just have to learn not to focus inwards so much. Just enough to keep the priceless humility that makes you so irresistible. Does that make sense?'

Hearing his lover speak to him this way rekindled the lost boy's waning positivity. His ego was being inflated, of course, and he was used to being surrounded by sycophants these days, yet such comments from his dream girl were worth much more than any others. His adolescent fantasies of a partnership with Lynn Dyson was now well within his reach on every level, as unbelievable as it still seemed. He could envision it clearly, and even better, it appeared that now so could she.

'It makes perfect sense,' he agreed, grasping both her hands. 'It's what I've always wanted but never dared to expect. My fear is that I've been cocooned in my warped, little world for so long that I won't recognise myself outside.'

'So don't make yourself into someone you don't respect,' the insightful teenager offered in a matter-of-fact tone. 'That way, you'll want to recognise yourself. I'm going to have a shower. Are you joining me? I want to hear more about the soup. Have you been writing?'

Jeff smiled, his eyes following her lithe form as she twisted her legs off the bed and jumped up. How had he got so lucky? He had just made love to a goddess who was prepared to stand by him and help him figure out who he was going to be. Springing enthusiastically to his feet, the reinstated world-changer followed her into the bathroom.

'It's not that I'm scared of stepping outside my comfort zone,' he continued, cool water running onto his chest as they lathered themselves with soap. 'I'm used to that. Tactically, at least.'

'Tactically?' Lynn laughed. 'What does that mean?'

'You know. Trying new things, like performing on stage, writing a book, movie scores,' the erudite artist explained. 'And drugs too, or exotic booze. I'll try anything at least once. There's no problem with that.'

Taking him by surprise, the athlete grabbed the shower head and directed the jet straight into her boyfriend's face. 'Yes, well... You need to be careful about that particular comfort zone. My dad's not going to take too kindly to finding out about some of the things you try.'

'Spoilsport,' Jeff teased, wrestling the slippery nozzle from her hand easily and returning the favour. 'But you're right. I will be careful.'

'Good. Thanks,' his wise girlfriend was satisfied, her mood solemn enough to make her point. 'I don't want to have to say goodbye, Jeff. Not now. Not now we're on such an exciting journey.'

Both lungfuls of air suddenly exited Jeff's chest cavity, and he stopped in his tracks. The water continued to gush over his head and shoulders, but he had heard her words perfectly clearly. He understood what his soul-mate was telling him. Neither lover wanted to relinquish the happiness they had found with each other, yet their life singular was entirely his to lose. She was Bart Dyson's daughter alright!

Jeff wiped the grin off his face and began to rinse the shampoo out of Lynn's hair. She leaned back into him, and the compassion in this simple gesture melted his heart.

'I hear you,' he responded with alacrity. 'It's my responsibility not to fuck this up, I know. You're right to remind me, and I hope you'll keep reminding me. I'm just a man, angel. I know I've got a hell of a long way to go, but you have my commitment. Complete and undying.'

The blonde beauty manœuvred around, leaned forwards onto his chest and kissed it tenderly, while determined arms reached around her and twisted the shower taps off.

'And I'm just a woman,' she whispered. 'I'm no more perfect than you are.'

'Oh, you are,' the emotional man smiled, kissing her forehead. 'You're so much more perfect than I am.'

Feeling guilty at having lectured her mysterious Catholic Argentinean Polish Jew unnecessarily, Lynn stepped out of the bath and grabbed their towels. Wrapping herself in one, she hopped up onto the vanity and sat silently watching her strapping and bristly hero dry himself off and turn his mind to shaving.

'Jeff?' she ventured after a minute or so.

'*¿Sí?*'

'How do you define perfection in a person?'

Her handsome sage exhaled slowly, leaning heavily against the vanity. 'Whoa!' he smiled. 'That's a heavy subject for a post-coital shower. I'm guessing there's a connection somewhere with soul soup?'

'Yes, I think so,' the nineteen-year-old grinned back. 'Are you rescuing me, by any chance?'

Jeff snatched away her bath towel and swung it overhead like a cape until it swirled over the beautiful woman's head and covered her like a ghostly cartoon character. Chuckling at the comforting sight, he lifted the edge away from her face and enveloped her in its fluffy volume.

'Do you need rescuing?' he asked. 'From yourself?'

Lynn nodded. There were tears in her eyes. She let the man she loved so much lead her back into the bedroom, surprised when he kept going. Her knight in shining towel walked her all the way to the piano, where he invited her to sit down next to him. He began to pick out a few chords, feeling a torrent of words stream into his head, demanding to be sung to his thoughtful *confidante*.

'In my opinion, perfection is an unattainable state,' he mused. 'The process of becoming perfect is what's real. How we strive to be who we need to be to make each other happy, I guess. Or maybe we all start out perfect when we're born, and then some of us gain imperfections along the way while others don't.'

The song evolved through trial and error, tears and laughter. What was often viewed as weakness might sometimes be an admission of an untapped strength, he proffered. Everyone's vision of perfection must be different, she re-joined.

'A man picks a woman because he thinks she's perfect,' the village idiot recited over his lover's expert accompaniment. 'Whereas a woman picks a man because she wants to turn him from work-in-progress into perfection.'

The teenager frowned, allowing his words to sink in.

'The trick is to determine whose perfection you're after, angel. You want to help me to become who I want to be and not necessarily your idea of perfection. Not simply what you want me to be.'

'Do I?'

'Yeah,' Jeff kissed her pouting lips and nudged her sideways. 'You do. You're enlightened. You see the vision of what can be, beyond the obvious of what others see now. That's our souls talking, angel. Across time, pointing us in the right direction, when things don't seem clear.'

'Is that why some people take more risks than others?'

'Maybe,' her lover shrugged. 'Or more likely because they're just plain stupid.'

Lynn slid off the piano stool and dropped onto the floorboards, giggling at her clever man's vacant stare. 'To think you're about to start a PhD... I mean, is that how certain people calculate risks? By looking into the future?'

'I doubt it,' Jeff shook his head. 'We can't learn from the future. That's impossible, baby. Only the past. And yeah, enlightened people probably do take more calculated risks. Old souls aren't afraid to fail, because they see failure as a means to an end. Learn from our mistakes, and all that jazz.'

Australia's princess listened spellbound to the song which literally wrote itself as her no-good boyfriend pieced it together, with the peal of a commoner's *concerto* ringing throughout the apartment. She couldn't help but recognise herself as he painted a picture of someone without scars; someone who played by the rules. It was a magical lesson, and they were learning it right there, together.

More than two years ago, during their conversation about sexual mercenaries, this mysterious man had encouraged his muse to challenge convention, and the sixteen-year-old hadn't possessed the maturity to understand. Now, in the renaissance of their life singular, the nineteen-year-old understood perfectly.

'I get it,' she nodded, tears rolling down her cheeks. 'What we might think of as perfection is actually pretty superficial, isn't it?'

The wise man nodded. He loosened the towel around his waist and took hold of one corner to wipe his face, where his own tears were mixing with droplets trickling down from wet hair. Lynn raised herself gracefully up from her position on the floor and sat next to him on the piano stool again.

'I will chase the future with you,' she promised. 'There's nothing I'd rather do. Nothing in this whole world, Jeff. And who cares about my dad? Whatever happens, we're not going to say goodbye. I'm sorry I spoke like that. I judged you based on the old rules; the conventions, as you said before. They're outdated and invalid these days. That's not the world I want to live in either.'

'Nice work,' her lover croaked, leaning into her body. 'You know what I want?'

The young woman shook her head, suddenly childlike.

He smiled and continued. 'I want us to sail close enough to the edges of the Earth, just so we can look over the side and see if there's anything there worth pillaging. Let's never close our minds, Lynn. You're right. We'll make ourselves into people we respect. That way, the soup'll stay hot and spicy.'

The gorgeous superstar laughed. 'And tasty.'

Growling, Jeff kissed her passionately, licking his lips as he let her breathe. 'Yep. Very tasty. I want us to learn as many of life's lessons as we can. Hopefully not all as hard as some we've already learned. And there's no point learning something that someone else already knows.'

'Except if you learn it from a different perspective,' his student countered. 'You're bound to feel overwhelmed to begin with, but I can tell you're excited too.'

'I am. Without question, I am. But what's the bloody point just watching from the sidelines, angel? The world is our lobster.'

'Oyster!' the amused woman jumped to correct him, laughing aloud again. 'Not lobster!'

Jeff winked. 'I know. I couldn't resist. I had this really daggy teacher in high school who thought he was being funny when he said that. I couldn't miss such a ripe opportunity to lob it in.'

'*Lob* it in?' she echoed, groaning. 'Please... No more plays on words.'

'I'm just trying to focus outwards,' the comic attempted to justify his actions. 'Stop being so critical.'

'Argh!' Lynn groaned again. 'I can't win! You twist everything round to suit yourself. But just think of the talks you could give through Childlight and The Fellowship to people who are going through what you did. You can tell them first-hand how you fought the symptoms and came out the other side stronger. It's an inspirational story.'

The Sydneysider shook his head and smiled, his chest instantly tightening. 'I guess so. I'm sorry. It's a bad habit, I admit. It's hard to find my story all that inspirational when I'm in it.'

'Of course,' the empathetic woman agreed. 'I get that. But it is. If you'd come to speak at my school when I was twelve or thirteen, it would definitely have left an impression on me. Kids need people like you to give them direction.'

'And this kid needs someone like you,' Jeff reached across and held his girlfriend's face in his huge, gentle hand. 'I could only have done this with you, angel. Truly. I won't leave that section out of my speech. You're the vital ingredient.'

'So tell them to find whomever they decide they need. That's what you could advise other kids. Don't be afraid to ask for help from someone you can trust.'

'Jesus! We can be the dream team, you and I. Your organisational skills and steadying influence, and my wild imagination and persuasiveness. How about it, partner? We can change the world, bit by bit.'

The sportswoman lifted her right hand for a high-five. 'You're on! Sounds fantastic. You're the front end of the pantomime horse, and I, unfortunately for me, am the back end.'

Slapping her hand in mid-air, the young man laughed at the funny image which had been conjured up. 'Yeah. That is somewhat unfortunate,' he frowned. 'I won't tell anyone, I promise. I'll be your passionate, parasitic front-man, and you can take care of everything in my wake. Does that sound fair?'

The teenager knew her ambitious and unpredictable boyfriend was only half joking, but she was more than happy with this arrangement. After living her childhood firmly in the public eye, she no longer craved the limelight half as much as he did.

'Not entirely, but where do I sign?'

'Here,' her handsome stranger indicated his heart. 'Here's where you sign.'

His dream girl kissed the spot he had singled out, before reeling back. 'Wait a minute,' she ventured, crossing the room to the coffee table and returning with a pen.

Parting the hairs on his chest, Lynn scrawled something on his skin and signed her name with a flourish. Scowling at the weird sensation, her man was unable to read her writing upside-down.

'What does it say?' he asked, trying to twist himself round to read it.

'Go and have a look,' she laughed, pointing into the hallway.

Gathering their towels around them, the happy pair made their way back through the bedroom and into the *en suite*. Gazing into the bathroom mirror, Jeff deciphered the words "Bring it on!" written backwards, with the superstar's reversed autograph beneath.

'Cool!' he shouted behind him, feeling like a sixteen-year-old again. 'Can I get this tattooed on?'

The slender blonde pushed herself lazily off the doorframe, whence she had surveyed her exuberant boyfriend's reaction in amusement, approached the mirror and witnessed her reflection being bear-hugged.

'If you want to. You'll have to shave your chest.'

'Or get it done somewhere less hairy.'

Stepping forwards, the young woman took hold of his sides, under the ribcage, and turned him round, looking up and down his body. 'Oh, yeah? Where, for example?'

He smiled. 'Good point.'

'Would you like a tattoo? Seriously?' Lynn asked. 'We should both get one, as a celebration of going to London and starting our life singular.'

Pleasantly surprised that this refined, former private school girl should suggest such an unconventional thing, Jeff was instantly sold on the idea. 'D'ya wanna? Would you?'

'Why not?' the tennis champion answered. 'I need to challenge convention too, don't I? What design would we have? Exactly the same or two complementary things?'

They stood and examined their naked selves in the bathroom mirror. The tall man joked that Lynn might go for LOVE and HATE across her breasts, at which the beauty gazing back at him stuck her very regal tongue out as far as it would go.

'A fat cat?'

'A scrawny, mangy cat, more like,' her boyfriend countered. 'No, I know... What about our initials, back to back?'

Leaning over the basin, he breathed heavily on the surface of the mirror and drew a "J" and an "L" side by side with his finger. The stencil quickly faded away, but not before both had seen the transient letters formed in such a way as to resemble a figure One. The passionate songwriter repeated the process for good measure.

'Yes, I love that,' his beautiful best friend nodded. 'Us, but singular. Perfect! They could probably choose a typeface that'd look like a one but still be recognisable enough as different letters.'

'Font,' the technologist corrected. 'They're called fonts nowadays. Move with the times, girl. And then we could even use the design as a logo for anything we did together, with a matching photo of us sitting back to back. How about that?'

Lynn laughed, slapping his arm hard, as she was steered into position for a demonstration.

'There! A naked photo of us back to back for promotional purposes. Yeah. Your mum and dad'd love that...'

'No!' she squealed. 'Now you're getting a bit carried away, aren't you? You're our self-appointed marketing manager now. Cathy wouldn't be very pleased.'

'Fuck Cathy! She works for me, not the other way round.'

'Do I work for you too then?' the young star asked, teasing him for his effusive arrogance.

'No, you don't,' the pretender became suitably restrained, receiving another smack on the arm.

'I'm just kidding, he who would be King,' his dream girl chided. 'I love the idea. We should see if anyone's open today. Do tattoo artists go on holidays too?'

Jeff's imagination was racing, fired up by this most unequivocal show of support for their future together. However, by the time they had walked back into the bedroom, his face had turned serious again.

'Are you sure about this? I mean, what if I die and you want to hook up with someone else?'

Lynn hugged him. His instability had left him crestfallen again, and she instantly pictured his happiness score taking another nosedive.

'You're not going to die,' she disputed, 'and even if you did, I'd still want a memento. It's no different for me than it is for you. It would depend where the tattoo was though, obviously. We haven't even discussed that.'

'Right. Excellent point also,' Jeff sniggered, relaxing a little.

He still couldn't quite believe what they were contemplating. This was a very big step, even for him. The twenty-two-year-old caught his breath as he remembered he still hadn't called Gerry back on the topic of whether he would ever consider getting married, as he had promised to do before they left Sydney.

Lynn beckoned her handsome boyfriend across the room to join her on the bed. Standing over him, having let her towel fall to the floor, she drew shapes with her hands to demonstrate various possible locations for their convention-challenging adornments. Listening, watching and feeling her glide around him, the hot-blooded lover became lost in a fantasy world of entwined limbs and touching body art. He became quickly aroused again and reached out to arrest her flight of fancy.

'You can't do this and expect me to concentrate,' he warned the incredibly sexy woman, dragging her down on top of him again.

Their lovemaking was peppered by suggestions of tattoo spots and frequent collapses into fits of laughter. When they finally relaxed down onto the bed breathlessly, they had also come to a decision.

'So! Is that it then?' the slender teenager asked, flicking her hair back over her shoulders, her breasts rising and falling enticingly as she moved.

Jeff kissed her again, taking her blazing body into his arms. Pushing him off playfully and with both index fingers working together, she drew their new symbol onto his left pectoral muscle, five centimetres or so above his nipple, where there was less hair. Jeff nodded, shrugging.

'And mine'll be on my shoulder blade, so that they touch when I sit in front of you,' she finished. 'Is that what you want?'

Her lover was speechless for a moment, a lump forming in his throat. 'Are you sure?' he searched his girlfriend's eyes. 'That's truly amazing. And I'm still going to get him or her to trace your other message, if you don't mind me having a bald square here for a while.'

He put his hand over the words she had written earlier. The impromptu autograph which had sparked this whole inspiring episode had now faded almost to nothing with the sweat of body contact.

The young woman kissed him on the very spot. 'Let's do it.'

'No, angel,' Jeff hesitated, gripped by a rare, rational resistance. 'Let's sleep on it, and if we both still want to do it in the morning, we'll go. *D'accord?*'

'*D'accord, mon ami,*' Lynn agreed. 'See? That's the new Jeff talking.'

***

Their fourth night back in the Melbourne apartment after the game-changing events of Boxing Day was fast approaching, and with it, renewed apprehension about potential nightmares. Lynn had cooked dinner, and they had spent the evening catching up on paperwork and preparing for their departure. Every so often one of them would catch him- or herself thinking how momentous these last few weeks had been, and how equally important the next few months promised to be.

Already the dynamics of their relationship had begun to change. Jeff no longer followed his dream girl around the apartment, anxious not to let her out of his sight in case she disappeared again. He had even elected to return to the pub before dinner, to watch the last session of the day's cricket and to say goodbye to some of his university mates prior to leaving the country. Although Lynn realised this was perfectly normal, she couldn't help but worry that she may be in for a reality check soon.

Were need and love two sides of the same coin for her damaged man? Would his devotion to her fade with his dependence? If they were to reach the point where he was so well fixed that he no longer needed her, the young woman wondered, would he still love her?

'I'll always need you,' the incredulous man maintained when questioned over dinner.

'No, you won't.'

'I will, angel,' the world-renowned playboy nodded insistently, taking her hand. 'I need you because I love you, not the other way round. I've loved you since before I needed you, and I'll love you forever. You don't have to worry about that, and we can argue about whether I need you or not all the way into our eighties.'

'Our eighties?' his girlfriend exclaimed at this response so peculiarly out of character. 'Wow! You're definitely changing. You've never projected yourself so far into the future before. For how long have you been picturing yourself in your eighties?'

576

Her coy flatmate shrugged and grinned. 'Since right now, I guess! Since you catapulted my sorry ass into the future.'

Chuckling at his expression, Lynn picked up their empty plates and carried them over to the sink, knowing better than to sensationalise things too much and risk having her poor boy slip back into the old indulgences.

'*I* don't even do that,' she confessed. 'Now you're wishing your life away in a whole new way. That's a big shift, Jeff. Do you really think we'll be together in our eighties?'

'Hope so. Don't you?'

The superstar returned to the kitchen table and accepted her nonchalant boyfriend's invitation to sit on his lap. He wrapped his arms around her.

'Yes, I do hope so,' she answered, kissing him. 'It's lovely. I just never thought I'd hear it from you.'

'Can you be happy without me?' he asked, changing the subject back again to mask his own unease.

'That's want, not need,' Lynn countered. 'Being happy isn't necessary to survive. You know that only too well.'

'Yeah, but would you be happy enough?'

'No, absolutely not,' she shook her head, 'but that's because I *want* to be with you. More than anything else, but it's still a want.'

'OK,' Jeff frowned, unsure where their argument was going. 'Wellbeing then? That's need.'

'Yes, I'll give you that. That's Maslow, isn't it?'

'Sure is, baby,' the amateur psychiatrist raised his hands in the air triumphantly. 'OK! I need you for my wellbeing. I will always need you. But I sure as hell love you too and I'll love you forever, Lynn Dyson. I know this for a fact because I want to make you happy above everything else. To make your dreams come true, and all that corny codswallop, as old father Blake would say.'

'It's not corny codswallop! What is codswallop anyway, corny or otherwise?'

'I'm fucked if I know the answer to that, my dear,' came an accurate impersonation of Gerry's dad, with the added expletive thrown in for effect. 'Quaint old Irish custom is walloping cod. Something straight out of Monty Python, I reckon.'

'OK! That programme's weird. I'll love you forever too, Jeff,' his girlfriend assured him, hoping she wasn't giving the impression this was all one-sided. 'But do you want to make me happy so I stay with you?'

Jeff closed his eyes, feeling a wave of panic wash over him. Where was she going with all these questions? A number of hours had passed since an attack had taken hold, and it took him by surprise. He breathed deeply for a moment, resting his pursed lips on the soft skin of Lynn's neck.

'Before, yes,' he murmured, after a short pause, 'but not now. I want to make you happy because I love you.'

'*Ditto*,' she agreed, turning round and kissing his very fervent lips.

'It's not all about me, angel.'

'No, I know. I just wanted to hear it from you. I want to know exactly where I fit in your life.'

'Where you fit?' his face reflected the horror behind his words. 'Are you doubting us? After this afternoon?'

It was the young woman's turn to be serious. 'No. It's just that I was thinking earlier that once you're all normalised and totally in control of your life, you might start behaving like my friends' boyfriends,' the courageous woman blurted out. 'And I don't want to be in that situation. You know, having arrangements broken at the last minute and not knowing where you are. All that playing around... I've been spoiled and I've got used to it.'

'So stay used to it. You will always be spoiled,' the handsome man cut her off with a disarming smile. 'You were born to be spoiled by me, *mi Regala*. Many, many moons ago.'

'Was I?' she asked, not knowing whether she was being sweet-talked or if this was truly her soul-mate calling. 'I don't think so. I bet you say that to all the girls...'

'Right,' Jeff scoffed. 'Well, if you won't believe me, how can I help you with your insecurities, ma'am?'

His girlfriend pouted. 'Do you really mean it?'

The flamboyant performer threw his hands in the air. 'Jesus Christ! Yes, I really mean it! I've infected you. I've transferred my anxiety to you. That wasn't supposed to happen. Angel, you are and always will be the most important thing in my life. That's just the way it is, take it or leave it.'

'I'll take it,' the happy woman jumped in, sensing some desperation creeping back into his voice. 'What was it? *¿Tómelo o déjelo? Gracias.*'

The half-Argentinean laughed. 'Well remembered! That was a while ago. Subject closed?' he enquired, flexing his ankles and bouncing numb legs underneath her weight, rendered somehow heavier by the earnest conversation. 'I've got work to do, you realise.'

'Yes, you have. OK. Let's forget it. I'm sorry. I know what it took for you to let me go to the US, and I know you want the best for me. Let's just agree on both need and love being part of our future, shall we?'

The couple stood up and embraced each other fiercely. The air had cleared magically by itself, and Lynn walked over to the sink to wash up their dinner dishes. Jeff followed her, dutifully picking up a tea towel like the well-behaved, domesticated flatmate he was endeavouring to become, and leaned on the counter pensively.

'Can I ask you a question now?'

'Of course.'

'Do you want me to stop smoking?' he asked, feeling a distinct pull towards the cigarette packet sitting on top of the refrigerator, taunting him at eye level.

'No,' she smiled, following his eyes. 'Jeff Diamond's meant to be hard-edged and vice-ridden. That's who you are.'

The rock star leaned over and planted a kiss on her soft, glowing cheek, while at the same time shaking soap suds from a wet saucepan all over her. She squealed, escaping from his slippery grasp and running to the other end of the kitchen.

'Not sure vice-ridden is quite where I should be aiming, but thanks,' he smiled. 'I like that.'

'I fell in love with someone hard-edged and vice-ridden,' Lynn added. 'It's very sexy.'

'See?' her man turned, impersonating her earlier tone while looping the tea towel around her neck and pulling her close into his body. 'How can I not love you when you behave like that? You're nymph-like when you play with me. It's unbelievably on-turning.'

His dream girl giggled, returning to his side and hugging him. 'Well, it would hardly show much integrity if I supported your public image but then forced you to be Mister Clean at home, would it?'

'You could,' Jeff countered.

'Yes, I could, but I don't want to. It's who you are.'

'So how's this?' he span her round to listen to his suggestion.

'How's what?'

'I know you don't want to be breathing in my second-hand smoke all the time,' he insisted. 'You've removed the clouds from my sun, so it's the least I can do to stop covering your life with a grimy film.'

'But you don't want to give up,' the spirited woman interjected.

'I know,' he laughed, putting his hand over her mouth to silence her. 'And if you let me finish, I'll tell you I'm not going to give up. I'm just saying I'll smoke outside, except when we've got smoking company.'

'So will that mean you'll smoke less?'

'Sure,' the swarthy Mediterranean brute nodded. 'That's the secondary benefit. Having to leave you every time I want a ciggie'll be a disincentive, so it'll gradually wean me off. That's my theory anyway. And who knows? One day I might want to give up altogether.'

'I love you, my beautiful, vice-ridden, black stallion,' Lynn swooned, pulling him by the hand into the lounge room. 'You've got work to do.'

'I have.'

The remaining evening hours passed in relative silence, both immersed in their various last minute tasks. Jeff was finishing off a batch of lyrics that he had promised to a fellow songwriter in Los Angeles, and his new secretary had taken it upon herself to write a funding proposal for a Childlight centre in Brisbane. From time to time, she would look up and catch him staring dreamily at her, only to have him look away *post haste*.

'Do you feel tired yet?' she asked, reading the glowing, red digits on the video recorder.

After over forty hours of solid sleep, it was hard to gauge which time zone the new man's body clock was set to. He had already run ten kilometres earlier in the day, before spending at least an hour in the gym and several more working, but he still had no real idea what time it was.

'Not really. You go to bed, if you want to. I might stay out here for a while. Is that OK?'

Lynn stretched, yawning. 'I will. It's after eleven, and I need to get going early in the morning. Thanks for a great day. It's really good to see you so happy.'

Jeff walked her to the bedroom, fending off mounting anxiety. 'Thanks to you too, angel. I am happy, especially with what's happening to us. I have to keep pinching myself. I can't actually believe I'm hearing some of the things you say. It's like I'm replaying my teenaged fantasies. I'd love to know what really brought us together.'

Lynn hugged him. 'You mean like some force from outer space?'

'No,' he mocked, smirking.

It did sound ridiculous, he had to admit.

'Before you pack me off to the loony bin, that's not what I mean. But you have to wonder why you agreed to go out with me that first time, don't you?'

'Look, mate!' the feisty nineteen-year-old insisted, pushing him out of the bedroom. 'Stop overanalysing and read a book or something. I was asked out by a tall, dark, handsome man to a play I wanted to see. We had a few laughs, we were on the same wavelength, and there was a physical connection. That's what brought us together. And then we fell in love. That's pretty much how it's supposed to happen, isn't it? It's normal.'

Her mystery man turned in the doorway to argue, but his chest met two palms pushing forwards with the strength of an Olympic athlete who had been training all day.

'Stop talking and get out, Plato. I love you and look forward to waking up next to you at about seven o'clock tomorrow morning.'

'Jeez! OK, OK. I get the message,' Jeff complained, eventually being given permission to kiss his concubine goodnight. 'Spenser would be closer, but Plato's good too. Sleep well, my gorgeous, alien angel. I'll do my best to comply with your wishes.'

As the door closed in his smiling face, the happy philosopher shrugged to himself. Lynn's was a perfectly good explanation, and quite possibly all there needed to be to it. That was what happened to most people, he surmised, and certainly considering animal evolution too. A physical attraction first, followed by sufficient compatibility to make a life together. So what compelled him always to look deeper? Why was he constantly driven to find greater meaning and hidden layers where perhaps there was none? Maybe all this soul-searching wasn't necessary. His partner obviously didn't think so. Both lovers had found what they were looking for, by whichever criteria they used to judge their prize. This was normal, his beautiful best friend had said, and who was he to think he had the monopoly on being right?

Seated back in the dimly-lit lounge room, with the doors to the balcony open to let in the night's cool breeze, the intellectual was in two minds whether normal was really what he sought at this stage. He agreed with his flatmate's earlier opinion about focussing his energy and passions on that which was important for him to achieve. However, right now, the concept felt very foreign and unnatural to him. He was determined to stay on course towards recovery, but the pull inside was strong and almost oppressive. Gravity the troll was not ready to wave his white flag just yet.

The songwriter moved to the balcony with the only guitar not already on its way to London and lit his first cigarette of the evening, whistling a melody and strumming along. Another new lyric had been running around his head for a couple of hours, and the resultant song took shape in the short time it took for its composer to smoke the one cigarette. Of course he was going to get used to this new way of living and thinking. How could he reject it after a matter of days, when he had beaten a path to its door for as long as he could remember?

'Get over yourself,' he whispered into the humidity. 'She loves you. Ça va être formidable. '

The other phenomenon totally contrary to Jeff was the fact that he didn't feel in the least bit tired. He had always been tired. In fact, sometimes he had felt as if exhaustion defined him. But now he wasn't tired, so what was he supposed to do? Jesus, it was like growing up and learning basic life skills all over again. How screwed up was that? He had a good teacher though. Somewhat callous tonight, he recalled with a smile.

Despite the straightforward way in which Lynn had accounted for how they had ended up together, the romantic simply couldn't let go of the notion that destiny or fate must have played a part. How many teenaged boys would have dreamed about meeting Australia's favourite superstar? Countless. How many wrote fan letters? Thousands, probably millions by now. He had seen the sacks full of mail she received these days. And how many men regularly tried to get backstage after a concert to meet her? Hundreds at a time.

So why, among all those other fans, had it been he who decided that she was more than a pretty face with an amazing body and the voice of an angel? Why Lynn Dyson and not one of the other good-looking film stars or singers whose posters lined teenagers' bedroom walls? Jeff Diamond had dated a significant number of beautiful, intelligent women in his relatively short lifetime but would never, ever have trusted anyone other than his *Regala* with his secrets, nor allowed any other lover to help him recover from the effects of his traumatic childhood.

Whether destiny had prodded a random tearaway from Canley Vale or whether said tearaway had prodded destiny, there simply must be other factors at play than "How it was supposed to happen." Even the eternal cynic, Gerald Michael Joseph Blake Junior, keeper of his worldly goods and knower of all things cold and commercial, had postulated that there was something more to his VIP client's situation than purely boy meets girl.

'Shit!' the twenty-two-year-old cursed out loud.

He hadn't rung Gerry back. How selfish of him. He had been so caught up in the aftermath of the Big Sleep that he had kept postponing the call until it was too late. What was it that his friend had wanted to know again? Whether he would ever get married? And Jeff had told the hesitant hedonist to ask him again when he was sober.

Well... Not a drop of drink had passed the alcoholic's lips since the few beers he had enjoyed in front of the last session of cricket with his mates, and it had been over seventy-two hours since he had smoked any dope. This afternoon he and Lynn had decided to get matching tattoos. For Christ's sake, wedding rings could be twisted off at a moment's notice!

So what was marriage anyway? What significance might marriage have for him beyond the deeper bond he and Lynn shared? They were already living under the same roof and talking about being octogenarians together, and had even made a pact to be the first pantomime horse to change the world. What difference would a ceremony and signatures on a register make to that?

What a formidable set of in-laws he would gain... Fuck! No, thanks. Surplus to requirements.

He and Lynn would have legal access to each others' fortunes. Big deal.

He could share his name with her if she wanted to. Yeah, maybe that would be kind of nice, but equally immaterial in the grand scheme of things.

Sliding the glass door shut behind him and relishing the silence of his newfound calm contemplation, Jeff wondered what his dream girl's view of marriage might be. It was one of those perennially avoided topics between "serious" boyfriends and girlfriends, under-discussed yet over-imagined. Gerry's current predicament was the only reason he and his gorgeous flatmate had had recourse to utter the word in each others' presence. Nonetheless, it was a well-known fact that women loved weddings and the thought of being married, and he saw no reason to believe that Lynn would be atypical. Furthermore, she was too well-bred ever to raise the topic herself.

However, the rock star felt fairly sure the chart-topping champion currently reclining in his bed would consider marriage at nineteen to be detrimental to her professional image.   She was ambitious and therefore slightly unconventional in this respect. She had never complained about the prospect of living in London "in sin", and neither was she afraid of bringing negative publicity or stigma upon herself or the prestigious family name by being in a *de facto* relationship. At least, she hadn't mentioned it. The world was about to enter the last quarter of the twentieth century, and no-one could accuse the post-Californian Lynn Dyson of not being independent and progressive.

The marriage preoccupation with which the affable accountant was struggling was far different though. The age-old legal union under God was an oft-prescribed antidote for the unfortunate side effect of original sin which had been visited on him. And Gerry Blake was certainly a non-practising Catholic who regularly indulged in a large amount of practice at being both original and sinful. He, like Jeff to a lesser degree, had been brought up with the doctrine of the priests and nuns in primary school and church. Guilt, shame and atonement had been their staples while growing up. For all his flaws and superficiality, faced with the onset of parenthood, even the indomitable Irishman would feel compelled to serve his penance on some level.

Approaching this ethical hill, the clear-headed thinker's brain shifted gear, now sitting at the piano and staring out at the darkness and the myriad flickering lights beyond his balcony. What decent person would wish to inflict bastardhood onto an innocent child? It shouldn't matter these days, but it did. Even in the mid-seventies, people were somehow still curious to discover who were the illegitimate ones. Whether it was to administer pity, scorn or ridicule, these kids were singled out for one of the few attributes they had no power to change. Adults who found themselves unexpectedly expecting could negate such impropriety by marrying, should they choose to, whereas an unborn child lacked the wherewithal to force its parents to legalise its very existence.

A conclusion was forming. The machinations of his mind reminded Jeff of the songwriting process, back where he had started out after having been sent packing from the bedroom. Marriage was something that should be reserved for when one needed to make that final commitment, which surely had to be the age-old and very primal decision to create the next generation.

That was what he would tell his troubled mate, the old soul decided. There could be no better reason for his friend to get married than to give his child the best start in life. Hopefully in years to come, the marriage certificate of its parents would no longer be such a vital artefact for a child. Regardless, it was his considered opinion that Australian society still expected one today.

And good, old Gerry Blake definitely intended to be a pillar of Australian society, even though currently he was little more than a dancing pole in a Thai brothel. Even if he and Heather were to divorce some years hence, their child would not be a bastard, and his mate would have done the honourable thing by him or her.

The young man stared straight in front of him, gripped by a strange feeling of foreboding. Fatherhood was an intimidating prospect. Jeff's own father had made a complete mess of it, both through ignorance and in the pursuit of selfish, ill-gotten gains. Yet poor parenting notwithstanding, if his devout Roman Catholic grandparents hadn't insisted that this good-for-nothing, immigrant Polish Jew marry their pregnant daughter, Madalena's unwanted baby brother would never have been born. Sitting in his comfortable city apartment, with the best arse-end of a pantomime horse that ever lived sleeping peacefully no more than twenty metres away, the closet intellectual suddenly became a big fan of marriage.

It was patently obvious to the Sydneysider that taking one's eye off the ball as a father could have disastrous consequences. He only had to cast his mind back to all those messed-up, under-educated, directionless kids he had seen on the bus to Canley Vale a few months ago. Most probably had fathers like his, who didn't give a damn as long as their offspring didn't get in the way.

And then there were fathers like Gerald Blake Senior and Bart Dyson... also Senior, Jeff realised... who were highly intentional fathers. They moulded and flexed and conscripted and pressured their children into the successful progeny they had planned. This brand of fatherhood was better than the first, since it was a type of no-expense-spared husbandry. However, there were still more destructive aspects to it than the afflicted man cared for.

This type of overbearing parenting wasn't solely the domain of the rich either. The child inside shivered as he remembered a Taiwanese student he had befriended in the psychiatric hospital, whose parents deprived themselves of all but life's bare necessities in order to send their only son to medical school. The unfortunate boy had ended up attempting suicide because he couldn't cope with the pressure of his studies.

So what was in between? There had to be a middle ground, where children could be nurtured and encouraged to succeed, but to succeed in a life that they had been shown how to choose for themselves. There was nothing wrong with being pushed to do well. It was a lot better than the inattention of his own parents, which was no direction whatsoever. But to give life to an individual and then try to create him or her in one's own image was morally wrong in Jeff's book.

So far, the prolific composer had only written one song that had projected him forward as a father, and that was "Roads of Stones". That song had been written in nineteen-sixty-eight, he figured. He had turned sixteen, uncelebrated and rebellious, during the time of the student revolutions in France and the Soviet invasion of his father's homeland. The inquisitive adolescent had been fascinated by the vagaries of a law which finally bestowed upon him the legal right to have sexual intercourse with a human female, long after his own iniquitous *début*. By this invisible starting line, the young man had assumed the legal eagles in their infinite wisdom had intended him now to be old enough to sustain a mature relationship with a woman, and thereby be responsible enough to rear a child together as a family.

But just how wise were these lawmakers in reality? Who in their right mind would rule a sixteen-year-old boy suitable father material? But then again, how old did one need to be to act responsibly on behalf of a dependent? Was it even a quality measurable by age? The teenaged loner had owned a cross-breed German Shepherd for a while, until it had been shot by the butcher down the street for stealing. He had looked after it fairly well, but it wasn't a child. It hadn't needed much in the way of encouragement or education, and yet looking back, what he had given that dog was about the same as he had received from his own parents: food, water, shelter and the occasional game or scolding.

The dog had escaped the abuse however, he rued.

So where did love figure in these golden rules? Age-appropriate, as Sarah Friedman's research questionnaire had repeatedly qualified. Jeff had loved that dog in his way, provided it with affection and attention. Funny how love was always omitted when it came to the judiciary... Why was that? Was it because it was too hard to quantify, measure or even to describe, and hence the powers-that-be had taken the easy way out? How defeatist this was, simply to omit altogether the very factor which made all the difference! His parents had probably loved him enough in accordance with a deficient legal definition, as did Lynn's and Gerry's awe-inspiring patriarchy.

And there lay the crux of his dilemma, and hence one to which Childlight could easily turn its mighty hand in the future. Sitting in the dark, the millionnaire brought down a precipitous verdict not to sell the Stones Road flat, prompting his fingers to find some more soft chords. He had written in "Roads of Stones" that his son had visited his childhood home, as Lynn had reminded him when they were there. Something had made him write a child into his future. Perhaps it was the same something which had made him buy two tickets to see "A Streetcar Named Desire" on the million-to-one chance that his path might cross with that of a certain golden-haired saviour? Something decidedly abnormal...

Well, would you look at that? One in the eye for Miss Irony for a change. There he was, back where he had started just before Lynn had gone to bed. Whether by destiny or design, it was a perfect circle.

The imaginative wanderer was positive that his beautiful best friend would want children of her own someday. She would be the most amazing mother, with her boundless patience and gritty determination. She was also a born teacher. He thought back to the techniques she had used on him. There was a lot of her father in her, he recognised, but with a gentler, more compassionate overlay. She engineered situations for him to experiment safely, encouraging and testing him over and over until new behaviours became second nature.

Lynn's kids would be independent and highly motivated, yet loving, respectful and oh, so tolerant, just like their mother. Jeff knew he taught more through storytelling than engineering. He would plant so many seeds in their young heads and talk through the hypotheticals until they formed solid opinions, but parenting from his amazing partner would be more directly experiential. This could be a great combination, but hadn't he always known this?

Decision made. Jeff concluded that he would be proud and honoured to be the father of Lynn Dyson's children. And therefore, to give them the best start in life, he would get married someday. He would ring Gerry tomorrow and let him know his sober, considered position on the subject.

The contented man felt confident that he had focussed outwards for long enough to allay his fat cat fears, and Lynn was fast asleep, so she would never know. It was almost one o'clock in the morning, and his brain was beginning to tick more slowly.

'Hey, angel. I'm tired,' he whispered. *Well done, mate.*

The new man climbed into bed next to the future mother of his future children and slipped his arm around her. 'I love you.'

Drowsy lips kissed his hand. 'I love you too. Sleep well,' she murmured.

***

Six-fifteen, Lynn saw on the clock beside her head. All was well to her left, by the looks of things. She had a vague recollection of her man coming to bed but wasn't sure if she had dreamed it. She slid out of bed and went to put the kettle on.

'Good morning,' Jeff said, rolling over. 'Are you coming back?'

The beautiful blonde bent over and kissed him. 'Yes. Morning. Do you want tea?'

'Good. Yes, please. How very normal.'

Indeed, normalcy reigned supreme in the Diamond-Dyson residence as their life singular commenced another bright morning. A mug of tea was being placed on Jeff's bedside table when he returned from the bathroom.

'What time did you come to bed?'

'Just after one,' he replied. 'You spoke to me. Don't you remember?'

His flatmate nodded, climbing back into bed. 'Yes, I think so. Uneventful night then?'

Was that a trace of regret in her voice? 'Are you disappointed?'

'No, of course not,' Lynn squeezed his arm. 'It's great. I'm going to have to strike nightmare abatement services off my job description.'

'Boring, isn't it?' Jeff smiled, moving her hand to something he hoped she would find more interesting. 'It's been like that since I came to bed.'

His girlfriend was shocked. 'Really?'

'No!' the comic chuckled.

She was still naïve sometimes, and he loved it.

'I'd have woken you up by now if that was the case, don't you worry!'

Seeing his dream girl lying naked beside him, looking as if she belonged there, it put the intellectual in mind of another slow transformation taking place. He turned towards her and gathered her in close to his body, feeling a strange sort of serenity behind the arousal gnawing at him to move faster.

'You know what I thought would take me a while to adjust to, but it hasn't?' he began, fondling Lynn's left breast with a covetous hand and kissing her shoulder.

'No,' she giggled and twisted around to face him, playfully grabbing his penis. 'What's that?'

'Hey!' her lover objected. 'Take it slowly! I thought it was only me who'd been waiting all night.'

The smiling face kissed his lips, stroking him as she pressed herself against the whole length of his body. 'I can feed off you too, can't I?' she challenged, staring into his eyes expectantly.

'Sure. Any time. But when you're dating... well, for men anyway... there's always that drive to make sure you get your rocks off at some point in the finite period available while you're together. Otherwise, what's the point? You know?'

Lynn nodded, climbing on top of him. 'Yes, I know only too well.'

Jeff shook his head, smiling. He must have been very demanding, he took from her look of resignation.

'Yeah. Sorry, angel. That's exactly what I mean. Now we're living together, that's no longer necessary, and I didn't think I'd get it, but I do.'

'Sex on tap,' the beautiful blonde suggested, sitting astride her man.

'OK!' the lustful twenty-two-year-old responded, taking hold of her hands from where they were fondling his chest. 'I wouldn't have put it quite like that, but since you're offering...'

The passionate couple made the most of the morning sunlight, slowly losing themselves in pleasure. Today was New Year's Eve, and tonight was Gerry's big party, where they were part of the evening's entertainment. There was a rehearsal at five in the afternoon, which meant the rest of the day was their own.

'How do you feel about the tattoos this morning?' Lynn asked the spent man breathing heavily beside her.

'Fine. I like the idea. You?'

Lynn stretched her right arm over her opposite shoulder and pointed to the spot which they had picked out the previous afternoon. 'Just there?'

'Yep. Pretty much,' the musician affirmed, kissing the skin next to her fingers.

'I'm just wondering about my dress for tonight, and whether it'll be all sore and red and ugly.'

'Aha! Excellent observation,' Jeff agreed. 'We don't have to do it today. We don't have to do it at all, if you've changed your mind.'

The sexy woman looked him in the eyes. 'No, I haven't changed my mind. I want to do it, but I don't know how long it'll take to get the desired result. To heal, you know.'

'Me neither,' the songwriter acknowledged. 'We could go in and discuss it with them, and then decide later.'

'I know...' his girlfriend announced. 'Why don't we get temporary ones drawn on? Do you think they could do that? It would be like a test drive. Then if we don't like them, we'd know, and it wouldn't be too late.'

How frightfully sensible, her lover smiled. 'You know, it's so subtle...'

'What is?' Lynn asked. 'Don't you like that idea?'

'Yeah. It's a great idea,' he replied, shaking his head from side to side and making her smile. 'I mean this conversation. There's such a fine line between the impetuous act of a normally rational person, and the compulsion that I previously would've shown. I'd have said, "Fuck it! Wear a different dress," but your solution's so much better.'

Lynn kissed her man's forehead as he lay staring at the ceiling in the half light of the bedroom. 'You're so gorgeous. Stop thinking about everything. I've got to get going. What are you doing today?'

Jeff opened his eyes, and groaned when he remembered the pledge he had made before coming to bed.

'Hmm... I have to go and see Gerry. I remembered at midnight that I never returned his call. There's heaps of stuff to sort out before we leave, so that'll be most of the morning gone. Then I need to get a haircut, and all that mundanery.'

'Shall I meet you at Gerry's office after training?' she asked, organising her things and heading for the shower. 'There's a girl at the gym' who's covered in tattoos. If she's in today, I'll ask her where the best places are.'

'*Excelente*,' her man agreed, half asleep again. 'Hey? D'you know if your bank account's going to be working when we get there? The last thing we want to be doing is carrying around huge wads of pound-cash because we can't get access to our money.'

The worldly sportswoman laughed, pinning her hands on her hips. 'What a turnaround between us! I'm worried about tattoos, and you're worried about money. Right-oh, boss. I'll find out today.'

Jeff wagged a finger at her. 'Stop thinking about everything,' he scolded.

***

Gerry was on the telephone in the reception area of Blake & Partners' recently refurbished offices and juggled with the receiver as he attempted to shake hands with his biggest client, much to the amusement of the flawlessly turned-out young ladies at the desk. Jeff slapped him on the back on the way to his sumptuously appointed corner office. The door was open, so he entered alone and waited, hands in pockets, surveying his manager's commanding view over Flinders Street station and southwards towards the bay. It was another blisteringly hot day, and there were several tourist ferries on the river, taking people to Williamstown or on other Yarra cruises.

'Mate! Nice haircut,' Gerry shouted, closing the door. 'Where the hell have you been the last few days? You're running out of time. When do you fly?'

'Yeah. Sorry,' the younger man apologised. 'Friday. I was going to ring yesterday but I didn't remember until midnight. Didn't think you'd appreciate a call then.'

Gerry picked up a large bundle of files and envelopes, snorting his dismay. 'Shall we get some lunch somewhere?' he suggested. 'I could do with getting out of here. You can pay.'

The striking pair left the building via the back entrance into Flinders Lane and crossed into DeGraves Street, where the lunch crowd was buzzing with holiday chatter. They found a table inside one of the well-established Italian restaurants, ensconcing themselves in a quiet corner. Most customers had elected to dine outside and enjoy the sunshine, giving the recognisable men-about-town an opportunity to talk freely without being hassled.

'My answer's yes, by the way,' Jeff announced, picking up the menu.

His old friend was instantly dumbfounded. 'Say what? Yes to the marriage question, you mean?'

The star nodded, pouring his beer slowly into a long, tilted glass. 'Yep. Surprised?'

'Gobsmacked!' Gerry exclaimed. 'Is this your own work, or has Lynn put the hard word on you?'

'All my own work, mate,' his client closed the menu, having chosen his meal already. 'But not for a while though.'

'Shit! Now you're piling on the pressure,' the executive complained, looking pale. 'Mum's been at it too. And Jack. I'm going to cave, I can tell.'

The waiter took their order and asked for Jeff's autograph, which he graciously supplied on one of his manager's Stonebridge Music business cards.

'But why would it be caving?' he asked. 'You shouldn't do it if you're just bowing to pressure. You need to do it because you've convinced yourself it's the right thing to do.'

The suave accountant took a handwritten letter out of his pile of papers and handed it to his pseudo-brother. 'Look what Mum sent... Can you believe she *wrote* to me? If you've got something to say, say it to my face, old dear.'

The musician scanned the first couple of paragraphs. 'This is private, Gez. I'm not going to read it,' he said, handing back Celia's letter. 'She's written to me before too. She cares, that's all. It's the old-fashioned way.'

'It is the right thing to do. I know that,' Gerry hinted at acquiescence. 'Would you do it? In my position, I mean.'

'Christ, mate!' Jeff scoffed, tapping the handle of his fork on the table. 'How should I know? In exactly the same situation, yes, I think I would. For the sake of the kid. You're not involved with anyone else; Heather's an attractive, intelligent woman, and she's going to be the mother of your child. Would it be that bad? And you'd have sex on tap, as my angel so delightfully put it just this very morning.'

Their bowls of pasta arrived, and the new man tucked into his *con gusto*, amazed at how much his appetite had increased since he had returned from Sydney, covering the sauce with more than a generous helping of parmesan cheese. He wound his fork through the sticky spaghetti and fixed his friend with a hard stare. On the other side of the table, the older man pushed his lunch away from him, his own hunger fading due to the topic's enormity.

'No. Not that bad,' he conceded. 'Sex on tap? Lynn really said that?'

'About us, not you. Don't panic, Blake-san. We don't devote much air time to your sex life.'

Gerry sniffed, flicking the distasteful comment to one side. 'We wouldn't be exclusive to each other. Neither of us wants it, and I just don't think I could give up the freedom. But you're right about the child. That's what really matters, isn't it?'

Jeff nodded. 'Damned right, it is. Even if you don't stay together. Even if you give it three years or so then get a divorce, at least your kid'll have a rightful claim to your name. You'll have developed that all-important connection that can endure a graceful exit from your relationship with his or her mum, and then you'd have a legitimate case to stay involved if you want to. And who knows? You might.'

'Three years?' the sullen Irishman had a distant look in his eyes. 'For fuck's sake, that's an eternity. Just think how long two years in the wilderness was like for you.'

'Yeah. You're right. But you'd hardly be in the bloody wilderness. If Heather's not demanding you be faithful, you'd have the best of all worlds, mate. One year then? Six months? Jesus! It doesn't matter how long. And especially if you're both free to see other people. You'd just need to be able to divide your week between dad-time and fun-time.'

'Yeah, but what would that do for my rep'?' the ladies' man asked, realising he was backing himself into a corner.

'What fucking rep'?' Jeff laughed aloud. 'You're a legend in your own lunchtime, you bastard. The women you date don't care 'bout no rep', man! And even if they did, most women love kids. It'd be like having a puppy. A real draw-card. Instant bedroom pass.'

Gerry pondered this new angle. 'Hmm... Maybe you have a point there. And I am going to be lonely while you're swanning around in old London town.'

'Is that right?' the celebrity jeered. 'Since when have you ever been lonely? When's the baby due anyway? Depending on the timing, you could come over for a few weeks, and we could take the rally car up to the Lake District. It'd be great.'

The businessman began to warm to what he was hearing. His friend was correct. Life wouldn't be all bad on that basis.

'End of April. Springtime in Paris,' he dreamed, adopting a mock romantic tone. 'Yeah. That might work. Heather's mum's going to be staying with her for a few months when the baby's first born, so I could scarper safely. I'd be useless anyway. What do I know about new babies?'

Jeff lifted his empty glass and filled it from one of the new bottles of beer which had arrived at their table. He didn't know anything about babies either, yet last night he had decided he would have at least one. Jesus! Him, a family man? Who would have guessed?

'Mate, no-one knows anything about new babies, especially Heather. She'll be shitting herself, so even if you're useless, at least you'd be there and useless.'

'So what does Lynn think about all this?'

'Don't bring Lynn into it,' Jeff pointed his fork in Gerry's general direction as a warning. 'We haven't talked about it.'

'OK. Let me put it another way,' the accountant persisted, starting on his spaghetti at last. 'If Miss Dynamite told you today that she was pregnant, what would you do?'

'Miss Dynamite? You old charmer. I wish I'd thought of that! Is it mine?' his client rebuked. 'Hypothetically, I mean...'

'Yes, you idiot. Of course it's yours.'

'Good. I'm hypothetically relieved then. Yes, certainly. I'd ask her if she wanted to get married. It's different for us. We're already committed, so it wouldn't be that big of a deal. It won't happen though, because we're careful.'

'Very funny,' Gerry frowned, decidedly queasy. 'One slip up in over ten years isn't bad. I'm surprised it hasn't happened sooner, to be honest. How come you've escaped?'

'Careful, mate. Fuck carefully.'

The two men changed the subject, needing to finalise a number of commercial decisions and schedule obligations before the millionnaire jetted off to the UK. Their conversation became more relaxed after a couple more bottles of beer and the prickly subject of parenthood had been temporarily filed away, before they were eventually moved to dissect the form of the entire Australian cricket team in advance of the Sydney test.

'Shit!' Jeff suddenly remembered that his beautiful best friend had told him she would be meeting him at Blake & Partners after training. 'Lynn's probably up in your office now.'

With the hands on his watch tripping past one o'clock, the superstar paid the bill to an awestruck waitress before handing the receipt to his manager. 'That's yours.'

The two men thanked the staff and acknowledged the waves and smiles of their fellow diners as they emerged from the upper level and stepped out into the street. It was another particularly sticky day, and Gerry loosened his tie. While wandering back towards 333 Collins Street, his client confessed to their plans for the rest of the day.

'We're seeing someone about getting tattoos this arvo.'

His friend's eyes almost burst out of their sockets. 'You're what? Where?'

'That'd be telling,' the rock star answered with a boyish grin. 'And it's harder to get rid of a tattoo than a wedding ring, mate. So the ball's back in your court.'

'Jesus, Mary and Joseph!' the businessman lost all colour in his face again. 'I envy you for being so sure. Hey! Ship ahoy!'

Jeff followed his friend's hand as it pointed ahead. Sure enough, Lynn was walking towards them, hair in a ponytail and her sports bag over her shoulder.

'Hello! I wondered where you were. I went upstairs, and they told me you'd gone to lunch.'

Feeling proud, the luckiest man alive kissed the stunning woman in broad daylight and watched her embrace his old friend too. She looked so relaxed and confident, and instantly he felt his libido switch into overdrive. Moreover, the thought crossed his mind that grumpy, old Gravity was nowhere to be found. Previously, the troll would have jumped on any such delicious awakenings and done his best to give him a metaphysical cold shower.

Standing in the street with his best mate watching his every move, the horny celebrity was almost disappointed. However, by the way Lynn was responding to his touch, she was most definitely not disappointed.

'Apologies, angel. We got talking, and well... You know how it is...'

The athlete took his hand. 'Did you tell Gerry what we're up to this afternoon?'

'He did indeed,' the older man replied. 'It's bloody brave of you. What happens if you go off him?'

Lynn shrugged. 'Or the other way round?'

LORRAINE PESTELL

Countdown To London

Arriving at the hotel for Blake & Partners' fancy New Year's Eve extravaganza, Lynn Dyson and Jeff Diamond ably fulfilled their duty as celebrity greeters, wooing the upmarket crowd with their professional charm and the occasional private confession. Cathy Patterson had made sure only a handful of entertainment industry reporters had been given access, and the couple schmoozed them all while cocktails were served.

As usual, one of Gerry's senior partners commandeered the prettiest girl in the room, leaving Jeff to face the press on his own. Previously, her sudden absence would have triggered an involuntary downward spiral, which at first he waited for. After a minute of silent preparation, all the while responding to questions flying at him from all angles, he finally allowed himself to relax, realising that he was perfectly alright on his own.

'Absolutely not,' the rock star smiled. 'I'm looking forward to a long series of regular one night stands, stretching out over the next sixty or seventy years. It's going to be immensely gratifying.'

From several metres away, Lynn glanced across at the sound of feverish female voices, instantly figuring her playboy boyfriend to be at its core. She excused herself to return to his side, in a mixture of jealousy and protectiveness, and her reappearance was met with another round of joyous whoops. Thinking how utterly delicious her man looked in his tuxedo, she joined the others in ogling his chiselled jawline freshly-shaven and the long, noble neck above his bow tie. She was filled with pride when picturing the first of two tattoos healing under a crisp, white shirt. He looked hotter than hot, and didn't he know it!

'What did I miss?' the young beauty asked, rubbing his chest over the tender site.

For once, Jeff had nothing to feel guilty about. The sign of an angel now adorned his body forever. He kissed his beautiful best friend on the cheek, so as not to smudge her make-up so early in the evening, and squeezed her slim waist tight against his hip.

'Debbie asked me if the rumours were true about us living together in London,' he began, catching the eye of the Woman's Weekly reporter and grinning from ear to ear.

'Yes. But that's old news, isn't it?'

Several of the other awestruck female guests jostled to listen in to their not-so-private conversation. The journalist repeated what she had asked the imposing songwriter, to gauge his girlfriend's reaction.

'No, that wasn't what the fuss was about,' she told the blonde singer. 'I asked Jeff whether it'll be difficult to give up all the one night stands and instant gratification that he's infamous for.'

This time, the young man gave into a modicum of embarrassment as his irresistible flatmate heard the screaming and excited chatter at close range.

'And what did you say?'

'Ah, you know… Something about having over half a century of steamy one-night stands ahead of us. That OK with you?'

Lynn cringed a little inside, knowing full well that London would be her long-awaited opportunity to shed her goodie-two-shoes image with Australia's media posse. For now however, what should she say? Her parents were unlikely to get wind of any comments made for the women's magazine for a week or so, by which time the youngsters would have long flown the coop. And she could hardly lie, could she?

'One night stands?' the young woman frowned. 'But you're such a morning person.'

With that, his dream girl slotted her arm through his and led her quietly overwhelmed dinner partner away, leaving high jinx behind them. The rest of the evening proceeded in much the same vein, with the boy from Canley Vale riding high on their combined happiness. The boss and his famous hired help were the perfect hosts, wowing existing and prospective clients with their charming personalities and entertaining conversation. With the charity auction and other fundraising efforts well supported, many new business relationships were cemented, all lubricated by festive cheer.

Gerry and his date for the evening, the flame-haired Natasha, joined Lynn Dyson and Jeff Diamond on the stage at about three minutes before midnight, and they had all linked arms for the countdown. Waiters made sure they each had a full glass of champagne. When the moment arrived, the *Maître d'* signalled fifteen seconds and continued to mark off the remaining ticks with each wave of his ceremonial arm.

'Ten!' Lynn's voice rang out.

'Nine!' Jeff was next.

'Eight!' It was Gerry's turn.

'Seven!' Natasha's.

'Six!'

The sequence cycled again until the handsome rock star's rich baritone shouted 'One!' and the host completed the process at the top of his voice.

'Happy New Year, everybody!'

Jeff embraced his stunning partner almost reverentially up on the stage, to sentimental gasps and rousing cheers of delight from their audience. Guests and band all wished each other their New Year greetings in whichever way they saw fit and downed their bubbly with similar effusiveness.

'Happy London Year!' the romantic shouted into the tennis champion's ear, raising his glass of champagne to hers. 'Here's to us.'

'Happy London Year to you too!' Lynn echoed, kissing him without inhibition.

Still officially on duty however, the blissful duo immediately broke apart and took up their *cabaret* positions. As they had rehearsed behind the scenes earlier, Gerry and Natasha filed off stage right, and Lynn nodded to the drummer to start their final scheduled number. Jeff banged out the chords to "Auld Lang Syne" on the piano, before they shifted into the lyrics that had been written especially and hastily for the evening, an adaptation of the traditional Scottish folk melody for their largely Anglo-Antipodean crowd. Within a few bars, a large number of couples rushed to the wooden floor in front of them to partake in the first dance of nineteen-seventy-five.

The executive host applauded wildly and wolf-whistled as the song drew to a close, very grateful for the famous pair's assistance in making his gala *soirée* reach its successful conclusion. He was sorry to see his good friends depart overseas but was also keen to seize his chance to fly north to Cairns and finally lay claim to the new boat. Natasha had agreed to fly up with her boss, excited at the prospect of cruising down the east coast in such luxury.

Returning to the stage and grabbing the microphone, Gerry shook his mate's hand warmly and gave the stunning blonde a robust, alcohol-fuelled hug. 'Ladies and Gentlemen, please put your hands together one more time for our special guests tonight, Lynn Dyson and Jeff Diamond!'

The rest of the throng applauded and stamped their feet, while the star performers reminded everyone to thank the band as well. They all took several bows, and calls for *encores* rang out all around them. Exhausted, Gerry thereafter called the proceedings to a close, and one by one, everyone trooped off the stage.

The aspirant travellers made for their table and graciously began to sign autographs for the long queue of people who had already gathered nearby. Meanwhile, the remaining band members and the staff at the opulent Collins Street hotel, situated only a block from Blake & Partners' Victorian headquarters, were being thanked heartily by their host for having worked hard all night. Eventually, the majority of guests drifted away, and the clean-up effort commenced.

Right on cue, Lynn spied her older brother in the doorway of the ballroom and went over to meet him. 'Happy New Year, June,' the young woman said brightly, kissing the enormous man on the cheek.

'You too. Did it go well?'

'Yes, thanks,' she replied. 'How was your party?'

'Excellent, yeah. I've just dropped Julie back home. Shall we get going?'

Melbourne's Best and Fairest footballing hero was quickly surrounded by eager admirers, having arrived to drive his sister back to Benloch in preparation for their family's arduous day of competitive deliverance for the coming year. The siblings frowned at each other and sighed comically, foreshadowing the long day ahead.

Seeing the matching pair together, Jeff broke away from a humorous conversation he had been sharing with their rowdy bunch of session musicians to join his girlfriend and her brother.

'H N Y, Junior,' the larrikin greeted the new arrival, grasping his hand and shaking it vigorously.

'Of course!' the huge hulk laughed. 'And you too, mate.'

'So you've come to take her away,' the dark-haired celebrity moaned, looking glum and feeling glummer. 'Can you pick someone else instead?'

'Yes. OK,' Junior scoffed. 'Dad'll never notice the difference. You guys always get me into strife. Are you ready?'

'No,' Lynn replied, putting on her own sad face. 'But I'll come quietly.'

The trio strolled back to the small salon which the couple had used as their makeshift dressing room for the evening. The sexy singing sensation changed in a flash and emerged dressed in jeans and a light jumper, with her bags packed. Reversion from performer to flatmate at once made her boyfriend's heart soar and his sex drive leap into action, yet all thoughts of further advances in the dawning potential of this New Year were futile. Back in the cavernous shell of the ballroom, Lynn introduced her brother to Gerry.

'I'm so going to miss you tonight,' Jeff told his dream girl. 'I forgot how to be on my own already.'

'I'll ring early in the morning,' she promised. 'I'll miss you too. Heaps. Just think of next week and you'll be fine.'

Panic reared up behind her boyfriend's eyes. 'One more dance?'

'There's no music, you idiot.'

'Upstairs, I mean,' the comic fought to quell his overreaction.

Lynn raised her hand to his shirt, applying just enough pressure through the dressing over his smarting tattoo to send shockwaves through his chest. The simple communicative act, indecipherable to anyone else, served to flood his mind with sensual input, as the only option available to her.

'No, Jeff. I love you. You'll be OK,' she reinforced, her heels high enough to kiss his lips without standing on tiptoes.

'Cheers. I know. Good luck, angel. Hope it's not too tough tomorrow.'

The lovers embraced once more for luck, and the tall, handsome stranger watched the love of his life leave with her brother, embibing her compassion into his veins like a drug. Regardless, to his disappointment, even before they were fully out of sight, Gravity had raced to grab his heart, and a figurative wrestling match broke out between the old adversaries. Jeff turned away from the doors, feeling rather sick, and headed back to what remained of the party and in search of some entertainment.

While Gerry continued to attend to the last few guests, in full-on schmooze mode, one of the country's richest men set about assisting the hotel staff to stack chairs and roll away tables into storage off to the side of the function room. It felt just like the old days, he rued. Anything to delay having to go back to the apartment alone.

'D'you fancy another drink in the bar before we call it a night?' he asked his manager and the leggy redhead, who were by now tangled in each other and balanced precariously on a dining chair.

'No, thanks, mate,' Gerry answered. 'We're heading back now. I'm shagged out.'

'No worries. I'll do the same.'

'Listen, mate. Thanks so much for everything,' the host reiterated, standing up and embracing his dispirited friend, of course none the wiser as to his mood. 'You and Lynn really made this evening swing. Fantastic job, mate.'

Jeff slapped the hard-working businessman hard on the back. 'It was a pleasure. Everyone had a good night. Book us for next year, if you want. You'll have to talk to my agent.'

'Right you are,' Gerry laughed. 'Does that go for the girl too?'

'The girl?' his friend exclaimed, shaking his head. 'Oh, you'll pay for that when she hears...'

With only a handful of curious heads turning as he walked towards the reception desk, the famous musician left the hotel through the same anonymous rear fire exit of which Lynn and her brother had availed themselves, before slinking unnoticed past a larger group of casually-dressed adults who were waiting on Collins Street for the celebrity couple to emerge from the party. Men and women, he noticed, in roughly equal number; not groupies but genuine fans. He took this as another sign that he and his dream girl had been accepted as an item. The couple wasn't so naïve not to assume a certain number of their more objectifying devotees to be hostile towards the union, since it cancelled out any mystique around either star's accessibility. However, the proportion caught up in the Christmas romance of the decade far outnumbered the dissenters.

And so it was that Jeff Diamond, multi-millionnaire, philanthropist and most popular entertainer in present-day Australia, came to be walking through the streets of Melbourne alone at two-thirty on New Year's morning. The clubs and pubs along Bourke and Russell Streets were bursting at the seams with happy drunks, and hordes more people roamed the streets in search of either a taxi or another party. Having shed his bow tie and opened his shirt, and with his dinner jacket hooked over his shoulder, the dark man with the darkening heart did his best to stick to the dark laneways in order to avoid becoming drawn into any further revelry, no longer confident in his ability to refuse any time-wasting and sinful stopgaps.

What a start to the year! On his own again. *Oh, well... Not for long*, the young man sighed, still disconcerted by how quickly he had found himself sliding downwards.

Snap out of it, Jeff scolded himself. The journey from last New Year's Day to this had taken the superstar far and wide, and from deep, dark despair to a brightly-coloured, telescopic paradise. At the same hollow juncture, last year's model would have paid no mind to detouring right about now and ending up finding a room with a total stranger to while the rest of the early hours away in superficial, carnal pleasures. This year's model clung to his resolve, frantically engaging all five senses to call up a lumbering Jumbo Jet at full speed on the runway.

The new man went straight back to his own apartment, turned the key quickly in his front door, flashed his metaphorical sword at the demons which had been weakened by the love of his good woman, turned on the television without even bothering to find out what was showing, kicked off his shoes and promptly fell asleep on the couch, still dressed like a cabaret clown.

Unfortunately, not long afterwards, Jeff awoke with a start when his watch crashed onto the glass top of the coffee table. Fighting for breath, he sat up on the couch, taking a few minutes to remember where he was.

'What the fuck?' he shouted angrily at the slowly retreating images.

***

It felt as if the elegant but troubled man in the creased white dress shirt and black suit trousers had only recently managed to doze off again when the telephone rang on the side table behind his ear. He had no idea of the time, but judging by the brightness streaming in from the balcony, it had been light for a number of hours already.

'Hello?' he said, turning down the television's volume and attempting to sound enthusiastic.

'Jeff, it's me,' came Lynn's voice down the line. 'You don't sound too good. What's up?'

'Hey, gorgeous. How're you going?'

His girlfriend's telepathic powers didn't need to work too hard to realise that things hadn't gone too well since she had left the party. 'Bad night?'

600

'Ah, yeah. I'm OK,' her boyfriend sniffed, fighting to stay positive. 'It's just not the same when you're not here, but it's all good now.'

'Did you dream again? Sorry.'

Jeff was annoyed the feebleness in his voice was so hard to dislodge. 'Don't be. You have to be able to leave me alone sometimes, you know, angel. Don't beat yourself up. The nightmare was nowhere near so intense, and you were in it this time. At least I seem to have more success protecting you before I wake up screaming, and the door was pretty much OK. Life's good, baby. What's it like there?'

'OK. That's not so bad,' the patient woman encouraged him. 'It's going to be great to get out of Australia, isn't it? I didn't talk to anyone last night. Just went straight to my room and crawled into bed. I'm willing to bet that by the time we're coming back from London, you'll be pretty straight. It's bound to take time to figure out what all the different triggers are. How's your head? Did you party on much longer after I left?'

'About an hour, maybe,' the reformed transgressor replied, 'and then I stuck around to help tidy up for a bit. I was home by three. My head's a bit sore, but I'll live.'

'I'm ringing with a request, actually,' Lynn broached, drawing a deep breath, 'from Mum and Dad.'

'Oh, yeah? What sort of request?'

The young woman continued. 'They'd like you to join us for dinner this evening. They want to give us some sort of proper send-off.'

'Firing squad?' the comic offered.

'No!' Lynn was a little annoyed by the swift, sarcastic retort, but understood his reaction. 'Don't be so mean. They're adjusted to things now. They're happy for us to be going to London together. Really. Dad's impressed with your PhD subject. I think they want to mend some bridges before we leave the country. Please will you come?'

Jeff sighed, knowing it was the right thing to do. He wanted peace and harmony to break out too, but his pride was stubborn. He expected Big D would be the same. No doubt this cosy family dinner idea had been cooked up by the women to smooth the waters, and this was as good a reason as any to accept his fate.

'Sure,' he agreed. 'For you, anything. As long as we can go to the dam before dinner.'

Lynn giggled. 'OK! You drive a hard bargain. I think I could handle that. What are you going to be doing today?'

The ungrateful songwriter felt a lump in his throat. His *Regala* always made things better. He should ditch his petty grudges once and for all.

'Working on a few last minute things this morning, then I'm having lunch with Suzanne. She wanted to catch up with both of us before we left, but we're going to run out of time. Do you mind?'

'No, of course not. It's a good idea. Tell her I'm sorry I couldn't make it.'

'Thanks for what you did last night, by the way.'

'With the tattoo?'

'Nope. Jeez, I need you here,' the sportswoman heard her boyfriend's voice crack.

'Hey... You're OK, aren't you? Not long now,' Lynn geed him up. 'Get some breakfast. I'll see you about five, five-thirty. Please could you bring something for me to wear? All my stuff from here's already gone. Pick something appropriate.'

The twenty-two-year-old scoffed. 'You trust *me* to pick something appropriate? Brave woman!'

'Hmm... On second thoughts... Oh! How's your chest?'

The party boy rolled his shoulders, causing his pectoral muscles to flex. Now she came to mention it, he was indeed aware of a dull pain but had forgotten its cause. The couple's first visit to the tattoo parlour had been enlightening, and he had shown no hesitation towards shaving his chest and exposing fresh skin to the noisy needle. He pressed tentatively on the dressing which now covered the precious signature.

'Oh, yeah. It's a bit sore. I haven't looked at it yet, so I've no idea what it's come out like. How's yours?'

It was Lynn's turn to laugh aloud at yet another wisecrack subtly delivered, for her appointment with the tattooist was not until the day after tomorrow. Her insides fluttered at the mental image of her gorgeous lover, hands akimbo, intent on fondling her breasts. He never missed an opportunity to deal her a veiled compliment. She was very lucky, and couldn't wait to tell him so once they were face to face and skin on skin in the seclusion of their own private oasis.

'Very funny! You're feeling better then. My chest's about to get a big work-out, so treat me gently tonight.'

'OK! It'll be my absolute pleasure. I'll pack the kid gloves,' her lover gave her his best audible smile. 'Hope it all goes well today. Knock 'em dead, angel.'

'Thanks. I will,' Lynn responded. 'See you later. I love you so much.'

'I love you too. And thanks for working your magic. See you at five-ish.'

***

The borrowed Holden Kingswood transported Jeff along the gravel driveway up to the house for the first time in over two years and the last time for another. He had mixed emotions at being back at Benloch, unable to purge the sacrificial lamb image which Gravity had planted into his psyche. He and his gorgeous angel had shared some blissfully happy times here, albeit a long while ago, before her parents had found out who he was. Since then, the family farm had been out of bounds; a self-imposed exclusion zone.

The determined world-changer was prepared for a confrontation but also anxious for his dream girl to see he was keen to make peace. It was all about the moral high ground again. Why was he so pig-headedly principled? Why did it matter what the senior Dysons thought of him? Lynn's was the only opinion that mattered; not her parents'.

The Dyson-branded vehicle gained the young man easy access through the gates, and he struggled to suppress a smile when a *bona fide* cowboy stepped out of the hut and checked his driver's licence. Everything was unusually quiet when he arrived at the house, in contrast to the sound of much activity coming from somewhere behind it.

Jeff walked around the side, back towards the garages and the courtyard. The lawn was lush, bordered with many brightly coloured rose bushes in full bloom, a well-watered oasis among the yellow dryness of mid-summer. Still no sign of human life-forms however, with the noise now coming from beyond the reception centre. He rounded the corner to find a funfair in full swing, with adults and children absolutely everywhere. Of course, he remembered. Today was the annual staff party for those who worked on the settlement and at Admin, in true "Lord of the Manor" style. Lynn had mentioned this generous benefaction a while ago, and he had dismissed its quaintness at the time without further deliberation.

The famous star suddenly heard his name being called from up ahead, assuming he was about to be ambushed by a fan or two. It turned out to be Rick Pelten, the farm manager, looking relaxed and weather-beaten. They shook hands.

'Long time!' Jeff grinned. 'How's the family?'

'Great, thanks. They're around here somewhere. I hear you're off to London with the lovely Lynn.'

'Sure am,' the musician confirmed, his smile widening to an arrogant smirk. 'Not a bad gig, eh? What's new with you guys?'

'Fancy a drink?' Rick asked. 'I was just going to get one.'

The two men strode towards the beer tent, which was in use as much as shelter from the hot sun as for refreshments. Standing at a high table, the lifelong farmer leaned forward as if he were about to impart a deathly secret.

'The big man's certainly changed his tune lately,' he said. 'About you and Lynn, that is.'

Jeff stared at him quizzically. 'Oh, yeah? Why are you telling me this?'

Rick stepped back and put his hands up, bemused by the young man's response. 'Jeez! Don't be so defensive, mate. I'm telling you something you want to hear, I reckon.'

In truth, the twenty-two-year-old wasn't sure how to react. The unwelcome nocturnal visit from his old foes had left him unhinged and shaky, and he was sickened by an overriding sense of being back behind enemy lines. He barely knew Pelten, and yet Lynn's father had obviously seen fit to share some fairly personal information with his right-hand man, about which the hot-headed rock star wasn't entirely comfortable. Exactly how far had the news of this investigation spread?

'Sorry, Rick. I wasn't aware I was a hot topic between you two.'

'Fair dos,' the older man replied. 'I forget it's so long since you've been here. It feels like last week to me. I've been around so long, you know. We all had dinner a couple of weeks ago, and Bart played a tape of an interview with you and Michael Parkinson that he'd got hold of. You're an impressive bloke, mate. I know some of the reasons he wasn't too keen on you hooking up with Lynn, but I gotta tell ya, you're well in now.'

This was good news after all, Jeff admitted. Vindication even, but at the expense of hearing it from a stranger who really had no right to know. The recalcitrant swallowed his pride. He guessed that Rick was Bart's sounding board, just as Gerry was his.

'Thanks, I guess,' the celebrity acknowledged after a short pause, and raised his half-empty stubby. 'I look forward to hearing what he has to say tonight, in that case. Lynn told me they want to mend bridges and give us a send-off. I feel like I've been summoned to the king's court. Apologies for being suspicious, but there's some bloody sensitive information floating around that I'd hoped would be kept confidential.'

Rick slapped the younger man on the shoulder, appearing not to have understood a word. His ruddy rancher's face hinted at an ethos based on a much simpler life where one dealt with problems by brute force and plain speak. Romantic notions of sophisticated vendettas and being called to face off against an adversary for the sake of harmonious relations were baseless in his world. He turned his own beer bottle upside-down and waved it in front of the rock star's tired eyes.

'One more?'

Jeff nodded, letting the subject ride. No wonder Lynn was so keen to escape this cloistered existence. In its way, it was every bit as suffocating as Sydney's western suburbs.

'Cheers, mate.'

He watched his stout but strong drinking buddy return to the bar. It certainly promised to be fascinating to hear what the great man had to say this evening. Obviously his investigators had drawn a blank, and if Gerry's dad's testimony stood up... and the tearaway multi-millionnaire had no reason to believe it wouldn't... then there was no case for this Catholic Argentinean Polish Jew to answer. He was infuriated that it had come to this, but what the hell? He and Lynn were leaving in a few days' time, and he knew she would rather go with her parents' blessing than without.

'Are you guys coming to the dinner tonight?' Jeff asked Rick when he returned, interested to know who would be in the audience when the showdown commenced.

'No. It's just family, I gather,' the older man replied. 'Listen, mate. Don't be offended at what Bart's done. I hardly know any details and I'm a pretty private person too, so I understand you not wanting all and sundry knowing your personal info'. You have to understand that Bart and Marianna want the best for Lynn. I'm sure you understand that. You're a smart bloke.'

The songwriter cocked his head to one side, waiting in muted impatience for the fatherly advice to be fully dispensed. If he were half as smart as the pundits suggested, he would do well to pay heed to this well-meaning bystander who evidently felt compelled to slip him some valuable intelligence.

'The boss doesn't eat humble pie very often, so this is a bloody big thing for him. One thing I've learned over the years working for big man Dyson is that respect has to be constantly earned. He never takes people for granted, and it still gives him the shits when I expect too much from him.'

Jeff smiled wryly. 'Thanks for the heads-up, mate. Truly. And I'll be respectful, don't worry. But more for Lynn's sake than his.'

Rick raised his beer bottle to the cool and influential musician. He had known the Dyson children all their lives, and couldn't quite believe that this hypnotic, long-haired Bohemian was actually about to take his favourite one away.

'Good on ya, pal,' he let out a boisterous guffaw. 'Actions speak louder than words anyway. You'll look back and laugh in a few years. Lynn's grown into a real beautiful woman, hasn't she? You're fucking lucky, mate. She could have her pick of any bloke in Australia. The world even. Not surprised you want to give her a good time!'

Jeff exhaled the caustic air from his lungs, somewhat irritated by the farm manager's bawdy insinuations. It was definitely perfect timing for him and his beautiful best friend to be flying away. He knew damned well how lucky he was and certainly didn't need to have his street-kid nose rubbed in the dirt by this second-hand news merchant. He had fought hard to set himself on an equal footing with these people, and nowadays there was precious little luck involved.

The statuesque star rattled the drained green bottle on the table, choosing his words carefully. 'I don't have that chip on my shoulder anymore. It's onwards and upwards. Lynn's made her choice, so watch this space. Thanks again for the advice, Rick, and for the beers. I need to find me a beautiful woman. See you around.'

'All the best, Jeff,' the farmer replied sincerely, shaking the Sydneysider's outstretched right hand. 'Enjoy London. Too bloody cold for me!'

The pretender left the shelter of the beer tent and began to walk back through the busy paddock, pausing for a satisfying cigarette. A moment later, he spotted a barefoot Anna Dyson on her way back from the gymnasium, swinging her running shoes by their long laces. Although she instantly recognised a familiar face, she took a moment to place the man standing in front of her, with his long, dark hair and broad grin, leaning on one of the farm's many white utes.

'Jeff! I haven't seen you forever!' the young girl called out, running into his arms like a long-lost friend. 'I didn't know you were here.'

What a welcoming sensation after the conversation the young man had just finished... 'Hey, beautiful!' he said, shaking the girl's shoulder gently. 'Great to see you too. What's new?'

'Lynn's going to London,' the little girl was eager to impart, 'and I'm going to visit her in April because I'll be at the Worlds.'

'World championships? Well done! That's fantastic,' Jeff gave her a high-five and squeezed her arm muscles playfully. 'You're getting very strong. Stronger than me, I think.'

Anna laughed and tried to wrap her small hands around the twenty-two-year-old's well-developed biceps. 'Don't think so. Did you know Lynn was going away again?'

'Yep,' the songwriter replied. 'I'm going too. We're going to study.'

'Oh, good! She'll be very happy about that,' Anna told him, swinging around and putting on a dreamy air. 'She loves you.'

The visitor chuckled. 'Is that right? That is good news, I agree. I love her too. I thought that was all yucky stuff for you.'

His girlfriend's younger sister hit his hip with her arm deliberately as she completed another circle. 'It *is* yucky,' she responded indignantly, pulling a face as she came to a stop.

'Where are the others?' Jeff asked. 'Are they in the house?'

Anna pointed back towards the sports hall. 'Everyone's in there. There's a big meeting about scores and next year's goals. It's boring, and my bit's finished, so Mum told me I could go to the fair. Have you seen it?'

Jeff looked at his watch, wondering how long this meeting was scheduled to continue. 'Shall we go together?' he asked. 'D'ya wanna go on something scary?'

'Oh, yes!' the gleeful child shouted. 'Please, please, please!'

Without inhibition, the little gymnast grabbed the handsome stranger's hand and immediately began to pull him back towards the source of the loudest noise. He stubbed his cigarette out in the ashtray, laughing at her childish enthusiasm.

'OK. I'm coming. Hold your horses!'

Anna slipped her hand in his as they walked. Jeff wondered if he should let it go, given what some people must think of him around here. He was already stealing away one Dyson daughter, and now here he was, hand in hand with the other. She was only eight years old, and her exuberance seemed innocent enough. Jesus! Why was his life suddenly littered with kids? It was like being haunted by the future, just when he had managed to shake off the ghosts of the past.

'So what are your goals for next year?' the musician asked, swinging her arm. 'Junior world champ'?'

'Yes, and entry in the seniors,' the youngest Dyson told him without affectation. 'I've got to train with the seniors next term. I can't wait. I know I can do it, but it'll be hard work.'

The intelligent man smiled to himself. *So it all starts again*, he thought. Robust compared to Sandy, Anna still seemed too tiny to be competing with adults. He imagined the conscientious schoolgirl once the summer holidays were over, holed up like Lynn had been, in her studio apartment atop the Dyson Administration building, and travelling robotically from training to school to training. Her burgeoning life would be spent doing homework, falling into bed and then having the whole thing start again, day after day after day. She wouldn't argue. Of course it was what she wanted. He didn't doubt that, but neither could he help but wonder what else she might want. At her age, it was all the girl knew to want.

'It's winter in London, isn't it?' came the girl's next childish question, clearly recounting an earlier conversation with her sister. 'It'll be freezing, and Lynn's going to miss the summer.'

'That's true,' Jeff affirmed. 'You'll have to send her photos of the beach and the hot weather to make her jealous.'

The blonde girl giggled, skipping along without a care in the world. 'That's funny! I will send some. We're going to Hervey Bay next week for holidays.'

'Hey, that sounds great. What about this one?'

The pair had reached an enormous structure called the Spider, belching diesel fumes from a steel engine cage. It had long, steel limbs which raised its revolving pods up and down as the whole thing turned. The new arrival hoped he wasn't committing some new family sin by encouraging Anna to go on it, having no idea how frightening this ride might be to an eight-year-old. Turning somersaults on a ten-centimetre-wide wooden beam must also be somewhat terrifying, but the duty of care currently sat fairly and squarely with him.

Anna was keen though, still pulling on his hand. 'Yes! It looks brilliant. Come on!'

Jeff sighed and waved the youngster on ahead, watching her spring up into the pod effortlessly. He was flying out soon, and he concluded that the fairground staff must be well aware of this little lady's identity, as would anyone milling around. No-one raised any objections while the motor turned the mechanical arachnid's legs, and the whirling contraption gradually built up speed.

The gymnast wasn't fazed at all. Her sister's boyfriend watched a capable pair of hands grip naturally onto the safety bar and realised she knew exactly what she was doing. This was one independent kid.

'Sit back, you dare-devil,' he urged. 'It's going to go much higher.'

The ride went on for a good three minutes, and his young charge was having fun. She laughed as her long ponytail whipped her pod-mate's good-looking face as they span, before grimacing when he spat the ends out of his mouth. They had a commanding view of the homestead in the foreground from their dizzy heights, and the songwriter noticed how nice it was to be in the company of someone who demanded so little from life.

'There's Lynn!' Anna cried out, pointing down below. 'Look! There she is.'

Feeling slightly off-colour as his eyes swept over the crowd below, Jeff soon located the stunning female form. The youngster was shouting her sister's name at the top of her voice, causing everyone to look up. After some searching, Lynn's eyes met theirs and she waved. Junior, Sandy and Marianna were all walking back together too, making their way towards the house.

'Do you think your mum'll be annoyed about you being on here?' the accidental child-minder yelled to Anna above the cacophonous din created by the wind, the exposed engines and the blaring fairground music.

'This is so much fun!'

The girl's innocent reply hardly helped, but Jeff didn't bother to push her for a better one. The ride was slowing down, so facing any consequences would be unavoidable as soon as they descended to ground level. Whyever was he so nervous?

'Oh. It's stopping,' Anna moaned, disappointed. 'Can we go on something else?'

The young man shrugged. 'Depends what the others are doing. They might need us to come back to the house and get ready for dinner.'

As diverting as this was, his mind had already switched to the quite different type of fun he had been anticipating all morning, involving the bigger sister out by the dam. The ride attendant opened the door of their pod, and the precocious girl jumped out. She ran into her mother's arms.

'Look! It's Jeff!' she shrieked, pointing backwards over her shoulder. 'He took me on the Spider. It's really fast. Can we go on something else, please?'

Lynn held her hand out as the visitor landed back onto solid ground. He feigned vertigo, falling into her embrace and latching on for a long, steadying kiss. She looked tired but extremely happy to see him. Much the same as his own state, as it happened.

'Mmm... That's better,' he swooned, reluctantly freeing his beautiful girlfriend's lips from his and shaking his head appreciatively. 'Hi, everyone.'

The charismatic musician stepped to one side and gave Lynn's mother a kiss on the cheek, watching with arrogant curiosity as she eyed him up and down. He could tell that on some level she wanted what her daughter had. Marianna had always given him this impression, even in those early days. His mind wound back to the concluding moments of their bizarre meeting in the Georges' Food Hall, when he remembered toying with the idea of transporting the sophisticated woman to her fantasyland just for fun. His heart skipped a thankful beat. How glad he was to have thought twice about such a stupid move! He really had been one crazy, deranged son-of-a-bitch in those days...

'Missus Dyson, good to see you again. Thanks for inviting me to dinner.'

The lady of the manor was all smiles. Fame hadn't changed this young man's charming manner, whatever his motives might be.

'You're welcome, Jeff. Glad you could come,' the dignified woman replied, turning to her little daughter. 'What were you doing taking Jeff on such an alarming ride?'

Anna looked up at her sister's boyfriend. 'You weren't scared, were you?'

'Petrified,' he answered, winking back.

Lynn squeezed his hand, receiving a most appealing grin in return. She couldn't wait to be alone with her beautiful, black stallion again. He looked relaxed enough, even though it was clear the night had not treated him kindly.

'You're very good with her,' she whispered, as the group strolled behind the others to the door at the end of the kitchen corridor.

Before her man had a chance to respond however, their new calm was again destroyed by a whirlwind of teenaged girls screaming as they ran over.

'Jeff Diamond! I can't believe it's you!' one of them shouted. 'Can we have our picture taken with you?'

The rocker's equally famous girlfriend smiled at the rowdy scene. The fans' intrusion was an excellent opportunity for her mother to see that this gorgeous man of hers was so much in demand these days. She stepped back and let him oblige the fans with a photograph or two. The cheering bunch soon ran off, delighted with their unique piece of memorabilia.

Once inside the air-conditioned mansion, the family members dispersed to their respective rooms to prepare for dinner. The former nobody from Canley Vale entered the all-Australian princess' bedroom for the first time in over two years, excitement coursing along every nerve.

'Nothing's changed,' he murmured.

Sweet memory after sweeter memory of his virginal starlet nourished his fervour. He took the grown woman in his arms, and they kissed passionately, pressing their bodies closer and closer. The philosopher silently acknowledged the untruth in his impulsive statement, gazing around while lapping up their shared urgency. Everything had changed.

'Sorry things weren't so good last night,' the tired athlete said. 'I missed you.'

'Thanks. I missed you too. So much. I'm OK. Just dead keen to get out of here now.'

The nineteen-year-old looked at Jeff's watch, twisting his left wrist around until it burned. Yelping, he wrestled it free and grabbed hungrily for her waist, swearing when she was too quick. Lunging at her again, his libido in full flight, this time he managed to catch hold and leave her in no doubt.

Lynn giggled, running her fingers along the outline of his erection through his jeans. 'It's too late to go to the dam now. Sorry we were so late finishing.'

Jeff put on a dejected look. 'D'you mean to tell me you're going to renege on your side of the deal? I drove all this way on a promise and now all I'm going to get is dinner?'

The compassionate woman cupped his face in her hands, kissing him gently on the lips. 'And a ride on the Spider.'

'Very funny,' her mystery man smiled, clutching his playmate's slim contours. 'Take me to bed, big sister.'

'I need a shower first. I've been running around for most of the day,' Lynn warned, deliberately taking off her shoes and socks as slowly as she could.

Impatient eyes cautioned her. Her guest didn't give a damn. There was only one thing that mattered right now, and by the air pressure building from both sets of lungs, their shared attraction was plainly obvious.

'No. I haven't got time for that,' he snarled, restlessly shoving his hands into his jeans pockets. 'Where's your tennis skirt. Are you going to put it on for me?'

The temptress shook her head. Without speaking, she then took hold of her t-shirt by the hem and whipped it off over her head, reaching agile arms behind her back to unfasten her sports bra. Jeff looked on, mesmerised by her tanned, nymph-like body as it became progressively more nude, and began to unbutton his shirt.

'That's much better,' he approved. 'Fuck the tennis skirt.'

'You did, I seem to remember,' his dream girl responded slightly coyly, sending his hot-blooded passion soaring to boiling point.

Lynn led her aroused lover back towards the bed, and they fell onto it in a tempestuous embrace. Jeff was thrilled by how much his sexy minx liked to play with his urgency. It was so provocative, and he immediately had to rein in his raging desire to make sure he satisfied her first.

'That feels so good,' the young woman moaned as his fingers brought her close to orgasm. 'I love you so much.'

Tipping her expertly over the top, his engorged penis thrust into her and began to move with serious intent, his left hand caressing her flushed breast. The scabs were hardening over his brand new tattoo, and he shivered as tender fingertips brushed over them. His breathing escalated, loud and sensual in her ear, punctuated by slowly-articulated words of love which suspended themselves heavily in the air above their heads.

'Is this what you want? You are the best, Lynn. The only and the best.'

The couple stretched their long-awaited encounter for as long as the testosterone-charged man possibly could, collapsing together as he came with a loud roar. Reclining in ecstasy once more, exposed and replete in her childhood bedroom, the sophisticated celebrity gave him a tender kiss.

'That was wonderful,' she whispered. 'We can go to the dam tomorrow morning, if you want, before we leave.'

Jeff nodded without opening his eyes. 'How about after dinner? In the dark?'

'Too scary,' Lynn declined. 'It'd be pitch black. We might fall in and not be able to get out.'

'You, scared?' the songwriter teased. 'Your little sister'd come with me...'

'Ooh!' the slender blonde made a face, sitting up to examine her inked-in pledge again. 'Are you trying to make me jealous? I'm too old for you now, am I? You're a cradle-snatcher. There are laws against that, you know.'

Her boyfriend rolled his eyes. 'There are laws against all sorts of things,' he countered. 'I hope to break a few more once we get to London. What time's dinner?'

'Soon. We'd better get ready.'

The teenager made her way to the *en suite*, quickly followed by her joyful shadow. She had her father's face on again, and he knew exactly why. He who had been the master manipulator for so long was regularly being outdone these days, which amused him nearly as much as it spooked him.

She tossed him the shampoo bottle. 'I hope you don't expect me to bail you out of jail when you've broken all these laws.'

Jeff smiled, tensing up. 'No, because I'm not going to get caught. Let's not even go there, huh? Not 'til we're in the UK.'

Lynn cut her loveable rogue some slack, knowing full well he would be worried about dinner. 'Sorry.'

'It's fine, angel. I'm just tired and oversensitive. Ignore me.'

The happy couple were the last to arrive at the formal dining room that evening, Bart Dyson's voice booming ever louder as they approached. He was in a bullish mood after a successful day counting the previous year's many triumphs and the sure-fire future accolades which he and his troupe of *élite* sporting heroes would plunder. Lynn and Jeff's joined hands sneaked a quick boost of encouragement. In his rush to remove her clothes, the visitor had forgotten to update his girlfriend about the earlier conversation with Rick Pelten. There wasn't time now, and all would be revealed soon regardless.

'Good luck,' she whispered.

'You too,' he replied, kissing her cheek.

Bart immediately switched his attention to the handsome pair as they entered. 'Aha! Here are the wanderers,' he announced, walking towards them with open arms.

He kissed his elder daughter on the lips before turning to her nervous suitor. 'Jeff Diamond,' he bellowed. 'Welcome back.'

Big D placed his left hand on the guest's right shoulder and energetically worked his right hand. Jeff matched his vigour, looking the big man straight in the eyes.

'Sir, how are you?' he responded, not quite as loud but with supreme confidence summoned from somewhere deep within.

'Very good, Jeff. I'm well, thanks. Drinks? What can I get you two?'

Lynn put in an order for a vodka and tonic, and the relieved songwriter opted for his favourite whisky and dry ginger ale. Bart shouted across the room from the drinks cabinet.

'Jeff, I hear you had a cage built for your Aston Martin.'

The popular musician looked at his blonde *confidante* and smiled wryly. She appeared slightly concerned, and he raised a hand to communicate that he was ready.

'Yes, I have,' he confirmed. 'I didn't want it roaming around while I'm away. It might get up to no good. It's more than a cage. It's in a shipping container. It can't even see out.'

Big D was impressed. The young man had come prepared for a fair fight, and he was pleased.

'Good man,' the statesman said, handing him his cocktail just as Marianna appeared at the dining room door.

'Dinner will be in ten minutes, everyone. Bart, I'll have a vodka too, please.'

Jeff surveyed the scene as Lynn chatted idly with her mother. Junior and Sandy were deep in conversation too, which was gratifying for the new arrival to see. Anna had disappeared to help the housekeeper in the kitchen, which left him and Lynn's father unavoidably face to face.

'So... A good day today? All prepared for the year ahead?'

'Absolutely, thank you. We're in good shape,' Bart responded. 'It's a bit of a consolidation year, this one. Montreal next year is our main focus.'

'Already?'

The intelligent musician was intrigued with the fact that his girlfriend's control freak father actually seemed happy to follow someone else's line of conversation this time. His, at that! This had never happened before, and the inquisitive researcher decided to see how long he would be allowed to steer this particular ship.

'Anna tells me she's competing with the adults this year. That's amazing.'

Bart fixed his dark-eyed adversary with a friendly glare. 'Yes, indeed. We're pushing her very hard because she's responded positively in the last twelve months. It turns out she's quite a bit stronger than Lynn was at the same age.'

Ah, Jeff's brain turned. *Interesting tactic...* Could it be that the Olympian was making the big sister into a scapegoat for his own capitulation? Was Anna a better prospect for him to focus on now, in order that he might justify allowing his elder progeny to leave the fold? The world-changer wasn't prepared to let the older man off with this.

'Is that right?' he replied. 'Perhaps the training for a gymnast is more technical than Lynn had. And she needed to focus on music as well.'

Bart frowned, resting a weighty hand on the Sydneysider's shoulder. 'Nice. You are a good reader of men, Jeff. You might have a point regarding the music, but I can't give you the other argument. Anna trains harder than Lynn ever did.'

Jeff raised his glass, knowing he wasn't qualified to push this debate any further. 'It was worth a try. All work and no play, and all that...'

Before either sparring partner had a chance to throw another metaphorical punch, Marianna interrupted. 'Come on, everyone. Please take your seats.'

A trolley was wheeled in by Helen and another, younger woman who looked remarkably similar to the jovial housekeeper. The cynical guest opted for daughter rather than clone, although lingering parallels with Josef Mengele were never far from his mind in this house. The family tucked in to a hearty roast dinner, despite the fact that it had been close to forty degrees Celsius that day. Junior proposed a toast to the coming year, and everyone drank to it enthusiastically, Lynn and Jeff perhaps for different reasons. Conversation soon resumed around the table, and the special guest leaned in to talk to his girlfriend quietly while the others tackled their meals.

'I forgot to tell you...'

The intrigued beauty shifted sideways to bump shoulders. 'What?'

The rock star continued, the cuteness of her raised eyebrows dealing his insides another delicious kick-start. 'When I got here this afternoon, I ran into Rick Pelten. We had a couple of beers, and he told me your dad's going to eat humble pie.'

'Oh, wow. That explains it. He's been really nice to me all day,' Lynn responded, nodding. 'I suspected something was up but thought maybe it's just because we're going away.'

'He doesn't know I've seen Rick, presumably,' the young man continued. 'D'you think I should come clean before he starts, or would that embarrass him?'

The elegant celebrity touched his right wrist with the heel of her left hand, fork to fork. 'That's very kind of you. You don't have to.'

Her boyfriend winked. 'I don't want to leave on bad terms any more than you do. What should I do?'

'Telling him would be the Jeff thing to do.'

Spirits were high throughout dinner. Junior was leaving for New South Wales to take on the day-to-day management of the family's second property at Narrandera. He had agreed to take Sandy with him for the remaining weeks of the school holidays, once the rest of the family returned from their trip to the picturesque coastal town just north of Brisbane. The eldest Dyson offspring had recently met a new girlfriend and seemed quite taken with her, confiding in Lynn that he might be asking her to move up there with him.

Wine flowed in its plenty, and tongues were loosening accordingly. The reforming reprobate was making a valiant effort to limit his consumption, determined to stay in control of the situation and to please the love of his life. The new Jeff was no less proud than the old one, having at last grasped the value of investment outside the millions of dollars channelling through his ragamuffin life, these days leaving him considerably calmer and more measured in his approach to everything.

Helen and her slimmer offsider returned to clear the plates after the main course, and then to serve the sweets and a raft of cheeses. Bart coughed and clinked his wine glass with a dessert fork, and the pure sound from the crystal chimed around the room.

'Can I have everyone's attention, please?' the great man opened. 'Today has been a very good day, and tomorrow, we enter a new era for our family. Both Junior and Lynn are starting new chapters in their own rights, and we need to acknowledge their coming of age. Your mother and I are very sorry to see you leave our clutches but are also excited by the opportunities that lie ahead of you.'

He turned to his elder son first. 'Junior, you've proved yourself this year as a fine businessman running Narrandera from down here. Your helicopter licence is certainly going to come in handy, my lad! I'd like to propose a toast to Junior and the Narrandera settlement. Raise your glasses, please.'

Everyone at the table lifted their wine or water glass, depending on their age. 'Junior and Narrandera!'

The blond footballer thanked them all politely, saying how much he was looking forward to being his own boss. Ever a man of few words, he referred the audience back to his father.

Of course, Bart was ready to continue. 'OK. Thanks, son. Now, before we wish Lynn on her way, I'd like to say a few words to Jeff.'

The formidable father looked purposefully in the direction of the dark-haired superstar. The younger man stared him down without changing his expression. Marianna glanced at Lynn and then at her *beau*, smiling ever so slightly.

'Nearly three years ago now, I believe, our beautiful sixteen-year-old fell in love with a tall, handsome stranger, as young ladies are wont to do. Now let me tell you, as a father, it's very tough to see yourself replaced by someone else. By a younger version of yourself, at that.'

His daughter's very adult hand sat on Jeff's leg under the table. Affectionately, she squeezed his thigh.

The imposing patriarch carried on. 'Lynn, your mother and I recognised fairly early on that this relationship was very special to you. Far more than the first love most girls fall for. But you were still a child, and we were keen for you to grow up before you gave your heart away, hook, line and sinker. We didn't want to see you squander your future for the sake of a love affair. However, what we hadn't anticipated was the tenacity of someone driven by as much deep-seated ambition and passion as this man here.'

Still the visitor's expression didn't change, and the big man forged ahead unfazed. 'We've discussed before, Jeff, that in my position, it's my duty to protect my family and our reputation. Naturally, I have resources at my disposal capable of finding out who's who, and unfortunately we weren't happy with the information that came to light. So we had no choice but to effect a separation, and we assumed you would both move on with your lives.'

The young woman's hand tightened its grip on her boyfriend's leg, feeling its muscles twitch under her palm. After a couple of seconds, his own hand descended on hers and smothered it in incredible warmth. She looked into his eyes and only saw serenity. The old Jeff was fading fast, and the replacement Jeff was even more irresistible than his predecessor.

'You both behaved very maturely and honourably, for which we were grateful,' her father went on. 'And when we saw Jeff's career take off as strongly as it did, we felt better about things. But as soon as Lynn was back in Australia, we put two and two together fairly quickly. I'll be frank with you, Jeff. I really didn't want someone with your background associated with my family.'

'I know that, sir,' the dissident songwriter acknowledged. 'And I understood. Believe me, I understood. My own grandmother won't let me inside her house.'

The others chortled politely, not at all certain of why they were laughing. Junior glanced from his father to his sister's poker-faced lover and then back again.

'What exactly is Jeff supposed to have done? Are we allowed to know?'

'That's for this man to decide,' Bart snapped, 'and certainly not a discussion for tonight. Suffice to say, I seriously underestimated you, Mister

Diamond. The first thing you said to me when we met in my office to discuss this matter was something to the effect of "So the sins of the father are the sins of the son." You exposed me at the outset, and I didn't like it, but it impressed me nonetheless. In fact, everything about you impresses us, and obviously impresses Lynn too.'

The pretty nineteen-year-old raised her glass to her father. She had been waiting for this speech for a long time and shot her big brother a compassionate smile. They were both escaping, and by the looks of things, not a moment too soon!

Still Bart continued. 'So while I was sending private investigators out in Sydney, you were appearing on chat shows all over the world, inspiring many with your ideas, exploits and of course, the music. And damned well showing me in the process that the sins of *your* father were very definitely not the sins of his son. You've never backed down from me, and that's probably the quality I admire most. My sons know I expect that of them, and if they're looking for a role model in that regard, they need look no further.'

Jeff exhaled sharply. Such unprovoked and unexpected praise took him by surprise. Sweet vindication indeed. He nodded to Big D respectfully.

'Then in early November, I exchanged a 'phone call with a gentleman by the name of Gerald Blake, whom I believe is your manager's father. A most enlightening conversation that had a profound effect on me, I have to say. It enabled me to see exactly what my astute daughter has obviously been able to see from Day One. Therefore, I… And I speak on behalf of my wife too, I'm sure…'

Marianna motioned her agreement and smiled at the young couple, looking as though she too wished to throw her two cents in. The Olympian was not finished however.

'We would like to apologise to you, Jeff, and to you, Lynn, for the lack of faith we showed in your relationship and in the potential power of your partnership. Jeff, I welcome you into this family in whatever capacity you both desire. I know you're going to treat Lynn with the respect she deserves, and I have no doubt that you'll both go from strength to strength.'

Bart's hand moved to lift his wine glass, and those assembled at the dinner table collectively breathed a sigh of relief that the speech was over. Jeff leaned back in his chair and put his arm around his lover's shoulder, hurriedly piecing together an appropriate rebuttal. Lynn shuffled her chair closer just as he began to speak.

'Whoa! I'm not sure where to start,' he coughed. 'Thanks very much, sir. Thanks, both of you. There's no apology necessary. As I said before, I understand why you did what you did. I didn't like it one bit, but I understood. But if you insist on apologising, then I'm very happy to accept it.'

Marianna intercepted her husband before he moved in with his next volley. 'Excuse me, Bart. I'd just like to add my own few words to this, in that I know how hard it was for the two of you to be torn apart when you were so much in love. I felt so guilty but believed we were doing the right thing. Lynn, darling, I hope in some way you can take some solace in now knowing for sure that you have met the man of your dreams, and not merely the first man who swept you off your feet.'

Jeff caught the patient teenager's eye, guessing that her guarded temper would be seriously tested by her mother's comment. Her face was smiling, but he could tell she was seething underneath. A fierce pride swelled his chest, feeling her body tip forward to respond.

'Thanks, Mum,' the unflappable teenager acknowledged. 'Like Jeff, I've come to understand why, but I didn't actually need to sleep with other men to be able to recognise how fine a man Jeff is.'

'No. I know that now, dear,' Marianna nodded. 'I'm sorry. I really am.'

Bart clinked his glass again. 'So let's bring this to a close by wishing Lynn and Jeff huge success and happiness for their coming year in London. I know you'll make the most of big city living, and we hope you'll allow us to come and visit occasionally. It is important that you two get away from us, in the same way as we're keen to see Junior leave our stronghold. You're destined for greatness, all of you, and I'm getting as much, if not more than I bargained for. Let's drink to nineteen-seventy-five and all our futures.'

'Nineteen-seventy-five and all our futures!' was the chorus from around the table.

Anna began to clap, which was the signal for the rest to lighten up and join in. Jeff kissed Lynn hard on the lips, causing the youngest family member to shout maniacally for them to desist.

'Well done,' the boy from Canley Vale whispered to his dream girl. 'Couldn't have said it better myself. We really must leave the country as soon as possible.'

Lynn grinned, and the lovers clinked glasses once more.

***

The family adjourned after dinner into the courtyard for coffee. Anna and Sandy were keen to spend as much time with their elder siblings as they could before they departed. The start of this New Year represented a changing of the guard of sorts. Bart and Marianna sat apart from their children, also taking stock of the day.

At a suitable break in conversation, Jeff put his hand on Lynn's shoulder and kissed the top of her head. 'Back soon.'

The contented singer watched the man she loved approach her parents and accept their invitation to sit with them. Nice move, she thought. He had genuinely come in peace, and she realised how much of a step forward this was.

'I just wanted to say thanks privately,' the humble man began, extending his hand to shake Bart's. 'They were very kind words, sir, and I appreciate the sentiment.'

Big D reciprocated the gesture eagerly, gripping the superstar's wrist with his left hand for good measure. 'You're welcome, Jeff.'

Marianna smiled sweetly from the other side of the table. 'Are you looking forward to your stay in London?'

The ambitious musician nodded. 'Oh, yeah. Very much. It's perfect timing for me and an amazing opportunity to learn from someone I admire greatly. And I think it'll do us both good to escape for a while, to be honest.'

Bart agreed. 'Yes. We were only saying that yesterday. Since Lynn returned in September, it's been a peculiar time for all of us. Coming to the realisation that she's not our little girl anymore; that she has a mind of her own which is very firmly made up.'

'That's true,' Jeff affirmed, smiling. 'And I haven't made it easy on her either. I don't know how much she tells you, but it's a challenge living with me.'

Marianna giggled. 'I can't imagine that!'

The self-confident lothario wasn't sure if the elegant lady was being sarcastic, choosing to overlook the flirtatious comment. His reserve paid off though, to his delight, since Bart's curiosity had also been piqued.

'What exactly do you mean, darling?'

Slightly embarrassed by her husband's wish to expose her, Marianna hesitated and chose her words carefully. 'Well, just that after two years apart and so many stories in the press... All your hit songs that were obviously messages about our daughter, and for Lynn too... It must have been quite intense getting back together.'

Jeff smiled knowingly. That wasn't exactly what the practised politician had meant, he surmised, but a stealthy diversion instead.

'It's been a wild ride, that's for sure,' he agreed. 'Lynn's been amazing. I've learned a lot from her in the last few months.'

Bart looked inquisitive. 'How so?'

Looking over at his beautiful partner, immersed in an innocent board game with her siblings, the proud man answered. 'I've no idea what you and Gerald Blake spoke about a few weeks ago, but he told me you'd contacted him. Who grassed him up, by the way?'

The Olympian chuckled. 'Who grassed him up? The police, actually.'

The blonde singing star turned around on hearing the laughter, unable to make out what her boyfriend was saying. His casual wave renewed her comfortable happiness, communicating that all was well.

'OK. Good,' Jeff continued. 'That's what I expected. He and his wife, Celia, have been like parents to me, but always from a distance on my part. I didn't even know how much they knew about me until this Christmas. Before I met your gorgeous daughter, I had no reason to trust anyone. No-one ever believed in me until she came along, and it finally made me wake up to myself. I'd always had plenty of bright ideas and knew exactly who I wanted to be. I just had to learn to open up. She showed me that it doesn't hurt to be a bit vulnerable every now and again because there are people out there who care. Celia and Gerald Blake are people who care.'

Marianna rested her hand on the young man's, causing his blood pressure to surge without warning. 'Lynn has told me about your struggle with PTSD. It's an awful thing. Dreadful nightmares and inexplicable fears. It's terrible how the mind plays tricks on people.'

'I didn't know about this,' the elder statesman said to his wife, a little confused. 'You've been harbouring secrets with our daughter while I held an open investigation?'

The dowager pouted at his indignant stare. 'You never asked me for a statement.'

'Good thing too,' Bart replied. 'You're as far under this man's spell as Lynn is.'

Their elder daughter heard her name again and excused herself from the game. Jeff invited her to sit on his lap while they talked, continuing where he had left off. He felt more than a little uncomfortable that Marianna had edged too close to him, figuratively speaking, but was also pleased to be able to converse with the Dysons in this honest way.

'But from tonight it's clear to me I've still got some learning to do. I need to learn forgiveness. This priceless woman's taught me about looking forwards and not back, but it's hard to look forwards when you're holding so many grudges.'

Big D nodded. 'Yes. I agree with that.'

'Sir, I bumped into Rick Pelten earlier, and we shared a couple of beers. He told me you'd seen a tape of the Parkinson interview I did last year. I was glad to find this out, because that's certainly one of my finest hours so far! It took me a long while to accept that people were never going to take me at face value, given who I am and where I come from, and it used to make me so incredibly angry. But now I know that proving myself is not actually that difficult. It has a good side effect too; helps me validate myself to myself.'

Lynn pecked his cheek. 'He's his own harshest critic!'

'Very important to stay that way too,' Bart said. 'Complacency is the root of all evil.'

Jeff looked at his beautiful best friend. 'Self-satisfied fat cats!' they proclaimed in unison.

The nineteen-year-old tennis champion laughed and rubbed the front of her boyfriend's shirt, ready to relieve her parents of their vacant stares. 'Jeff was only saying a couple of days ago that he was keen to keep hold of some of the jagged edges he used to have, so that he didn't sell out and become a self-satisfied fat cat.'

'Oh, for heaven's sake! Welcome to the world of Bart Dyson,' cried the long-suffering wife almost hysterically. 'You two need to have a long chat some time. That's one of his pet obsessions, if you pardon the pun.'

'Brandy or something, Jeff?' the older man asked, standing up from the outdoor table. 'Lynn, what would you like? Is there any more coffee, Marianna?'

Bidding the youngsters to stay seated, the young woman's parents left them to prepare the next round of drinks.

'Thanks so much for doing this,' the teenager said, her voice both kind and august. 'I know it's tough, given what they've done, but it means a lot to me to see you going out of your way to get on with them.'

'It's not tough at all, you gorgeous creature,' her humble partner countered, shifting her tall athlete's frame off his lap and onto the chair next to him. 'Except my leg's gone numb. You're too heavy, muscle-woman! It's a learning process, that's all. Rick told me something earlier that rang true. He told me that he still gets caught out taking your dad for granted, even after all the years he's been working for him. And while we were talking, it dawned on me that I do that to people too. I definitely do it with Gerry, and probably with you too. I don't give people many breaks, do I? And I don't give myself breaks either. I expect things to work perfectly every time, but how are people supposed to know what's going on in my head...'

'...unless you tell them?' the muse finished her ardent activist's question for him.

'¡Justamente!'

'I know this isn't what you want to hear just now, but you're frighteningly alike, you and Dad. I've only just noticed how much. I hope you guys can become friends. I think it would be an awesome partnership.'

Her boyfriend frowned, as yet unconvinced but prepared to give it a go. 'OK. Not as good as ours though. I'm not going to get a tattoo with him.'

Lynn looked around. 'Shhh! I haven't even told Junior about that.'

At that moment, Bart returned with a tray of liqueurs and glasses. 'Pour yourselves whatever you like. You too, Junior. Kids, let June out of the game, please.'

Jeff poured three generous glasses of VSOP cognac. Marianna brought out the coffee shortly afterwards, and the adults gathered round. The guest offered his cigarettes to the family of fitness freaks, receiving as many takers as he expected. He lit one anyway and moved to one side so that the smoke would blow away from the others.

'We're going to miss these warm evenings,' he rued, smiling at the blonde, tanned farmer's daughter he was set to transplant into the London fog. 'You're going to wish you were in Hervey Bay with these guys.'

'No, I won't,' Lynn shook her head. 'Not with you looking so sexy like that, smoking and drinking, all relaxed.'

Her father put his hands over his ears. 'Please, my girl! Not in front of the parents. Remember we're still only just coming to terms with the whole idea.'

***

'Hey! Let's get out of here,' Jeff suggested, grabbing Lynn and spinning her round in front of him. 'Look at the moon. It'd be fantastic out by the dam now.'

The teenager followed her gorgeous lover's gaze across the paddocks between the buildings. He was right. The hillside was bathed in moonlight.

'It does look nice,' she agreed.

'Please?' the insistent man whined childishly. 'Last chance for a year.'

'OK! If only to shut you up. We're not going to swim, are we? It'll be freezing.'

The younger children had already been dispatched to bed, and the couple issued their excuses to the rest of the family and headed towards the garage. Lynn selected a rug and a water bottle while Jeff backed out one of the utes. They drove along the track without the need for headlights, making for the creek. The car windows were wound down, and they could hear faint noises as they drew closer.

'We're not alone,' the driver said, pointing ahead to a mob of aboriginals milling around by the dam.

'Oh, sorry,' his loving passenger sighed, thinking her man would be disappointed at having to turn back.

'No. Don't be sorry. It's perfect. They won't mind if we join them, as long as we don't cramp their style.'

The young woman was surprised. 'Are you sure?'

'Yeah,' her boyfriend reassured. 'They'll have been drinking since the funfair. They'll welcome us. Don't be scared. It's not like the city, where the aborigines are all bitter and twisted. They love being out here as much as we do.'

The intrepid city boy stopped the ute about fifty metres from the revellers and shut off the engine. The pair jumped out onto the loose sand in their bare feet, feeling themselves sink in the cool, velvety layer. He took Lynn's hand, sensing her nerves at being out of her very proper comfort zone.

'Life's very exciting with you,' she told him, cuddling into his arm.

'Why, thank you, ma'am. Glad to be of service.'

He motioned for his favourite friend to sit down on the edge of the revellers' circle, which was a trick the new world traveller had learned while visiting various African tribal ceremonies. At first no-one seemed to notice them, and he lay down behind the gorgeous blonde and tempted her torso down to lean against him. After a while, one of the men approached and offered them a single beer bottle. Jeff accepted it with thanks, taking a large gulp. He passed it to Lynn, who took a somewhat smaller mouthful. The man then beckoned for them to come closer into the inner ring, so they moved up as directed. The others clapped and cheered, inviting them to join their party.

'Good drinking night,' one of them shouted.

'Sure is,' the handsome visitor agreed. 'Cheers.'

'You Lynn D?' one of the older women asked.

The beauty nodded. 'Yes, I am. This is Jeff.'

The women whooped and clapped as one by one they recognised the swarthy, dark-haired celebrity.

'Jeff Diamond. He sing good too. We heard 'bout you! You two goin' together then?'

The proud man put his arm around his young lover. 'Yep. We are.'

'Your daddy know?'

Lynn nodded, chuckling and feeling safe in warm arms.

The moonlight cast a white glow over the whole scene, allowing them to see quite clearly. There was a group of children playing closer to the water, and some teenaged boys further away scrapping, quarrelling and drinking. An old bath sat off to one side, full of ice and beer.

'That's a lot of grog in there,' Jeff said to the men, pointing to the tub. 'Is it all for tonight?'

'Yeah. It's from her daddy. Get some more.'

It would be impolite to turn them down, the comic joked quietly to his wide-eyed girlfriend. He got to his feet and helped himself to two more bottles out of the makeshift refrigerator. Before sitting down again, he removed his shirt, screwed it up into a ball and tossed it in Lynn's lap. Dressing for dinner at Benloch demanded many more airs and graces than did their new hosts.

'Cheers!' he yelled back, twisting the top off one bottle and handing it to his awestruck companion, while keeping the other for himself. 'You OK?'

Swooning at his sincere wink, the sportswoman felt unbelievably tired yet was beginning to enjoy this new experience immensely. 'Yeah. It's great!' she gushed. 'You're perfectly gorgeous, Jeff Diamond. I feel like I'm on the edge of the world and looking over, just like you described the other day. I love watching you interact with everyone.'

One of the women ran over and thrust a guitar into the rock star's hands. 'Sing for us, mate, eh? "Lay It Down"! "Lay It Down"!' she chanted the name of one of the star's biggest hits.

The famous duo looked at each other. It was an impromptu request at the end of a long day, but one they were happy to honour. The guitarist dug his half-full beer bottle into the dry soil and struck up the opening chords. An instant audience appeared, ready to dance and sing along. Both musicians clambered to their feet, and the friendly crowd engulfed them in a matter of seconds.

Jeff moved effortlessly through a medley of his most popular songs, each one louder than the last. Lynn poured beer down his throat every so often and sang background vocals, joining hands with the women and children. Someone shouted out "Donna Jade", causing the nervous man to hesitate and check with his co-star to seek her approval. He still felt guilty every time he sang this song, even though it was arguably the best melody he had ever written and people absolutely loved it. The glint in the carefree teenager's eyes was all the encouragement he needed, and the showman led everyone in a rousing rendition of the well-known instrumental opening riff.

Eventually sick of the sound of his own voice, the polished performer segued into the introduction of "Two Tickets To Paradise". The good-humoured songstress by his side flashed her entrancing, blue eyes again and instantly sprang into action, following this with two more recent chart-toppers. The children quickly caught on to the well-known tracks, and Jeff watched the crowd closely as he drove the various rhythms with the guitar. He signalled for a cigarette from one of the men by pointing at his packet and lighter which were lying on the ground.

The beer kept flowing, and the songs kept coming. Eventually Lynn caught her boyfriend's attention and made a throat-cutting gesture to signal she had had enough.

'OK, folks. One more, and that's it!' the Pied Piper shouted to their enthusiastic crowd, who objected most strongly.

'"Everlasting"?' he yelled to his fellow entertainer, who nodded.

Just as at the Blakes' on Boxing Night, they found it virtually impossible to do the song justice with only an acoustic guitar. Dissatisfied with its limitations, the performer abandoned the old, scratched instrument and danced with his dream girl instead, leaving the tune to run along supported only by vocals and enthusiastic clapping. No-one cared how rough it sounded. At the end, they held their arms high in the air, denying the loud pleas for more, and finally flopped down onto the ground breathing heavily. The crowd kept singing, a raucous *pastiche* of several different hits over the top of one another.

'This is the best ever leaving party,' Lynn shouted above the noise. 'I'm so glad we came.'

Jeff nodded. 'Yeah. Not quite what I had in mind.'

The celebration eventually petered out, and the romantic man looked at his watch. Just after midnight. The moon was still high and bright, and the stars were glittering. He wrapped his dream girl up in his arms.

'I'm going to love you forever and ever,' he whispered, brushing his lips against her neck.

The young woman turned round, only to be swallowed by an earth-shattering kiss. 'Thanks. Same from me to you. You're so amazing.'

'D'you want to go soon?'

Lynn nodded. 'Yes. In a minute. These guys'll probably party all night. I'm exhausted.'

'You must be. So am I.'

They stood up to leave, brushing the grass and sand off their clothes. A few of the younger children rushed up to hug their entertainers, and the sleepy adults waved and shouted their thanks and goodbyes. The couple waved back as they walked to the ute, climbed in and drove slowly away round the edges of the paddock. The moon lit the tracks all the way back to the house, and it wasn't long before Jeff was turning the ute into the garage.

'So how do we make city people as happy as that?' he asked, as they climbed the back stairs. 'What's the secret to keeping that simplicity?'

His star pupil shrugged, tiredness hampering her every pace. 'Don't ask such complicated questions at this time of night. Community? Music? Family? Who knows? All of the above.'

'Yeah. That's got to be it. And how much money did that cost? Next to nothing.'

Seeing the washed-out expression on his gorgeous girlfriend's face, the world-changer let the subject be. They would think further on this problem another day. He didn't even pester her for sex, even though their next blissful dam encounter had now slipped by twelve months. Life was different now, the new man decided. This pantomime horse was investing in the future, for the future, wasn't it? He no longer needed to seize every opportunity as if it were his last. This picture of perfection would be here tomorrow, and the next day and for the majority of their tattooed days to come. So what if he was horny? He had to learn to take things slowly and savour life's anticipation.

Lynn sunk her head into the pillow, mystified by the apparent inaction behind her on the other side of the bed. Pleasantly surprised that Jeff was allowing her to climb into bed unmolested, she turned over to make sure nothing was wrong. The lovers kissed tenderly and wished each other a good night. With a parting wink, he turned the light out, and she fell asleep.

Inked In

Australia's darling awoke to the sound of knocking at her bedroom door. It was insistent and with no pattern, and she guessed it was Anna coming to wake them up. Jeff was still sleeping beside her after another unbroken night. He would be a very happy man today. Slipping on her bathrobe, the tousle-haired young woman went to open the door. The impatient knocking was now accompanied by a high-pitched voice trying not to shout.

'Lynn, are you awake? Lynn, can I come in? Open the door.'

Sure enough, the littlest Dyson was standing in the doorway.

'What's the matter?' her big sister asked.

'Junior's leaving,' the girl answered, frustrated that it had taken so long to attract some attention. 'You have to come and say goodbye.'

'OK. Thanks. I'm coming,' Lynn responded. 'Go on down. We'll be there in a minute.'

Shooing Anna away, the teenager walked back to the bed and gently touched her boyfriend's shoulder. 'Hey. Wake up.'

She kissed his forehead and repeated the instruction. One eye opened. Then all at once, he growled and grabbed her, causing her to fall down on top of him and scream.

'You bastard! Were you awake all the time?'

'Might've been...' Jeff answered, feigning innocence. 'I could hear you talking at the door. Who was it?'

'Anna,' his flustered playmate replied. 'Junior's leaving. Want to come and say goodbye?'

'Sure thing,' the handsome man nodded. 'What time is it?'

'I don't know. Haven't even looked. Wow! It's after nine-thirty. I can't believe we slept that long.'

Neither could her grateful bedfellow. 'Did you have to wake me up during the night?'

'No. Unless I did it in my sleep,' Lynn smiled. 'The first thing I knew was Anna knocking.'

The elated songwriter reached for her again, this time more sedately. '*¡Excelente!* You're the cure, my amazing angel. It's definitely you who makes me sleep.'

'Great advert for a girlfriend!' the young woman exclaimed, pulling away from his eager kisses and reaching for last night's clothes. '"My girlfriend puts me to sleep."'

Jeff laughed, watching her draw quotation marks around the aired testimonial. 'Sounds like a very abrupt ending to a beautiful relationship. Like those female spiders that poison their mate after sex.'

The big, blue eyes shot theatrical daggers his way, as if to say, "Don't tempt me." The couple dressed quickly, and the happy nineteen-year-old ran her fingers through her boyfriend's thick hair to stop it from sticking out in all directions. She then put her own long locks up into a ponytail.

'You look great! I want a photo of you just like this,' she cajoled.

Her lover's eyes travelled down to his boxer shorts. 'Like this?' he queried. 'See what happens when you play with my hair?'

Lynn smiled coyly. She fetched her camera from the table.

'Smile!'

The off-duty rock star posed and pulled faces while his own private groupie snapped away. 'I have to get some of you too. Pre-London pictures.'

'Later. We've got to get downstairs. Is it safe for you to go yet?'

Out in the wide gravel driveway in front of the neo-Georgian homestead, Junior was busy loading the contents of his room into a van, aided by his younger brother. Jeff helped them to carry the rest of the boxes and bundles of clothing, whistling away the last dregs of his hangover. Bart was nowhere to be seen, and Marianna busied herself by making sure her firstborn was loaded up with sufficient supplies for his six-hour trek north-north-east across the border into New South Wales.

'Where's Dad?' Lynn asked her mother.

'Good morning!' Marianna said, amused by the young couple's precipitous descent. 'You've had a lazy start to the day. Your father's on a call. He'll be here in a few minutes.'

'Where did you guys go last night?' Junior asked the dark-haired musician as they crossed the threshold in opposite directions for the umpteenth time. 'You made a swift exit. You didn't stay in the house, did you?'

'Nope,' Jeff answered. 'We ended up having a *corroboree* up at Coldwater Creek in the moonlight. It was fantastic, mate. We went up there to be alone, but gate-crashed a party with about thirty aboriginals instead. We gave them a free concert, and they gave us free beer.'

'Wow! They're up there at night?' Junior stated the obvious, not needing an answer. 'I've never been to the dam in the dark. That would've been magnificent. It was almost a full moon last night.'

626

Their guest nodded. 'It was pretty cool. Will we see you in London at the end of the season? You have to come over. I'd like to buy you a few beers, now your dad and I have smoked the peace pipe.'

'Yeah. That'd be great. Don't know when I'll get a chance to come over, but I'd love to.'

The huge footballer smiled. He liked his sister's boyfriend a lot. He was a really genuine bloke. With the remaining small bags on board, the loading was finally finished. Junior slammed the rear doors and threw his wallet and some paperwork onto the passenger seat.

'I'm off, Mum. Is Dad still on the 'phone?'

Marianna sent Sandy in to find his father. 'Tell him Junior wants to get on the road now, please.'

Bart and his younger son arrived after a few awkward minutes when no-one really knew how to fill in time. 'Good luck, son,' the statesman boomed, slapping his namesake on the back and shaking his hand ferociously. 'Drive safely. Watch out for the 'roos on the Newell around Jerilderie. They come out of nowhere.'

Bigger D thanked his father for the advice, having driven this road many times already. He caught his sister's eye, figuring that the hushed exchange between her and her city slicker boyfriend would undoubtedly include the fact that their dad trotted out these exact pearls of wisdom every single time the family had travelled this particular stretch of highway.

When it came time for the parting farewells, Lynn gave her brother a big hug. Jeff noticed she had tears in her eyes, appreciating vicariously yet again the pull of family which he had never known.

'Have fun up there,' she told him. 'Be careful when you fly that chopper.'

The eldest Dyson kissed his sensible sibling on the cheek. 'Thanks, sis. Good luck in the UK,' he said, also reaching to shake her suitor's hand. 'And you, Jeff. Stick together, you two. Hope to see you in London.'

The whole family waved as the white van emblazoned with the Dyson logo crunched slowly down the long driveway. Marianna was crying, and Bart did his best to console her.

'And it'll be you two next,' she lamented to her rapidly maturing daughter, wiping tears from her eyes and turning to Sandy and Anna. 'Please don't grow up, kids.'

Lynn squeezed her former renegade's hand as they made their way back through the front door. 'How things change, huh?' she whispered.

The sultry visitor nodded but said nothing, even though he had been thinking the very same thing. It hadn't been too long ago that he had been read the Riot Act by his girlfriend's father, and now her mother was mourning their departure.

'Have you two had breakfast yet?' Marianna asked from over their shoulders.

The pair looked at each other and both stifled a laugh.

'No, we haven't,' Lynn answered. 'We'll go and get showered, and then make ourselves something. Don't you do anything, Mum. We can do it.'

The joke had not been lost on Bart, who shook his head and masked a smirk. His wife had clearly missed the *innuendo*, and no-one cared to enlighten her in her heightened emotional state.

'I'm sorry,' Jeff apologised, still chuckling as the lovers climbed the sweeping staircase. 'I caught your eye just at the wrong time. I could see you were thinking what I was thinking, and couldn't keep a straight face. Your dad noticed, did you see?'

His girlfriend slapped his arm. 'Get upstairs, you sex maniac. You can't be trusted! Your eyes are just too talkative.'

That was a nice thing to say, the poet thought. He liked the idea of talkative eyes, instantly feeling the rush of a new song forming in his head. They walked the length of the long corridor hand in hand until they reached the second-last door on the right.

'So what's for breakfast?' he asked, closing the bedroom door behind them.

They broke into a fit of amorous laughter again, and Lynn hugged his tall, aroused frame. 'Did you want to go back to the dam?' she asked, pressing herself provocatively against his fast-rekindling passion.

The eager lover kissed his compassionate girlfriend long and hard. 'No,' he breathed heavily against her neck. 'Let's leave the memory of last night alone. It was one of those special moments in time and it'll seem far away very soon.'

The nineteen-year-old was overjoyed with his forward-thinking response. She led him towards the bed, and they fell onto it, rushing to touch each others' skin.

'I hope Julie moves in with Junior,' she mused.

Jeff squinted his displeasure. 'Hey! Concentrate.'

The young woman giggled. 'Sorry. At least I was only thinking about my brother.'

'I'm not sure that makes me feel any better,' he responded in jest, kissing her breasts and stomach.

'He's lonely, that's all. He's very jealous of us.'

'OK, OK. I appreciate his position, but can you focus, please?' the joker pointed to his own chest.

Sliding down the bed, out of reach of his long arms, Lynn grabbed his huge penis and put it into her mouth, beginning to flick his foreskin sensually.

'Ahhh... That's better,' Jeff groaned, before crying out as a set of sharp teeth clamped down on his shaft in an act of evil, perverted dominance.

Their playful encounter continued until neither of them could wait any longer. The nubile sportswoman pushed her man onto his back and climbed on top of him, riding his whole length until she came. The look on her face as she orgasmed sent him off too, both needing to remind themselves to keep the noise level down for fear of being overheard.

'London, here we come!' the delirious musician called out, still breathing heavily. 'I hope the new apartment is soundproofed.'

'Who cares?' the teenager replied, stroking the dark, flaking scabs which were beginning to reveal her signature on her boyfriend's muscular chest.

'You will,' the confident lover insisted, chuckling at her uncharacteristic brazenness. 'As soon as one of the neighbours mentions hearing something, you'll want to move out.'

The celebrity blanched. 'That's true. Is this still sore?'

'No. Only when you touch it,' he smiled, instantly seeing her lift her fingers clear of the tender spot. 'How long have you had this bedroom?'

'Err... Not sure. This house was finished when I was four, I think. Or five. Why?'

'No particular reason,' Jeff replied, his voice suddenly distant. 'I was just picturing you as a little child, being the only one in such an enormous room. You must've looked very cute, tucked up in bed.'

'Gerry's situation has really got to you, hasn't it?'

The philosopher nodded. 'How did you know? You're right. It has.'

'Do you think he's going to change his mind about marrying Heather then?' the gorgeous blonde wondered aloud. 'Is that what you were talking about over lunch the other day? I thought you looked more serious than usual.'

'Spot on,' her lover affirmed. 'I gave him a bit of a lecture. You know... Moral blackmail. I'm so good at that. I've got to stop. I think he might be swaying back towards her, but I'm not sure she'd still have him.'

'Would you fly back for the wedding?'

'Christ! I never thought of that,' he muttered, feeling exposed. 'I'd have to, I suppose. After making such a scene about it, I'd hardly be allowed to pike out. I'd never hear the end of it. That's an interesting question. Would you come with me?'

The young woman smiled, equally anxious. 'If I were invited.'

'Oh, you'd be invited,' her tamed stallion replied softly, staring deep into her eyes. 'You bet your life you'd be invited, my beautiful tattoo co-recipient.'

Lynn kissed him. 'Then I'd have to go too. Hey! We're running out of tattooing hours. Shall we get moving?'

The couple showered together in double-quick time and packed their things. Downstairs in the kitchen, they made themselves coffee and a bite to eat, keen not to repeat the drama of Junior's protracted exit. The lady of the house was working in the office with her husband when their elder daughter knocked on the door.

'Come in,' Bart looked up and smiled when he saw his daughter followed in by the man who had proved himself worthy.

'We're leaving soon,' Lynn announced.

Marianna looked at the couple from over her spectacles. 'Right-oh, dears. One question before you go... We'd like to come to the airport on Friday, if that's alright?'

Jeff nodded, seeing his girlfriend's hopeful eyes. 'That'd be good.'

Relieved, the pretty celebrity gave her mother a kiss. 'Thanks, Mum. Thanks, Dad.'

'I'll pull the car round to the front,' the Sydneysider announced, recognising a need to make himself scarce temporarily.

The tall, Mediterranean-looking thief of hearts rounded the Olympian's massive desk, and the big man stood up. Two impressive leaders shook hands firmly, reconciled at last. The young musician thanked his girlfriend's mother and father again for accepting him, hugging Marianna and promising to keep their little girl safe and happy. Seeing tears well up in her eyes again, the sensitive guest turned and left the office.

Lynn thanked her parents too, once Jeff had left the office. 'I'm really glad you're starting to like Jeff. He's amazing. We're going to be so happy in London, I can just tell. And the fact that we're leaving on friendly terms is so perfect.'

The elegant lady agreed, as did her husband. 'He is a fine man, young lady,' the proud father told her. 'I was wrong to doubt your choice.'

The three remaining adult Dysons struck out for the front entrance together. Jeff had already loaded their belongings into the car they had borrowed from Admin after the Aston Martin had been secreted away in its secure container.

'I've got a few cars like that,' Bart quipped.

'Really? Well, you can have this one in a few days too,' the comic replied, holding the door open for his passenger to climb in.

'You have beautiful manners, dear,' Marianna observed. 'Drive carefully. See you on Friday.'

Lynn wound her window down and held her hand out to her mother. 'Thanks, Mum. I'll ring you before then anyway. Bye!'

The car drove off, following the same initial path as Junior's van.

***

The incessant buzzing of an oversized robotic mosquito filled the dark, claustrophobic room, growing more and less insistent in waves as the drawing took shape. Jeff felt positively nauseated as he watched the tattooist's needle dig deep into Lynn's shoulder. She was chatting away happily however, only wincing every now and then when the sharp pen took her by surprise. He knew exactly what she was going through, having sat in the same chair just two days prior, and he would be changing places with her again in half an hour or so.

'Where do you go to learn how to give such pleasure?' the handsome superstar joked with the tattoo artist, who was himself covered in body art.

There had been no second thoughts on the drive back from Benloch. The shape of their two initials back to back in the shape of a figure One had been quickly sketched by the artist, and its creative architect was pleased with the way the simple and amply singular "work of heart" was taking shape so far on the smooth skin of his girlfriend's shoulder. They had laughed about adding a tiny pantomime horse to their order, somewhere hidden, until they realised how hard it would be to explain it away to doctors once they were in their eighties. The finished design had soon been transferred from the tracing paper, only two centimetres tall on Lynn's shoulder blade, whereas Jeff's would be twice the size.

When the buzzing finally stopped, the stunning teenager looked in the mirror which was held up behind her shoulder. She smiled back at her lover, who could see she was ecstatic with the result, even though the skin around it was red raw and enflamed.

'It's fantastic,' she said dreamily. 'Do you think so?'

Jeff nodded. He wanted to cry but would save that for later. Someone had just carved his initial in Lynn Dyson's skin. How unbelievable was that? He kissed her instead.

'You're gorgeous. And it's gorgeous.'

A faint noise made the smiling man stir, sensing movement beside him. A tall, willowy female placed a full cup of coffee down on the desk.

'Christ Almighty, Kizzo, what are you doing?' Jeff started, shaken rudely from his pleasant dream.

'What are *you* doing?' his daughter had an uncomfortable smirk on her face on seeing her father's hand move adroitly away from his crotch.

Thank Christ! The disappointed father cursed under his breath, feeling a distinct shrinking sensation inside his pants. What *had* he been doing? Embarrassed more for the impressionable seventeen-year-old than for himself, he levered his long legs off the desk and dropped his feet heavily onto the floorboards, sitting up and thanking her for forcing him to take a break from writing.

Robbed of yet another delectable encounter with his beautiful best friend, Jeff closed his eyes and attempted to drift back into the dream before it skulked away. Kierney pulled up a chair next to him and began to read the latest paragraphs on the computer's screen.

The forty-four-year-old smiled, as tears leaped into his eyes. His close shave had reminded him of the time the Diamond family had been on a flight going somewhere or other, when his four-year-old gipsy girl had fallen asleep with her head in his lap. "Watch where your mind wanders to," Lynn had whispered, raising eyebrows laden with suggestive allusion, her hypnotising, blue eyes dancing.

'Ew!' Kierney frowned, glancing over as her father emitted the faintest chuckle. 'Now what are you grinning about? Mamá'll be jealous she's missing out on all the fun.'

'Oh, no, she's not,' her father countered, leaning over and hugging his daughter hard. 'It was she who reminded me.'

The teenager watched the tired author rub his chest vigorously, regretting waking him from what must have been a satisfying spiritual *rendezvous*. She didn't know if his "JL" tattoo really did itch so frequently with special messages from her mother, or whether her ever-thoughtful papá simply employed it as a prop to help push her through her own grief. Either way, it didn't really matter. The mere idea of an enduring connection seemed like a nourishing experience to the famous couple's enchanted offspring.

'What were you dreaming about? Mamá, obviously.'

Her father nodded, still with his eyes closed. 'Yep. Mamá, obviously, but only to begin with. Your presence must have changed the course of the dream, because all of a sudden I was doing the tattooing myself, and on a baby.'

'On a baby?' Kierney repeated, her voice shrill with incredulity. 'I'm sorry if I made that happen, but why the hell would *you* be tattooing a baby?'

Jeff shrugged, his chest tightening with emotion. 'How should I know? I'm guessing the baby was you, infiltrating my head again.'

'No, not necessarily,' the gipsy girl almost whispered. 'What if it's Mamá's soul telling you she's been re-born? Telling you to get a move on…'

The author smiled, shaking his head. 'Don't even go there, *pequeñita*. That was my first thought to, but I wanted to spare you my madness.'

'But you don't have to. I love the idea. I want to believe in it.'

'Well, don't, please,' her dad turned his attention to Indie, who failed to offer an opinion either way. 'It's not likely, and you've been talking off and on about getting a tatt' lately, so I guess it all merges into one bizarre story inside here.'

The widower tapped his ancient head a couple of times and sighed, gulping down his coffee. 'Jesus, Kiz, I was tattooing your mamá everywhere. It said, "I love you, I love you, I love you," all over her skin. She was smiling up at me and pointing to where I should go next, and then she turned into you as a tiny baby, and I was scrawling all over you too with that bloody needle.'

'What were you tattooing on me?' the elfin beauty smiled.

'The same, I expect. I don't know,' her indignant father shrugged, pushing his chair back and standing tall to stretch his back. 'You woke me up!'

The rambunctious golden retriever jumped up at his master, excited at the prospect of some activity, and landed a heavy paw directly in his groin. Kierney chuckled, her face screwed up as she imagined the discomfort caused by the wayward paw.

'Bloody hell, Indie,' Jeff gasped, sitting down again. 'Well, that's put paid to any more lascivious fantasies, boy.'

The widower grinned at his pretty daughter while the pain radiated through his mid-section and down his legs, watching the Labrador wagging his tail furiously.

'Bloody dog!' they shouted in unison.

***

The incessant buzzing of an oversized robotic mosquito filled the dark, claustrophobic room, growing more and less insistent in waves as the drawing took shape. Jeff felt nauseated as he watched the tattooist's needle dig deep into Lynn's shoulder. She was chatting away happily however, only wincing every now and then when the sharp pen took her by surprise. He knew exactly what she was going through, having sat in the same chair just two days prior, and he would be changing places with her again in half an hour or so.

'Where do you go to learn how to give such pleasure?' the handsome superstar joked with the tattoo artist, who was himself covered in body art.

There had been no second thoughts on the drive back from Benloch. The shape of their two initials back to back in the shape of a figure One had been quickly sketched by the artist, and its creative architect was pleased with the way the simple and amply singular "work of heart" was taking shape so far on the smooth skin of his girlfriend's shoulder. They had laughed about adding a tiny pantomime horse to their order, somewhere hidden, until they realised how hard it would be to explain it away to doctors once they were in their eighties. The finished design had soon been transferred from the tracing paper, only two centimetres tall on Lynn's shoulder blade, whereas Jeff's would be twice the size.

When the buzzing finally stopped, the stunning teenager looked in the mirror which was held up behind her shoulder. She smiled back at her lover, who could see she was ecstatic with the result, even though the skin around it was red raw and enflamed.

'It's fantastic,' she said dreamily. 'Do you think so?'

Jeff nodded. He wanted to cry but would save that for later. Someone had just carved his initial in Lynn Dyson's skin. How unbelievable was that? He kissed her instead.

'You're gorgeous. And it's gorgeous.'

The tattooist covered the tender area on Lynn's shoulder with a dressing and gave his famous customers some instructions on how to treat their wounds over the next few days. The thirty-hour flight to London would be uncomfortable every time his favourite sports star wanted to switch position, he warned. The location of Jeff's version would be much easier on him for the duration of their journey.

After another hour, the larger tattoo was finished too, much to the young man's relief. His dream girl had teased him every time he exhaled or swore when the needle strayed to a bonier part of his sternum, doling out maximum embarrassment by kissing her poor soldier better in front of the amused professional. Finally able to put his shirt back on, the millionnaire paid the bill and thanked the artist profusely, and the inked duo ambled back to their apartment through the city they were on the verge of vacating.

'That's it!' Lynn announced, throwing her arms in the air. 'You're stuck with me now.'

Jeff trapped her both hands in his and brought them together, leaving them hovering between their hearts. 'And you with me, lady. It's the only thing I ever really wanted.'

The blonde singer kissed him, and he flinched as she touched his shirt by accident.

'Oh, sorry! We're going to have to treat each other very carefully over the next few days. No more rampant sex.'

Her lover looked perturbed. 'You never told me that was part of the deal.'

Lynn laughed. 'Non-rampant sex is OK. Don't stress! I'm sure you won't let me go without.'

The couple reached the top floor of the building, and the nineteen-year-old sensed some nerves gathering in her partner once more. She chose to say and do nothing as Jeff's fingers dipped into his pants pocket to retrieve the front door key. Still holding her hand, he slotted the key straight into the lock and turned it a quarter turn to the right without apparent hesitation. The door released the key back to his fingers as it swung away from them. At his behest, the refined young lady calmly walked in past her chivalrous knight, and he followed in silence. She heard the door click shut behind her, but that was all.

'OK!' the boy from Canley Vale declared in subdued triumph after a few seconds. 'That was good.'

'¡Excelente!' the ecstatic young woman replied. 'I could feel you tense up, but there was no wild look in your eyes as you crossed the threshold. Did the images stay away?'

The anxious millionnaire breathed deeply, trying to neutralise his pulse rate. 'Not completely, but pretty low-level. Thanks for acting normally. It was just what I needed.'

With only one day to go until their flight to London, the celebrities' respective levels of excitement and anticipation were building as quickly as their realisation of how much was still left to do. Most of their belongings had already been sent on ahead, but there remained some last minute laundry and packing to finish and a whole slew of unscheduled requests for television interviews and photography shoots they felt unable to spurn.

'Do you realise this'll only be the third time we've flown together?' Jeff reminded his girlfriend, while unloading the washing machine. 'You know, in many ways, we still hardly know each other.'

Lynn was busy ticking off items from her checklist of last-minute tasks. 'Yeah. I suppose you're right,' she agreed. 'It's been such a cyclonic few months that it does still feel very new and exciting. For me, when we got back together, it was really like starting again because so many things had changed from before.'

'Really?' her boyfriend challenged. 'I think you feel that way more than I do. I mean, I agree that so much has changed about our lives. But for me, it was just like getting my old friend back, only more sophisticated. Was I really that different?'

The pretty singer sat thinking for a few seconds, quietly rejoicing at the complete lack of paranoia on display today. 'You weren't different, but my perception of you had changed, I think. Before, we did simple things. Dating. Just having fun. Lots of talking, like we still do, but probably less about things that affected us directly. Do you know what I mean?'

The handsome man nodded. 'Yeah, I do.'

His dream girl continued. 'Whereas now... or since September, anyway... we've been so stressed out about beating the odds to stay together that everything became really intense.'

'Ha!' Jeff gave an exasperated sigh. 'Jesus Christ! You're not wrong there. That's why I'm keen to stop all that once we get to London. All my fault too. I was driving that intensity because I was so scared I'd lose you again. All the travel, the shit with your dad, getting my past out of my system... Now I just want things to calm down so we can live a normal life. You do your thing, I'll do mine, and then we can each come home and tell each other what's happened. No pressure. Just loving each other.'

The sportswoman sprang out of her chair to hug her gorgeous partner. 'I'm so glad to hear you say that. That's my dream for London too. Not to say I haven't enjoyed every minute of the last few months with you. I have. But we just can't sustain that sort of intensity, can we?'

'No,' her soul-mate agreed, kissing her forehead. 'And we won't have to, I promise. I already feel less extreme, since Christmas, at either end of the scale. I don't have that same anxiety I used to have every time you disappeared from view. I'm finally at the stage where I'm confident you'll come back. Up to a point anyway, but give me time... I know there'll be tomorrow and the next day. Before, it was like I had to extract every last ounce of you out of every day in case I never saw you again.'

The caring teenager smiled. 'I know. And I tried to deliver what you wanted, but it really wasn't helping, was it? I'm not going anywhere, and we've got the tattoos now too. I absolutely, absolutely don't want to go anywhere. And now even Dad's got the message that we're here to stay, which makes it that bit easier still.'

Jeff pushed his beautiful best friend back to arms' length and shook his head defiantly. 'Oh, baby, don't say what you did didn't help. It did help. Bloody oath, it helped heaps,' he countered. 'At the time, it saved my life. I'm serious...'

Lynn looked into his dark, doleful eyes and saw a man trying so desperately to stay positive on a journey which was not yet over, doing his best to stop himself drifting back into the clamouring clutches of those memories that had clung on to him for so long. She let him say what he needed to say.

'At that time, you saved my sanity. Be sure of that, angel. Without you, I would've gone over the edge again in September, like I did the previous year.'

A spontaneous kiss interrupted the healing adolescent's frantic account, telling him to snap out of it or else. The tall, dark stranger smiled at his wise therapist.

'However,' he announced assertively, 'that was the old me. That's why I had to get you to fix me, because to carry on like that would've destroyed us both eventually, wouldn't it?'

The solemn woman nodded. 'Yes, I think so.'

Jeff flinched. It cut him inside to hear these four simple words, but he needed her to speak the truth nonetheless.

'You helping me in the short term wasn't helping *us* for the long term,' he echoed his girlfriend's thoughts, forcing himself to absorb the pain and move on.

'But now it doesn't matter anymore, all that,' Lynn assured him. 'Even now, you're much more in control than you used to be. Don't you think? You're not at all like how you were when we went to New Zealand for your birthday, for example.'

'Manic, you mean?'

The refined celebrity frowned at the adjective's negative connotations. 'I suppose so. It was like someone had lit a fire under you.'

'Was it?' smiled the boy from Sydney's west. 'I don't really perceive it until I'm sliding down. Didn't? Don't? Shit! Who knows?'

His patient lover grabbed his hand, which had started to shake again. 'Didn't, Jeff,' she emphasised. 'You didn't perceive it. Now you're just excited, and it's gorgeous. Much easier to share in that.'

Gradually feeling less of a basket case, the twenty-two-year-old exhaled. 'Rather than being run over by it?'

'Yes, exactly!'

'That's your fault,' the determined man said in an accusative tone, eyebrows raised.

Lynn raised her hand to object. '*Our* fault.'

'No, angel,' her biggest fan shook his head harder and for longer. 'It's *your* fault. End of story.'

Tears welled up in the young woman's eyes, and the pair embraced, lost in their own thoughts of how far they had come and what lay ahead.

'Jesus, I'm so bloody impatient to go,' Jeff smiled. 'I'm trying to keep a lid on it.'

'Well, don't worry about it. I think you're doing fantastically. So much so that sometimes I think you've gone cool on the whole thing. Does it feel weird?'

Her irresistible and enigmatic stranger stretched his arms out again and gazed into his dream girl's piercing pools of pure paradise. Did it feel weird?

'No, not really,' he answered. 'Behaving any other way now would feel weird.'

Lynn leaned forward on tiptoes and planted another kiss on waiting lips. 'Wow! That's huge, Jeff.'

'It is?' he asked, his eyes dropping down to below the waist, making the innocent teenager giggle in embarrassment.

'Yes,' came her nonchalant reply, sending shivers down the aroused man's spine.

Their bodies locked together again, drawn closer by shared desire. Her boyfriend took hold of her right hand and placed it over his instant erection, which she was only too inclined to stroke through the thick material of his jeans. It felt so good to be so close.

'D'you *wanna* use it?' he invited.

'Of course! But not yet. Too much to do.'

'Christ, you're a hard taskmaster,' Jeff lamented, winking. 'But to answer your question, I have fleeting trips to the dark side, but on the whole I'm the new me now.'

He picked up the laundry basket as if to draw the conversation to a close, before immediately returning to his smiling flatmate. 'And one other thing,' he started, shaking a comedic finger.

'What's that?' she giggled. 'Why am I not surprised there's one other thing?'

'I'm not going to ask you for sex every five minutes anymore,' he proclaimed, 'like I'm constantly having to validate myself. To prove I'm useful, you know... I coped OK last night without it, and even slept through 'til morning.'

'You did the other night too, when you stayed up after I went to bed,' Lynn reminded him.

'Yeah. That's right,' he agreed, unleashing a lecherous grin. 'Although, Christ Almighty, I was raging for it that night! I so nearly, nearly woke you. I'm surprised my dick didn't wake you independently.'

His girlfriend frowned. 'How do you know it didn't? Maybe you missed all the action?'

Jeff smiled, content that they could find humour in something which was still occasionally difficult for them to navigate. He unbuttoned his shirt and examined the dressing over the fresh tattoo on his chest. Lynn brushed her fingers lightly across the older one, and he flexed his pectoral muscles, making the most of the pleasurable sensation. The scabs were beginning to lift off, and they could almost make out a dark green string of joined-up lettering on two lines.

'Bring it on,' she read aloud, retracing the lettering.

Her boyfriend held his arms out as if to welcome her into his world, and the thrilled emigrants hugged each other. Everything was working out so perfectly.

'It's going to be hidden soon, once the hair grows back,' the tennis champion remarked, kissing the uncovered tattoo. 'It's already spikey, like your chin but a bit softer.'

Jeff gently scratched his day-old shadow across his girlfriend's silken cheek, rotating his face until their lips met. 'You believe in the new me, don't you?' he asked, once more unsure of himself. 'Could you honestly see it when I told you who I wanted to be? Is it going to be what you want?'

Planting her hands on her hips, Lynn pointed to the bundle of wet clothes on the kitchen floor. 'That lot'll be dry before it gets hung out at this rate,' she said sternly. 'And that's two other things, not one. Yes, Jeff, I absolutely believe in the new you. I always have. I saw how much you wanted to change. Needed to change. I loved you heaps before, but I'm convinced it's going to be even better in the future. Now do *you* believe *me*?'

The man with fire in his heart picked up the laundry obediently and turned on his heels. 'I guess so, boss. Don't look back. Isn't that what you said?'

'Yes. Not until we're ready to write our autobiography, I suppose.'

'*Our* autobiography?' he repeated, his eyes flashing at the thought of this intoxicating hand grenade of a presumption.

'Sure,' his dream girl smiled. 'If we're committing to one life singular, then we can only write one autobiography. I'm surprised you're surprised.'

Jeff leaned against the doorframe, light-headed and euphoric. 'I shouldn't be. Every time I think I know you off by heart, you go and say something so totally cool like that. It's a fantastic idea, angel, and I love you. Now get back to work.'

End of Part Three

If you enjoyed reading this book, please take the time to tell your friends and leave a review on Amazon and Goodreads.

Book 2 in the series, "A Life Lived", was published in December 2014. Full details can be found at http://lorrainepestell.com.

So this was it… Lynn and Jeff, two celebrities driven to change the world together, had grasped their life singular with both hands and were not about to let go. They had the Midas touch, gifted through the virtues of reciprocity and a deepening understanding of right versus wrong.

Mirroring the black jetstone ring which lived on the handsome man's right hand, the prospect of turning two into four filled the couple with excitement. Never in his wildest dreams had the no-good street kid imagined himself as a father. His own had given him nothing. So much less than nothing, in fact.

Should Jeff settle that score? Was it worth disturbing the paradise they had planned, where their well-established careers showed no sign of slowing down and their hard work yielded so much for so many? Surfacing past wrongs and holding people to account for setting them right were part and parcel of letting go, his dream girl had insisted. And who was he to argue? She had been right all along.

As the book's extraordinary chapters continued to document the achievements of their life singular, the solitary author cried and smiled in equal measure through the arrival of a small boy with blond, curly hair and the sultry gipsy girl who could see inside his soul from the moment she was born. Lynn had given him two new friends who must now be steered through their young lives, learning their own lessons about the endless pursuit of love and wisdom.